# The Memory of Souls

ALSO BY JENN LYONS

*The Ruin of Kings*

*The Name of All Things*

# The Memory of Souls

Jenn Lyons

A Tom Doherty Associates Book

*New York*

THE MEMORY OF SOULS



A Tor Book
Published by Tom Doherty Associates
120 Broadway
New York, NY 10271

www.tor-forge.com



The Library of Congress Cataloging-in-Publication Data is available upon request.

ISBN 978-1-250-17557-1 (hardcover)
ISBN 978-1-250-17556-4 (ebook)

Our books may be purchased in bulk for promotional, educational, or business use. Please contact your local bookseller or the Macmillan Corporate and Premium Sales Department at 1-800-221-7945, extension 5442, or by email at MacmillanSpecialMarkets@macmillan.com.

First Edition: August 2020

Printed in the United States of America

10 9 8 7 6 5 4 3 2 1

*For my mother, Alexandra.*

*I miss you.*

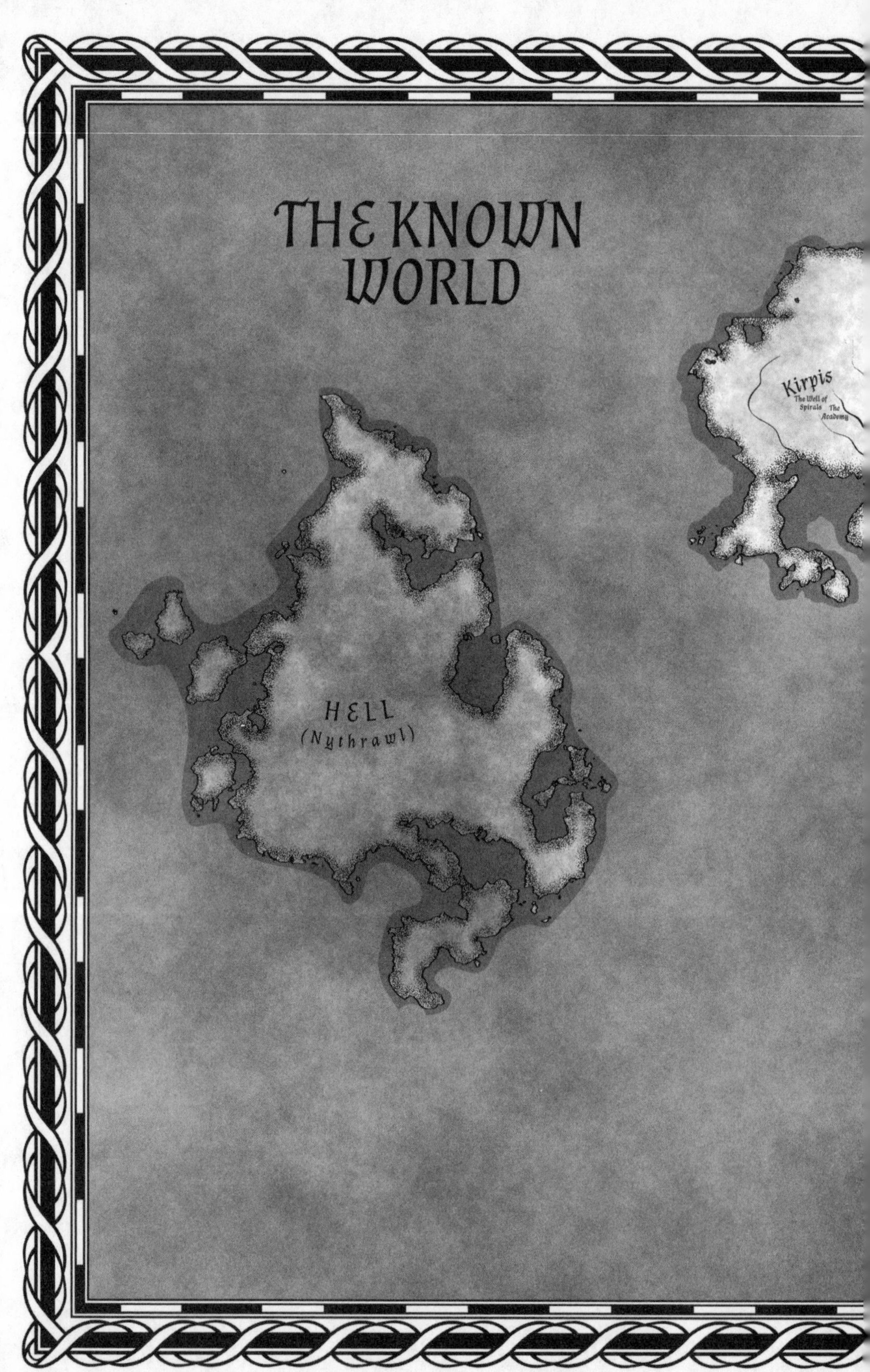
THE KNOWN WORLD
Kirpis
The Well of Spirals
The Academy
HELL
(Nythrawl)

Shadrag Gor
Drakon Reach
Yor
Raenena
Kazivar
The Great Steppe
Jorat
Wintersea
The Grazing
Lake Jorat
Atrine
Kumisha Bay
The Dragonspires
Marakor
Eamithon
Kulma Swamp
The Capital City
Khorvesh
Stone Gate
The Korthaen Blight
The Quarry
The Mother of Trees
Devors
Seraval
Galla Sea
MANOL
Zherias
The Desolation
The Maw
Kishna-Farriga
DOLTAR
Bahl-Nimian
The Free States

# The Memory of Souls

# Foreword 1

*Your Majesty,*

*Enclosed is my chronicle of recent events, as well as Senera's accounting of events leading up to Atrine's destruction.*

*And I am asking you to not read either of them.*

*I realize this seems an odd request, but time . . . oh, time . . . is a luxury we don't have at the moment. What I am asking is that you read the attached summary of Senera's book and then come immediately, without a second's delay, to the tower on the island in center of Rainbow Lake. The Crown and Scepter know the way.*

*We need your help. I need your help. I do not have time for you to read either book. Once you are here, and not before, only then will we find you the time necessary.*

*We'll steal it if we have to.*

*You should know I've given a copy of this chronicle to Senera. There is little point in keeping it from her; she has it within her power to divine the contents. I'm hoping my gesture of "friendliness" will convince her that acquiring her own copy is unnecessary. Because her copy is not complete, and it is of vital importance that it remain that way.*

*The fate of the whole world rests on this.*

*Always your faithful servant,*
*Thurvishar*

What led up to this:

Two days after the Capital City Hellmarch, your own ascension to the Quuros throne, and Kihrin's recovery of the sword Urthaenriel, Kihrin D'Mon traveled to Jorat to find the Black Knight. As plans go, it needed work; I believe it amounted to "anyone Duke Kaen and Relos Var hate this much must be someone I'll like."

He found Janel Theranon, former Joratese Count of Tolamer, who had bribed a House D'Aramarin Gatekeeper to make sure Kihrin crossed her path. Since Kihrin had Urthaenriel, Janel wanted to recruit him to slay the dragon Morios, which she believed would soon attack Atrine, second-largest city in Quur. Why did she believe this? I'll get to that in a moment.

Janel knew Kihrin because she'd helped Return him to life. He didn't remember her and, believing this a con, attempted to leave. He failed. The dragon Aeyan'arric, Lady of Storms, had arrived, trapping everyone inside. So Kihrin agreed to at least listen to Janel (and her Vishai priest confidant, Brother Qown) explain how the current crisis came to be and why she needed Kihrin's help.

It seems several years earlier, Janel had encountered Relos Var, who had been fomenting unrest in the Jorat region. Var's plan seemed to be multipronged; he was sneaking disguised Yorans into the duchy, destabilizing the power structure with spurious witch hunts, and summoning real demons to be trapped and eliminated. His main provocateur was a Doltari wizard named Senera whom he'd given a Cornerstone called the Name of All Things, which allows Senera to answer any question.

Besides trying to warn her Joratese superiors, Janel became determined to recover a magic spear named Khoreval, which she believed could kill Aeyan'arric. Unfortunately, it was owned by Relos Var's "boss": Duke Kaen of Yor.

Janel contrived to get herself kidnapped and taken back to Yor, with an unintended companion as Brother Qown was also taken (and gaeshed as a hostage on Janel's good behavior). Janel won over both Kaen and his undead wife, Xivan, and spent the next several years trying to find a way to steal Khoreval. In the process, she learned Kaen had the spear because he intended to use it to kill the dragon Morios when it woke from under Lake Jorat. (So then Janel had two dragons to kill.) She also secretly passed messages to both Teraeth (yes, our Teraeth) and her own agents working to undermine Kaen's plans. (This last under the guise of a Jorat persona known as "the Black Knight"–the same one Kihrin sought.)

During this time, Janel learned several important facts. First, Duke Kaen kept the god-queen Suless as a gaeshed slave. Second, Janel's father was General Milligreest (a fact that Duke Kaen intended to exploit). And third, Janel was also the daughter of Tya, Goddess of Magic (a fact that Relos Var *was* exploiting). Janel herself used this last bit of information to help steal Khoreval, and together, mother and daughter slew Aeyan'arric.

While Janel told this story to Kihrin, she had an attack of conscience and admitted the truth to him: Relos Var had later captured both her and the spear again. She had been dragged before an enraged Duke Kaen, who ordered her death for her betrayal. Before the god-queen Suless could enact this, however, something happened: Kihrin destroyed the Stone of Shackles. Suless, freed from her gaesh, destroyed Kaen's palace and almost everyone in it, but Janel, Qown, and a few others managed to escape. When Relos Var returned, he revealed that Khoreval[1] alone wouldn't be able to kill Morios (or Aeyan'arric, who would return). The only way to do so permanently was to simultaneously kill both the dragon and their matching Cornerstone. "Fortunately," he knew the location of Morios's Cornerstone. The only piece missing was Urthaenriel.

That's where Kihrin came in.

I'm sure Kihrin would have told Relos Var to get lost, except Morios did rise from Lake Jorat and did start destroying Atrine. So Kihrin agreed to help, a decision I know he now regrets. While Janel, Senera, and Relos Var dealt with the dragon, Kihrin, Qown, and myself (yes, I was part of this) agreed to travel down under Lake Jorat to the dead god-king Khorsal's flooded throne room, where the Cornerstone Warmonger waited.

And Kihrin had been right from the beginning; it was all a con. The dragon existed, the threat existed, but Senera had sabotaged the signals we'd created to time our strikes, so Kihrin, thinking Morios had been slain, destroyed what he thought was Warmonger. Instead, it was an ancient warding crystal, one of eight, used to keep Vol Karoth imprisoned and sleeping. Its destruction didn't free Vol Karoth, but he woke from his slumber. When Kihrin tried to confront Relos Var, Qown betrayed us and ambushed Kihrin.

Relos Var and Qown took Urthaenriel and left, having accomplished everything they wanted. (Teraeth later rescued both Kihrin and myself from drowning under Lake Jorat.) The rest of us, yourself included, were left to clean up the mess.

In terms of Relos Var's goals, I would say it was a complete success. It certainly opened the path for what's followed, because Relos Var knew exactly how the Eight Immortals would respond.

He was planning on it.

[1] Was Khoreval recovered? I know Morios broke the spear in two and the pieces fell into Lake Jorat, but . . . never mind. I suppose we have more important problems right now.

# FOREWORD 2

*My dearest, Senera,*

*I originally thought to address this volume to Empress Tyentso. After all, she does need to be updated on the rather startling events happening outside Quur's borders.*

*Those events will come to roost on her throne as well.*

*However, it occurred to me that I can do nothing to keep you from reading this chronicle. I am well aware of what the Name of All Things can do. You may be required to write down the answers to questions in full, but there is no rule that says you must do so at a moderate and sedate pace. I also know those spells, as well as how to reach Shadrag Gor.*

*When you have finished reading, ask yourself this for me, as one equal to another: If Relos Var didn't know this could happen, what else doesn't he know? And if he did know, just how much of his true motives has he hidden from you? He believes that only he can save the world and has followed that belief to its most narcissistic and grandiose conclusion. Thus, no matter how much he values your support, you will always be expendable to him.*

*It's not fun to be a wizard's toy, is it?*

*Believe me, I know.*

*Think on this and ponder the possibility that saving the world doesn't have to mean sacrificing your soul. Consider the idea that Relos Var might be* wrong. *What will you do if you discover all these atrocities he has had you commit were never necessary, but rather a failure of imagination?*

*Your most respectful and admiring enemy,*
*Thurvishar (that D'Lorus brat)*

# PART I

## Rituals of Night

Kihrin found Thurvishar in the library, or rather, the three thousand years of accumulated detritus that had passed for a library to a bachelor who had never once considered that another person might need to look through all his centuries of research. Books littered every room of the tower, along with notes, diagrams, junk, and objects whose purpose and providence were unfathomable. Kihrin had no idea how most of it hadn't rotted away, besides the obvious: magic. But then, there was rather a lot of magic here. The walls stank of it, the floors vibrated with tenyé sunk into every pore of granite and quartz. The stone was a battery for wizardly power, although not enough power.

Never enough power for what they needed.

The D'Lorus Lord Heir didn't look up from his reading. "May I help you?"

A bang made Thurvishar glance up as Kihrin dropped a large, heavy book on the table. Kihrin had to shove a stack of papers out of the way so Thurvishar might actually be able to see him as he spoke. "Are you going to write another one?"

Thurvishar paused, then closed the text he'd been reading. "I'm sorry. What was that?"

"Are you going to write another book? Like the one you wrote about finding Urthaenriel?" Kihrin gazed at him intently.

"Technically speaking, I didn't write—"

"You *did,*" Kihrin said. "You may have had those transcripts, but you can't tell me you didn't make up large chunks of it. Senera wasn't wrong about that." The golden-haired man paused. "I think you need to do it again. You need to write another book."

Thurvishar straightened. "To send to Empress Tyentso, you mean?"

"Sure, that too." Kihrin drummed his fingers on the book he'd returned. "I just think if we don't, *they* will." He didn't clarify who "they" were, but it was obvious: Relos Var and his associate, Senera. And likely his new apprentice, Qown.

Thurvishar studied the book under Kihrin's fingers and pursed his lips. "So I take it you finished both accounts, then?"

"Yeah," Kihrin said. "And I think your conclusions are right."[1] Then the young man sighed. "But I want . . . I want to cover what's happened since then. I know you were there for almost all of it, but I keep thinking that there's something we missed. Something we could have . . . I don't know. Something we could have done differently." He shook his head. "I keep telling myself that it didn't have to end this way."

"Kihrin, are you–" Thurvishar grimaced. "Are you going to be all right?"

"What do you think?" Kihrin snapped, and then he stopped himself, exhaling. "I'm sorry. But no. No, I don't think I'm going to be all right at all. Maybe never again."

Kihrin picked up a page from the stack of papers he'd moved earlier, and glanced at it. When he realized what it said, he raised an eyebrow at Thurvishar.

The wizard cleared his throat. "I may have already started. But I was going to ask you for your input, I promise."

Kihrin's mouth quirked. "No time like the present."

[1] Naturally.

# 1: An Interruption

## *(Thurvishar's story)*

When the gods descended on the Atrine ruins, they interrupted an assassination.

Thurvishar hadn't perceived the danger at first. Yes, soldiers had been pouring through the eight open magical portals set up on a small hill next to Lake Jorat, but he'd expected that. A mountain-size dragon had just finished tearing the second-largest city in the empire into rubble and fine quartz dust, with an incalculable body count. Morios had attacked the army right along with the civilian populations—populations now panicked and displaced. Of course there were soldiers. Soldiers to clean up the mess left in the attack's wake, soldiers to help with the evacuation, soldiers to maintain a presence in the ruined, rubble-strewn Atrine streets. And the wizards? They needed to render Morios's body into something so discorporate the dragon couldn't re-form himself and start the whole messy apocalypse all over again.

To add fuel to the fire, the damaged dam holding back Lake Jorat, Demon Falls, had begun to fail. When the dam blew, Lake Jorat would empty out. *Millions* would die, if not in the flooding itself, then by starvation when Quur's breadbasket[1] found itself twenty feet underwater. The wizards would focus on stopping such a catastrophe.

In hindsight, Thurvishar had been too optimistic; he'd assumed the Quuros High Council would care about saving lives.

Janel's fury alerted him, furnace hot, a bubbling cauldron usually locked away behind a fiercer will. He felt Kihrin's anger a moment later, sharp and lashing. Thurvishar paused while discussing spell theory with an Academy wizard and looked up the hill. The same soldiers he'd ignored earlier had set up a defensive formation. They weren't dressed as normal soldiers. These men wore the distinctive coin-studded breastplates of a particular sort of Quuros enforcer.

Witchhunters. He couldn't see who they surrounded, but he made assumptions.

[1] That is to say, the farmlands of Marakor, which lie below the falls.

urvishar debated and discarded opening a portal to their location. hat might provoke the very reaction he sought to avoid.

So instead, he ran.

What he found when he arrived qualified as a worst-case scenario. No one tried to stop him from pushing to the front. He was, after all, Lord Heir to House D'Lorus. If anyone had a right to be here, he did. More witchhunters gathered in this one area than he'd ever seen before. They didn't stand alone either; he recognized Academy wizards in equal number as well as High Lord Havar D'Aramarin and several Quuros High Council members.

All for three people: Kihrin D'Mon, Janel Theranon, and Teraeth. Neither Kihrin nor Janel held obvious weapons, and while one might argue they didn't need them, with this many people?

The outcome seemed predictable.

"What is going on here?" General Qoran Milligreest pushed aside several witchhunters as he strode into the confrontation's center.

"It seems our thanks for helping is to be a prison cell." Janel clenched her fists.

"Vornel, what's the meaning of this?" Milligreest turned to a Quuros man without acknowledging his daughter.[2]

Vornel Wenora, High Council member, snorted at the general's question. "I should think it obvious. We're dealing with a threat to the empire. Which is what you should have done."

"Threat to the empire?" Qoran pointed toward the giant metal dragon's corpse. "*That* is a threat to the empire. The impending rupture of Demon Falls is a threat to the empire. These are children!"

Thurvishar scanned the crowd. The witchhunter minds stood out as blank spaces, as did some wizards and all the High Council. But where was Empress Tyentso?

Vornel shrugged. "So you say, but all I see are dangerous people who are a grave threat to our great and glorious empire. This is the man who killed the emperor and stole Urthaenriel. Then we have a witch who flaunts her powers in public and a known Manol vané agent. Yet for reasons I cannot begin to fathom, you've done nothing to put a stop to them. Why is that, Qoran?"

"Because I understand priorities!" the general replied.

Thurvishar raised an eyebrow at Vornel. While the accusations had merit, they missed the truth by an astonishing margin. Plus, none of the High Council members were giving Thurvishar so much as a glance,

[2] He hadn't acknowledged her for the twenty years she'd been alive prior to this moment; why start now?

when he was the far more appropriate target for their anger. Vornel's accusations seemed disingenuous, less true outrage than a savvy councilman sensing a perfect opportunity for a power play, and too arrogant, petty, or stupid to temper his ruinous timing.

Councilman Nevesi Oxun, old and thin with silvering cloudcurl hair, stepped forward. "It doesn't matter, Milligreest. By unanimous vote—"

"Did I vote in my sleep, then?" Milligreest growled.

"Nearly unanimous,"[3] Oxun corrected. "If you act to prevent us from doing this or interfere with these men in their lawful enforcement, we will be forced to conclude you've fallen under the sway of foreign powers and remove you from the High Council."

"How dare—"

Kihrin started laughing. Thurvishar grimaced and glanced away.

Of course. Tyentso.

"You don't want us, do you?" Kihrin said. "You couldn't give two thrones about *us*. But Tyentso? *She's* the one you think is a 'grave threat to the empire.'" The young royal, still wearing a Quuros soldier's borrowed clothing, held out his hands. "If you geniuses think Tyentso's stupid enough to show herself now with all these witchhunters present, I've got a gently used bridge by the lake to sell you."

Thurvishar's own anger rose. Kihrin had called it. The High Council considered Janel and Teraeth inconsequential. They might have regarded Kihrin more seriously if they studied the Devoran Prophecies. But they cared a great deal that the new Quuros emperor had somehow managed to insult them all by being born a woman.

If they had their way, she'd have the shortest reign of any emperor in recorded history.

"I wouldn't start forging deeds to bridges just yet, Scamp." Tyentso appeared on top of a nearby tent, balanced there through literal magic. "I might be that stupid. Or maybe just that cocky." She waved the Scepter of Quur—currently wand-like—to trace a delicate path in the air. "This is a fun toy. I want to practice."

"Men, kill her—"

Which was when the gods arrived.

Seven blazing pillars of light slammed into the earth next to the confrontation. The men who had been standing there—witchhunters, wizards, soldiers—vanished. Thurvishar liked to think those men found themselves transported to a safe location, but he couldn't verify that

[3] A High Council vote requires a two-thirds majority, so while Milligreest's vote as Acting Chairman counts as two votes and can break any ties, Vornel's cabal might easily have had sufficient votes without his.

suspicion.[4] But he knew the beings who stood there—had been standing there—when the light dimmed enough to see again.

The Eight Immortals had arrived.[5] Every single person within sight—high lord, soldier, wizard—went to the floor.

No one could doubt their identities. Their aspects seeped into the air around them. Galava dressed in spring green, plump and lush, the ground beneath her feet blooming flowers. Argas, mathematical formulae visible around him like a halo. Tya, her rainbow dress of veils shimmering as her fingers crackled with magic. Taja, dressed in silver, playing with a single coin. Ompher, looking less like a person than an animate statue carved from rock. Khored in red, raven-feathered, holding a glass sword. And last, Thaena, dressed in shroud white, crowned in burial roses.

To a one, they were all furious.

"Are we interrupting something?" Thaena's voice echoed the sound a mausoleum door might make as it scraped against a tomb floor.

Silence lingered on the hillside for several awkward beats before people realized the Goddess of Death had asked a question to which she expected an answer.

Empress Tyentso rose. "I believe the High Council were trying to murder me, my lady."

"And us as well, Mother." Teraeth shrugged at Tyentso. "They wouldn't have wanted witnesses, Ty."

"Oh, good point."

"Now this was all a misunderstanding—" Vornel Wenora stood.

"Silence!" Khored thundered. All sound stopped, everywhere. Even the background noises faded into quiet. "Vol Karoth has woken. An evil you have forgotten, but if he is not re-imprisoned, an evil you will come to know too well."

"Every time this has happened before," Argas explained. "Quur's emperor has been given the job to re-imprison him."

"In fact, this duty is the sole reason Quur exists."[6] Ompher's voice wasn't loud and was, strangely, much less rocklike than Thaena's, but it reverberated through the ground, all around them, all at once. The god looked toward Atrine then, frowning. In the distance, a grinding noise echoed, but no one dared look away from the Immortals to see the source.[7]

[4] And, sadly, still cannot.

[5] I admit it offends my sensibilities that the official title for the Immortals doesn't line up with the actual head count. But then I can't very well call them the Seven Immortals, can I?

[6] Not technically true, but given the circumstances, I felt it unwise to correct an angry god on a matter of semantics.

[7] Ompher repaired Demon Falls. Nice of him, all things considered.

Every eye on the clearing shifted, from the gods to Tyentso.

She swallowed and stood a little straighter.

"If you would prefer someone else to be your champion . . . ," Vornel Wenora began to say, "we'll make your will done. Happily."

Thaena said, "We are satisfied with Tyentso, but less so with what we've arrived to find. You orchestrated this, and you persuaded the others." Thaena's expression could have felled armies. "You are interfering with *the fate of the whole world.*"

"I was protecting–"

"Look into my eyes," Thaena ordered.

Vornel met the goddess's stare. He didn't hold it for more than a second before he looked away, shuddering.

Thaena made a gesture then, like brushing away a cobweb.

Vornel Wenora fell down–dead.

The Goddess of Death turned to Nevesi Oxun. "Have I made my point?"

The whites of the councilman's eyes formed a ring around his irises. "Yes, goddess."

Khored turned to the crowd. "This is not the time for coups or rebellions."

The Goddess of Luck added, "Nor invasions. We shall not be sending the Quuros army south into the Manol Jungle. This time, our emperor will serve us best by fortifying the empire."

"Do what you must to end the Royal Houses' squabbling," Thaena said. "It tires us."

Thurvishar exhaled. The Royal Houses might not appreciate several ways their infighting might cease. Tombs were seldom political hot spots, after all. And Tyentso might prefer that solution.

The empress bowed her head. "I will, my lady."

"And one . . . last . . . thing." Tya stepped forward, speaking for the first time. She addressed the Academy wizards and the witchhunters. "I have also grown tired of something."

Janel's eyes widened at the expression on her mother's face.

"We have let you rule yourselves as you will," Tya said, "but humanity's need has become too great for us to overlook your foolishness anymore. We have no time for this." Her expression wasn't kind. "Congratulations, you have succeeded in eliminating the witch threat, because this day forward, they don't exist. *Witches* no longer exist. I am changing the definition. No more licenses. No more persecuting wild talents. Anyone who can touch the Veil will be allowed to do so, regardless of sex or lineage."

The confusion and disbelief in the wizards spiked so strongly, Thurvishar heard their thoughts even through any talismans or protections.

No one protested out loud, but a stubborn defiance rose up. Eliminating the license system would destroy the Royal Houses, defenestrate the witchhunters, cause confusion and anxiety for the Academy. The Royal Houses depended on their magical monopolies to survive. What the Goddess of Magic had just declared . . . it might not break them right away, but the time would come. If anyone could use magic, *any* magic, without fees, restrictions, or fear of the accusation of witchcraft, then the Court of Gems would soon find itself unnecessary.

The Royal Houses wouldn't accept such a change, even if the Goddess of Magic herself flew down from the heavens and ordered it–which she had.

"Disobey us at your peril," Thaena warned. "We have no more patience or time. Our next meeting will not be so friendly."

With that final warning given, the light flashed again. The gods vanished.

As did Thurvishar, Kihrin, Janel, and Teraeth.

They reappeared in a wondrous locale. The cavern loomed so large, Thurvishar didn't recognize the space at first. In the massive chamber's center hung a fiery orange ball, while islands floated in a plane around that central pivot. The entire group, eleven in all, had appeared on the second island, large enough to hold ten times their number. Seven chairs had been set on the ground, not in a circle as one might expect but in a random pattern. A translucent sphere of red, violet, and green energy encased this floating island. Still more glowing notations hung in the air between the islands, floating in circles around them, not labels as much as mathematical formula.

Thurvishar looked again. The islands varied in size. A scree of boulders and rocks wrapped crosswise around the floating island like a bracelet. Past that marker, small fiery dots moved beyond, embedded in a *rotating* cavern wall. It was, he realized, a sort of mechanism, the heavens' movements modeled in abyssal stone.

As Thurvishar looked around in astonishment, the seven Immortals fanned out over the space. Some sat. They all looked tense and anxious and even frightened. The mortals remained standing, although Kihrin looked like he was contemplating turning invisible and jumping.

It was . . . uncomfortable . . . to be so close to these beings. Like sticking his fingers too close to fire, too close to ice, against a blade's edge, the sparking arc of lightning–all at the same time. The tenyé snap felt so strong, Thurvishar presumed the Immortals could only gather for any length of time in a place like this, clearly Argas's sanctified ground just as Ynisthana had once been Thaena's.

Thaena turned to her son and demanded, *"What happened?"*

Before he could answer, Janel fell to her knees. "It's my fault, my lady. I should have seen through Relos Var's trickery."

Thurvishar's mouth twisted. He knew a great many high lords who couldn't see through Relos Var's trickery. High lords and–as he gazed around the figures standing on the island–at least eight gods.[8]

Kihrin scoffed. "Now hold on. Did you smash Vol Karoth's prison open and then lose Urthaenriel? Because I remember it happening differently."

Janel's posture tightened.

Thaena's eyes flashed as she motioned for Janel to stand. So much as glancing in the goddess's direction filled Thurvishar with a deep and profound dread. Never had her existence seemed more a promise. Thaena's body vibrated with an anger barely held in check.

Meanwhile Taja, Goddess of Luck, picked up a chair, walked forward several steps, then flipped the chair around and sat on it backward. Argas scowled as if she'd just handed him a personal insult. "Must you?"[9]

"I don't care whose fault it is," Taja announced, ignoring Argas's reproach. "What a shocking idea. Relos Var tricking someone into doing the dirty work for him. I'm so surprised." She put a hand to her cheek.

Galava, flowers blooming as she paced, gave Taja a reproving look. "This is no time for jokes, child." She stopped as Ompher approached, not walking so much as sliding along the ground, and put his arms around her.

"He's not free," Teraeth murmured. "Not yet."

Kihrin said, "I felt him wake. I *felt* it."

"Awake isn't the same as *free*." Khored removed his red helmet, revealing himself as a black-skinned Manol vané underneath. "Vol Karoth is still trapped in the center of the Blight."

*"For how long?"* Thaena's voice boomed through the great and echoing chamber. "How long when we know Relos Var is working to shatter the other seven crystals and let Vol Karoth loose on the world? How long when we know that bastard has Urthaenriel?" She cast a hateful stare at Kihrin. "Well done, by the way. Did you just hand the sword over, or did he have to make an effort?"

Kihrin flinched.

"Stars," Taja said. "You are *such* a bitch when you're frightened."

Thaena whirled to face her, eyes blazing.

The tension vibrated in the air, clung to the nerves like ice crystals.

8 Yes, eight. I include S'arric here, whose naïveté regarding his brother's treachery landed us into this mess in the first place. I'm sorry, Kihrin, but it's true.

9 I suspect the chairs were in some special order, one I didn't have time enough to study and discern during our brief visit. This smacked of a long-standing grudge.

Thurvishar had never seen gods fight before; he never wanted to. They seemed to be seconds from open violence.

"I'm terrified," Tya admitted. She wrapped her veils around her, eyes far away. "Vol Karoth killed us so easily, as powerful as we are, and it was *nothing* to him." The Goddess of Magic stared at Kihrin. "We didn't know what had happened, you see. All we knew was that something had gone wrong–a giant, cataclysmic explosion. And then . . . there he was. A hole in the universe. He knew just what to do. He killed Taja first, then Galava and Thaena . . ."

Galava made a small, hurt noise and grabbed Ompher's hand.

"Enough." Thaena's voice sounded tight and strained.

Argas shook his head. "It's different this time." The god studied Kihrin. "You being here, now, makes it different. We're not the ones who can destroy Vol Karoth. You are. We just need to buy you enough time to do it."

"Me? I can't imagine–"

"You and I, we used to be friends," Argas gestured toward the two goddesses who had nearly come to blows, Taja and Thaena. "Did either of them tell you how the two of us were friends?"

"No, I–" Kihrin's gaze narrowed. "Wait. I *do* know you. Not from some past life either. How do I know you?"

Argas grinned. "Used to come by the Veil to check in on you when you were a kid."

It was Taja's turn to glare. "Damn it, Argas. We had this conversation! You promised you'd stay away from him."

Argas's laughter was mocking. "*You* promised. I just didn't bother correcting you."

Kihrin sighed and ground a thumb into his temple. His voice low, he muttered, "I'd make a joke about the parents fighting, but . . ."

Thurvishar contemplated Janel and Teraeth. "But for some of us, it happens to be true."

"Yeah," Kihrin agreed.

"So what's the plan now?" Teraeth said, trying to turn the conversation back to something living on the same continent as productive. "The Ritual of Night?"

Taja and Khored both shared a look.

"That can't be necessary," Taja said.

"It's been *necessary* for every other race," Galava said. "And it's necessary this time too."

"The ritual's never been anything but a delaying action–" Khored started to say.

"It's different now," Argas said. "Vol Karoth is different. He's weaker now." He pointed to Kihrin. "This might be the first time where destroying him is possible, but not if he escapes before we can figure out a way. We have to keep him locked up. Just a little bit longer will do."

"What," Janel asked, "is the Ritual of Night?"

"It's the ritual that turns an immortal race mortal," Thurvishar answered. "Four immortal races used to exist, and now only the vané remain. That's because the ritual has been used three times before, each time to repair Vol Karoth's prison before he could free himself."

"Oh."

"We need breathing room," Thaena said. "And I mean to have it. It's long past time the vané paid–"

All seven gods stopped whatever they'd been doing, or had been about to say, and looked up and to the side. As if they all stared at the same object, something the mortals in the room couldn't see.

"How long before the demons breach into the Land of Peace?" Khored asked.

"Ninety-eight percent chance they don't move in for another five minutes," Taja said, "and then an 86 percent chance they rush the Chasm."[10]

"My people are there," Thaena said, "but they won't hold for long."

"Then we're out of time," Argas agreed.

Tya turned to Janel. "We won't be able to provide support. With Vol Karoth's awakening, the demons have retreated from their Hellmarches–it made them too easy to find–but they're laying siege to the Land of Peace, trying to reach the Font of Souls. Don't expect us to be in any position to come to your aid."

Janel's expression darkened. Thurvishar reminded himself to ask for a detailed explanation later.[11]

"If the Font falls," Galava said, "our future dies with it."

Thaena's mien turned nasty as she addressed her son Teraeth. "Terindel should have done his duty millennia ago. Since he wouldn't, it's your job to ensure his nephew Kelanis does."

Thurvishar looked away. It would be the final tragic act in a play that had taken four thousand years to unfold. The vané would become mortal; the last great race would die. Yes, it would buy them time, but . . . well, it would be time paid for at a horrendous price.

"What if he says no?" Kihrin asked.

"He won't say no," Thaena answered. "He won't dare. I've guaran-

[10] I'm fascinated by this, since I would have expected Argas to be the one citing numerical statistics. But perhaps this is Taja's realm because they are *odds,* never mind the mathematics involved.

[11] Evidently, there is a single location in the Afterlife that is a wellspring for souls–both new and reincarnated–on their way to the Living World. One presumes that without it, reincarnation would be impossible and death a much more permanent affair.

teed that. I removed your mother from the throne so there wouldn't be a repeat of Terindel's sin."

"Right." Taja's smile was equal parts bitter and sad. "So at least that part should be easy."

Kihrin studied the goddess for a moment, expression uncertain, before he turned to the others. "I hate to be the person pointing out the soup's cold, but are we the best choice for this? For example, I'm pretty sure Teraeth is the only one who speaks vané."

*"Voral,"* Tya corrected absently. "The vané and the voras always spoke the same language."

"See?" Kihrin said. "I don't know even the right name for the language."

Argas grinned. "I'll fix that."

# 2: The Wounded Sky

*Kihrin sat back and exhaled.*

*"You do have to talk, you realize," Thurvishar said. "Unless you'd rather I just continued. I'm fine either way."*

*"Just thinking how funny it is that I never want to start where everyone else does." Kihrin chewed on his lip, eyes distant.*

*"Where would you start?" Thurvishar asked.*

*Kihrin drummed his fingers on a stack of papers, formulas for some arcane bit of mathematics almost no one in the whole world comprehended anymore. Although–no, that wasn't right. The dreth probably taught classes in it somewhere.*

*"The Blight," Kihrin said.*

*Thurvishar closed his eyes, opened them again. "Because everything starts and ends there?"*

*"At least it does for me," Kihrin answered.*

### (Kihrin's story)

I opened my eyes. Sulfur-laced clouds overhead, battling across a wounded sky. A sick, dull pain throbbed inside my head, so it took a moment to realize it wasn't my imagination; I was lying down while the world lurched past me. The air smelled rotten and tasted sharp, acids layered like fine mist making my eyes water and my throat choke. The humidity made my clothing and hair stick to my body. In the distance, an insistent croon beckoned.

As soon as I saw those clouds, my pulse soared and the throb worsened. I knew where we were, and it had been a long time since this had been a place that knew any joy.

I sat up and looked around. I had been tossed into a slowly moving wagon. Next to me lay three people, all still unconscious: Teraeth, Janel, and Thurvishar.[1] Our kidnappers hadn't even bothered to change our

[1] What Kihrin actually said here was "Teraeth, Janel, and *you,*" but I thought that might be

clothing from the ornate stuff we'd been wearing when we had been ambushed, although they'd taken our weapons.

Two animals pulled the wagon. Nothing I recognized–some ungulate with striped hindquarters.[2] Since no one held the reins, every few steps, they paused to nip at the grass, which is why we'd been traveling the same speed as a land-bound starfish. Mind you, there was no grass to nip–just thorny bush and slick, gelatinous slime. It all looked inedible. It was all likely toxic.[3]

"Taja!" I shouted what could only laughably be called a prayer to my favorite goddess before I stopped myself.

She wasn't going to show herself. Not here. Not this close to where a now wide-awake Vol Karoth cracked his knuckles, preparing for round two. The Manol Jungle had been the closest the Eight had been willing to travel, and even then they'd taken a risk. We were on our own.

I shook the others. "Wake up. Wake up, damn it."

Janel roused first, to my surprise. I suppose the fact it was daytime helped. Waking her was impossible at night.[4] She rubbed her eyes before she reached for weapons she didn't have anymore. "What happened? Where are we?"

Before I could answer, Teraeth woke, followed by Thurvishar.

I took quick stock of our very fancy, very useless wagon: no food or water. Which meant whoever had put us here hadn't intended on us surviving the experience. "At a guess, I'm going to suggest someone in the vané court wasn't so keen to let us talk to the king." I rubbed my forehead. "How did they get us?"

"Poisoned darts." Teraeth looked offended over the whole matter. He offered Janel a hand; she stared at him oddly as she ignored the offer and clambered from the wagon, followed by Thurvishar.

Teraeth pulled his hand back.

"Do we have any idea who's responsible?" Janel hesitated. "It wasn't the king, was it?"

"If Kelanis had been involved, I rather doubt he'd have smuggled us from the palace in secret," Thurvishar said. "Our kidnappers took care to avoid being seen."

We paused.

---

confusing under the circumstances, so I've edited out any second-person references from here on out.

[2] Okapi, or some relative thereof.

[3] Exceedingly so. There are a rather astonishing array of poisons and toxins to be found in the Korthaen Blight.

[4] Because her souls travel to the Afterlife when she sleeps at night.

"You were . . . conscious?" Teraeth's question wasn't idle considering Thurvishar's skills at magic.

Thurvishar pretended to find a spot on his silk robe. "No. Kihrin can tell you; I don't react to drugs in what you might consider a typical fashion. I experienced periods of near lucidity. That doesn't mean I was *coherent*."

"So who dumped us here?" Teraeth gestured around us. His voice sounded rough.

"Vané?" Thurvishar said. "I don't remember much. One of them was a woman with blue hair."

"Queen Miyane?" Teraeth looked over at me as if I had any way to confirm the guess.

I felt a sting in my throat that had nothing to do with the air. "Or my mother. She has blue hair too."[5]

My answer made everyone pause. Khaeriel's whereabouts were unknown and she'd been notoriously opposed to ever performing the Ritual of Night when she'd ruled the vané. Now that she'd escaped enslavement, I expected her to try to retake her throne. She probably had allies and contacts in the royal palace. Enough, perhaps, to ambush the messengers sent to see the Ritual of Night completed.

"If your mother did this"–Teraeth gestured to our surroundings–"then you may need to reassess your relationship. Putting us here is tantamount to a death sentence."

"Literally so," Thurvishar said. "I believe the vané call this the Traitor's Walk."

I exhaled. "I can't discount the possibility that yes, she did this. A child she never knew versus her own immortality? Maybe that wasn't even a hard choice."

"We'll have time for finger-pointing later," Janel said. "Right now, we have bigger problems: food, water, surviving for long enough to make it back to civilization. Any civilization. This *is* the Korthaen Blight, isn't it?" She looked around, at least as much as she could, given the cracked, craggy terrain.

"Pretty sure." I gave Janel a curious look. I had expected Teraeth and Thurvishar to recognize our location. But Janel? She'd never been to the Blight before, but only in *this* lifetime. In her last lifetime, she'd embarked on a rather epic quest into this region.

She was starting to remember.

I knew the Blight because I'd been here once before a few years

[5] In point of fact, she didn't by this time, but Kihrin had no way to know that. Hair color isn't much of an alibi for a race that can alter their appearance so swiftly, in any regard.

earlier, when I'd transported myself to the ruined city of Kharas Gulgoth, where Vol Karoth's prison lay. Once was enough; I'd know those clouds and burning tang in the air anywhere. I'd survived before because three of the Immortals had personally shown up to escort me back out. That wasn't going to happen this time.

Teraeth picked up a rock and threw it in frustration. "Oh, this is absolutely the Korthaen Blight. Damn it. I'm wondering if the king even knew we'd arrived to see him." The pack animals still wandered from scrub bush to scrub bush, forcing everyone to walk after the wagon if we didn't want to lose it.

"Perhaps not," Thurvishar said, "but he soon will. I'll open a gate and return us to the Capital. Once there, we can contact the Eight again and decide how to handle this next. Does that sound reasonable?"

There was a beat of silence. Then I realized Thurvishar was waiting for us to give him permission.[6] "Yeah. Great idea. Do it."

"Please," Janel added. She looked down at her red silk outfit with obvious exasperation. "Why couldn't they have waited for us to be dressed properly before drugging us and dumping us out here?"

The vané had been hospitable. That was the galling thing. No one had ever said, "No, go away." They had instead welcomed us in; insisted we would see the king as soon as he returned to the Capital; and that in the meantime, we needed appropriate clothing for the court. At which point they'd spent the next week or so throwing sumptuous attire at us, mostly so we could wear something nice at all the parties they'd invited us to attend.

Janel's outfit resembled traditional western Quuros attire, but only to someone who'd never seen traditional West Quuros attire. So while she wore a raisigi, hers clasped tightly around her breasts and then fell in panels of transparent silk, which deepened from orange to dark crimson. Her kef pants had panels missing at the hips joined by a thin chain of interlocking gold salamanders. The outfit didn't even faintly resemble outdoor attire, although at least she wore boots.

That was better than Teraeth or I could claim. We wore sandals, in addition to silk vané robes so thin I found myself glad the fashion required layering them.[7] The only reason Teraeth wore anything that could be described as more than "formal jewelry" was because he'd wanted to make sure he could conceal all his knives.

Teraeth sighed. "At least the silk is worth a fortune."

"I'd rather be naked and still have my sword," Janel said.

[6] When one has grown up knowing that disobeying an order means death, certain instincts become quite difficult to break.

[7] In fact, the layering is optional. The vané don't seem to have nudity taboos.

Thurvishar held out his hands as he began casting the complicated spell that would get us out of this death trap. I wasn't surprised our would-be killers–whoever they were–had assumed we wouldn't be able to escape the Blight. There weren't more than a hundred people in the whole world powerful enough to open freestanding gates–and most of those were god-kings. I can count the number of mortals who can pull off that trick on my hands with fingers left over.[8]

Fortunately for us, Thurvishar was one of those people. Dumping us into the Blight without food, water, or weapons would have been fatal if we'd been stuck there.

Except nothing was happening.

"Um, Thurvishar?" I cleared my throat to catch his attention.

He stopped moving his fingers. "That . . . didn't work. Let me try this again–"

"Thurvishar, look up." Janel's voice sounded soft and urgent.

I looked up too. The clouds above our heads had turned from sickly yellow brown to silver gray, flickering with rainbow colors: reds, greens, violets.[9] The clouds seemed to be boiling.

"What the hell is–?" Janel started to say.

"I know that sky." Teraeth's eyes widened. "Everyone under the wagon! *Under the wagon right now!*"

Janel grabbed the nearest person–Thurvishar–and pushed him down. At the same time, Teraeth yanked me down. I didn't need the incentive, but I was happy to take all the help I could as I scrambled under cover.

Something thumped to the ground nearby. A second sound followed the first, then another, until it echoed like violent rain.

"What–" I turned my head to look.

A sword slammed into the ground, point first, impaling itself. A dagger sank down next to it, vibrating. Then another. Not all the weapons fell point first, but anyone outside without cover could expect to be bludgeoned or stabbed to death in short order. As if to punctuate the point, animal screams rang out, cut mercifully short.[10] Metallic sounds rang out all around as weapons crashed into metal already on the ground.

"Swords?" I said. "It's raining *swords*?" I remembered Morios, the dragon Janel had slain, but he'd breathed clouds of wind-whipped metal, more like razor-tipped metal shards. These were actual, honest-to-gods swords, complete with wire-wrapped pommels, cross guards, and blood grooves.

[8] Kihrin does know rather a lot of people powerful enough to open gates, though, doesn't he?

[9] Tya's colors. I find that fascinating.

[10] It's fortunate they'd died quickly, before they could bolt and drag the wagon away from us.

"This time," Teraeth agreed. "At least it's not raining acid."

"Or poisonous spiders," Thurvishar added. "I've read an account–"[11]

"Yes, you read *my* account–"[12]

"Kihrin!" Janel grabbed my misha and pulled me toward her, just as a sword found its way through a crack in the wagon's wooden floor and sliced all the way down. It missed me by the finest of margins.

It also meant I was pressed against Janel, which, to be honest, wasn't unpleasant at all. Janel seemed to realize how provocative the new position was the same time I did and started to smile.

"Are you hurt?" Teraeth asked.

I looked back over my shoulder, past the sword, and met Teraeth's eyes. He looked scared, which wasn't an expression I remembered ever seeing on his face before.

Teraeth's worry shook me out of any temptation to flirt. I let out a small prayer to my goddess, even though I knew it wouldn't do any good.

Taja was *busy*. Or hiding.

I'm not sure which idea bothered me more.

[11] Atrin Kandor brought troops into the Korthaen Blight the last time Vol Karoth woke. And then took them right back out again.

[12] Yes, I suppose I had forgotten Teraeth actually is the reincarnation of Atrin Kandor.

# 3: Witch Hunt

*Thurvishar paused, looking over the account, then set it aside. "I'm not sure where I want to start next."*

*"What about Senera?" Kihrin asked, grinning.*

*"I'm sorry?" Thurvishar narrowed his eyes and didn't seem amused.*

*"Senera. You know . . . white skin, black heart? I don't see the appeal personally, but . . ." Kihrin leaned over the table toward Thurvishar. "You like the color black a lot more than I do."*

*"I have no idea what you mean," Thurvishar said stiffly. "Anyway, I don't have an account from Senera for how her part in this began."*

*Kihrin laughed and sang out, "I don't belieeeve you."*

*"It's true." Thurvishar waited for a moment under Kihrin's intense scrutiny, then sighed and reached for a different sheaf of papers. "To have a complete version, we must start with Talea."*

### *(Talea's story)*

The ground began to shake rhythmically.

Talea pulled a spear from the Forgurogh clan soldier who had been foolish enough to think running at her screaming obscenities would somehow make him impervious to damage. She stepped over his body and locked stares with Bikeinoh, another Spurned. The Yoran woman looked every bit as confused as Talea.

"What is that?" Talea asked.

The older woman shrugged.

The meeting had gone wrong almost from the start, turning into an ambush. Xivan Kaen, Duchess of Yor, had been trying to deal with the Yoran clans declaring independence after her husband's disappearance and presumed death, but there were problems. Three problems, specifically. One, the clans hated the fact that Xivan Kaen wasn't a native Yoran. Two, Xivan was a woman, and Yoran men were apparently delicate snow flowers who didn't know how to handle being given orders by a woman. And lastly, Xivan Kaen was dead.

Under normal circumstances, none of these issues were insurmountable.[1]

But the Forgurogh clan had been sheltering the god-queen Suless. Xivan had hoped they might parlay and convince the clan to give Suless up. In hindsight, they should have expected the ambush.[2]

The ground continued to shake. A head peeked out from behind the snow-covered rocks of the icy pass where they had arranged the meeting. That blue-white, bearded head was roughly the size of an entire polar bear. The body attached to that head scaled proportionately. And he wielded a whole pine tree torn up by the roots.

"Ice giant!" Bikeinoh called out. "Gods, I didn't think were any still left alive."

Talea noted the creature's dried flesh and desiccated eyes, the cheekbones and skull fragments visible under rotted flesh. "I'm pretty sure there still aren't. Run!"

The giant moved in slow, ponderous strides, but it also made the ground jump with each step. When it swung that tree, it didn't have to be accurate. Even the Forgurogh ran before the indiscriminate attack. It made zero attempt to sort friend from foe, or more likely, to an animated ice giant corpse, everyone qualified as foe.

Spurned arrows sank into its chest to no effect.

"Save your arrows!" Talea screamed. Something had to be done. But what? Trip it?

That didn't seem completely ridiculous. Cutting the tendons on its feet might slow it down, depending on how it had been enchanted or possessed by a demon. There was only one way to find out.

Just then, a figure emerged from the southern cliffs flanking the pass: Xivan. The woman made a running leap at the ice giant. She sailed through the air in a perfect arc before landing on the giant's back, just behind his neck. Xivan held a long black sword in one hand, which she raised to the side and swung in a slashing motion. Although the sword hadn't started out long enough to decapitate the ice giant in a single pass, by the time Xivan finished, the blade had more than doubled in length. It cut through the giant's dead flesh and bone as if the creature were made from goose feathers and children's rhymes.

Xivan rode the giant's body down to the ground, jumping off just before the fall made the entire pass shake. The black sword–Godslayer, Urthaenriel, whatever one called the cursed thing–returned to an acceptable length as Xivan sheathed it.

[1] To be fair, that last one would be a deal-breaker for most people.

[2] Suless is the god-queen of treachery and betrayal. So yes. Yes, you should have.

The Yoran duchess brushed an imaginary snowflake from her cloak and walked in Talea's direction.

She always took Talea's breath away. Of course, most people wouldn't have agreed. Xivan's appearance varied widely. Her dark Khorveshan skin either looked as dried as old leather or like that of a young maiden spending just a little too long out in the snow–sweetly red-cheeked–depending on how recently she'd fed. She wore her dark curls matted into locks held back by silver clasps. Her eyes were white. That last bit was the only part of her appearance that looked Yoran, if for all the wrong reasons.

"Report," Xivan said to Talea as she walked past her lieutenant to the meeting site, now littered with bodies.

"Casualties still to be determined," Talea said, "but we did capture Chief Mazagra.[3] We brought him here for you to question."

"Any sign of the Bitch Queen?"

Xivan meant the god-queen Suless. She almost never called the goddess her real name. To be fair, "Bitch Queen" was one of Suless's actual titles, but Xivan meant it with a lot less respect than the average Yoran devotee.

Talea shook her head. "No, none, but I'd be surprised if she wasn't watching."

They'd been forced to take a keen interest in all the old stories, god-king tales, and fables about Suless. They'd learned to take those stories at face value. Yes, Suless could enchant minds. Yes, Suless could steal souls. Yes, Suless could use wild animals–the crows and the snow hyenas, the white foxes and ice bears–as her spies. They couldn't afford to underestimate the goddess.

"I would also be surprised," Xivan admitted, casually making a rude gesture to the tree line for emphasis. She paused before the tent where the meeting would have occurred if the other side had played the situation honorably. Arrows riddled the fur-covered oilcloth canvas, which was also on fire. Xivan walked past that raging inferno until she reached a woman holding down a screaming man dressed in furs and hardened leather armor. Other women raised shields over him to protect him from arrow fire.

The Spurned had assumed Mazagra's own men would be perfectly willing to kill their leader to keep him from falling into enemy hands.

"Stop struggling," Xivan ordered, "or I'll tell Nezessa to break your arms. She wouldn't have to try hard."

True enough. Nezessa was their strongest member.

[3] A minor Yoran clan leader. I have no particular records on him.

The Forgurogh clan chief looked at Xivan with disgust and spat to the side. "I have nothing to say to you, whore."

"Oh, that's not true," Xivan said. "For example, you *will* tell me where Suless went." She crouched next to the chieftain, settling back on her heels. "Let me be clear, Mazagra–I don't need you to tell me. I'll find out on my own. All we're deciding here is whether or not I exterminate your entire clan as an object lesson to the others."

His eyes widened. "You wouldn't dare."

"What stories has Suless told you?" Xivan laughed. "Did she say I was weak? Did she tell you I was soft? That I would go easy on you because my soldiers are women?"

Talea laughed at that one. So did all the Spurned nearby.

"My husband, Azhen, destroyed an entire clan once," Xivan continued, "and I can't help but remember how effective that tactic proved. People took him much more seriously afterward. Are you volunteering to be that example? People will be whispering about what happened to the Forgurogh clan for years."

He flinched. Talea noticed and knew he would break long before Xivan lost her nerve. And she knew Xivan had noticed as well.

"You don't know what she'll do!" Mazagra said. "She's our goddess. You can't defy a goddess!"

"Watch me." Xivan stood up again and walked off to the side.

Talea followed. "What do you want to do with the clan?"

Xivan scowled. "Azhen had such plans for these people. He wanted to show them a better way than all this senseless violence, this belief only the strong can rule the weak. He wanted Yorans to become better than the barbarians the rest of Quur thinks they are. And for that, they hated him."

"Yes, Your Grace." Talea had her own opinions about the duke, but she kept them to herself. Maybe Azhen Kaen had been different once, before Suless had gotten her claws into him. Xivan remembered some younger, more vibrant Azhen Kaen when she reminisced about her husband, but Talea had never known that duke.

But maybe she wasn't giving him a fair chance. Talea didn't always understand the nuances of Yoran culture. On the other hand, she didn't think the Yorans more barbaric than the Quuros.

Rather, she thought the Yorans were amateurs at the game by comparison.

Xivan noted Talea's expression. "I'm whining again, aren't I?"

Talea grinned. "Not at all, Your Grace." Her expression sobered. "But the clan?"

Xivan sighed. "Oh, I suppose we have to prove the Yorans right. Rule is only for the strong and only through fear." She waved a hand contemptuously. "Kill all the men. Let the women and children go with a warning we'll do the same to any clan who shelters the Bitch Queen. Let the word spread."[4]

Talea's stomach clenched. She'd known from the start this would be the answer, but she didn't like it. "Yes, Your Grace."

"Oh, don't give me that look. I know you don't approve. I don't approve either. But maybe if we kill a few more now, fewer will have to die later."

Talea said nothing.

Xivan stared at her. "Out with it."

"I just wish we were better than this. Better than what the Quuros Empire would do. I hate we're doing the exact same thing–solving our problems with a sword's edge."

Xivan's flat, unwavering stare made Talea lift her chin defensively. "I didn't mean to imply you're not doing a good job, Your Grace."

"You don't need to imply it. Go right ahead and say it. It happens to be true. I wish I knew a better way." Xivan unbuckled her sword belt and passed it, sword included, to Talea. "Hold this for me. The fight made me hungry."

Wordlessly, Talea buckled Urthaenriel around her waist. She hated the damn thing, but she also appreciated the honor of being entrusted to carry it when Xivan could not. For example, Xivan couldn't carry Godslayer and feed at the same time. She couldn't even be near Urthaenriel and feed at the same time. Using magic near the sword was impossible, and Xivan's vampiric soul-devouring qualified.

Xivan started to turn back toward the clan chief, undoubtedly first on the menu, but then paused. "Oh. And, Talea? Find Relos Var. I need him."

"Yes, Your Grace. Right away." Talea hurried off, grateful Xivan had provided an excuse to leave before the slaughter began.

[4] It seems uncharacteristic for a Khorveshan woman to spare other women for any typically clichéd reason. Certainly she wouldn't have done so under a belief they needed protection. It's far more likely she was playing to misogynistic Yoran attitudes regarding the sanctity of motherhood.

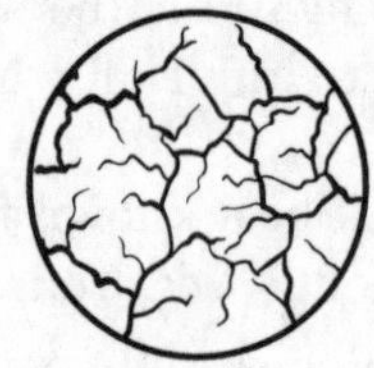

# 4: The Korthaen Blight

*Kihrin was grinning when Thurvishar took a break.*

*"Stop," Thurvishar told him.*

*"I didn't say a word!" Kihrin protested. "Anyway, it's funny about the sword."*

*Thurvishar regarded him and waited.*

*"Urthaenriel's always been silver when I've held it, but for Xivan? Black. Curious, don't you think?"*

*Thurvishar looked thoughtful. "I suppose you're right. That is odd. Perhaps it's the sword's way of commenting on Xivan's status as an undead being."*

*"Wouldn't the sword be white, then?"*

*Thurvishar pressed his lips together and didn't answer.*

*"Anyway, I'll continue."*

***(Kihrin's story)***

When the "rain" stopped and we climbed back out from under the battered wagon, metal weapons littered the ground. Sword, spears, daggers, every kind of knife. The two pack animals–whatever they'd been[1]–now resembled butchered meat.

I turned to Janel. "Could you complain about not having any food or water next?"

She smacked my arm. "It doesn't work that way."

"How will we know unless we try?" I picked up a sword. "Do the weapons just . . . stay?" The weapon seemed surprisingly well made. I wouldn't have felt stupid buying such a sword at market. Of course, the cursed sky had only dropped blades on our heads, not scabbards. Carrying the damn thing safely was going to be a challenge.

"No," Janel said, "but they'll last for a few days. Long enough for us to escape the Blight."

"How would you know?" Teraeth twisted his mouth. "Was this something you learned from Xaltorath?"

[1] Still okapi.

Janel gave the man a sideways stare. "If you must know, I'm starting to remember my last life."

Teraeth swallowed and looked away. Abandoning the conversation, he removed a thin silk robe he'd been wearing and bent down by the two slaughtered pack beasts. He began scavenging meat, butchering further when necessary.

Honestly, I'm glad he'd thought of it. Who knew how many days would pass before we could make our way out? This might prove to be our only food.

"So no gates," Thurvishar said. "Noted."

"That's not normal," I said. "That definitely didn't happen the last time."

Janel shrugged. "The last time, Vol Karoth was still asleep."

I exhaled. She had a point.

"What does that mean?" Thurvishar asked. "Vol Karoth is changing the laws of magic?"

"Not exactly," Teraeth said. "Try looking past the First Veil." He looked apologetic. "Sorry I didn't warn you. I haven't been back here in this lifetime."

Thurvishar concentrated. A moment later, he made a low noise and shut his eyes, as if he'd caught himself looking into the sun. "Veils," Thurvishar cursed. "What was that?"

"Vol Karoth's corruption," Teraeth answered. "Now, the last time I journeyed here–in *my* last life–I wielded Urthaenriel, which stopped me from looking past the First Veil myself. But I'd brought other wizards with me, and they never stopped complaining. Vol Karoth distorts the magic for miles around. No one should use magic." He gave Janel a significant stare.

She scowled. "You mean my strength."

"I mean your strength."

Janel paced back and forth, hands clenching and unclenching, as if psyching herself up for a fight. "Well, I'm going to try something–*not using my strength*–so everyone be prepared to dive back under the wagon."

"What are you going to do?" Teraeth seemed prepared to give a lecture on weapon safety. "This is not the time to experiment."

She ignored him as she bent down over the pack animals' remains. Janel scooped up a gory handful and dipped her braided laevos[2] hair into the blood.

[2] A *laevos* is a traditional Joratese hairstyle that mimics the horse manes–a single strip of hair across the top of the head. It's considered a mark of prestige if one can grow a laevos naturally, although most nobles probably shave and pretend they don't need to or, like Janel's family, pay an exorbitant fee to House D'Mon for a permanent modification.

I raised an eyebrow. "No, really. Mind explaining what you're doing?"

"Hold still," she told me as she approached. "I know, it's disgusting, but trust me."

"Always," I said.

Her ruby eyes softened as she smiled at me. Then she reached up and drew something on my forehead with the blood-soaked tip of her hair.

The air stopped scorching my throat.

"This is that sigil, isn't it? The one we used at the tavern?" I inhaled deeply. I'd personally experienced this sigil once before when Aeyan'arric the ice dragon had sealed off the tavern we'd been inside.[3] The smoke had down-drafted right back into our living space, and we couldn't leave since a dragon waited outside . . .

Janel looked up at the clouds, waiting. We all looked up.

Nothing happened.

"Good," Janel said. "Whatever is causing this doesn't seem to count the sigils as 'magic.'"

"Sigil?" Teraeth asked. "What sigil?"

"It's this glyph thing," I ever-so-helpfully explained. "It either conjures air or purifies what's there. I'm not sure which."

Thurvishar rubbed a knuckle against his chin. "Did Senera teach you that?"[4]

"Taught?" Janel laughed. "No. More like Qown–" She flinched, as though uttering the name itself hurt.[5] "We realized what she'd done and copied her. Now let's paint you two, and you can copy the mark to draw on me. I don't know how long it will last–likely until the symbol wears off. Given what I'm using for paint, not long."

"Perhaps we'll be able to make charcoal later, if we can find something to burn," Thurvishar agreed as she drew the sigil on his forehead.

"The cart will burn, but I don't feel like carrying planks with me," Teraeth said dryly.

"Stand still," Janel ordered. "You're too damn tall as it is." She painted the increasingly familiar glyph on Teraeth's forehead while resting one hand on his arm for balance.

Ever since I'd woken, I'd been hearing this low droning noise. Almost a croon. And it had been easy enough to ignore while we were all in fear for our lives, but now that we'd had a chance to catch our breaths, the noise became intolerable.

[3] Senera compiled a chronicle of those events. See the attached copy.

[4] I hadn't yet read Senera's account.

[5] She's referencing a Vishai priest named Qown, who has since sided with Relos Var. See Senera's account.

"Don't you hear that?" I asked.

They all stared at me blankly.

"Hear what?" Teraeth asked.

I pointed in the direction where I thought the noise originated. "That sound. It's like singing? A humming? Something. It's coming from over there."

"Uh, Kihrin . . . ?" Janel's voice sounded worried and far away.

I turned around. The other three all stood fifty feet away. I blinked. "Hey, why did you all walk . . . away . . . ?" The wagon sat right next to them, the dead pack animals, the deadly weapons on the ground. My friends hadn't moved.

I had.

I looked back toward the sound. I didn't remember walking toward it.

I heard footsteps. Teraeth took my arm. "Okay, then, let's get you back over here."

I'd apparently started walking again.

"What is happening?" I let Teraeth lead me back, but I could feel my feet trying to turn. The impulse to reverse course felt overwhelming.

"I don't know," Teraeth said, "but I don't like it. I'm going to be honest here—you're starting to scare me."

"Let's not go that way," I suggested as we returned to the others.

Janel raised her head. "Do you hear that?"

"Not you too," Teraeth said.[6]

She waved a hand at him, looking irritated. "No, not whatever Kihrin's hearing. *Listen.*"

I stopped, trying to ignore the crooning noise. Almost immediately, I heard distant shouts, yells, a low, graveled rumble.

"Battle," Janel said.

As soon as she labeled it, I heard it too—someone was fighting. Angry yells, shouted directions, the quick drum of running feet.

Janel picked up a metal javelin from the ground, balanced it in one hand, and grabbed a sword with the other. Then she jogged off in the direction of the fighting.

"Wait," Thurvishar called after her. "Shouldn't we try to find out what's going on first?" He turned to Teraeth and me for support.

"Janel, come back here right now!" Teraeth yelled after the woman.

She paid no attention.

"I could have told you that wasn't going to work," I said.

Teraeth gave her fading silhouette an exasperated stare. "Damn it, woman."

[6] In Teraeth's defense, I had the same reaction, wondering if whatever was affecting Kihrin might have been a perversion of the sigil magic Janel had used on us.

"We'd better follow." I immediately started doing so.

Teraeth grabbed my arm. "You're going the wrong way," he said.

I'd started walking toward the droning again. Even though I was breathing in clean air, I suddenly felt like I was choking on it. I had a terrible suspicion the noise had to be coming from the Blight's center, from Kharas Gulgoth, where Vol Karoth waited.

I nodded, feeling shaken, and let Teraeth lead me after Janel.

# 5: A Wizard, a Duchess, and a Soldier

***(Talea's story)***

A storm gathered in the west as the magical gate opened. That spiraling, glyph-filled portal settled into quicksilver glass, broken only as three people stepped through: two Quuros men and a white-skinned woman. Talea recognized all three: Relos Var, Qown, and Senera.

Qown and Senera were dressed for the cold weather, but Relos Var, just . . . ignored it. As if he didn't notice the frozen Yoran weather.

Relos Var always reminded Talea of a high lord. It didn't matter that she'd never once seen him dress like a royal or that his eyes were an entirely normal brown. Like most royals, he moved like he was the most important person in any space. Unlike most high lords Talea had ever known–oblivious to all the "lesser" servants and slaves around themselves–Relos Var always noticed her. Every time he observed her, she felt valued, appraised, measured.

And then dismissed, with the gentlest of smiles, as utterly inconsequential.

Talea possessed no illusions concerning her place in the grand scheme of things. She wasn't the child of a Royal House or a divinity. No prophecies mentioned her. She wasn't anyone's chosen hero and she would never, she knew, be a great leader. But she could *serve* a great leader and be proud to do so. That had to mean something.

Relos Var looking at her like that? It was just rude.[1]

The second man, red-cheeked from the cold, pulled his furs more tightly around himself. Relos Var's apprentice, Qown, stepped so far inside the other man's shadow, it was easy to miss his presence. The last person was Relos Var's former apprentice, the wizard Senera. One might be forgiven for thinking she was Yoran given her skin pallor. Whereas most Yorans were ice white, winter white, sometimes glacier blue or storm-cloud gray, Senera was the color of cream and fresh-churned butter. A legacy of her Doltari ancestry.

[1] Oh, Talea, I am not at all convinced you are inconsequential. Var is making a mistake to think so.

Talea waited, resting easily with one hand on Urthaenriel. She kept her distance from the magic portal. Talea didn't think Urthaenriel would disrupt a gate while sheathed, but why take the chance? She absolutely wasn't going to draw the damn thing. She'd done so once—just once—and had been nearly overwhelmed by the insatiable urge to kill every mage anywhere near.

A definition that included almost all the Spurned.

Once Senera had closed the gate, Talea stepped forward and gave the trio a short, respectful bow. "It's nice to see you again. Thank you for responding so quickly, Lord Var. The Hon is most eager to speak with you."

"Why, thank you." Relos Var was at least always polite. He eyed her with unusual wariness. "Where is she?"

She wasn't the cause of his unease, she realized at once. It was Urthaenriel.

"The main cavern," Talea answered. "I'll take you—"

Var turned on his heel and marched up the path toward the Spurned camp.

So much for always being polite.

After a moment's startled hesitation, Qown and Senera followed. Talea cheerfully fell in next to the white-haired wizard. "How is your puppy?[2] Did you give her the bones I sent you?"

Senera glanced at her sideways. ". . . she's fine, thank you."

"Oh, I'm glad to hear it. Things haven't been so great here. The parlay with the Forgurogh clan—they were sheltering Suless—didn't work out. Ambush. Suless animated a dead ice giant. So that was exciting. We had a few injuries, but no fatalities, so we were lucky there. Unlike the Forgurogh clan. Are you hungry? Do you need anything? I'm sure I could find you some tea . . . ?"

Senera turned back to Talea and raised a finger.

The soldier paused, head cocked to the side.

"Stop talking," Senera said.

"I was just being friendly." Talea didn't take Senera's rudeness personally. She'd known the woman for almost four years, and in all that time, Talea couldn't remember seeing Senera smile. The wizard struck Talea as desperately unhappy. That's why she'd been so happy to hear about the puppy.

In Talea's opinion, Senera was a woman in desperate need of a dog.

Qown cleared his throat. "I'd love some tea."

Talea widened her eyes in mock surprise. "But, Qown, I *assumed* you

[2] Rebel would be around four years old by this point? But I suppose Talea likes to think all dogs are "puppies."

would want tea." She winked at him and then stage-whispered, "In Senera's case, she also needs friends."

Senera's eyes narrowed. "I do *not.* Just take us to Kaen."

Talea grinned again and pointed after Relos Var. "That way. And everyone wants friends. Some people are just too stubborn to admit it, hmm?"

Senera stormed off, and Talea grabbed Qown's arm with her own. "Let's go find the tea. I don't suppose you brought any sunflower candy?"

Qown looked startled. "Oh no, there wasn't time to make any. I'm so sorry–"

Talea inclined her head toward him. "I'm teasing. But I did make the mistake of sharing the last batch you made, and now the other women won't stop bothering me. You do realize you're the only man who has an open invitation to come visit us anytime you want?"

Qown blushed adorably. "I didn't, I mean . . . I'd stopped making it. It was Janel's favorite. I didn't realize she'd been sharing it."

"For years now. It's like eating a sweet cloud." Talea's smile faltered for just a moment. She didn't know exactly how events fell out in Atrine, but parting with Janel after Suless destroyed the Ice Demesne had made it clear enough the Joratese knight wasn't coming back–another sin she laid at Relos Var's feet. Talea already missed her. "Anyway, we're here."

Inside the cave, Spurned prepared for the storm. They took storms seriously in Yor. Talea was probably the only member (outside of Xivan herself) who hadn't been trained in snowstorm survival techniques since childhood. Everyone else was stacking firewood, gathering supplies, preparing sleeping areas in the back.

Xivan Kaen stopped her conversation with Bikeinoh when Relos Var entered. In the dim lighting, few would notice anything amiss with Xivan. She looked fully alive and spectacularly beautiful, a Khorveshan woman in her midtwenties instead of someone twice that age who'd been dead for half of it.

It was almost worth holding Urthaenriel to see Xivan looking so perfect.

"Relos, thank you for coming. I realize you're probably . . . busy." Xivan stepped toward the wizard, tilting her head in his direction. "I need your help finding Suless. We seem to have lost her. Again." She scowled as she made a "give me" gesture to Talea with two hooked fingers.

Talea unfastened the sword belt and gladly handed Urthaenriel back.

Senera crossed her arms over her chest. "You mean you want *my* help."

The corners of Xivan's mouth turned down. "I don't care if I need the help of two startled rabbits and a drunk hyena as long as it results in Suless dead." She glanced over at Relos Var. "You want that too, don't you?"

"Oh, ever so much." Relos Var seemed amused by the exchange. "She has interfered with my plans too many times. I see no reason to expect she's going to stop. Best to remove her permanently." He smiled at Senera. "If you'd be so kind, Senera."

Senera sat down at the table.

"I must warn you–" Senera began.

"I know," Xivan said. "The stone's answers are literal."

Senera glanced up at the duchess. "Yes."

The pale-skinned woman pulled a small dark-gray inkstone from her bodice and retrieved an ink stick from her belt pouch. She pulled her favorite brush from its normal place as a hairpin.

Senera wasn't just a normal wizard, if such a word as *normal* could ever properly be attached to *wizard*. She owned a Cornerstone, one of the few great artifacts. Hers was less combat-oriented than most, but it was still precious. The Name of All Things did just one thing, but it did it better than anyone, including gods.

It answered questions.

The process had a certain slow elegance to it. The Name of All Things would not be rushed. So Senera sat down and ground out the ink, moving the stick against a slick of water in the smooth stone. She took the time to make the ink properly, in the style so different from western Quuros inkwells and crow quill pens.

Talea set a teacup down next to her.

Senera paused from grinding the ink and looked sideways at Talea.

Talea's smile was impish. "You're welcome."

Qown made a strangled sound as Senera deliberately dipped her brush into the tea to wet it.

*"Thank you,"* Senera said.

Senera then swirled her brush against the ink and then began to write. Talea found this part fascinating, since apparently while she used the artifact, the wizard could no longer lie in answers she wrote down.

Talea had so many questions she would have loved to ask.[3]

Senera finished writing her answers and studied the result.

Talea looked over the woman's shoulder. "The Vale of Last Light. Where's that?"

"Doltar." Relos Var frowned.

[3] While some questions would probably have been quite mundane, I have to admit Talea sometimes surprises.

"That glyph means Doltar," Senera explained, tapping on the symbol in question with the end of her brush.

Talea didn't hide her surprise. "You mean where you're from?"

Senera's look could have cut flesh. "I'm *from* the Capital of Quur."[4]

Senera looked over her shoulder at Relos Var. "Suless knows what the Name of All Things can do. And she knows there's an excellent chance Xivan will have our assistance. If I were her, I wouldn't stop moving."

"No, I wouldn't either," Relos Var agreed. He inclined his head to Xivan Kaen. "But the question is, what do you intend to do?"

Xivan returned his stare coolly. "I intend to remind you none of my women can open a gate, so if you want Suless dead, I'm going to need a little more help than a magic sword."

Var laughed. "Indeed. That would probably be a helpful reminder. You should do that." Xivan's expression started to darken as it began to seem like Var would make her repeat herself. "Very well. Senera, I want Suless destroyed. Make it happen."

The white-haired woman frowned. "But, my lord, the Capital–"

"Never fear. Qown and I will be taking care of matters in the Capital."

The priest blinked, surprised. "We will?"

"Oh yes," Relos Var said. "You might even enjoy yourself." He clapped the other man on the shoulder. "Healers are in great demand at the moment. I have plans."[5] He glanced back at Senera. "Don't give me that look. I know why you want to return to the Capital. Your plans will have to wait."[6]

"Why not? They've waited this long." Senera's expression was so bland one might have missed the bitter note to her voice. Senera drank her tea, oblivious to Talea's choking laugh.[7] She then turned to fully face Relos Var. "So you want me to just . . . pop them down to the Doltari Free States, where we neither speak the languages nor know the customs? And while we're there, track down a renegade god-queen through the city-states of who knows how many *other* god-kings, all the while carrying the sword infamous for killing the same god-kings?"

Var smiled. "Nothing you can't handle, my dear."

[4] Which is true. I've researched this enough to know Senera was born to slave parents Inalea and Vimor, both owned by House D'Jorax and kept in the Upper Circle. Both parents are deceased, as are their specific owners, as well as anyone who ever owned Senera herself. I'm sure that last part is just a coincidence.

[5] This tells me Relos Var isn't done picking on House D'Mon.

[6] I admit to some curiosity about what Senera might want to accomplish, and how.

[7] I do hope Senera dutifully cleaned out her brushes between uses. Or that she likes the taste of ink.

Talea grinned at Senera. "But bonus–we'll have time to get to know each other."

"How positively delightful," Senera said. Through clenched teeth.[8]

"I feel just the same," Talea replied.

Xivan said, "So we're agreed. We leave at once."

[8] One might be tempted to think Senera isn't being entirely honest here. Surely not.

# 6: Briar and Bone

***(Kihrin's story)***

The fighting turned out to be both closer and farther away than I'd originally thought. Several deep crevasses and valleys separated us from the battleground, distorting the sound into something distant and muted. Those same crevasses and valleys made reaching the battle surprisingly difficult.

We'd almost caught up to Janel when a large form rose up from the next canyon over, then slammed back down on whomever it fought.

The creature was animate, but I hesitated to call it *alive*. Rather, it looked like an enormous serpentine skeleton, held together by a web of connective tissue, dried tendon, and dead flesh that shifted and merged with each movement. The monster existed in a constant, never-ending state of simultaneous decomposition and regeneration. The only color I'd seen had been the glowing blue dots of its eyes and the green vines tied around its massive wings and long neck.

Oh, also it was several hundred feet tall and so large it could probably smash most enemies by stepping on them. And its shape was depressingly recognizable.

"That was a dragon, wasn't it?" I asked.

Janel started running. Toward it, naturally.

"Shit," Teraeth cursed.

"That's Rol'amar!" Thurvishar shouted as we all started running after Janel.

I remembered the name. Relos Var had referred to Rol'amar with unusual loathing, but it didn't mean Rol'amar would want to be our friend. Dragons, as a rule, were no one's friends.[1]

At the canyon trailhead's crest, the path dropped down. The crusted Blight floor transformed into hot springs and scalding, bubbling pools filled with liquid that probably wasn't water and definitely wasn't safe.

[1] Particularly Rol'amar. Sadly, he seems even less sane than most dragons, likely the result of being in indescribable pain for millennia.

The canyon continued, following an arrow-straight hard stone floor whose shape scratched at my mind with nagging familiarity.

I mainly paid attention to the dragon. The creature's pure awe-inspiring size emerged as we drew closer. He wasn't as large as Morios, the metal dragon who had devastated Atrine, but he was easily Sharanakal's equal. Fighting a creature like that seemed impossible, but I knew it had been done before.

At least it had been done before with *other* dragons.

A morgage band fought the beast. They weren't doing a great job, since bodies littered the ground all over the canyon's base, but I admired their stubborn determination. As a morgage woman in the back of the canyon raised her arm, something green glinted in her hand. She shouted; leafy vines shot up from the canyon floor and looped around the dragon's bones. The vines drew fast and grew from places lifeless just moments before. Some vines broke—okay, most vines broke—but enough stayed in place to slow the dragon. The morgage warriors seemed to be buying enough time for their people to retreat.

Janel threw her javelin, a perfect arc flying through the air. The weapon hit directly in the center of a glowing blue eye. Then it flew right through the dragon's open eye socket, slammed against the far wall, and did no damage to the dragon at all.

But Janel did catch the dragon's attention.

"That's Rol'amar," Thurvishar repeated as he came to a panting stop next to Teraeth and me. Thurvishar was shockingly well muscled for someone who spent his life sitting in libraries reading books, but he wasn't used to sustained exertion.[2] "You can't kill Rol'amar. Nothing can kill him. Rol'amar isn't *alive.*"

"There has to be a way," Teraeth said. "All dragons are vulnerable to something."

"Oh, so is Rol'amar," Thurvishar replied. *"Magic."*

I only half paid attention. After Janel's failed attempt to spear the dragon through the eye, she'd kept moving forward. She was running toward a dead morgage woman lying on the ground.

No, Janel was running toward the baby lying next to the corpse. A baby still alive. With an undead dragon about to bring his whole foot down on the mother's corpse, the baby, and Janel.

"Damn it." I ran down into the canyon after her.

"Kihrin!" Teraeth screamed after me, but I didn't pay any attention to him either.

Janel slid between the dragon's toe claws, tumbled, and stood, scoop-

[2] That's . . . fair.

ing up the baby as she ran. The dragon lunged, but a dozen vines tied his head. He couldn't reach down far enough to bite her.

I dove to the side to keep from being crushed. When I tumbled back up again, I used the dragon's foot to steady myself, bracing my hand against the bone.

I wondered if all magic would backfire. What the morgage woman was doing looked like magic. And dragons were magic—or really, chaotic magical distortions.[3] Still, I suspected Janel had ignored Teraeth's instructions not to use magic to make herself supernaturally strong. No chaos storm had shown up yet. Maybe only certain kinds of magic were the problem?

And what sort of magic would mess with a dragon who was already dead?

I set my hand back on the dragon's foot and concentrated on healing. Instead of the normal feeling of warmth, a black miasma spread out from my handprint. Bone turned to ash, flaked off, began to float away.

The dragon reacted immediately, letting out a deafening roar.

I blinked. That hadn't been healing. That had been the opposite of healing. Which I figured meant my hunch had been right.

The dragon raised its foot and started to slam it back down again. On me.

I ran.

The morgage hadn't been idle while I was distracting Rol'amar. The woman in the back had continued to summon up plants and vines, so I ran in her direction. A thorny briar welled up from the ground behind me, an impenetrable hedge as high as the valley wall. Even the dragon had to pause. I slid into the dirt next to the morgage. A warrior pulled me to my feet, saying something thick and guttural in an unknown language. Argas may have blessed those of us who didn't know how with the ability to speak the vané language,[4] but nobody had contemplated the possibility we'd end up facing morgage in the Blight.

Thurvishar and Teraeth, being a little less suicidal than Janel or myself, had skipped attacking the dragon and had instead made their way over to the main morgage line. They were attempting to help the injured.

[3] I believe dragons have a similarity to the chaos storms of [illegible]en Blight—and the same origin.

[4] I'm getting ahead of myself here, but this is just a variatio[illegible]e imprinting techniques the gods use when Returning their angels.

"I hurt it," I gasped as I joined them. "I think healing acts the opposite against it."

A roar and a staccato of wet snapping sounds met my proclamation. I turned back to see the dragon breaking free from the vines.

A vine whipped backward, flicking against a morgage as fatally as a spear wound. Others immediately rushed to his aid.

The whole battle might have gone differently if we could have used magic—if the morgage could have used magic. Other than however the lead morgage sorceress was creating that extraordinary plant growth, my own attempt at "healing," and maybe Janel's strength, other attempts hadn't worked out so well. Another morgage woman tried to cast something, only to fall down to the ground choking, her yellow-green skin turning an ugly purple.

Clearly, casting magic was still a problem. Except when it wasn't.[5]

The canyon floor, with its unusually straight angles, caught my attention again.

It seemed familiar. But why? I'd never been in the Blight before, except for that brief trip I'd taken to Kharas Gulgoth when I was sixteen.

I couldn't shake the feeling I knew this place.

"Wait," I said.

No one paid any attention.

"Let's just be thankful the damn dragon doesn't breathe fire or choking gas or something," Teraeth said.

Thurvishar gave him a pained look.

"It doesn't do that, does it?" Teraeth said.

Thurvishar pointed to the ground near the dragon's skeletal feet. Dead morgage warriors were beginning to stand back up again.

"Oh," Teraeth said. "I should have known."

"There's a tunnel at the end of the canyon." I knew it was true. Somehow.

No one heard me.

"Everyone ready!" Teraeth had a knife in each hand as the dragon began to tear through the final bits of bramble and thorn. He looked grim.

I sighed. Then I shouted, "*We need to retreat!* End of the canyon. *Right now. Go!*" I started backing up in case anyone misunderstood me.

Janel turned to me. "Is it defensible?"

[5] Events often seem random when we lack the context for proper interpretation. In this case, we weren't taking into account how our own personal tenyé might shield us from chaos effects. In short, personal magics still worked. Anything at a range? Disaster.

"Very." I stopped to pick up a wounded morgage woman. Fortunately, she was unconscious, so she wouldn't stick a knife in my ribs. I hoped. "But we need to reach it first."

Janel nodded, then turned to the morgage and screamed out something low and guttural. *She* spoke morgage.

Where had Janel learned to speak morgage?

I answered myself immediately. She'd learned morgage the same way I knew we'd find a tunnel at the end of the canyon. Janel Theranon didn't know how to speak morgage, but in Janel's past life as Elana Kandor, she must have picked up the basics.

The lead morgage woman responded, calling out to her people. She must have thought whatever Janel had yelled out a fine idea, because she wasted little time making it happen.

I couldn't help being impressed by the morgage. What I had originally taken for chaos and disorganization proved to be anything but. The Quuros imperial army would have envied their formation skills. The men covered for the women. The women picked up children, packs, supplies. As one, the morgage retreated down the canyon. A morgage man came up to me, and although I didn't understand him, he clearly wanted to take the woman from me. I let him. He had a lot of poisonous arm spikes.

The morgage leader–who *also* seemed oddly familiar–raised her hand higher. The green flare I'd seen glinting from her hand originated from a large green gem she held. Plant growth exploded from the canyon walls, forming a second thorny hedge filling up the crevices between the dragon and us.

As Thurvishar moved backward, he said, "Healing the dragon hurt it, you said? And it didn't cause any backlash?"

"I'm fine, and no chaos storm," I said. "But I'm not sure it's the dragon's vulnerability. I think the Blight itself is what's twisting everything. You tried to teleport us away, so instead it teleported a bunch of something else to us. I tried to heal, so maybe instead I destroyed."

"That is an interesting hypothesis. I wish we had more time for research. I'm not sure how wise it would be to try healing magic from this range, anyway."

"Wouldn't kill him, anyway, would it? Not permanently. We don't have its Cornerstone. Wait, we don't, do we? Please tell me it's the green gem that woman's holding." I didn't think Relos Var had been lying when he said the only way to kill a dragon was to destroy both it and its matching Cornerstone at the same time. My "brother" saves the lies for when it really matters.

Of course, since Relos Var had stolen Urthaenriel from me, I didn't have a way to destroy a Cornerstone, but one problem at a time.

"No," Thurvishar said, "it's not. Rol'amar's Cornerstone is the Stone of Shackles."[6]

"Oh, isn't that nice? Rol'amar and I know all the same artifacts."

The dragon roared as he seemed to finally realize we weren't just repositioning ourselves but engineering an escape.

As we approached the spot I remembered, I ran to the front. I ignored what would happen if my memory proved faulty or if, more likely, a thousand years of wear and natural disasters had sealed the entrance.

I started examining the walls. The chiseled stone sides didn't seem familiar, but the angles–the way the walls framed sky, that turn there, the slope over here . . .

It had to be here. It had to be.

Then I saw it. Smooth gray stone, partially covered by scrabble and rockslides. "Thurvishar!" I shouted back. "Thurvishar, I need you!"

Several morgage who'd followed close behind me started shouting. I didn't have to speak their language to suspect they were demanding I materialize whatever miracle Janel had promised. I did my best to ignore them, which wasn't the easiest thing to do when the average morgage male stood two feet taller and twice as wide. And seriously, let's not forget those poisoned arm spikes.

Thurvishar ran over to me. "What is it?"

I pointed to the cliff. "I need you to clear this rock away."

Thurvishar looked at me like I was surely the stupidest person ever born. "I can't use magic, remember?"

"You can. Put your hand on the rock, flush up against it. Then try it."

Thurvishar's expression was skeptical, but he placed his hand against the rock face and closed his eyes. He must have found concentrating difficult, what with the shouting morgage and the roaring dragon and the real probability we only had only seconds to live.[7]

The rock face exploded in fine ash and debris.

The morgage nearby shouted in surprise, then covered their faces and started coughing. Thurvishar and I were fine, thanks to our air sigils.

"What the hell are you doing–?" Teraeth's voice cut off as he ran forward.

The falling rock revealed a panel set into the smooth gray stone. I slammed my hand against the square, which depressed with a soft click.

[6] We need to track down what happened to that. Did it re-form in the Arena? Somewhere else? Who has it now? And what happens when someone who hasn't been told gaeshe are no longer possible tries it anyway, and it *works*?

[7] He's exaggerating. I'm sure we would have lived for at least a minute.

A grinding noise sounded from inside the wall. The gray stone slid down into the ground, revealing an opening easily large enough to pass a burly morgage male, but far too small for a dragon. Beyond, stairs led into darkness.

"One miracle, as requested." I ran down the steps.

# 7: Walk into a Bar

*Thurvishar chuckled and shook his head. "You do realize how lucky we were, yes? Because you were quite wrong about how the magic worked there."*

*"Ah well. No harm done, right?" Kihrin cleared his throat. "Yes, yes, I know. Thank Taja—" Kihrin stopped himself.*

*An uncomfortable silence followed.*

*Thurvishar picked up his papers and began to read.*

***(Senera's story)***

It was winter in Kishna-Farriga.

The three women—Senera, Talea, and Xivan—arrived in a location tucked away on a rooftop with a shielded street view. Relos Var had shown Senera the location years ago, in case she'd ever needed to come there herself. She'd made a few trips, but had found the many customs too strange to feel comfortable.

Senera had brought her pet dhole, Rebel, because this seemed like a long-term mission. And also because while Senera could have hired someone to look after her dog, Rebel could only be considered domesticated by the most generous standards. Her pet tugged at her leash, excited to be outside, a little nervous at the noise and activity from the nearby cobblestone street. Behind them, rows of brightly colored buildings comprised the largest city on the continent, the famous trading port and entrepôt that drew the rich and poor, gods and mortals, free men and slaves. All came to be either its beneficiaries or its victims.

The city smelled almost sweet and clean, welcoming woodsmoke and baking smells carried along with the ice and snow. It was a lie. Most of the year, Kishna-Farriga smelled like dead fish, unwashed bodies, and naked greed—in contrast to her birth city, the Capital City of Quur, which always smelled like spices, sunbaked tile, and despair.

The port city was shockingly covered with snow, which hadn't done much to slow down activity on the docks. Merchant ships plied back and forth, delivering their wares and picking up new cargo before sailing out again. The snow did, however, simplify Senera's job. The trio hadn't even needed to change clothing before they'd headed through the portal to their destination.

Senera had made Xivan and Talea disrobe temporarily before their arrival. Underneath their fur-lined tunics and thick winter coats, they now wore several new glyphs marked into their skin—a glyph for understanding languages and, in Xivan's case, a glyph to hide her unique status as a deceased but still entirely animate being.

Of course, neither glyph would be worth the ink Senera had used to paint them if Xivan or Talea decided to draw That Damn Sword (Senera's private name for Urthaenriel). The thing made her skin crawl. She honestly didn't know how anyone could stand to hold it.

"Why can't we go directly to the Vale of Last Light?" Xivan asked.

"Because I've never been there before," Senera responded.

"Yes, I suppose that makes sense." Xivan gazed at the scene before her. "I admit I thought Kishna-Farriga would be more . . . I don't know . . ."

"Whiter," Talea said.

"Whiter?" Senera raised an eyebrow. "There's snow everywhere."

"No, I didn't mean—" Talea bit her lip.

Senera sighed. Oh. That kind of "whiter." "No, that's farther south. Kishna-Farriga has had too much contact and intermingling with Quur, Zherias, even the Manol.[1] Even once we're farther into the Free States, you'll find a mix of skin tones. Trust me when I say none will be as 'white' as a Yoran's coloring."

"Let's find shelter," Xivan said.

Senera knew the duchess couldn't possibly be cold. More likely, she was showing consideration for her two mortal companions. Or just realized standing around in the snow acting like the cold was someone else's problem didn't qualify as normal behavior.

Senera pointed. "There's a tavern over there."

Honestly, Senera wanted to go inside as quickly as possible. Not because of the cold but before she spotted a slave ship, or some wealthy merchant enjoying his newest purchase, or the next slave batch being taken to the auction house.

Before Senera succumbed to the perpetual burning desire to level significant swaths of a city like Kishna-Farriga to the ground. A tempta-

[1] Which means the "average" Kishna-Farrigan can be expected to be a mélange of all Four Races, since between their proximity to the dreth homeland, their proximity to the Manol, and the high percentage of Zheriasians who claim voramer ancestry, a little bit of everything's been thrown into the mix.

tion made all the more problematic because she was powerful enough to carry through on the impulse.

She loathed this city almost as much as she hated Quur.

Conversation stopped as they entered the tavern and gave themselves time to adjust to the poor lighting. Senera pursed her lips and again considered the possibility Taja just didn't like her. The tavern chatter died; a room full of dark-skinned Quuros sailors turned to regard them.

While more egalitarian than its equivalents in Quur, Kishna-Farriga often sheltered travelers. In this case, they'd walked into a bar that catered to Quuros visitors and Quuros tastes. Every woman in the room worked there in a "professional" capacity–either selling drinks or themselves.

Next to her, Talea tensed.

Xivan headed for the bar.

Noise started up again, but regular conversations didn't resume. The entertainment had just arrived. "Hey there, pretty things, why don't you come over here?" "Well, now, ladies, come to keep an old man warm?" "How much for all of you?"

"I assume you take Quuros metal?" Xivan asked the bartender eyeing them warily from behind a polished wood counter.

The bartender chewed the question over. "I can. But no dogs allowed in here."

Xivan pushed three thrones across the counter. "Three plum wines. Keep the change, and forget the dog."

Three thrones was significantly more than plum wine should cost even considering the import costs and whatever the current exchange rate happened to be.

"Three wines coming right up." Then he paused. "No disrespect, but you ladies sure you're in the right place?"

Talea snorted as she sat down. Backward, so she faced the tavern. She rested one hand on her sword pommel while she kept the other on a dagger hilt. For anyone with a lick of sense, everything about the Spurned warrior screamed, "If you touch me, I will kill you and then use your flesh as bait to catch my dinner," but these people didn't seem sensible. All the Quuros sailors likely saw were three women who'd come in alone, never mind that two of them wore mail and made no effort to hide their arsenals.

Senera didn't sit. They weren't going to be here that long.

Xivan smiled at the bartender's question. "It's out of the snow, so yes. Now perhaps you can help answer a question?"

A drunken sailor sauntered up. He seemed the sort of large, wide fellow who comfortably won any bar fight he might happen to pick.

Talea stood and blocked his path.

"Hey, rose petal, now you're a pretty thing, aren't you? Come sit over at my table. I've got a lap you could warm up nice." He grinned as he looked Talea up and down.

"No, thank you," Talea said.

Senera rolled her eyes. She really was just that nice to everyone, wasn't she?

"Go sit down," Senera told the man.

"Bitch, I wasn't talking to you."

Senera exhaled. She'd been in situations where diplomacy and her goals had required her to play nice, pretend to be meek, act like the good little slave. She excelled at it.

She wasn't playing by those rules today.

"Do you have any idea how many bones are in the human hand?" Senera asked the man.

He blinked at her. "What?"

"Hey there. Hello. Could you maybe not kill anyone?" the bartender asked Senera. "I just cleaned up this place."

Senera glanced back at the man, mildly surprised. He'd actually recognized the real threat. "I'm not going to kill a soul," she reassured him. "And since you asked nicely, I won't even spill any blood."

Meanwhile, the sailor had focused his attention on Senera rather than Talea. "Damn woman, those are some fine shakers you got there. Hey, Grakire, come over here. Maybe we can get two for one."

"My mistake," Senera said. "I was too subtle. What I should have said was, 'Sit your ass back down before I break every fucking bone in your hands, so you can't jerk yourself off unless your friend Grakire helps.'"

The sailor blinked at her, dull bovine confusion. "Shit, a little girl like you? I'll show you–"

The sailor stepped toward her; Rebel lunged forward, growling. And that's when the sailor made the worst mistake of his entire life.

He started to kick the dog.

Before he had a chance to finish the motion, he began screaming. A sound filled the air, like someone breaking a bundle of small branches, all at once. A popping, snapping sound. His hands visibly distorted as he held them to his chest, sobbing.

Talea moved for her sword as men around the tavern stood, angry murmurs filling the air.

Xivan didn't draw her sword. She didn't seem interested. She picked up a mug of plum wine from the counter and drank while watching the crowd.

Senera glared, hands on hips. "Do you lot think I couldn't do the same to you? Sit down and finish your damn drinks. We don't want trouble, so don't make any."

The tavern stilled.

If they hadn't been proud, drunken fools, they might have listened to her. But they were drunk. They were Quuros. And they were most certainly fools. They just couldn't stand the idea of some Doltari woman telling them what to do. Which struck Senera as incredibly witless in a land where you never knew if a god-queen had just walked through the door.

Again: fools.

Not everyone stepped forward at once, but three men seemed eager to avenge their fallen comrade.

Senera broke their kneecaps. It was easier than trying to do the finger bone trick to three men at once.

They fell to the ground, which naturally made them scream all the louder. The men behind them paused as it finally started to sink in they'd pay dearly for a victory. Assuming they could win at all.

Which they couldn't.

"Go. Sit. Down."

Chairs scraped across the floor as various customers remembered they'd left games and drinks unattended or they had something better to do.

"I never liked Mabrik, anyway," one man muttered.

Then everyone returned to their drinks and conversations. Someone, possibly the previously mentioned Grakire, collected Mabrik and took him back to another table, while others helped remove the last three fallen men.

Xivan turned back to the bartender. "So how does one get to the Vale of Last Light from here?"

"The Vale of Last Light?" The man was visibly taken aback. "Why would you want to go—" He paused and glanced over at Senera, at Talea, and apparently leaped to conclusions. "What I mean is, you take the main road east toward the mountains. It's just nestled at their base. Can't miss it." He made a face. "I can't imagine why anyone would want to go there, though. It's not a nice place."

"That's all right," Senera said. "We're not nice people."

"Thank you." Xivan nodded to Senera and Talea, and all three left together.

Rebel wagged her tail and rubbed up against Senera's leg.

"Is that going to happen everywhere we go?" Talea asked Senera.

"Oh no," Senera said. "Most bartenders aren't nearly that helpful."

# 8: The Underroads

***(Kihrin's story)***

As soon as I set foot on the fourth stair, lights turned on in the vast room beyond. The chamber revealed looked as large as the D'Mon Blue Palace's banquet room, which had previously taken top marks as the largest interior space I'd ever seen in my life.[1] Columns filled the room at regular intervals, leading down to a floor decorated with repeating black and white tiles. Several pillars sported cracks and visible damage, but the room didn't seem to be in any danger of collapse. Toward the far side, dirt and silt had slowly invaded from corridors branching off, giant round tunnels leading into darkness. The invading dirt hadn't done any harm other than covering the tile floor. Benches sat spaced around the room, but nothing else that might be considered furniture.

In the old days, there would have been more. There would have been magical constructions, enchanted wagons, people. Now, only dust and shadows remained.

"Come on." I took the stairs two at a time and ran for the panel at the bottom. The controls to close the door again. Rol'amar might not be able to reach us inside the chamber, but the roaming dead the dragon animated most certainly could. I also didn't know if the dragon would be able to smash his way inside, but I had hoped we could all hide before he noticed where we had gone.

The morgage ran inside, setting up a defensive line with the women and children in the center. Despite this gender-based protectiveness, the morgage woman with the green gem and Janel herself came through the door last.

"Shut it!" Janel yelled.

I hit the panel.

Nothing happened.

There was stunned silence.

I hit it again.

[1] I suspect the Octagon's main auction room is larger, but frankly, I'd have blocked it from my memory too if I could.

Gears grinding echoed through the room as the doors began to close.

Every living being in the room exhaled.

"What were you thinking?" Teraeth rounded on Janel immediately. "If you go running off every time you hear a fight—"

Janel reached out, grabbed Teraeth's neckline, and jerked him down to her eye level.

I looked around, concerned with spectators. With the immediate danger of "undead dragon" passed, or at least literally out of sight, the morgage turned their attention to us.

Those stares were not universally friendly.

Morgage traditionally rewarded intruders into the Blight with death. I'd be hard-pressed to say whether they hated Quuros or vané more.[2]

"Shut. Up." Janel growled at Teraeth through clenched teeth. "We'll talk about what I did and why later, but right now, I need to be in charge, and you need to act like I'm in charge. Do you understand?" She tilted her head and raised her voice so it echoed through the hall. "Don't be in such a hurry to be an old woman. I can think of better uses for that mouth."

Teraeth was so stunned, he just stared at her. Then he started to make an angry reply. Started to, but then he too noticed the morgage giving us ugly looks. His eyes swept from side to side, taking in the scene, and then he knelt before Janel. "Please forgive me." He bowed his head.

I could feel the pause in the air, the hesitation.

. . . and then the morgage stopped paying attention to us. They returned to treating their injured, assessing the casualties.

"What just happened?" I asked Thurvishar.

The wizard didn't seem to understand any better than I did. "I'm not . . . I'm not sure. Except have you noticed this group seems to be matriarchal?"

"Yeah," I said, "but I'm pretty sure the group I met the last time was too." I eyed the leader, the one carrying the green gem. She had black skin with a silver-scaled stripe down her face. "Wait . . . you know, I think this *is* the same group. That's the morgage woman I met in Kharas Gulgoth last time."

"Extraordinary," Thurvishar said.

I had a feeling our D'Lorus friend would have been hip deep in note-taking if only he'd had ink and paper with him.[3]

Several hulking morgage men made their way over to us, or rather,

[2] It's no contest. They hate the vané much more.

[3] As if the lack would be a deterrence. A wizard of my ability and a little thing like paper is going to stop me? Please.

over to Janel. "The Dry Mother will see you," one said in surprisingly good Guarem. "Just you."

Janel laughed. "Do you think I was a boy yesterday? My husbands come with me."

"Husb–" I started to say.

Teraeth stepped past me. "Just go with it." He adapted fast after his bad start. Teraeth stepped before Janel, openly spinning a dagger. Getting into someone's personal space as an intimidation technique was a language he spoke well. For some reason the size difference didn't seem to matter so much.

A morgage man grunted, then shrugged, popping out the spines along his forearms. "Just one husband."

Janel rolled her eyes. "And I say all of them. If another woman wants to contradict me, tell her to come to me and explain her reasons."

Several more morgage stepped up. They had their weapons out: spears, javelins, and those spines on their arms. Poisoned spines, I reminded myself. Several morgage growled, nose tentacles twitching.

Janel stretched one shoulder, then the other, as if warming up for a fight. "Do you want to do this?" She asked the question rhetorically; clearly, she already knew the answer. Janel grinned, her expression almost shockingly feral.

She'd been raised in a culture that relished fighting. She wasn't necessarily faking her enthusiasm. I suspected the same was true for the morgage; more giant men circled us. Not a single one stood shorter than seven feet tall.

"Great," I muttered. At least I had a sword.

A woman's voice rang out, saying something in the morgage tongue. The men reacted immediately, and they all sighed and began putting away their weapons.

"Fine," one said grudgingly. "*All* your husbands."

"You might just die an old woman yet." Janel smiled. The morgage man grinned in response and ducked his head in what could be easily interpreted as a bow.

We followed Janel. I still carried a naked blade, but the morgage didn't seem to think that unusual or, more importantly, rude.

The men escorted us to the woman with the green gem, which now sat nestled against her bosom. Up close, the gem sparkled yellow green, the color of new leaves or fresh grass. Chrysoberyl or peridot.

And it *had* to be a Cornerstone. She hadn't had it with her the last time I'd encountered her; she'd have used it against Relos Var.[4] Same black skin, same distinctive silver scaling down her face, and same

[4] I do find myself curious where she acquired it.

spikes and spines where hair would have been on a human. This time she wore armor, small overlapping bronze plates reminiscent of fish or dragon scales.

She grinned as we approached. I wondered if the morgage considered the expression friendly.

"It's been a long time since we've met a human leader who knows our ways," she said as greeting. "I'm Bevrosa, formerly guardian of the dead city, now keeper of the Spring Stone, Wildheart."

"Baelosh's stone," Thurvishar whispered to me.

The name sounded familiar, and then I remembered why. Emperor Simillion had stolen his star tear necklace from Baelosh's hoard. I put a hand to my neck. In all the excitement, I hadn't noticed the necklace missing. Our kidnappers had apparently decided they just couldn't stand to let those priceless gems escape. Well enough. I put recovering it near the bottom of my to-do list.

"I'm Janel Theranon," Janel answered. "We did not mean to intrude into your lands, but we have been abandoned here by vané who wish to ensure no one enacts the Ritual of Night."

All talking in the hall stopped.

"Huh," I whispered to Thurvishar. "I guess they *all* understand Guarem."

Bevrosa's smile faded. "You are the Eight's children?" Her gaze examined us then and stopped on me.

I waved at her.

"I know you," the morgage leader said to me. "You trespassed into the dead city."

"Yeah, not by choice," I responded. "Thanks for helping out with Relos Var. And, you know, not killing me." Her people *had* tried to kill me. One even went so far as to put a spear through my leg. After the fact, though, I realized this particular morgage band seemed to think their sacred duty was to keep interlopers from poking around too close to Vol Karoth. No one had thought to tell them I was on the "okay list."

Although, now that I think about it, I'm pretty sure I should *never* be on the okay list.

Bevrosa's expression turned wary. "You . . . you should not be here. This is not safe."

Janel cleared her throat. "We don't intend to stay. We must return to the vané and make this right, but we have no supplies, and thus we need your aid. We realize you have little to spare, but I hope you understand our need."

Bevrosa turned to the side and snarled something in her own language. The men scattered, presumably to gather what they could spare.

Bevrosa turned back to Janel. "It's a bad time to be in the Blight."

She grinned. "Never is it a good time, but still . . . Warchild has awoken." She pointed in my direction. "That one needs to leave. Now."

I bit back on a protest. Leaving immediately fit all our plans. With the fighting over, I heard the droning again, but softer now, quieter. I hadn't found myself walking in any particular direction without realizing it. It was an excellent sign.

Teraeth started to say something. I nudged him in the ribs and shook my head.

"Is that why you were moving south?" Janel asked. "Are you trying to leave the Blight?"

The morgage woman nodded. "The time of guarding has ended. No one who stayed near the holy city still breathes. We have taken our sons and our husbands and we'll travel as far as we can, but soon the whole world will not be large enough to hide us if you cannot convince these weak vané to do their job." She spat to the side in punctuation.

"We know," Janel said. "But we're going to make things right–"

The room changed. All existence slowed down, time itself stretching out like a drawn piece of wool thread spun fine. Sound blunted as if I'd ducked underwater. Except the droning sound I'd been hearing since I'd woken condensed, sharpened, became recognizable.

It was speech. It had always been speech.

*Come back. Join me.*

Vol Karoth appeared in the hall.

# 9: A Murderer's Hands

*Kihrin stopped. "Do you think there's a kettle around here? I'd love some tea."*

*Thurvishar stared at him.*

*Kihrin grinned. "It's a bad habit I picked up from Janel. Anyway, it's not like you don't know what happened. You were there too."*

*Thurvishar rolled his eyes and then pointed to the end of the cluttered room. "I believe I saw a kettle on that other workbench—honestly, I have no idea how anything was ever accomplished in this mess. You'd think a wizard of his caliber would at least be organized. I suppose he must have just known where everything was." Thurvishar started to continue, but then set his papers aside. "We should skip the rest of Senera, Talea, and Xivan's story for now."*

*Kihrin frowned. "You're not going to finish?"*

*"Oh, I'll pick it up again later, but in between this and when we become involved, it's more of the same, really." Thurvishar grimaced at his notes as though the paper itself was somehow culpable. "They traveled through at least ten more city-states. Always the same story—arriving in town one step behind Suless. I believe it's a tale that would probably grow stale with repetition."*

*"Oh, sure. Plus, there's only so many times you can hear, 'Please, scary lady, stop hurting me,' before you kind of get the point." Kihrin then laughed outright, to Thurvishar's indignation.*

*Thurvishar vindictively grabbed another folder. "All right. Then let's try this one. I think you'll find it interesting."*

*"Why do I feel like that's a threat?"*

*Thurvishar smiled.*

***(Khaeriel's story)***
***Two months earlier . . .***

The sound of buzzing bees and chirping birds paused as a hole opened in the world. The shimmering iris of chaotic energies flared out in spinning harmonies, disgorged two shapes, and then snapped shut before vanishing as though it had never been.

The birds resumed their songs. The bees traveled to new flowers.

The two shapes resolved into two figures: a woman, standing; a man, prone and floating in the air. The woman was tall and beautiful, vané through and through, with long blue hair and silver-dusted skin. The man was darker, his height more difficult to guess, but he matched in a fashion: dressed in blue the same color as his eyes, her hair. The woman raised an arm, gesturing toward vines and old rocks resting against the trunk of an enormous Manol sky tree.

They were near the jungle outskirts, where warm gold-green shafts of sunlight still reached the floor. Farther in there would be no light at all as the canopy crowded out the sky, but here the world existed in happy birdsong and monkey noises, the smell of loamy earth, sweet orchids, and decay. Farther in, protections against opening exactly the sort of gate Khaeriel had just created existed, but this little pocket fell outside the barrier roses' normal wards.

"The shelter is still here," Khaeriel told her companion. "How fortunate for us."

Therin D'Mon couldn't move and certainly couldn't answer. His bright blue eyes looked glassy and drugged, open but unfocused.

Khaeriel gestured again, and the jungle vines parted to reveal a door, neatly hidden behind a leafy curtain. She walked over, placed her hand against the surface, and waited.

A small *click* signaled success; the door opened fractionally.

Therin floated in after Khaeriel when she stepped inside. The door closed behind them.

Several irregularly shaped rooms comprised the safe house hidden under the huge sky tree's roots. A tall human or normal vané could stand upright in the chambers without difficulty. Khaeriel gestured toward a low, flat bed in a side room; Therin's body moved there before floating downward and resting. He made no movement at all besides breathing.

Khaeriel sat down in a chair and, for the first time, let herself look as tired and harried as she felt. She spent a long time staring at her hands, while the air lingered still and cool and silent. After twenty-five years, they still didn't feel like her hands.

Probably because, in the most literal sense, they weren't. They were the hands of a murderer, the hands of an assassin.

Well. She'd kept that tradition alive, had she not?[1]

A shudder rippled through her as she remembered Quuros royals, dead at her hands. She shunted the thoughts from her mind like rogue demons of guilt, but these demons weren't so easy to exorcise. The enemy, she reminded herself. The D'Mons had been her enemies. Sla-

[1] I believe I can now definitely say Khaeriel, or Miya, was indeed responsible for the D'Mon massacre during the Capitol Hellmarch.

vers and supporters of a corrupt and evil empire. Not one had deserved mercy.

Khaeriel could only hope she one day believed that.

She had been there when Galen D'Mon was *born.* When so many of them had been born. Lives cut short indeed, first by Gadrith, then by her own hand. Who would have ever suspected she would be the one to finish the job the necromancer had started? But when the gaesh had vanished–when she had finally been freed from the soul chains binding her–she had wreaked vengeance.

She remembered Kihrin's corpse, tossed on a sacrificial altar, and steeled her will.

Therin still did not move; indeed, could not move. Even the most primitive thought was beyond him, a necessary precaution against casting spells.

Khaeriel sat down on the bed next to him and waved a hand over his face.

His blue eyes focused on hers, sharpened, turned venomous. Therin started to say something, do something.

Khaeriel waved her hand again and placed him back under paralysis.

She returned to the main room, searching until she found a small box on a shelf. Opening the box, she removed a blue robin's egg from a fine nest of twigs and fibers.[2]

She crushed the egg in her hand.

When nothing immediately changed, she exhaled slowly. She waited.

Nothing.

She laughed to herself after a dozen minutes crawled by. Relos Var was busy. It was to be expected.

Khaeriel returned to the bedroom where Therin waited.

Therin was a problem.

After Khaeriel had slaughtered Therin's family before his eyes and bound him in magic, she had told the high lord he would never hate her half as much as he hated himself. But Khaeriel wasn't so sure. Hadn't she given Therin a visible symbol to blame? Who would fault him for choosing to hate her? Therin would be in his rights to never forgive her.

And if he did blame himself? Well, she couldn't count on the idea he wouldn't one day chose to act on that self-loathing. That he might indeed take it to a point where moving on to the next life would seem like the natural solution to all his woes. Which brought her to the real problem: *Khaeriel needed him.*

She hoped she wouldn't. She hoped her plans to retake the throne

[2] Father Zajhera gave Qown a similar egg. Sloppy of Relos Var, wasn't it?

wouldn't require the last true heir of Kirpis vané royalty. Gaining a Quuros high lord's cooperation–proud, arrogant, willful–would have been almost impossible even under the best circumstances. But when she had spent twenty-five years as his slave? Twenty-five years unable to disobey a single order? Twenty-five years of meek, quiet, ever-so-obedient service?

He'd never follow her orders. Not unless she took *steps*.

So Khaeriel steeled herself to commit the evening's second atrocity.

She sat down next to Therin, held his head in her hands, and began weaving an enchantment.[3]

[3] It should be noted enchantments are both difficult to perform, unreliable, and incredibly dangerous. She's centuries old, so I suppose she'd had time to practice, but still . . .

# 10: Vol Karoth's Shadow

*"Seriously?" Kihrin narrowed his eyes at Thurvishar. "My mother?"*

*Thurvishar smiled. "You're not even slightly curious what happened to your parents?"*

*Kihrin scoffed. "Fine. I'll admit I am a little curious. But I didn't need . . ." He sighed. "Anyway, where did I leave off? Oh right, everything had just gone to hell."*

### *(Kihrin's story)*

No one could truly *see* Vol Karoth. He formed a man-size hole cut from reality, a silhouette of absolute, perfect blackness. His appearance offered up the final, absolute proof of my worst nightmares: Vol Karoth was *free.*

As Vol Karoth appeared, everything around him died.

It all happened without warning. I couldn't even be sure how many died. A morgage group had been sitting near the spot where he appeared, and then they simply . . . weren't. I didn't think they'd had time to dive out of the way. Four morgage men standing too close started to scream before they disintegrated, falling to ash. The pillar's stone edges flaked away; the floor crumbled under Vol Karoth's feet. The universe itself cringed at his presence. He was anathema.

I felt sick. The black flaking ash mimicked what had happened when I'd touched Rol'amar. It looked exactly the same, which implied I'd been wrong about why I'd been able to hurt the dragon.[1]

Judging where Vol Karoth's gaze fell was unimaginable. Gauging his expression was unachievable. It was impossible to discern any information about him at all.

But I knew: Vol Karoth was looking at me. The silhouette reached out a hand in my direction.

*Come to me. Join with–*

[1] So very, very wrong.

Time sped back up. The voice stretched back out into an indecipherable low drone.

"Kihrin!" Teraeth tackled me to the ground.

I'd started walking forward, you see.

Screams and shouts rang out. No matter how brave the morgage might be, this was different. Who could fight Vol Karoth? This wasn't something you could kill or defeat. This wasn't someone you could slay. Vol Karoth didn't even have to try to kill. All he had to do was *exist.*

Bevrosa stared at Vol Karoth with wide, panicked eyes and then turned back to us. "You're all Hellwarriors." She said it like both accusation and revelation.

"So it would seem," Thurvishar replied.

"Follow the tunnels," she ordered. "I don't know where they lead, but we'll hold the line for your retreat. Take the food and water and go." Bevrosa looked directly at me. "He mustn't take you."

Janel started to protest but then simply nodded. "Thank you." She picked up the packs the morgage had dumped at our feet and began walking backward toward the tunnel.

"That's not him." I said the words aloud as soon as I thought them.

"What?" Teraeth pulled me to my feet, but didn't release me. Words cannot describe how glad I felt he didn't let me go.

"Vol Karoth's not here," I insisted. "That's an echo."

Teraeth scowled. "That echo is going to kill everyone here if we stay."

I shook my head. "If he were really here, it would already be too late." I grabbed Teraeth's robe. "We need to leave right now."

"I'm *trying,*" Teraeth growled. This proved the second time I could remember seeing Teraeth look scared, and I wasn't enjoying the experience any more with repetition.

Teraeth kept a firm hand around my waist, another on my arm, as we ran.

"No, wait!" I called out. "It's the other way! We need to go the other way!" Panic lanced inside me; the pure certainty the way to safety lay behind us.

"No good," Teraeth said. "That way takes us past Vol Karoth. Not happening."

I looked back over my shoulder. Bevrosa stood tall, Wildheart in hand, summoning up plants that crumbled to ash before they reached within ten feet of Vol Karoth. She couldn't possibly win this fight or even survive it. But she still fought.

I didn't know I could ever be that brave. I could only marvel at the morgage tribe, and mourn them too. I didn't think they could survive this. I wasn't sure we could either.

Then Teraeth led me into the tunnel, where millennia-old stonework blocked the morgage tribe's fate from my view.

I couldn't tell how long we ran. Small globes embedded in the tunnel walls provided minuscule amounts of light, enough to see the ground but not much more. I felt like these lights hadn't turned on in response to our presence, like the lights in the main hall outside, but had just always been on. Always on, for millennia, since before Karolaen's destruction and Vol Karoth's creation.

Apparently, the voras really knew how to weave a spell.

I couldn't hear Vol Karoth's droning plea anymore. "He's gone." I stopped running. "Wait. Let me catch my breath. It's safe."

"Oh, thank the gods." Thurvishar bent down and put his hands on his knees, chest heaving.

"Are you sure?" Teraeth asked me. He hadn't released me yet. I didn't want him to. He felt safe.

Still, I removed his hand and leaned back against the curved tunnel wall. "Yes, I'm sure." I felt sick, not physically but soul-sick, numb. No matter how one measured such things, I'd had a bad couple of months. I was still reeling at how quickly everything had gone wrong.

And how much of it had gone wrong by my own hand.

"Are you all right?" Janel asked.

I stared at her.

She winced. "I'm sorry. That was a stupid question."

I took deep, slow breaths. "I'm the one who's sorry. I didn't know he could home in on me like that. I just didn't think–"

"Vol Karoth's never been free from his prison at the same time you've been free from him," Thurvishar said. "Every other time he's escaped, your souls were still trapped. No one could have predicted how he would react to your absence. Personally, I would never have assumed this would be his response."

"He wants me back," I said. "That's the droning sound I'm hearing: Vol Karoth calling to me. He's just speaking too slowly for me to understand what he's saying."

Thurvishar raised an eyebrow. "Slowly? Oh, now that is interesting."

Janel crouched down and began rifling through the packs she had grabbed, separating supplies and cloth bundles. "Is it?"

"I've seen similar sound distortions while trying to communicate magically with someone while I'm inside the Lighthouse at Shadrag Gor," Thurvishar explained. "Remember, time moves extremely fast there. That's the whole reason why Empress Tyentso couldn't contact you"–he pointed to Teraeth—"after you followed Darzin there.[2] She sent the message, but in comparison to your perception of time, you didn't recognize it as speech."

"But time's moving normally for me," I said.

"Indeed. So it must be *Vol Karoth* who is experiencing a slowed temporal state. In fact, I'm wondering—" Thurvishar blinked.

"What?" Teraeth said. "I don't like it when you get that look on your face."

"I'm wondering if the gods were mistaken," Thurvishar said. "Khored said Vol Karoth is awake but still imprisoned. But what if the imprisonment is nothing more than this slowed temporal state?"

"Oh Veils. As if I wasn't already having nightmares." Teraeth glared.

"You did ask," Thurvishar said.

"I just wish I could say you're wrong, but I can't."

"I get that a lot."

"An echo," I insisted. "A mental projection. He wasn't really there."

"He shouldn't have been there at all, Kihrin. The Eight told us that with a crystal destroyed, he was awake, but still imprisoned. I don't think that's true."

I swallowed bile. "You think he's free?"

"Not free, exactly. But what if the 'prison' isn't what we assumed? What if the voras trapped Vol Karoth by freezing him *in time*? Technically, he was never trapped, time just moved so slowly for him that seconds became eons. With a crystal shattered, time is moving faster for him. Why, he might even take a step in a few months. That's why he hasn't gone on a rampage yet or even left the Blight. This explains so much."[3] Thurvishar started to look excited.

"Thurvishar." I gazed at him dully. "He moved faster around me."

Thurvishar started to say something and stopped himself. "Yes, so it's just as well we're leaving."

Janel dropped satchels and waterskins on the ground. "There," she said. "One for each of us. That way if we're separated, we won't starve or die of thirst right away." She made a face. "Although to be honest, what the morgage consider food isn't for the fainthearted. Trust me when I say we'll want to eat the meat we took from the pack animals first. Also, we're a little light on blankets, so let's hope it stays warm down here."

Teraeth turned to her. "Can we talk about what happened back there?"

She paused. "Which part? There are so many options."

[2] If I understand, the plan to kill Gadrith hinged on being able to magically communicate with each other, which failed because no one knew about Shadrag Gor.

[3] If only that theory had been correct. Alas.

I pinched the bridge of my nose and prayed Teraeth wasn't about to do what I thought he was.

"You running headlong into a damn dragon without so much as a word to the rest of us," Teraeth said. "What did you think was going to happen?"

And there it was.

Janel cocked her head and stared at him. "Ah, I see. So you mean the part where I ran forward because I knew the only way the morgage would share food and water with us would be if I–the only 'woman'–impressed them with my bravery. Good to know." Her voice was deceptively mild. "You do realize why morgage targets are always female, don't you? They think they're attacking our leaders."

Janel wouldn't use the word *woman* to describe herself normally. By her culture's definitions, she wasn't a woman even if she admitted to being biologically female. It made for some interesting semantical discussions.

"I know how voramer physiology works, thank you," Teraeth snapped.

"So what exactly is your problem?"

I sighed. Teraeth hadn't made any secret about being interested in Janel romantically. But he seemed to be having trouble coming to terms with the idea Janel didn't need to be placed on a pedestal and protected. Which honestly made me laugh; under other circumstances, she would have been exactly Teraeth's type, no pedestal required.

Of course, she was my type too. So that was awkward.

Anyway, Teraeth needed to drop it. And Teraeth would absolutely not drop it.

"You put us all in danger," Teraeth insisted.

"I put us all in danger?" Janel pointed back up the tunnel. "Were you with us back there? Vol Karoth showed up for a drink and a friendly chat. *I* put us all in danger? Say that again."

Teraeth's eyes narrowed. "That business with you being in charge–"

"Oh, so that's what really upset you." Janel picked up her waterskin and a satchel. "Not running ahead, but claiming idorrá over you."

Teraeth frowned. "I don't even know what that word means."

"Oh, it's a Joratese idiomatic expression . . ." Thurvishar started to say, but he trailed off as he noticed me making frantic slicing motions across my throat. "But that's not important right now," Thurvishar said in a much softer tone.[4]

[4] As I was saying, the word *idorrá* is a Joratese idiomatic expression that in the original Karo means leadership and influence over an area and group–people, property, livestock–which an individual protects and thus has authority over.

"You should have consulted with us," Teraeth insisted. "I'm used to him running off without warning–" He pointed to me.

"Hey," I said. "You usually have a little warning."[5]

"–but I can't babysit both of you," Teraeth continued, locking glares with Janel.

She stood nearly a foot shorter than he, and yet she still took up all the space. I found myself reminded of her father, High General Qoran Milligreest. Mostly of her father's temper.

Did the room seem warmer just then? It seemed like it to me.

"Babysitting? Who told you I needed a babysitter? Who made that your job?" Janel flicked a thumb and forefinger against Teraeth's chest. "Listen up, because I am only going to explain this once: I do not need your permission to do the right thing." She smiled, though not in a friendly way. "Now that I ponder the matter, it occurs to me I do not need your permission *for anything.*" She slung her waterskin over her shoulder. "Rest's over. We should keep moving." Without waiting for us, she began walking down the tunnel.

I wasn't wandering anywhere near that argument, and she had a point about moving, so I picked up my supplies and followed. After a brief hesitation, Teraeth and Thurvishar did as well.

Teraeth caught up to me and sighed. "She is *definitely* starting to remember our past life together."[6]

5 Depending on one's definition of "little."

6 Honestly, given Joratese cultural standards, Teraeth upset Janel entirely on his own merits.

# 11: Not a Love Story

***(Therin's story)***
***Twenty-four days earlier . . .***

When Therin woke, he lay in a bed covered with pale green silk sheets in an irregular room with no windows and with walls made from cob, carved with trees, leaves, and summer flowers. The air smelled fresh and verdant. The softest pink glow, emanating from small crystals hanging from the ceiling, lit the room around him. Where was he? Not the D'Mon palace. Possibly not even in Quur.

He felt weak and ravenously hungry, both signs of serious injuries healed magically. He pulled himself up, pleased at being strong enough to accomplish that much.

Miya–Miya, who was so beautiful that after twenty-five years his breath still caught in his throat every time he saw her–sat on the edge of the bed, next to him. A tray of food rested next to her, ample evidence his awakening wasn't unexpected. Therin didn't recognize the dishes.

Miya smiled and touched his cheek. "How are you feeling?"

Panic finally overtook him. "Wait, what happened? Where–?"

"What's the last thing you remember?" Her hand pressed against his shoulder, a strong suggestion to stay in bed.

Therin didn't try to fight her. Everything was hazy, with scenes of unspeakable violence presenting themselves in lightning flashes and then dissolving before comprehension could thunder home, but he remembered . . .

Gadrith. He remembered Gadrith and Xaltorath and his son Kihrin's body lying on an altar, a gaping wound where his son's heart should have been. He remembered rage and pain and the knowledge he had been betrayed.

"Did we lose?" he asked.

"I suppose that would depend on one's definitions," Miya admitted after a long beat. "If you mean the Capital is naught but a smoking ruin and the D'Mons are . . . gone . . . then yes, we lost."

His breath shuddered in his chest as he fought to wrestle with grief and anger and all the rage of a lifetime. "Everyone? The entire family?"

"Your daughters were absent," Miya said, "so there is no reason to think them dead. I do not know what happened to your . . ." She paused. "I do not know what happened to Darzin, if someone dealt with him or not. I thought it best to remove you from the city; this is the second D'Mon attempt at a coup in twenty-five years, and this one started a Hellmarch. I doubt the council would ignore that."[1]

Therin's heart was twisting into pieces. He didn't remember . . . but he remembered enough. More than enough. The guilt was crippling. Kihrin had tried to warn him, hadn't he? And he hadn't listened. How many people had his pride killed?

"Gadrith?" he finally asked.

"Emperor," Miya answered in a voice so cold and flat it made him shiver. "But," she added, "emperor for how long? That I do not know."

"What do you mean?"

"Look at your wrist."

He didn't understand what she meant at first. Then he realized what he wasn't seeing around his wrist: Miya's gaesh, a small silver tree medallion. He felt a moment's confusion, wondered if someone might have stolen it or if it had somehow been lost in the fighting. In all the years he'd known Miya, the talisman holding a piece of her soul had never once left his wrist. She couldn't have removed it herself; the gaesh prevented it.

"How . . . ?" Therin couldn't put his thoughts into words. "Who took it?"

"Not stolen," Miya said. "Destroyed. It disintegrated. I am not gaeshed anymore–the missing fragment of my soul returned. Someone destroyed the Stone of Shackles. How, I do not know. I cannot imagine Gadrith doing so, so perhaps someone has finally slain the villain. Of course, this is conjecture. I cannot know for certain."

Therin's stomach knotted. "Why am I here?"

Miya frowned. "I explained–"

Therin almost picked up her hand, but stopped himself at the last second. "No, I mean, not just why did you bring me here? Why bring me *anywhere*? If you're not gaeshed anymore, why *wouldn't* you leave me to face the High Council's anger? Why are you still here with me? Why rescue me from the council at all? You weren't with me of your own free will. That can't be so easy to forgive."

[1] Honestly, that's almost a reasonable explanation. I rather suspect the High Council would have had some unpleasant questions had Therin stayed.

Miya stared at him, open-mouthed. Then she looked away and laughed, light and sweet, the most beautiful ringing of crystal bells.

"Don't misunderstand," Therin said, "I'm glad you're here, but–"

She shifted the tray over to the bedside. "You need to regain your strength. You should eat."

"Miya–"

She stared straight into his eyes. "I am not bound to answer your questions anymore. So eat, or I will be cross with you."

Bemused, Therin reached down toward a dish. Fruit of some kind. It tasted like a ripe tart berry, although the flesh more closely resembled mango. Next to that, something like sugar floss, tasting sweet and creamy, with a hint of vanilla. The banana was more recognizable, except it tasted like lime. The only meat dish consisted of dense lobsterlike flesh, covered in a savory brown mushroom sauce. He almost asked her what the last dish was, but decided against it. It was delicious, he needed the protein, and he'd do himself no favors if its provenance made him squeamish.[2]

He reached for the goblet and discovered it too contained fruit, this time juice, coconut-like in taste.

Sag bread for eating was absent, just a spoon and a slender, delicate fork, four-pronged and distinctive. He'd have taken it as a sign they were in Kirpis, but the food . . .

"This is the Manol?"

"Yes."

Therin took a deep breath and concentrated on eating. The Manol. The heart and home of the vané people, unwelcoming to foreigners. Especially unwelcoming to Quuros. He wouldn't have been surprised to discover trespassing was a capital crime.

When he finished, he pushed the tray aside, amazed at how much better he felt. "So now I've eaten. Can we revisit why you're helping me instead of all the other things you justifiably should be doing instead? I find myself surprised to still be alive, to be honest."

That made her laugh again. Miya leaned over and kissed him on the nose. "Idiot. You truly cannot guess?"

All the air fled the room. Therin's throat threatened to close on him; he lifted a knee to hide how that simple touch had made him stiffen like a teenager. "No. No, I can't. I have guessed wrong before–"

*"No," Kihrin interrupted. "Absolutely not. This is not happening."*

*Thurvishar stopped reading. "Pardon?"*

[2] It's a type of caterpillar. Apparently a delicacy and, surprisingly for the Manol, not poisonous.

*"If this narration is about to describe my parents having sex, I don't need to hear it. Ever.* No one *needs to hear it. In fact, remove all those scenes." Kihrin pointed to the papers.*

*Thurvishar narrowed his eyes. "No."*

*"No, it's not going to turn into my parents fooling around?" Kihrin looked skeptical.*

*"No, I'm not going to stop* reading *a scene just because it involves physical intimacy between two people who happen to be your parents." Thurvishar rolled his eyes. "Veils, Kihrin, I wasn't planning on going into detail."*[3]

*The wizard continued reading while Kihrin contemplated plugging his ears.*

A flicker of pain crossed Miya's face. "You didn't guess wrong," she said, "but holding my heart is not the same as trapping my soul. How could I ever tell you yes when I could never choose to say no?"

Therin stared at her, hardly daring to breathe. She couldn't mean . . .

He closed his eyes and cursed himself, cursed himself a thousand times as the worst fool. Never, he thought, had there been a greater idiot than himself.[4]

Therin lifted a hand to her face, tucked a strand of her hair back behind her ear. He couldn't speak right away, his voice trapped in his throat. Regret choked him mute, thinking back to the early offers he'd made to free Miya, always refused,[5] and how he'd gradually stopped asking.

He'd stopped offering because he'd been terrified she'd finally accept.

"I'm sorry," he whispered. "I'm so sorry for everything I've put you through."

His apology caught her off guard. An animal sob escaped her throat while tears sprang up in her eyes.

Then her mouth came down against his, violently, as if he were the antidote to all her poisons. She fell into his arms, and no guessing was necessary. He wrapped his arms around her, leaving her mouth only to gasp for air and slip down to her jaw, her neck. She was everything he'd ever wanted, knowing the wish unobtainable. Events had taken on the cloak of dream. Impossible. Glorious.

"No," he whispered, lowering his hands from her body.

"What?" Miya seemed to shake herself awake, staring at him in shock. "No?"

[3] Not graphic detail, anyway.

[4] I mean . . . I'm sure that's technically not true . . .

[5] I suspect initially Khaeriel must have refused because she saw the need to adjust to her new body and relearn her magical skills. House D'Mon must have offered her reasonable safety. It might have even seemed *clever.*

"Tell me you want this," he said. "No guessing. No assumptions. Tell me you want me to make love with you."

Miya exhaled, her relief obvious. "Gods, yes," she whispered as she tore at her clothes. She hadn't even finished undressing fully when she pushed the sheets off his body and straddled him.

"Goddess," he corrected, reverently. "Miya–"

Therin instantly knew he'd done something wrong. She froze.

"What's wrong? Am I hurting you?"

She shuddered and drew a deep breath before shaking her head. "No. No, it is fine." She finished lowering herself and pulled her raisigi off her body, revealing breasts he had been dreaming about for over twenty years.

His body would have betrayed him a hundred times if he hadn't used magic to force the issue. He wanted this too desperately, too fervently, and it had been too long. He was damned if he would spend himself in minutes. He kissed the tears from her skin, unsure if those tears were hers or his. The pain and horror of the last day–the last day he remembered, anyway–was all too fresh, too shocking. He had lost everything.

Therin didn't care as long as he had her.

# 12: Four Branches

*Kihrin showed Thurvishar a rude gesture.*

*Thurvishar chuckled. "Oh, it wasn't that bad."*

*"Easy for you to say; those weren't your parents."*

**(Kihrin's story)**

We reached a crossroads in the tunnel, four branches stretching out into darkness. The air smelled wet and musty; the temperature a steady balm compared to the heat above. It was still claustrophobic. I found myself glad the tunnels had been originally built to house large carriages; it kept me from curling into a little ball, screaming.

I don't like enclosed spaces.

Teraeth turned to me. "Which way?"

I shrugged. "Like I know? I lost track when we didn't take a left turn at Vol Karoth."

"We could walk in circles if these tunnels connect the wrong way," Janel said.

No one disagreed with her, but no one had any suggestions either.

"Do you think we're far enough away for you to open a gate?" I asked Thurvishar.

"Do you want to take the risk if we're not?" Thurvishar shook his head. "We don't have anything to use as cover this time."

Mentioning the sword-dropping chaos storm reminded me of the weapon I still carried. The metal now looked pitted and corroded.

"How long did you say these weapons would last?"

Janel shook her head. "I had thought a few days, but they seem to be degrading faster this time."

While Janel and I spoke, Thurvishar walked to the crossroads and squatted down, putting a hand on the stone ground. He tilted his head to the side as though listening to something beyond normal hearing.

Thurvishar stood. "South is that direction." He pointed down the right tunnel.

"How do you know that?" I asked.

Thurvishar gave me a look. "I'm half-dreth."

"Oh, right." I knew almost nothing about dreth except they lived underground, but it seemed reasonable they'd be sensitive to direction–a handy talent if one never saw the sky.

I was glad I wasn't *any* amount dreth.[1]

"We shouldn't tarry." Janel walked forward. We followed her, continuing what was starting to seem like an endless trek.

I wasn't sure when we should stop. We had no way to judge day or night. We'd stop when we were tired.

"Question for you, Janel," I said, mostly to make conversation.

"Yes?"

"Why is being an old woman a compliment to those morgage? I mean, you told that warrior you hoped he died an old woman and he just blushed at you, like you'd said he was cute."

"I'm going to scout up ahead," Teraeth announced.

I frowned at him, although at least Janel didn't take the opportunity to point out he certainly hadn't "consulted with the rest of us," despite his lecture earlier. Teraeth jogged ahead into the dark tunnel.

"It's a funny thing about morgage." Janel scratched her chin. "Did you see any little girls back at the camp?"

"I wasn't paying attention," I answered. "And I'm not sure I could tell a baby girl morgage from a baby boy morgage."

"You'll never have to. Baby girl morgage don't exist."

I blinked. "I'm sorry. What was that?"

Janel nodded at my surprise. "Morgage babies are born male. Always. So all morgage children are boys. I know how odd that sounds. It threw me off too."

Thurvishar cleared his throat. "I hate to be a pedant, but we've met morgage women. A new and novel experience for me, although I knew from Kihrin's transcripts they existed. Bevrosa is undeniably female."

"Yes," Janel said, "but she wasn't born female. No morgage is. All these morgage baby boys grow up into strapping young morgage men, expected to prove their bravery, protect the tribe, attack their enemies, and impregnate as many women as they can, whether said women are willing or not." She made a face. "That last part isn't a stellar commentary on morgage culture, lest you think we've horribly misjudged them all these years. After they've proven their worth and are covered in battle scars, they will settle down and become women. Literally become women. They physically change. And those women lead the tribes–

[1] I will attempt to not take that personally.

because it's assumed they have the most experience and wisdom–as well as have more baby boys, this time as mothers. I shudder to think what would happen if a morgage doesn't want to perform their societal duties, but I shall assume that is *also* not a fantastic commentary on morgage culture."

"What?" I actually stopped walking. "No, seriously. *What?*"

"I'm with Kihrin on this one." Thurvishar too turned to face her. "What?"

Janel shrugged. "It's not difficult to understand. Morgage have two biological sexes, but they experience them sequentially. They're born male, and if they're lucky, tough, and smart, in various combinations, they'll die female. To them, this is perfectly normal. Thus, 'May you die an old woman'–a morgage blessing."

I blinked and shook my head.

"That's amazing," Thurvishar said. "No wonder the scholars at the Academy never deciphered morgage social structures. That's . . . that's stranger than any theory I've run across, including old Professor Dogal's drone theory. Do you know if this trait is a morgage-specific mutation? Were the voramer like this as well?"

I stopped cold.

"You don't think–" I racked my brain to remember if I'd ever met a male voramer. Not many voramer existed since they'd sacrificed their immortality for the Ritual of Night. Only two, as far as I knew: Thaena and Galava. Both were women. Sharanakal was male, but he was a dragon now. It probably didn't count.

Thurvishar looked thoughtful. "I wonder how many generations it takes for that particular trait to breed out."

I met his stare. Thaena had two children besides that dragon: Khaevatz and *Teraeth,* both half-vané and half-voramer. If being half-voramer was enough . . . [2]

I remembered the earlier conversation–okay, *argument*–between Teraeth and Janel. When she'd been explaining morgage women were always in charge and he'd retorted he knew perfectly well how *voramer* physiology worked. How angry he'd been and how little sense that had made.

"An auctioneer at the Octagon once offered to sell me a half-morgage girl . . ." I bit my lip. "But who knows if he was lying."

"Perhaps it doesn't always breed true," Thurvishar suggested.

I swallowed. "You're saying there's a chance someday Teraeth is going to . . . change sex?"

[2] I admit to still being curious as to how this would work. As a voramer, Teraeth should transition to female at the appropriate time, but vané can be any gender they wish.

Janel tilted her head toward us as she passed us. "Being female is no curse."

A whistle sounded from up the tunnel.

"That's Teraeth," I said.

We all started running.

# 13: The Strongest Claim

***(Khaeriel's story)***
***Twenty-three days earlier . . .***

After, Khaeriel nestled in Therin's arms, a task far less onerous than she'd expected. To her delightful surprise, Therin had proved a talented lover. He hadn't been the last time, but he'd been drunk and brutish, oblivious to any pleasure but his own. This time, it had been as different as jungle from desert.

She sighed happily as Therin's fingertips traced patterns against her skin.

He kissed her cheek. "I'll get a message to Qoran. I'm sure we can work out a deal to keep the council happy—"

She sat up, sliding away from him. "No. I will not speak to the council. And we need to talk about what you called out earlier."

"'Oh gods, oh gods'?"

"No, before that." Khaeriel bit her lip. Stars. He was *smiling.* He had a beautiful smile.

"'I love you'?"

Khaeriel nearly choked. The enchantment was working so much better than she ever could have expected. A lovely warmth spread over her . . . and a flutter of apprehension. It might be working *too* well. "You didn't say that," she whispered.

"No wonder you wanted to talk about it then. Unforgivable lapse on my part." He reached over and ran a finger over her cheek. "I love you," he said again.

A new feeling came over Khaeriel: loathing.

Not loathing for Therin. She should have been happy to know her spell had taken so fully, but instead, Khaeriel felt shame. Was this so different from what had been done to her? Worse, for even if she'd have died for disobeying an order, she'd still been allowed the dignity of her own emotions, her own hate. Instead of contempt for the woman who'd massacred his family, Therin was enthralled.

Used without knowing it.

Khaeriel had never hated herself as much as she did precisely then.[1]

"Hey." Therin sat up and reached out to her. "That wasn't supposed to make you cry."

She wiped her eyes. "It's not you, it's . . ." She cursed herself as his face transitioned through a dozen emotions, including fear. Khaeriel floundered for a quick, believable lie. "I don't deserve to feel this happy."

"You don't–?" Therin laughed darkly, then pulled her back into his arms. "Oh gods, I understand. I do. It's been a terrible couple of days and I–" He shook his head. "I am such an idiot. It's all my fault. I *know* it's all my fault. If I'd stopped Darzin when I should have–" Therin shuddered. "You're the only thing keeping me sane."

"I have done things, Therin. You don't . . . you don't know."

He squeezed her. "It doesn't matter. Whatever it was . . . who cares? I'm far from perfect myself, as you are well aware. If you can forgive me for what I've done, then nothing you could possibly have committed is unforgivable either. Maybe that makes us a good match. We are well past the age when we expect our lovers to be perfect and without flaws."

Khaeriel pulled back so she could see his face. She had to focus. "I meant earlier, when you called me Miya. I did not wish for you to call me Miya, because that is not who I am. Literally. I am not Miya. I have *never* been Miya. The entire time we have known each other, I have never once been the woman whose name you've called me."

His smile faltered. "What? I realize that's a nickname . . ."

She inhaled deeply. "The real Miyathreall died before you and I ever met. The woman who gaeshed me originally"–Khaeriel wasn't yet ready to reveal it had been her grandmother Khaemezra, better known as Thaena, Goddess of Death[2]–"also prevented me from telling you certain things. Or showing you. I was not lying when I told you Miya was Queen Khaeriel's handmaiden. But only because Miya was *my* handmaiden. And also my murderer."

Therin blinked at her. "I don't understand."

"I was wearing a necklace–an artifact–called the Stone of Shackles," she explained, then laughed blackly. "I didn't know what its power was! Which was to switch the wearer's soul with their murderer's. Miya was an assassin my brother sent to kill me.[3] When she did, I ended up in her body, but I have always been Khaeriel."

He flinched at the Manol queen's name. Khaeriel's heart fluttered with fear, wondering if the words had triggered a latent memory of the

[1] And deservedly so, in my opinion. There's a *reason* enchantments are considered black magic.

[2] As Therin was once a Thaenan priest, I suspect that was wise. It would have sidetracked the entire conversation.

[3] Afterward, Miya's sister married the king, so that's interesting.

first time she'd said the name, where everything had ended with blood and death. Enchantments were tricky in their early stages.

Therin shook his head. "I don't even know what to say. Really? The vané queen? No one ever recognized you? It's not like I avoided taking you out in public . . ."

"I just explained this. I do not look like Khaeriel right now; this is Miya's body, and as much as I made it my own, I was never allowed to change the outward guise."

He tilted his head, squinted his eyes in confusion. "Made it your own? I still don't understand."

"My race is mercurial. We choose our appearance. Perhaps it would be best if I demonstrate. Would you like to see?"

". . . yes?" he said.

She pulled herself fully onto the bed and crossed her legs under her, breathing deeply as she put herself into the proper meditative state. What she attempted was usually done slowly—over the course of weeks, if not months. Doing so quickly invited insanity, something any mimic could confirm.[4]

Still, Khaeriel didn't have weeks or months.

She still took several excruciating hours, though. She didn't allow Therin's gasp to disturb her concentration, although it confirmed the process was working. After so many years, she'd been concerned she'd lost too much sense of self to ever return.

For a vané, the physical body was mutable. Taken to the most ridiculous extremes, the same ability created the mimics, but it had been fourteen thousand years since anyone had been foolish enough to imprint a vané with that kind of shape-shifting proficiency.

When she opened her eyes again, they were not blue but gold, bright as her gold-spun hair, both almost luminescent against her dark bronze skin. She knew her face, her body, every part of her, all looked different. If Khaeriel had her way, she would never appear as Miya—or anyone else—again.

One might well note the similarities in her appearance—her cheekbones, her jawline—to certain D'Mons: to Pedron, to Tishar, and to her son, Kihrin.

Therin stared. "Are we . . . are we related?"

Khaeriel smiled. He had noticed. "As Khaeriel, I would have been, yes. Cousins, twice removed. Close, but humans would not consider it incest. No vané would."

She saw him doing the mental gymnastics, putting the pieces together. He knew more vané history than most Quuros, even most

[4] I've been told rushing the process is also exquisitely painful.

Quuros scholars. There had only been one vané in the family tree before Khaeriel–a slave girl named Valrashar. So for that relationship to have worked . . .

It meant Valrashar's father had to have been Khaeriel's uncle, the infamous Terindel.[5]

"The stories have lied, you understand," Khaeriel admitted. "I loved my father, but he twisted history to support his reign, as rulers often do. The truth is my father usurped his throne from his brother, Terindel, and then used his new position to marry the Manol vané's ruler, Khaevatz. To eliminate their threat, Terindel's wife was executed and his daughter sold into slavery." She laughed bitterly. "You might say my younger brother, Kelanis, is simply upholding a venerable family tradition."

"I'm related to Terindel the Black?" Therin was having trouble absorbing the news.

"Yes," she answered. "He was your great-grandfather. Which makes you"–she caressed his face–"my darling, the true Kirpis vané heir. Whereas even if I discount my father's claim, bought as it was with dishonorable coin, no one will deny that I am Queen Khaevatz's firstborn child. So you are the true Kirpis vané heir, and I am the true Manol vané heir"[6]

Those lovely blue eyes turned calculating. "You want to retake the throne."

"Yes, I do," Khaeriel said. "But not alone. The two of us, together. Our claim is stronger than Kelanis could ever hope to match."

"But I'm not vané."

"Do not waste your time worrying over inconsequential details, my dear. No one will care when we are through."

Therin seemed skeptical, but didn't pursue the matter. "And then what?"

Khaeriel smiled as she slipped back into his arms. "And then we raise an army, invade Quur, and burn that entire accursed empire to the ground." This was the final test of how well the enchantment had taken, for if she could convince him to agree with her, she knew Therin was hers. If his loyalty was to Quur, to his old power base as high lord, he would never agree to such a plan. He'd try to talk her out of it. He'd hope he could make her see *reason*. Even if he had someone managed to

[5] This is a good time to point out once more that Teraeth and Kihrin are not in any way related to each other in a biological sense. Just in case you may have been concerned.

[6] What this makes Kihrin is quite the political knot. Kihrin does have a strong claim to the Kirpis vané throne through his father. His mother's status is more open to debate.

defy her enchantment, she knew him well enough to be confident that she could spot him out if his enthusiasm was a charade.

Therin buried his face in her hair and smiled. “Yes,” he whispered. “That plan works for me just fine.”

# 14: The Sand Daughters

***(Kihrin's story)***

We found Teraeth crouched down behind a broken slab thrusting up from the tunnel floor. The area beyond was the first time we'd stumbled across any signs of decay or neglect; the floor and ceiling were missing large sections, while a steady stream of sand made islands among the rubble. The wet smells of the tunnel had been replaced by the scent of hot sand.

Teraeth threw us an irritated look. "I meant join me, not imitate a herd of elephants while you did it. You used to be a thief, Kihrin. Did you forget how to be quiet?"[1]

"Oh, my bad. I thought you were in *trouble,*" I said.

Teraeth scowled as he turned back toward the rubble. "We're all in trouble. Settle down for a minute and see what's blocking our way."

We crouched down behind the rubble and waited. We didn't have to wait for long.

Undulating flesh broke the surface in a smooth arc, then descended again.

"What the hell is that?" Janel asked.

"A tentacle," I whispered. "A large tentacle. Is that a sand kraken? Is there such a thing as sand kraken?"

Thurvishar exhaled. "The evidence of my eyes suggests yes. Although it's not as large as the Daughter of Laaka you described meeting while you sailed on the *Misery.*"

I gave the wizard a look. I sometimes forgot he knew far more about my life history than I found comfortable.

"I can't guarantee there's only one," Teraeth said. "It's hard to tell."

"What are kraken vulnerable to?" Janel asked.

"Fire-breathing dragons," I answered, "but I left mine on my other island."

"It's worse than you know," Teraeth said. "Considering how it's hid-

[1] It's as if Teraeth had forgotten he called us to him by *whistling.*

ing under the sand, I don't think it can see—which means it probably hunts by vibration."

Thurvishar stood. "That means it already knows we're here."

Teraeth might have been mistaken on sand kraken hunting techniques. As soon as Thurvishar stood, a tentacle shot through the gap in the floor and wrapped around his torso. Naturally enough, he screamed.[2] The creature moved with extraordinary speed, but at least this kraken's tentacle didn't have spikes replacing suckers. Small comfort, though.

Janel swung her blade at the creature's outstretched arm.

Her sword broke, the loud crack echoing through the tunnel.

"Damn it," she said. She dove for Thurvishar's waist as another tentacle emerged from the sand to help drag the kraken's new prize back to a presumably waiting maw.

I swung my sword at a tentacle as well. I didn't expect it to hold up better, but it was all I had. My sword didn't break, but it also didn't do much good. My blade's deteriorating edge didn't make a mark on the creature's tough, scaled skin.

Teraeth had started stabbing. He was on his fifth dagger, with four crumbling blades littering the ground at his feet. At least he'd accounted for several severed tentacles, but there seemed to be an endless supply.

Then a tentacle wrapped around my sword arm and yanked me up into the air.

"Shit!" I cursed.

"Oh, to hell with this." Janel's black hands lit up with fire as she placed them directly on a tentacle. A nightmarish animal yowl filled the air.

I was pretty sure we'd just made the kraken angry.

The sand began violently boiling. Something emerged. I noticed the resemblance to an octopus's head, although nothing so wet or moist. This looked like some mad god had taken an octopus and modified it for a life in the desert. More tentacles emerged, heading straight for Janel.

Thurvishar dove for her and pushed her aside. They both fell to the ground beneath the whipping tentacle. "I'm so sorry," he said at once. His face was pale. "I acted on instinct."

"You're the last person I expected that from," Janel said, grinning. "I'll let it pass this time." Her eyes blazed red as she rolled to her feet. She was . . . enjoying the fight.

I couldn't say the same for myself. The tentacle smashed me against

[2] It was more of a manly bellow. Fine. I screamed.

the ceiling, knocking the wind out of me. As I struggled for breath and something resembling a plan, I heard Thurvishar say, "Protect me. I'm going to try something."

As he said the words, a tentacle grabbed Teraeth and flipped him back.

"But . . . ," Janel protested, looking between myself and Teraeth, not sure whom to rescue first.

"Please do it!" Thurvishar crouched down and placed both hands on the sand pile. "I learned this from Tyentso."[3]

Teraeth managed to brace his legs against the monster's beak. His legs strained with the effort, but I knew it wouldn't be long before he'd succumb and find himself pulled straight into the creature's waiting maw.

A tiny part of me that had never stopped being a minstrel wondered just what this thing ate when random Hellwarriors didn't happen along.

Another tentacle lashed out at Thurvishar and Janel. She picked up a piece of fallen ceiling, a chunk easily half her size. It must have weighed several hundred pounds. She swatted the tentacle away like the stone was a delicate silver serving platter from the main table at House D'Mon.

The tentacle lashed at her again, while my own continued to play a rousing game of Smack-Kihrin-Against-the-Wall.

As I had little I could do other than push vainly at the appendage grabbing me, I had a moment to look at the monster. Chitinous plates covered it, with gaps allowing the limbs to bend. For all it mattered, this beastie had to be less maneuverable than a Daughter of Laaka.

"Whatever you're doing, do it *faster*!" Janel yelled as she ducked under a tentacle that tried to ensnare her.

Thurvishar ignored her. A faint thrumming began to fill the air. The sand began to vibrate, grains cascading down the slope from where the kraken had emerged.

Suddenly, Thurvishar jerked his hands back. As he did, a wave of . . . something . . . emanated from where he had been touching the sand. The resulting mass shifted, flowed, morphed, and then solidified. In seconds, the sand had become solid glass.

"Pretty," Janel said, "but I'm not sure how it helps . . . ?"

The transformation didn't seem to be stopping the kraken. The amount of creature free from the sand included far more mouth and tentacle than I was comfortable with.

"Wait for it," Thurvishar said, holding his side as he slowly backed away. Sweat ran down the side of his head.

[3] Sort of. I knew it was *possible* because of Tyentso. Not precisely the same thing.

The sand kraken flexed the tentacle holding me aloft, but then, as it prepared to brain me against the wall, it screamed. The deafening sound echoed in the tight corridor space. The tentacle unfurled, dropping me back to the ground.

I looked up. Blood dripped from all the gaps in the monster's carapace. Each time it moved, it flinched and screamed. More blood poured out.

The kraken stopped moving. It wasn't dead. I could tell from the way its eyes followed Teraeth as he escaped its slack grip and climbed down. "What did you do?" he asked Thurvishar.

"Glass." Thurvishar looked pale, drained, exhausted. "The creature lives under sand . . . it had to be coated in the stuff. So I turned all the sand around us into glass." He cleared his throat, embarrassed.

"And the chaos storms?" Teraeth asked.

"I took a chance," Thurvishar admitted.

"Took a chance . . ." Teraeth rolled his eyes and muttered under his breath as he walked over to find salvageable daggers.

"Now it can't move or it will cut itself into ribbons," Janel said. "Nicely done." She slapped Thurvishar on the back.

Noise rumbled through the tunnel as the air around the monster sparked in violet, red, and green flashes.

"Chaos storm," I said. "Run!"

No one needed to be told twice.

# 15: A Foundation of Lies

***(Khaeriel's story)***
***Fourteen days earlier . . .***

Khaeriel looked up from writing as Therin knocked at the open door. It seemed like the last few days had been filled with nothing but letters and codes and carefully worded messages as she tried to organize what allies she still might possess without alerting her brother.

She welcomed an interruption.

Therin stood there, grinning at her. She marveled at what a difference a few weeks had made. He seemed at least a decade younger, the years melting from him along with his stressful burdens.

She set down the quill and turned toward him. "How long were you watching me?"

"Not long," Therin admitted. "Actually, you have a visitor. He showed up out of nowhere–literally out of nowhere–and asked for you *by your real name.*"

Khaeriel blinked. "What?" She suppressed a flutter of panic. Her safe house had been well hidden, and few vané knew it existed. Fewer still would have any reason to suspect her presence there. She could count the possible candidates on one hand. Would an enemy have given Therin a polite introduction and request to speak with her?

"What does he look like?" She crossed over to him.

"Quuros, medium height. Average." Therin raised an eyebrow. "Is there a problem?"

"Relos Var," she exhaled. "Finally." Khaeriel put a hand to Therin's cheek. "There is no problem. He is an old friend. But it might be best if you wait here. Relos can be reticent around people he does not know well."

Therin frowned. "I've heard Relos Var's name before. Not in a good way."

"He has become infamous in certain circles," Khaeriel said, "but we shall need his assistance if our plans are to succeed."

Therin's expression turned wry. "I suppose it wouldn't do to spurn his help just because he has a reputation for being a provocateur against the Quuros Empire, would it?" He kissed her cheek. "Good luck."

Khaeriel grabbed Therin, turned the chaste kiss into something a little more memorable, and then walked outside.

Relos Var waited in the small clearing near the root shelter. He looked the same as she remembered—an average-looking Quuros man who might have been anything from a merchant to a cobbler. He had a penchant for well-crafted boots, but otherwise wore functional, practical clothing that leaned more toward drab than fashionable.

But no, looking closer, something seemed different. Relos Var looked haggard. His appearance hadn't changed; this was something more ephemeral.

"Your Majesty." Relos Var bowed as soon as she entered the clearing.

"Oh, stop," Khaeriel said, but his dramatics always made her smile. "I would ask where you have been, but from the look on your face, I will take it as granted you have been busy."

"More than I can say," Relos Var agreed. "I came as soon as possible." He paused and gestured toward the root shelter. "But if I may, Your Majesty—what friend would I be if I didn't point out your present course is extraordinarily ill-advised."[1]

"The safe house? It should serve for a few more days—"

"Therin D'Mon, Your Majesty." Relos Var shook his head. "Really? *Therin?*"

Khaeriel's cheeks flushed. "He is a direct descendant of Terindel. Why shouldn't I use him?"

"Teraeth is a direct descendant of Terindel too. A much closer descendant. Yet we both know why you're not using *him.*"[2]

She dismissed the idea with a flick of her fingers. "Teraeth is a direct descendant of Mithraill. I know how the Stone of Shackles works. If I didn't, I wouldn't need Therin. And I can handle the politics, thank you."

Relos Var sighed. "Khaeriel—this isn't about politics. This is about you. This is about you making a tragic mistake. He can't possibly be here of his own free will. I saw the mess you left behind in the Capital. Therin D'Mon would never overlook that under normal circumstances."

"I've enchanted him."

Relos Var stared at her.

Khaeriel swallowed and looked away. "He has free will, he's just madly in love with me. And he doesn't remember the last several hours after the Hellmarch started."

"You repressed memories too?" Relos Var seemed even less thrilled.

"Yes."

[1] It makes me uncomfortable when I find myself agreeing with Relos Var.

[2] Because he'd say no?

"That won't last. Souls *never* lose memories. Not permanently. Once his memories return, the shock will break any enchantment you've placed on him. An enchantment cannot overcome trauma forever."

"I want his cooperation, Relos. I will have it."

"That's not what's going on here. You can lie to yourself but not to me." The wizard shook his head. "Damn it, Khaeriel. You picked a hell of a time to fall in love."

Khaeriel's mouth fell open. "*Me?* You seriously think I'm in love with–" She looked around to make sure Therin hadn't picked a particularly poor time to eavesdrop. Khaeriel lowered her voice. "You honestly think I am in love with the man who kept me a slave for a quarter century? Do you have any idea the indignities I have suffered at his hands? And you are hardly one to judge. What was that Marakori witch's name? The one you were so taken with a few decades ago? Did *she* have any choice in the matter?"[3]

Relos Var didn't seem inclined to rise to the bait. "I am not saying you can't have him; I am saying if you think you can have him *like this* without consequences, you are playing the fool. The truth will tell. The truth *always* tells. I am saying this to you, not as a coconspirator or an ally but as a friend; remove the enchantment and tell him the truth. Tell Therin you weren't in your right mind. Perhaps he'll believe you. Perhaps he'll even forgive you."

"I will not–"

"By my word, Khaeriel, if you don't, I promise you'll regret it. As you said, he has free will. An enchantment isn't a gaesh. If someone comes along and tells him the truth, this charade is done. Do you think our enemies don't know what happened? Do you think *Thaena* doesn't know? Even as we speak, she is Returning the House D'Mon members *you murdered*. And while you enjoy your pleasurable idylls in this picturesque bower, Vol Karoth has been released. I don't need to tell you what that means."

"No." Khaeriel felt panic well up in her. "I thought we would have more time."

"I can only assume certain forces had reason to hurry the schedule," Relos Var said blandly.[4] "So we don't have more time, and you're going to need to move now to stop your brother from doing something we will all regret–enacting the Ritual of Night."

Khaeriel closed her eyes and exhaled. "You have truly brought me a bouquet of sorrows today, do you realize that?"

[3] Depends on one's definition of *choice*.

[4] Of course, this wasn't technically a lie, was it? He just left out the part where *he* was the "certain forces" he'd just mentioned.

"Then let me give you two gifts to lighten your heavy heart." Relos Var snapped his fingers, and a triangular package appeared on the ground next to him.[5]

Khaeriel recognized it: the harp Valathea.

Queen Valathea.

"As per our agreement. I assume you'll know what to do with her."

Khaeriel ran a reverent hand over the harp, feeling the tuning pegs even through the cover. "Yes, yes, I most certainly do." She raised her eyes to look into Relos Var's. "Two gifts?"

"The second gift is knowledge," Relos Var said. "Your son, Kihrin, is alive."

She stared at him. The air in the clearing seemed to vanish, and she couldn't draw a breath. The daggerlike pain in her heart was paralyzing. Relos Var had a faint smile on his face, a twinkle in his eyes, the look a man thoroughly enjoying the response his pronouncement had elicited.

"That is not funny."

"It wasn't meant to be," Relos Var reassured her. "I've spoken with him. He's alive."

"Darzin and Gadrith sacrificed him to Xaltorath. I saw the body. No one comes back from that."

"No one before Kihrin, you mean," Relos Var said. "For reasons I don't understand and honestly would love to, Xaltorath didn't eat Kihrin's soul or turn him into a demon. Instead"–he brought his fingers to his mouth and made a puffing motion–"they let him go. Your son found Urthaenriel. He shattered the Stone of Shackles. He killed Darzin, then slew Gadrith with that same sword, while Gadrith possessed the body of my . . ." Only on the last word did Relos Var stumble. "–of the emperor. I told you years ago your son would fulfill the prophecies. He is doing so, and honestly, without much help from me at all."

"Then he's going to come here." It wasn't a question. She simultaneously felt elation and pure terror. Her son was alive . . .

. . . which meant her sins became even less forgivable. Excuses evaporated. And now he was on a collision course with her–and with his father.

"He's already here. Of course, King Kelanis is unlikely to drop everything to see him, even with the Ritual of Night involved."[6] Relos Var tilted his head.

Khaeriel fought to keep from hyperventilating. "Does he know? About me? About . . . what happened?"

[5] I assume he'd cloaked it with an illusion? Summonings don't work like this, but Var does love his dramatic gestures.

[6] No indeed. You should have seen the spectacular bureaucratic runaround the vané gave us.

"I'm sure someone must have told him by now."

She inhaled.

"So now I must ask this question: Does this change anything? I'd be surprised indeed if you hadn't been plotting vengeance against those responsible for Kihrin's death. Now that you know Gadrith and Darzin are dead, does this change your plans to retake your throne?"

Khaeriel's eyes widened, and then she laughed out loud. "No. Gods, no. My brother still betrayed me, had me assassinated, sentenced me to the Traitor's Walk. He will pay for that. And Quur–Quur still has a great deal to answer for."

"True." Relos Var started to walk away, raised his hands as though to call upon the energies to open a gate, then paused and turned back to Khaeriel. "Do you know what the real problem with immortality is?"

Khaeriel blinked. "I am not certain I understand your point."

Relos Var walked back to her. "Immortality. You're a few hundred years old, so I'm sure you think you've seen it all, that you know all the answers. You haven't, and you don't."

She flushed again. "I am almost five hundred years–"

Relos Var waved a hand. "And I'm over fourteen thousand years old. I am older than humanity's presence on this world."

She closed her mouth. She forgot sometimes. Forgot Relos Var matched the vané's race for age.

"Fourteen thousand years old," Relos Var repeated. "And let me spell this out–the problem with immortality isn't that you forget things. It isn't that you grow bored–there is always something new to learn. It isn't even watching the people you love who aren't immortal die–that's tragic, but loss is part of life. No. None of that. It is watching the people you care about make the same *stupid* fucking mistakes again and again and again."

Khaeriel scowled. "I am in control of this, Relos."

"Are you, though? I just watched a good friend throw his life away because he too thought he was in control. He very much wasn't.[7] Don't follow in his wake, Khaeriel. Nothing about *your* situation will end in anything but tears if you ignore my advice. If nothing else, lies make a poor foundation for love."[8] He pointed to the root shelter and presumably to Therin, just to make sure she caught his point.

Khaeriel pulled herself up. "I'm a grown woman. I can make my own decisions."

A resigned look came over the wizard's face. "As you say, Your Majesty. But please at least consider my words. I vastly prefer it when my friends die of something other than the fickle whims of tragic farce."

[7] I assume he's referring to Duke Azhen Kaen of Yor. He can't have meant Gadrith.

[8] Honestly, who knew he'd be so sensible about this?

"You may *go,* Relos."

He opened up a gate and left.

After he'd departed, Khaeriel stood there for a moment in the clearing, thinking, hands resting on the curve of Valathea's neck. She exhaled slowly.

"I got to admit, ducky, that's a tough call. Personally? I think the old man has a point."

Khaeriel spun around. A woman Khaeriel hadn't seen in twenty years stood at the end of the clearing. Not since she was Khaeriel's handmaiden–the same handmaiden Khaeriel had sent off with the Stone of Shackles and a mission to deliver her infant son to friendly allies. She looked the same too, a beautiful young Quuros woman with honey-colored skin and doe-brown eyes. Impossible after twenty years, but Khaeriel knew better than to think her mortal.

By all the stars, she even wore the same dress.

"Lyrilyn? But it's not Lyrilyn anymore, is it?"

Talon grinned. "Yes and no. Can we talk?"

Khaeriel didn't hesitate. "Talk? Of course."

The vané queen attacked.

# 16: Travel Inconveniences

***(Kihrin's story)***

I grabbed Thurvishar's elbow and pulled him into a full sprint down the tunnel. Behind us came a vicious electrical whine while the sand kraken screamed. I didn't know what effect the chaos storm had taken, and truthfully, I didn't want to know; I just wanted to be outside the area of effect.

After my sides started to cramp and I was out of breath and gasping, I finally slowed down. I hadn't been running my fastest, mind you; Thurvishar was lagging behind.

Teraeth held up a hand. "That should be enough."

"Do you think we've escaped it?" Janel asked.

"I think if we were going to be caught in the storm, we would have by now."

Janel leaned her back against the tunnel wall and slowly slid downward. She pulled out her morgage waterskin, took a drink, and grimaced.

I also drank and immediately knew why she'd made the face. I mean, it was technically water, but its cleanliness was debatable.[1]

"We might as well stop here." Teraeth sat down. "Sleep for a while if we can. Who knows how long we'll have to walk until this tunnel ends? But if we meet any more sand kraken, I'm going to see if they're any good to eat."

My laughter was strained. If we met up with any more sand kraken, we were all going to die.

"This is . . . not ideal," Thurvishar said.

Janel smiled. "I do love your gift for understatement."

But Thurvishar hadn't just been making a commentary about our current predicament. Thurvishar was looking down at his long robes, dark gray rather than his usual House D'Lorus black. A darker color stained the cloth at his waist.

[1] Which I now find curious, because Bevrosa did have Wildheart. Perhaps she didn't realize the full extent of its abilities?

"You're bleeding," I said.

"I'd quite brilliantly tucked a dagger into my belt, you see." Thurvishar explained. "So when the kraken grabbed me . . ." He looked pale. "In hindsight, that may have been a tactical error."

"Oh hell. Teraeth, help me remove his robes." I scrambled over to Thurvishar's side to see how bad the damage was.

Pretty bad. While the dagger hadn't created a deep stab wound, the edge had sliced down efficiently. Thurvishar had bled the entire fight since, easy enough to ignore with everyone fighting for their lives. If he'd been smaller, he'd probably have bled out long before he'd turned all the sand into glass. It was a wonder he hadn't gone into shock.

Teraeth grabbed my wrist as I started to bring my hand near the wound. "You said healing does the opposite here."

I met his eyes. "I was wrong. That's not what happened earlier. And he's going to die if I don't heal him, so let's go with the option that gives him a chance. You two should be prepared to run."

I slipped my vision past the First Veil and looked over Thurvishar. The Veil didn't look like what I expected; instead of the normal rainbow auras, chaotic eddies filled the world, flickering ugly fractal whirlpools. The chaos grew stronger in one direction, and I knew—absolutely knew—that if I followed it back to its source, Vol Karoth waited at its center. The farther from that monster, the less the effect. I paused a moment, waiting until the eddies around me weakened before I lowered my hand to Thurvishar's side.

My mother had briefly tutored me while I'd been with the D'Mons, but I'd learned far more during my stay on the Black Brotherhood–controlled island of Ynisthana. Tyentso had enthusiastically endorsed being able to put one's injured companions back together—or oneself—if the need arose. And wouldn't you know it? Turns out I have a talent for healing.

I relinked the cut arteries and veins, pulled out a bacterial infection that had already begun to spread, and finally gave Thurvishar the energy he'd need to finish restocking his blood supplies. I felt pleased with myself. Miya would have been proud.

Except her name wasn't Miya. It was Khaeriel. I tore my thoughts away from my mother.

By the end, Thurvishar regarded me with those blacker-than-black eyes, weak but smiling. "I can't even fault your technique. Thank you."

I smiled at him. "You're welcome. You should sleep, though. You need to recover your strength."

Thurvishar nodded. "I doubt I'll be able to, given the bedding accommodations, but I'll try."

"Ha. I think you'll find your body disagrees with you on that–" I broke off as I caught the scent of roasting meat.

I looked behind me to see Janel had heated the stone floor, using the hot surface to cook. I felt a moment of panic, but Janel had either been lucky or she'd worked with small enough sections to avoid the chaos effects. Maybe Teraeth had helped, because he was the one actually roasting the bits of pack animal, carefully flipping the meat to cook both sides.

"Fortunately, these don't need much seasoning, but I'm afraid we'll need to eat them Kirpis style." He wrapped a piece of meat in cloth salvaged from a silk robe and handed it to Thurvishar.

"What's Kirpis style?" I asked.

"Just *imagine* it tastes good."[2]

"I'm just glad you're here, Teraeth," Janel said. "I've never cooked anything in my life. I'd have probably burned it all to char."

That earned her one of Teraeth's rare bright smiles, the sort with the power to make clouds part and the sun shine after a month of storms. I didn't look away in time when Teraeth caught me staring. For just a moment, our eyes met.

"Catch." Teraeth tossed me a piece, still piping hot.

I bounced the roast meat between my hands until it cooled, and then tucked in. No spices. No seasoning. It was the most delicious meal I'd ever tasted. No imagining required.

I suspected that had more to do with my hunger than the meat quality.

We ate all the meat Teraeth had butchered. There seemed little point in letting it spoil when we had no way to preserve it. Well, no way that wasn't risky.

We just had to hope we'd escape the Blight before we all starved to death.

"I think I know why Thurvishar's spell backfired," I said after we'd finished our dinner and sat around, cross-legged in the dim red tunnel light.

"You mean the way you knew why Thurvishar's spell backfired last time?" Teraeth reminded me.

"You can't expect someone to explain that correctly on the first try," I said. "Anyway, whenever I look past the First Veil, the whole region seems . . . corrupted. Chaos clusters float all over. Here's my theory: the larger the spell, the greater the chance you'll hit a cluster. And a gate covers a pretty large area." I purposefully didn't mention what I'd done

[2] That really is an excellent description of almost all Kirpis vané cuisine.

to Rol'amar or how closely it resembled what Vol Karoth himself did to the people and objects around him.

I was trying desperately not to think about that.

"So is a human body." Janel cleared her throat. "I haven't intentionally been using my strength, but . . . wouldn't I have run into a cluster too?"

"Really? That's your idea of unintentional?" Teraeth raised an eyebrow at her.

Janel ignored him.

"Not necessarily, Janel," Thurvishar's sleepy voice said. "You have a strong aura without talismans, which may provide a buffer. If your sense of self protected you, that might explain why. It's the same reason we're taught not to target armor at the Academy or why someone looking to kill a sorcerer will often use daggers instead of swords. Daggers are small enough to be protected by their wielder's aura."

I glanced over at Teraeth. I'd always assumed he used daggers because they were easier to hide. Then I poked a finger at Thurvishar. "You're supposed to be sleeping."

Thurvishar chuckled, which turned into a groan. "You're still talking. Besides, one of you might be wrong."

"Sorry, Thurvy," Janel said.

The glare he cast in her direction was so adorably irate I had to fight not to burst out laughing.

"If that's true," Janel said, "we'll probably be fine as long as we only cast magic while looking past the First Veil, only affect a small area at a time, or only use it on our own bodies."

"That still takes far too many risks," Teraeth said. "We should perform magic as little as possible."

"Obviously," she snapped.

Teraeth's eyes narrowed. "What is going on with you?"

"Oh, so we *are* going to talk about you second-guessing or contradicting everything I do or say? I assumed we were skipping that conversation."

"Wanting you to be more careful is not contradicting everything you do or say," Teraeth said. "You're being reckless even by your standards."

"Maybe I just don't appreciate you treating me like a child." Her voice rose at the end before she shook her head and gave the prostrate wizard a guilty glance when he sighed. "Sorry, Thurvishar."

Teraeth blinked at her, then stood. "I'm treating you like a child. Right." He turned to me. "I'm going to stretch my legs." He stalked off into the darkness.

"Let me know if you find a babysitter out there," she called out after him.

The silence felt tense and awkward after Teraeth left.

"You realize he treats everyone like that, right?" I finally said. "I mean, far be it from me to take Teraeth's side, but he's not singling you out."

Janel scowled. "It feels like he is."

I studied her for a minute. "Is this really about Teraeth?"

She folded her arms over her chest. "Of course it is."

I raised an eyebrow and waited.

Janel exhaled, a deep shuddering breath. "Okay, fine. Maybe it isn't. I just can't believe I let him use me like that. He turned me into bait, made me the lure so he could steal your cooperation, which you never would have done otherwise. I let him make me a fool. And then he took Qown–"

The *he* Janel meant wasn't Teraeth. *He* was Relos Var.

"You know what Relos Var said to me, right after I'd smashed the control crystal and freed Vol Karoth?" I chuckled darkly. "He said, 'Don't feel so bad. A lot of very smart people fell for it.' Implying I wasn't one of those 'very smart people.' The jerk." I shook my head. "It wasn't your fault."

"I know," she said. "But that doesn't make it easier to accept. He turned me into a game piece, something to be used and discarded. I'll never forgive him."

"More than fair," I said. "He turned me into Vol Karoth, so, you know . . . I'm the last person who'll suggest you should. But . . . do you want to talk about Qown?"

Janel stared at the far wall, although I doubted she focused on it. "I just don't understand. I didn't see it coming. I didn't . . ."

"I think Qown tried to tell us," I said. "We just didn't . . . we didn't understand the message. You once told me Var had groomed you, but he was really grooming Qown. Relos Var is the leader of Qown's religion, after all. And even the stories Qown told us didn't paint Var in a bad light. He was always so nice to Qown. Always brought Qown his favorite foods. Relos Var opened up to him, entrusted secrets to him, made him feel special. Who wouldn't have responded to that? I would have."[3]

"I just wonder if some enchantment–" Janel clenched her fists in her lap and then slowly released them, finger by finger. "I don't want to believe Qown left of his own free will. I want him to be under some spell." She shook her head. "I know that wasn't what happened. Qown thinks he's doing the right thing. Somehow."

"Hey, I don't want to believe my mother massacred every D'Mon she

[3] And did. It just wasn't Relos Var who did the grooming. What did you *think* was happening on Ynisthana?

could get her hands on, but . . ." I made a face. "I am so sorry. I know what Qown meant to you."

*"Means,"* Janel corrected. "He *means* a lot to me. Qown's my best friend, Kihrin. He sacrificed so much for me, never asking anything in return. Did I take him for granted? If I had just been there for him . . ."

I moved over, sitting down next to Janel, and put my arm around her. I wouldn't have under most circumstances, but she came from a culture a lot more comfortable with physical contact than my own.

Janel turned her face into my chest and held me tight.

The tunnel light's faint red glow reflected against Thurvishar's eyes, and I knew the wizard wasn't yet asleep. He watched us both without comment or movement.

Down the tunnel, out of sight, I felt Teraeth's presence. I knew he'd stopped and turned around. That Teraeth watched us from the dark.

I held her close and tried not to let it bother me.

# 17: Vows of Loyalty

***(Khaeriel's story)***
***Fourteen days earlier . . .***

Khaeriel summoned up winds and gestured, pulling the mimic high up into the air. She began aligning her thoughts to create lightning, impossibly hot electrocution to stun even such a creature as this.

But Talon didn't fight back.

The mimic just sat there, looking almost serene as the winds tossed her skyward. She made no move to free herself. No move to attack Khaeriel. The only sound she made was a prolonged "Wheee!"[1]

Khaeriel didn't lower her to the ground, but she lessened the gale forces.

"I come in peace, you know," Talon called out over the howling wind.

The door to the root shelter opened, and Therin stuck his head out. "What is going on out–" He gaped at the figure hovering in midair. "Who is that?"

"Aww, ducky, I'm so disappointed you don't recognize me," Talon called down. "Really, it hurts my feelings. I'm sad now."

"Go back inside," Khaeriel told Therin.

"Yeah, because that's going to happen," he replied and kicked shut the door behind him.

Khaeriel scowled but didn't protest his defiance either. An enchantment was not a gaesh, she reminded herself. "This is the mimic who infiltrated our house. The same mimic who worked for Darzin. She cannot have good intentions."

"Oh, you are so wrong," Talon said, "but hey, I get it. I do. I wouldn't trust me either. Darzin trusted me, and look where it got him. By the way, I just love what you've done with your hair."

"I am going to rip you into small pieces now," Khaeriel said matter-of-factly.

"Shouldn't we at least listen to what she has to say?" Therin cupped a

[1] I have zero trouble believing this.

hand over his eyes and looked up to the mimic's spread-eagle form. He frowned, and shook his head, as if trying to clear it.

"Yes," Talon agreed. "Shouldn't you at least listen to what I have to say?"

Khaeriel felt more concerned with the look on Therin's face. Holding the mimic aloft copied what she'd done to Therin, in the fight she'd made him forget. Khaeriel might well trigger a flashback if she continued.

Khaeriel lowered Talon to the ground. "Very well. Talk. But if I do not like what you have to say, I am killing you. And please believe I know all possible ways to kill your kind."

"Oh, I believe you," Talon said. "After all, you did create me. Not *you* you. More of a general vané you."

"A costly mistake," Khaeriel growled. "And I do not *like* what you are saying."

Talon sighed. "You used to have a better sense of humor. Has anyone told you that? You'd think weeks of marital bliss would have put more of a smile on your face. Ah–" She held up a hand to forestall Khaeriel's attack. Instead, Talon prostrated herself on the ground before her.

"What are you doing?" Therin asked.

Talon lifted her head. "Isn't it obvious? I'm pledging myself to my queen. My full and total loyalty. I promise I have never stopped being loyal to you, Your Majesty. Not once. Now that you're free, I want to continue to help you in any way you see fit."

Khaeriel continued to stare at Talon. "You cannot be serious. I cannot trust a mimic. I certainly cannot trust any oath you would give me."

"Then trust my well-developed self-interest," Talon said. "I am . . . familiar . . . with the prophecies, and I know current events enough to know Vol Karoth is awake now."

"Wait, what did you just say?" Therin said. "Vol Karoth's awake?"

"Oh, hey, ducky, you know who Vol Karoth is," Talon said, grinning. "You really are better educated than most Quuros, aren't you?"

"I only just found out about Vol Karoth myself," Khaeriel admitted. "I was going to tell you as soon as I came back inside."

Talon continued, "The next step is for the only unaging race's declared leader to enact the Ritual of Night, which will strip the immortality from the vané in order to re-imprison Vol Karoth. At least for a little while."

Khaeriel's gaze turned cold. "I will never allow the Ritual of Night to be enacted."

"Oh, I don't want it done either! I can't help but notice the length of Vol Karoth's imprisonment grows a little shorter each time, and we're almost out of immortal races. What will the gods want us to give up next time, I wonder?" Talon pulled herself up to her knees and placed a hand over her heart. "Now, I may be insane and dangerous and, I admit, a little too fond of unorthodox cuisine,[2] but under my charming ever-changing exterior, I *am* vané.[3] I don't want to be mortal." She stopped smiling. "I refuse to be mortal. Which means I can't support King Kelanis, can I?"

Khaeriel looked over at Therin. "Would this be a mistake? Would I be making a terrible mistake if I suffered her to live?"

He frowned. "I hate myself for saying this, but she might be useful."

"So is a fire until the moment it flares out of control," Khaeriel said, but she lowered her hand. "Very well. Let us discuss how you may serve your queen."

Talon clapped her hands together in delight.

[2] Unorthodox, *cannibalistic* cuisine.

[3] Technically. Physically, anyway.

# 18: Bad Dreams

*Kihrin shook his head. "Yeah, that was a mistake. A huge mistake. Friends with Relos Var and she spared Talon's life. My mom has the worst judgment."*

*"They didn't know Talon like we do," Thurvishar said. "And the last time I saw your parents, I was hardly in a position to warn them."*

***(Kihrin's story)***

The morgage had only given us two blankets. The tunnel wasn't cold, but we weren't keen on sleeping on naked stone ground. So we spread out our blankets and made ourselves comfortable with a very Joratese sleeping arrangement–huddled together. I'd insisted Janel sleep next to Thurvishar, because her body temperature ran so volcanically hot she'd keep him warm as well as a fireplace. I'd ended up sleeping next to Janel by virtue of calling dibs before Teraeth returned to camp. And once Teraeth did return, he curled up next to me.

Later, a hand on my shoulder shook me awake from the nightmare I'd been having.

"Hey." Teraeth's mouth quirked. "Some of us are trying to sleep," he whispered.

"Sorry," I said. "Bad dream." I slowly blinked further awake. I felt Janel's body against me, back-to-back, and Teraeth had turned on his side, propping his head on his elbow as he watched me.

"What about?" Teraeth whispered.

"I'll give you one guess. It rhymes with *soul sailcloth*."

"Cold clam broth? What an odd thing to have a nightmare about." The red glow from the tunnel lights limned his face. His eyes looked dark in that light, but I remembered enough to trick myself into seeing the green in them.

I chuckled in spite of myself as I shifted on the thin blanket to fully face him. "If only."

His expression turned serious. "I hate watching you go through this. I wish I could do something. Anything." Teraeth reached out and lightly touched my jaw, the stubble on a face that had badly needed a shave for several days now.

Funny how one touch changed the whole conversation. It felt like nighttime. It felt like those early-morning hours when inhibitions hide and the surreal gossamer of if-onlys and possibility–so clumsy and fragile by daylight–transform into action. We do things at night we would never dream of doing when the sun is watching.

I moved a finger across his cheek, just to see if the skin was as perfect and soft as it looked. He smiled and started to lower his head toward mine.

And then I made it go wrong. A fluttery panic welled up in me. I couldn't quite tell its source, if it was excitement or anxiety or a mixture of the two, but Teraeth's eyes widened. He jumped to a conclusion about what my reaction meant. Teraeth looked hurt and frustrated, just this side of angry. His eyes narrowed.

Next to us, Janel groaned in her sleep.

Teraeth and I stared at each other for a split second, our attention sharpening, and then we both turned around. Janel flinched, the way one sometimes does with a bad dream, and murmured something unintelligible under her breath, followed by a low, terrified *no.*

Janel was having a nightmare too. Except Janel didn't have nightmares, because Janel didn't dream. Where another person might sleep, Janel's version resembled death, a state of slowed bodily responses while her twin souls roamed the Afterlife.

Yet here she was, *dreaming.*

I touched her shoulder the same way Teraeth had touched mine, while Teraeth leaned over me to gain a better angle. I shouldn't have been able to wake Janel, but only if it was indeed night. Her body seemed to know the difference no matter her physical location. Yet I had a feeling something else was happening here.

Her eyes flickered open. "What?"

"You were having a bad dream," I told her.

Janel's eyes widened. "I was . . . what?" She lay there for a moment, still breathing fast, then blanched. "How lovely. So this is what I've been missing all these years."

"I'm going to assume Vol Karoth is interfering with your ability to shift your souls into the Afterlife," Teraeth whispered.

Janel sat up. "So much for trying to contact Arasgon."

I mentally slapped myself. I'd forgotten–yet again–Janel's ability to communicate with her fireblood companion in the Afterlife. Theoretically, she might have been able to get word back to the Eight Immortals, although what they could have done with us in the Blight wasn't clear.

Still, I hadn't thought of it. Janel had–but it wouldn't work if she couldn't reach the Afterlife in the first place.

Teraeth said, "You know, when I was little, if I had a nightmare, I'd crawl into bed with my mother. Sounds corny, but it always helped." Teraeth patted the blanket between us. "Why don't you shift over? Thurvishar'll be fine, and we'll protect you from any more bad dreams." He smiled at her. I think Teraeth meant it as an apology for earlier in the evening.

I winced in sympathy. I understood his sentiment, echoed it myself, but it was about to blow up in his face. *I'll protect you* was a phrase one didn't casually say to Janel Theranon. The youthful anecdote only made it worse, emphasizing a child role. Thurvishar might have pulled it off because Janel didn't consider him a "stallion,"[1] and so wouldn't have taken his offer as a challenge to her authority. Qown? Oh yeah. Qown could have gotten away with it easily. But probably not me, and *definitely* not Teraeth.

Janel blinked at him, just once. "I'm fine where I am."

I rubbed my neck and sighed. Janel looked annoyed; Teraeth looked confused. And I didn't feel like playing referee and explaining how they were screwing up.

"We all have plenty of ammunition for nightmares. I'm only awake because I was having my own." I smiled at Janel. "Let's just . . . let's try to get some rest."

Her glare softened, and she nodded.

I settled back down next to her. I knew I had an angry Manol vané assassin behind me, but this wasn't the time or place to fix things properly. I motioned behind me with my free hand, beckoning Teraeth closer. It was the best I could do.

Teraeth settled in next to me. We all tried to find sleep one more time.

No god-king tale I'd ever learned at my adoptive father Surdyeh's knee ever prepared me for being stuck in an ancient voras tunnel with barely any food, water, or privacy.

That last bit was becoming a problem.

When I woke up the next morning (or what may or may not have been morning), Janel, Teraeth, and I had all shifted positions. Janel's chest pressed up against my back. I'd turned around, facing Teraeth. He'd managed to wrangle one arm under my neck–possibly under Janel's too–and I'd wrapped a leg over his. Teraeth had thrown his other

[1] Should I be offended by that? I'm honestly not sure.

arm over my chest. One of my hands rested on Teraeth's hip. Everyone was fully dressed, but Manol silk seemed damn thin in such close quarters.

And since we'd just woken, I could definitely say Teraeth hadn't begun any voramer-style shift in gender. He was still very male. The proof pressed into my thigh, and I was returning the favor. Fairly normal for waking up in the morning–only the part where I had woken in another man's arms was new.

Fortunately, Teraeth kept sleeping, which meant this only had to be incredibly awkward for one of us.

I untangled myself and slowly crawled from the makeshift bed. Teraeth shifted and made a noise–I'd probably woken him despite my best efforts. Janel slept on–she seemed to be a deep sleeper even when she wasn't magically catatonic. It seemed safer not to say anything, so I stood and ungracefully tripped my way back up the tunnel to the latrine.

The "latrine" wasn't anything more than a spot in the tunnel far enough away from camp so we wouldn't have to smell the result. Since we didn't have a safe way to dig a hole or even clean ourselves, it was all thoroughly awful.

Disease might well do us in long before starvation if we didn't escape these tunnels soon.

As I returned, Teraeth passed me, making no indication anything embarrassing had happened a few minutes earlier. I avoided eye contact, still feeling embarrassed. Teraeth had long since established himself ready and willing to sleep with anyone or possibly anything; the only person he seemed to want a deeply committed romantic relationship with was Janel. At least I assumed so; he'd lied to me about Janel and had even gone so far as to propose marriage to her once.[2] So as long as I didn't make it a big deal, Teraeth wouldn't take it personally if I told him I wasn't interested.

I reminded myself, quite firmly, that I wasn't interested.

After Teraeth returned, Janel left, and when Janel returned, Thurvishar left. I gave Thurvishar one last checkup, careful not to get anywhere near the injury with my filthy hands. I thought I'd closed it all up properly, but I'd have hated to be wrong.

"You're as ready as you'll ever be," I told him.

"And we can't wait for me to make a full recovery," Thurvishar said.

"That too."

Nobody mentioned how grim this had become. We all knew.

2 Admittedly, said proposal happened in the Afterlife, and I'm not convinced Teraeth was serious, but I suppose I can understand why Kihrin might have come to a different conclusion.

We didn't run, knowing we couldn't afford to work ourselves into exhaustion. Rather, we walked until forced to stop: by cramping, or hunger, or on several occasions, blisters. Then we'd pause, take care of the issue, and keep moving again.

Time didn't have much meaning after a while. We weren't sure how long we'd been walking. We just knew when we were too tired to keep going. We had several more sleep cycles; no one had enough energy to chatter or flirt. The morgage had given us dried jerky strips (I didn't know and didn't want to know its origins) and pickled grubs. We forced ourselves to eat both. I cursed that I had never asked Master Lorgrin, head physicker back at the Blue Palace in Quur, to teach me that trick for summoning water. Lorgrin had been right; it would have been extremely useful.

On what I suspected was the fourth day, we saw light up ahead.

"Teraeth–"

"I see it too. Let me scout up ahead." The Manol vané sprinted off ahead. We slowed, but nobody stopped.

I heard a dull roar.

"Is that water?" Janel asked.

We looked at each other and then picked up our pace. When we caught up with Teraeth, the tunnel ended precipitously at a large iron grate letting in sunlight. We all heard running water, but we couldn't see any.

"That grate isn't original construction," I commented. "It looks vané."

Teraeth nodded. "The tunnel doesn't end cleanly. I'm guessing the vané just put a big cap over the end lest a monster escape the Blight. Unfortunately, it's going to do a fine job of keeping us from escaping the Blight as well."

"I believe we may be far enough from Vol Karoth," Thurvishar said. "Please allow me." He walked up to the grate, put his hands against the metal, and it simply peeled back to the side, like it was paper-thin instead of three inches of solid steel.

"I'm suddenly reminded why we keep you around," Teraeth said.

"Thank you. I think."

I peeked outside. "We may have a different problem."

The water came not from a spillway but from an actual waterfall, fifty feet away, where the same cliff the tunnel had broken through swept into a wide arc heading away from the Korthaen Blight to the north. The problem was the forty-foot drop to the lake below us.

Basically, it was a long way down.

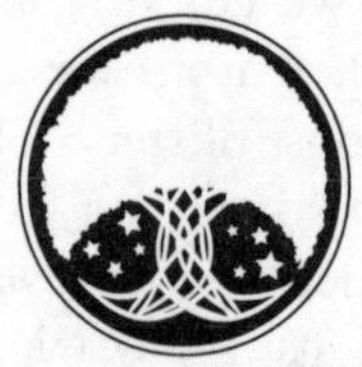

# 19: The City in the Way

*Thurvishar shook his head. "I don't believe you're in any position to say a word concerning your parents' bedroom habits."*

*Kihrin raised an eyebrow. "Excuse me?"*

*"You had no problem describing your own physical arousal," Thurvishar pointed out. "How is that any different from Therin and Khaeriel?"*

*"I'm not afraid of erections, Thurvishar. I just don't want to imagine my* father *having one."*

*The wizard reached for his tea as he shook his head. "I suppose. I just can't believe I slept through that."*

***(Therin's story)***

Therin suspected he was slowing Khaeriel down. As someone used to being one of the most powerful people in Quur–and therefore all the world–he didn't enjoy the realization. But if he hadn't been there, Khaeriel would have embarked on her schemes immediately, solidifying allies, renewing ties, implementing plans to retake the throne. Instead, she'd taken the time to give Therin a crash course in voral, the vané language, as well as the simplistic spells every vané knew. These spells included ways to see in the dark, discourage insects, and save oneself from a messy death if one happened to stumble off a high bridge. Vané seldom visited the jungle floor–the whole reason Khaeriel had kept a safe house there.

And if he hadn't been there, their next trip wouldn't have been necessary at all.

"It is called the Well of Spirals," Khaeriel explained to him. "You might consider it a holy place. It is where we train our children."

"And why are we going there?" Therin asked. "Last I checked, we didn't bring any children with us, even if we have been practicing making more." He could make that joke now. The news Kihrin wasn't dead had lifted a weight Therin had only identified by its absence.

Khaeriel smiled at him over her shoulder. "That is not the well's only purpose. All will be made clear soon enough."

Opening a gate was impossible due to something called a *barrier rose,* so they were riding a velsanaund, which looked a lot like a horse-size iguana. Velsanaunds had been specially bred to more easily navigate their jungle home's tree-filled environs; Therin could only imagine how terrifying they would be in combat.

Of course, they didn't actually have a velsanaund, although Khaeriel had warned him feral velsanaunds did exist in the jungle.

So they were riding Talon.

Therin was trying not to think about it.

The dappled yellow-green light he had grown used to at the Manol's edge rapidly darkened as the tree canopy closed in overhead. The ground cover grew scarce as the sunlight dimmed, until they were running in a maze of trees, dark, elegant towers jutting from the ground all around them. The scent of flowers, loamy earth, and a smell he could only describe as "green" wrapped around them, occasionally punctuated by the resin spice of tree sap. Therin never noticed the tree roads begin. One moment they were still running on the floor, and the next minute the giant lizard–*Talon,* he reminded himself–had leaped up and around onto a series of branches he could only assume had not grown so conveniently by chance.

After that, they were never less than thirty feet above ground, which rapidly became never less than thirty feet above water as they entered flooded jungle. The air felt sticky, riotous with wildlife. Few creatures in the Manol lived at ever-flooded ground level–everything either survived underwater or made their homes in the canopy.

That included the vané.

When they finally reached the vané city, it dazzled. The canopy had been manicured away from tall, thick trees, so sunlight flared like gold against the sculpted green leaves. Wrapped around the trees, webbed through the branches, a lacy network of buildings lay like jeweled bracelets against perfectly sculpted arboreal limbs. Stained glass windows blazed ruby, emerald, or amethyst in the afternoon sun, while floral scents, bright insect shells, and butterfly wings crafted a tapestry too complex and wondrous to take in all at once.

"Gods," Therin said, stunned.

"This is a small city," Khaeriel told him, "and not what we're here to see. Unfortunately, it's in our way."

"'Unfortunately'? What does that mean?" Dread clenched Therin's stomach, but he didn't understand why.[1]

As if in answer, a wall of violet energy manifested across the bridge. Talon came to a screeching halt.

[1] Because of that whole D'Mon massacre, I imagine. Relos Var *did* warn her.

A vané with dark green skin and lighter ombré green hair stepped from a building. Therin couldn't tell if they were male or female.

"Stop," they said in voral, which Therin barely understood.

Khaeriel dismounted, still holding the harp she'd been clutching to her like a child. "It's good to see you again."

The person narrowed their eyes, then widened them again. They started speaking too quickly for Therin to follow.

Therin dismounted as well. He may not have understood the conversation, but it didn't seem to be a welcome home with open arms.

"Please," Khaeriel said.

Therin knew that word, anyway.

The vané had an unpleasant expression on their face; it didn't give Therin hope for a peaceful resolution. Then he noticed a building across the way start to glow from inside, followed by screams and a giant eight-armed spider creature emerging from the doorway.

A demon. A demon lighting the tree on fire.

The vané turned back to Khaeriel.

"I had nothing to do with this," she protested.

Whether the vané believed her or not, they thought the demons a greater threat. With one last worried look in their direction, the vané ran off to fight the new invaders.

A tear in reality opened at the magical barrier blocking them from exiting the bridge, and a new demon emerged. Easily ten feet tall, a monster of a creature with the head of a massive tiger and giant eagle-like claws instead of hands and feet. If it had a gender, it wasn't obvious, although the bulging muscles and size would be easy to interpret as "male." It seemed . . . familiar, but then, there have been a lot of demons running around ever since the gaeshe were broken.

The demon spotted the two of them, seemed to do a double-take, and then diverted, heading in their direction.

**I KNOW YOU,** it snarled. **I MET YOU AND YOUR FRIENDS AT FEONILA.**

Khaeriel turned to Therin in confusion, which was when he realized the demon was speaking to him personally. At first, he had no idea what the monster was talking about, but then the memory clicked into place.

"Feonila?" Therin scoffed. "You're that demon we killed . . . ? It's been thirty years!"[2] He scowled.

**I HAVE NEVER FORGOTTEN.**

[2] I found a reference to a group of travelers confronting, exorcising, and banishing a demon in the town of Feonila, near Stonegate Pass, approximately thirty years previous. They never left names, but based on their description, I suspect it may well have been Therin D'Mon, Qoran and Nikali Milligreest, and Sandus.

"Talk about holding a damn grudge . . ." Therin drew his sword. "Which one were you again? Fegasor?"

**BEZAGOR!** the demon roared.

"Whatever. Truthfully, you weren't that memorable."

Khaeriel made a tsking sound, which Therin was quite certain had probably accompanied her rolling her eyes at him.

The demon growled and extended its claws. Its bird feet made clicking sounds on the wooden floor as it ran forward at him.

Khaeriel summoned winds while Therin came forward with his sword. He swiped the blade through the air, and a red line opened across the demon's stomach. Bezagor looked down at himself and snarled. The demon waved a hand; the wound closed.

Therin clamped down on his desire to grimace; he'd have remembered if the demon had been capable of doing that last time. "It's not going to go any better for you this time than it did the last."

**IT'S BEEN THIRTY YEARS. I HAVE FEASTED ON A THOUSAND SOULS SINCE THEN.**

As Therin focused on opening cuts on the demon's body, a shadow stepped out of one of the doorways of the tree and darted forward. Therin didn't notice it until Bezagor, knocked backward by one of Khaeriel's attacks, stumbled. The shadow pounced on the misstep, sliding silently behind Bezagor with a curved sword. He carved away one of the demon's arms as if it were made from paper.

Therin looked the man in the face and flinched. He'd expected a Manol vané, someone good at stealth and lethal with a sword. But this wasn't a man at all; it was another demon. The shadows surrounding the man were literal, spiraling off him in umbral whorls, pooling at the demon's feet as the creature took advantage of Bezagor's distraction. His face was hidden by an eyeless ceramic mask. The shadow demon paused. He might have been staring at Therin, but it was hard to know for sure.

Therin would have expected gloating or insults. That would be normal for a demon. From this one, though? Silence. The demon gave him a single nod and then continued whittling away at Bezagor.

But Bezagor didn't fall so easily. **I WILL DESTROY YOU ALL!** Bezagor screamed. Blue flame spiraled out from his body even as an arm composed entirely of fire sprouted from the stump.

"Therin, run!" Khaeriel shouted.

Just as Therin took a step back, the fire raced out to his position. He could feel an icy chill through the soles of his shoes, a sharp, numbing, frostbite-like pain. Then a screaming ball of scales and claws leaped at the tiger demon. Tentacle-like appendages sprouted from its back. Talon screamed, "Go now! This is your chance!"

Khaeriel grabbed Therin's hand while she picked up the harp. "This way."

Therin saw Talon was right; the magical field blocking their way had vanished.

He heard Bezagor let out a hissing scream. A second scream belonged to Talon, although he couldn't tell if it was pain or pleasure. Therin felt a pang of remorse, quickly suppressed. He didn't understand what would possess Talon to make a heroic gesture, but this wasn't the time to question it.

The shadow demon never made any noise at all.

They ran up the wooden ramps placed around the city, darting in between buildings to avoid the rampaging demons. The whole city burned. Therin assumed the vané possessed some fantastic magics for dousing fires, but the fact the demons were killing anyone who tried complicated matters.

Khaeriel led Therin through a metal archway–the only metalwork he'd seen so far–and then the ramp began descending. In fact, he began to understand how the city might be "in the way."

The city trees had been joined together so a hollow area–approximately forty feet in diameter–had been created in the center of the giant trunks. Silver gutters caught the rainwater and channeled it in a spiraling pattern around the inside area, while thick branches, wide enough to walk down, creating a ramp spiraling down to the bottom.

Khaeriel walked down without hesitation, clutching the harp. After a few moments, Therin followed.

As they walked farther down the ramp, the light dimmed again, until the glowing lanterns hanging from branches and walls provided the only illumination. Then too many lights glowed from the walls–too many to be lanterns. They looked more like stars. That resemblance became more pronounced the farther down they walked, until they reached the bottom. Then the stars began to move.

"Should I be concerned?" Therin asked.

"No, this will take but a moment."

The stars began to whirl, faster and faster until they formed a wall of pure white light, searing blindness into his eyes before the stars fell away.

And then they were somewhere else.

# 20: They Hunt in Packs

*"The vané Gatestone system is just so much cooler than ours," Kihrin grumbled.*

*Thurvishar sighed. "You're not wrong."*

***(Kihrin's story)***

Teraeth and I examined the cliff face surrounding us. The tunnel jutted out several feet, which made swinging back to the rocks challenging. Vines and plant life clung to the cliff itself, which looked sturdy enough to support a climber's weight. But appearances can be deceiving. The waterfall itself seemed safe enough; I doubted its wake was strong enough to pull anyone under.

Teraeth looked over at me. "What do you think?"

"For you and me? Easy. For these two?" I gestured toward Janel and Thurvishar. "I don't think so."

"I can climb." Janel crossed her arms over her chest.

"I'm sure you can," I said, "but this is a little more specialized than what you're used to doing."

"I'll just open a gate," Thurvishar said. "We're not in the Blight anymore."

"Oh! Right. Sure, go for it." I stepped back to give the man room.

Thurvishar concentrated as he cast the spell.

Nothing happened.

"This isn't funny anymore." Thurvishar looked utterly offended. "I'm actually good at this, you realize."[1]

We all waited, but no chaos storm presented itself.

Teraeth made a face. "I'd bet metal we're inside the barrier roses again."

We all groaned. The whole reason the Eight Immortals had to open the gate themselves to the vané capital city was because a vané magical network–the barrier roses–stopped gates and teleportation. Which,

[1] I really am. You know how difficult it is to open a gate without a Gatestone.

while pretty fantastic from a defensive standpoint–the whole reason, in fact, Emperor Kandor had been forced to invade the Manol the old-fashioned way–was proving inconvenient on a personal level.

"Wait." I turned to the others. "How long were we unconscious? I mean, transporting us to the Blight must have taken weeks . . ."

"We'll know once we're back," Teraeth said, shrugging.

I returned my focus to our present dilemma and pointed down to the lake. "Anyway, I'll climb down and see if the water in the lake is deep enough for jumping."

"I'll go." Teraeth gave Janel a quick glance.

I frowned. "Hey, who was the professional burglar?"

"I'm the better swimmer." Before I could make any further protest, Teraeth swung out, leaping over to the vine-covered cliff face.

Janel sighed.

I tried to keep Teraeth in sight, but the angle of the tunnel walls made it difficult. Teraeth climbed down until he'd almost reached the lake and then simply dropped. I waited for Teraeth to surface.

He didn't.

We waited. The lake's surface didn't still–not with the waterfall and steady lake outflow–but the water took on a quiet air.

"Teraeth?" Janel shouted down. "Teraeth!"

"Shit." I took several steps back.

Thurvishar must have sensed my intentions. "You don't know if it's safe. What if the same thing–"

I was already jumping.

I hit the water feetfirst, the roar of falling and landing cutting off abruptly as water rose over my head. All sound muffled, the light turned green and glassy. Searching for Teraeth proved impossible through the muddy churn. As I surfaced, a hand grabbed my wrist and pulled me up.

I gasped for air. Teraeth surfaced with me.

"You actually jumped?" Teraeth said. "Why would you do that? You had no idea why I hadn't come up for air!"

I flushed. "I was worried about you. You're such an asshole!" I shoved water in Teraeth's direction in pure frustration; I didn't have the leverage to punch him.

"Guilty as charged," Teraeth said mildly. "I mean, I'm flattered, but don't do that again. I can return from the Afterlife a lot easier than you can."

"Fuck you." As I treaded water, I shouted up, "False alarm. He's fine!"

"Yeah, we see that!" Janel shouted back. "So how do we climb down again?"

"You won't have to. We'll leave the water so we're not in your way!" I shouted.

"It's easy," Teraeth said. "Plenty deep. Just jump feetfirst."

"No!" I corrected. "Feetfirst, keep your arms out when you jump, and bring them down to your sides as you hit the water. Try to keep your body straight."

"I'm suddenly not feeling so confident," Janel admitted.

"You'll be fine," Teraeth said.

"Janel?" I called up. "Don't use your full strength when you jump. You don't want to land too far out, understand?"

"Uh, Kihrin?" Janel's voice wavered.

"Yeah?" I shared a look with Teraeth. I had a sinking feeling I knew her next words. *Don't say you can't swim. Do* not *say you can't swim.*

"I can't swim," Janel called down.

"Seriously?" I shouted. "Wasn't your family castle right next to a river in Jorat?"

"Yes, but I never swam in it! I didn't even know how to swim in my past life. Elana grew up in a desert!"

Teraeth sighed. "Honestly no excuse."

"Fine," I called to her. "It's fine. Not a problem. We'll swim off to the side. Thurvishar, you go next. You can swim, right?"

"Yes, I know the basics!" Thurvishar shouted.

"Great!" I decided against clarifying if he meant *in theory.*[2]

Teraeth and I swam to the side. I hadn't seen any predators—one factor in our favor. I'd learned to swim in the Senlay River next to the Capital City, but the trick to doing so had always been making sure the crocodiles were someplace else.

"You're going to do great, Thurvishar. Take a running leap. Keep your arms out to start."

I thought Thurvishar might be having an attack of nerves. Then he vanished from the tunnel, and a second later, a dark flailing shape jumped into the air and plummeted down to the lake.

Thurvishar didn't bring his arms down in time, but he also didn't scream, which had to count for something. Teraeth helped him make his way to the shallow end of the lake, which Thurvishar managed without any incidents.

So that left Janel.

"Okay, so you saw what Thurvishar did, right? It's that easy!" I shouted. "We're here to pull you from the water, so there's no reason to be afraid."

"I'm *not* afraid!" Janel yelled down.

[2] The theory proved to be sound, didn't it?

I took a deep breath. "Of course you're not."

Teraeth cupped his hands over his mouth and made chicken clucking sounds.

I turned and looked at him in disbelief.

Janel jumped.

She hit the water like a spearpoint, went under, and came back up immediately, flailing in pure panic. She choked and breathed in at least some water.[3]

I pulled her from the lake. As soon as Janel reached land she spent several minutes on her hands and knees coughing, before giving Teraeth a murderous glare while he continued to tread water.

"No, we can't kill him," I told her. "Teraeth's the only one who knows the way back to the Mother of Trees."

She laughed as she settled down on her side. "At least I'm cleaner now."

I decided this would be a poor time to point out her silk clothing had turned transparent. I certainly didn't mind. Besides, given Joratese nudity taboos, or lack thereof, Janel probably wouldn't care.

And that issue with the clothing proved true for all of us.

Teraeth waved from the water. "Hey, want to help me with this?"

"Help you with what?" I asked.

"The crocodile I killed earlier and lodged under this rock!" Teraeth shouted. "I figured we'd cook it for dinner."

I looked at Janel. "The crocodile he killed earlier. Of course."

Thurvishar sighed and scrubbed his face with his hands.

That evening went a lot better than previous ones.

True, our clothing was tattered, our footwear condition laughable, and we had no weapons worth the name. We possessed only a theoretical knowledge of our location in the Manol, Thurvishar couldn't open a gate, and we were too close to the Blight to expect the Eight to answer our prayers.

Don't think we didn't try. Even with the warnings the Eight had given us that they'd be too busy to respond, we still tried. I prayed to Taja, Janel prayed to both Tya and her patron god, Khored. The closest we came to an answer was Teraeth, who blinked as if slapped and announced Thaena had been too busy to talk–she'd been in the midst of battle.[4]

But even if we didn't have a way to contact the Eight Immortals, we had food and fresh water, and most importantly, magic *worked.*

[3] Had we been thinking, we'd have redrawn the air glyphs, but we were all fighting off exhaustion by that point.

[4] Presumably with the demons invading the Land of Peace.

So accommodations were made. I pulled water from green wood we gathered until it turned dry enough to burn. Janel had a fire going in no time. Thurvishar knapped a razor-sharp knife from local stone, and Teraeth used it to skin and dress the crocodile. Thurvishar even repaired our shoes (that crocodile was proving handy).

Teraeth cooked again, mostly because he was the only one any good at it. Under his care, the crocodile meat tasted so fantastic, I almost forgot where we were.

By the time we finished eating, it was dark. The jungle sounds echoed around us with intimidating cacophony. I struggled not to flinch at every noise.

Teraeth rescued a wooden stick from the fire and drew a map on the ground with its burned end. "So this is where we are," he said, pointing to a long river running just underneath the Korthaen Blight. "And we need to be here." He draw an *X* to the southwest. "That's the capital, the Mother of Trees, and King Kelanis's palace."

"I'm no expert on such things, but I think that's going to take a while," I said.

Teraeth gave me a look. "No kidding. But I'm more concerned about traveling all the way down there and finding ourselves in the same situation."

Janel grimaced. "There's no guarantee whoever kidnapped us the first time can't do the same thing twice."

"Exactly," Teraeth said. "How do we strong-arm our way past the bureaucratic maze that trapped us before?"

Thurvishar studied the map. "Do you have a suggestion?"

"Yes, I do." Teraeth circled another location, southeast of our current position. "This is Saraval. There's a Brotherhood chapter house there—"

"Out in the open? Do they have a sign on the front door? Is it black?" I couldn't help myself.

Teraeth rolled his eyes. "No. The Black Brotherhood is illegal in the Manol."

I tilted my head. "I'm sorry. What was that? I could've sworn you just said the Black Brotherhood isn't legal among the vané."

Teraeth rubbed his jaw. "It's considered a cult. Most vané don't worship gods, so to the eyes of most vané, we're just a band of uh . . . fanatics."

"Huh. Imagine that," I said.

*"Anyway,"* Teraeth continued, "more important than the chapter house, there's also a gate there to the Well of Spirals." He gave that last pronouncement significance, then sighed when we all stared blankly. "It's a holy place."

"You *just* said the vané don't worship gods," I pointed out.

"Fine," Teraeth said. "It's sacred."

Janel paused from chewing a piece of crocodile meat. "That means the same thing."

"Revered, then. My point is the caretakers there have the authority to contact King Kelanis directly. We can cut right through all the bureaucracy and go straight to the top."

"Great," I said. "That's starting to sound like an actual plan."

"Anything else we should know?" Thurvishar asked. He'd been letting us talk, saying nothing, but watching us with studied care. He looked like a man who already knew the answer to the question he was asking.[5]

"Yes," Teraeth said. "Only the vané are allowed to step a single foot near the Well of Spirals," he explained. "Janel and Thurvishar would be arrested. Or killed. Probably the latter."

"What about Kihrin?" Janel pointed to me.

"Kihrin is more vané than human," Teraeth said. "He can pass."

"Janel and I don't need to go," Thurvishar said, "as long as Kelanis receives our message."

"What is the Well of Spirals?" Janel asked.

Teraeth made a face. "It's complicated. Without it, the vané wouldn't *be* vané. Babies are sent there to learn their first spells–"

*"Babies?"* Thurvishar all but sputtered.

"They're imprinting them," Janel murmured. "They must be."

We stopped and looked at her.

"What was that?" I asked her.

Janel started poking the fire with a stick of her own. "If you're good at body magics–the way any god-king would be–you can modify a child's development to ensure they'll be able to use magic. You can even give them a sympathy toward specific spells guaranteeing they'll develop them as 'witch gifts.'" She casually added, "Pretty sure either Tya or Xaltorath did that to me."[6]

Teraeth's expression fought between pride and annoyance. "I . . . am not going to confirm what might easily be considered a state secret. The vané have dedicated our existence to biological magical study. We literally created our own race; the Well of Spirals is the tool we used."

"Created your own race?" I blinked at him. "Explain, please."

"You know how god-kings have been responsible for creating races? The thriss, firebloods, centaurs, and so on? Well, that. Except it was a group of voras sorcerers, not a god-king, and they did it to themselves. The vané created the vané." Teraeth shrugged. "That's how they escaped becoming mortal when the voras did."

[5] I didn't know the specifics regarding the Well of Spirals, but I suspected.

[6] If not both. And the witch-queen Suless made changes as well.

"And we're asking them to give that up," Thurvishar mused.

"It's that or we *all* die," I protested. "Vol Karoth's not going to spare them just because they've been around for a long time."

Teraeth held out his hands. "We're not the ones who need convincing. But if you were unclear why a faction inside the court might not like us? Now you know."

I leaned back against a log. "Right. Well, one disaster at a time, I suppose. Let's figure out how to reach Saraval first. We'll just have to–" I paused as a clicking noise emanated from the jungle.

Several clicking noises. Surrounding us.

Why did that noise seem familiar? Then it came to me, in a rush of dread. "Wait. I know that sound . . ."

Teraeth sat still. "This is important: no one move."

To Janel's and Thurvishar's credit, they followed orders. And I didn't need to be told.

"What is *that*?" Janel asked.

She must have seen the first of the reptiles–about the size of a hunting dog, with a mouthful of teeth and wickedly sharp claws on its hind legs. The creature ran on those back legs, and it moved fast. The drake stared at Janel with keen, intelligent eyes, tilted its head, and trilled.

"That's a drake," I answered. "Problem is–"

A dozen creatures ran into the clearing.

"–they hunt in packs," I finished.

# 21: The Soul in the Harp

***(Therin's story)***

The sunlight dazzled off soaring white alabaster spirals, arching overhead to highlight perfect blue sky.

Not teal. Not blue green. Blue.

Therin and Khaeriel stood in a meadow, surrounded by low flowering hedges next to a wide reflecting pool. The air smelled of sunlight and spring flowers and the sweet, pure tang of conifers. Opposite the reflecting pool, several man-size topiaries stood at attention, densely covered with flowers.

"The sky's the wrong color," Therin said. "So's the sun."

Khaeriel smiled at him and touched his cheek. "No, they are not." Sunlight shimmered off her golden hair. "We simply have a longer memory than the Quuros."

His eyes kept being drawn to their surroundings. Just where were they? This was no jungle; the temperature felt mild. Was this an illusion?

They were not alone. Figures in long yellow-green robes moved through the area, checking plants, looking at flowers, and being quite mysterious. No one carried weapons, but the vané were so proficient with magic as to render the idea redundant.

A priest with dark ruby skin serenely approached them. Therin didn't truly know if he was a priest, but he acted like one. Therin liked to imagine he had some experience in that area.

Therin expected his presence to upset the priest. Therin was, after all, a human in a place where humans weren't allowed.

The priest's eyes landed on him and then moved on. He didn't realize Therin wasn't vané. That wasn't to say the priest had no reaction. Just not to *him*.

"You dare impersonate our dead queen?" he demanded of Khaeriel.

"Impersonate?" Khaeriel laughed. "Oh, you have jumped to an incorrect conclusion. Now stop being so dramatic. I am here to request a tsali transfer."

Therin furrowed his brow. He knew what tsali stones were. Indeed, the attendant wore just such a crystal. He knew vané used them to hold the souls of dead loved ones before sending them on to Thaena's realm, but . . .

Khaeriel didn't own a tsali stone.

"You are not Khaeriel." The priest raised an imperious eyebrow.

Therin started to reassure the priest in some manner, but stopped himself. His lack of language skills would give him away.

"Shall I prove my identity?" Khaeriel gestured; the priest spun up into the air, choking.

"Uh, Khaeriel, my darling . . . ," Therin said softly, "I'm sure you know the local etiquette better than I, but don't we need him? For whatever you're trying to do?" Watching her push the man into the air was almost physically painful. Something about the act itself . . . every time he saw Khaeriel commit violence with magic, he flinched. As if expecting the blow to fall on him. His mind shied from shadows and half-remembered pains.

Khaeriel let the priest go. He fell to the ground gasping.

"Your Majesty?" A woman's voice. Another priest stepped forward. She reassured the others, "Everything's fine. No cause for alarm." She bent down next to the priest. "Morasan, don't play the fool. That is clearly Queen Khaeriel."

The new priestess was a pastel creature, all soft blues with indigo shading, a bluebell reborn as a woman. "Please forgive him, Your Majesty."

Khaeriel smiled. "Damaeris, how lovely."

The man, Morasan, rose to his feet still holding his throat. He glanced over at Therin, started to say something, and then closed his mouth. He didn't look happy. Which was fine. Therin didn't *feel* happy.

He just didn't understand why.

"How can we help Your Majesty today?" Damaeris asked.

"As I told Morasan, I wish to request a tsali transfer," Khaeriel explained again.

"Of course," the priestess agreed. "If you'll give me the tsali?" She held out her hand.

Khaeriel set the harp down next to the priestess. "This particular tsali stone takes an unorthodox form. But I see no reason why that should prevent it from working."

"Oh," Damaeris said. "I . . . see."

Therin stared. The harp was a tsali? He had always assumed tsali were gems, that they *had* to be gems. Theoretically, though, other vessels might hold a soul under the right circumstances. If this harp somehow contained a vané soul, then it technically qualified. He racked his brain for everything he could remember about that damn harp. His old friend Qoran Milligreest's family had owned the antique for generations, but

Qoran never made a big deal about it. Qoran's cousin Nikali, on the other hand . . .

Qoran once joked about selling off his musical instrument collection to pay a gambling debt, and Nikali had threatened to duel him on the spot. He'd been serious too. Which Therin might have dismissed as pride in the family music collection, if Therin hadn't long since concluded Nikali was in fact a vané just pretending to be human.

Behind them, a soft whirring noise rose, like someone twirling a weight on a string. Then a blue-haired vané woman with silver-brushed skin appeared a few feet away. Therin's eyes widened. He could hardly fail to recognize her, considering how many years she'd served as his seneschal.

Miya.

*"Lady Miya–" Therin's grandson had said.*

*"That's not my name," Khaeriel had replied.*

Therin flinched as the memory shredded into vapor before he identified it. The woman couldn't *be* Miya, because Khaeriel was standing next to him. Khaeriel *still* wore Miya's body, even if it looked different now. That left one candidate who not only knew what the original Miya looked like but could impersonate her.

Therin walked over to Talon. "What kept you?"

"Apologies, Your Majesty." Talon gave a half curtsy to Khaeriel.

Khaeriel waved a hand in acknowledgment and returned to talking to Damaeris.

Therin fought to keep his breath under control. His heart was running for its life.

Talon studied him. "Uh-oh."

Therin took a deep breath. "What do you mean, 'uh-oh'? What happened back there?"

Talon shrugged. "Oh, I just wanted to find out if I could eat a demon. I guess that's a curiosity that's going to have to go unsatisfied." She returned to studying Therin. "And 'uh-oh' means you are standing on the edge of a cliff, ducky. So. The question is: Do you step off?"

A shudder passed through him. "I don't know what you mean."

"No, you don't. But you're so close, Bright-Eyes." She looked around the clearing. "Now this place brings back memories. It's been a few millennia."

The shudder passing through Therin that time was easier to understand. Because Bright-Eyes had been Ola's nickname for him, decades ago, when Pedron had decided that the thing Therin needed to polish the sanctimonious edge off his halo was his own slave . . . [1]

[1] And later, I should note, Ola used the same nickname for Kihrin.

He remembered Kihrin's warning that Talon had been impersonating Ola. He knew enough about mimics to understand they could copy anyone, but to copy someone perfectly . . .

"I didn't kill Ola," Talon whispered softly, answering the question even as it formed in Therin's mind. "I *loved* her."

"Would that have stopped you?" Therin asked.

Talon flinched then. She didn't answer but gestured toward the glade. "This is Well of Spirals," she said. "The holiest of holies. People think the Mother of Trees is the vané's spiritual heart, but no, it's this right here." Talon paused. "I was born here, you know."

Therin glanced at her. "Were you really?"

"Okay. I was *created* here. Oh, heady days back at the founding. People did all sorts of things we shouldn't have. Played with concepts we didn't understand." She gave him a peculiarly solemn look. "Do you realize we're in Quur?"

"What?" Therin forgot to keep his voice down that time.

Khaeriel looked back. "Is everything all right?"

"Everything's fine. Sorry." He waved a hand at her, and Khaeriel returned her attention to the two priests. They were rigging a cradle in which to rest the harp next to a flower column.

Therin turned back to Talon. "Quur? Are you serious?"

"Oh yes," Talon said. "This is the great Kirpis forest." She grinned at the look on Therin's face. "Oh, come on. You honestly think you Quuros ferreted out all the vané's dirty little secrets? Invasion or not, human eyes have never seen some parts of the Kirpis." She paused. "Well, until now." Talon gave Therin's arm a whack. "Lucky dog."

"Don't ever touch me again," Therin said. He examined the impossibly beautiful meadow, frowning. "I don't understand, though. Don't the Manol vané have their own—whatever this is?"

"Oh no. There's only one Well of Spirals," Talon said. "And no matter how bad tensions grew between the two countries, no one ever restricted access to *this*. No one would dare." She leaned toward him. "You know, all you have to do to escape is just . . . run. The Academy isn't far from here. You'd make it in less than a day."

"Why would I want to run? I'm not a prisoner." But the open meadow suddenly felt claustrophobic, stifling. The priests giving him suspicious glances took on the aura of guards.

"I am loyal to Khaeriel," Talon said, apropos of nothing. "But I have limits." She chewed on her lower lip. "Letting Ola work independently as a courtesan—most royals wouldn't have done that. Most wouldn't have let her buy her freedom. Easy enough to just take the star tears from her and be done with it. No one would have thought less of you." She snorted. "No one 'important' would have thought less of you."

"And as a thank-you, Ola betrayed me." Therin didn't quite understand why Talon was saying this to him. Even if she possessed Ola's memories, for him, those memories held only pain.

"No," Talon said. "She didn't betray you. But you *were* betrayed. By people quite a bit closer to you than Ola Nathera." She watched Khaeriel talk. "So much closer."

"Nothing you say isn't a lie. Why would Miya–"

*That's not my name, she said.*

Therin didn't finish the sentence.

Talon leaned in close. "You're almost there, Bright-Eyes. Remember the old days? You, Qoran, Nikali, and that wide-eyed farm boy from Marakor . . . remember when your father Pedron decided to *do* something about you . . . ?"

Therin inhaled sharply. Because he indeed remembered what it had been like. Pedron hadn't wanted to gaesh him, so he'd used something else. He remembered the way his mind shied away from the wrong subjects, the way he forgot conversations and people important to him. The way the whole world had seemed to distort–

The sharp final sound of bones breaking, echoing through the Great Hall. Screams.

A neck, snapping.

"Thaena help me," he whispered. The trouble with enchantments wasn't in breaking them. That was easy. The difficulty was only in identifying they existed.

"Ah yes," Talon whispered. "There we go. Think of this as my way of saying thank you on Ola's behalf. You gave Ola her freedom. Now I'm giving you yours."

Therin stood still and tense, fists clenched at his sides as the memories scraped his mind with hurricane winds. The disbelief as the killing had started. The pain of Khaeriel's words, even more hurtful than her magic. The horror of listening to her kill everyone, being unable to stop her. The knowledge he'd earned that outcome. That her anger was . . . justified.

Therin closed his eyes as tears slid down his cheeks.

"And now that you've stepped over the edge," Talon whispered, "do you fall or do you fly?"

Therin knew better than to run. No sharp, sudden movement that might draw Khaeriel's attention. While the priests would object to Khaeriel throwing around magic, her earlier demonstration stood as testimony to the fact they wouldn't object *much.* He glanced around. The glade had to be surrounded by illusions. Khaeriel couldn't see past them any more than he could. Once he walked to the other side, he'd be invisible.

He slowly stepped backward. Each step mired in a nightmare of worry Khaeriel might turn and spot him, recognize his intentions. One priest noticed, but other than a frown in his direction, the man hadn't drawn attention to Therin's movement.

Talon–

Therin choked back bitter laughter. Talon had turned *into him.* If Khaeriel looked back, she'd see Therin standing there. She might not look past the mimic to see the real Therin slowly retreating into the tree line.

After the trees closed around him, Therin turned and ran.

# 22: Under a Verdant Sky

***(Kihrin's story)***

The drakes made a slow circle around us, moving back and forth.

"Are they waiting for us to run?" Thurvishar asked nervously.

"Maybe," Teraeth said. "But there's one other possibility–" He raised his voice and shouted out a greeting in thriss.

After a moment's silence, thriss voices answered.

"Don't attack," I whispered to Janel.

"Why would I–?" She tensed as a half-dozen thriss walked into the campfire light. "Oh."

The thriss looked basically human, if covered in snake scales and possessing snake heads. I've always considered any variations largely cosmetic.

"I didn't know any thriss lived in the Manol," I said to Teraeth, keeping my voice light and conversational.

"Are you kidding? All the thriss live in the Manol. Where do you think they went after Quur pushed them out of Khorvesh?" Teraeth said something else to the thriss, which I followed well enough to recognize as a polite introduction.

The Black Brotherhood had a large thriss contingent, since the thriss had switched from worshipping their god-king Ynis to worshipping the god responsible for Ynis's destruction: Thaena. It made a strange sort of sense.

Anyway, Teraeth and the thriss continued talking for several minutes.

Meanwhile, Thurvishar attempted to feed crocodile meat to a drake, who crept forward as cautiously as a feral cat. Thurvishar didn't even lose a hand in the process, which was impressive.

Teraeth stood. The tension lessened. A thriss stepped forward and clapped Teraeth on the shoulder.

"This is Vsizinos," Teraeth explained to us, "a cousin of Szarrus's. He's heard of us."

To underscore the point, the thriss in question gave me a broad grin, opened his arms, proclaimed, "Sligoltho!"

I groaned even as Teraeth laughed.

Janel leaned over to Thurvishar. "What did he just say?"

"Monkey?" Thurvishar offered tentatively, unsure of the translation. "Apparently, there's a golden-furred monkey found in the Manol . . . ?"

I pinched the bridge of my nose. "One of my weapons instructors, Szarrus, gave me the nickname. One I thought I'd escaped when I *blew up the island I lived on at the time.*"

Teraeth grinned. "That wasn't you. Don't take credit for the Old Man's temper."

Janel's eyes lit up. "Monkey? They call you Monkey? That's much better than Scamp. Can anyone join this club and call you Monkey?"

I gave her a serious look. "No."

Teraeth slapped me on the shoulder. "Come on, Monkey. They've offered to take us to their village. Let's go sleep in real beds tonight."

I can't fault thriss hospitality.

The "village" ended up being quite large—easily a full town anywhere in Quur. Farther into the jungle, the houses sat on stilts to escape the floodwaters. This close to the edge, everything rested at ground level.

Thriss preferred daytime, so most townsfolk were sleeping when the hunting party returned with us. A few heads peeked from windows. At one point, a door slammed open and a tiny thriss ran out and attached itself to a hunter's leg, to much amusement and laughter all around.

I'd never seen a thriss child before. None of the thriss on Ynisthana had been raising families, so I'd only met full-size adults. I couldn't determine the child's sex, but if I'm being honest, I have that problem with grown thriss too. Either way, the kid was adorable.

The thriss brought Teraeth's crocodile as well as other animals they'd hunted with the drakes' assistance.

Since it was late, we skipped any greeting ceremony. The thriss showed us a room with four rush-covered wooden beds. I fell asleep the moment I lay down, didn't wake once the whole night.

The next morning, they treated us to a magnificent breakfast of wild bird eggs and crocodile meat, along with coffee and a yeasted thriss breakfast bread called *shorva* I'd grown to love during my stay on Ynisthana. We knew we needed to rush, but Thurvishar insisted we take the time to recover from our ordeal. None of us fought his logic.

All day, I found myself grateful for thriss generosity. They provided us with food, baths, and clothing. Someone lent me a razor sharp enough for shaving. Teraeth, who held a near-to-holy status among the thriss, had explained the urgency of our quest. Yet I'm sure they would've helped us even if they'd never heard of Thaena; the thriss were not a stingy people.

Of course, what they considered clothing, others might call armor: layered stiff leathers and specially cured leaves treated until iron hard. The thriss made their clothing in pieces they laced or knotted together with thread, so no tailoring was necessary. Their weapons were particular to thriss sensibilities as well, since the thriss used curved swords similar to the Khorveshan style.[1] Daggers were ever present.

I was readying a pack when Teraeth made a strangled noise next to me. I looked up to see what was the matter.

Janel was the matter. Oh gods, was she ever the matter.

The thriss had given her typical thriss clothing, which she'd modified to satisfy her propriety. So a snakeskin raisigi she'd bound as tightly as possible to mimic a Joratese bodice, sturdy boots, and tight leather kef. Most thriss preferred a knee-length skirt or a split loincloth, but she'd somehow managed to find pants. Even though it had been a while since she'd ridden a horse (which had to be killing her)–and who knew when the opportunity would arise again?–she'd still insisted on riding-appropriate attire. Just in case.

She'd also convinced our hosts to give her jewelry–how, I had no idea–carved crocodile teeth and various shells. She'd taken those pieces and woven them through her laevos. She wore more bracelets on her wrists, cords around her neck. Joratese stallions expressed their masculinity through jewelry and body ornamentation.

I don't think it struck either Teraeth or myself as excessively masculine.

We both stared.

The funny thing was, her clothing in the Blight had been more revealing. This was more distracting–although Teraeth's bare legs were doing a fine job of competing for that prize.

I found myself feeling uncharitable as I reflected on how Teraeth had lied to me about Janel. He'd known her for years before she and I had ever met. Known her, courted her, and never once suggested he knew us both. Even though those damn prophecies talked about Janel and me ending up together. Even though he had known the link between us in our past lives. Even though he knew Xaltorath had hunted me down and slammed Janel's existence into my mind for reasons I still couldn't fathom.

I walked over to Teraeth and clapped him on the shoulder in exactly the same way the Manol vané had done to me the night before. "Remember what you told me four years ago?"

Teraeth tore his gaze away from Janel. "You may need to be a little more specific."

[1] I suspect it's exactly the opposite, and Khorveshans use curved swords in the thriss style.

I smiled. "Four years ago, back on Ynisthana. I was falling over myself for a woman not too dissimilar to the one standing right over there. You offered me some sage advice. I'm curious if you remember what you said."

Teraeth narrowed his eyes. I couldn't tell if he remembered or if he just smelled the trap. And I was feeling in a nasty mood, so there was most definitely a trap.

I leaned over to Teraeth's ear and whispered, "She's not for you."

Then I walked away.

# 23: Lost in the Woods

***(Therin's story)***

Therin found two problems with traveling through the Kirpis forest to reach the Academy.

First, he hadn't stepped a foot inside a forest in over twenty years.

Second (although probably related to the first), he was lost.

The Kirpis's giant conifers soared beautiful and majestic, so tall they blocked out the sun. Which meant Therin had no idea what direction he faced. Even if he had, he didn't know what direction he *should* face. Presumably south, but "south" allowed for walking a thousand miles to his death without food, water, or anything resembling appropriate clothing.

He knew something of wilderness survival. When he'd been younger and still convinced of his own immortality, he and his friends had actually marched into the Blight on a dare. They hadn't stayed long–but that they'd survived at all was an achievement. And they'd left the Blight with one additional person–a vané slave Therin had bought rather than see executed.

Khaeriel.

He found himself stopping at every odd noise to make sure it wasn't the vané sorceress in pursuit. He still couldn't believe–

Oh, but he could. Therin had no trouble understanding why Khaeriel had enchanted him. He was insurance in case whatever tactic she tried to regain her throne didn't work. Her first plan clearly involved that harp. Therin might have discovered the details if he'd stayed, but . . . that hadn't been an option once he remembered the truth. The only idea worse than Khaeriel enchanting him was Khaeriel repeating the act once she discovered he'd broken her spell.

No, what confused Therin was Khaeriel sleeping with him. An enchantment made such behavior irrelevant. It gained her nothing.

Well. It had probably gained her another child, but if she'd wanted that, she *still* hadn't needed to sleep with him. Given House D'Mon's specialty, Khaeriel knew how to impregnate a woman without sex. They both did. She hadn't needed to bed the man who'd kept her a slave for a quarter century.

Maybe keeping him in her bed had been revenge. A private revenge, each time reveling in Therin's inability to refuse.

But she'd needed no enchantments to ensure his cooperation. For Khaeriel, the only word Therin knew was *yes.*[1]

When Therin heard wolf howls in the distance, he started to give serious consideration to just what the hell he was going to do. Find a clearing, right? And something about dry wood . . . which he'd best attempt before it grew dark. He could create mage-lights, but since those were visible from a distance, he didn't want to risk jeopardizing his location when Khaeriel began her search.

Therin started preparing the fire spells he knew. Not many. At least Galen had been smart enough to marry someone from House D'Talus . . . He flashed to Galen's murder. Therin shuddered and then growled at himself. It had been almost a month. Who knew what had happened in his absence? House D'Mon might be gone.

Galen and Sheloran had been inseparable, but they hadn't been in love. Therin found himself hoping against hope he'd been mistaken, because without a D'Mon to petition the Black Gate for Galen's Return, Sheloran was Galen's only chance. He wasn't so naïve as to think his daughters[2] would do it, even if returned to the Capital. Why Return a nephew to be high lord when they could do nothing and let one of their own sons be high lord instead? No, it would have fallen to House D'Talus to have their daughter Sheloran Returned, and on her to petition for her husband, Galen . . .

"Damn it all, Thaena," Therin said out loud. "Don't refuse Galen just because she doesn't love him."[3]

Therin heard a raptor scream. He looked up in time to see a large golden hawk alight on a tree branch and cock its head at him. Since his family's symbol was a golden hawk, he couldn't help but notice. But then, hawks lived in forests. Seeing one didn't mean the gods had started answering his prayers for once.

Then, to Therin amazement, a blue-winged jay circled around him, chirping merrily before landing on his shoulder. Therin eyed the creature in surprise. This was not a message from Thaena. As a rule, Thaena didn't use living creatures for that purpose.

But birds didn't normally behave like this either.

Several other birds joined the first, flying circles around him or land-

[1] Poetic, but hardly true, given the whole "kept her as a slave" side of their relationship.

[2] He has two: Tishenya and Gerisea. Neither have lived in the Capital City in years.

[3] I once described their marriage as loveless, which is true from a definition of sexual attraction, but I believe Galen and Sheloran love each other as family. That's more than many marriages can claim.

ing on nearby branches and singing in loud counterpoint with each other, all focused specifically on him. A rabbit scrabbled from the brush, twitched its nose at him, and then darted back through the trees. Several birds (but not the hawk) followed the rabbit, while others hopped on tree branches in that direction and resumed their song.

"Uh . . ."

A fawn peeked its head out on tiny, delicate legs, regarded him with liquid eyes, and then leaped back into the forest.

A few seconds later a tiger—a *tiger*—repeated the process.

"Yes, all right, already," Therin groused. "I get the message. I'm walking *that* way."

As he followed the tiger, the forest around him changed. The leaves turned greener, the ground lusher. Soon he walked on a carpet of flowers and delicate leaves. A space in the trees formed a clearing.

And in that clearing sat a goddess.

She couldn't be anything else. Her skin gleamed a delicate shade of jade and she was dressed in a gown of petals. Her beauty shone alien and wild, staring at him with quicksilver eyes without pupil or iris. And if he had any doubts concerning her identity, the way the flowers bloomed from her mere presence—the way the animals sheltered near her—left little doubt in Therin's mind. No, not Thaena.

Exactly the opposite of Thaena.

He bowed to the Goddess of Life. "I am humbled and grateful."

"Well, hello, Humbledandgrateful. I'm Galava."

Therin stared.

*"And* you're adorable," Galava said. "Thaena really should have led with that one. I assumed you'd look older."

Therin had no idea what to say.

"Don't talk much, do you? Are you hungry? Oh, you must be. Come, dear boy. Sit with me and eat, drink. You're safe now." Galava said this without a trace of irony, even with a tiger at her side.

Therin supposed he'd be in more danger sitting next to one of the palace cats. And it seemed unwise to refuse. He sat down cross-legged next to the goddess. "Thank you."

"Oh, this must have been difficult for you. Here—" She reached behind herself and handed him a gourd with the top cut off. The liquid inside tasted of honey and spice and effervesced against his tongue. If House D'Laakar had the recipe to this, they'd be the richest house in Quur. He couldn't tell whether or not it was alcoholic, but it felt like it *should* be.

The thought led to a second, more troubling one: he hadn't had a drink in . . . how long was it? A month. Not since the Hellmarch. Not since his family's massacre. Not since the day he lost every single son.

No. All his sons but one. Kihrin was still alive.

Therin stared into the cup, mutely noted the mirrorlike reflection of tree leaves. A flower sprouted, bloomed, and began shedding petals in minutes. When was the last time he'd gone so long without wine or brandy? Why hadn't he noticed?

He'd started drinking after his wife, Nora, died and hadn't stopped. Therin had become quite expert at sobering spells when they were needed and letting himself float in a numbing abyss when they were not. The situation hadn't improved after Kihrin's kidnapping. How in all the world could he have failed to notice what had become a ritual foundation of his existence?

The obvious answer: because Khaeriel had distorted his need into a leash. Khaeriel knew all his weaknesses: that one had never been subtle or well hidden. *She* had become his drink and his drug, his addiction to which he would have gladly returned again and again.

"Are you all right, dear child?" Galava's voice was so kind it made his eyes sting just to hear it.

Therin forced himself to set aside the gourd with some effort. "Perhaps some food?"

Galava's eyes crinkled with her smile. "Naturally."

She waved a hand. A feast appeared in the clearing. Not just for him—the tiger had been given a haunch of meat, and the fawn sat before a small mountain of acorns, mushrooms, and fresh fruit. The birds flocked to little delicate shells filled with seeds. Had he searched the trees, Therin felt certain the hawk was eating too, although probably not the rabbit.

He picked up a mango and bit deep. Therin was hungry enough that it would've been the best thing he'd ever tasted even if it hadn't been the best thing he'd ever tasted. He saw guava and goldenberry, sugar apples and peray seeds, bananas and more, every single one deliriously good. Soon his fingers were a sticky mess. He knew and didn't care that juice dribbled off his chin.

But as he wiped his face with the back of his sleeve in a manner that surely would have made his tailors faint, he studied the goddess who had saved him. Those eyes made it difficult to gauge her expression, but she patiently watched back. And waited.

"Thank you," Therin finally said. "Don't think I'm not grateful, but . . . why would a goddess show up to rescue me? I'd think you'd be too busy for that."

"You did pray, you know." She looked past him, as if staring at someone just over his shoulder, and frowned.

"I didn't—" Therin stopped and looked behind him. No one was there.

Had he prayed? Possibly . . .

Galava held out a hand to the tiger, who rubbed its chin against her. "Truthfully, it's less about you than Khaeriel. I hope your ego can handle that." She tilted her head. "Do you know what the Ritual of Night is?"

Therin sipped his drink as he considered her words. "It sounds familiar, but I can't say I'm placing the reference."

"You probably learned about it back at the Academy–it's been a while," she said. "I'm sure you realize most offerings to the gods are burned because destruction frees tenyé. But that is not the only way to harvest tenyé. Loss is even more effective."

"You mean sacrifice."

"One definition of sacrifice, yes." Galava rolled her eyes at the tiger as it made a chuffing noise and started to roll over on to its back. "No, I'm too busy to play right now." She turned her attention to Therin. "Many years ago, a demon was imprisoned in the Korthaen Blight. A demon who is, in fact, the reason for the Korthaen Blight's existence."

Therin straightened. He knew what monster the Blight imprisoned. He'd never approached, though, because even the foolishness and immortality of youth had its limits. His friends and he hadn't traveled *that* far into the Blight.

Galava continued, "Keeping this demon imprisoned requires extraordinary tenyé reserves. So, a long time ago, one of the Four Races–the voras–devised a ritual to pool together enough tenyé. And the quality they agreed to sacrifice was their immortality."

Therin winced. "Oh. Right. *That* Ritual of Night. I had it confused with the other one." One of his history professors had droned on about it. It had been enough to send him to sleep every time.[4]

"That other Ritual of Night is a lot more fun." Galava winked at him. "Now, this ritual uses a figurehead symbolically linked to the race in question. A monarch works quite well. First, the voras gave up their immortality. Then my people, the voramer, gave up ours. Last time, the vordreth did so. And that leaves only . . ." She trailed off.

"Only the vané," Therin said.

"Yes. Only the vané." She smiled sadly. "The whole reason we removed Khaeriel from power was because she'd made it clear she had no intention of enacting the Ritual of Night."

"We? *We* removed Khaeriel from power?"

"Oh no, dear boy. You had nothing to do with it." Galava's expression turned impish. "But Thaena and I are a different matter."

[4] Oh, I see Therin D'Mon has taken classes from Professor Tillinghast too.

"It worked. She's not queen."

"Yes," Galava said. "But there have been"–she waved a hand airily–"complications with King Kelanis. The people we sent to handle the situation have run into obstacles.[5] Which Khaeriel might exploit to reclaim her throne–especially with your willing assistance."

Therin let the sticky leavings of a sugar apple fall from his fingers. "So that's why you're helping me." A bitter taste fought with the sweetness lingering on his tongue. "Why haven't you just killed her if you don't want her queen? You and Thaena are both *gods,* after all." Revulsion filled him, dark and ugly. Horror, at the idea that these beings might want Khaeriel dead. That he could do nothing to save her if they decided to act on that desire.

Something almost as sour as horror as he realized he'd still try.

"Kill her?" Galava widened her eyes. "Oh no. Thaena might not be happy Khaeriel refused to perform the ritual, but Khaeriel *is* her granddaughter. Thaena's wrath has limits."

The whole world tilted as if they were at sea. Therin choked. "Khaeriel is Thaena's *what*?"

Galava's laughter sent the birds into flight from the trees.

He felt unbalanced, unmoored–and glad he was already sitting. "I didn't–I didn't know."

"Why would you have ever thought, 'Oh, that lovely vané I just bought–I bet she's queen of the vané, and also Death's granddaughter'?" Galava's expression turned somber. "But I can't help but think Thaena isn't so upset at Khaeriel's refusal as she pretends. Khaeriel does so take after her grandmother–they have a similar temper[6]–and the ritual is fatal to whomever performs it. I suspect Thaena would rather lose Kelanis than her favorite granddaughter."

"Right. Favorite granddaughter." Therin still felt dizzy at the idea. Then a red flash of anger rose through him, leaving behind only scorn and ash. "How favorite could she possibly be, if Thaena left her to endure slavery for twenty-five years? If she'd had any other high lord as her owner . . ."

"True, but I assume that's the reason Thaena sold her to you." Galava stopped herself. "Hmm. It's possible I wasn't supposed to mention that."

He'd been wrong to think himself immune to any future shocks. Therin could only stare at the goddess while his mind flung memories and conclusions at him like an angry, accusing mob. It was one thing to gaesh her favorite granddaughter and hand her over to someone for safekeeping, a prisoner taken to a jail without bars. Quite another thing

5 Ah, Galava. Not even going to mention Therin's own son is one of those people?

6 Truer words have rarely been spoken.

to do so to a Quuros royal, even one who was a Thaenan priest. What had *that* gained Thaena? What were the consequences?

Kihrin. Kihrin had been the consequence.

In which case, had his late wife, Nora, really died from childbirth complications? He'd always viewed that fact with incredulity given the capacity and quantity of healers who had been attending her–or had she died because Thaena had simply *killed* her to clear the way?

Therin picked up his gourd and drank deep before he scowled at the liquid. "This isn't alcoholic, is it?"

"No, dear boy. I thought it best."

"It's that stupid prophecy, isn't it? Pedron's damn prophecy. That's why . . ." His jaw clenched. When he thought of all the people Pedron D'Mon had killed–no, when he thought of all the people *his father,* Pedron, had killed so Pedron and Gadrith D'Lorus could chase after some fool's quest for godhood and ultimate power . . .[7]

Galava reached over and picked up his hand. "Poor boy. I know it's scant consolation, but it seems to have worked. And your son Kihrin's grown up to be such a nice young man."

"Of course he has," Therin scoffed. "I had nothing to do with raising him." He raised the gourd to her with his free hand. "If I asked for a cup of wine nicely . . . ?"

Galava squeezed his hand and ignored the question. "Listen to me, dear boy. Darzin wasn't your fault. Sometimes our children don't turn out as we might like, no matter what we do or say. My children–" Pain shone raw and ugly on her face, pushed out by a forced smile. "Xaloma was always such a sweet child, I never thought Sharanakal would leave a library except to go to a concert, and Baelosh . . ." She paused. "All right. Baelosh was always a bit of a troublemaker. But in a nice way.[8] Now? It hurts to think of them. I *mourn* them."

Therin set his cup to the side. "I don't . . ." He shuddered and started again. "I don't feel . . . anything . . . about Darzin." He swallowed with a throat suddenly dry as the Quur Capital streets in summer. "No, that's

[7] Pedron D'Mon and Gadrith D'Lorus had followed a section of the Devoran Prophecies referring to the Four Fathers (possibly forefathers–it's controversial). Apparently, the Eight Immortals *also* attempted to fulfill the same prophecy–but with greater success. It's not an idea I find pleasing, since it suggests divine intervention guided my own conception, rather than my parents falling in love.

[8] Which means that in millennia-long history of the Immortals, Galava was involved with both Thaena and Ompher at various points. She and Thaena had two children, Sharanakal and Xaloma, while she and Ompher had one child, Baelosh. All three children are now dragons. Since both Thaena and Galava are voramer, it's anyone's guess who was the father and who the mother in that particular relationship. I suppose it's inconsequential as anything but this–a footnote.

not true. I feel relief. If I had just done something . . ." He closed his eyes. "Bavrin and Devyeh are really dead, aren't they? Not just dead but–destroyed. Gadrith destroyed them."

Galava hesitated a moment before answering. "Gadrith devoured Bavrin's lower soul, so Bavrin's upper soul had no way to cross over to the Afterlife. So yes, he is . . . gone. Devyeh, however, was simply murdered. He's in the Land of Peace." She squeezed his hand. "It's unlikely anyone will think to petition for his Return, but he'll be reincarnated. I'll make sure he ends up someplace nice."

"Thank you," Therin murmured. "That's kind." He felt a flash of hate, directed firmly at Quur, the Capital, and every single Royal House. He wouldn't have minded at all if Khaeriel invaded and burned Quur to the ground. They all deserved it. Himself included.

But it was hard–even as he sat in the Kirpis forest being comforted by a goddess–not to hate the Eight Immortals just a little too. For all the manipulations. For all the unwillingness to intercede. For not *doing* anything about Quur. He didn't dare look at Galava lest she see it in his eyes.

"So . . . ," he finally said, looking away. "I'm not helping Khaeriel, as you wanted."

"Are you really . . . *not* . . . helping Khaeriel? Are you so certain?"

Startled, he turned back to face her. "I–"

Galava released his hand, sat back on her heels. "You have more cravings than just wine, dear boy. I wouldn't judge you for returning to her, even after all she has done to you, and all you have done to her." She examined him with those silver, alien eyes. Nothing about her seemed friendly in that moment. "But if you do, understand Thaena's patience has limits. She *will* kill Khaeriel rather than see the ritual go unfulfilled. So if you want to save your lover, keep her from the throne. One way or another, she wouldn't wear her crown for long."

Therin flushed. He'd ordered Shadowdancer threats to Watchmen guards handed down with more subtlety. *Your husband loves you very much. Why don't you help him make better decisions about who to arrest?*[9]

"But why?" Therin finally asked. "Why is this ritual so important the Eight Immortals even need it? You're *gods*. If this imprisoned demon bothers you so much, re-imprison him. Why do you need to drag the vané down to the same level as the rest of us?"

Her small nostrils flared, the first and only time he'd seen anything like anger in her expression. "I wish it were so easy," Galava said, "but

[9] Therin D'Mon controlled the Shadowdancers, an entirely illegal underworld organization operating in the Capital City. Given that his son Darzin wrested control from his father, it's unclear who controls them now.

is it fair that every other race—your people, mine—have made this sacrifice while the vané refuse? There must be a balance." She laughed, but not with any joy. "They wanted so badly to be separate from your people. The vané enchanted themselves and changed themselves until they made that desire reality. But there is a price."

"I don't understand," Therin said. Was she saying the vané had once been *human*?[10]

"Perhaps you might try faith?" Galava suggested. "Kelanis will die, yes, but not forever. He will be reborn. All vané will be reborn, no different from what happens to humans, morgage, dreth. We only need a time—enough time for the prophecies to play out. The Ritual of Night buys us that time."

Therin examined the goddess, finding himself feeling . . . shaken. Shaken and angry. Because if Galava, Thaena, and presumably all the other gods felt the only solution was to put their own faith in the Devoran Prophecies, it meant that, ultimately, they waited on a mortal to save them—to save *everyone.*

More specifically, they were waiting on *his son* to save everyone. Therin honestly didn't know what the appropriate emotion was in reaction to that idea. Pride? Anger?

Maybe terror.

"All right," Therin said carefully. "Faith it is. Thank you for—" He gestured toward the food, the clearing. "And for explaining matters to me."

"Would you like me to send you back to Khaeriel now?"

Therin hesitated. He wasn't ready. He needed time to clear his head, to figure out what he wanted. "If you don't mind, I'd rather return to the Capital."

Galava blinked. "You won't be able to help there."

"I won't be able to help if you send me back to Khaeriel before I'm ready either."

The goddess studied him for a long beat before she leaned over and kissed him on the forehead. He felt like a ten-year-old with his mother. "I understand. Be good."

"That's not really in my nature—" The world flashed, fell into darkness, and then blazed up in a glory of light . . .

Therin D'Mon was back in the Capital City of Quur.

[10] Again, that's a matter of definition. And frankly, true for all the Four Races. We are all "human."

# 24: Conversations in Wicker

***(Kihrin's story)***

We left that evening.

I had expected to wait until morning, but the thriss insisted. The transportation the thriss had provided traveled just as well in the dark as during the day.

I'd also assumed we'd journey by boat. The thriss had a different plan. As the sun set to the east, the thriss presented us with our rides: lizards.

They were not normal lizards. They reminded me of anteaters, with long pointed noses and black button eyes, but dragon-like scales covered their bodies. They walked on their hind legs. Their front legs ended in long, sharp claws. And each lizard stood roughly as tall as an elephant.

They moved faster than they looked, could run for hours, and climbed trees with spectacular agility assuming the tree proved large enough to support them. I'd have assumed no such trees existed, except the Manol Jungle paid no attention to my assumptions. The trees in the Manol were big.

Really big.

However, one didn't "ride" the lizards. Well, the driver did, hanging on or sitting on the moolthras (as the thriss called them) as appropriate. The passengers rode in a large basket on the lizard's back, making the creature look like it wore an adorable backpack. Passengers spent the trip strapped into the baskets and lying down, except when climbing left them effectively standing.

I let out a long, nervous breath when I saw those baskets. They didn't look that large. I noticed another problem, but I didn't say anything. Teraeth saw the problem too.

He just didn't see the trap.

"I'll ride with Janel," Teraeth said.

I shook my head. "Not how I would have played that one."

"What's that supposed to mean?" Teraeth asked.

Janel raised an eyebrow. "Oh? You'll ride with me, will you? Just like that."

Teraeth paused. "I mean . . . if it's all right with you?"

"In fact, it's not," Janel said. "And I must say I've grown tired of the back-and-forth."

"Janel, if I've been out of line, I apologize." Teraeth looked panicked.

"I mean the back-and-forth between you two." Janel pointed to Teraeth and me. "I won't be your scorecard so you can figure out who wins. Thurvishar, would you mind if I rode with you?"

"It would be my honor." Thurvishar bowed.

"Thank you." She gathered her pack and walked over to the thriss waiting to help her into a basket.

I turned to Teraeth. "Wow. You're supposed to be good with women?"

Teraeth growled as he grabbed at his own pack. "Shut up."

When the thriss helped me shimmy into our basket, I immediately regretted it. Logically, I knew I had enough room to move around. The belts were for my comfort, not my restraint. I wasn't trapped.

I dearly, desperately, and completely hated it.

I closed my eyes and told myself I was someplace with wide skies and freedom and plenty of space. Not bound by anything. Free.

I didn't realize I'd been making noises until the lizard started moving. Teraeth, sounding much less angry, asked, "Are you all right?"

"I'm fine," I said through clenched teeth.

"Sure. You sound fine."

I didn't answer. Neither of us spoke for some time after that.

"I don't like small spaces," I said.

"What?"

"I don't like small spaces," I repeated. "I think–I just–when my soul was trapped inside Vol Karoth, I couldn't move or speak. I had no power, no choice. I couldn't control my body, because it's his body now. Which is funny, because I used to like being tied up–okay, you didn't need that much information."

"Oh no. Please tell me more about your kinks. I'm interested."

I half laughed and let another stretch of eternity march by.

"I haven't forgiven you for lying to me," I said later.

"Lying to you?" Teraeth sounded outraged. "I've never lied–"

"When you first told me how you knew about Janel. You *lied*."

Teraeth snorted. "Oh gods, I just knew you'd bring that up. Technically, I did not–"

"Shut up with that 'technically' bullshit. You purposefully led me to a wrong conclusion, and when I did, you made no effort to correct me. You deceived me. You didn't know about Janel because I talked in my sleep; you'd already met her in the Afterlife. Hell, you'd already kissed her–"

"How do you know that?" He sounded appalled.

"She told me! I even remember when it happened. That first day on Ynisthana when I saw you perform a Maevanos. You danced on that altar, practically naked, before you plunged a dagger into your own heart. When you Returned from being dead, you had a huge smile on your face. I asked you why, and you said you'd just been reunited with your *wife*."

"What was I supposed to say?" Teraeth replied. "Hey, you know that girl? The one you've never met but you're completely obsessed with because a demon fucked with your mind? I've been dating her in the Afterlife. She's the reincarnation of my past life's wife, and I'm still smitten. She has no idea who *you* are, though, so I'm not going to introduce you."

"Asshole."

"Still guilty. And by the way, it was both. You *also* talk in your sleep. Kalindra told me. That's how I knew Janel was important to you."

"Go to hell."

"I'm quite certain I'm already here."

At some point, the lizards began climbing, leaving us standing. It helped. I felt like I had some control when I had gravity under my feet and not my back.

"What are we going to do about Janel?" Teraeth asked.

I laughed–not a nice laugh, if I'm being honest.

"I'm serious."

I shook my head. "I don't think that's up to us. She's going to have her own opinion." I looked over toward him; even I couldn't see Teraeth clearly in the dark. "You know what I don't get? How someone who goes wild for independent, self-assured women–Kalindra, Tyentso–keeps treating *this* one like she's a fragile doll. You heard she killed a dragon, right? Two dragons? Have you slain a dragon?"

Teraeth sighed. "My memories of her are screwing me up."

"Elana Kandor marched into the Korthaen Blight–while pregnant with *your* child–and demanded the morgage stop attacking Khorvesh. And the morgage *agreed*. How meek could she have been?"

"I guess I didn't know her."

"Yet you married her. Was it an arranged marriage or something?"

"Marriages were . . . different back then. I married her because she was pretty and I liked her singing and she had good, strong childbearing hips. We didn't talk."

"Wow. Really? So you would just come home from your latest conquest, rape your pretty wife with the nice, wide hips, and leave again?"

"It wasn't rape!" Teraeth protested.

"I wasn't there, so how would I know? But I'm pretty sure the only difference between being a wife and being a slave in Quur is who gets the money from the sale.[1] And if she didn't have any choice in the matter, how exactly is that not rape again? Oh, right, it was legal. *Technically.*"

Teraeth let out a long, shuddering breath. "I'm screwing up."

"Well, far be it from me to tell you what you're doing wrong," I said spitefully.

"Oh, fuck you."

"You wish," I snapped.

I had a half second to recognize the sound of a belt being unbuckled before Teraeth shifted over and pressed me back against the lizard saddle with his hand at my throat. "You son of a bitch," Teraeth hissed. "You know what the worst thing is? Worse than failure, worse than that moment when you realize you've screwed up irrecoverably, the arrows are falling, and you'll *never* be able to make this right? Watching the two people you love fall in love with *each other.* Don't you think it fucking kills me every time I see you hold her hand, every time she cries in your arms, the way you laugh and smile at each other? And who am I supposed to be jealous of? I've spent four years trying to win either one of you over, and it took you both one day—*one whole day*—to forget I existed."

An impossibly heavy weight settled on my chest. My throat closed up. *The two people you love* echoed through my head as the refrain to a song I couldn't stop replaying.

"Teraeth—"

"Fuck you. I don't want to talk about it." Teraeth's voice hitched, someone trying as hard as they could to hold back tears. Teraeth pulled away, moved back over to his side of the basket, and buckled himself back in.

"Teraeth—" I didn't know what to say. I resorted, desperately, to quoting Teraeth's own words. "You had to know you were never going to own her."

Teraeth laughed, the sound blending with the choking sob that followed. "That's a goodly part of her charm," he whispered, which had been my response four years before. Then he added, in a voice so soft I barely heard it, "Yours too."

I didn't know what to do. I felt gutted. Everything ached, a swirling vortex. I leaned back and exhaled slowly. Everything seemed broken and ugly. All I wanted—desperately wanted—was to fix this. To somehow make it right. Except I didn't know how. I wasn't even sure what "fixed" looked like. What did I want?

[1] Sadly accurate.

Teraeth had never made a secret of the fact he wanted to coax me into bed with him, but Teraeth welcomed *anyone* into his bed, at any time, for any reason. We were still friends, but Teraeth saw no problem with sleeping with his friends too. I did. That was that. I'd shoved our relationship into a corner I never had to examine.

Teraeth's confession . . . gods, was he really saying what I thought he was?

"I wouldn't assume she's falling in love with me," I finally said. "She's . . . she's Joratese. They like physical affection. It doesn't mean anything romantic. But she's a stallion–every time you try to protect her, what you're saying is she belongs under your idorrá, your authority. That she *needs* your protection. That's not the way they do things where she's from. She's going to fight you. She can't stop herself. She has to put you in your place."[2]

"Idorrá?" Teraeth's voice was faint. "I *conquered* Jorat. You'd think I'd be more familiar with their culture."

"It's been five hundred years. Whatever culture existed when you stopped by has changed. You should ask Janel to explain it to you. She'll do a better job than I would. I barely understand it myself. Mind you, I don't think the way they do things is a healthy basis for a relationship. That whole idorrá/thudajé business. It's all superiors and subordinates. If one person's dominant, the other person *has* to be submissive. I don't know. I guess I'm just enough of a romantic to think that's great for bondage play and terrible for love."

Teraeth actually laughed. Just a tiny bit of the ache in my chest eased. "You know, sometimes I forget you grew up in a brothel. I keep thinking you're inexperienced because you're such a prude."

I choked out a laugh. "Prude? I'm not a prude."

"Oh, you're a prude," Teraeth said. "Apparently, you're just not naïve."

"Not about the act itself. Love? Sure. I've no clue what I'm doing when it comes to love."

"None of us do," Teraeth said. "Obviously."

"Look, I realize we have a lot to discuss–" I paused. "I need time."

"At least you're still talking to me. That's a start."

"Yeah," I said. "I suppose it is."

We didn't travel nonstop. The lizards halted every few hours at regular rest stops along the tree line, seemingly designed for all functions one

[2] I've spent some time thinking about why Janel doesn't seem to hold Kihrin to the same standards. Then I realized the obvious answer: she went to Kihrin for help. Kihrin *does* have idorrá over Janel. I wonder if Kihrin realizes?

might require except food—which we'd brought with us. We stretched our legs, took care of necessities, ate, and drank.

I couldn't tell when day broke, because even outside the baskets, we'd moved under such a dense canopy, no light made its way to the jungle floor. That floor turned glassy smooth as we entered a flooded area, the real ground somewhere under thirty feet of water. The temperature dropped from lethal hot to humid and warm.

I made a special effort to include Teraeth when we stopped for breaks. Not to ignore him, not to snap at him, not to fight with him. While I wrestled with my emotions, I knew one thing: I wouldn't help the situation by showing Teraeth his heated confession had been a mistake. I wanted Teraeth to be honest with me.

Even if it complicated my life a hell of a lot.

Still, I would have been lying if I didn't think our relationship had turned uncomfortable. I couldn't ignore the situation, but I also didn't want to confront it. Thurvishar threw us the occasional worried look, but otherwise said nothing. Janel acted like everything was fine.

She was either oblivious to the subtext or didn't think her opinion would help.

We napped while traveling, sleeping fitfully. The moolthras moved with a surprisingly smooth gait, but it still jarred me awake more than once.

One of those times I noticed Teraeth had been watching me sleep.

"Okay, that's not creepy," I murmured.

"Sorry," Teraeth said.

He didn't sound even slightly sorry.

"Answer a question for me." I yawned, turning over on my side while I readjusted my belts.

"Yes?"

"What are you going to do after you save the world?"

Teraeth stared at me.

I raised both eyebrows. "Oh, come on. What are your plans? We save the world, re-imprison Vol Karoth, defeat Relos Var, destroy the demons, fix all the bad things. What happens next?"

"I . . ." Teraeth's voice trailed off.

Teraeth had never planned on "what happens next." Teraeth's whole world must have been prophecies and special destinies since childhood, learning his chosen status on his mother's divine knee. Or maybe just remembering it from his past life.

"What would you do?" Teraeth asked in lieu of answering.

"Hmm. I used to think I'd open a tavern, but really I just wanted to give my father a nice retirement. I was going to be the world's greatest thief. No guarded vault or dragon hoard would be safe. Now? I don't know. I might tag along after Janel. Pretty sure if this all sorted itself out tomorrow, she'd be right back in Quur overthrowing the empire. *She* has ambition. A hell of a lot more than I do." I paused. "You can't tell me you wouldn't enjoy tearing down the Quuros Empire."

Teraeth laughed. "If we ask nicely, the current Quuros emperor will help. I've just been fighting this for so long . . ." He sighed. "More and more, I wish I didn't remember who I used to be. People shouldn't remember their past lives. It hasn't done me any favors."

"Sure. It's more than a little awkward to realize your father in this life used to be married to your widow from your last one. That would unnerve the hell out of me."

Silence descended, walked right past pause, and settled firmly into stunned to stay awhile.

Oh no.

"So . . ." I cleared my throat. "No one's mentioned that?"

"No, funny how that just hasn't come up in idle chitchat." Teraeth paused. "Wait, are you joking? Because if you're joking, well done. You *got* me. I jumped at that, hook and bait." He paused. "Oh gods. You're not joking."

"No. Sorry. Not joking. Doc told me about it back on Ynisthana. He married Atrin Kandor's widow, Elana. Which I suppose is a sort of revenge. You took his country; he took your wife."

Teraeth exhaled.

Then he started laughing.

The laughter verged on the hysterical, to the point where Teraeth started coughing. I reached over and slapped him on the back, fighting laughter myself. Not because it was funny but because that sort of laughter is contagious.

"My mother has a wicked sense of humor," Teraeth finally said.

"You know, the stories don't give Thaena nearly enough credit for that." I was about to ask Teraeth if he was okay—although that seemed unlikely—when our ride slowed. The thriss steering the lizard tapped the top of the basket.

I understood their language enough to get the gist: *climb out, you need to see this.* Around the same time, a change of wind or just proximity carried a new scent: burning wood.

When we climbed out, we stood before a bridge arching over gigantic trees grown together into a larger whole. Each tree loomed so large the buildings jutting from their sides seemed like natural extensions rather than man-made constructs. The walkways joining them looked like lace.

And all of it was burned to a husk.

# 25: The Culling Fields

***(Therin's story)***

Galava had a sense of humor. The goddess transported Therin to the Capital City, yes, but specifically to the temple district. To the Temple of Thaena. She'd put him in the white-and-red robes of a Thaenan priest. And removed all his weapons.

"Subtle," he muttered under his breath as he stumbled into the night air. A funeral had been in progress–apparently, the funerals had been running nonstop–and no one noticed when he appeared in the back.

He stole a sallí cloak from the wall and left.

The stench of smoke and burning stone assaulted his lungs, not a sweet hearth fire scent but devastation, burned flesh, lives destroyed. This was no faded tragedy, weeks old. This was ongoing. Who knew how long it would take to rebuild? House D'Kard wouldn't do it for free, which meant huge swaths of population in the Lower Circle were now homeless. Some Royal Houses would snatch up the available land at bargain prices.

Therin pulled his sallí cloak hood over his head. He knew what he *should* do: go to the Blue Palace, present himself, pull his house back together. It wasn't even a long walk. He could be back home in minutes.

Yet Therin stood there, ignoring the familiar heat rising from white cobblestones. He couldn't make his feet move. This was his duty. He was High Lord of House D'Mon. He needed to return. He was responsible for one of the twelve Royal Houses of Quur.

Which was the problem, wasn't it? He was *responsible.*

The word tasted ashy in his mouth, yet sharp enough to cut–accusation, obligation, duty, curse. *You'll never hate me half as much as you hate yourself,* Khaeriel had told him.

Maybe she'd had a point.

Therin forced himself to move, but he hadn't gone far before he veered off the road, down a worn stone path leading into the Upper Circle's center. A few hours wouldn't make much difference when he'd been missing so long. He needed someone to talk to. Also, a drink.

He could fulfill both goals at the same time. So instead, he let his steps lead him to the Culling Fields. The infamous tavern had survived the destruction better than most buildings. Perhaps the tavern's hardy construction was to blame, but Therin suspected isolation more likely. The real destruction here would have happened inside the arena, with magical fields protecting the nearby buildings. And the Black Tower, where the Quuros army headquarters had likely been a more appealing target.

A few singe marks marred the walls. Glass had been broken. Ruined furniture had been piled in the back. Still, the bar looked remarkably intact and shockingly busy for an afternoon, even assuming a lingering late-lunch crowd. He wasn't the only person who needed a drink.

Therin walked to the bar. A young woman dressed in men's clothing directed workmen conducting repairs. He recognized her: Taunna Milligreest, Doc's adopted daughter.

Taunna addressed the craftsmen. "The glass measurements must be precise. We can't just–"

"Excuse me," Therin said. "My apologies for interrupting, but I must speak with Doc."

Taunna looked back at him. "And where have you been that you don't know Doc hasn't been around for years?"

Therin leaned back, surprised. It's true he hadn't seen Doc for a while, but he'd just assumed . . . It seemed impossible Doc was gone. "He hasn't? But I–" He started again. "Do you know where I can find him?"

"No, I don't," Taunna said. "Now do you want to order something? Otherwise, you should go."

A server walked up to Taunna and said, "We're out of the white pepperleaf. I'm going to go fetch another tun from the basement."

Taunna wiped her hands on the cloth at her belt. "No, leave that. I'll take care of it."

"Oh, I don't mind."

"I do," Taunna said. "It's not up for debate. Go look after your tables. The D'Mons are still waiting on their drinks."

Therin froze.

He shifted so his hood cast a shadow over his face and slowly scanned the bar. There, in the back, Therin spotted him.

His grandson Galen D'Mon. He sat at a table piled high with open books. Galen's chair had been pushed up against its neighbor to form a larger seat, which he shared with his wife, Sheloran. The two leaned against each other, back-to-back, facing in opposite directions. Therin might have taken it to mean they weren't on speaking terms except they physically touched, as though each was the wall the other used for support.

Sheloran appeared much as she ever did–all curves and sensuality, dressed in a blue silks beaded with sapphires. She sat in earnest conversation with a woman roughly the same age, dressed in the Khorveshan style. It took Therin a moment to realize the other girl was Eledore Milligreest, the high general's youngest–no. He corrected himself. The high general's only child, after Jarith's death.[1]

Eledore put her hand on Sheloran's arm, adjusting the royal's grip as if Sheloran held an imaginary sword. The two women smiled at each other and started laughing.

Galen was also in the middle of a conversation, although in his case with a slender young man with long, shiny black hair who wore D'Mon blue. Their animated discussion seemed to concern the open books on the table. If Therin had to guess, he'd say Galen had finally gained a start on the magic lessons Darzin should have given him years earlier.

Galen looked happy. Therin wasn't sure he'd ever seen the boy happy before. It was like watching the sun peek from behind storm clouds.

Therin inhaled and turned away.

Doc not being here had shaken him. *Doc* wasn't his real name, of course. Therin had first met Doc using the name Nikali Milligreest, already famous for his skill with a sword. But even after Nikali had faked his death and started hiding in plain sight, he'd never once left the Culling Fields. The only time he'd ever shown any interest in anything other than the arena–

"Oh," Therin said out loud. "He must have gone looking for Valathea."

Taunna turned back. "What did you just say?"

Therin exhaled. "Just thinking about where Doc might have gone. You said you didn't know."

She gestured to the workmen. "Wait right here." Taunna crossed the intervening space between them, grabbed the front of Therin's robes, pulling him down to her height, so their faces were close. "Valathea. How do you know that name?" she whispered.

"Doc and I are old friends," Therin answered.

"Then what's his real name?"

"Nikali." Therin whispered the word.

"His *real* name."

He hesitated. "I don't know it. But I know he's vané."

She let him go and studied him. "You have blue eyes."

"Ogenra can be priests too," Therin answered.

Taunna's mouth quirked. "And I'd say there's a pretty strong family resemblance. All right. Follow me." She called over to the same waiter

[1] Only because Therin didn't know Janel Theranon existed at this point.

who'd been by earlier. "Going down to the basement, if anyone asks." Without turning to see if Therin followed, she walked to a side door–one that thankfully didn't take him past Galen's table.

Therin followed, feeling bemused. If Doc *was* here, why had she lied?

Taunna led him down a flight of stairs in the back, into a basement haunted by the pungent vinegar odor of wines and alcohols stored in cool, dark places for decades. She searched the shelves before lifting up a wooden cask and hiking it over her shoulder. Then Taunna snagged a key ring off a hook and tossed it to Therin. "He's in the wine cellar in the back."

Therin caught the keys. "*What?* Why do you have your father locked up in the basement?"

"That was his idea." Taunna paused at the doorway. "He returned right after the Hellmarch. A couple of times a day I throw some food back there, but he's not eating much."

Therin crossed his arms over his chest. "That doesn't explain why he's locked inside."

"So he doesn't kill our customers," Taunna said as though it should have been perfectly obvious. "He's not safe to be around right now. I mean, really not safe." She added, "Emperor Sandus's death hit him hard. I guess they used to be close."

Therin felt his stomach sink, leaden. Oh. "I didn't . . . Yes, they were close."

"If you're an old friend, I'd take it as a favor if you'd talk him out of committing suicide like this, because it's not fun to watch. And try not to let him kill you." She eyed him speculatively. "He shouldn't. He's always had a thing about not killing family."

"Wait, what do you mean–"

But she'd already left.

Therin contemplated chasing after her before he decided Doc could answer the questions himself. Then, as he turned to the wine cellar door, he stopped himself.

*He* was the one who was going to sober up Doc? Ridiculous. But if his old friend had been down here binge drinking for weeks, the chances Doc flirted with alcohol poisoning, liver disease, chronic undernourishment, possibly total systemic failure . . .

So Therin was going to have to be the responsible one, wasn't he? He sighed and unlocked the door.

Darkness lurked on the other side. Therin might have thought the room empty had not, at precisely that moment, a bottle crashed to the ground, followed by a muffled curse.

"Hey, asshole," Therin said loudly, "what are you doing sitting in the dark?"

"Dark?" Doc's voice answered, low and menacing and utterly malicious. "Oh no, old friend. From where I'm sitting, it's the last bright day this gods-forsaken planet ever saw. But don't take my word for it. I'll show you."

And Therin's whole world changed.

## 26: The Well of Spirals

***(Kihrin's story)***

Dead and injured vané littered the ground. Other vané hurried from group to group, treating the traumas. Putting out literal fires complicated attempts at healing. And it all seemed incredibly familiar.

It reminded me of the Capital Hellmarch.

I rushed forward to see if I could help, when vané soldiers spotted us first. And to be fair, the thriss clothing and animals only meant so much when at best only one of us–maybe two depending on how they viewed me–was vané.

The soldiers headed in our direction.

"Let me handle this," Teraeth said.

"By all means," Thurvishar responded.

Teraeth stepped forward, bowed, and began speaking in low murmurs.

After a few minutes, Teraeth returned. "I have good news and bad news. The good news is they're not thrilled by outsiders, but we're clearly not demons. That's what attacked here."

I said, "So demons don't have any problems with the barrier roses?"

Teraeth grimaced. "So it would appear."

"Lovely," Janel said. "What, then, is the bad news?"

"We're still under arrest," Teraeth admitted.

"What?" I looked behind us. Guards now stood at the end of the bridge we'd just crossed. More soldiers were arriving as reinforcements.

"Not all of us are vané," Teraeth explained. "Even if we have every reason to be here, they're going to follow orders. They're surprisingly apologetic about it. I'm flattered."

"I'd settle for being less flattered and more not arrested," I said.

"Trust me on this." Teraeth wagged a finger. "Let them do their jobs." He turned to thank the thriss for their help.

The two thriss saluted us, hopped back on their rides, and left across the bridge. The vané soldiers didn't try to stop them.

Teraeth turned to us. "Come on, let's go."

No part of me calmly accepted turning myself in to the watch or whatever passed for the authorities in the Manol. That was never a good idea. I'd spent too many years living in a town where justice came on the edge of a gold coin tossed to a Watchman. No situation was ever so quarrelsome that the addition of the guard wouldn't make it a thousand times worse. The Watchmen were always the enemy. I edged away.

"Kihrin," Teraeth said. *"Trust me."*

I stopped myself and exhaled. "Okay."

We stepped forward and let the vané put us in chains.

The vané took our weapons. They patted us down. They even found the knife I'd turned invisible. Then they tied our hands and marched us around Saraval's spiral until we reached a structure that looked like a municipal center.

Since I was under arrest, I wasn't feeling as sympathetic to Saraval's citizens as I should have been. To my eye, the damage looked superficial, less like an invasion than a raid. Demons had popped in, burned and killed everything they could, and then vanished before reinforcements arrived. With the demon invasion, no one noticed us entering town except for the soldiers–everyone else had their own problems to preoccupy them.

The soldiers escorted us down a dark hallway, which looked like it dug into the giant trees themselves. The room we entered looked forbidding and not designed to engender goodwill, tailored for violent interrogations. I contemplated turning invisible and making a run for it, but I'd have to leave behind the other three. That was purely unacceptable.

Then the soldier leading me untied my hands.

"Sorry," the man said. "We had to make it look good."

"What?" I turned around. The vané were untying everyone.

The guards set our impounded weapons on a table.

Janel rubbed her wrists. "What just happened?"

Teraeth raised his hands and gestured to the surrounding room. "May I present one Black Brotherhood chapter house, as promised."

I blinked and looked around. The vané smiled. Several wandered into other rooms to take care of other duties. "Right. May I have my weapons back?"

A soldier pointed. "Everything's on the table."

We immediately retrieved our weapons. Thurvishar stayed where he was, but Thurvishar wasn't carrying anything more dangerous than a food knife on him.[1] Teraeth didn't have nearly as many weapons in the

[1] I must admit the idea of carrying sharp objects near my belt is a deeply uncomfortable thought for me at the moment. For some reason.

pile as I knew he carried on him. I suspected the soldiers hadn't completely stripped the vané assassin–professional courtesy.

"So the demons," Teraeth said. "Just a lightning raid, or were they after something?"

"Not sure," a soldier admitted. "Possibly a distraction. Someone used the spiral path without authorization."

Teraeth froze. "Someone snuck into the Well of Spirals?"

"The former queen, no less," the vané said. "King Kelanis is there with his people right now on the off chance she returns."

I stood up. Teraeth's plan to make contact with King Kelanis at the Well of Spirals looked like it was going to take us even less time than expected. "Take us there. Right now."

# 27: Dark Sun

***(Therin's story)***

There'd been no transition, no warning. One second, Therin had been walking into a dark basement, and the next moment, he was outside. Well, technically outside. He stood on a balcony, looking over a city.

A clearly magical city, woven from marble and porphyry, alabaster and chalcedony. Graceful towers reached for the sky. Broad thoroughfares resembled parks more than streets. Flowers, trees, and greenery lined the streets.

But now the flowers were wilted and singed, the plants browned at the edges. Huge crowds of vané stood in the middle of the colonnades, staring upward. Therin wondered why they focused their attention on the balcony, but then he realized the people were looking up at the sky.

Therin looked too. Doc was right; the sky looked stunningly bright, almost white behind the glowing iridescence of Tya's Veil. The sun resembled what he'd seen at the Well of Spirals too—small, yellow, too blinding to look at directly. What he saw also looked . . . misshapen, as though some nameless god had pinched an edge and pulled. Some force sparked and arced along Tya's Veil, sending out bursts of light along its rainbow sheen. The fire blooms exploded, beautiful and celebratory, but their presence clearly engendered wild-eyed panic in every other onlooker.

"What the fuck is that?" someone said next to him.

Therin took a step back, because the man standing next to him . . .

Well. The man standing next to Therin looked like his father, Pedron D'Mon.

The resemblance wasn't perfect. This vané man dressed in purple and gold silks, embroidered with enough flowers and jewelry to make a Quuros royal blush. His skin was too pale, but the gold hair looked the same, the cheekbones, the shape of the nose. The resemblance was uncanny, right down to body posture.

Which meant, if what Khaeriel had said about Therin's ancestry was true, that this could only be Terindel the Black, presumably named for reasons other than his appearance.

He remembered Taunna's words: *I'd say there's a pretty strong family resemblance.*

A second person stood next to Terindel, a woman, one of the most vané-looking people Therin had ever seen. She resembled nothing so much as a blend of flower and human, with violet cloudcurl hair and a heart-shaped face too perfect to be real. Her gown of layered silks fell about her body like elaborately beaded petals, so ethereal her movement made them dance around her as she tucked herself against Terindel's side. "I don't know, my love," she said, "but nothing good. I've sent a message to the Guardians. Hopefully, we'll know more soon."

"If it's an attack," Terindel said, "I'd like to know who's responsible."

"Tya is," a deep voice said, "for which I'm grateful."

All three–Therin, Terindel, and the woman–turned at the sound of the voice.

Ompher and Taja stood in the room's center. Therin recognized the two gods, even if he'd never seen them in person before.[1] Ompher somehow stood on the pinnacle of a mountain even inside a palace and theoretically not in contact with the ground, while Taja's silver hair and wings were iconic enough for easy recognition.

"First Preceptor Valathea." Ompher bowed to the violet-haired woman before turning to Terindel. "Your Majesty."

Valathea left her husband's arms and crossed over to hug Ompher. "Oh, stop it. You don't have to use that silly title. You haven't taken orders from me in a thousand years. *What happened?*"

"The eighth ward failed twenty-two minutes ago," Taja answered flatly. "Vol Karoth's awake."

A shocked silence settled over the room, muffling the noise of the crowds outside.

Valathea grimaced. "Grizzst warned me it was failing, but I thought we'd have more warning."

"So did we," Ompher said.

"What–" Terindel scowled. "What does *that* mean? Explain it to me like I'm the only person in this room actually born on this planet."

Taja turned to her companion. "You'll explain it better than I would."

The literally stony-faced man nodded. "There isn't much to explain. S'arric–" Ompher paused, scowled, and corrected himself. "*Vol Karoth* is still trapped by the seven remaining wards, but has access to his powers. We can only assume he decided to free himself by pulling down enough raw power from the sun to obliterate the wards from outside. So he's caused a massive coronal eruption and is dragging the entire plasma plume directly to the planet's surface." He gestured toward the balcony

[1] Technically still true.

door. "What you're seeing outside are just the solar winds impacting the shield Tya put up as soon as she detected the change. The plume itself won't reach the planet until tomorrow."

"Tya said it's moving faster than should be possible," Taja added.

"Oh, how nice," Terindel growled. "Any other good news while you're here?"

"The dragons are going to start rampaging any second, which is a problem because Baelosh and Gorokai are both near the Kirpis forest," Taja answered, "not that it matters, because Tya doesn't think her barrier will be strong enough to stop the main coronal wave from breaking through if Vol Karoth's still awake when it reaches the atmosphere."[2]

Valathea made an incoherent noise. Ompher smacked one of Taja's wings.

"What?" the Goddess of Luck said. *"He asked."*

"You're saying we all have less than a day to live." Valathea looked like she might be having trouble breathing. "That the plume that S'ar–" She caught herself. "That Vol Karoth created will destroy *all life on the planet.*"

"In fact, it will destroy all life, knock the planet from orbit, and annihilate at least one moon," Ompher gently corrected. He made a face. "Probably Hara. It's mostly ice. Additionally, whatever Vol Karoth did has caused some sort of deep systemic damage to the sun. We don't yet understand the consequences, but let's survive this apocalypse before we worry about the next one."[3]

Therin's gut wrenched. He didn't understand all of what they were talking about, but he understood enough. The absolute helpless dread on every face in the room would have made the point clear regardless. Two gods were in the room, and they looked like they'd been handed their dooms.

"So. We need to repeat the Ritual of Night," Terindel finally said.

Valathea turned to her husband. "The Ritual of Night *failed.*"

"The Ritual of Night failed after two thousand years. We don't need nearly that long." Terindel looked past his wife to the two gods. "I assume you've already thought of this and that's the reason you're delivering this news in person."

[2] One assumes that this "barrier" is Tya's Veil, which indicates it has a far more important purpose than giving poets a thematic device. Remind me to say thank you to the Goddess of Magic at some point.

[3] In point of fact, it changed the color and size of the sun, shortened the length of our year, and did indeed destroy a moon. The seasonal and atmospheric changes were catastrophic, and it's unlikely humanity would have survived without the magical protection of the Eight Immortals and various god-kings. And all this while Vol Karoth was still imprisoned.

"We're also here to deal with Baelosh and Gorokai," Taja said, "but yes."[4]

"The others are talking to the leaders of the other two immortal races," Ompher elaborated. "We don't expect to be the ones who'll choose which race has the honor of being next."

"Oh, so you *do* remember you're not gods," Terindel said. "I was starting to wonder."

"Terindel, you're not helping," Valathea chided. She then turned back to place a familiar hand on Ompher's arm. "Thank you. I know it's not easy to be here when you could be looking for your son. I only hope that after this crisis is over, you *will* remember you're always welcome to stop by. I've missed you."

Ompher looked embarrassed and also grateful. "Thank you. I hope to have the opportunity."

Taja gave the room a little wave. Then both gods vanished.

Therin waited for the vision to end, but it didn't.

"Doc?" Therin asked. "What the hell did I just see?"

"I would like to throw up now," Valathea announced.

"Doc!" Therin looked around the room, but if Doc was there in more than spirit, Therin couldn't see him. He walked around the room, hoping whatever magic his friend was using wasn't going to let him fall and knock his brains out against a wine rack.

"Spoken for all of us," Terindel said, "but I need you to go north and talk to Elgestat. I'll send Kelindel to see Queen Shahara. Maybe we can draw straws to figure out who specifically wins the honor of being fucked."

She worried on her lower lip for a moment before reaching up, putting her hands on Terindel's face, and giving him a kiss. "At least the group in question will still be alive."

"Have you been to a human city lately?" Terindel said. "The very fact that they're calling themselves human without a sense of irony–" He shuddered. "As though the rest of us *aren't*."[5]

"Be patient with them, love. They don't remember." Valathea clutched his hand. "If it is to be our lot, I'll help you with the ritual when I return."

Terindel nodded, his expression tight. He loosened his robe's collar and traced his fingers along the edge of the blue crystal tsali there.[6] "I'd expect nothing less."

[4] Gorokai is Taja's father, and Baelosh is Ompher's son. See the chart in the back.

[5] It would certainly explain why all the Four Races seem to be able to interbreed. I'm sure whatever word Terindel was using to mean *human* is probably not the same word we use now, but the meaning was likely the same.

[6] Ah yes. The Stone of Shackles.

Everyone watched her leave the room, Therin, phantom memories, and Doc from wherever he was. After she left, the illusionary king turned back to another vané, a white-skinned man so pale he looked albino. "Gather the Founders in the main hall. We'll set up the Ritual of Night there."

The vané blinked at him. "I'm . . . I'm sorry? I thought we're calling for an alliance meeting . . . ?"

King Terindel snorted. "Have you ever heard of the vordredd deciding on any course of action in less than twenty-four hours? The voramer aren't much better. Elgestat and Shahara will still be arguing about who's going to be the lucky bastard who gets to commit suicide when the sun's fires turn all life on this planet to ash. I'm not waiting. We'll perform the Ritual of Night as soon as I've sent my brother away. If you have a problem with that, participation is strictly voluntary."

The other man's gaze turned thoughtful. "This desire to rush things wouldn't have anything to do with the *queen* volunteering, would it?"

Terindel ignored the question. "She won't be gone long, so let's get started."

"Wait." Therin had to assume whatever illusion Doc had cast allowed him to see Therin, even if the reverse wasn't true. "Galava said the vané were the last race left who could cast the Ritual of Night. How is that possible if Terindel already did it?"

The illusion vanished.

Therin found himself back in the Culling Fields wine cellar. A dim sourceless light illuminated the room, which held an impressive number of wooden racks and a smashed pile of glass bottles next to a startlingly handsome black-skinned Manol vané man. His clothing was torn, filthy, and wine-stained. A shiny emerald-green tsali stone glimmered around his neck.

Therin had never seen the man before in his life, but he recognized the tsali stone. Doc never went without it. And while it was nice to have his suspicions about his friend confirmed, Therin still had questions. A lot of questions.

"Who *are* you?" Therin asked. "You can't be Terindel . . ."

"Oh no, I very much *am* Terindel. I'm just not wearing Terindel's body anymore. Haven't been saddled with that dead weight in almost five hundred years, in fact." The man threw Therin a wry grin and raised a wine bottle in a salute. "Here's to the vané civil war, friend."

"And you're also Doc? Nikali Milligreest? How does that all work?"

Doc shrugged. "Blame the Stone of Shackles. Lucky me, though. Turns out my killer was prettier than me."

Therin might not have caught the reference if he hadn't had it explained in great detail to him by Khaeriel. Therin cocked his head. "And here I always consoled myself that you were an ugly bastard."

"Aw, you didn't think Doc was sexy?"

"Oh, absolutely. Wasn't a day that went by I didn't think to myself I should have my guards go fetch that barkeep 'Doc' from the Culling Fields bar so I could have him perfumed and brought to my bedroom. Spice things up a bit."

Doc began laughing. He pointed a finger at Therin. "Don't deny it; you thought Nikali was hot."

"*Everyone* thought Nikali was hot," Therin corrected. "That's why you ended up in so many duels."

Doc leaned back in his chair. It looked like it had been a while since he'd moved from it, although Doc made it seem deliberate and regal, a bit of intense lounging rather than a drinking binge. "It's nice to see you, Therin. Now mind explaining why the fuck Galava was confiding in you about the Ritual of Night?"

"Can we talk about you being gods-damn Terindel the Black first? Because we've only been friends for thirty years. That should have come up in conversation before now."

"I don't really want—"

"Maggot brains, how long have you known you're my *great-grandfather*?"

Doc paused. "Technically, you dank harpy, I stopped being your great-grandfather long before you were born. This body is not related to you." He winked.

"Slime breath, that's semantics. Answer the question."

"Dog breath, you can't—"

"No. I already used breath."

Doc sighed and rubbed his nose. "Remind me not to play this game with you when you're sober and I'm not."

"Just answer the question."

"I suspected from the moment I laid eyes on you, but didn't know for certain until I met the D'Mon high lord. Pedron looked a lot like me, you know. Old me, anyway."

"If that illusion was what you used to look like, then yes, he most certainly did."

Terindel chugged a healthy gulp of his wine bottle. "I'd always assumed my daughter—your grandmother—had been executed. Turns out she was a gaeshed slave living here in the Capital the whole time—*centuries*—and by the time I'd finally figured it out? She'd already died." Doc saluted him with the bottle. "Your turn, pus worm. Answer my damn question."

"Because apparently, Vol Karoth's awake again," Therin said. "Galava wanted to make sure Khaeriel didn't try to reclaim the throne and then refuse to do the ritual."

"No." Doc's green eyes widened. He followed his first pronouncement with a round of blistering expletives. "Aw, fuck me. It won't work. Someone needs to stop them."

*"Stop who?"*

"Whoever! My brother's children–Khaeriel, Kelanis–whichever poor idiot they con into performing the ritual." He leveraged himself to stand, wobbled, and started to list. "Shit!"

Therin walked over to him. "I didn't think you were actually drunk, but you are, aren't you?"

"Of course I'm drunk," Doc replied. "I'm just incredibly good at it." He raised a finger. "Hundreds of years of dedicated practice."

"And here I thought I'd found one thing I was better than you at doing."

"Aw, don't be like that. I can't help it if I'm gifted."

Therin smiled thinly. "Well, for your next trick, you're going to dedicate yourself to sobering up." Therin wrinkled his nose. "And bathing. Then we're going to talk."

"How about instead"–Doc stood up quickly–"I tell you to go fuck yourself." His eyes rolled up into his head as he collapsed to the ground.

Therin sighed. "Great."

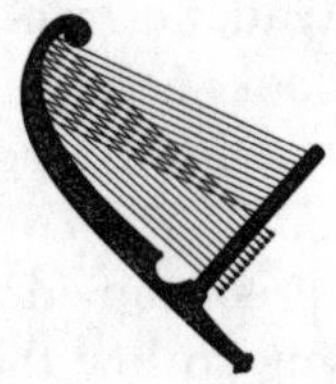

# 28: The Oldest Vané

***(Kihrin's story)***

I'd always wondered why the vané tolerated a defensive shield that cut off magical transportation.

They hadn't.

They simply had their own Gatestone network. Maybe not the same as what House D'Aramarin created back in Quur, but close enough.

When Teraeth and I appeared at the Well of Spirals, we came alone. Everyone agreed it best to leave Janel and Thurvishar back in Saraval. Our task was no less urgent than it had been two weeks before,[1] but we didn't think it would help our cause any to have two of us arrested for trespassing as humans in a place where no human was allowed to go.

I wasn't sure about my own presence, but Teraeth assured me I was more vané than not, no matter where I'd grown up.

At first, I thought we'd arrived in a manicured garden, but the longer I stared, the odder it looked. It was as if someone had taken a single, lovely little garden scene–reflecting pool, flowering hedges built in fantastic shapes, delicately wrought hanging lamps–and then duplicated it exactly a thousand times so it filled up the entire meadow with the same scene repeated. Around each garden area swirled a collection of vané in all colors, wandering in identical green robes. The sky overhead was darkening with the setting sun, the clouds limned pink and orange against a sky without a trace of green.

"The sky . . ."

"Is the wrong color, I know. It's an illusion."

"What is this place?"

"Now that is a long conversation." Teraeth used the tone he saved for moments when he had no intention of explaining something anytime soon. Or preferably, ever.

"No, really," I pressed. "What is this place? Why would my mother come here?"

[1] Technically eighteen days, so two weeks and two days, approximately.

Teraeth didn't answer. Instead, he grabbed my arm and pointed with his chin to a garden scene. "Look. Over there."

A crowd had gathered at a reflecting pool. I couldn't help but notice the crowd included royal guards and someone I assumed was likely King Kelanis. They seemed preoccupied with a flowering hedge bent over toward the pool, dropping so low the flowers nearly touched the water. Next to the manicured base sat a triangular . . .

I blinked. "Taja! That's my harp!"

Teraeth whispered, "No, no, no. Don't just walk over there. We still don't know–"

I ignored him. For the better part of four years, the mystery of what had happened to my harp, Valathea, had haunted me. Seeing that harp here, in a place where it had no business being, brought it all back. I couldn't ignore that.

Maybe it wasn't the same harp. Maybe all vané harps looked the same. How many had I ever seen, after all? Just Valathea. But the closer I walked, the more convinced I was that this was the same harp General Milligreest had given me, later stolen.

Honestly, I didn't even pay attention to the fact King Kelanis stood *right there.* To be fair, he didn't pay attention to me either.

The flowers touched the water. The entire hedge broke apart, spilling flower petals down into the pond–

–along with a naked woman.

I stared, because this defied any definition of normal I possessed. The flowers sank into the dark waters and vanished. The topiary, free from its cargo, straightened again.

The woman had pale white skin, with lilac fingertips and violet cloudcurl hair. Her slender face looked delicate as porcelain. She landed in the water, curled up in a fetal position, and made inarticulate noises. The water wasn't . . . water. It didn't flow right, or rather it flowed far too well. The liquid slipped off her body, leaving her flesh above the water perfectly dry. Small rainbow flashes flared up over the liquid, then dissipated as mysteriously.

Teraeth joined me. "There's a problem. We need to leave right now."

The woman in the water put her hands over her head and whimpered.

"There's a problem," Teraeth repeated, his voice urgent. "We'll come back later."

I sensed movement behind us, and a second later, a woman's voice said, "Well, what have we here?"

Teraeth cursed under his breath. I looked back and froze.

It was Queen Miyane.

At least, I felt safe assuming this was Queen Miyane. She dressed entirely in a gown formed from silver knotted links–too intricate to pass as "simple" mail–interwoven with delicate enameled blue orchids the same color as her hair, cropped to just below her jawline. Silver dusted her dark skin, and, her eyes shared their color with the deep blue sea. A blue diamond drop rested in the center of her forehead, sparkling in the setting sun.

Queen Miyane, potential suspect for the person who ambushed us and left us in the Blight. A whole lot of royal guards stood by her side.

Her eyes narrowed as she regarded us. "I didn't expect to see you again."

Teraeth stepped forward. "It has been a few years, Your Majesty."

Right. Teraeth had met the queen. I never had. At least not while conscious.

So this was a problem.

Queen Miyane could order her soldiers to remove us before the king even realized we were there. And then we were back at square one–more likely worse, since she wouldn't be content with exile this time. Unless we caught the king's attention . . .

I casually ran my hand across the harp's strings.

It made the same sound I'd fallen in love with the first time I'd heard it–the most beautiful silver tone.

The king looked up; our eyes met. Kelanis was a slim, pretty man with dark bronze skin, green eyes, and copper cloudcurl hair he wore short and trim. He looked a lot like his deceased mother, Khaevatz, if a bit lighter in coloring due to his Kirpis father.[2] He wore long silk robes whose color and cut suggested falling leaves. The robes opened in the front to reveal more sumptuous needlework, sewn on to body-hugging silks.

Kelanis's eyes widened, and he motioned for us to approach. Queen Miyane sighed and turned back to us, gesturing. "Shall we?"

The soldiers with her made it clear this wasn't a request. Still, we were about to see the king, which meant our job was almost over. Even if Kelanis didn't believe his wife had arranged our original kidnapping, he'd still know the Immortals expected him to complete the ritual.

Teraeth seemed about to protest, so I grabbed his arm. "Of course," I said. "We'd be delighted."

The crowd's attention fixated on the woman in the pool, but they parted for the queen. Kelanis returned his focus to the woman in the water.

"Give her a moment, Your Majesty," a vané in long green robes told

2 While Kihrin never meet Khaevatz in person, he did "see" her through one of Doc's illusions while he trained with the swordmaster.

the king. "Rarely have I seen a tsali dormant for this long. Valathea needs time to adjust."

"Valathea?" I said before I could stop myself.

"Focus," Teraeth whispered.

The king stepped away from the pool and took a towel from an attendant. He wiped his hands as he smiled at Miyane. "Now what have you found, my dear? These couldn't be the messengers trying to reach us so urgently, could they?" He looked at us and blinked. "Why are you dressed like thriss?"

"Because they were kind enough to offer us a change of clothing after we clawed our way out of the Korthaen Blight, Your Majesty," Teraeth said.

"Don't ask us how or why we ended up in the Blight," I added, "because we've no idea. It seems someone didn't want us to reach you." I somehow managed to not look at Queen Miyane. Besides, there was always the chance we were wrong. Or she'd been framed. Thurvishar's drugged memory of a hair color hardly constituted definitive proof.

"I see." King Kelanis studied us, clearly concerned. "I was told there were four of you. Did your friends not survive?"

"No, they're—"

"They were injured," Teraeth said. "We left them back with the thriss."

I didn't correct him. I could see the logic in lying. We didn't know who'd done this. We didn't know if the guilty party was present.

"This is all distressing," King Kelanis said. "We will naturally have you put under our protection. I will not see this happening again."

"That's not necessary," Teraeth said. "We're not going to be here that long." His whole body had tensed, as though he planned to pull knives or run or both.

I could only agree, but . . .

"Apologies if this is inappropriate, but what's going on with the woman?" I pointed toward the lavender-haired figure in the pool.

The king seemed taken aback. "Oh yes. You were not raised here, were you? Please, step forward. See for yourself."

Teraeth put his hand to his neck and clutched at the arrowhead necklace he wore. He stared at me as though trying to communicate telepathically, but other than sensing his fervent desire to leave, I didn't understand what he wanted. I gave him an apologetic half smile and stepped forward beside King Kelanis at the pool.

"Do you know what a tsali is?" King Kelanis asked.

Attendants were helping the young woman step from the pool, giving her a green robe to wrap around herself. She reminded me of a newborn foal, struggling to take her first steps, eyes not quite focusing.

And maybe it was my imagination, but I did feel like I knew her. Which made no sense.

"Yes," I said. "I'm familiar."

"The woman there"–the king pointed to Valathea–"her souls were trapped in a tsali. But we have transferred her souls into a new body." Kelanis leaned toward me. "I am excited to meet her; she is my aunt. We all thought her dead. She was supposed to have died out in the Blight."

"Grown her a new body . . ." In my shock at the idea, I turned to face Kelanis fully.

Which was when I noticed his necklace and finally understood Teraeth's warning. King Kelanis wore a necklace of star tear diamonds. But not just any necklace of star tears.

My necklace of star tear diamonds.

Kelanis notice my stare and smiled softly. He touched one of the jewels. "Can you blame me?" he said. "I didn't think you'd miss it. After all, you were supposed to have died out in the Blight too."

The sound of unsheathing blades made me glance away. All the soldiers had drawn their swords. Queen Miyane in particular had hers lying across the smooth skin of Teraeth's neck.

We'd all assumed King Kelanis wouldn't have bothered to hide our kidnapping if he'd been involved himself.

And as it happened, we'd all been wrong.

# 29: The Bathhouse

***(Therin's story)***

After confirming Doc hadn't given himself a concussion, Therin sobered the man up using magic, forced him to eat something, and dragged him to a bathhouse.

All the Royal Houses had their own private bathhouses, but enough rich merchants, wizards, Voices, bureaucrats, and priests lived in the Upper Circle to create their own demand. So Therin took Doc to one of the less exclusive bathhouses, too easily accessible to be exclusive enough for a royal, but not seedy enough to appeal to the same princes who might be looking for a fun time slumming.

Therin had tried to pay extra for their own room, only to discover private rooms were unavailable at any price. A rumor had spread that since demons liked fire, water provided protection; all the bathhouses had been filled to capacity since. Therin didn't think it mattered; in his experience, some businesses always fared best when everything else was at its worst. The brothels, the bars, gambling houses, and social halls like bathhouses would do all the business they could stand and more as people tried to forget how terrible everything was. Mostly by gossiping about how terrible everything was.

Crowds created their own odd kind of privacy, the clamor of the flock as effective a wall of secrets as the hush of isolation. Eventually, having been steamed, soaped, and folded like the wash, Therin and Doc reaching the soaking stage. They jammed themselves in a small corner of a steaming pool filled with men, old and young, who grappled with their own private griefs. Everyone else in the pool thought Therin sat next to someone who looked like what he'd grown used to seeing Doc looking like—a taller-than-normal Quuros man with a bald head and a comfortable middle. Heavens only knew what they thought *he* looked like. But for Therin, Doc looked like a stranger—a beautiful vané with green eyes to put any House D'Aramarin member to shame. Which was deeply weird. Therin wondered if Sandus had known what Terindel really looked like. It would have explained some things. The crowd gave them an unusually wide berth, likely because they imagined a great deal more people lingered in this corner than happened to be true.

"You know, I came looking for you because I . . . I needed someone to talk to," Therin finally said.

"What happened with Miya this time?" Doc said. He floated entirely submerged except for his face and the floating strands of ebony hair spiraling out like silken thread.

Therin made a noise not unlike a laugh and knocked his head against the tile wall. "Her name isn't even Miya. It's Khaeriel." He raised his head again. "But you knew that, didn't you?"

"Some secrets aren't mine to tell."

Therin bit back on the urge to say, "Since when?" or the very appealing alternative, which was to try drowning the man. The whole reason he'd gone to the bathhouse (besides the fact that Doc had stunk like a man drinking for two weeks straight) was for the same reason any royal met with dangerous people in a bathhouse—so they wouldn't be armed when a fight broke out. Somehow, Therin suspected that precaution would prove only a minor inconvenience to the former vané king.

"She enchanted me." Therin scowled. "I don't mean metaphorically. She kidnapped me and tried to warp my mind so I'd . . ." Therin didn't want to explain the particulars, how she'd twisted one addiction into a different kind. "I escaped, Galava found me, and that's how I ended up back here."

Doc's voice sounded sleepy and not particularly concerned. "So what's the problem?"

"I'm still in love with her."

Doc stood, pushing his hair from his eyes as steam rose from his body. No one else in the room reacted. To their right, an old man suddenly broke out into sobbing crying, and a much younger man—probably a grandson—put his arms around the other man's shoulders, eyes full of misery. Everyone else in the pool began studiously admiring the artful ceiling tiles.

Doc turned around. "No surprise. You've always been in love with her. Fortunately, you're perfect for each other, since you're both terrible people." Doc sat back down again, this time on a bench across the way. "But hey, since I'm also a terrible person, I've always liked that about you."

"She *slaughtered* my family, Doc."

"And clearly that's important to you," Doc replied, "since you're here mothering me and not back at the Blue Palace actually giving a shit about them."

Therin felt each word twist in his gut. But if the words cut, it was only because the truth had sharpened them. Therin had practically turned somersaults at the Culling Fields to keep his grandson from spotting him. "I suppose I deserve that."

"Let's not forget you kept Khaeriel a slave for how many years? And then there's Kihrin. I seem to recall you literally wouldn't allow her to acknowledge Kihrin was her own child. That is . . . not good, Therin. Not good at all. I don't know if anyone's told you this, but you're an asshole."

Therin frowned. "What? How do you know that?" He waved a hand. "Not the asshole part. That's common knowledge. I mean how did you know about the rest of it?"

"Because Kihrin told me." Doc wrinkled his nose. "Oh yeah, I should probably mention I haven't been around here for the past few years because I've been off on a tropical island training your youngest how to use a sword. He's pretty good. Unfortunately, he's going to need to be."

Therin stared at the man. "What?"

"Oh, come on. With everything else that's happening right now, that had better not be the thing that throws you."

"Just–okay." Therin rubbed his nose. "I guess–thanks? I'm told Kihrin killed Gadrith."

"That is also my understanding." Doc frowned over where several loud, boisterous men were starting to intrude into their cleared zone. They began having an animated, push-turning-to-shove conversation with empty air–no doubt the result of whatever Doc was making them see.

"–and probably made it stick this time, unlike *some* people."

Those green eyes focused on him again. "Again, fuck you. And you have no idea if he made it stick. I thought I'd made it stick too." But Doc straightened, splashing water as he pulled a leg under himself. "Wait. That's not right. Sandus killed Gadrith, not Kihrin."

"Gadrith wore the Stone of Shackles," Therin explained. "Sandus *did* kill Gadrith–and you know what happened next. And Kihrin killed–well, it wasn't Sandus."

"How? If Gadrith had the Stone . . ."

"The Ruin of Kings,"[1] Therin said. "Kihrin found the sword."

Doc's whispered curse was so quiet, Therin almost didn't hear it. Then Doc started laughing. He didn't stop for a long time. There was some private, dark jest at work that Therin simply didn't have the context to understand. A joke Doc found not at all funny.[2]

[1] Urthaenriel, Godslayer, and so on. The sword has a lot of names.

[2] I believe that Doc had stayed so close to the Capital City for all these years because he wished to find Urthaenriel in the hopes it might be able to cure his wife's "curse." He only left

Therin didn't ask him to explain the punch line. He just asked, "Do you have a son?"

Doc stopped laughing.

"Because after the conversation I had with Galava–" Therin rubbed his forehead. "I still can't quite believe I casually spoke to one of the Eight in person."

"Trust me, you get used to it."

Therin let that comment fall into the water and drown an early death. "It's pretty clear to me Gadrith and Pedron weren't the only people trying to force that damn Four Fathers prophecy. And apparently, you were right to be skeptical Gadrith ever sired a child–Thurvishar D'Lorus was never Gadrith's son–he's Sandus's. So I can't help thinking that means all four of us have a son out there somewhere."

Doc went back to leaning his head against the side of the pool. He didn't answer.

Therin sighed and contemplated calling for a cup of wine. The vendors were doing terrific business selling drinks and snacks to the bathers looking for any reason to linger. Except if he did that, Doc would want one too, and damn it, at least one of them needed to stay sober.

But then Doc surprised him and answered the question after all. "Yes, I have a son. And yes, he's the right age, and yes, he's involved in all this garbage. His mother's made sure of it. Qoran's got some tadpole running around out there too. Honestly, the shock would be if he didn't, considering how many beds that man was always skipping through."

"So where have you been hiding yours?"

"Ah, now who's forgetting the prophecy? His mother never told me. I had to find out by meeting the little brat in person."

"Ouch. Takes after you that much, does he?"

"Oh yes. He's a top-grade dick." Doc raised an eyebrow. "Want to switch? I like *your* son."

"I wouldn't know," Therin said. "I hardly know the kid." He scowled. "I suppose I should say I hardly know the man."

"Trust me, he's a hell of a lot better than either of us. Honestly, I have no idea where he gets it from."

"You're too kind."

"Have you *met* our family?"

"Apparently, no, I haven't. For fuck's sake, I just found out that Khaeriel's grandmother is Death herself."

"Heh, yeah . . . that–that's not even half of it."

"You're not really a Milligreest, though, right? Even though you used

---

the Capital to train Kihrin, and managed to not only lose Valathea a second time (when the harp was stolen from the Devoran priests) but also his chance to claim the sword.

the name when we first met? I'm not secretly related to Qoran? Because I'd rather not be."

"No, no. I'm just that crazy uncle that's been around forever. Not related to Qoran or–" His expression fell.

Therin knew exactly why.

"I'm sorry about Sandus," Therin finally said. "I had assumed you'd gotten over him. Or did you two rekindle things after his wife died?"

Doc's eyes opened all the way. "You knew about that?"

Therin scoffed. "Of course I knew about that. Everyone knew about that. You practically handed out signed confessions every time you snuck into each other's tents while we were traveling. You honestly think I never noticed?" He paused. "Okay, Qoran probably didn't notice. He's always been adorably oblivious about some things."

"There's no way you saw anything," Doc protested. "I was using–" He gestured to the tsali around his neck. "I was using magic. You never saw me sneak into Sandus's tent."

"No," Therin said, "but I still knew. Body language always gave the two of you away, and you may have been using magic to conceal what you look like, but you often forgot to hide that just-kissed flush you and Sandus used to show up around the campfire wearing. And how old was Sandus? Literally fresh off a farm in Marakor? The lovestruck stares he would send your way . . ."

"Shit." Doc scrubbed a hand over his face. "Yes, we rekindled things."[3]

"Figured as much. Generally speaking, people don't go on several-week benders over old friends dying. Old lovers are a different matter."

"It kills me that last time we spoke was a fight," Doc said. "I was so angry at him."

"Let me guess–you'd found out he asked Qoran to give Valathea to my son."

Doc's eyes were too bright as he nodded. "Exactly so. I demanded he get her back. Which, uh . . ." He barked out a harsh laugh. "He did. But before I could come back and claim her, I find out Sandus has been murdered and someone *else* has stolen the harp I'd originally ordered stolen in the first place."

"Wait. *You* were the one who stole Kihrin's harp?"

"Technically, I'm pretty sure the Devoran priests did that." Doc pointed an angry finger at him. "She's not Kihrin's harp. I like your kid, but she doesn't belong to him."

Therin thought back to his experiences with Khaeriel, delivering the harp Valathea to the Well of Spirals earlier that day. Hell, had it *really*

[3] Oh, well, that's . . . interesting.

only been earlier that day? He dismissed Doc's comment with a hand wave. "Fine."

"Now what was that you said about stopping the Ritual of Night?" Therin asked. "Because that's exactly the opposite of what the Eight Immortals want."

"With all respect, the Eight Immortals can suck my cock," Doc replied easily.

Therin stared.

"Oh, have I offended? Did you decide to rekindle things with the ol' Pale Lady? Couldn't help but notice how you were dressed . . ."

"I just think maybe a little reverence . . ."

Doc leaned forward from the bench so quickly, he sent a wave of water splashing against the side. "No. Absolutely not. They're not gods. And I know they're not gods because I'm old enough to remember when nobody worshipped them. When nobody would have even *thought* to worship them."

Therin decided to let that pass for the moment. He didn't know how old Doc was, but . . . old. Older than the Empire of Quur seemed obvious enough. Maybe what Doc said was true, but it seemed hard to imagine. "So you were going to explain how you performed the Ritual of Night when everyone else says you refused? Or was that just a fantasy of how you wished it had gone?" Therin frowned. "But–the business with the sun. You refused to perform the Ritual of Night during Atrin Kandor's reign . . . the sun didn't look like that five hundred years ago."

"No, but it looked like that fifteen hundred years ago. That's when I performed the ritual. Tried, anyway. It just didn't work." Doc shrugged. "As it happens, Queen Shahara of the voramer drew the lot to do it. And she performed the ritual perfectly, and the voramer lost their immortality. Never saw Thaena as angry in my life as the day her people became mortal. She didn't make any secret of the fact she thought it should have been the vané."

"So why wasn't it?"

"I messed up a glyph. Screwed up my own heroic sacrifice. It happens." His green eyes were dark and bitter.

Therin couldn't tell whether or not he was lying.

"Okay, so you didn't have time, the voramer had to step in and do it instead, fine. But why doesn't anyone seem to know that? Why does everyone think you refused?"

"I do not want to talk about this," Doc said.

"I do," Therin replied.

"I believe the technical term for your situation is *tough shit.*"

"Yes, but I know where Valathea is." Never mind that Therin happened to be telling the truth; he also knew that this tactic wouldn't exactly endear him.

Doc growled, "You son of a bitch. Seriously?"

"My son is apparently in the middle of this mess, and I have gods and my best friend telling me two very different stories that don't add up. So yes, seriously. Help me understand why you think the Ritual of Night is a bad idea–something beyond the death of people performing the ritual and your race becoming mortal. Do that and I'll tell you where you can find your damn harp."

Doc's glare was decidedly unfriendly. "Fine. I don't want them to perform the ritual because it won't work. It won't work for them, exactly the same way it didn't work for me. It *can't* work. There's no happy ending to any story where that ritual is performed a fourth time."

An ugly sense of dread settled over Therin. "What do you mean?"

"I *mean,* that's all the explanation you're getting. You don't know Thaena the way I do. You don't know what she's capable of doing when she feels betrayed, and I promise you, when this is all over, she's going to feel betrayed. Even if no one actually did."

"I don't know Thaena?" Therin scoffed. "She's my goddess!"

"And she's the mother of my son," Doc retorted. "Turns out when people talk about sleeping in Thaena's bed, it's not always a metaphor for dying."

Therin's mouth fell open. "Uh . . ."

"Now where the fuck is my wife?" Doc's expression suggested he had run out of patience.

Therin was so in shock from that particular reveal–worse, in its way, than the whole grandmother thing with Khaeriel–that he answered instantly. "The Well of Spirals."

Terindel's eyes went very wide and then very narrow. ". . . why?"

"I honestly don't know, but when Khaeriel took it there, she told the attendants the harp was an 'unconventional' tsali stone."

Every trace of expression fled Doc's face.

"What am I missing about that, Doc? I mean, even if that's true, what are they going to do about it at a vané temple? It's not like Thaena will Return her. Even if her souls are intact, which after five hundred years seems unlikely–"

"It's a tsali stone?" Doc wasn't asking Therin the question. "All this time, I thought it was a curse . . . I've been trying to break a *curse.*" His expression was a curious mixture of horror and something Therin couldn't quantify. Not hope exactly, but some related emotion that wanted to make friends with hope. "A tsali stone? That's the easiest thing in the world to fix . . ."

"No, it's not. She doesn't have a *body.* You'd need both Thaena's *and* Galava's consent."

Doc splashed his way over to Therin and grabbed him by the shoulders. "No, you don't. That's what the Well of Spirals *is*, my friend. It's where my people go when we want new bodies, and we use tsali to keep our souls safe until we make the transfer. Don't you see? They're bringing back my wife!" The Manol vané started laughing. "Come on, then. We're going to the Well of Spirals."

Therin grabbed the man's hands. "You, maybe. I don't know if you remember, but that's where Khaeriel is. And in spite of how I feel about her, I also have to acknowledge she's unlikely to be happy with me right now."

Doc scoffed. "Nonsense. The Well of Spirals is the last place in the world where you're going to find Khaeriel. She's too smart to stick around–I guarantee you someone already alerted her brother, and he's shown up with soldiers on the off chance she had an attack of stupid. It'll be perfectly safe."

"Perfectly safe when I'm a known associate of hers? They're not morons, Doc."

"Pssh. The odds we'll see the same people you encountered are so small it's a leaf in the forest." He hopped out of the pool, not bothering with wading through the crowds to the shallow steps. "Come on, Therin. Let's go! When was the last time you left the Capital City?" He paused before Therin could answer. "When was the last time you left the Capital City of your own free will?" Doc pulled a towel off a shelf and wrapped it around his waist. "Remember when we used to have fun?"

"Remember when we almost ended up dead on numerous occasions?"

Doc clapped Therin on the arm. "That's called *fun.* And trust me, after the first thousand years or so, you learn to enjoy it."

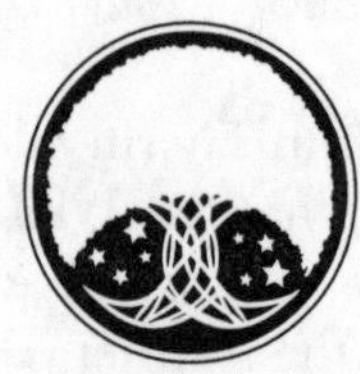

# 30: Cycles of History

*Kihrin blinked. "Your father and Doc . . . ?"*

*Thurvishar tilted his head. "So it would appear."*

*"Wow." Kihrin clearly fought back laughter. "I suddenly understand where Teraeth gets it from."*

***(Kihrin's story)***

I consoled myself that at least they hadn't captured Janel and Thurvishar.

Which was when the meadow where we'd appeared flashed with a blinding light. A second later, soldiers moved in our direction, dragging Janel and Thurvishar between them. Both looked unconscious.

I prayed they were just unconscious.

Teraeth still focused on the king and on Queen Miyane's sword. "Oh, I see. This was all about deniability. If we couldn't identify who sent us into the Blight, we couldn't snitch on you to the gods after we died—" He broke off as the soldiers pulled Janel and Thurvishar into the circle where we stood. His face took on that calm I associated with the worst and most murderous aspects of the man's temper, that moment just before the poisoned knives appeared.

"A plan that has unfortunately come to naught," Kelanis said. "Given how many royal family members have survived being sent on the Traitor's Walk, I am honestly starting to wonder why we even bother." He pursed his lips as he regarded Teraeth. "I must admit it feels odd to have an uncle so much younger than oneself."

I blinked, then looked over at Teraeth. It hadn't occurred to me, but Teraeth *was* Kelanis's uncle. I somehow didn't think it would bring Teraeth any clemency.

Seriously, *this* family was proving themselves even worse than the D'Mons.

King Kelanis snapped his fingers before Thurvishar and Janel. A shudder passed through both as they visibly woke. Whatever magic had kept them asleep hadn't fully left them; they couldn't stand without assistance.

"Thank you." Thurvishar didn't sound grateful for some reason.

Janel lifted her head. She didn't say a word, but she glared swords and mayhem at the vané king.

"I hope you are all intelligent enough to realize the Eight are not in any position to rescue you at the moment," King Kelanis said. "And with all the wards here in this place, they would be unlikely to hear you even if you called out to them."

Thurvishar raised his head, tried to focus. "Why do this, Your Majesty? We didn't come with an army to try to force you to do what you promised." He ignored or didn't notice the annoyed glare Teraeth gave him.[1]

"True," Kelanis said. "I gave my word. Now, I have broken it. Alas." King Kelanis tilted his head as he examined the D'Lorus wizard. "But I lacked important information when I made that promise, so I refuse to be bound by an oath made under false pretenses."

"What false pretenses?" I asked. I glanced over at Teraeth. He didn't seem to be about to try anything rash, at least for the moment, but I was worried; his instincts ignored self-preservation. Previously, his mother would always resurrect him. This time, though? Probably not.

Kelanis turned back to me. "I have always considered myself a historian. Making up for my young age, I suppose. The first time they performed the Ritual of Night, Vol Karoth stayed imprisoned for over two thousand years. Remember that number. The second time they performed the ritual, it imprisoned Vol Karoth for a thousand years. This last time? Just over five hundred years. Are you noticing the pattern? The next Ritual of Night buys us *two hundred and fifty years*. We vané will lose everything—our culture, our history, our knowledge—for two hundred and fifty measly years. Meanwhile, I die, and all the Founders who help me perform the ritual die. That is a price too dear for such meager returns; I refuse to pay it."

"It buys us time," Janel said. "Time we can use to plan and find a solution—"

*"You have had three thousand years!"* King Kelanis screamed.

Silence descended on the Well of Spirals. No one uttered a word. The acolytes at the well itself all stopped their activities. Everyone stared. In the distance, a crow cawed from a tree.

King Kelanis calmed himself, smoothing the creases on his robes. "The Eight Guardians have had over three thousand years, to be pre-

[1] It honestly hadn't occurred to me I was downplaying Atrin Kandor, although even Teraeth would admit that as methods of coercion go, invasion was not particularly successful.

cise. The Eight Guardians have known about the danger imprisoned in the Korthaen Blight for millennia. Yet no solutions have been suggested. No one has even offered up a good theory on dealing with Vol Karoth. Just books of dubious prophecies and no plans at all. Every time a race gives up their immortality, people sigh with relief, go back to their lives, and *forget* the clock is still ticking. So perhaps it would be better motivation if the danger stayed imminent. Perhaps a little pressure is what the Eight Guardians need, what we *all* need, to solve this problem."

"Huh," I said. "That's a really good point."

King Kelanis spun back toward me. "What was that?"

I shrugged, or at least as much as I could with two guards holding my arms. "I hadn't thought about it like that, but now that I've heard your position, I think you have a good point. Maybe you're even right. The Ritual of Night doesn't buy us much, does it? And even you're giving the ritual too much credit. Because if there's anything to this prophecy business, well, events are in play *now.* So what do we gain? A few months? A year? I'm sure the demons would love it if we re-imprisoned Vol Karoth. They'll go right back to Hellmarching. Clearly, we need to find a different solution, because this one is, at best, temporary." I chewed on my lower lip. "I'm just not sure what we can do."

"Is that so?" King Kelanis's expression turned unreadable.

"Yes," I said. "It honestly is."

The king walked over to me and grabbed my throat. Kelanis turned my head from side to side. "You remind me of someone. Who could that be?"

My friends gave each other uneasy looks. I had to hope no one was about to say or do something rash. Especially Teraeth. Or Janel.

Probably not Thurvishar. At least we had one person with us who was levelheaded.[2]

I tried to ignore the fingertips digging into my skin. "I can't imagine who, Your Majesty. I was born in Quur." I looked down as far as I could without moving my head. "I didn't know you were into this sort of thing."

Okay, so *or myself* should have been added to that list. I could actually *hear* Teraeth roll his eyes.

To my surprise, Kelanis laughed.

The king released me and walked away, chuckling. Then he turned back. "Your mother was just here, you know. You missed her by less than a day."

My throat dried. When we'd shown up at court, I'd introduced myself as, well, Kihrin D'Mon. I'd played up the role of a Quuros royal

[2] Thank you.

prostrating himself before vané might, figuring the idea would tickle their pride. I'd never suggested, not even once, I might be related to vané royalty. The last thing we'd wanted was to complicate negotiations with the mistaken belief I schemed to claim the vané throne.

"My mother?" I tried to sound skeptical. "With all due respect, Your Majesty, I don't think so. My mother was a D'Mon family slave."

Kelanis smiled. "Not bad." He pointed at me. "I almost believe you. Khaeriel's a fantastic liar too. I'm sure you get it from her." He paused. "You do realize your tenyé betrays your ancestry?"

I cocked an eyebrow. "Again, Your Majesty, that's unlikely–"

The king slowly pointed a finger at Queen Miyane, who winked at me. At no point had she moved her sword away from Teraeth's throat.

"Shit," I muttered. Because Queen Miyane *was* sister to the assassin who'd murdered my mother. Miyane was my aunt by blood, because my mother had ended up permanently residing in said sister's body before I was born. The Stone of Shackles and all that.

My tenyé would indeed give that away.

The king shook a finger at me, like a teacher scolding a student. "I did not discover the Stone of Shackles' true nature until I searched through old family records. Historian, remember? I found this fascinating account of a voras wizard giving a Cornerstone to my uncle Terindel. But what happened to the Cornerstone after Terindel's 'death'? It has been left in a jewelry box, discarded as a trinket–one claimed by my sister. By the time I pieced together the truth, it was too late to do anything but hope your mother had died in the Blight. And yet, here you are, nephew. Such a shame about the timing. We would have thrown you such a party."

"Surprise . . . ?" I said weakly.

Teraeth leaned away from the blade's edge. "This doesn't change anything. Kihrin has no claim to your throne; we've committed no crime. Why execute us when all you have to do is refuse to cooperate?"

"Now, now. The humans did trespass here," King Kelanis pointed out.

"That's not worth killing them over," Teraeth responded.

"Let's not make matters even worse than they are," I said. "Teraeth's mother is Thaena, and Janel's mother is Tya. There's refusing to conduct the ritual, and there's killing their *children*."

"You can't use us as hostages if we're dead," Janel added.

"What about him?" King Kelanis pointed to Thurvishar. "I suppose his mother is Taja?"

"No, I'm just pretty," Thurvishar offered.

Okay, so maybe *all* of us belonged on that list.

Kelanis paced before us. "No one would argue this is a fantastic situation. And you are quite right. Killing you would likely not help me. Turning you into tsali, however—"

"No!" Janel said.

Several well attendants looked in our direction.

"Darling," Queen Miyane said, "not *here.*"

He tilted his head in her direction. "You make an excellent point. No sense upsetting the attendants. And if Khaeriel refuses to leave hiding to reclaim Valathea, perhaps she will for her son."

I grimaced. Great. Perfect. "You know she didn't raise me, right? And I can count the years I've spent with her using one finger? Half of one finger? I wouldn't assume she cares that much."

"For your sake, I hope she does. Your execution will be both public and excruciating. It would be a shame if she refuses to turn herself in and I'm forced to carry it out." The king motioned to his guards. "Take them to the Quarry. And be gentle with this one. He is a prince, after all."

# 31: Trying to Rule an Empire

***(Therin's story)***

When Therin and Doc reached the Capital Gatestone, a large sign across the front said, "Closed to the Public." Evidence of angry crowds, fighting, and riots lingered in scattered litter and debris. Chains barred the entry. No obvious guards stood watch, but it seemed unlikely that there weren't people watching from rooftops lest anyone return intent on causing more trouble.

Therin gestured. "That's a problem."

"Oh, you think so? Any other obvious facts you'd like to share?"

Therin ignored his friend's sarcasm. "The Gatestone system must have been so overwhelmed, they've shut down everything but essential traffic. And we don't qualify unless I reveal who I am or"–Therin shrugged–"go to Qoran, which is as good as revealing who I am."

Doc snapped his fingers. "The emperor can help."

Therin raised an eyebrow. He'd heard stories about the new emperor while in the bathhouse–people wouldn't shut up about it. He'd even heard the emperor was a woman, someone named Tya-something? He didn't remember.

"Why would the emperor let us within a thousand yards of her?" Therin asked.

"Because I'm an old friend." Doc grinned. "And so are you."

Therin paused. "You're not going to tell me, are you?"

"I thought you liked surprises."

"Since when have I *ever* liked surprises?"

"Oh, good point." Doc shrugged.

The bastard still didn't tell him how Therin knew the emperor.

Therin had only rarely visited the Soaring Halls. The imperial palace was nothing more than a marble mausoleum housing a collection of paintings and statuary, echoing with the ghosts of dead wizards. Emperors rarely lived there; Sandus never had. The last Therin had checked, the High Council imperial liaison, Fayrin Jhelora, had turned the palace into his personal bordello.

At least, that had been the case previously.

The doors stood open when they arrived. Despite the late hour, people bustled about in a steady stream. One would have thought this was the High Council chamber, which Therin wouldn't have expected to be this busy. National emergencies, after all. Military personal, witch-hunters, priests, and all manner of people walked with purpose in their stride.

Therin stopped and blinked at the sight. This new emperor wasn't expecting to *rule* Quur, was she?

"Don't gawk." Doc grabbed his arm and dragged him inside.

The soldiers there saluted.

Therin narrowed his eyes at Doc. "Tell me you're not impersonating Qoran."

"Okay, I'm not impersonating Qoran. Any other lies you'd like to hear? I've got plenty. Here's a fun one: our sons are absolutely, definitely *not* in love with each other."

"It's a capital offense to impersonate–I'm sorry. *What did you just say?*"

Doc laughed as he strode inside the palace like its owner. His impersonation of High General Milligreest was fantastic even without the illusion.

The Soaring Halls were as beautiful as Therin remembered, the product of a thousand years of craftsmanship, spellwork, and Quuros ego-stroking. Even he found the palace excessive. Someone had hauled an ornate marquetry and gilt-covered table over to the main entrance and set a chair behind it. Fayrin Jhelora had ignored the chair, instead sitting cross-legged directly on the table. He was staring off into space, head resting on one hand, chatoyant opal eyes focused on nothing in particular.[1] He seemed to be contemplating the entertainment possibilities of chewing off his own fingers.

"Where's the emperor?" Doc barked out.

The scandalously young council member raised his head and blinked. "Oh my. Hello there."

Doc cocked his head. "The emperor," he repeated.

"Right," Fayrin said. "Of course. Won't you follow me, General? She's having dinner." He glanced at Therin, then returned his attention to Doc.

"Fine," Doc said.

The man hopped off the desk and shouted out, "Take my place, Glaris. I'll be right back." He sighed. "I simply can't believe I'm covering the front door like a damn doorman. I swear, you host one orgy in the imperial bedroom and you're never forgiven . . ."

[1] Fayrin Jhelora is an Ogenra of House D'Jorax.

Therin chuckled. Besides his reputation for obscenity, Fayrin was famously open to the highest bidder on council votes, which Therin himself had exploited. The man didn't have an ethical bone in his entire body. Therin wouldn't have trusted him to empty chamber pots, let alone screen palace visitors.

Presumably, the new emperor would learn, one way or another.

They walked through the palace, past soldiers, bureaucrats, wizards, and to Therin's extreme surprise, a shocking number of witchhunters. Then Fayrin reached a set of double doors, already open. Two soldiers stood at attention.

"Your Majesty, you have a visitor!" Fayrin Jhelora shouted out.

A woman Therin recognized turned around. She stood before a large map of the empire, painted along a wall. Small lights on the map flared into brightness before fading again. Some lights stayed on, while others shifted their location. She held a piece of sag bread wrapped around spiced meat in one hand and gestured with the Scepter of Quur using the other. People filled the room, bunched up over tables, poring over records, writing out letters, and then handing them to heralds, who promptly sprinted from the room.

Another person, standing next to her, also turned.

Qoran Milligreest.

"Oh, now this is a touch awkward," Fayrin said. "The high general is here to see the high general. Only which one's the real high general, I wonder."

Therin's stomach twisted. Qoran was a friend, but there were limits . . .

But everyone else just looked confused. A similar expression crossed Tyentso's face, quickly suppressed. She waved a hand. "You're thinking too much, Fayrin. Thank you for showing them in."

High General Qoran Milligreest raised an eyebrow. Unlike the High Council member turned doorman, Qoran took notice of Therin. And recognized him too.

Fayrin didn't hide his surprise. "You don't want them executed? I'll happily call for the guards–"

"Out, Jhelora." Tyentso pointed toward the door. "Everyone, I need the room. Thirty minutes, then come back."

"Oh, fine. Never let me have any fun." The liaison sighed dramatically.

Everyone else dropped whatever they'd been doing and shuffled out past Therin along with the liaison, who shut the door behind him.

Qoran immediately stalked across the room. "Therin? You're alive, what happened–" He paused and stared at Doc. "Who are you?"

"Oh, no one important."

"Raverí?" Therin said. "*You're* the new emperor?"

Tyentso looked like she hadn't slept well in weeks, and neither had her tailors. The embroidery on her agolé must have weighed as much as a small child. "You don't have to sound so damn shocked. And call me Tyentso. Everyone here's adorably oblivious to who I used to be. Let's keep it that way."

Therin scratched his head. He hadn't seen Raverí–Tyentso–since . . .

Well, since she'd helped free him and his family from Gadrith's animated dead. He never expected see her again. Something to do with being a magic-using woman is a country where that was a death sentence.

"What happened?" Qoran repeated.

Therin waved a hand. "What you probably heard. Miya's gaesh broke, and she . . . reacted as I suppose one might expect. I escaped from her this morning and made my way back to the Capital."

Qoran looked him over carefully. "Why are you dressed as a priest?"

Therin smiled and spread his arms. "Someone's idea of humor. Look, I'm happy to see you, Qoran, but I'm here to see the emperor." He pointed to Tyentso. "We need to use a Gatestone, but since they're closed down, we need a writ."

"Why?" Qoran asked. "You're a high lord. It's your right."

Therin exhaled. He didn't want to have this conversation.

The new emperor caught on more quickly, but then she knew more about running away. "You're not coming back?"

"No."

Qoran's expression mimicked someone who'd just stepped in something foul and sticky. "What? Don't you understand what your house is going through? They need you back. The empire needs you back."

"The empire's done just fine without him so far," Doc said.

General Milligreest scowled at the vané. "Who are you again? Use proper names this time, before I have you arrested."

Doc pressed his lips into a thin line. "Oh, come now, Qoran. Surely, your mother told you what I really look like. You've always known I wasn't Quuros."

Qoran looked at Doc as if seeing him for the first time. "Nikali?"

"As it happens. But you know that isn't my real name either."

Qoran closed his eyes for a moment. "So you're . . . you're going back home?"

"It's been a few years since your mother asked me to watch over you," Doc said gently. "The family doesn't need me anymore."

Qoran seemed to search for the words before finally saying, "Have you told Taunna?"

"I told Taunna four years ago, old man."

Qoran snorted. "'Old man'? You're one to talk."

Therin bit his lip as he watched the exchange. He'd never figured out just how much Qoran knew about Doc. Quite a lot, as it happened.

Qoran focused his attention on Therin then. "He has a homeland. And so do you. This one, here. Reclaim your position as high lord."

"Don't feel like it," Therin said. "Besides, I have things I need to do."

The high general stared at him. "What sort of things?"

"Prophecy things," Doc said. "You know, the end of the world? That stuff."

An ugly look came over the high general's face. "Hmm."

"You remember the Devoran Prophecies, don't you?" Doc continued. "Lucky us, turns out we get to do what Gadrith and Pedron couldn't. Or rather, our kids do."

Qoran gave Tyentso a dirty look. "Don't."

Tyentso put a hand to her chest. "What? Me rub in the fact I've already told you all this? And I like your daughter, Qoran. I like her a lot."

"She's revolting against the empire," Qoran growled. "She's . . . she's started a *rebellion*."

"Has she, though? Because no one's explained to me how anything happening in Jorat is illegal." Tyentso added, "Anyway, the empire could use a good rebellion."

"Must I remind you that *you* are emperor?"

"Must I remind you that you're the only person on the fucking High Council who seems to believe that?"

Therin cleared his throat. "Fayrin Jhelora seems to be fine with it."

Both Tyentso and Qoran said simultaneously, "He doesn't count."

Doc walked over toward a table loaded with food and helped himself to a plate. "So we need a writ to get past the guards at the City Gatestone. Or use a military Gatestone. Either way works. We just need to go to the Academy."

Tyentso squinted at them, shutting one eye. "Do I want to know why?"

"Nope." Doc started eating.

Therin was tempted to do the same. He'd eaten when he'd forced Doc to do likewise, but that had been hours before.

Instead, he leaned against the table, eyed the map of the empire, and started thumbing through the open book next to Tyentso. "There's stuff involving the vané happening right now. And while it affects everyone else in the world, I'm reasonably sure the vané won't want the emperor of Quur involved–" He faltered as he picked out names in the text. His son Kihrin's name. Other equally familiar names. "What *is* this?"

"A book. Seriously, you made it all the way to high lord?"

Therin ignored the quip as he turned the book back and looked at its cover, but there wasn't anything like a title or embossed stamp. "No, really, what is this?"

Tyentso waved a hand. "Thurvishar D'Lorus threw it together. It's, uh . . ." She made a face. "It's a chronicle." She waved her hands vaguely. "Not important right now."

"It's a load of absolute garbage," Qoran Milligreest snarled.[2]

"How would you know? You haven't read it," Tyentso reminded him.

"Who's had time?" he groused.

"How'd he have time to write it?" Therin asked. "This is . . ." He flipped through the pages again. It wasn't small. It had to haven taken months.[3]

"Funny you should mention time," Tyentso said. "But that's another story. Please tell me you're not trying to interfere with what the kids are doing. Let them do their job."

Doc and Therin blinked and looked at one another, then back at the emperor. "What the kids are doing?" Therin asked.

"Well, the Eight showed up at Atrine and sort of . . . took them," Qoran Milligreest said. He pointed to Therin. "Your son, a young woman—"

"Oh, just say *daughter*. She's your daughter," Tyentso said. "How can you be *this* embarrassed by adultery?"

"It's not—" Qoran cleared his throat. "I would remember if I'd slept with the Goddess of Magic!"

Therin had been through so much, he found Qoran's proclamation only faintly startling. "You slept with Tya?"

"Not that I remember!"

Tyentso looked over at Doc and grinned. "Isn't he adorable?"

"Quite. Was my son there?" Doc asked.

She nodded. "Yes. Thurvishar too."

"So the whole group, then." Doc sighed. "How much do you want to bet the gods sent them down to the Manol to make sure Kelanis performs the Ritual of Night?"

Qoran Milligreest scowled. "The Ritual of what?"

"Oh, the state of education in Quur today," Doc murmured. "I'm afraid our kids have just stepped into giant piles of shit. But we can help; just take us to the Academy."

"I don't know if anyone has pointed this out, but I'm a little fucking

[2] I take offense.

[3] Almost six months, in fact. And yes, I pulled it all together in Shadrag Gor, so in terms of real time, it took just under a day. I'd just delivered it to Tyentso, in fact, when Brother Qown contacted me and asked me to help with the situation in Atrine.

busy at the moment," Tyentso said. "I'm certainly not going to act like your personal carriage driver."

"No one's asking you to," Therin said. "A writ to use a Gatestone is more than sufficient."

Tyentso picked up a fresh sheet of paper from a secretary's desk.

"What is that, anyway?" Therin pointed to the wall. "I mean, obviously a map, but what are the lights?"

"Demons," Tyentso answered as she began to write.

Therin felt a chill. That was a lot of lights. "I thought the gods were fixing that."

"They're doing their part," Qoran said, "but they can't be everywhere at once. And something else is killing demons too. I'm not yet quite sure what, but any demon who stays in one place for too long tends to"–he pulled his hands apart–"disintegrate. We're not sure why."[4]

"It's nothing I'm doing," Tyentso agreed. She blew on the paper to dry it and then handed it to Therin along with an additional envelope. "That should get you access to the Gatestone."

"What's the envelope?"

"The price for my help. While you're there, please hand that over to Dean Filoran." She smiled with a snake's charm. "It's an invitation to a party."

Therin raised an eyebrow. "You're throwing a . . . party?" That hardly seemed like a thing she'd do with the empire falling apart around them.

"Oh yeah, all the high lords will be there." Tyentso laughed wickedly. "It should be memorable."

Therin paused. Ah. He understood. This wasn't a party. This was an object lesson. Tyentso was absolutely going to try to rule the empire–she just had to teach the high lords to know their place first. "Please don't take this the wrong way, but I'm glad I'm not resuming my old duties as high lord."

She stopped laughing. "Oh, Therin. You wouldn't have been invited."

"That's *very* kind of you."

"My pleasure," Tyentso said. "Now, would you mind getting the fuck out of here? Some of us are trying to work."

"Of course, Your Majesty." He bowed to her, ignoring her surprised snort. "Word of advice, if I may?"

Her eyes narrowed. "Go on."

"Recruit Lady D'Talus to your cause. She's been the real power behind that family for years."

Tyentso seemed to relax a little. "Thank you. I'll keep that in mind."

[4] Oh, this is a piece of information I wish we'd known. I suspect Vol Karoth is the reason why.

"Try not to be idiots, either of you," Qoran said. "I've lost enough family."

Doc laughed. "Don't worry. Nothing's going to happen to us. We're too pretty to die."

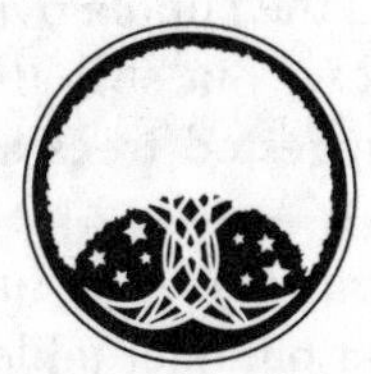

# 32: The Quarry

***(Kihrin's story)***

I had no idea where they took us, only its name: the Quarry. For a race notoriously fond of green, living things, I didn't think a name suggesting a hole in the ground was a good sign.

We ended up in a circle at the end of a long marble hallway. "This way," a soldier said, before the royal guards half escorted, half carried us to a doorway. Most of the soldiers then left, leaving behind two guards for each of us.

This was the lightest our guard had been since our capture.

A soldier opened the door. "Step inside, please."

A cushioned room lay beyond. Not cushions on the floor–the entire room was padded.

Teraeth kicked the door guard in the throat, while using momentum to yank his arms from another guard's grip. It seemed a shame to waste the opening, so I slumped down and turned invisible. Surprised, a soldier released my arm. I punched him in the groin, then stole the water from the other guard's lungs (I'd learned the trick from Tyentso), and claimed his sword. Janel threw her guards into the wall, where they struck the marble to the sickening melody of cracking stone. Thurvishar's soldiers tripped over their own feet and fell sprawling.

"Come on. Let's see if we–" But I never heard Teraeth finish the sentence.

Without warning, everything turned black.

I woke to find myself slumped in a comfortable chair. My clothing and equipment had been replaced by a simple gray cloth tunic and drawstring pants. My feet were bare. Also, my jaw hurt, probably because I'd hit myself on the marble floor when I'd fallen unconscious.

I wasn't tied up. I wasn't shackled. Teraeth, Janel, and Thurvishar were there, similarly attired, starting to wake.

As far as I could tell, we'd been taken to a palace.

Gold and gray threaded the white marble walls. Breathtaking murals and bas-relief filigree covered the cupola over our heads. Intricate stonework lace covered the windows but still allowed light to spill through. The view in the distance suggested trees and beautiful vistas. I heard birds singing.

Not far from where we sat, someone had laid out a banquet table, covered in white silk. On that banquet table–

My eyes widened.

Roasted meats trimmed with vegetables cut to look like flowers. Dark red pomegranate glazes covered succulent game birds. Rice cooked with saffron and precious herbs. Stuffed dumplings shaped like rare animals. Whole salmons, sharks, and sturgeons steamed and then garnished with spices layered to look like scales, jeweled with caviar beads. Tarts of every description, oysters, soups, stews, baked breads, and cakes piled high. Perfectly ripe fruits and fine wines sparkled gemlike next to steaming trays of fragrant tea.

A man stepped before us.

A vané man, of course. Kirpis vané specifically, with pale skin and shifting blue-green cloudcurl hair. His eyes were mismatched–one blue, one green. He was also the most muscled vané I'd ever seen, opting to forgo the typical vané preference for thin and lithe.

He was still pretty, though. Rebellion has its limits.

"Welcome to the Quarry," the vané man said. "I'm your host, Rindala. I'm here to make your stay as comfortable as possible. If you have any concerns, don't hesitate to come to me."

I blinked. Quur didn't have many prisons as a rule. Criminals were either fined, executed, or sold into slavery. The exceptions weren't nice places. They weren't nice places *at all.*

"Nice to meet you, Rindala, but I have to ask: Are we in the right place?" I looked around. I didn't see any soldiers. It was unnerving.

"Oh yes," Rindala said. "Unfortunately so. Obviously, we can't allow you to leave, but that's no reason to make your stay unpleasant. The Quarry's goals aren't punishment. I always make sure everyone enjoys their stay."

"What happened?" Janel rubbed her eyes. "What knocked us unconscious?"

"Sleep gas," Rindala answered. "We prefer to administer it when you're not in a position to injure yourselves, but you lot were stubborn. I find the intake process so much less humiliating when new prisoners are unconscious for the experience. Please, enjoy the food. You must be hungry."

Teraeth took the first bite, so to speak, sitting down at the table and helping himself to several dishes. He ate with enthusiasm before looking up at Rindala. "This is phenomenal. I commend your skills."

Our host smiled with pride. "Thank you. I made sure to include Quuros dishes." He motioned to the rest of us, who hadn't started eating. "We've never had Quuros guests before in the Quarry."

I studied the amazing spread. "You cooked all this?"

"I created this, yes," Rindala admitted. "Banquets are a personal specialty."

"He's a dreammaker," Teraeth said. "You might as well eat."

"Yes, please," Rindala said. "I want you to enjoy yourselves."

Thurvishar sat down and began eating. He didn't seem to be enjoying the food, though. He lifted a forkful of beautifully golden rice and critically watched it fall. "You actually *like* this?" he asked Teraeth.

"Ah now. Why are you making this so difficult?" Rindala asked Thurvishar. "This is a great honor. My services have been commanded by royalty."

Thurvishar turned to us. "It's just porridge. This isn't real."

"How is enjoyment not 'real'?" Rindala asked. "If you can taste it, smell it, touch it, see it, hear it? If it satiates you, body and soul, how isn't it real?" He paused. "But you're actively blocking me. I'd much rather you enjoyed yourself."

"The food isn't real?" I could smell it. I could see the steam rising from the plates, juices flowing from meats. I was salivating.

"Oh no," Teraeth said. "The food is real. *Haerunth*. It's a grain the Kirpis developed. Incredibly nutritious. You can survive on haerunth alone indefinitely. Most Kirpis do." He continued eating. "Honestly, I'd never guess this wasn't traditionally cooked. You're fantastic, Rindala. I hope they're paying enough."

"His Majesty is generous," Rindala admitted, "but your appreciation of my skills warms my heart."

I couldn't tell if Teraeth was laying it on so thick because he wanted to cozy up to Rindala or if he was sincere. Finally, I sighed and sat down to eat. Janel did as well.

"Oh, sweet fields," Janel murmured after biting into a tart. "I think this might be the best thing I've ever eaten."

Rindala beamed.

I decided Teraeth had understated his praise. The venison was perfectly tender, so flavorful. Each dish I tried tasted better than the last. Teraeth, Janel, and I began comparing dishes, suggesting new ones to each other.

Thurvishar ate his rice, a child who'd been told he couldn't leave the table until he cleaned his plate.[1]

As I enjoyed what was without question the most delicious meal I'd

[1] I'm not inclined to allow myself to be vulnerable to telepathic intrusion just to enjoy a meal.

ever eaten, I considered our situation. Which wasn't great, even if Rindala seemed nice.

"Rindala?" I asked.

"Yes, Your Highness?" Rindala rushed over to me immediately.

"The king told you who I am?"

"Ah yes," Rindala said. "My sincerest condolences on the execution. Hopefully, it won't come to that. I'm rooting for you."

". . . thank you," I replied. His weaponized sincerity was a little off-putting. "Would you mind telling me about the prison itself? Can we expect to be housed together? Will there be guards?" I had certain expectations for guards in prisons. Not good expectations.

The other three at the table slowed their eating as they listened.

"Oh, naturally there are guards," Rindala said, "and you'll be housed separately." He nodded to everyone. "It's for your protection."

"Right. Naturally." I leaned toward him. "I wonder if you might indulge me. If it wouldn't cause any trouble for you. Just in case it does come to that, and they execute me, it would mean the world if I could spend my last days with my lover. You understand."

"Oh," Rindala said. "Yes, I see. I assume someone here is that lucky person? Which one?" The vané looked at the other three people sitting at the table.

"The woman," I said.

"Then worry not, Your Highness. I'll make sure she stays with you."

I nodded to him. "Your kindness is appreciated."

As I turned back to eating, I noticed Janel and Teraeth both slaying me with proverbial daggers.

"Seriously?" Teraeth whispered.

"It's not what you think." Which it wasn't. As much as I'd have loved to spend time with Janel, I'd never heard of a prison where the people in power didn't abuse the people without it. Rindala seemed nice enough—too nice, creepy nice—but that's because I knew this wasn't a spectacular hotel. One friendly warden (or concierge, or dreammaker, or whatever) didn't convince me the prison guards would be so altruistic.

We were all in danger, but the Quuros seemed especially vulnerable, and Janel most vulnerable of all. Since she found her souls locked in the Afterlife once she slept, Janel wouldn't wake no matter what someone did to her in the meantime.

Which made me wonder. How did her body know when to wake up again? Did some portion of her souls remain behind? Could she be tricked with an illusion? Of course, the illusions here were extraordinary. Everyone in the Manol seemed to automatically know how to cast fantastic illusions. So good. It had to make navigating the cities awkward, though. How did you know if a bridge really existed? What if nothing was real? Would I even notice?

What was I talking about again?

"Are those sesame cakes?" Thurvishar asked. "I love sesame cakes." The wizard grabbed three cakes at once and began to eat.

Janel swayed in her seat and blinked.

I looked down at my plate. With effort, I tore my thoughts away from contemplating how the vané created the magnificent sheen on their ceramics. "They drugged the food?"

"Of course they drugged the food," Teraeth agreed, smiling blissfully. "Drugged it to the gills."

"As I said, Your Highness," an increasingly blurry Rindala told me, "everyone here *always* enjoys their stay."

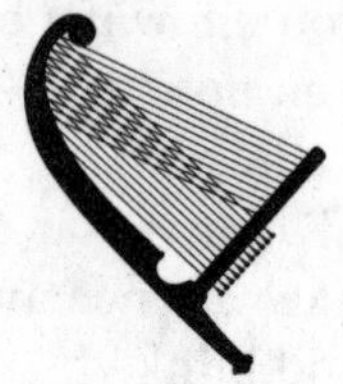

# 33: The Nature of Power

***(Therin's story)***

The soldiers at the Gatestone asked them no questions after Therin and Doc presented the writ from the emperor, nor did any of the wizards on the other side.

The Academy hadn't changed since Therin had last visited. Admittedly, he hadn't stayed long. Wizardry hadn't suited him, or at least so he'd thought. So instead, he'd joined the church, ironically to learn the same things he would have otherwise learned at school.

"Should we hire horses?" Therin asked.

"Horses won't like where we're going. Parts of the Kirpis are so dense a horse is useless."

"And you expect us to do better?"

Doc only laughed.

Later, Therin began to understand what Doc had meant. They'd simply walked into the woods. Everyone at the Academy knew about the vané ruins near the school.[1] Everyone knew how dangerous and foolhardy going there was. Still, every year at least one poor idiot always took the professors' warning as a dare and never came back.

Apparently, the ruins' haunted reputation owed its origin to vané traps and spells more than ghosts.

Doc knew the way, and after pacing out a certain distance, he knelt and wiped away a section of soil. "Stand over there." He pointed to a corner of stone wall as he did something.

Therin looked around. The indicated area was circular and vaguely familiar. Then he identified the original of that feeling. This resembled the bottom of the pit in Saraval, the one that had led . . .

"Are you fucking kidding me?" Therin said. "There's a working gate here to the Well of Spirals? That the Quuros could have used to invade the Manol *at any time*?"

[1] These are the same ruins where Gadrith murdered Phaellin D'Erinwa and where Tyentso later met Phaellin's ghost.

"Careful there, grandson," Doc said, grinning. "You're forgetting to call yourself Quuros too."

He slid his hand across the stonework in a peculiar way, then sprinted over to join Therin. The light swirled around them, flashed, and then they stood in the blue-sky-covered meadow Therin remembered.

As did a great many soldiers.

Therin forced himself to stay calm. They weren't in any danger; Doc had almost certainly cloaked their presence so the soldiers wouldn't even know they'd arrived.

This belief lasted all of two entire glorious seconds and ended with a ring of metal as the soldiers advanced on them with drawn weapons.

"What are you showing them?" Therin whispered.

"Oh . . . us," Doc said. "Chainbreaker only works on someone if I know they're there. Makes it awkward when traveling through something like a Gatestone."

"Or a *door,*" Therin whispered. "Why didn't you mention this beforehand?"

"You didn't ask," Doc said with a shrug.

Therin stared daggers at him. "Are you kidding?"

The first soldier inspected them closely, then lowered his blade in what he probably meant as a reassuring gesture. Therin was not reassured.

"Apologies," the man said, "but the well is temporarily off limits."

"It's the Well of Spirals," Doc said. "You can't deny us entrance."

Therin stared at both vané as they spoke voral. He knew they were speaking voral. He also knew his understanding of voral matched a vané child's. He shouldn't have been able to follow their quick exchange.

Therin understood them *perfectly*. He made a mental note to thank Galava—assuming he survived this.

Doc's mild reply didn't sit well with the lead soldier. "Yes, I know." The vané flushed with either embarrassment or anger. "That's normally the case, but I'm under orders."

"Orders from whom?" Doc's voice burned. His hand drifted toward his belt as if seeking the pommel of his sword. "Someone's overstepped their authority in a spectacular fashion."

Therin wasn't the only one to notice his friend's wandering hand. The soldiers tensed, weapons that had just begun to drift into relaxed poses snapping back into threatening postures. The lead soldier's lips twisted, but before he could unleash a snappy retort, a woman interrupted them.

"Captain, is there a problem?" Therin couldn't see the speaker through the wall of irate vané until she pushed her way through. He barely covered his startled shock; it was Miya, or Talon pretending to be Miya.

He immediately corrected himself. This wasn't Miya. Her short-cropped blue hair and shimmering silver-chain gown suggested another identity. She pursed her lips in a way Miya never did. The eyes were different, the cheekbones. This could only be Miyathreall's sister, Miyane. Queen Miyane.

"Your Majesty." The soldiers grounded their weapons and bowed deeply. The captain continued to speak. "A pair of petitioners. I was sending them away, but one of them seems to think he is a part-time advocate."

Doc snorted.

Queen Miyane looked them over closely. "And what brings you to the well this day?" she asked, giving Doc a second look.

"It's my mother's Death Day," Doc said. "May I ask why the well is closed?"

"Just for a few hours," the queen reassured. "There was an incident earlier. A matter of treason." Her blue eyes flitted between them again, a faint furrow creasing her brow. "I don't believe I have had the pleasure. What are your names?"

"Mithraill," Doc said, indicating first himself before pointing at Therin. "And my friend Montherin."

Therin plastered a dumb-but-pleasant smile on his face, the kind he used at parties he'd long since stopped caring to attend.

"Mithraill." The queen rolled the name around on her tongue. "That name sounds familiar."[2] She waved a hand in airy dismissal. "Return in a few hours. You may finish your pilgrimage then."

"With all respect, Majesty," Doc said, his voice flat and hard, "you cannot deny us access to the well. Not for any reason."

Therin glanced sideways at his friend. He knew Doc's moods. This level of anger used to result in Doc's enemies dead on the Arena floor.

Queen Miyane drew herself up, her expression furious. Then she laughed. "I see what you mean," she told the captain. "A part-time advocate indeed." To Doc, she lifted her chin and said, "You are brazen." Her amused expression drained away, leaving her face as cold and hard as marble. "Contradict me again, and I will have your hand. Then you may visit the well to have them grow you a new one."

Therin nudged Doc. "We can come back later."

Doc ignored him, his focus solely on the queen. "I said, 'With all re-

[2] It seems unlikely Queen Miyane ever met Mithraill since he died before her birth. However, she may have heard stories from other vané. Mithraill, of course, is the man who slew King Terindel during the vané civil war, and thus swapped souls with Terindel because of the Stone of Shackles.

spect,' and I'll say it again: With all respect, since when does the king have any authority over the Well of Spirals?"

"He does *not,*" the queen said, eyes flashing. "But he has authority over traitors, especially those who choose to shelter here."

Therin cast a brief look around. The crowd by the pool ignored the confrontation, preoccupied with Well-of-Spirals-y tasks. That left the soldiers facing them (Therin counted fifteen) and a score more who could easily reinforce them. Things wouldn't go well for Therin and Doc if a fight broke out.

Yet Doc seemed to want just that.

"At the risk of being called an advocate a third time in one afternoon, and with continued respect to Your Majesty, the king most certainly does *not,*" Doc said. "The Well of Spirals is outside vané control or politics, both Kirpis and Manol. It is open to all, at any time, and it Cannot. Be. Closed. Except by order of the chief attendant, a thing that has only happened twice ever."

"Do we really want to pick a fight with the queen?" Therin asked sotto voce. Louder, he said, "Why don't we bow, apologize, and come back later? The well isn't going anywhere."

"I believe we're past that point," the queen snarled.

Doc continued, "The king has no authority to shut down the well. Most especially not a king is who nothing but the usurper son of a usurper!" With that, he drew his sword.

Therin experimented with Zheriasian swear words he seldom had opportunity to practice.

The guards sprang into action.

And attacked each other.

Seven guards attacked the other seven as if they stood in a fencing line learning their forms. The fifteenth guard, the captain, saved his madness for the queen.

All was chaos. Therin turned, expecting to see Doc wading into the fray. Instead, his friend stood perfectly still, sword held loosely in his hand, concentrating intensely as he watched the scene.

"Nik–Doc–Mithraill–damn it, why can't you pick one name and stick with it–*what* are you doing?" Therin reached for his own sword before remembering Galava hadn't given it back to him.

"Shh," Doc said. "It's not easy controlling this many at once."

*"What in the name of Nythrawl's frozen heart is going on here?"* a voice thundered from behind the tumult.

Therin froze, astonished. The fighting stopped instantly.

That voice hadn't asked for respect. That voice hadn't demanded obedience. That voice had simply expected both, to such a degree it seemed inconceivable respect and obedience would *not* be granted.

Therin followed the solders' wide-eyed gazes to the voice's source. He expected to see an Immortal, or at least a god-queen. Instead, he saw a vané woman. Beautiful, to be sure, but one might as well call the ocean wet. She didn't seem impressive enough to have been the source. Indeed, she leaned on an attendant as she hobbled forward on unsteady legs.

Therin turned to Doc to ask the woman's identity. He blinked and looked away quickly. Seeing such naked joy, longing, pain, and hope on his friend's face was uncomfortable. Besides, Therin had his answer.

Only one person could elicit such a response from Terindel the Black.

Doc's wife, Valathea, released the attendant and crossed her arms over her chest. "Well?" she asked at a normal volume. "Care to explain why blood is being spilled in the most sacred spot in the entire world?"

Quiet settled over the well, nestled among the perfectly shaved grass and flowering hedges. The queen looked all around, wild-eyed. She stared not at but *through* where Doc and Therin stood. "Where did they go? They were just here!"

Therin turned to his friend; Doc was still concentrating.

"I asked a question," Valathea said.

"I owe you no explanations, Founder," the queen growled. "We were attacked, obviously." She studiously ignored the fact her men had been attacking each other. "Captain, take the Founder somewhere safe."

"This is the Well of Spirals," Valathea said, her tone suggesting this was all the safety one should ever need. "And yet I've never seen this many soldiers taint this land with their presence. Explain why I shouldn't report you."

She hadn't directed the last sentence at Miyane; she addressed Doc.

"I'm not Mithraill," Doc said. "I know who I look like, but please, let me explain." His voice cracked from the strain, his eyes desperate.

Valathea examined Doc with a hateful gaze. That stare slipped once, to look at Therin, before returning to Doc's face.

*Gods,* Therin thought. *Valathea knows who killed her husband. She knows who Mithraill is. And my moron of a best friend is letting her* see *us as we really are.*

Valathea opened her mouth and started to say something, but Queen Miyane beat her to it.

"Report me?" Queen Miyane said, her tone incredulous. "Do you have any idea who I am?"

Valathea blinked. She made a moue at Doc before turning back to the queen. "As a matter of fact, I haven't the slightest idea."

"I'm Miyane, queen of the vané!" Clearly, Miyane found the idea of a vané not recognizing her intolerable, even if said vané had spent the last five hundred years as an inanimate object.

"I'll assume you're my nephew's wife." Valathea sounded bored.

". . . yes." Miyane visibly searched for some more scathing retort.

Valathea gestured toward the well. "Perhaps the attendants might live up to their titles and see to your people? As you said, whoever those men were, they're no doubt long gone."

"I'll find them," Miyane growled. "They can't have traveled far. No one's left by a gate." Then she paused, hand pressed against her arm. "One of them called my husband a usurper son of a usurper."

"Did he?" Valathea said. "How interesting."

"That sounds like something one of your husband's loyalists might say." The queen's eyes narrowed with suspicion. "Do *you* know those men?"

"The ones who fled, you mean?" Valathea raised an imperious brow. "Yes. But he was no friend of mine nor of my husband. I recall him associating with Queen Khaevatz." She tilted her head. "Surely, you noticed he was Manol vané."

"I do not appreciate your tone," Queen Miyane said.

Valathea studied the woman, her expression placid. Then she said, "Allow me to give you a piece of advice, as one queen to another–"

"By the Law of Daynos, you're no longer queen," Miya retorted.

Valathea laughed. "How adorable of you to think a label defines authority. Since you're family, here's a lesson for free: if you choose to demonstrate power, make sure you can follow through. The problem with a bluff is someone may call you on it." She gestured around, to where attendants still lingered, now watching the scene. "How many witnesses would you like me to summon when I appear before parliament?" Valathea smiled at the flash of panic on Miyane's face. "Neither you nor my no doubt perfectly legitimate nephew have power here. And we both know it. *So leave.*"

Queen Miyane stood very straight. She seemed about to order something unpleasant, but just then, a guard moaned. The queen took stock of her wounded guards, some with serious injuries.

"Fine." Her face wrinkled in distaste. "But we will return to collect you later. His Majesty wishes to speak with you."

"I shall count the seconds," Valathea said.

As the queen and her people swept away toward the gate, it was impossible not to feel like Miyane was the underling sent packing by her ruler. From the scowl on Miyane's face, she felt the same.

After Miyane left, Valathea announced, "It's a lovely day. I think I'll go for a walk."

# 34: In the Dark

***(Kihrin's story)***

I felt great.

I didn't even care when the guards collected me the second time or when they dragged me down several flights to the slummier section of the Quarry housing actual prisoners. The room where we'd eaten sat in a building perched above a stone pit. Some enterprising artisan had carved prison cells into the defunct quarry's walls. Lovely, artistic cells, each a tiny dollhouse carved from marble. A pulley system provided the only entrance, controlling a vertical moving platform.

Well, in theory, it was the only entrance. I told my guards the walls would be child's play to climb. They smiled at me. Then I oohed and aahed over the long drop while the guards kept me from wandering over the edge.

After some eternity of gazing in rapt wonder at the way the setting sun cast shadows against the rocks, at the stone's sublime beauty–how had I never noticed marble was that beautiful–they tossed me into a cell.

The small room's ceiling provided enough clearance for most vané to stand and not an inch more. A bed dominated the room, with a commode and basin for washing in a corner. The latter two objects were built into the cell and couldn't be moved. A drinking cup sat on the basin's edge. Mage-light lit the room, no brighter than starlight and the soft glow of the moons. A stone underpinning provided the foundation for the bed, fixing it in place. Given the warm jungle air, the lack of bedding seemed unlikely to prove an issue.

What an amazing bed, I thought as I lay down. Definitely the most comfortable I'd ever known. Better than any bed in the Blue Palace. This was less a prison than a den–the sort of place where one paid good metal to lie down on satin-strewn pillows and drug oneself senseless. I'd known such places growing up in Velvet Town. Never as a customer, because they were all the sort of locale where the owners would rob a customer down to their underwear. Worse than that, in many cases. And Ola hadn't approved of drugs. At least, she hadn't approved of drugs for me. She'd been fine about drugging her customers, especially when she did so without the customer's permission.

Rindala proved good to his word. A minute after the guards escorted me into the cell, the door opened again. Janel stumbled inside before the door behind her closed and locked.

Light flickered off the red highlights of Janel's black hair as she stood there, looking lost and furious and more perfect than any goddess. She slowly examined the room until her gaze reached me. "You."

I lay there, feeling like I should say something, maybe apologize, although the misdeed requiring an apology escaped me. I'd done something, although I couldn't put my finger on exactly what. I was just glad she was there.

"I'm mad at you."

I waited.

Janel cocked her head to the side. "Why am I mad at you?"

"I don't really know." I scratched my head. "Um. Hmmm–Teraeth? Wait. Hey, do you know where–" I forgot the question. I grasped for petals of memory fluttering about on the wind. And why did I have to figure out why Janel was angry while she stood there looking so intoxicating?

Then Janel dragged herself onto the bed. To be fair, there wasn't room anywhere else. I hadn't made any space for her, she crawled on top of me, like a cat who'd decided to lie down in a rival's spot and paid no attention to the fact that said spot was already occupied.

And then the time for rational thinking was officially over.

I wrapped her in my arms, held her close, and spent some small measure of eternity smelling her hair. Even through the drugged stupor, excitement and panic fluttered through me, but flinched from my grip whenever I tried to pinpoint their cause. Something about us both being here, together, in no condition to enforce the normal boundaries between us.

I felt her lips at my neck, teeth grazing along a tendon, then she whispered, "I don't need . . . your protection."

I barely heard the words, distracted by her lips, by the tingling thrill of her teeth along my skin. Faintly, what she'd said filtered into comprehension.

Of course Janel didn't need my protection. Why would she think that? Wait, did she need my protection? I tried to focus and shifted my weight under her so I could look her in the eyes. "You do when you sleep."

"That's not–" Janel made a face. "That's not the point." She blinked at me, and I could tell she was having just as difficult a time focusing as I was. "Do you remember C'indrol?"

I frowned. I had no idea who she meant. "Who?"

"C'indrol," she repeated.

The name sounded familiar, but damned if I remembered why.

"It's who I was before Elana." She grinned wickedly. "They *liked* you." To emphasize the point, Janel slipped her hands under my flimsy gray tunic, then trailed and dipped down under the edge of my drawstring pants.

I grabbed her by the wrists and–

*Kihrin paused.*

*Thurvishar sipped his tea and raised an eyebrow. "You don't have to talk about anything you don't want to, you realize."*

*"It doesn't bother me," Kihrin said. "Teraeth thinks I'm a prude, but that's because his definition of inhibited is refusing to attend orgies. It's not just my privacy I'm putting on a display here."*

*Thurvishar picked up a set of papers next to him. "Would it help to know I already have Janel's account?"*

*Kihrin blinked once at the wizard, slowly. "You what now?"*

*Thurvishar cleared his throat. "I'm not sure if it even occurred to Janel you might consider this an indiscreet topic of conversation. If you like, we can skip all this."*

*Kihrin took the papers from Thurvishar and began flipping through them. He stopped at one point and grinned broadly before schooling his expression into something more serious. Finally, he gave them back and cleared his throat. "There's one or two points I should probably clarify. Especially with what happened afterward."*

Janel once broke her fiancé's arms after he tried to claim dominance over her. If I'd been thinking clearly, I wouldn't have responded in a manner so easily mistaken for the same. But clear thought and I weren't on speaking terms. Fortunately, in that stunned moment of surprise when I flipped her over onto her back, I had enough presence of mind to whisper, "Reins or saddle?"

She relaxed under me. If you'd asked me when I was sober, I'm not sure what answer I'd have given about my own preferences, but I'd have confidently expected Janel to be a prefers-to-be-in-charge type in the bedroom. Especially since in her culture, dominance and submission were two sides of a coin that never landed on its edge.

But as I pinned Janel's arms over her head, she looked up at me and whispered, "Saddle."

That was the last word either of us said for some time. I'm not sure how long. Time stopped having any meaning. Eventually, after, we fell asleep.

Which is when everything went completely, utterly wrong.

* * *

I don't know what time it happened. Later. I thought it was nighttime, but enough soft light filtered through to suggest the moons had risen. I fell a lot less drugged. Almost rational, or at least cognizant enough to realize Janel and I had just done something we'd both regret.

Okay, *regret* was the wrong word. This *complicated* matters. I was still trying to figure out what to do about Teraeth. Once he found out Janel and I had escalated our relationship . . . well. I didn't know how he'd react. Teraeth had been fine when we'd previously argued over a woman, but this was *Janel.* Teraeth wasn't rational when it came to Janel.

Then again, neither was I.

Janel slept next to me, effectively catatonic, looking peaceful. I hoped she was fighting the good fight in the Afterlife. She was probably still directing the rebellion in Jorat. No reason to stop that just because the Eight Immortals had asked her to go save the world, right?

Then I noticed the opposite corner of the room had grown . . . darker. The more I focused on it, the darker it became, until I couldn't believe how absolutely black that space had become. The void almost had a form, looked human . . .

Vol Karoth stepped through the wall.

I jumped in front of Janel's body, as though I could shield her. But then I felt the pull.

Vol Karoth held out his hand.

The sense of longing, the sense of need, was more than I could stand. The sense of being . . . incomplete. I'd be welcomed back. I'd be accepted.

*This was the only love I'd ever need.*

I reached out to take Vol Karoth's hand.

# 35: Lost Loves

***(Therin's story)***

"Seeing you again," Doc said. "I never dreamed–"

Therin cleared his throat. "Explain first, then gush."

Valathea had slowly, carefully walked out past the tree line, turned, and waited. Therin and Doc had joined her. No one tried to stop her. Therin suspected that no one dared.

She sat down on a log and adjusted her dress. "Yes. Please explain. Because unless you're a mimic, I fail to understand how you're not Mithraill when you look exactly like my husband's *killer.*" She stared at her hand. "Honestly, the only reason I didn't turn you in is because I've discovered I'm even less fond of our new queen."

"Who knew she'd turn out to be such a massive bitch," Therin said.

"Do you remember a necklace Terindel used to wear? Blue stone, around this big?" Doc held his fingers apart. "Wizard gave it to him. Swore it would save him from being killed?"

"Yes," Valathea said. "I also remember it didn't work. But thank you for the reminder. I should see if Grizzst is still alive so we can talk."[1]

"No, it worked," Doc said. "Grizzst neglected to explain how 'save' meant the stone would swap the souls of its wearer with that of their killer. But technically, I didn't die–I just ended up wearing Mithraill's body."

Valathea's violet eyes widened. "If this is your idea of humor, I find it in poor taste."

"No, I swear." Doc went down on his knees next to her. "Valathea, it's me, Terindel. I tried to find you, but by the time I did, you'd been turned into a harp and . . ." He gulped air, his expression miserable. "If you're wondering why I never changed back, it's because it seemed safer with everyone searching for Terindel. Then I grew used to it and–"

Valathea put a finger against his mouth to quiet him. "What's my name? My *voras* name?"

[1] I honestly can't tell if she meant talk or "talk."

Therin blinked. *Voras* name? Why would she have a voras name?

"A'val," Doc said instantly. "Your personal name was Athea."[2]

Valathea raised her hand to her mouth. Tears began spilling down her cheeks.

Then they were in each other's arms, lips pressed together, oblivious to Therin's presence.

Therin cleared his throat. "You know, I should give you two some space. I'll be over here." He gestured vaguely toward the forest. If they heard him at all, they didn't indicate it. He walked away from the pair and leaned against a tree, looking out into a forest he apparently had more ancestral connection with than he'd ever imagined. It would certainly make for interesting dinner party conversation with the Duke of Kirpis.

Therin saw a looming problem on the horizon, a test of loyalties he had no idea how to navigate. His best friend, who didn't want to see the Ritual of Night enacted. His goddess, who did. Khaeriel's goal to reclaim the throne. Doc's probable wish to do the same now that he had Valathea back. And hovering over it all, his son Kihrin, the prophecies, and the literal end of the world.

Leaves crackled behind him as someone approached. He turned to see Valathea, Doc on her heels, grinning like a schoolboy who'd just been given free rein in a bakery.

"And who are you?" Valathea asked.

"Love, this is Therin, a good friend." Doc voice grew somber. "Also our great-grandson."[3] In answer to her unasked question, he added, "Valrashar's gone. I'm sorry."

Valathea froze. Her composed joyful expression cracked and fell away, leaving something wounded almost beyond endurance underneath. Therin's mouth dried and his throat felt thick. Her grief was painful, in no small part because it was so familiar.

Therin had seen six of his children die, each death a hammer blow against a thick glass plate, until finally, with Kihrin's death, he'd shattered. And while Kihrin had returned to him, the boy's older siblings were gone forever. Therin ached to think of it, a dull, empty hurt trapping the breath in him, bringing tears to his eyes. Would it be worse to only have one child and lose her? Or was it more that she'd only been hurt once compared to his half-dozen times?

Or was it useless to juxtapose such moments of loss against each

2 If I'm remembering Senera's notes correctly, A'val is mentioned in one of Janel's flashbacks—as one of C'indrol's friends.

3 Technically, just Valathea's great-grandson since Doc is in a different body now, but I'm sure it doesn't feel that way.

other when each one was its own fatal wound? One stab to the heart killed as easily as six.

The former queen of the Kirpis vané picked up Doc's hand in hers and squeezed it. Then she started to pull away, straighten, and compose herself. Doc made a noise and pulled her into his arms.

Therin turned away a second time and tried to ignore the sound of the woman sobbing. He prepared another retreat, again to give them some privacy if this time for a different reason.

"No, no, wait." Valathea backed away from her husband, wiped her hands across her eyes. "We've no time for this. There's a young man we need to save. Someone caught up in that 'treason' matter Miyane babbled about. If he is who I think, then the whole world's fate may depend on finding him before your extremely foolish nephew can execute him."

"What?" Doc turned to Therin of all people. "Who?"

Therin scoffed, then cleared his throat in an entirely unsuccessful attempt to hide how infectious Valathea's tears had been. "Why ask me?"

"Oh, I shouldn't think you'd know him," Valathea said. "His name is Kihrin."

"We're leaving, right now." Therin began walking toward the Well of Spirals the moment Valathea finished her explanation.

Doc made a face. "Agreed, but first things first."

Therin stopped. "They have my *son*. And for that matter, they have your–" He broke off since Valathea was standing *right there*.

Doc sighed.

Valathea raised an eyebrow at her husband. "Your–what?"

"My son," Doc said. "They also have my son." He held out his hands. "It's not like I've had a chance to tell you."

"No, I don't suppose you did." Valathea's expression still looked haunted, not yet recovered from the earlier grief. She sniffed. "Who's the mother?"

Doc hesitated.

Therin wondered if this might be yet another good time to wander off. The only thing more embarrassing than being this close to a friend having an intimate moment was being this close a friend having a screaming fit with their spouse. The latter seemed imminent.

"Khaemezra," Doc said.

Therin frowned, because Doc had said–

"Thaena?" Valathea's voice held the whisper-smooth edge of a sharpened razor sliding against one's throat.

Therin rubbed his temple. He reminded himself he was no longer a Thaenan priest. And he still hadn't sorted through his feelings regarding a goddess capable of having lovers, children, and all these secrets.

Maybe Doc was right to claim she shouldn't be worshipped as a goddess at all.

"It made sense at the time?" Doc wrinkled his nose.

Valathea pulled herself up.

"I hate to interrupt," Therin said, "but can we go rescue the kids now? You two can argue later. I'm sure Terindel has all sorts of skeletons in the closet for you to be upset about."

Doc glared every dagger in the world at him.

"I'm not jealous." Valathea's protest was a soft tiger purr. "But my husband and I have always had an understanding–"

"I'm going to stop you right there," Doc said, "before you say something you'll find embarrassing later. Also, Elana Milligreest."

Valathea paused midsentence as if Terindel has said the final command word in a complicated enchantment. "Ah."[4]

"Uh-huh. Exactly."

Therin resigned himself to being able to understand voral clearly and yet still having no idea what anyone was talking about. He pinched the bridge of his nose. "Rescue. Kids. *Now.*"

The two vané stared at each other for a long beat, and then Valathea picked up Doc's hand and kissed his fingers. "He's right. We'll discuss this later."

"If you say so," Doc said as if that wasn't a conversation he probably wanted to put off until after the end of the world, "but let me go first with Chainbreaker. Just in case my nephew or his wife have come back with soldiers."

"They'll be in such trouble with the Founders if they keep this up." Valathea tsked.

Therin resisted the urge to ask who the Founders were. Priorities.

"Fine," he said. "Let's just do this."

[4] I believe the point of this exchange is that Valathea had an (admittedly brief) affair with Elana Milligreest while they traveled in the Korthaen Blight, prior to Valathea's transformation into a harp. Terindel would presumably have found out after he married Elana.

# 36: The Way No One Expects

***(Kihrin's story)***

*"Taja!"* I woke screaming.

I sat up in bed. Janel still slept. The room looked empty. We were still in prison. On the plus side, there was no sign of Vol Karoth, and I felt exquisitely sober. So just a nightmare.

"Well, this isn't ideal, is it?" Taja said.

I looked up. This time, the goddess standing by the door wasn't the little girl I'd last met. Now she was a full-grown vané woman, although with the same silver hair.

"Am I still dreaming?"

She wrinkled her nose. "No, my dear. I snuck away. Just for a few minutes. If I'm lucky, they won't notice." Taja looked around the room and tsked, then walked over to the bed and studied Janel. "She looks like her mother, doesn't she?" Taja glanced up at me. "You took precautions, I hope?"

I scrubbed a hand over my face. I had a ring that prevented unplanned pregnancies. My vané lovers back on Ynisthana had thought it adorable, but it had seemed like a sensible precaution considering the human women who'd lived there.

But King Kelanis's people had taken my jewelry when they'd dumped us into the Blight, never mind the second capture.

I sighed. "Nope."

Taja winked at me. "Maybe fortune will smile on you. Just this once."

I hoped that meant she was swinging the odds in my favor. "Thank you." I pointed at the cell door. "I don't suppose you can do anything to help with this?"

"Now what kind of friend would I be if I showed up and did nothing to help?"

"Thank you," I repeated again.

The Goddess of Luck paused. "I realize it's been a few years, but you *do* remember what we talked about, when you first arrived on Ynisthana? About black waves and the things people will do to survive?"

"I remember. You told me when that wave finally falls, it will be fast."

Taja pressed her lips together. "And it has been, hasn't it?"

I blinked. "I suppose . . . I suppose it has, yes."

"You're going to see that people–normally good people–will justify ugly deeds if they think it means their survival." She touched my cheek. "That doesn't mean they're right. Don't blindly accept solutions born of fear. You're smart enough to find better solutions."

I felt a chill as I remembered Taja chiding an upset Thaena. Was that who Taja meant?

Was that who Taja had meant *all along*?

"Am I smart enough, though? Because I've got to be honest, Taja, I don't feel that smart right now. I feel . . . swept up in the tidal wave. Out of control. Tricked. When I lived in the Lower Circle, we used to call people like me *gulls,* Taja. We'd take them for everything they had." I looked away. "Innocent people have died because of me."

"No, people have died because of Gadrith. They've died because of Suless. They've died because of Xaltorath and Morios and Relos Var. They've died because of monsters. You may have provided a few opportunities, but don't take credit for their sins. They earned those deaths, not you."

"But–"

"Do you honestly think Relos Var didn't have his own candidate picked out to wield Urthaenriel? That he wouldn't have used them to destroy the Stone of Shackles? He likely had Morios sleeping under Lake Jorat for centuries in anticipation of tricking someone into destroying that warding crystal. However–" Taja held up a finger for emphasis. "However, he had no way to know we were going to reincarnate *you*."

I frowned. "Yeah, about that . . . this body wasn't random, right? You picked it out to match the prophecies. So if I hadn't volunteered, whose soul would've been here instead of mine?"

Taja raised an eyebrow. "I have no idea. Some other volunteer. Maybe Simillion would have ended up reborn as Kihrin D'Mon instead of Thurvishar D'Lorus.[1] But you understand my point, don't you? If you'd never been born, it only means someone else's hand would've wielded that sword. Don't for one second think all this wouldn't have happened. Relos Var had it all planned."

A hand had tightened around my heart. "How am I supposed to win against someone like that? He's eight moves ahead of me."

"So use that. Kihrin, you're smarter than your brother gives you

[1] Oh, now there's an uncomfortable thought.

credit. While he's an overconfident know-it-all who isn't as clever as he thinks he is. You know what Ola would do with someone like that."

I chuckled. "She'd take him for everything he's got. The ones who think they're too smart to con are the easiest to con."

"Exactly," Taja said. "Remember his screwup got us into this mess. Relos Var isn't immune to making mistakes." She squeezed his hand. "I should go, but never worry. Your help is about to arrive."

"Okay, but what–"

Taja was already gone.

Someone rapped on the cell door. A guard's voice called out, "Your Highness, we're coming in. Someone wants to see you."

I scrambled to dress. "Wait!" I kissed Janel on the cheek before running to the cell door. At the last second, I remembered to fake being drugged. "Yeah? What?"

"Step out," the soldier said. "Now, please."

"Kind of early, isn't it?" I walked outside. The Quarry looked rather beautiful, with lanterns set up to light the path so guards didn't trip and hurt themselves. The sky was turning violet with the approaching dawn's light.

Mind you, the cries echoing through the Quarry sounded less peaceful.

I did have a moment of worry considering how loud Janel and I had probably been. We'd been in no condition to understand *quiet*. I just had to hope people had been too drugged to pay attention.

I *really* hoped Teraeth had been too drugged to pay attention.

I wore my best impersonation of befuddled while the soldiers led me back to the warden's house (or whatever they called Rindala's palace). The soldiers brought me to a room filled with the lovely furnishings a vané of means might use for receiving guests, especially a dreammaker compensated generously by King Kelanis. They stood me in the room's center, next to a couch.

They hadn't tied my hands, but then why would they? It's not like I'd cause trouble.

"Behave and do what you're told," they told me before leaving.

I started to wonder what this was about–formulating some unpleasant suspicions–when a second door opened.

Valathea stepped through.

At least, I thought she was Valathea. Pale skin and violet cloudcurl hair, delicate, beautiful features. She wore a slender, elegant gown of beaded purple silks, which rustled as she moved.

"Valathea? That is you, isn't it?"

She coolly crossed to me, pushed my chest until I fell backward onto the couch, and then straddled me, throwing a leg to either side. Which wasn't the behavior I'd expected.

As I tried to push her away, her form flowed, changed, and settled in a different, much more disturbing form. I still recognized her, though.

Before I could escape, Talon grabbed my wrists and held them over my head.

"Hey, ducky. Miss me?"

## 37: The Star Court

***(Therin's story)***

Returning to the Well of Spirals proved easy. If Doc missed anyone with Chainbreaker's illusions, they didn't call for guards. Neither King Kelanis nor Queen Miyane showed themselves.

But as soon as they passed back through the vané equivalent to a Cornerstone gate, Therin noticed a different problem.

This wasn't Saraval.

They stood at ground level, and the weather remained temperate and mild. This city wasn't burned, but had long since been abandoned. Great swells of ivy grew up over otherwise surprisingly pristine walls. It looked like the same city Doc had shown Therin using illusions, the Kirpis city he'd once ruled.

Valathea raised an eyebrow at her husband.

"This is the only undefended gate I know back to the Manol," Doc explained. "Plus I need to pick up a few things."

"I wouldn't exactly call it undefended," Valathea said. "And Therin might be able to pass safely, but you won't."

Therin felt a flash of unease as he realized what they were talking about. The city had struck him as familiar the first time he'd seen it, but without the overabundance of wildlife and weeds, he hadn't possessed the context to identify it. "Wait," Therin said. "Is this Serafana?"

Both vané paused.

"Yes," Valathea answered, "it is. I admit it's upsetting to see it this way . . ."

"We used this place for practice," Therin said. "I mean, the Academy sends students here to show them how dangerous wards can be. No one's ever made it inside."

"Yes, that's because we didn't want them to," Doc said. "We always held out the hope we'd come back." He scowled at the cityscape surrounding them. "It was either ward the place or destroy it."

"While I'm thrilled you went with option A," Therin said, "no student of the Academy has successfully breached the defenses here in five hundred years, and there's a Quuros military contingent stationed here to make sure no one tries on their own."

Doc shrugged. "Yes? Unfortunately, to return to the Manol, we'll need a gate the Manol vané aren't guarding. My palace is the only option."

Therin started to ask how the Manol vané wouldn't know about this and immediately corrected himself. If he had a secret way into another Royal House's grounds, he wouldn't have told them either. "This remains the most heavily trapped land in the whole world. How do we plan to get past all this?"

"You don't," Valathea said. "I do. And then I'll lower the wards for you."

Without waiting for them to respond, she began walking from the "building" where they'd arrived (really an outline of columns) toward what was clearly the palace. Everything was still and quiet, save for birdcalls and the wind rustling through the leaves.

"It's fine," Doc said, tapping the fingers of one hand against the palm of the other. "She'll be fine. The Eidolons won't attack her."

"Eidolons?" Therin raised an eyebrow. "You mean the Watchers?"

"Sentries," Doc said. "Wards. They're–" He made a vague gesture toward a roof.

A statue stood there, as if watching over the city ruins. It resembled a giant hooded robe filled with nothing but shadow and darkness, so concealing that the figure within couldn't be discerned. The stonework was cunningly wrought to resemble fabric. Even after centuries, it looked freshly carved. Two gigantic wings made from stone sprouted from the creature's back. There were more statues besides–winged lions, serpents, gryphons. All of them seemed too new to match the city's wear.

Therin recognized the statues from his short-lived student days. They stayed inanimate as long as no one trespassed into the city proper. Then they proved all too capable of devastating action. Every student knew stories about the poor idiots who thought they'd found a way to sneak into the vané city and came across the Watchers instead. And never came back.

One of the hooded stone figures began to move.

"Doc, they're activating," he told his friend. "I hate to point this out, but centuries of Academy student meddling might have messed with who these constructs recognize as safe."

"What?" Doc looked over, surprised. "That's not possible. Valathea is cleared to enter–" The statue spread its wings. "No!" Doc ran after Valathea.

"Oh hell." Therin ran after him.

Valathea hadn't gotten far. She'd paused at a broad thoroughfare, both feet on a rosette carved into the road. Ahead of her, a winged stone lion prowled the streets, tail twitching. To the side, the stone Eidolon they'd seen earlier approached. It clearly didn't think she was a friend. "Terindel, no–stay back!"

"Like hell I will. The cleared wards have been reset."

"Yes," Valathea said. "I noticed. If only I could cast spells."

Therin slid his sight past the Veil and looked at the creature. It was indeed stone, or rather a cement mixture of limestone and clay. Unfortunately, dealing with inorganic monsters wasn't his forte. He did best with living monsters. And he didn't know if Doc could use illusions on such a creature. Therin suspected no.

Therin looked around. There had to be something . . .

Trees. They were surrounded by trees.

Therin cast an unsubtle spell, wrenching a nearby redwood's base, weakening the cell structure so the tree became too heavy to support itself. A loud, cracking boom sounded through the forest as the tree came crashing down. Toward them.

"This isn't helpful, Therin!" Doc shouted. He grabbed Valathea and ran.

"No, wait!" she screamed.

Small lights bloomed into brilliance all around them, the entire promenade space filling with glowing threads reminding Therin of nothing so much as Watchmen trip wards. As soon as Doc saw them, he drew short, stopping just a hair's breadth before he interrupted a magical beam.

The ground shook as the tree fell onto the path behind them, smashing the statue.

If only that had been the only Eidolon.

A robed stone Eidolon flew in their direction. As it closed, the Eidolon gestured toward Doc with both full, thick sleeves–still absent of limbs–and a massive flurry of delicate rose petals poured out. The huge mass moved like a living thing. Therin didn't need to be told this wasn't a good thing.

"If you have a plan on how to deal with this," Therin shouted, "you might want to do it now!"

Doc looked back over his shoulder and spotted the crushed winged lion. "Therin, put your hand on the statue's head!"

"What? But why?"

"Just do it, hag head!"

Therin wasn't thrilled about this idea. Running back to the tree put him closer to the robed Eidolon advancing on their position, closer to the petal storm. But he had to trust Doc knew his business. Therin ran to the broken statue and set his hand on the lion's forehead. A soft glowing light sprang up from the lion's stone forehead, outlining Therin's hand and highlighting his finger bones.

"Now what?" Therin shouted back.

"Now order the other statues to stop!"

Therin did . . . and the statues stopped.

They froze into position, hovering, every single one looking in Therin's direction. The petal cloud paused midair, each delicate flake spinning idly in position even as the mass kept its shape.

The forest settled into quiet again.

"What just happened?" Therin retreated to Doc and Valathea.

"You were right," Doc said. "Some enterprising Academy student must have modified the wards to allow Quuros royals to control the security grid. Except they didn't turn off the previous restrictions. So the only one capable of resetting the wards was someone who's both a blood relative of the Kirpis vané royal family *and* a Quuros Royal House. Which isn't either of *us*."

"Would you mind terribly shutting off the wards?" Valathea asked. "We shouldn't stay here all day."

"How do I do that?"

She pointed to the Eidolon hovering in midair. "Go tell it we're your friends and are to be allowed access. Then tell it to reset the defenses to their original parameters."

So Therin did this thing.

Afterward, they went down a stone-lined road to the main palace.

Therin found the condition of the grounds amazing. True, plants had grown up all over the place, with vines covering the buildings, but no plants had broken up sections of road or toppled walls. No stonework had degraded. Paint had faded, wood had rotted, any furniture had long since turned to dust and dirt, but the shell lay perfectly intact.

Once they entered the main palace, Doc held up a hand. "One moment. I'll be right back." He ran down a narrow hallway.

"Should we follow . . . ?"

Valathea looked both concerned and curious. She seemed to have no more idea what Doc was up to than Therin did. "He'll be right back."

Doc returned a few minutes later, carrying a small metal box, the surface enameled to look like a starry night sky.

Valathea's eyes widened. "The Star Court? You're bringing the Star Court?"

Doc nodded as he shoved the entire box into his pack. "Consider it insurance. I think the time's come."

"What's the Star Court?" Therin asked.

Both Doc and Valathea paused, as if they'd just been caught in an embarrassing and compromising situation.

"It's a funny story," Doc said. "Remind me to tell you sometime."[1]

"For now," Valathea said, "the transport circle is this way. Let's return to the Manol, shall we?"

[1] Funny as in odd, not funny as in humorous.

# 38: Hell's Daughter

***(Janel's story)***

As soon as Janel fell asleep, she realized she'd made a mistake.

Under normal circumstances, she fell asleep in the Living World and immediately woke again in the Afterlife ready to fight, convinced she'd be attacked from the start. It had been over a month since she'd seen any significant demon presence in the Afterlife, so she'd let down her guard.

When she woke this time, Xaltorath ambushed her.

Janel screamed as the demon's claws raked down her body.

***SLOPPY, DAUGHTER. I TAUGHT YOU BETTER THAN THIS.***

Janel growled as she dodged backward, blood splattering all over the blackened moss underfoot. Xaltorath looked female at the moment, but her gender and appearance were subject to whim.

Xaltorath stepped to the side, revealing another demon, human-looking except for the shadows draped over him like cloth, an eyeless ceramic mask covering his face. Janel hadn't noticed him on the ground, with arms and legs bound in magical energy. Janel forced her focus back on Xaltorath, coming in for another strike.

Janel summoned sword and shield. "I thought you were hiding from Vol Karoth."

***HIDING? NOW, WHY WOULD I DO THAT?*** The demon queen sounded insulted.

"All the other demons are." Janel lashed out with her sword, scoring a hit on Xaltorath's arm. The wound closed immediately, but what shocked Janel was that she'd scored a hit at all. She didn't savor the victory. Janel drew a white-hot fireball into her hand and threw it at the demon, then attacked again. "No matter. I owe you for gaeshing me."

***I SAVED YOU.***

Janel scowled. "Why would you do that?" She readied her sword. "Never mind. Don't bother answering. You'd only lie."

Xaltorath lashed out with clawed hands, one after the other, laughing. Janel leaped into the air as the demon's tail tried to tangle her legs, then rolled to the side to avoid another swing. Janel imagined she was whole, unwounded.

Souls were malleable. Janel had always known that, but at the same time, souls in the Afterlife followed rules not unlike the Living World. They could suffer damage that seemed like bleeding, injury, death. A soul that sustained too much injury might cease to function. Death, in the Land of the Dead.

Janel realized she didn't have to blindly accept those rules.

The long parallel slashes in Janel's side closed as if they had never been. Janel summoned fire around her sword and came at the demon. This time, she pushed one of Xaltorath's arms out of line and chopped her sword down against the other.

Black blood splattered as one of Xaltorath's limbs fell to the ground.

Xaltorath didn't seem either hurt or offended. She grinned. ***IN THAT CASE, I'LL STOP BEING SO EASY ON YOU.*** Xaltorath paused, flexed, and the arm simply reappeared. Then three more sets grew from her sides. This time, each hand held a nasty-looking weapon—swords, hammers, maces.

"Oh, you've got to be kidding me," Janel said.

The demon closed again, this time with eight limbs attacking, deflecting, feinting, driving forward. Any thrill Janel tasted in her temporary success died quickly. Xaltorath scored a deep hit across Janel's thigh, another against her shoulder. She healed the wounds as fast as she could, but it was growing harder to convince herself she was uninjured.

Even as she managed to close the larger wounds, the small ones accumulated. Xaltorath proved relentless. Finally, a hammer swing crashed into Janel's head, making the universe spin, her vision turn black. The world tilted and slammed into her.

Janel woke on the ground, not remembering how she'd gotten there.

Xaltorath's clawed feet stepped in front of her face.

***YOU KNOW WHAT YOU HAVE TO DO.*** Xaltorath dragged the bound, masked demon into Janel's field of vision. The demon struggled, but it clearly couldn't escape its magical chains.

Janel's lip curled. Now she understood why Xaltorath had brought another demon.

When a demon caught a human soul, they didn't have to eat it. They could instead *infect* it—but only in the Afterlife. To Janel's knowledge, it was never done to a living person, simply because the souls of living people never reached the Afterlife.

Except Janel. Xaltorath had found a way to infect her even though she was still a living person. Janel should have become a demon herself, should have become a corrupt creature of malice, feeding on heat and pain. But since she refused to consume other souls, refused to make other demons her food, she'd never finished her transition into a bodiless, rampaging monster of darkest evil.

Xaltorath had tired of waiting.

"Never," Janel whispered. Blood flowed down a cut on her face.

***SO STUBBORN. YOU HAVE ALWAYS BEEN SO STUBBORN.***

"Go to hell." Janel coughed up blood. Her broken ribs' jagged edges stabbed inside her, a screaming sharp pain.

Xaltorath sat down on the ground next to Janel. ***WOULD IT HELP IF I TOLD YOU *NOT* TO EAT THE DEMON?***

"No." Janel pushed herself up to her feet. Most demons lacked anything resembling subtlety, choosing forms monstrous, gory, and obscene. This one was almost elegant, had taken a form suggesting concepts far scarier than predatory animals. Shadows, darkness, the unknown.

Had this been any other encounter, she'd have enjoying killing him.

But not to make Xaltorath happy. And certainly not to further Xaltorath's plans. She stared down at the demon. She couldn't make out much detail about him with the way the darkness curled up around his form like black incense escaping a brazier, but he wore a weapon–a sword–that Xaltorath hadn't bothered to take away. Rare, in demons, but not totally unknown.

Janel reached out to touch the edge of that mask. Would there be a face behind it? Probably not. Or it would be something terrible. That was, after all, the way demons worked.

**KILL ME.** The demon's voice was a whisper, its tone the blackest despair. Janel had never heard a demon beg before, but that's what this was.

"Ask me again next time," she whispered. Janel unsheathed the demon's sword and sliced twice–at the magic binding his wrists and ankles–freeing him. "Run!"

Which he did.

Xaltorath growled in anger, grabbed Janel by the shoulders, yanked her around. ***STUPID IMP. I MADE HIM JUST FOR YOU.***

Her words almost distracted Janel. Almost. Because as much as Janel knew how demons worked, as much as she understood how the infection spread, she'd never seen Xaltorath create any other demons. Just her. Xaltorath ordered other demons, controlled other demons, ate other demons, but she never *created* other demons.[1]

The sharp pain of broken ribs, the jagged, awful spikes of agony

[1] I suppose that's possible. Xaltorath might think of it as creating potential rivals. Alternately, since she had previously tried to hide the fact she was not bound with the other demons, it's equally possible she avoided creating demons who would inherit that immunity.

with each breath, set Janel to rights. As the demon queen grabbed Janel by the throat, Janel set both her hands on her "mother's" wrists and concentrated. If Xaltorath would make it impossible for Janel to survive without succumbing to her demonic taint, Janel wasn't going to feed on some newborn brother.

She'd pull the energy from Xaltorath herself.

Janel must have caught Xaltorath off guard. The demon lurched backward, but not before an outpouring of healing tenyé rushed over Janel. Tenyé and . . . something else. Memories. People. So many souls. Janel reeled from the impact, the disorientation made worse because of their power and familiarity. God-kings. God-queens. Janel tasted the souls of Immortals.

Janel recognized Khored. Her own mother, Tya. Galava.

Thaena. Relos Var.

*Suless.*

Then Xaltorath threw Janel across the field, breaking the connection.

***NOW, THAT WASN'T NICE. YOU CAUGHT UP MORE QUICKLY THAN I EXPECTED. MUST BE MY INFLUENCE.***

"What are you talking about?"

***YOU'RE STARTING TO REMEMBER TOO MUCH. WE CAN'T HAVE THAT.***

Janel writhed on the ground. She hadn't killed Xaltorath, hadn't pulled souls from the demon queen. That was the only explanation she could come up with for why the corruption hadn't taken her. She'd pulled power, but only that.

But what she'd pulled . . .

"How–?" Janel stared at the demon. "How could you possibly be–?" She bit down on the desire to declare what she'd learned impossible. How could Xaltorath have consumed the Eight Immortals? *Impossible.* And yet somehow, Janel had felt their presence among the legions Xaltorath had devoured over the course of her existence.

"I don't understand."

Xaltorath chuckled as she cracked the knuckles of one set of arms, the other six still spiraling out from her body. She walked toward Janel. ***NO, OF COURSE NOT. HOW COULD YOU?***

"You can't have devoured the Eight Immortals. They're still alive."

***NOT RIGHT NOW. BUT ONE DAY? OH, THAT'S DIFFERENT.*** The demon gazed down at Janel fondly. ***SHOULD I MAKE YOU FORGET OR JUST DESTROY YOU AND START OVER?***

A shudder spread over Janel. "Start over? Isn't it a little late for that?"

***OH, I'VE DONE IT BEFORE.*** The demon shrugged. ***THE LAST TIME, I LEFT YOU ALONE. I LEFT YOUR PARENTS ALONE. EVERY NIGHT, YOUR MOTHER, TYA, WOULD VISIT

AND TEACH YOU MAGIC. YOU WERE LOVED. YOU WERE HAPPY.*** Xaltorath snorted. ***SULESS ATE YOU ALIVE.***

Janel's eyes widened in horror as she finally realized what Xaltorath implied: that this had happened before, that Xaltorath had absorbed the souls of Khored, Tya, and others not because she'd eaten them now but because she would do so *in the future.* Janel had always heard demons possessed an incomprehensible relationship with time, but she'd never seen anything to support the idea. The prophecies were too vague to guarantee veracity. She'd never met a demon who could travel through time.

But if they could? If demons could not only perceive time but move through it . . . ?

"No. No, you're lying. If you could go back in time and start over whenever you didn't like how something turned out, you'd have already won. No one would be able to stop you."

***HAVEN'T YOU NOTICED? NO ONE CAN STOP ME.*** Xaltorath grinned down at Janel. ***IT'S NOT AS EASY AS YOU MIGHT THINK. DO YOU HAVE ANY CLUE HOW HARD IT WAS TO TRICK ATRIN KANDOR INTO MARRYING YOU? I HAD TO MAKE HIM THINK IT WAS HIS IDEA."

Janel blinked and then scrambled backward, heart pounding. Xaltorath lied. She knew that a thousand times over. And yet . . . "What? Atrin Kandor? But you–" Janel narrowed her eyes. Elana Kandor–no, *Elana Milligreest*–hadn't been anyone important until the most famous emperor in Quuros history[2] had picked her as his wife just prior to marching off to his death in the Manol Jungle. It was the events that happened after: Elana traveling through the Korthaen Blight to beg the morgage to stop their invasion, Elana freeing S'arric's soul from his imprisonment inside Vol Karoth, Elana returning to Khorvesh to help rebuild her shattered and war-torn dominion. Because of *those* deeds, the Eight Immortals chose Elana as one of their champions, had her reincarnated as Janel. And here was Xaltorath, claiming she'd orchestrated it all.

And so Janel was reduced to a question she loathed. "Why me? Why would you want Kandor to marry me?"

***WE'RE DONE TALKING.***

Janel tried to fight. Xaltorath batted her sword away with ridiculous ease. The demon grabbed her waist, lifted her up, and two of those hands landed on either side of Janel's head. Janel started to scream . . .

Janel opened her eyes. What had just happened? She didn't remember.

She scrambled to her feet; Xaltorath stood just a few feet away. "What are you doing here? I thought you were busy hiding from Vol Karoth."

[2] Excuse me. One of the most famous.

Xaltorath grinned. ***SOON HE'LL BE HIDING FROM ME.***

Janel felt a shudder tear through her. Then she recognized a familiar sensation: her body in the Living World beginning to stir. But hadn't she just fallen asleep?

Janel woke.

# 39: A Counterfeit of Royalty

***(Kihrin's story)***

I stared in shock at Talon. Then I growled, twisted under her, and tried to throw her off.

Unfortunately, her strength beat mine handily. Plus, she wasn't holding my hands so much as wrapping tentacles around them.

"Talon, let go of me!"

"Shhh. You don't want the guards to show up."

"Oh, I think I do." I tilted my head back and started to yell.

"But I'm here to rescue you." Talon slapped a hand over my mouth. Note she grew an extra arm to manage it. "I'm betting your mother will forgive me if I bring you back to her."

I stopped struggling. "Mother? Which one?" My words were unintelligible through her hand, but I knew Talon understood me.

I wasn't just being a smart-ass with that question. Talon had *eaten* my adoptive parents, Ola and Surdyeh, adding their personalities and memories to her "collection."[1] She operated under some entirely false delusions concerning our relationship, at times indicating she thought of herself as my mother.

Considering our relationship has been sexual on at least one occasion, words can't even begin to describe how uncomfortable that idea makes me.

Talon leaned in close. "Queen Khaeriel. I'm working for her."

I eyed her suspiciously. *My mother isn't this stupid.*

"Ha, you'd think that, right? But mimics are just so useful." She beamed at me. "Oh, it is good to see you again, ducky. Honestly, you're lucky I found you."

I slumped back against the sofa, defeated. Lucky. Right. This was Taja's "help."

"Taja? What? Taja didn't send me." Talon suddenly looked nervous.

*I'm not leaving without my friends.* I mumbled that too, but the net effect was thinking it at her. She heard me fine.

[1] Talon uses this term to refer to the collection of personalities she's absorbed.

Talon scrunched up her nose and leaned in close. "Speaking of, which one did you just have sex with?" She sniffed. "Oh. The girl." Talon tilted her head. "Wait. She's *that* girl, isn't she? The one you told Morea about. Oh, I've been waiting *so long* to meet her."

*Stay away from her. Now remove your slimy tentacles and let me go.*

"Oh, come now, ducky. I think we can–"

The door opened behind us.

Talon didn't have time to hide her monster nature; she was a three-armed woman sitting on a couch with tentacles growing out from her back. The mimic released me and whirled around. The tentacles turned with her, tips sharpening to points like knives as they raced toward the source of the interruption.

"Run!" I shouted. I rolled off the couch and turned invisible. No sense making things easier for Talon if I could help it.

I saw the woman standing in the doorway. Pale and fragile and colored like violets.

Valathea. The *real* Valathea.

Talon paused with her claws inches from the woman's face. The mimic looked oddly shocked. Valathea? Not so much.

Valathea's expression never changed. She seemed neither startled nor afraid. She tilted her head to the side and regarded Talon like a bird examining a worm. The room fell quiet, a standoff I didn't understand at all.

"Now put those away," Valathea said, "before someone's hurt."

Talon's lip curled. "Don't threaten me. You're in a new body. There's no way you've adjusted quickly enough to cast spells."

Valathea smiled. "But I'm not in a new body. I'm in *my* imprinted body. An exact duplicate down to the smallest cell, every neural pathway grown to exacting standards under instructions I left centuries ago. I could cast spells from the moment I opened my eyes."

One of Talon's tentacles quivered. "You're bluffing."

Valathea's expression turned serene as she raised two fingers. They were disturbingly long and delicate, with lilac fingertips and slender purple nails. "Shall we find out together?"

Talon stared. Her expression faltered.

Then she ran.

Really, Talon flew, because a second after she started running, she shape-changed into a raven, banked, and flew out the same open door Valathea had just entered.

Valathea watched her go, then stepped into the room and shut the door behind her.

"Kihrin?" Valathea scanned the room. Then she paused. Her gaze backtracked and settled on the spot where I stood, leaning against the wall with my arms crossed over my chest.

She smiled.

"You can see me," I said.

"I can see you," Valathea agreed.

The door I'd originally used opened, and guards poured through. "Founder? I am sorry, but there seems to be some confusion . . ." The guards looked around the room. Unlike Valathea, none of them noticed me.

"Yes, I would say so," Valathea said. "Perhaps one of you would care to explain what a mimic was doing here?"

"What? A mimic?" The lead soldier was appropriately horrified.

"When I entered the room, a mimic sat on that couch." Valathea pointed. "I came here to question the young prince, but instead, you give me a mimic? Did you think I wouldn't notice, or did you simply not realize Prince Kihrin had been replaced?"

"Uh . . ." The soldier's eyes widened.

"I am sounding the alarm," another soldier said.

"Yes, I think you'd better," Valathea said.

"Please stay right here," the first soldier said. "We will find out what is going on. I will station someone right outside this door in case the mimic returns."

She made a shooing motion with one hand. "Go on, then. Station away."

He opened the door for the other soldiers, then closed it as gently as he could, as if afraid he might wake a sleeping baby.

Valathea turned back to me.

"I need to free my friends too," I said quietly. At least one vané soldier stood just on the other side of that door. "Know any spells for that?"

"I used to, but what I said to that mimic earlier?"

"Yes?" I had a sinking feeling.

"I was bluffing." Valathea shrugged apologetically. "It's almost the truth. This body has been prepared especially for me, so I'll recover all my magical aptitude in just a few short days. Normally, it takes months."

"I see." I took a deep breath. "Any other ideas?"

"Hmm. My husband and your father are dealing with the soldiers your uncle garrisoned here, but that only solves part of the problem." She tapped an elegant, too-long finger against her upper lip.

"Wait. Terindel? And my father—" I lowered my voice. "My father's *here*?"

"Yes, looking for you. I told him you might need a little help. I hope you don't mind."

"No, I don't mind at all."

"Even so, a distraction might help. Especially a distraction that provides us an excuse to leave quickly.'" Valathea held up the same finger.

"Terindel and your father will find your friends, but you're the one in the most danger."

I'd rejected that same justification from Talon, but from Valathea, it made so much more sense. Or maybe I just trusted her more.

Trusting her was naïve. I knew that. I'd never known her as a living, animate being. I had no idea what she was like, if she could be depended upon, what her motivations might be. I didn't even know if she was telling the truth about Doc and Therin. I knew she was Doc's wife, and after his "death," she'd been sentenced to die in the Korthaen Blight. The same sentence we'd been given, just with a lot more soul-chaining to make sure she never left.[2]

Maybe she deserved that sentence. Doc had never been coy about admitting he'd done terrible things as the Kirpis king.

Oh yeah. She was also my great-great-grandmother.

"Okay," I finally said. "But we still need that distraction."

Valathea tilted her head. "Do they still use knockout gas on prisoners they bring here? No scent. No warning. One second lucidity and then the void?"

I nearly asked her how she knew that, but the answer was obvious; she knew for the same reason I did. They'd used it on her. Valathea must have been a "guest" here—a prisoner waiting for her own execution in a drugged-out stupor. Just like me.

Except no one had come to her rescue.[3]

"Yeah," I said. "They do."

The woman smiled—serene, soft, wicked. "It's extremely flammable."

I grinned back at her. "Is that so? They should be careful. It would be a shame if there were an accident."

Leaving the room proved easy; Valathea opened the door and asked a soldier (there were three, not one) to bring her tea. While she held the door open, I slipped out.

It took me longer to steal the keys from an overseer and find the storeroom, which sat on the far side of the house. I was glad, since I didn't know how big a fire I'd cause. The vané stored the sleep gas itself in large glass containers with wide lids. I wasn't sure how the containers themselves were transported or how they forced the gas into the main hallway. Bellows of some kind? Magic?

[2] And she didn't leave—not as a human being, anyway.

[3] I believe Terindel was dealing with the shock of being extremely injured and trapped in an utterly unfamiliar body with no ability to cast spells at the time. And of course, the surviving members of the Kirpis side of the civil war had either surrendered or were running. No one would have been in a position to help the queen.

It didn't matter. If I could set the gas on fire without blowing myself up, we'd be golden. If I screwed up, I'd find myself dead or captured.

Captured was the same as dead, just delayed a bit.

I slipped my vision past the First Veil and checked; the containers were glass.

I scouted the warden's house until I found the kitchen, whose main function seemed to be providing a place to cook porridge. I ran into a slight snag because all the plates proved to be simple wooden trenchers instead of elegant ceramics and glassware. Finally, I located a glass wine goblet in a receiving room. I brought it to the kitchen, where I used ash, water, and the goblet's reflective surface to mark Janel's air sigil on my forehead.

I had to work fast. I located a large bag of haerunth grain and scooped it into the wine goblet, followed by an ashy piece of charcoal from the hearth. Another layer of haerunth followed on top. Lack of air would eventually smother the charcoal. I had a small window of effectiveness.

I snuck back into the storeroom, avoiding guards, and set the wine goblet on the floor. Then I closed the door behind me and got out fast.

If I'd done everything correctly, nothing would happen. In fact, without any further interference, the charcoal would snuff out long before it burned through the top layer of haerunth.

But I had every intention of interfering.

I worked my way back down the hall and set up a safe distance away. Guards didn't often pass through this particular hallway, which was important.

I sat down, took a deep breath, and began to sing.

It wasn't really singing, mind you. It was wordless, for one thing, a soft drone. And I used magic to cheat. I could have done this more easily with a musical instrument, but the theory remained the same. I slowly built up reverberating sound layers, casting out the vibration like a net, crafting a subtle disharmony devastating to a single material like granite or iron.

Or in this case, glass.

I wasn't sure it was working until I heard a thump and a strange sound. Loud, and then muted, as if I'd dunked my head in the bathwater. Then the shock wave had me stumbling backward.

Okay. So the explosion was a little larger than I'd intended.

I regained my balance and hurried back to the receiving room, where Valathea waited. I remained invisible, naturally.

I arrived just in time for the show.

Rindala was trying to calm an increasingly uncalmable Founder. "Lady, please, I promise you–"

"Bring my carriage around immediately," Valathea said. "I refuse to stay here another minute. Another second. Do you hear? I'm leaving at once." Her gaze swept past me, but I knew I'd been seen.

Rindala knew he was beaten. "Of course. We will naturally send word when the situation is better under control, Your Majesty–" Rindala stopped himself. "My apologies, Founder."

Valathea studied the man. Then she reached out and touched his cheek. "I remember you. You came down with us from the Kirpis, didn't you?"

"Yes." Emotional volumes wrestled in that single word. "Please be careful. My heart would break if any harm befell you now that you're back."

"Thank you. It gives my heart joy to see your friendly face. Even if I'm no longer queen."

"You'll always be my queen," Rindala whispered. Then louder: "I'll have your carriage brought around immediately. If I may?" The warden offered Valathea his arm.

"Again," Valathea said. "Thank you."

They walked out of the room.

I followed right behind them.

# 40: Bas-Reliefs

## *(Janel's story)*

Janel opened her eyes. She immediately slammed her hand down against the mattress, hard enough to make the whole thing jump. "Damn it!"

Something had happened with Xaltorath. Janel didn't know what, but she knew she was missing time.

Then she simultaneously realized two things. First, her inner thighs ached.

Second, she was alone.

Janel sat up. The room wasn't large enough to miss Kihrin's absence. She looked behind herself and immediately felt a fool. Did she think Kihrin had fallen behind the mattress?

The smell of sex and sweat lingered in the air, mixing with the odor of cold, dusty stone. No sign of blood or violence, but anything could have happened while she had been in the Afterlife.

"Irisia, please, I need your help." Janel called out her mother's name, her mother's *real* name.

Nothing. No response at all.

She didn't know why she'd expected otherwise.

Then Janel noticed a rainbow shimmer sweep over the stone sink. She blinked, but it remained, a chatoyant sheen against the marble. Something new.

She'd avoided drinking the water for fear their jailers had drugged it. The effects clearly needed to be renewed regularly–she woke feeling only slightly woozy–which meant regular dosing. The drinking water and food seemed obvious.

Janel went over to the sink, which included a single spigot from which flowed a thin stream of water. Not fantastic for washing, but enough to give a prisoner drinking water. Janel stared at the stream with the intensity of a starving cat eyeing a sleeping rabbit. Was the rainbow glimmer on the stone meant as a warning? Or meant to say the water was now safe?

There was only one way to find out.

Janel picked up the cup, filled it, and drank. Then repeated the action.

Her tongue felt like a jungle insect had crawled inside her mouth and died, but the light-headed wonderment of the previous night didn't return.

Janel sat on the bed, collected and dressed herself, then considered the night before. To say she was annoyed with herself was a vast understatement. It's not like she hadn't wanted to have sex with Kihrin, but she'd also wanted to do so while sober. Especially for their first time.

Kihrin had seemed enthusiastically willing—she dimly remembered him asking the questions *she* had forgotten—but she still found herself furiously angry at Kelanis for putting them in a situation where their intentions toward each other could ever be in doubt. And then there was Teraeth . . .

Gods, Teraeth. Janel felt torn between wishing Kihrin and Teraeth would just fuck already to being terrified of where she'd fall in their lives once they finally did. Whatever had possessed her to involve herself with two stallions who didn't understand her culture or place within it?

Except she knew that too. What had possessed her were the echoes of other lives, the seeping memories of wounded souls and loves she'd inherited rather than earned. S'arric. Kandor. Men she'd never known and yet whose shadows fell across her heart. Counting the moments until they realized what they had with her was nothing more than a fading reflection.

Janel shook off her fugue. She drank some more water, used the commode. Finally, she returned to the sink, grabbed the sides, and yanked the entire basin right off the wall.

Water surged into the air. Janel dropped the stone basin and returned to bed, curling up against a wall as still drugged. A flood pooled inside the room, washing out under the door.

It didn't take long for someone to respond.

The door opened. A vané guard tipped his head inside, spotted her, then motioned for someone else to join him. The second man raised an eyebrow at the sink. "What . . . happened here?"

Janel ignored the question and rocked back and forth, not looking at them directly. One guard was Manol vané, the other Kirpis vané. She knew she could take them if she had the advantage of surprise.

The Manol vané approached her. "Come on, then. Everything's fine. You're safe now." His voice was soothing. He held up his hands, as if trying not to startle a deer.

When he reached the bed, the vané bent down and tried to put an arm around her. She twisted, grabbed, and slammed his head into the stone wall.

Or rather, she tried. Janel wasn't fast enough. The guard grabbed her arm, arrested her swing, and then forced her down to the bed. Her strength meant nothing to him. How?

"Oh, for fuck's sake," he growled. "Would you *stop* that?"

She had zero intention of stopping anything, but the sharp snap of his voice flashed through her with recognition. She stared up at the man's face. *"Terindel?"*

The illusion vanished in tattered wisps. She still lay on the bed; no one had touched her.

Doc[1] leaned against the wall he'd been holding up with a shoulder, while his chestnut-haired companion stayed by the door, watching out for interruptions. They both dressed in guard uniforms, but with closer inspection, she noticed the bloodstains left by the original owners.

Therin watched Janel with idle curiosity. "Do you know her?" he asked his companion.

Doc's mouth quirked to the side. "No, not at all. I'd say my reputation precedes me, but not many people know what I look like these days."

"It's a long story." She clambered out of the bed, although it meant squeezing into a space that now held two more people than its original builders had ever intended. "And nothing would please me more than to go into greater detail," she lied, "but might we first find my friends and leave?"

Therin pointed toward the still-gushing plumbing. "How did that happen?"

"How do you think it happened? I ripped it off the wall."

He blinked at her. "Gods, how old are you? Sixteen?"

"I'm *twenty,*" she corrected. "I'd ask how old you are, but I'll simply assume *ancient beyond belief.*"

Doc started snickering.

"Shut it, you. You're the old man here," Therin said. He turned back to Janel. "You're also not drugged. We were told they keep the prisoners insensate."

"I was given an antidote," Janel said.

He held up a vial of a wine-colored liquid. "Looks like we won't need this, then."

"Maybe for the others?" Doc said. "Let's go." He started to reach for Janel for real.

At least, she thought he was. Chainbreaker made it hard to know for sure.

"Wait," Janel said. "Do you know where they've taken Kihrin? When

[1] Yes, I realize Janel has no reason to call Terindel *Doc,* but I have decided to continue doing so in the interest of consistency.

I woke up, he was gone." Even as she asked the question, she realized she'd assumed they'd know who Kihrin was.

"My wife's taking care of that," Doc said. "Don't worry."

"They put you in the same cell as my son?" A wry smile formed on Therin's lips.

Janel found herself looking at the bed, at the state of her clothing, at the unmistakable scent lingering in the air. Well. No sense trying to pretend nothing had happened.

"Your son–" Janel floundered, her brain unwilling to make the proper connections, until she realized the man's amused, twinkling eyes were indeed the same blue as Kihrin's. "You're High Lord Therin D'Mon."

"You don't need to make it sound like a disease."

"Don't I?" She tilted her chin and put her hands on her hips.

Doc started laughing again. Janel's glare in his direction just made his laugh harder. He pointed a finger at her. "You're Qoran's daughter. The one Tyentso was talking about."

"Since I wasn't there for your conversation with Tyentso, I've no idea if she meant me." Janel scowled. "But yes to the first statement."

Therin cleared his throat. "Much as I would love to continue this conversation about how Qoran is going to first murder my son and then me, she's right. We need to go."

"Hold up there," Doc said as Janel started to leave. "It'll look better if we're pulling you."

"Then do so."

She had no idea why Therin D'Mon seemed to find her impatient retort so humorous.

They "dragged" her outside, walking at the normal, determined pace of two guards in no particular rush. The dawn light was turning the morning sky green, and fog lingered at the tree line, spilling down the quarry sides to wander along the stone paths like ghosts.

"I don't remember where they put Thurvishar or Teraeth," she admitted. Janel didn't stop talking–she'd been running off like a wild horse the night before, so she didn't think any watching guards would find chattiness unusual.

"Not a problem," Therin said. "We've already checked with the guards."

"Give her the antidote," Doc said, "and we'll throw her in the next cell. Should look like a prisoner transfer."

"The two cells at the end there," Therin said.

"You don't have a key?" Janel asked.

Doc laughed. "As a matter of fact, we do." He gave her a vial as Therin unlocked the cell door. They pushed her inside and closed the door behind her.

For a second, she wondered if they'd made a mistake, but then her eyes adjusted to the light.

Teraeth lay on the bed with his elbow under his head, eyes half-lidded, reminding her of a jaguar lazing about on a hot afternoon. A particularly beautiful jaguar. Her breath caught at the sight.

His gaze sharpened fractionally. "Are you real?"

"Fortunately for you, yes." She knelt next to him. A small cup sat by his side–clearly, he'd been drinking the water.

"Oh." He pondered her with a deep, serious regard. "Has anyone told you that you look just like this woman I married?"

She stopped and made a face. Lovely. Just perfect. "*You* weren't married to anyone. Atrin Kandor was. You live your own life now."

"I was an idiot. I was the biggest idiot." He paused. "Did I ever apologize?"

"No, you didn't. Since that was another lifetime, I don't require any. You haven't done anything wrong to *me*." She held up the vial Doc had given her. "I need you to drink this."

"I'm so sorry."

Janel inhaled. While she'd started remembering her past life, Teraeth had always remembered his, with perfect clarity. Which wasn't a good thing, in her opinion. This whole past-life business had proven more annoying than useful.

"C'indrol," Janel murmured. She looked away, frowning. Who was C'indrol?

"Who's that?" Teraeth asked.

She bit her lip. "I have no idea. I don't remember."

"Oh. Okay, then." He shrugged.

Janel scowled. She'd asked Kihrin about the name the night before. But today? She'd forgotten the context.

She thrust the bottle at Teraeth. "Drink this."

"Oh, I shouldn't." Teraeth whispered sotto voce, "I think they're putting something in the water."

"That's why I need you to drink this," she repeated. "Can you do that for me?"

"I don't want to," Teraeth said.

Janel sighed, resisting the urge to roll her eyes. Taking a deep breath, she thumbed off the cork and said, "I understand. I couldn't convince Kihrin to drink his either."

"Give me that," Teraeth said.

She handed him the vial. He drank it in one go, gasping. "Holy–That's disgusting." Teraeth closed his eyes, made a face, and then shook his head violently from side to side.

"I suspect that's on purpose." Janel set the bag down. "Get dressed. We're leaving."

"What's that?" Teraeth reached for her, rather than the change of clothing.

"What?" She didn't understand what he could possibly mean, then his fingers touched her hip, where the drawstring pants had settled low enough to uncover the love bite left there the night before. "Oh."

Teraeth traced the pattern of ruptured blood vessels with a fingertip. "Kihrin did this." It wasn't a question. The Manol vané looked at her with hooded eyes, his mouth quirked in a smile. Far from being upset or jealous, he looked aroused.

She bit her lip as a shiver swept over her body.

Janel made a soft noise. Much as Teraeth had been driving her to the brink of frustration lately, his touch left her dizzy. She clasped her hand over his, which had started to hook two fingers over the gathered fabric. "We don't have time for this."

He stood slowly, cupped his hand against her cheek. "We might have a little time."

She reached up until her lips almost met his. *"Your father,"* she whispered, "is waiting outside this cell, and I don't know where the guards have taken Kihrin."

Teraeth stopped smiling and removed his hand. "You're right; such a shame we don't have time for this."

She pushed the uniform and mail into his hands. "Your father brought you a present. I know it doesn't make up for all those missed birthdays, but let's applaud the effort."

"What did you make me drink? The antidote?"

"I assume. That present is from *Kihrin's* father, also outside."

His laughter was midnight dark. "Oh, this just gets better and better." Teraeth dressed quickly and, much like his father, looked the part perfectly. He threw her a wary, worried look. "Does my father know who you used to be?"[2]

"Who I–?" Janel lowered her voice. "Oh. Kihrin *told* you." She reminded herself to have a long talk with Kihrin once they'd escaped this mess.

"In his defense, he thought I already knew." Teraeth paused. "So does Terindel–?"

"*No.* And let's keep it that way."

Teraeth exhaled. "Nothing would make me happier." He eyed the club that had been included with the outfit, rolled it around his arms a few times experimentally. "This'll do."

[2] See *Elana Milligreest/Kandor,* whose second husband was Terindel.

"Good. Let's leave. We still need to find Thurvishar–"

A bell started ringing somewhere in the compound. Then another.

The door to the cell slammed open, and Doc stuck his head inside. "Come on, you two. I'm guessing they found the bodies."

"Father," Teraeth said.

Doc waved a hand. "Yes, yes. Heartfelt, tender family reunion later.[3] Hurry!"

Teraeth grabbed Janel by the arm and pulled her outside, acting for all the world like another guard dealing with a prisoner. Hopefully with the alarm, no one had been watching for long enough to notice they'd gained a guard or question why three guards would be needed for a single prisoner.

A guard shouted at them. "Forget that one! We need everyone up top!" The guard promptly ran off, paying no more attention to them.

"Should be at the end," Therin said, pointing.

They moved as quickly as they could without running. When they reached the door, Janel reached out and broke the lock before Therin found his key. She raised an eyebrow at Therin's stunned surprise. "It's quicker this way."

Teraeth smirked at the two men. "We'll be right back."

Janel and Teraeth ducked inside the cell, both expecting to grab Thurvishar and leave. Instead, they both stopped and stared.

Teraeth slowly closed the door behind him.

The prison cell, if it could be called such, had a beautifully polished floor inlaid with black and white marble to form an orchid flowering from a book–the symbol of House D'Lorus. An elaborate sink and commode lined one wall, both more ornate than the plain built-ins from their cells. Above the sink hung a polished silver mirror. A full marble Zaibur board with all the pieces and an eggshell-thin chalcedony goblet rested on a small marble table. A high-backed marble chair had been pushed under the table. A crystal chandelier hung from the ceiling, mage-lights sparkling as they lit up the corners of the room with rainbows.

Most *palaces* weren't this ornately decorated.

And the walls–the walls had been shaped into sumptuous bas-reliefs. Writhing dragons–each one different–encircled the wall where the bed attached, while the wall behind them had been turned into a montage of the Eight Immortals. A celestial map decorated the opposite wall, charting the planets, stars, and innumerable constellations. An open passage broke the pattern of that wall, complete with a lighted stairway.

Also, the room was empty.

[3] I doubt that for some reason.

Teraeth opened the door again. "Get in here."

Janel walked over to the open passage and waved a hand through it. It wasn't a trick–a tunnel led straight back into the quarry bedrock.

"What the–?" Doc said as he and Therin stepped inside.

"You know, this is the last place I'd have expected to see a symbol of House D'Lorus," Therin D'Mon said. "How on earth did this happen?"

"The obvious answer is Thurvishar," Janel said. "I'm just not sure *why*."[4]

"That's you, Janel." Teraeth sounded awed.

"What?" Janel turned back around.

The last stone wall had been carved with a bas-relief of seven figures, all posed in heroic stances, as if frozen just seconds from running off to fight evil. The one that Teraeth touched was indisputably, unmistakably Janel, carved in stone. But other likenesses were also recognizable.

"Not just her," Doc said. "You and Tyentso too. I don't recognize the others."

"I do," Janel said, breath catching. She pointed at each in turn. "That's . . . Talea." She inhaled. "And that's Relos Var's minion, Senera." She ran her fingers over the last one's surface. "This is Xivan Kaen." She shook her head. "He's made it look like we're all on the same side."

"You think Thurvishar did all this?" Teraeth sounded dumbfounded.

"Who else could have done it? I cannot imagine how, but it seems unlikely the vané put him in a cell personalized with family crest and *escape tunnel*." Janel shook her head.

"Where's Kihrin?" Therin said. "I'm surprised there's no carving of him."

"Gods," Doc said. "Look *up*."

Behind the chandelier, an enormous dragon had been meticulously sculpted, sparkling like opal in the reflected rainbow spray. It was locked in battle with another figure–a black silhouette, roughened and turned matte so it somehow reflected no light at all. The black figure held an equally black sword, and since both carvings drank the light, it seemed as though man and sword merged.

No one said a word. In the background, the alarm bells continued to ring.

"I've seen the dragon before," Janel finally said. "That's Relos Var."

"But the silhouette–" Teraeth started to say.

"That's *not* Kihrin," Janel insisted.

"No. It can't be." Teraeth exhaled forcefully.

"Well, this is . . . something," Doc said. "And in case you're curious, no, none of this is an illusion."

[4] I would tell you if I knew.

Janel looked up the stairs. Each step's riser was mage-lit, illuminating the passage. Here too the walls were decorated, but nothing so grand or illustrative as the bas-reliefs below. Janel choked off a hysterical laugh as she began climbing the steps. "He made handrails. *Handrails*."

Teraeth followed her. "Note to self: Thurvishar does nothing by halves. Also, I'm asking him to build my next house."

Doc's laughter echoed up the long passage.

Thurvishar had also made landings. Each had benches and little alcoves whose purpose eluded Janel until she realized they were reading nooks, apparently existing for no other reason than Thurvishar couldn't imagine going that long without stopping to read something.[5] Then they turned a corner and the stairway opened onto the jungle floor, near the edge of the quarry grounds.

Thurvishar sat on the ground, studying a flower. He wore an elegant black misha and kef trimmed with silver thread, with matching boots, nothing like the prisoner garb they'd been issued.

Thurvishar looked up and beamed a wide, happy, deeply drugged grin.

"My friends!" He held out his hands. "You must join me. I was about to have a picnic." He pointed. "We're having flowers."

Janel blinked. Thurvishar was still drugged. He was *still* drugged? She'd assumed he'd thrown off the effects, or he'd faked eating the food, or something . . .

The whole point of drugging their food and water had been to keep their thoughts too disorganized and scattered for spellcasting. Except Thurvishar had gone right ahead and kept casting spells. And had done so *beautifully*.[6]

"Oh, how interesting," Therin said. "He's still drugged."

Teraeth pointed to the tunnel. "Thurvishar, you're up in the clouds right now. How the hell did you manage all that? Handrails?"

"Oh! Thank you for reminding me. I need to fix those. They're not the right shape." He started crawling on his hands and knees back to the tunnel entrance.

"Oh no you don't." Doc caught the man by the neck of his robes. "There's no reason to go back there right now. Or ever."

Teraeth was trying desperately not to laugh. "Have you practiced casting spells while, um, . . . blissful?"

"Oh yes." Thurvishar grinned. "This reminds me of finals week, my first year at the Academy. We were all so . . . so stewed. Beyond stewed. We were supposed to animate a dead frog, and Mazor D'Aramarin

[5] Guilty.

[6] Honestly, I'm just as much at a loss as anyone. I'm chalking it down to being half-dreth.

made the damn thing twelve feet tall." He began laughing at the memory. "Never did figure it out. You should have seen the dean's face . . . It breathed *fire.*"

"Oh yes," Therin said. "That does bring back some memories."

"Well," Janel said, "this is . . . delightful. We would, all of us, love to hear about your unexpectedly drug-filled Academy years, but first, drink this." She uncapped the last vial and held it out to Thurvishar.

"Oh? Sure." He took the vial and tipped it back into his mouth. He winced. "Oh, that tastes like book paste and shame."

A few seconds after he drank the vial, Thurvishar blinked, his eyes widened, and then he focused on the group. "Oh."

Janel smiled. "Welcome back."

Thurvishar brushed himself off. "Thank you." He cleared his throat. "Did I do anything?"

"You redecorated," Therin said. "Bit unorthodox, but who am I to judge? And don't worry; I won't tell House D'Kard."[7]

"Oh no." Thurvishar looked extremely embarrassed.

"There is no need to blush," Janel said. "I've never seen its like."

"And just so you know," Teraeth said, "I really do want to hear about your college years." He stage-whispered, "They sound fantastic."

"He's kidding," Doc said.

Teraeth shook his head. "Oh no. I'm not kidding. I'm hoping he remembers recipes."

Janel crossed her arms over her chest. "We need to find Kihrin."

Just then, an explosion lit up the trees behind them, coming from the Quarry.

"Easy." Teraeth pointed. "He's that way."

[7] They control the stonemasons.

# 41: Old Loyalties

*"Really?" Kihrin blinked at Thurvishar. "What was the deal with the carvings?"*

*Thurvishar shrugged. "Honestly, I don't have the faintest clue. I remember creating them, but for the life of me, I don't remember why."*

*"Huh."*

### *(Kihrin's Story)*

Rindala escorted Valathea to where an elegant gold-trimmed carriage waited, drawn by a team of the kind of animals that had pulled our wagon in the Korthaen Blight. I still didn't know what they were called,[1] but evidently horses weren't a local resource. Several bags had been strapped to the carriage, and one object in particular caught my attention: a harp case. I knew it contained a double-strung harp with silver strings. My harp. Or rather, Valathea's now-empty tsali. Its presence struck me as morbid, like carrying a corpse. Not just anyone's corpse, but your own corpse, after you'd moved on to a different body.

Rindala kissed Valathea's hand and left. He winked at me as he walked away.

My eyes widened. What just happened?

How long had Rindala been able to see me?

Rindala paused to ask a soldier out front a question. While they spoke, the soldier wasn't looking when the carriage dipped from my weight.

I climbed inside and sat down across from Valathea. The carriage's graceful curves reminded me of plants without showing a single leaf.

I exhaled as the driver set the animals into motion, pulling away from the prison entrance. That didn't mean I turned visible. Not yet.

"He could see me," Kihrin said.

"He's one of the greatest dreammakers who's ever lived," Valathea

[1] Still okapi.

said. "Of course he saw you." Her expression turned morose as she stared outside the carriage window. "I fear he'll come to some trouble because of this."

"Maybe you just gave him the excuse he needed."

"Perhaps so." She continued brooding out the window.

I tilted my head, staring at her. She seemed so familiar. Then I realized why. My throat tightened, and I made a low noise under my breath.

Valathea looked back at me. "What is it?"

"You . . . I'm sorry. I just realized–you remind me of my aunt Tishar."

"Given your expression, should I assume she's no longer alive?"

"You would be assuming correctly, yes. I'm sorry you never had the chance to meet her."

Valathea looked faintly bemused. "Why would I–" A cloud passed over her eyes. "Would we have been related?"

"She was your granddaughter."

Valathea sat very still for a moment. "Yes, I was told my daughter had died. I take it Tishar was one of her children?"

Tishar's mother had been Valathea's daughter, Valrashar. I nodded. "Yes, I'm sorry."

She waved her fingers in the air. "It's fine. I suppose it explains why I liked you."

That made me pause. Because it was one thing to meet this woman who was in theory my great-grandmother and quite another to, well . . .

"Were you really . . . I mean . . . ?"

The corner of her mouth quirked. "Was I that harp?"

I swallowed. "Yes."

She leaned forward in the carriage. "Yes, I was. I even have a few memories. Not many. Not often. Like flashes of lightning, single moments of light trapped between stretches of exquisite darkness." She leaned back again, idly stroking the velvet upholstery. "But I wouldn't forget you. Not with such beautiful fingers."

That last comment caught me off guard. I found myself blushing, with no idea what to say.

Just then, the carriage halted. Valathea didn't seem concerned.

"Expecting friends?"

"Oh no," Valathea said as the door swung open. "I'm expecting family."

*"Do you mind if I add a bit here?" Thurvishar asked.*

*Kihrin looked at him oddly. "You want to add a bit to my story?"*

*"Well, not to yours–I mean, it's a bit like the part I added with Janel. It just fits best here."*

*"I'll pour another cup of tea."*

**(*Rindala's story*)**

Rindala walked back inside and began assessing his options. None of them appealed.

"Warden." A soldier rushed up to him, running and out of breath. "We finished the head count. Everyone is accounted for except three of the four prisoners brought in yesterday. Also there, ah—" The woman licked her lips nervously. "I suspect you will wish to see one of the cells for yourself. *Vandalism* does not quite do the matter justice."

Rindala stared at the woman. "*Three* of the four?"

"Yes, Warden," she said. "The prince remains. We moved him to a new cell because of water damage to his old one. We found him wandering. His companions were forced to leave him behind."

Rindala looked back toward the front door, toward the coach he imagined running as far and fast from the prison as possible. He turned back to the soldier. *Three* of the four.

"We should check on our guest," Rindala said.

A few minutes later, Rindala stood outside Prince Kihrin's cell. To all appearances, the young man Rindala had met the previous day slept soundly. Rindala checked for an illusion.

There was none.

He pressed his tongue against the inside of his teeth and considered.

Rindala found himself in a moral quandary.

He knew perfectly well Kihrin had escaped with Queen Valathea, but admitting that would also mean admitting he'd let them stroll out of his prison. And then there was the matter of this imposter's true identity, although he thought the answer obvious.

The soldiers said Valathea had reported a mimic.

Just because his queen engineered the prince's escape didn't mean she had *lied*.

But what to do about it?

There was only one reasonable answer.

"Do you want us to move him again?" the woman asked.

"Hmm?" Rindala smiled warmly. "Oh no. Unnecessary. But do send a message to His Majesty. First, give him my sincerest apologies. Inform him of the breakout, reassure him we still have Prince Kihrin in custody, but relay my belief his friends will return for him. I strongly advise we move the prince to a more secure location. The Mother of Trees, perhaps?"

"Yes, Warden." She ran off to deliver the message.

If King Kelanis did as Rindala suspected, he would move the prince before nightfall. That new location wouldn't necessarily be the Manol capital, but given that the king intended to publicly torture and execute the young man, it was only a matter of time before they were in the same room together.

And that's when things would turn *interesting.*

"I never did like Kelindel . . . or his damn son," Rindala said.

He walked back to the lift.

# 42: Rainbow Dragon

*"Oh, so that's what you meant," Kihrin said. "You know, people really need to stop calling me* prince.*"*

*Thurvishar raised an eyebrow. "I doubt that's going to happen."*

*Kihrin pouted. "Fine. I don't like it, though."*

*"No one said you had to." Thurvishar reached for a different stack of papers. "I think we'll skip your parents for the time being."*

*"Going back to Senera and friends, are we?" Kihrin didn't even try to hide his amusement.*

*"No," Thurvishar said primly. "I found some journals while we were cleaning up." He gestured around the room. "From the original owner, as it were."*

*Kihrin blinked at the man for a moment and then leaned forward. "What? Are you serious? He kept a journal?"*

*"He did," Thurvishar said. "Would you like to hear it?"*

*"Oh, more than anything," Kihrin said.*

**(Grizzst's story)**

The wizard Grizzst was climbing a two-hundred-foot rock cliff when motion flashed at the corner of his eye, a rainbow glimmer. He knew he'd messed up.

All his plans had hinged on spotting the dragon first, and instead, the reverse had just happened.

*Thurvishar looked up. "Yes."*

*"He wrote his journals in third person?" Kihrin didn't bother to hide his judgmental tone.*

*"You really must get over that quirk," Thurvishar told him. "There's nothing wrong with that point of view, and some people use it to distance themselves from otherwise uncomfortable situations."*

*"I'm just wondering: Are you sure Grizzst wrote this?"*

*Thurvishar stared at the papers in his hands. "No. I'm not. One might even make the argument it's unlikely he wrote this. But if he didn't–" Thurvishar paused. "If he didn't, Relos Var did."*

*"Okay." Kihrin leaned back. "Please keep reading."*

Grizzst froze. He would have prayed had there been anyone worth praying to. The Raenena Mountains were in the grip of winter–or rather, should have been. Instead, a giant murky lake thick with glacial meltwater filled the valley. Because of the lake, Grizzst had assumed he'd find the dragon on a nearby mountain peak.

But no. The dragon had wanted a bath.

Below him, the water roiled. The creature emerging from the bottom was an animated sculpture crafted from opal and satin, rainbow colors flashing iridescent as he spread his wings and took to the air.

Breathtakingly beautiful and crafted from pure malice.

The dragon landed on a lower mountain peak, craning his neck and hissing while he lashed his tail. Grizzst continued his impersonation of a statue. He would have exactly one chance at this, and if he messed it up, he might end up as something worse than dead.

Grizzst slowly inched a hand toward his pouch when the dragon screamed to shake the sky, twisted its head up toward heaven, and let out an enormous cone of blue-white fire that seemed to singe the clouds. The dragon spun that cone in a circle around him, blasting the trees, the ground, the lake, the rocks. It turned the entire valley into a cauldron of boiling water and steam, which Grizzst assumed was now also radioactive.

Grizzst had forgotten subtlety wasn't a requirement when you could just set the world on fire. Grizzst couldn't stop himself from uttering a curse as he was forced to release the rock and fall to avoid that deadly blast.

The dragon heard. His scream filled with triumphant rage.

Grizzst hit a rocky outcropping rising from the boiling water, dislocating his shoulder and shattering ribs. He'd prepared for such contingencies; spells reknit his bones as soon as they broke, but it still hurt with paralyzing, searing pain. He should have researched something to make him invulnerable to harm in the first place, but he'd underestimated the risk. Now he had a dislocated shoulder, which wouldn't heal until he popped it into place, which he couldn't do while he was using that arm to keep from falling to his death. And he couldn't use his other arm because . . . well, he needed it.

Wind slammed against him as the creature's wings beat toward him. He grabbed his necklace with his free hand, feeling as vulnerable as a kitten caught out in the open by a hungry wolf. Grizzst concentrated as he hung there, hoping this wasn't the last mistake of his misbegotten existence.

The dragon's shadow was so large it covered not only Grizzst but the whole valley.

The dragon reared his head back–and did nothing.

Grizzst rolled over. The dragon wasn't paralyzed, exactly. The creature had put all his legs on smaller hilltop islands for balance, and his wings played a gentle fan over Grizzst's head. But the monster wanted to lunge forward, breathe fire, bite, and rend. And couldn't.

Grizzst smirked a little and took the opportunity to catch his breath.

Grizzst used both hands to struggle his way to safety. He yanked his shoulder into alignment, letting the necklace fall back into position. It was a platinum chain, simple and clean, from which hung a brilliant white diamond, large enough for any set of crown jewels. "Took me a long time to find this," Grizzst said as he stared at the frozen dragon. "Searched the Blight for almost a century. I suppose it technically doesn't have a name, but I call it Cynosure. It lets me control dragons. Fun, huh? To be perfectly honest, I wasn't sure it would even work on you. Color me ever so pleased it does. Hello, Rev'arric. It's been a while."

Smoke rose from the dragon's nostrils while hate blazed behind his eyes.

"Oh, nice of you to pretend otherwise, but I'm sure you don't remember me," Grizzst continued in a pleasant, conversational tone. "We met at a conference on tenyé magnification systems. Well, I say *meet,* but you were lecturing and I was a student. That was before I flunked out of university." He shrugged. "What can I say? I discovered girls."

Grizzst liked to imagine the dragon silently cursing Grizzst's ancestors, but it was more likely Rev'arric was too insane to even comprehend Grizzst's words. He'd encountered a few other dragons, and their lucidity varied wildly. He actually held a fascinating conversation with Sharanakal once, but Rol'amar? Not so much.

"Turns out every dragon has a matching Cornerstone, and I'm pretty sure this Cornerstone is *yours,*" Grizzst said. "The reason you're so"–he waved a hand at the dragon's general form–"*you* is because you're missing it. So let's fix that, shall we? Because you and I need to talk."

Grizzst started building a bridge toward the dragon's head so he could get to work.

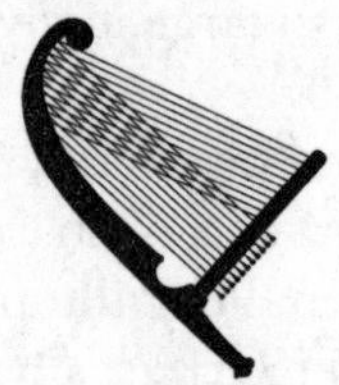

# 43: The Carriage Ride

*Kihrin paused. "Um, did Grizzst say what he did to restore Rev'arric?" He shook his head. "I mean, Relos Var."*

*Thurvishar sighed in irritation. "No. He did not. Which lends itself to your theory that Relos Var was the author, not Grizzst."*

*Kihrin exhaled slowly. "Yeah . . . although Grizzst is enough of an asshole that he could have left that out intentionally."*

*"True," Thurvishar agreed. "Nonetheless . . . I believe it's your turn."*

***(Kihrin's story)***

I was ready to turn invisible and jump from the carriage window when my father stepped inside the carriage and sat down across from me, next to Valathea.

I gaped. I wasn't imagining it. That was my *father.* He looked younger than I remember and he was dressed like a vané prison guard, but it was still High Lord Therin D'Mon.

"Dad?"

No sooner had I uttered that than Doc–or rather Terindel–followed. "Ah, you found Kihrin," he said to Valathea. "Good." He kissed her hand and put his arm around her as he made himself comfortable inside the increasingly cramped carriage compartment.

Teraeth entered next and sat down beside me. "You're never going to believe who we ran into." The smile he gave me suggested this was not okay and he was trying as hard as possible not to scream, commit murder, or both.

Thurvishar came next, eyes widening as he took in how large the carriage wasn't. "Ah, this is a bit–"

"Find yourself a seat," Valathea suggested. "We're all friends here."

Thurvishar cleared his throat and sat on my other side. He wasn't exactly what anyone would call a small man, and frankly, neither Teraeth nor myself were petite. This carriage looked like it comfortably fit six slim vané. Except where was . . .

Janel entered last. She could hardly fail to notice all six seats were filled.

"I'll see if I can help the driver." My father started rising.

"No need," Janel said. She closed the carriage door behind her and sat down between Teraeth and myself. Of course, there was no "between" Teraeth and myself, so she ended up sharing our laps–one thigh on Teraeth's leg, one thigh on mine. I shifted a little sideways to accommodate her. Teraeth did too. We each ended up each with an arm around her for balance, hands on each other's shoulders.

She smiled at us. "Everyone uncomfortable?"

"Oh, deeply," I said. "*So* uncomfortable."

"Good." She seemed to be contemplating what benefits might be gained from chewing on a mouthful of glass.

Doc put a hand over his mouth in an unsuccessful attempt to stifle laughter, and my father Therin wore a perplexed expression, like we'd told an inside joke he didn't have the context to understand.

Valathea tapped on the carriage ceiling. "We're ready," she said.

The carriage started moving, the rumble of the wheels jarring against the springs and jostling Janel in my lap. Which would have been fun, except see the part where my father was staring at me the whole time.

"Thanks for the rescue?" I said.

Doc nuzzled his wife's hair. "Thank Valathea. She's the one who told us Kelanis had arrested you."

"We were just starting to get to know each other, love," Valathea said. "I think I like him." Then her violet eyes wandered over to Teraeth. "So you must be my stepson."

Teraeth's hand tightened on my shoulder. "What gave it away?"

"You're too pretty to be anyone else."

Janel started coughing.

Valathea gave Janel a guileless smile.

"Darling," Terindel said, "would you mind *not* flirting with my son? He wasn't raised among the vané. Incest probably makes him twitchy."

Therin gave his friend a raised eyebrow. "And you're just fine with incest?"

Doc shrugged. "It's all relative."

My father rolled his eyes. "Why am I friends with you again?"

"I'm amazing in bed?"

I choked. *This is not happening.*

"Sure, that was it." Therin snorted. "You know this is why everyone kept challenging you to duels."

Valathea slapped her husband's arm. "I can't believe you've been having this much fun without me."

Teraeth's eyes met mine, his expression disbelieving. I'd be lying if I said I wasn't enjoying Teraeth finally–finally!–being embarrassed by someone else's flirting, but the fact I was every bit as discomforted dampened any amusement.

"Look, I'm sure this is all . . . so awkward," I said, "but we should probably talk about, uh–" I leaned back so I could look at Teraeth around Janel's hair while I frantically changed the subject. "Teraeth, Talon was here."

"What?" Teraeth nearly dislodged Janel, who balanced a hand against the carriage wall for leverage. "The mimic? What's she doing here?"

"Talon works for Khaeriel," Therin said. "At least, she's claiming to work for Khaeriel. I have some doubts as to her sincerity."

"Who's Talon?" Janel asked.

"An insane mimic assassin. I'll have to tell you the full story sometime." I studied Janel. If the previous night had upset her, I couldn't tell.

"I'm sure Empress Tyentso has finished reading through my annotated transcripts by now," Thurvishar offered Janel. "I'd be happy to let you read them if you'd like to quickly catch up on events. I tried to be thorough."

"Annotated–" My mouth dropped open. "Oh Taja. That damn listening rock. You actually wrote all that down?"

"He did," Therin volunteered. "I saw it on Tyentso's desk."

Thurvishar said to Janel, "It's not dissimilar to what Qown was doing with his enchanted journals."

Valathea cleared her throat. "Perhaps full introductions would be in order."

"Oh, um, right. Sorry. Everyone, this is Valathea. Valathea, this is Thurvishar D'Lorus, Janel Theranon, and I'm guessing your husband already told you about Teraeth." She clearly knew who he was. "I assume you know my father and, uh . . ."

Valathea smiled at me. "And my husband. Yes, one assumes I know him too."

Janel made a faintly strangled sound.

I shifted as best I could from the position I was in. "So I don't mean to sound like I'm not happy to see you," I said to Therin, "but what the hell are you doing here? And where's . . ." I grimaced.

"Where's your mother?" Therin said.

"Yeah. That."

He shook his head. "I have no idea. We parted at the Well of Spirals, after she ordered them to restore Valathea." Therin tilted his head in the delicate vané's direction. "Although I still don't know why she did that."

"Nor do I," Valathea admitted, "but I intend to send her a great many flowers. She left shortly after she realized you had fled."

My father nodded, his expression tense, and looked about to start brooding while he gazed out the window. As one apparently does in this family.

"Now we're going to the house of a dear friend of mine," Valathea said, "who'll be able to shelter us until we can decide on our next course of action."

"And this friend is . . . ?" Teraeth asked. I pinched his shoulder to remind him not to be rude, but he ignored me. "Apologies, but the last time someone was coy about given names, they turned out to belong to our enemies."

Janel pointedly ignored that.[1]

Valathea didn't seem offended. "His name is Dolgariatz. He keeps a summerhouse on the shores of Lake Eyamatsu. I'm sure he'll let us stay a few days while we regroup."

Teraeth pondered that. "Fine. Also, I have no idea who that is."

"He's a Founder," Valathea helpfully elaborated.

"We just need to contact the Eight," I said, "let them know Kelanis went back on his word."

Teraeth regarded the three people sitting across from us. "You know, we could use your help. Kelanis promised he'd be willing to enact the Ritual of Night, but now that the time's come, he's balking."

"Violently balking," Janel added. "We came as representatives of the Eight Immortals, but Kelanis drugged us and left us to die out in the Korthaen Blight."

Teraeth picked up the thread again. I honestly wondered if they'd been rehearsing this. They had their timing perfect. "I'm not thrilled about the idea of performing the Ritual of Night, but Vol Karoth has awakened. Kelanis must do the right thing. If you could put in a word with the other Founders, it might help."

Valathea once more turned perfectly still. "Vol Karoth is awake?" She turned to the two men sitting beside her.

"Apparently so," Therin murmured.

"Yes," Thurvishar said, "so if we're going to keep his cage from shattering fully, this way seems the most certain." He paused. "Well. Maybe."

Teraeth stared at him. "What?"

"Several passages in the prophecies suggest this attempt will fail. That this time, Vol Karoth will not be re-imprisoned." Thurvishar shrugged.

I frowned. I hadn't heard anything about this. "Which ones?"

[1] Teraeth was clearly referring to the events surrounding the destruction of Atrine and Janel's reticence to volunteer that Relos Var was involved.

Thurvishar said, "'When the last great people pay the debt of ages, demon due, none shall see the evil day when immortal rites are carried through.' Devoran Prophecies, book 3, quatrain 43. Or, 'Turn thy gaze toward the first tree, great king, for the queen of roses knows your lies. The dance over, no reprieves shall be given. The crystal, once broken, will never be made whole. The black sun's eyes open, and never again shall sleep,' from *The Sayings of Sophis*."

"No, no, no," Teraeth said then. "Those passages are talking about what happened five hundred years ago, when the vané were supposed to give up our immortality and refused. That's already been fulfilled."

"I'm not convinced that's true," Thurvishar said. "They apply just as strongly to what's going on right now."

"I don't believe that," Teraeth protested.

"Both of you, please. Don't put any faith in prophecies," Janel said. "Demons aren't in the habit of giving out *useful* information."

Valathea sighed. "I agree with the young lady. The prophecies are young as such things are measured. Only around three thousand years old. I don't even know what to say except nothing good can come of this." She squeezed her husband's hand. Therin stared at them both, a frown on his lips, looking like he was puzzling out some mystery.

Doc studied me. "You haven't said a word." He'd been quiet too. Maybe that's why he'd noticed.

I sighed. "That's because I think my friends are wrong."

"What?" Janel twisted, putting herself firmly in Teraeth's lap so she could glare at me.

Teraeth's fingers dug into my shoulder. "You're not serious, are you?"

"Completely serious." I didn't let go of Doc's stare. "I've been thinking about what King Kelanis said when he explained *why* he wouldn't do the ritual. He's right. Stripping the immortality from the vané when it only buys us two hundred and fifty years, at most, does seem ridiculous. Especially since the prophecies are coming to a head now. Not in two hundred years. Not in fifty. Now. Half the people sitting in this carriage won't be around in two hundred and fifty years. And if we go through with the ritual? None of us will be. So what are the Eight Immortals going to do? Keep reincarnating us? 'Oops, sorry, we brought you back too early. Let's just pull you back again in a few centuries.'" I made a face. "No, thanks."

A stunned silence met my speech. Mostly from my side of the carriage. Valathea wore no expression at all, and Doc looked almost proud. My father seemed worried, as though I'd just announced my lifelong ambition was kraken wrestling.

"That's . . . you can't . . . that would . . ." Teraeth blinked at me with those jade-green eyes.

I smiled. I'd actually rendered the man speechless. I'd always assumed that impossible.

"The Eight don't have anything else that can stop Vol Karoth!" he finally exclaimed in a rush.

"Is that going to change if we wait?" I said. "*Kelanis isn't wrong.* We've had over three thousand years. If the Eight Immortals were going to come up with something, don't you think they should have done it by now?"

"Well," Valathea said. "Isn't this unexpected."

"Let them work this out," Doc whispered to her.

I focused my attention back on Teraeth. "I'm sorry, Teraeth. I respect your mother. I do. But she's not thinking clearly. I can hardly blame her, but that doesn't mean I'm going to blindly follow her plan. Especially when her plan seems to be, 'Let's just do the same damn thing we've always done and hope we'll have a different outcome this time.'"

"Kihrin, how can you even say that?" Janel wasn't looking in my direction, but she was close enough that I still heard her. "You know what's going to happen if Vol Karoth breaks free, don't you? We all saw what happened in the Blight. What just a psychic projection of him can do. You won't be able to hide. He'll come after you. He always comes after you!" Her voice was a growl. "I didn't free you from him just to see him reclaim you."

Teraeth stabbed a finger in the air as though he were impaling someone's heart. "I'm not letting that happen. No way. If we have to lose our immortality, so be it."

I scowled. I appreciated their concern, overprotective and smothering as it was, but oh Taja, did it annoy the crap out of me just then. "There has to be another way. And yes, I'm aware he wants me. My nightmares won't let me forget. Vol Karoth thinks he isn't whole without me, never mind that the thought of being trapped inside that . . . thing . . . makes me want to scream *forever.* It doesn't change—"

"What are you talking about?" my father asked.

We all paused.

Thurvishar cleared his throat. "The prophecy about the Hellwarrior. The one that Gadrith was trying to fulfill—"

"It's you four," Therin said. "Galava explained it to me. But why would Vol Karoth want *you*?"

Valathea's mouth dropped open. "By the Veils. S'arric. I remember when you—" She blinked, shocked almost beyond words. "*You're* S'arric? Galava reincarnated *S'arric*? *How?*"

Therin looked over at her. "Was that supposed to answer my question? Because it didn't."

I shook my head and started mouthing *no*—I really didn't want to explain this.

"It's, uh . . . S'arric was, uh . . ." Valathea bit her lip. "Someone I worked with a long time ago. How did–" She paused, cocked her head. "How could this even be possible? I thought S'arric was still imprisoned inside the Blight. Imprisoned . . . along . . . with Vol Karoth."

Neither myself, Janel, nor Teraeth answered. I mean, where would one even start?

So naturally, Thurvishar took this as his cue to begin the lecture.

"Oh, it's fascinating," Thurvishar said. "S'arric's souls were freed–or really excised–from Vol Karoth's–"

"Thurvishar, you don't need to explain this," I said.

"Oh no," Valathea said. "I want to know."

Thurvishar cleared his throat. "S'arric's souls were freed by Elana Kandor, who sent S'arric on to the Land of Peace, where he slowly healed and eventually volunteered–as we all did–to be reborn and help fight this battle against Vol Karoth. But despite the fact that he's mortal now, there are lingering 'echoes' of his previous connection with Vol Karoth, which is intriguing."

"Volunteered *as you all did*?" Valathea's sharp eyes raked across us. "And who were the rest of you? Anyone I'd have heard of?"

"Nope," Teraeth and I said at the exact same time.

Valathea turned and looked at her husband.

Doc's mouth twisted. He gestured toward his son. "Khaemezra's sense of humor at play. Meet Atrin Kandor, my dearest."

"I'm not Kandor," Teraeth snapped. "Atrin Kandor died a long time ago."

My father's eyes widened as someone finally mentioned a name he recognized. Meanwhile, Valathea pursed her lips and contemplated her stepson before her vision focused on Janel. "So." She tilted her head. "You must be C'indrol."

Janel straightened. "What?"

"Ah, too far back. My mistake. Elana Kandor, then."

Valathea wasn't in a good position to see the way her husband's eyes widened, any expression momentarily locked away. He immediately began studying the carriage wall just over Thurvishar's head.

Janel was clenching her fists so hard, I feared she might cut into her own palms. "Yes," she said. "I was Elana."

"I suppose there's a kind of poetic justice to that." Valathea looked at Thurvishar. "And you?"

Teraeth frowned at the wizard as well. "It just occurred to me I don't know who you used to be."

"You never asked." Thurvishar chuckled. "Simillion."

"Simillion?" Janel blinked. "Seriously? The first Emperor of Quur? *That* Simillion?"

"That's the one. Your classic god-king tale of the farm boy who survives his family's massacre, finds a magic sword, and kills a bunch of evil god-kings with it before founding his own kingdom. Which he rules with a noble and generous heart." Thurvishar's mouth twisted. "Except in my version, I was murdered by the people I'd just saved, who dragged my body through the streets and turned that kingdom into the Empire of Quur." He looked me right in the eyes and said, "It turns out you don't automatically get a happy ending just because you're the hero of the story."

I felt like all the air had been sucked from the carriage. That was the moment, the very exact moment, that I realized something, and I knew it down to my toes.

I wasn't going to get a happy ending either.

Teraeth and Janel might finally work out their differences, be happy, grow old, have a mess of kids if they felt like it. Hell, Thurvishar would probably swing something like a happy ending, although in his case, there'd probably be fewer children and more libraries. But me? Inextricably linked by my very souls with a god/monster/thing so virulent, Vol Karoth's mere presence killed anyone near and made reality itself shrivel and flake away? Oh, there'd be no happy ending for me. My brother Relos Var had *fucked* me.

If I was lucky–if I was lucky and good and a lot smarter than my enemies gave me credit for–there might be an end. The kind of end without which there would be no happy endings for anyone else ever again.

I looked Thurvishar in the eyes and knew the other man understood. He knew what I was thinking. Exactly what I had just realized.

And he wasn't going to tell me I was wrong.

Valathea turned to Thurvishar. "Then we've met before as well. I knew Simillion. We fought side by side against King Nemesan."

I laughed bitterly. "You knew *all* of us, didn't you?"

"More than you realize or remember." The former queen of the Kirpis vané leaned back against the carriage cushions and smiled. "That makes this quite the reunion, then, doesn't it? I do believe I'm going to enjoy this."

"At least someone will," Teraeth muttered under his breath.

And no one spoke for a long time after that, each of us lost in our own thoughts. A whole carriage full of brooders, we were. Aunt Tishar would have scolded each and every one of us.

Eventually, the cadence of the carriage ride changed as it slowed and finally pulled to a stop.

The driver knocked on the roof.

"Oh good. After all this, I'm quite anxious to–" Valathea's voice trailed away as Doc opened the door.

We were next to a large lake, although if someone had told me this was a sea, I'd have believed them. An enormous sheet of teal reflected the sky above, so large that small waves lapped against the shore. A beautiful house had been built out over the water. But of course, that wasn't what made my stomach sink.

The archers did that. They surrounded us.

And they'd clearly been waiting.

# 44: Waking the Dragon

***(Grizzst's story)***

By the time Grizzst finished, the dragon was gone.

Or at least, Rev'arric didn't look like a dragon anymore. And because even Grizzst's dickishness had limits, he didn't force Rev'arric's shape to look radically different from his original body. Grizzst figured that would start their relationship on entirely the wrong foot. It wouldn't have been worth the laugh.

Well, probably wouldn't have been worth the laugh. Grizzst still didn't think it was fair for the bastard to be that smart *and* that good-looking.[1]

Grizzst took Rev'arric back to the tower, an enchanted piece of feldspar Grizzst had raised from a hot-spring lake millennia ago. He was fond of the place. In part, this was because it sat within the god-queen Dana's territory, who was almost tolerable for a god-queen, but also because no one bothered him there. The locals believed ghosts haunted the lake. Which was true from a certain perspective.

The dragon-trapped-in-a-man's-body didn't make any comment when Grizzst brought him inside. His gaze was unfocused; he didn't look *at* things as much as *through* them.

In hindsight, it had been foolish to think fusing the dragon with his Cornerstone would be enough to erase the last thirteen hundred years of mind-altered existence.

Grizzst rummaged around his main workroom until he found his favorite teapot. He wasn't used to having guests, so he even washed it before using it. He pulled out the brandy he'd been saving for a special occasion too.

Rev'arric pulled the cloak around him as he sat. Books and papers littered every surface, spilling out of bookshelves and used as impromptu tables. Grizzst didn't waste time contemplating his housekeeping skills.

[1] The implication here is that Relos Var has purposefully chosen to, in later years, look like someone nondescript and unremarkable. Which sounds like him.

He set the teapot, cups, and brandy bottle on a table before he pushed a stack of papers off a chair and pulled it around.

Grizzst sat down face-to-face with the man who'd doomed the world.

He had blue eyes. Grizzst wondered if Rev'arric had always had blue eyes and Grizzst had just never noticed. Probably. Most voras had red eyes, but that was solidarity and racial pride, not any insurmountable rule. It wasn't so difficult to change one's eye color. Vordreth had dark eyes, and voramer had silver eyes for similar reasons. Vané had . . . well, vané had whatever vané wanted to have. Fickle bastards.

Neither one spoke. Grizzst poured two cups of tea, added a generous dollop of brandy to one, and then handed it to Rev'arric.

Rev'arric drank the contents of the cup in one go. Either his draconic or voras nature meant he didn't notice the water was still scalding hot.

Rev'arric's hand fell to his lap. He stared straight ahead, stared at nothing.

Grizzst caught the teacup before it hit the ground.

"Rev'arric," Grizzst said. "Come on, asshole. I know you're in there. Wake up."

The man blinked and didn't answer.

Grizzst leaned over and snapped his fingers in front of Rev'arric's face.

No response.

Grizzst slapped him. Hard.

No response.

"Well, shit," Grizzst said. He slammed his hand against a table before leaning back. This hadn't been the plan. How long had he spent tracking this bastard down? And for what?

He'd had better luck trying to resurrect the Eight. At least that hadn't gotten his hopes up with false success.

They sat like that for the rest of the day, before Grizzst finally pulled the man-shaped dragon to his feet and put him to bed.

A month passed. Every day, Grizzst pulled Rev'arric from bed in the morning and put him back to bed at night. Grizzst fed him, dressed him, and cleaned him, no worse than other distasteful tasks he'd performed over the years. And still Rev'arric gave no sign he intended to engage with the world.

Which meant Grizzst had given up his favorite Cornerstone for nothing.

He set Rev'arric down beside a window while he debated his options. That debate mostly entailed pacing back and forth while he racked his brain for anyone else who could help. Maybe Dana, but he was loath to admit to anyone what he'd done. She wouldn't approve. Who would?

Then one day, he heard Rev'arric mumble something.

Grizzst turned around. "What was that?"

"Where's S'arric?" Rev'arric asked, louder.

Grizzst twisted his mouth to the side. "Oh, well, isn't this just going to be a fucking fantastic conversation."

Rev'arric blinked. "Who are you?"

"Grizzst."

Rev'arric actually looked at him that time, tilting his head. "Who?"

"A nobody," Grizzst elaborated. "An assistant spell engineer working at the Lesinuia power station, or at least I used to be. I suppose I became 'somebody' when I managed to survive your bullshit. Would you like breakfast? The village near here makes a mean spiced jam." He gestured toward a stack of flatbread, a bowl of honey, and a jar of minced spiced fruit. A plate and a knife sat next to them on a cleared-off section of rough-hewn table.

Rev'arric paid no attention to the introduction. "I don't remember what happened. I don't–"

Grizzst wasn't in the mood to be gentle. "What happened is you fucked up. You fucked up bad."

Rev'arric stared at Grizzst sideways. "No."

"*Yes.* Thanks to you, the Eight Guardians are gone, the rest of our people have an expected life span of around eighty years–if they're *lucky*–and voras civilization has collapsed like a ripped balloon. And your brother is . . ." Grizzst chuckled. "Hell, dead doesn't quite cover it. And as for you . . . do you even know what you are now?"

"I don't–" Rev'arric visibly shuddered and fell silent. He was about to slip right back into noncommunicative mode.

Grizzst had no intention of letting that happen.

He crouched down next to the "man." "So I'm curious what the fuck you were thinking, you know? I looked through your notes. Now I dropped out of university, but I still know basic ritual safety protocols. You, though? You went straight from theory to implementation. Who *does* that? Who does that and doesn't expect it to all go to shit?"

Rev'arric's eyes went from wide and shocked to narrow and furious in a split second. Then he growled, rose to his feet, grabbed Grizzst, and threw the man so hard he flew across his workshop and smashed halfway through the opposite wall.

"How dare you!" Rev'arric snarled. "I *couldn't* test my work. The Preceptors were revoking my access. I didn't have time for tests!"

"Oh. You're awake now. Good." Grizzst picked himself up and popped his dislocated shoulder back into place. Same one as back in the mountain too. He hoped it wasn't a trend. "But just between you and me, you should have taken the time."

Rev'arric rubbed his hand across his face. "Leave me."

"It's my workshop, so no. I don't think I will."

Rev'arric walked to the door. "Fine. I'll leave."

Grizzst turned his back to the dragon while he repaired the damage, pulling stones back into place. Over his shoulder, he called out, "Don't you want to know what happened to your brother?" He didn't check to see if Rev'arric stopped.

He didn't have to.

Rev'arric said, "I assumed . . ."

Grizzst looked back then. "Yeah?"

Rev'arric's gaze grew distant. "Since the ritual . . . deviated . . . from the expected result, I assumed he'd likewise . . . transformed."

"That's one way of putting it." Grizzst finished setting the final stone back into place. Then, knowing he had a captive audience, at least for a few minutes, Grizzst found his teapot and started making a new batch.

Rev'arric waited. To a point. "How would you put it, then?"

"Oh, well, he's not a dragon." Grizzst set the water to boiling with a finger snap and added his favorite tea, a wonderfully creamy floral variety he snuck into Laragraen to steal every few months.

A deep sigh from Rev'arric. "Then what is he?"

"Dead."

"Impossible." Rev'arric stalked back in his direction. "I made him unkillable."

"Oh, well, his body's unkillable. Sure. His body is playing permanent host to the avatar of annihilation, an eternally hungry, remorseless demon god who does nothing but consume: other demons, gods, reality itself, kittens. He doesn't really seem to care what's on the dinner plate. S'arric, though? S'arric's dead. I know what you were trying to do with your brother, but what you ended up with instead was a man-shaped black hole."

Rev'arric stared at him in horror. "You know nothing!" He turned away.

Grizzst waited it out. He had no desire to get into a debate with Rev'arric. He'd lose, even if he was right. That bastard was twisty with words. Grizzst hunted around for his teacups, washed them, and heated the ceramic to the right temperature.

Grizzst had almost finished steeping the tea when Rev'arric asked, "Out of curiosity, just what do you think I was trying to do with my brother?"

Grizzst shrugged. "Isn't it obvious?"

Rev'arric's gaze intensified, and then he scoffed. "No, it's not. And frankly, I doubt an 'assistant spell engineer' could even begin to comprehend my goals."

Grizzst put a hand to his neck and stretched to the side, cracking his spine. He exhaled in boredom. "Sure, Professor. Whatever you say."

"I'm wasting my time here." Rev'arric looked about to run again. That hadn't taken long.

Grizzst rolled his eyes. "You were trying to seal the Nythrawl Wound."

Once more, Rev'arric paused.

Grizzst continued, "Bet you figured the Eight wouldn't volunteer to suicide themselves for the good of the universe, so you were going to strip their powers away using blood relatives as proxies. Then you'd funnel all that vast cosmic tenyé into your brother, who you were setting up to contain it all, and then use the control link you made with his souls to puppet him into the Wound and close it from the other side." Grizzst smirked at the shocked look Rev'arric didn't manage to hide. "Like I said: *obvious*. Even for an assistant spell engineer who dropped out of college."

A long pause filled all the gaps in the room.

"If you think that's what I intended," Rev'arric finally said, "why would you cure me?"

"That's not a denial," Grizzst pointed out.

"Nor is it confirmation. I asked a question," Rev'arric growled. "Answer it."

"Oh well." Grizzst poured the tea, went to add more brandy, realized he was out, and threw the brandy bottle over his shoulder, where it rolled under a chair. He took his cup and sat down. Then he sprawled out, using a stack of books as a footrest, elbow on a table. "I cured you because your little ritual should have worked."

Rev'arric blinked. "Clearly, it didn't."

"Yeah, but it *should* have." Grizzst raised his cup of tea in a mock salute. "I went over every inch of your notes. Practically memorized them. I couldn't figure out where you'd screwed up the magic. Which is annoying, because it would have served you right if you'd dropped a glyph. But you didn't. It was perfect."

Grizzst could see Rev'arric resisting what must have been the overwhelming urge to say, "Of course it was." He could tell it took a real effort.

Instead, Rev'arric wandered over to the food and made a roll with the bread and jam. "I thought you said I'd fucked up."

"Oh, you did. You wouldn't have failed the ritual if you hadn't attempted it in the first place. Karolaen would still exist. The voras people would still exist. But the mechanics of the ritual itself weren't the problem. I'd bet you every rock in my lucky rock bowl it was the demons who corrupted what you were doing–those assholes were the problem."

"Demons . . ." Rev'arric paused, still holding up a knife loaded with spiced fruit. His eyes went distant again and stayed that way. The knife tumbled from his fingers.

"Oookay, we're not doing this again." Grizzst hopped from his seat and snapped his fingers in front of Rev'arric's face. The man blinked and focused. "Stay with me, Var."

Rev'arric set both hands on the table, visibly unsteady. "That's not my name."

"Yeah, well, trust me when I say your name can reliably be used in place of your favorite curse word from Tiga to Vela." Grizzst shrugged. "Anyway, we're not nearly intimate enough for me to use your personal name, and Rev'arric's a mouthful. So I'm calling you Var. Don't like it? Complain to my section boss. Oh wait, you can't. She's dead now thanks to you."

"She died in the explosion?" Rev'arric's eyes went unfocused again.

"No. Old age."

That particular fact brought a frown to Rev'arric's face. "What? How is that even possible? No one dies of old age. That hasn't happened since we came to this universe–"

"Oh no, I told you about this. Voras age just like I'm told we used to do back in 'in the old country.'[2] You see, after Vol Karoth–"

"Who?"

Grizzst rolled his eyes. "That's what everyone calls your brother, S'arric, now. Vol Karoth. The King of Demons? See why I think the demons have something to do with this? The *demons* call him that. Like they elected him president for life. Which is funny, 'cause he sure does like eating demons. Maybe they think that's just good leadership? Anyway, when the fallout settled, first thing your brother did was kill the rest of the Eight Guardians. Then he started killing everyone else. *Killing* might not be the right word. *Destroying* everything else. Finally, the voras Assembly worked up a ritual to imprison him, but what they used to power it"–he made a face–"aligned the voras with this universe fully, made everyone mortal."

"What? Why would they . . . ?" Rev'arric rubbed a thumb into his temple. "Of course. The tenyé yield of all that lost potential."

"Right. Incredibly big power surge. But now, as far as this universe is concerned, the voras here are full natives. We get treated just like all the other native species." He paused. "I mean, *they* do."

Rev'arric stood there considering that information. He returned to fixing the roll, then began eating it. The whole time, Grizzst just drank his tea, watched, and waited.

[2] I have on several occasions encountered this sort of reference, indicating we are not natives to this world but rather immigrants.

"And why are you still alive again?"

Grizzst shrugged. "After the cataclysm, I took up scavenging. Lots of us did. I just happened to be the lucky idiot who found this particular sword washed up on a beach. Made anyone who held it immune to magic." He didn't respond to Rev'arric's quickly concealed reaction, but he sure as hell noticed. "I actually had some morals back then, so I turned it in. Figured some brave fool could use it to keep Vol Karoth at bay while the Assembly did their ritual. Only turns out I'd volunteered myself to be the fool."

"Who could have predicted it?"

Grizzst ignored him. "So there I was, holding the damn sword when the ritual fired off and wiped out the brightest and best the voras had to offer. Didn't affect me at all."

"Naturally," Rev'arric said dryly. "You're hardly the brightest and best."

"Hey, fuck you. I was good enough to fix you, wasn't I?"

"I believe that stands as proof of your foolish bravery, not your intelligence."

"Hey, asshole, the correct response was: *Thank you.*"

"Fine," Rev'arric said, notably not saying, "Thank you." "But you haven't answered why you fixed me. I appreciate you recognizing the ritual should have worked, but *should have* and *did* live on different planets. And since I cannot imagine you've brought me back just because you're lonely and seek someone who understands the importance of basic hygiene and housekeeping, perhaps you might come to a point?"

"Hey, I bathed last week."

"And cleaned house last century."

"Feh, that's not true." Grizzst swung his arm, nearly knocking over a pile of books. "I cleaned up the place eighty years ago. Besides, I know where everything is."

"Who *hurt* you?"

Grizzst glared.

Rev'arric sighed. "Yes. I suppose I do know the answer to that question."

Grizzst stood up. "Anyway, yeah, I have a point. My *point* is that I've spent the last thirteen hundred years aiming at a single goal. One purpose. Only nothing's worked. Nothing. I've tried everything I can think of. I've tried things I knew couldn't possibly succeed. And I'm officially out of ideas. So I figured since you're the smartest asshole I know, you could take a stab at it. Because you owe me, and because I think you're going to hate what's happening to our people as much as I do. You may be an arrogant bastard, but no one can say you don't *care.*"

Rev'arric's expression turned wary. "And what problem is this?"

"Bringing the Eight Guardians back to life."

Rev'arric laughed, just once, loud and mocking. "Oh, I don't think so."

"Oh, well, you'd better start thinking so, Var, because we need them. We're running out of time. Vol Karoth's not going to stay imprisoned forever. His cage is eroding. And quite frankly, no matter how you feel about your first creations, they're a hell of a lot better than the god-kings."

Rev'arric stopped and blinked.

"What," he asked, "in all the Twin Worlds is a *god-king*?"

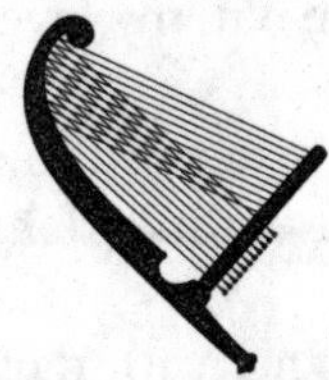

# 45: The House by the Lake

*"Okay, I take it back," Kihrin said. "Grizzst wrote that. Relos Var wouldn't want to come off as that much of an arrogant jerk. Whereas Grizzst would think describing himself that way was hilarious."*

*"Still, we don't know for certain," Thurvishar responded. "Which is something to keep in mind."*

***(Kihrin's story)***

After the Most Uncomfortable Carriage Ride in All History, I was happy to confront an enemy I could stab. Unfortunately, Valathea was having none of it.

She stepped from the carriage. "Put those away," she ordered whoever was outside.

I gave the others an uncertain look. It wasn't a huge leap to check for more people in the carriage, and given the open door, several archers could see us.

"If you will come this way—" a voice said.

"I'm here to see Dolgariatz. Is he here? Because if not, I'll just be on my way."

Another voice, male: "Valathea? Stars, is that really you?"

"Rather shocking, I know, but yes."

"I just never thought . . . I mean—"

Valathea laughed. "What, you thought you'd never see me again just because of a death sentence? I believe the Law of Daynos applies here."

The man laughed. "Of course. Relax, my friends. Valathea is my honored guest."

"Archers, Dolgariatz?" Valathea said. "Really?"

"There have been some . . . troubles. You are always welcome here. This is your home, after all. I have only been borrowing it."

"I'm completely in your debt. Also, I need someone to unload the carriage. Please be careful with the harp." Valathea tapped on the door and looked back inside. "Come out, my lovelies. I've someone you should all meet."

Thurvishar shrugged and stepped outside. I followed and then smiled to myself when Teraeth didn't offer Janel a hand down this time. He was learning.

Dolgariatz was a Manol vané, with dark indigo skin and silver hair braided with matching dark blue ribbons. As expected, he was beautiful, dressed in gossamer black silk robes embroidered with tiny silver stars. Crystals shimmered from chains hanging from his wrists and also from a decorated pectoral on his chest. One could easily miss the jewel-like mail hauberk and matching sword.

He raised an eyebrow at Doc. "Mithraill? It has been centuries. Where did you go?"

"Quur," Doc answered. "And I'm not Mithraill."

I could only assume Doc used Chainbreaker, because Dolgariatz's eyes widened. "What? No, what–?"

"Gari,[1] this is my son, Teraeth, and his friends Kihrin, Janel, and Thurvishar. And this is my friend Therin. You already know my wife." Doc was fighting a smile.

I waved.

Valathea claimed a stunned Dolgariatz's hand. "This is Dolgariatz, everyone. One of my dearest friends." She raised an eyebrow. "Even if he did switch sides on me."

"No, you cannot fault me for that. Kirpis winters are too cold." Dolgariatz looked at us, and his expression changed almost imperceptibly as he took in the prison garb, the guard uniforms. His gaze lingered on me.

"Well," Dolgariatz said. "Any friends and family of Valathea and Terindel are welcome here. Perhaps you would come inside and refresh yourselves? Have something to eat?"

Behind me, Janel whispered, "That depends. Will it be drugged?"

I fought to keep a straight face. "Thank you. We'd all like that."

The cottage looked small–much too small to hold all the soldiers roaming the grounds. Those soldiers had started slipping into the nearby jungle or positioning themselves behind bushes or trees near the shore. Their skills at hiding were impressive. So much so I suspected magic was involved.

Maybe we'd missed a larger building? Or maybe the cottage wasn't what it appeared.

Dolgariatz motioned for us to follow him as he walked past a wooden deck perfect for fishing or sitting down or whatever one did by a lake.

[1] I assume this is Dolgariatz's nickname?

Neither Doc nor Valathea gave a sign anything was amiss. I decided to give Dolgariatz the benefit of the doubt—for the moment.

My father caught up to me. "We need to talk," he whispered.

"Oh yeah. I would say so."

"I'm sorry," he said.

I almost tripped. "What was that?"

"I should have believed you. About everything. I'm sorry I didn't."

He kept walking, while I stopped and stared at him until Teraeth caught my arm. "Come on. Time for that later. I'm especially looking forward to the awkward family chats."

I laughed. "Liar."

"Do you think slitting my throat would be a good excuse?" Teraeth said pleasantly. "I'm prepared to find out."

"Don't." I punched Teraeth's arm. "Thaena's too busy to Return you, you know."

"Aww, but it's so tempting." Teraeth eyed his father. "Come on, I suppose. Food does sound nice."

Once we turned the corner, I saw the cottage wasn't a cottage at all. It was a three-sided cover for a ramp and a stairway leading under the lake.

"I thought the vané liked to live . . . you know . . ." I pointed up.

"In trees," Teraeth finished. "Above ground. Way above ground."

Valathea must have heard us. "That's what made this such a scandal. When you've lived as long as I have, one occasionally longs for novelty."

The tunnel looked spacious, with elegant stairs sweeping down to a well-lit corridor.

Double doors sat at the end of the stairs.

Dolgariatz turned around. "Please do not be alarmed. Trust me when I say what is behind this door is perfectly, completely safe."

"That's never a statement to inspire confidence," Teraeth said.

Dolgariatz grinned and pushed open the doors.

Another hallway lay behind, but only the floor was opaque. The glass walls and ceiling created the illusion of walking through water.

Doc said, "I honestly didn't expect this to still be here."

"You've kept this in wonderful condition," Valathea said. "I'm so pleased." She began walking down the corridor, gliding her hand across the glass, before she turned back. "This is quite safe, my lovelies."

"This is quite *gorgeous,*" Teraeth said as everyone followed.

The sunlight refracted through the water, casting floating shadows on the floor. Swimming fish added their own lazy shapes across the ground as they swam their daily routines. If I looked closely, I could see the seams, a thin metal mesh holding each pane. It all seemed . . . delicate. Beautiful, but fragile. It was lovely—as long as I didn't give too much thought to how much water floated above us or how this tunnel was five hundred years old.

I hurried through the corridor.

The flowing shadows continued past the end of the tunnel, meaning glass also encased the next room. Fantastic. I wondered if the whole house was the same way.

I walked forward. My father had stopped cold in the doorway, so I almost ran into him. "What?" I looked past him.

Dappled shadows, silk, and velvet-covered divans filled an elegant lounging area. A vané woman stood as we entered, wineglass still in her hand. Her skin wasn't as dark as Teraeth's or Doc's, but no one would think her Kirpis. Her skin had a golden sheen to it, as if she'd rubbed gold dust on herself. She dressed in a layered green silk gown embroidered with leaves. Her golden hair fell nearly to the floor.

"Therin," she said. A smile lit up her eyes.

My father turned around and left the room.

"Therin, wait!" She set down the glass and rushed to follow him. And then stopped as if a leash had snapped taut. "Kihrin?"

I didn't recognize her, but her voice seemed familiar. Then I realized why–she sounded like my mother. No. Not *sounded* like. I didn't know what to say. I didn't know how to react. I stared. This woman had murdered Galen, my nephews and nieces, every extended family member . . . if she didn't look anything like my mother, I still knew her identity. My father's reaction had proved that much.

But even as she reacted to my presence, her focus remained on Therin. As she started to push her way past us, Doc grabbed her arm. "Give him some space, niece. Also, if you enchant his mind again, I'll kill you."

Khaeriel stared at Doc for a beat before her eyes widened in recognition. "Ah. The whole family. Is my brother here too?"

"He wasn't invited."

"Let go of me," Khaeriel demanded.

I cleared my throat. Terindel sighed and let her go. "I'm serious. He'll find you when he's ready."

"Yes," Khaeriel said. "That is exactly my concern."

# 46: City of Snakes

***(Grizzst's story)***

The two men stood on a hill overlooking a city. The surrounding lush green jungle foliage thrived in the hot, damp air. Vines crawled over the black volcanic basalt buildings, covered with statues of serpents and a surprising quantity of flowers. The serpent theme continued from the diamond-like scales on roofs to the supports winding their way around towers. Giant lizards, not horses, drew the carts and wagons.

Even so, a city was a city was a city, full of wealth and poverty and people trying to live their lives. Prostitutes and gamblers, merchants and holy men. Grizzst waited for his companion to catch on to the fact they weren't just seeing a crowd of people wearing masks.

Rev'arric gasped. "Those aren't human."

"Sure they are," Grizzst said. "They used to be voras. Call themselves *thriss* now. Their souls are the same as any human's. They just happen to be humans with snake heads. And *this* is the problem with god-kings."

"Explain," Rev'arric demanded through gritted teeth.

"Easy enough," Grizzst said. "After the ritual went bad, well, everything else did too. The winter didn't end for a decade, the demons attacked wherever and whenever they liked, and after the Assembly locked up Vol Karoth, nobody lived past a century. But some spellcrafter from the old days cracked the code. She discovered how to become a passive receiver for tenyé. People could donate small amounts of tenyé. No big deal if just one or two did it, but when thousands did it, suddenly she was powerful enough to matter. Not as powerful as a Guardian, but powerful enough to fight off the demons. Keep the plants and animals alive. The answer to all our prayers, which was kind of the problem. What resembled prayer turned into the real thing."

"And the snakes?"

"They're just snakes." Grizzst shrugged. "The local god-king here is a fellow named Ynis, and he likes snakes. But when you're this powerful, when your people worship you as a god, why wouldn't you stick to a theme? You don't even want to know what Khorsal's done to his worshippers–he likes *horses*."

"Who devised this obscenity?" Rev'arric's distaste was so profound, Grizzst contemplated the possibility they should leave before the dragon did something rash.

"Someone named Suless. Heard of her?"

"No, I–" Rev'arric's eyes widened. "Wait. Su'less?"

"Yeah, that's the one. Nobody uses the apostrophes these days. Anyway, word spread of how she'd done it; any wizard strong enough to copy her did. Might have worked out except–"

"Power corrupts?"

"Yeah," Grizzst said. "And bodies can only hold so much tenyé at a time. That's the whole reason I haven't been able to bring the Guardians back. Their tenyé destroys any body I use to resurrect them. So the god-kings create these little projects to clear the excess out. Might be good stuff like making really hearty strains of rice. Might be stuff like, 'Hey, let's give my worshippers snake heads.'" He waved an arm toward the city.

"This is foul," Rev'arric commented.

"Who's going to stop them, hmm?"

"You have the sword." Rev'arric made it an accusation.

"I call it *Godslayer,*" Grizzst said.

Rev'arric scoffed. "Then why aren't you using it that way?"

"Because an immunity to magic doesn't mean much against armies, arrows, and swords. Plus, the god-kings are the only thing protecting us from the demons these days. I don't dare kill them as long as they're our only defense. Even the other races adopted the god-king idea. Maybe they don't worship their god-kings and build temples to them, but they need people powerful enough to stave off demon attacks. God-kings are powerful enough. Now do you understand why I want the Eight Guardians back?"

"I could fix all of this by taking Godslayer and using the sword for its original purpose: putting Vol Karoth into the Nythrawl Wound so he can seal it."

"That won't take care of the demons."

"Trust me. It will."

Grizzst noticed Rev'arric had no problem calling his brother *Vol Karoth.* Probably he liked distancing himself from the reminder of who that creature had once been. "I've been to the Nythrawl Wound, Var. It's not growing so fast matters can't wait a few thousand years. Whereas you haven't seen Vol Karoth. You think you can control him with that sword? I'm not so confident. And if you're wrong? None of us will live long enough to be worried about the damn Nythrawl Wound. Safety protocols, Var. That's why we need the Eight."

"You said he killed the Eight."

"He took them by surprise. They thought he was their friend. This time, they'll be ready for him." Grizzst waved his hand toward the city. "Besides, they can help with this. Or are you fine with what the god-kings are doing to our people?"

"No, of course not." Rev'arric stared out at the city, scowling. "And as much as I want to dismiss this as unimportant compared to the Nythrawl Wound and Vol Karoth, I'm not sure that's true. Do you have any idea what powers the god-kings are tampering with? Damnably, Su'less is smart enough to follow the research to its logical conclusion. That may be worse than these other dangers."

"Yeah, I just said–" Grizzst paused. "What do you mean, 'logical conclusion'?"

Rev'arric's lip curled. "Some avenues of exploration are too dangerous to be pursued.[1] Never mind. Forget I said anything." He turned to face the other man. "You're right. I owe you this much; I'll look through your test notes. Maybe I'll notice something you missed. I'm not fond of the Guardians, but even the worst of them would never stoop to this–" He flicked his fingers back toward the city.

"Okay," Grizzst said. "Excellent. Let's go." He rubbed his hands together and started walking toward the city.

"Wait," Rev'arric said. "Why are we heading into the city?"

"Huh?" Grizzst looked back. "Oh, because I'm out of wine. If we're going to go over all five thousand, three hundred, and seventy-two attempts, we're going to need more booze."

[1] Coming from Relos Var, that's saying something.

# 47: The Nature of Souls

***(Kihrin's story)***

I'd grown so used to every act of vané hospitality leading to an ambush, I found it difficult to enjoy Dolgariatz's generosity.

He hadn't skimped either. Guests had their own dedicated wing of the underwater lake house. Several walls of the room were made of glass, cleverly angled so no suite directly viewed into any other suite. Our rooms were complete with sunken baths and working plumbing, the beds so large we could have all shared the same one, had we chosen. So while everyone went off to rest and freshen themselves after traveling, Janel and Teraeth ended up in my room. It didn't feel planned as much as the inevitable result of none of us wanting to be left alone.

"I'm–" I pointed to the tub. "I really should go take a bath," I announced and felt a bit silly for doing so.

"Right." Janel blinked at the room as if wondering how she'd ended up there. Her gaze flickered over to Teraeth, back to me, then she abruptly left. The room grew quiet.

Teraeth could have made a sarcastic joke at my expense. "Looks like she's not for you either" seemed like the obvious and easy retort. He didn't.

I was so glad he didn't.

Instead, he asked, "Everything okay between you two?"

Which was the big question, wasn't it? I reminded myself to talk to Janel alone so we could sort it all out. Then I remembered Teraeth waited on an answer.

"I don't know," I said, because I didn't see the point in lying. I exhaled and shook my head. "I really just don't know."

"And us?"

The world spun; I felt unmoored. Also a hell of a question. I met Teraeth's green eyes. "Same," I said.

His face held no expression at all. "When you figure it out, let us know." Then he left too.

I was left standing there, trying to pull my pounding heartbeat back under control.

Someone knocked at the door. I raced to it, hoping either Teraeth or Janel had returned. Instead, I found a vané I assumed was either a servant or someone else living at the house.

He smiled and set my harp on the ground. "Founder Valathea said this was yours." Without waiting for my response, he retreated.

Bemused, I picked up the harp and brought it back into the room.

"I'm going to need to figure out a new name for you," I told it. "It would be pretty weird to keep calling you *Valathea* under the circumstances." I checked the tuning; the harp needed it desperately. It had never needed tuning before. Not ever. A sign, I supposed, that it was just a normal harp now. I made adjustments until I remembered my priorities–namely, taking a bath, shaving, and eating a meal that wouldn't be drugged. I hoped.

I wanted to linger in the bath, but I found I couldn't control my thoughts while I did. I found myself traveling roads ending in emotional destinations varying from awkward to terrifying. So I bathed quickly.

When I finished, Dolgariatz or someone in his employ had laid out several over-the-top, very vané outfits for me. Why wouldn't you provide a houseguest with ridiculously luxurious attire? I found some of the outfits uncomfortably revealing, not meant for public display. Although given what I knew of vané sexual proclivities, I couldn't discount the possibility the vané made no distinction.

I flashed back to my first days with House D'Mon, wearing clothing I could've sold to feed myself and my adoptive father, Surdyeh, for a year.

Some of the clothing proved eminently more practical: several fine shanathá mail shirts with matching swords. Sort of refreshing, honestly. My host evidently found it only polite to give me the proper attire for whatever situation I might find myself in: dinner, orgy, or war. If I had anything to say about it, I'd only need that first one.

I'd just finished dressing when I heard a second knock at the door.

"Come in," I called out, still hoping it would be Teraeth or Janel.

Instead, Thurvishar stepped inside. The Quuros wizard had changed from his mysteriously acquired black clothing to a set of layered silk coats, each a different shade of brown, starting with a shimmering burnt umber and ending in pale gold gossamer.

"I'm not sure I can handle seeing you in a color besides black," I admitted. "Although brown, so still neutral."

"I'd look fantastic in orange," Thurvishar said. "It's a shame I'll forever associate it with slavery."

"Maybe one day you'll have a reason not to anymore," I said.

"That will be a pleasant day indeed." Thurvishar tilted his head as he looked at me. "Might we talk?"

I gestured to a chair.

Thurvishar took a seat. "About what happened in the carriage . . ."

I sat down opposite him. "You didn't say anything untrue."

Thurvishar studied me. "I think both Janel and Teraeth are too blinded by their personal feelings for you to see the larger picture."

"Their personal feelings–?" I stopped as Thurvishar gave me *that* look.

"Please," Thurvishar said. "Just because I have no interest in that dance doesn't mean I'm blind to the way you three are stepping around each other."

I winced. "Right. Of course."

Thurvishar continued. "Teraeth and Janel aren't interested in performing the Ritual of Night to imprison Vol Karoth. They want to perform the Ritual of Night to keep *you* safe."

"Yeah, I caught that," I said. "But what can we do? And I'm not asking rhetorically. Is there a different solution?"

"We need more information," Thurvishar said.

I leaned forward in my chair. "I'm listening."

Thurvishar laced his fingers together in his lap. "I don't brag of it the way Teraeth does, but I also remember my past lives."

I made a face. "How does that work, anyway? Is there a tax you have to pay, a guild fee?"

Thurvishar leaned forward. "I learned it from Gadrith."

Suddenly I wasn't laughing. I straightened. "You *what*?"

"Gadrith was many horrible things, but he was *very* good at necromancy."

"Which might be considered one of those horrible things."

He gave me a tight-lipped smile. "I refer to ousology, magic involving souls. Since his witch gift involved the ability to create tsali, his research always leaned in that direction. He discovered why we don't remember what happens to us when we return from the Afterlife, either from being Returned or being reborn."

I blinked. "Uh, I always assumed Thaena did that. At least for the being Returned bit. I mean, divine servitors remember. Teraeth remembers what happens when he's dead. And for that matter, Janel remembers too."

He nodded patiently, having clearly gone into teacher mode. "You have it backward. Allow me to explain. Our souls store everything that's ever happened to us, in any life. The sum total of our cumulative experience. But–and this is an important caveat–there is no way to transfer that information back to a physical body. When you're alive, you only remember what you've experienced with your own senses in this lifetime. Just because your soul stores the memories doesn't mean your body can access them or will *ever* access them."

"Wait, so we just keep going through our lives adding books to a library we're never allowed to read?"

"That's a fantastic metaphor for the process. I'll have to remember that–"

"Thurvishar, focus," I said.

He cleared his throat. "Yes, basically. Under normal circumstances. It's possible for someone to be forced to 'check books back out,' so to speak. Force them to imprint spiritual memories back to their physical body. It's now obvious to me the vané do exactly that when they transfer a soul to a new body at the Well of Spirals, although only with the current 'book.' That's also what happens every time an angel dies and is resurrected. Healing their body also involves restoring the memories they experienced while dead. Since no one did that to you when you were Returned, you don't remember what happened while you were dead–at least, you shouldn't."

"Okay, but what about Janel? She isn't anyone's servitor, and she always remembers what happens to her in the Afterlife."

"Janel's case is interesting. Let's return to her later. Normally, this 'memory recovery' can only be accomplished by a second party, but Gadrith figured out how to do it *to himself.* He further refined the ability to remember his past lives as well. I learned the technique from him." Thurvishar paused. "I suspect he didn't intend to teach it to me, but I've learned a great deal of magic from him without his explicit permission."

I leaned back in my chair. "So what about Teraeth, Janel, and for that matter, me? We're all remembering our past lives, some quicker than others. Pretty sure none of us learned that trick from Gadrith."

"Indeed." A look of manic scholarly interest stole over Thurvishar's features. "None of you should be able to do this."

"And yet."

"No, seriously, I cannot emphasize enough how *none of you should be able to do this.* Janel shouldn't be able to enter the Afterlife at will and return with her memories intact. Since you were an Immortal in your past life, I suspected the rules might be different for you, but for Janel and Teraeth? No. Now, Thaena might be forcing her son to remember . . ."

"I don't think so. Teraeth commented how it surprised and irritated her that he remembers his past life." I waved a hand. "But what's your point? You think we need to fully unlock our past lives?"

His eyebrows shot up. "Oh, that's an idea." He must have seen the look on my face because he hastily answered the original question. "No, as I said in the carriage, in my past life, I was Simillion, proverbial farm boy turned hero. But he did have a mentor, someone old enough and knowledgeable enough to guide him. Mostly."

"I know this one. Grizzst the Mad, right?" These songs had been a foundational part of Surdyeh's repertoire. Grizzst had created the tools Simillion used. The old wizard had created the Crown and Scepter, as well as Urthaenriel–although I knew that latter claim was bullshit.

Oh, and Grizzst also bound the demons.

"He's not . . . He's not what the stories make him out to be."

I raised an eyebrow. "He wasn't mad?"

"Only if you mean angry. But the important detail for this discussion is that Grizzst knows more about Vol Karoth than anyone."

"I bet Relos Var would take exception to that statement."

Thurvishar smiled. "He can if he likes, but Grizzst always expressed strong opinions about Relos Var's, hmm, what did he call it? Oh yes. 'Inexcusably sloppy theoretical work and even sloppier safety standards.'"[1]

"I'm starting to like Grizzst."

"I find it odd none of the Eight have mentioned Grizzst, even though he'd be the expert on repairing the warding crystal."

I blinked. "Wait, he's still alive? I admit I used to believe him one of the Eight, but after I found out their real roster, I just assumed Grizzst was a god-king with an overblown reputation. You know, the hoary old wise man setting the hero on the path sort of thing."

"Oh no. Grizzst is . . ." Thurvishar laughed. "Not that. But my point is that when you don't know enough, the solution isn't to throw up your arms and say, 'Oh well, that's it. I can't figure it out'–you find an expert. You consult with experts. And for us, with this subject, that's Grizzst."

"Okay, I'm sold. Where do we find him?" I asked.

"I haven't a clue in all the world," Thurvishar said.

I stared at him. "So that might be a problem, don't you think?"

"Possibly, but if he follows his old habits, he'll be trackable."

"Go on."

Thurvishar's mouth quirked. "He's fond of taverns. Well, I should more accurately say he's fond of bars." He paused. "I mean brothels."

I laughed. "That does narrow it down, but do you have any idea how many velvet houses exist in the world?"

"Oh, you don't have to tell me. I believe I searched every single last one the last time I tracked down the man. I've figured out a shortcut this time. A bit unorthodox, but there's a god-king who can help us."

"A god-king of brothels?"

"Not exactly. He's new, which is shockingly rare these days. His worship has only just begun to spread into Quur." Thurvishar stood again. "We'll talk with the others. They may fight us on it, but I think we'd be

[1] Yes, yes, in hindsight perhaps Grizzst was protesting too much.

wise to find Grizzst. I realize he's not the nicest person. Or the friendliest. Or the most sanitary. But he's brilliant, and he's the only wizard operating at Relos Var's level. Only a fool would ignore him."

I nodded. "I think you're right."

# 48: Empty Glass Bottles

***(Grizzst's story)***

Rev'arric picked up the empty glass bottle, which glowed bright red, then white as it slagged molten and deformed. He shaped it, turning the glass into a glowing ball while it floated in midair. When he finished, the glass bottle was transformed into a thick glass tile. He pressed it against the tower's stone wall so it sank partway into the suddenly malleable substance.

"Are you going to do that with every bottle we finish?" Grizzst asked him. His topaz eyes looked glassy, but he only swayed a little.

"You don't throw them out," Rev'arric explained. Grizzst suspected Rev'arric was doing a much better job than he of hiding his intoxication.

They sat cross-legged in the tower basement. This area had been left free of bookcases or ornamentation, with two exceptions. A continuous inscription of carved glyphs ran from top to bottom along one wall. On the opposite wall, eight gems were set into stone. Seven of the jewels glowed, while the last rhythmically pulsed.

That last slowly blinking light had been the whole reason Grizzst had switched from his methodical experimentation to a foolhardy attempt to restore Rev'arric's sanity. That last blinking light represented the failing eighth ward on Vol Karoth's prison.

It meant he worked on borrowed time.

Rev'arric picked up an experiment summary and read it over. "Really? Sunflowers?"

"Piss off. I'd run out of ideas."

Rev'arric smirked. "It's unorthodox, I'll grant you."

"So what's this secret you think Suless might discover that's so dangerous?" Grizzst asked.

"Piss off," Rev'arric retorted. "It's better you don't know."

Grizzst started laughing. "You don't trust me!"

"I don't even like you." Rev'arric flung several pages at him. Then he started laughing at some joke only he understood.

"If I wanted to rule the world, Var, I'd have done it already and left you to go claw at mountaintops and chase gryphons. I wouldn't be trying to bring the Guardians back. I'd have made myself the damn god of wine and I'd have a temple in every bar from here to Damar-Valia. What I want most of all isn't power. It's a *vacation*."

Rev'arric stared at him. Finally, he scoffed under his breath. "One of my students," he explained. "My assistant, in fact. They developed a theory. God-kings, you see–"

"I swear to the Veil if you start explaining god-kings *back* to me . . ."

Var made a shushing motion with his hands. "It's passive. That's what I'm saying. God-kings need people to worship them, to donate tenyé, to maintain their power. My student believed that could be flipped. To *actively* absorb tenyé and do it independent of a physical body's needs."

Grizzst stopped laughing. "Wait. Wait–" He held up a finger. "Wait."

Rev'arric paused.

Grizzst stared at him.

"I'm waiting," Rev'arric said.

"Oh? Oh!" Grizzst slammed his hand to the ground. "That sounds like a demon. You just described a demon." He pointed at Rev'arric as emphasis.

"This was before the demons arrived," Rev'arric said. "Back in the early days, when we were adjusting to this world, learning its rules. Ousology was in its infancy."

Grizzst uncorked another bottle for himself. They hadn't bothered with glasses. "Before my time. I was born after the Veil ripped. So your student figured out how to become a demon? No, please tell me they didn't do that."

"No, no." Rev'arric also uncorked a new bottle and took a drink. "They listened when I told them it was too dangerous.[1] And it would be. I think it's possible, but you'd burn through incredible tenyé reserves to do the everyday tasks we take for granted." He swung his bottle by the neck. "Moving objects. Interacting with the world. Bodies are so . . . useful . . . for that. Very efficient, really."

"Plus, fun. Bodies are fun." Grizzst nodded in solemn agreement.

"Yes. That too. Anyway, sustaining that need would require massive tenyé consumption, and the trap–" Rev'arric leaned forward and lowered his voice, as though telling a secret. "The trap is someone might try to replace their lost tenyé by absorbing souls. And then it becomes an addiction."

"What? Why?"

Rev'arric gazed at him solemnly and raised a finger. "Math," he intoned.

[1] I rather suspect they did not.

"What?"

Rev'arric looked around as though expecting chalk or graphite to appear magically. "Give me that." He grabbed Grizzst's bottle.

"Hey!"

"I'll give it back." He gulped down an impressive quantity of wine.[2] Then Rev'arric poured the remaining wine into the other man's bottle before shaking his now nearly empty one. "So this bottle is me—"

"You've lost weight."

"This bottle is me," Rev'arric continued. "And the wine is my tenyé level. As you can see, it's almost empty. And even if it were full, I can only hold a bottle's worth of tenyé. Any more is wasted. Were I a demon—or one of my assistant's 'enhanced' souls—I might be tempted to attack someone else's souls for their tenyé"—he held up Grizzst's now full wine bottle—"and add it to my own." He waved a hand at the two bottles, concentrated, and watched as they slowly merged into a bottle twice the size. "But—I've doubled the size of my bottle."

"Yeah, about that—"

"I add the souls of my victim to my own, thinking it'll give me a larger capacity to hold tenyé. I'm clever, right?" Rev'arric was already shaking his head before Grizzst could answer. "No, no. I am not clever. I am stupid."

Grizzst pointed at the man, laughing. "Your words, Var."

Rev'arric actually giggled. "Okay, no. So the question . . . the question is, since I have absorbed your tenyé, is my tenyé reserve now full?"

"Of course not," Grizzst said. "You made the bottle twice as big. It's only half-full now."

"Right. Which I might interpret as 'hunger,' so I think the solution is to absorb a third person's souls. I think I'm fixing the problem, but in fact, I'm making things worse. Each person absorbed increases my capacity while diminishing my tenyé as a percentage of that total. I grow hungrier. Each time, an escalation . . ."

"That sounds like Vol Karoth," Grizzst said, no longer laughing.

"Yeah." Rev'arric stopped laughing too. "It does. Like you said, the demons corrupted the ritual." He chugged the oversize bottle before handing it back.

Grizzst rolled his eyes at the nearly empty bottle. He drained the rest, set it aside, and uncorked another one. "Yeah, how dare they interfere with you murdering your own brother and taking over the world. Rude."

Rev'arric exhaled a long, drawn-out breath and didn't respond.

[2] I don't know if he's technically a dragon when he's taken on a human shape like this, but such moments make me wonder.

"What are you going to do about that?" Rev'arric pointed to the blinking warding stone.

Grizzst gestured vaguely to the wall behind him, where the glyphs had been inscribed. "That's the Ritual of Night. It's how they charged the eighth warding crystal. I transcribed it from the working copy the Assembly created after–" He scowled. "After everyone died. Meant it to be a memorial."

Rev'arric raised both eyebrows. "That explains that. At least there's no chance you'll accidentally throw it out with the trash. If you ever threw out trash."

Grizzst ignored him. "Figured I'd make some rubbings, give 'em to the other races. Somebody's going to have to step up to be next if we can't figure out what to do about Vol Karoth before the warding crystal shuts down."

Rev'arric stood up and walked over to the wall. "I suppose you'll just substitute different racial glyphs." Rev'arric ran his fingers over several key spots. "It'll be a tragedy if they're ever needed."

Grizzst saluted with his wine bottle. "Hey, we can agree on stuff. Who knew? And this would be easier with Eight around."

"I doubt that," Rev'arric said. "They were good soldiers. The best. This solution requires more creativity." He pursed his lips. "Still, they would help with the demons. And the god-kings."

"Can you bring them back?" Grizzst contemplated sobering himself up.

"I don't know," Rev'arric admitted. "This was solid research. You were thorough."

"You must be drunk. Pretty soon, you'll admit I'm not an idiot."

"Let's not carried away," Rev'arric said. "You know, it's a pity Valathea's gone. We may not have been friends, but there was no one better at biological magics. Well, Su'less, but I'll assume she wouldn't be helpful."

Grizzst paused mid-drink. "What do you mean, 'it's a pity Valathea's gone'? You mean the Kirpis vané queen?"

"No, I mean–" Rev'arric frowned. "I expected her to have died of old age."

Grizzst looked confused. "No. What are you talking about? She's not going to grow old. She's vané. They're immortal. Four immortal races. Three now."

Rev'arric stared as if Grizzst had just told him a lie.

"No, really," Grizzst snapped. "Why wouldn't she still be alive? Last I heard, she married the Kirpis vané king."

Rev'arric cocked his head. "Kirpis vané king? That implies there's more than one."

"Because there is. But my point is she's still alive."

Rev'arric rubbed his temple. "Fine. I believe you. She's alive." He looked up and laughed.

Grizzst didn't understand what was so funny.

"I'll make you a deal," Rev'arric finally said. "I. Will. Make. You. A. Deal."

"When you say it like that, I don't think I should agree."[3]

Rev'arric laughed. "I'll help you. I won't try to free Vol Karoth yet." He sat down next to Grizzst. "I'll behave. If we succeed in resurrecting the Eight, I'll stay out of their way. I'll help you with anything you need. Research? I'm your man. Want a dragon to behave? I'll make them do so. Low profile, perfect gentleman."

Grizzst narrowed his eyes. "What's the catch?"

"There's a time limit," Rev'arric said. He pointed back to the wall. "Until the last race endures through the Ritual of Night. After that? You help me. You do what I ask. You, the Eight, Valathea–you have that long to solve both problems–the Nythrawl Wound and Vol Karoth. After that, I'm going to fix the mess the demons made."[4]

Grizzst leaned back. "Help me with anything I want?"

"I don't give sponge baths." He waved a hand at the room. "Or clean house."

Grizzst laughed but didn't otherwise respond. "So help me resurrect the Eight. Let's start there."

"Does that mean we have a deal?"

Grizzst exhaled. It would be centuries before this warding crystal failed. After that, three more races could perform the ritual and restart the clock. That meant what? Six, maybe seven thousand years?[5]

Surely, they'd find a solution by then.

"Deal," Grizzst said.

Rev'arric nodded. "Then you need to ask Valathea. I was serious about her skills. Convince her to help and she will almost certainly have useful advice. Although I would highly recommend that you never mention my name or admit to having ever met me. To say she is in all likelihood a thousand kinds of angry at me would be something of an understatement."

[3] You should've listened to your instincts, Grizzst.

[4] Oh, let's give credit where it's due. The demons may have created the Nythrawl Wound when they invaded our universe, but Relos Var is responsible for the mess named Vol Karoth.

[5] Unfortunately, Grizzst didn't calculate the fact that each use of the ritual seemed only half as effective as the one before. Even so, that left over three thousand years. It truly is embarrassing that the Eight weren't able to figure out a solution in all that time.

"Our deal was that *you* would help. What are you going to do while I'm gone?"

"Finish reading through your notes, for one. Then we'll see what we can do about fixing the world." He spread his hands and bowed in Grizzst's direction. "With proper safety protocols this time."

# 49: A Banquet of Vengeances

*Kihrin sighed loudly. "Oh, now that's a conversation it would have been nice to have known about."*

*Thurvishar nodded. "Indeed." He looked annoyed. "I still can't believe Grizzst was that gullible."*

*"Well, my brother is quite the charmer."*

***(Kihrin's story)***

"Are you saying you won't even consider helping?" Teraeth rested his weight on the table's edge as he stared at my mother. "What your brother's doing could doom us all."

I sighed, reached for a pastry, and leaned back in my chair.

Khaeriel and Therin had reached an equilibrium, but not a happy reunion. Their interactions with each other were brittle, fragile explorations onto thin, cracking ice. But at least they weren't trying to enchant or kill each other. Baby steps.

When we'd presented ourselves for lunch, I'd groaned to see a table once again laden with amazing food. Which I took to mean more haerunth porridge. Illusion or not, I never wanted to eat that stuff again. The problem wasn't the haerunth. The problem was the illusions and how they masked any other additions. Drugs, for example.

But Thurvishar (who had chosen to go without armor) blinked as he took in the lavish setting. "This is real. This is real?" He turned to Dolgariatz in surprise.

"Naturally. What do you think I am, Kirpis?" Dolgariatz smiled at Valathea. "No offense."

Valathea rolled her eyes at him.

So we sat down and ate a sublime meal of dishes I'd never eaten before, didn't know the names of, and loved with all my might. Succulent lobsterlike meats cooked in peppers so hot even I was impressed, fish fresh from the lake seared over scented woods, mushrooms soaked in aged vinegars, a wondrous selection of exotic fruits and greens and nuts of every description.

A perfect meal, except people had to ruin it all by *talking.*

It took no time at all for Teraeth and Janel to explain what had happened with King Kelanis, as well as their hope Khaeriel or Doc or somebody would lend them aid.

"Oh, not me," Doc had said. "Ask my niece for help. *I'm* not returning to the throne. Even if I could, I wouldn't want to. I'm done with crowns, thanks."

Teraeth's mouth twisted in a wry smile. "How nice–a bonding moment."

Doc snorted.

Khaeriel smiled as though she'd eaten something off. "If you want me to overthrow my brother so I will perform the Ritual of Night, I must disappoint you; I shall do no such thing."

Which is how we'd ended up in our present standoff.

I exhaled, closed my eyes, and sank back in my chair. I wanted nothing to do with this.

"Naturally, I want my brother removed," Khaeriel continued. "He assassinated me, after all, and he will answer for that. But putting myself back on the throne does not mean I will perform the Ritual of Night. Frankly, I am surprised to learn Kelanis came to his senses. While my feelings for him remain unchanged, I am gratified to learn he is something other than an idiot."

"How do you intend to get around the Law of Daynos?" Valathea asked the question with idle curiosity.

Khaeriel paused. "Honestly, I had hoped to solicit your services. If anyone can convince the Founders that a change of rules is needed, it would be you."

I sat up, refilled my wineglass, and snatched up a small sweet bundle I suspected was a grub. I didn't care; they tasted like caramels. "What's the Law of Daynos? For those of us who aren't thousands of years old."

"Thank you," Janel mouthed.

"The Law of Daynos," Dolgariatz explained, "says that while vané may have as many bodies as they like, passing from tsali to tsali, once someone truly dies and their soul goes to the Afterlife, it's legally final. Even if they are later Returned."

"The good news," Valathea said, "is that while a vané may lose assets and wealth, they also lose obligations and debts. As well as criminal judgments or . . . well . . . royal titles." She stared at Khaeriel. "You want me to argue the Stone of Shackles was a tsali transfer and not a true death."

Khaeriel nodded. "Yes. Personally, I have always considered the Law of Daynos a throwback we would do well to set aside, but I will settle for having it ruled inapplicable in my personal case."

"A little hypocritical, don't you think?" I sipped at the wine.

My mother's eyes widened. "Excuse me?"

Teraeth gave me his best "You idiot" stare and made a slicing motion across his throat. I ignored him.

I shrugged. "Your status as queen depends on royal blood you don't possess anymore. But now that you're no longer the biological offspring of Khaevatz and Kelindel, *now* royal blood doesn't mean anything? It sure did when you told me I was 'destined to rule' all those years ago."

Khaeriel turned and gave Therin such a clear "This is *your* son, do something" glare, I started laughing.

"Kihrin–" Therin frowned.

"It's a ridiculous idea." Janel let her knife and fork clatter against her plate. "Leadership and the qualities therein have nothing to do with bloodlines. The only argument to be made for the idea is that if you were raised as an heir perhaps–*maybe*–you were also educated in the skills needed to rule well."

"And thus we may assume your mother was not of noble blood," Khaeriel said.

Janel's smile turned wicked. "Why, no. She was a dancing girl."

I cleared my throat and coughed. Sometimes Janel enjoyed baiting people just a little too much. "Let's not go there."

"My lovelies," Valathea said, "what you must understand is that Terrin's line–of which we both do and do not have three generations sitting at this table–never claimed the throne because of vané belief in divine lineage. They do so because Terrin founded our nation and because the rest of us can't be bothered. We all have our hobbies. This family's hobby just happens to be *power*."

Khaeriel gave the older vané an odd look. I wonder if anyone had ever explained it to my mother like that or if her father, Kelindel, had given a different justification for their rule. Our rule, I suppose. At least by some definitions. The idea that most vané were too busy with whatever vané spent eternity doing to have any interest in politics fit with what I'd seen of the race. I could believe it.

"We're straying from the point," Teraeth grumbled.

"If the point had anything to do with the Ritual of Night," Doc said, "it's more like we abandoned it."

Valathea made a moue. "Any discussions of rituals are premature as long as Kelanis remains in charge, but do you truly want to overturn the Law of Daynos? Without it, we might hold someone responsible for sins committed in another life—isn't reincarnation, after all, just another way of being Returned?" She made a motion toward Teraeth, who looked uncomfortable.

"There's a lot more changing of diapers with the reincarnation version," Therin pointed out.

Teraeth pinched the bridge of his nose in pure exasperation. He turned back to Khaeriel. "So . . . Vol Karoth's not a concern? Not your problem? Maybe it'll help if I spell something out for you."

I straightened. "Teraeth, don't."

"They already know." Teraeth pointed at Doc, Valathea, and Therin. "It's just a matter of time before they mention it."

"Mention what?" Khaeriel gave Valathea a concerned look. "What is he talking about?"

The former Kirpis vané queen sighed. "In a conversation tangential to our discussion, it seems your son is the reincarnation of S'arric."

There was a moment of silence.

"I *still* have no idea who that is," Therin complained. "I assume you don't mean my great-uncle."

I laughed weakly.

Doc set down his goblet. "He was a god." He shook his head. "Not a god-king, mind you. S'arric was one of the Eight Immortals.[1] Your son was, in a past life, a peer to such luminaries as Thaena and Khored. S'arric, Lord of the Sun and Sky." Doc scowled at me, probably because I'd never explained any of this. He felt betrayed.

My mother let out a nervous laugh. "How would that be possible? I realize I am one of the youngest vané here, but I know the stories. The Eight Immortals are not called so trivially. My son cannot be one."

"That is not why it is impossible. It is impossible because S'arric *never died*." Dolgariatz examined me critically. "He was corrupted. What was light became darkness. What was life became death. He sits there still, in the center of the Blight, but no one calls him *S'arric* anymore." The Manol vané man crossed his arms over his chest and leaned back in his chair. "Any Manol vané knows who Vol Karoth is."

Khaeriel stopped smiling.

I sighed and drank the rest of my wine, which was outstanding.

My mother turned to me. "Is this . . . true? How could it be true?"

I sighed. "It's more complicated than all that. And . . . *god* is the wrong word. We weren't gods. Anyway, Dolgariatz isn't wrong exactly. S'arric's *physical* body is still immortal, still can't be killed. His soul,

[1] It's more than a little disingenuous for Doc to be calling S'arric by his "immortal" title here since he knows perfectly well none of the Eight were divine beings, but I suppose his goal was to shock.

though?" I thumped my chest. "Right here. Pity all the 'god' parts of that deal stayed with the original body."

Janel gave me a quick glance out of the corner of her eye, like I'd just told a lie.

I hadn't. At least, I didn't think I had.[2]

Teraeth turned back to Khaeriel. "When Vol Karoth starts roaming, you'd better believe Kihrin's the first person he's visiting. Something you might want to consider while you're telling yourself this isn't your problem and you have no 'reason' to enact the Ritual of Night." Teraeth tossed his napkin down on the table and stormed from the room.

"So dramatic." Valathea looked at Doc. "He gets that from you."

"He gets that from Khaemezra," Doc said dryly.

Valathea made a face. "Fine. He gets it from you both."

I stood up as well. "I'm going to, uh . . ." I paused and addressed Dolgariatz. "You don't happen to have a sparring room down here, do you?"

"Yes, I do," our host said. "Follow the right hallway to the end."

I bowed to the group. "Thank you for the truly exceptional meal, but if I may, I'll take my leave and go pretend to repeatedly stab Relos Var. I find it soothing." I left without waiting for a response.

Teraeth wasn't the only one who could be dramatic.

[2] And yet . . . I think it is, as he just said, "more complicated than that"–the fact that Kihrin could channel tenyé as a soul in the Afterlife has interesting ramifications. And we may need to consider redefining the definition of *demon*.

# 50: Petitioning the Vané

***(Grizzst's story)***

Grizzst approached the Kirpis forest. He came from the mountain side toward the north, mostly as a precaution. Last he'd checked, the Kirpis vané were engaged with a protracted war against the god-king Nemesan[1] to the south. Grizzst didn't expect the vané would welcome anyone who seemed "human." Thus, why he waited at the border, hoping for a peaceful entrance.

He'd been waiting for several weeks. This might have proven inconvenient if he hadn't become a reasonably competent sorcerer over the centuries.

Still, this had grown tiresome.

The vané knew he waited. He'd never visited the Kirpis, but he knew the vané had been least affected by the disaster. They still had their technology, their magical prowess, their memories, and their skill. He hated to admit Rev'arric's advice had been reasonable, but if Valathea knew all Var had claimed . . .

Unfortunately, the vané proved as unfriendly as Grizzst feared.

The forest itself was as beautiful as he'd heard. Giant redwoods soared into the clouds, with an occasional spruce or fir nestling in the gaps. The air smelled sweet with sap and sharp pine. Every so often, a deer wandered near the forest's edge, gazed at him blankly, and then wandered away again. A fox went so far as to sniff at his leg.

After several weeks of this, the vané grew tired of outwaiting him.

They attacked.

Technically, Grizzst had no warning. In reality, he had strung every bush and weed for a half mile in any direction with a fine web of tenyé-laden filaments. He knew the vané were advancing on his position long before they arrived.

He stood in a clearing, eyes closed, either asleep or deep in meditation. They had to know his occupation; no one who could see past the First Veil would miss his talismans, the way they sharpened his aura.

[1] Ruler of Laragraen, which is present-day Kazivar.

The vané had likely made certain assumptions. They certainly hadn't shown up to invite him inside for tea.

"Oh, let's not do this," Grizzst said. "I just want to talk to your leader."

They flooded the meadow with illusions in response, so powerful they clouded his sight even through his protections.

Grizzst sighed and lit the fuses he held. The fire sparked and trailed down the thin ropes he held like leashes, following the line back past grass and ferns to several dozen hidden pots, which caught fire. And then exploded into smoke clouds. Dismayed voices echoed through the trees.

He knew the vané would use magic. So he hadn't. They couldn't dispel the illusion of vision-blocking smoke because it hadn't been illusion. And he didn't wait for them to realize their mistake and summon a nice, strong breeze. So while they choked and gasped and dealt with the sudden lack of air, Grizzst attacked back.

As a truly flattering number of vané advanced, Grizzst gestured. Giant swaths of loamy ground vanished, revealing the carefully crafted pit traps underneath. And since the vané couldn't see where they were going . . .

Once most of them had fallen into the traps, Grizzst changed the smoke into something less friendly. He waited in silence, listening to the quiet thumps of vané falling unconscious. A few managed to stay awake long enough to work varying magics—the lightning bolt actually came frighteningly close—but they'd prepared to face someone using magic.

Which he had. Just not in the manner they'd expected.

He sighed to himself as he pulled everyone from the traps, made sure they'd live, and piled their bodies into a neat pyramid like stacked timber.

Grizzst also left a note.

It read, "I just want to fucking talk to your king." With the note, he left a small box, the metal treated with heat and chemicals so a flame-like shimmer licked up the sides.

He retreated back to the border and continued waiting. But this time, he sighed a lot and didn't bother hiding his impatience.

It didn't take as long the second time. A day later, a vané emerged from the forest. He didn't attack; he didn't cast spells. He was tall and so pale, Grizzst wondered if he might actually be an albino, with white hair and pink eyes. He wore matching clothing in white and silver and pale gray, with the net result of looking like a ghost.

"What does the stone *do*?" the vané asked.

Grizzst smiled. They'd opened the box. "I'll be happy to explain—to His Majesty."

That didn't make the vané angry. Someone had expected that response. The vané didn't mention the earlier attack. He didn't even suggest Grizzst should remove his talismans. Instead, he made an elegant motion toward the forest.

"Would you join us?" the lead vané asked.

It could've still been a trick, but they'd reached the point where Grizzst's next step was a leap of faith.

"Sure thing." Grizzst followed the vané into their kingdom.

# 51: Three Little Words

***(Kihrin's story)***

I wasn't surprised when the practice room door opened, but I'd expected Therin or Janel or maybe even Doc.

My mother walked through the door and closed it behind her.

I paused from practicing forms. "Yes?"

"I wish to talk," Khaeriel said.

"Fine." I sheathed Dolgariatz's loaner sword (which was nice). "Where do we start? Hmm. So many options. It's like a buffet of guilt and pain. We could talk about Talon, but I'm stunned to realize she's the least of my concerns at the moment. Hmm. Oh yes. I know. Why don't we start with you killing every D'Mon at the Blue Palace. Why don't we talk about *that*?"

Her eyes narrowed. "You were dead."

"What does that have–"

"It has everything to do with it," she said. "You were dead at Darzin's hands, who as far as I knew was still alive. Unpunished. Free. He had sacrificed you to a demon, and no one–not a single person there–had tried to stop him. So when I found myself free from that gaesh . . . I was so angry–" She swallowed and started over. "It happened. I cannot change it. I regret losing control."

"You murdered *Galen.*"

"I refuse to apologize for killing people who enslaved me for twenty-five years." She regarded me with all the calm reserve of a woman who had ruled the Manol for centuries. "You honestly blame me? Tell me you have not, while a slave yourself, felt such anger that you would have killed hundreds–nay, thousands–who would benefit from your existence as chattel?"

I paused.

*I would kill you all if I had a knife.*

I'd thought those words when they brought me to the auction block in Kishna-Farriga. Not one tiny bit of it had been in jest. I remember the impotent rage I'd felt waiting in the cages, one of hundreds waiting, trapped like animals. Not one of us able to do anything but wait to be sold, hoping against vain hope our buyers wouldn't prove cruel.

As if there were any other kind of buyer.

I let out a long, unsteady breath.

Perhaps the question I should've asked was how she could possibly have forgiven Therin. She obviously had. I said, "Explain to me how someone who was a slave for twenty-five years justifies hooking up with her old *owner.*"

I didn't understand either of them. But the sad truth was, I still cared about them.

"Oh, not you too." She rolled her eyes.

"Do you love him?"

Her gold eyes focused on me. "What does that have to do with anything?"

"You don't?" I fought back disbelief, battling with laughter. "You kidnapped a high lord and dragged him down here to be your . . . I don't even know. I don't want to know."

"Oh, by the trees, this was not revenge," she snapped. "Your father is heir to the Kirpis vané throne. I wanted him as a contingency plan in case the Founders refused to overturn the Law of Daynos. He has a legitimate claim to the throne." She clenched and unclenched her fingers.

"But . . . do you love my father?" I repeated, not willing to give up on the idea. "I get he's useful and the actual heir, and I'm going to try hard not to contemplate what that makes me, but *do you love him*?"

"Do I love him?" She scoffed under her breath and looked at a point somewhere over my shoulder. "We hurt each other so deeply. How can we ever openly acknowledge our vulnerability? We shielded our wounds, buried them. Admitting someone has power over you is not . . . easy."

"Oh, believe me, I know," I said.

Her gaze sharpened, and she looked back at me, eyes narrowing. "Is it the young woman? I noticed how you two looked on each other at dinner."

"Don't change the subject. We're talking about you."

She tilted her head. "Or is it your other friend Teraeth? I saw his face when we found your body back in the Capital. For that matter, the passionate plea he made in your defense over dinner." Khaeriel paused, tapping a finger against her lip. "Terindel's son. Hmm. *That* marriage would be quite politically advantageous . . ."

*"Mother."*

Khaeriel paused.

"We're. Talking. About. You," I repeated.

"Fine," she said in a tone of voice that meant everything wasn't fine nor was the conversation over. "None of this is why I sought you out. I would like to speak with you regarding Relos Var. Your words earlier left little doubt concerning your animosity, but I cannot imagine why you would feel that way."

I blinked. That was unexpected. "Um, because he's a monster? And besides the fact that's not hyperbole, he's a master manipulator and liar who's responsible for so many deaths, we could be standing here for years if I had to count them out. He's personally tried to kill me—"

"Kihrin, he would never do that," my mother protested.

I clenched my teeth. "I'd forgotten you two are friends. *He tried to kill me.* When he didn't win the bid for me in Kishna-Farriga, he absolutely tried to kill me."

Disbelief shone on my mother's face. "Kihrin, the only reason he was trying to buy you was because *I asked him to.* When we realized you were missing and began to piece together events, I went to Relos Var! Therin thought you had run, but I knew you would never leave Galen behind, certainly not like that. So I asked Relos Var for his aid. He said you had been kidnapped and sold to a slave ship heading to Kishna-Farriga. He went there to free you." She took a deep breath. "You cannot listen to Thaena. She is not to be trusted."

"She's your grandmother," I reminded her.

"Who gaeshed me and sold me into slavery!" Khaeriel said. "I am well aware of her qualities. I have known her far longer than you. She truly believes she is never wrong, and that is a dangerous quality in a monarch."

"She's not a monarch," I protested.

"What do you think a god *is*?"

"Relos Var is worse!"

"I am not sure of that," my mother said. "I am not sure of that at all."

I started to say something and then stopped. "Nice job."

She raised an eyebrow at me.

"You came really close to successfully changing the subject."

My mother scowled. "It is not changing the subject if you have exhausted the previous topic of conversation."

"It's two words," I said. "Yes or no? You've known my father for over a quarter century. Surely, you've figured out how you feel by now."

My mother clenched her fists at her sides and scowled at the ceiling for a long beat. "Fine! I hate him. He is the weakest man I have ever known. For twenty-five years, I watched him give up piece after piece of who he could have been, the great man he might have become. I watched him take a coward's path and hide from what he knew was wrong instead of doing something. Anything. There, you have your answer."

"If you hate him, why did you–" I glanced toward the door and stopped.

The door was still open.

My father stood just inside the threshold, leaning against the jamb. "Did I come at a bad time?"

"How long have you been standing there?" Horror lurked in my mother's expression.

"Long enough to hear your critique of my character." Therin walked over to us. "I'll need a moment with your mother."

"Why do I suddenly feel like leaving is the last thing I should do?" I fought down dread. I *knew* my father was capable of violence. And while I never imagined he'd unleash his temper on Khaeriel, that was before she slaughtered our family, kidnapped him, and enchanted his mind. I couldn't be sure what he was capable of at that moment. Anything.

"Therin, let me explain–" Khaeriel stood straighter.

"What's to explain?" His voice was so calm and soft. "Go, Kihrin. Some conversations are private."

"I don't think–"

"I promise I won't hurt her." He still wasn't looking at me.

I sighed. "Sure. Fine. I'd appreciate it if neither of you murdered the other. Think of the children, by which I mean me. I've already been an orphan once. I'd rather not repeat the experience." I walked to the door and slammed it shut.

I didn't *leave,* mind you. They were staring so hard at each other, neither was in any position to tell if I'd actually *left.* I hadn't. I'd turned invisible and slammed the door shut a second later. Risky, because my father wasn't wrong; some conversations should be private.

It's just that I didn't trust either one not to do something we'd all regret.

"Funnily enough," Therin said after a long silence, "it's not the idea you don't love me that feels like knives right now. It's the fact you enchanted me because you didn't think I was capable of forgiving you. *That* hurts."

Surprise flickered across her face. "What?"

"After everything I've done. After what I've done *to you.* You thought I was this much of a hypocrite? That I wouldn't understand? Or I wonder, am I overthinking this? Was it just that forgiveness requires apology, and your pride will never let you do that?"

"I slaughtered your family!" She glanced around the room then, as if assessing where she was and what tools she might have at her disposal if it did come to a fight. Quite a lot–it was the practice room, after all.

Weapons lined the walls. "What decent person would forgive me for such a crime?"

"Did you enjoy it?"

That brought Khaeriel's gaze back to my father. Her eyes narrowed. "What do you think?"

Therin laughed then, ugly and bitter. "I think you loved it. The surprise on their faces. The fear in their eyes. Don't think I'm judging; it's not like I don't understand, even if I 'take a coward's path,' which I'll assume refers to my drinking–"

She tried to protest, but Therin continued. "If you and I sat down and compared the number of D'Mons we'd slain, you wouldn't win the contest. And none of the family *I* murdered kept me as a slave. Yet I certainly liked the screams . . ."

"Stop it," Khaeriel said. "Pedron deserved every sword blow."

"True." Therin walked to her; she backed away. "But my hands aren't clean. I was a Quuros high lord, not to mention the criminal hobbies I inherited from Pedron.[1] I've killed a lot of people, and most didn't deserve it." Her back hit the wall. Therin framed her with his arms, hands resting to either side of her. "What decent person would forgive you? I don't know whether to be flattered or insulted. I've been a fiend all my life. I thought you *knew* that."

"I couldn't take the chance," Khaeriel said, "that you wouldn't help me."

"All right." He pulled his arms away from her, backed up. "Well, now, you don't need me. Terindel's agreed to help you and doesn't even want the crown. I'm superfluous." He paused and added, "I went back to Quur, you know. From the well."

Khaeriel didn't seem surprised. "I suspected. I assumed I would never see you again."

"And yet, you seemed happy to be proven wrong."

"I was happy to see you were still alive."

"The man you hate? I'm shocked at your generous spirit, my love."

Khaeriel looked away.

Therin's mouth quirked into something not quite a smile. "I'm not arrogant enough to think I'm that good in bed, not compared to all the vané boys and girls with centuries of experience. I'd amuse myself thinking you just enjoyed having me as a toy, except for one little thing: you never once told me you loved me."

"What?" My mother tilted her head, her confusion quite evident. "That makes no sense."

[1] Therin was head of the criminal Shadowdancers, who operated in the Lower Circle of the Capital.

"Why not lie to me while I was enchanted? If I'm just a tool to be used and discarded, why would you care whether or not you spun a falsehood around your feelings? It would've helped strengthen the enchantment. You should've lied. *Why didn't you?*"

"I have my pride," she said.

He shook his head slowly. "That's not it. Try again."

"What answer would you like to hear? Why not start there."

Therin smiled coldly. "You never said the words because they *wouldn't* have been a lie. And that's where your pride comes in."

"Because they wouldn't have been–?" She began laughing. "So now a refusal to say I love you means I *do* love you? The broken enchantment has clearly affected your mind."

"Nothing you said before was wrong, Khaeriel. I've been weak. I've taken the coward's way out, again and again. The easy paths expected of me were the paths I chose. And I'm done with it. I'm sorry for all the pain I've caused, to you and so many others. Truly sorry. I'm not going back to Quur."

"An apology makes it all better?"

"Oh no. It won't ever make it all better, which is something you'll learn when those screams come back to haunt you in the middle of the night. This isn't sums on a slate board. My good deeds don't cancel out my bad ones."

She stared mutely at him.

Therin spoke again into the silence. "How many times must I spell this out? You are my *soul,* Khaeriel. I love you. You're every good thing I cherish in the world, every reason I have to draw breath, the only reason I will ever need to smile. I'd pay that necklace of star tears or a thousand like them just to hear you laugh. It hurts to know you didn't trust me enough to tell me the truth."

"Yes, it is indeed such a mystery why I would ever think the man willing to *rupture my eyes* might not be willing to forgive me."

"Now, let's be fair, Khaeriel. You had just murdered my grandson."

"Said as if you'd ever given a damn about Galen."

He laughed darkly. "A fair point. But, Khaeriel, I'd forgive you anything. Anything. Including what you did to my family. All you have to do is ask."

She crossed her arms over her chest, looking simultaneously miserable and defiant. "So what do you plan now if Quur is no longer your destination?"

"That depends on you, my love. If you want me to stay, I'll stay. If you want me to stand by your side while you retake your throne, I'll do that. All I need from you are three little words."

"If you expect me to say–"

He counted off his fingers. "I. Am. Sorry. *Those* three little words. It won't fix what you've done, but at least I'll know I'm in love with a woman who still has a single redeeming bone in all her body. If I'm wrong, let me know now so I can have the dignity of a clean escape and the hope neither of us ever sees each other again."

"And if I don't love you?"

"Look me in the eyes, and tell me you don't love me."

She stared at him and didn't answer.

"This isn't about love," Therin continued. "This is about being adult enough to own our mistakes. Admit to me you made one, and maybe we can still have a future together."

Her stare was flat and cool. "Then leave. Because it was not a mistake, and I am not sorry." Khaeriel launched herself away from the wall and toward the door.

He watched her go and didn't make a move to stop her.

Therin just looked out at nothing, his expression distant. Then my father shook his head, sighed, and turned to me. "Eavesdropping is not the most endearing quality in the world, you realize."

I let out a dark laugh as I let myself turn visible. "I was afraid you might hurt each other."

"Oh, weren't you watching? We did." Therin walked to a bench and sat down. "Are you really this 'Hellwarrior'? Gadrith thought he was, and he killed so many people in pursuit of that."

I sat down next to him. "It's not just one person. There's more than one Hellwarrior."

He didn't say anything.

I sighed. "Yes, it's me. Destined to destroy the world. Save the world? Something like that. I forget."

"Destiny can go piss in Rainbow Lake," my father said.

That made me smile. "That's exactly how I feel."

"Still, it gives me some hope."

"What?" That wasn't even on the same continent as what I'd expected him to say.

Therin smiled. "If Gadrith had fulfilled the prophecies, it would have been an endless horror. He was a monster, body and soul." Therin clasped me on the shoulder. "But you? I've never been prouder of any of my children than I am of you. If anyone can figure out a solution to this mess, it's going to be you. Whatever happens, I believe in you."

I could only stare. It wasn't that I didn't hear the words. On the contrary, each word vibrated, sank into my soul, shattered me. But Therin spoke a language I only vaguely understood–I had to stop and puzzle over each sentence. Even then, it took a few seconds for the meaning to settle in, for me to realize my father was serious.

He misunderstood my widening eyes, the look on my face. "I know . . ." Therin scowled. "I know I haven't been there. I can't make apologies–"

"You don't need to. It wasn't your fault." My throat tightened until the words came out as a whisper.

"But I also don't regret what happened." He winced. "That sounded callous. I just think Surdyeh did a better job of raising you than I ever would have. At least, every other child of mine stands as testament to my poor parenting skills. If you're the only one who turned out to be worth a damn, it's probably because you *weren't* raised by me."

I wanted to tell him he was wrong, but . . . he probably wasn't. I'd never really known my brothers except for Darzin, but I suspect none of them were wonderful people. Having one's every whim and wish catered to at all times is probably not a recipe for sterling depth of character. At the same time, I'm not sure Therin gave his own father, Pedron, nearly enough credit for warping Darzin into what he became. Galen proved it didn't have to be that way.

I put my hand on top of his, paid no mind at all to the tears falling down my cheeks. The one thing Darzin had been good for was teaching me to embrace all the behaviors Darzin claimed as intolerable in a Quuros prince. Crying was on the list. So were more ephemeral qualities like mercy, compassion, and love.

Finally, I wiped my eyes. "Do you think she'll come around?"

"Your mother? I hope so. But I don't know." Therin stared down at his hands before speaking again. "Kihrin . . . Doc told me he already performed the Ritual of Night."

I blinked. "Obviously, he hasn't."

"He says he did. Not the last time. The time before that. Attempt number two. And he claims it didn't work, that he 'made a mistake' with one of the glyphs. But I think there's more he's not telling."

"That–" I shook my head. That contradicted every story about Terindel I'd ever heard.

Therin said, "I can't help but feel someone is lying to us about what's really going on. I'd hate to think it's one of my oldest friends, but I'd equally hate to think it's the Eight either."

"Easy," I said. "It's Relos Var. But the fact that I haven't *seen* Relos Var is starting to worry me."

"I've seen him recently. He gave Valathea to Khaeriel," Therin said, "as well as the news you were alive."

"Huh." I chewed on my lip. "I need to talk to Doc."

"Not today," my father said. "I doubt he and Valathea are going to leave their bedroom until at least tomorrow."

I laughed. "You're right. Of course not." I stood and spun back around before I'd taken a step toward the door. "Speaking of bedrooms, you don't happen to have a spare Blue House ring, do you? Kelanis took mine."

"Why would you need–oh right. *Janel.*" Therin seemed curiously relieved. "I swear Doc has such a strange sense of humor sometimes."

"What?"

"Never mind." Therin held out his hand. "I'll need a ring."

I pulled one of Dolgariatz's loaners off my hand, hoping the Manol vané wouldn't mind me keeping it for slightly longer than originally planned. I handed the ring to my father.

"I suppose I should at least be glad you're taking precautions," Therin said. "At least *this* time."

I glanced at my father's hands as he took the ring. Therin wasn't wearing any rings on his hands at all. And sure, Blue House rings didn't have to be rings, but they usually were. Therin would wear his as a ring, I was sure. It wasn't my business, but I couldn't help but wonder if in eight months or so, I'd find myself with another sibling.

Therin caught me staring, and his expression turned rueful. "That's . . . a different complication."

There was no point pretending I hadn't understood. "Is my mother pregnant?"

"Probably." He studied the ring, letting the silence settle over us before handing it back. "Whether she'll keep the baby is a different question."

I didn't know what to say to that.

"I should go," I said.

He nodded. I left him there, staring at the weapons.

# 52: The Kirpis Vané King

***(Grizzst's story)***

A hundred feet inside the forest, reality shifted. Twilight gloaming transformed, not to night but bright sunlight filtered by green canopy into soft yellow beams. The light falling on his head was velvety smooth, limning the edges of staghorn and maidenhair ferns. The rich smell of humus and sweet flowers mixed with the pine green scent. Everything lingered slow and gentle, as though they traveled in a place where time had no meaning.

They traveled for fifteen minutes before the vané ushered him through a transport gate. Which made sense; allowing Grizzst to know their capital's location would have been foolish.

Beyond, he found an alabaster-and-white-marble palace of soaring spires and piercing minarets.

Fake. All of it.

Parts of the palace were real, but illusions cloaked most buildings, making them more extravagant and sublime than the reality. More illusions created the scent of bluebells, honeysuckle, and wild herbs. The scene was as meticulously detailed as the most exquisite painting. The effort it must have taken to maintain this clever magical fiction was as impressive as if the decorations had been real.

They took him to a private parlor rather than the throne room. And by some odd back passages.

From this, Grizzst inferred King Terindel didn't want his court to know one of those filthy humans had invaded.

He sat down, helped himself to a drink, and waited.

"So what do you want?" A voice asked behind him. "I'll assume you didn't come here to give me a blue gem and drink my wine."

Grizzst stood up and turned. King Terindel was tall and pale-skinned with gleaming gold hair and blue eyes. He wore less finery than Grizzst expected, but still enough to highlight his rank.

Grizzst was probably supposed to bow. He didn't. Monarchies made his gums itch.

"Don't sell yourself short," Grizzst said. "It's really good wine."

King Terindel didn't look amused.

"I don't want anything from you," Grizzst said, "except an introduction."

King Terindel raised an eyebrow. "Is that so?"

"I've gone through a lot of effort to lie if it's not."

Terindel sat down across from him, elegant, effortless. He had the sort of poise that always made Grizzst long for a good supply of cow manure to throw. "And the stone?"

Grizzst shrugged. "It's called the Stone of Shackles, but name it whatever tickles you. It's yours now. It's a powerful artifact. Keep it on your person and almost no power in the universe can divine your location. In addition, it'll warn you when you're in danger, and should you die, it'll save your life. No strings attached. If you refuse to help me, keep the stone, anyway."

For a race who could only die through violence, Grizzst had just offered an appealing set of powers–but only because he hadn't told Terindel exactly *how* the Stone of Shackles would save his life.

Grizzst was playing a bit of a dirty trick, but he was only willing to part with so many of the Cornerstones in his lucky rock bowl. The Stone of Shackles was one.

"That seems an odd power set to be called the *Stone of Shackles*."

Grizzst shrugged. "I didn't name it."[1]

Grizzst had "recovered" the stone after Cherthog had lost his duel against the god-king Zakorus. Technically lost, anyway. Cherthog gained himself a handsome new body that day and lost himself a Cornerstone. But Grizzst had no intention of ever, ever wearing it.

"It's a royal gift." Terindel studied the blue gem, then the wizard, looking for the angle, the trap. He likely thought it was the obvious one: that Grizzst had lied about the stone's powers. "And to whom do you want me to introduce you?"

"I'd like to consult with your queen on a matter involving the biological arts."

Terindel blinked in surprise. "My wife is her own person. I'm not her gatekeeper."

Grizzst raised his hands. "That may be, but you *are* king. It seemed rude to approach her without clearing it with you first."

Terindel pursed his lips. "And what is this matter of biology?"

Grizzst hesitated.

"Did you think I'd allow you to approach *any* of my subjects without you first answering that question?"

[1] True. The stone was named by its discoverer, Cherthog, who used it to create his slaves, the first of which was the woman he forced to marry him, Suless.

Grizzst sighed. "It's complicated. The short version is I'm trying to resurrect the Eight Guardians."

Terindel's brows furrowed. "The Eight Guardians are dead."

"The Eight Guardians are trapped. It's not at all the same thing."

King Terindel gave Grizzst a hard stare that might have been more intimidating if Grizzst himself wasn't also millennia old. Then the vané seemed to deflate, leaning back in his chair, spreading his legs. It was as if he'd just pulled off King Terindel's mask and revealed a totally different person underneath.

"Then we have a small problem," Terindel explained. "Valathea left three months ago, and she hasn't come back."

"Left?" Grizzst wasn't sure he understood. "Do you mean she left you?"

"No," Terindel said. "I mean she left the city to go hunt a dragon. And she should've come back by now. So either you can wait for her to do that or . . ."

Grizzst sighed. "Tell me the last place anyone saw her."

# 53: The Memory of Souls

***(Kihrin's story)***

I found Janel later that afternoon in an interior room, with fewer windows looking out at the lake. Sunlight filtered down through transparent ceiling and the lake water to cast roaming shadows of swimming fish across the marble floor.

The room looked like an office or study, with full bookshelves and a mottled floor-to-ceiling mirror along one wall. Janel was studying a map that dominated the last wall. The map looked alien and unfamiliar until I realized someone had flipped a world map upside down, so Quur sat on the southern continent and the Doltari Free States lay to the north. A second continent labeled *Nythrawl* took up the left side. Interesting. Also weird.

I'll admit I was more inclined to stare at Janel. Gold rings and rubies threaded her hair, formed a choker around her neck. Layers of transparent red and gold silk fell over crimson scales that resembled jewelry more than armor. I found it funny; by my standards, she looked like everything feminine, and by hers, she was everything masculine.

Given the clothing Dolgariatz had provided me, the vané clearly didn't make a distinction between genders.

"Hey," I said as I walked into the room.

Janel glanced back over her shoulder at me. Her smile was so faint, I almost missed it. "Hey yourself."

I set down the harp just inside the doorway. "I thought we might talk about last night?"

Janel's expression went blank; she turned back to the map. "Why? Having regrets?"

"No! No regrets at all. What I can remember, anyway. Last night's fuzzy around the edges. I hope I wasn't too, uh"—I shifted uncomfortably—"rough."

"Rough?" She glanced back with obvious surprise. "Not that I remember."

"Good." I cleared my throat. "That's good."

"I'm the one who usually worries I might be too rough." Janel still wasn't looking at me. "What we did . . . was not–"

My heart started racing. Her tone was not approval–

"Neither one of us were in any condition to say no."

She exhaled. "That's the problem, isn't it? There are conversations one is supposed to have before sex. Etiquette to follow. Dorna would kill me if she knew what I'd done. At least you remembered to ask first. That's better than I managed."

"Wait. Are you mad at *yourself*?"

She looked confused. "Of course I am. I took advantage of you."

"You were drugged. We took advantage of each other." I walked around her until my back was against the map so I could see her face, her expressions. "But do you regret it?"

"Yes," she said softly. "I do."

*Shit.*

"I regret my memories are so . . . fuzzy," she continued. "It's not fair. I *want* to remember every moment."

Relief welled up to replace my panic. "Oh! Okay, good. Because I regret that too. But not the sex part. I don't regret that."

The room fell into quiet. She closed with me, put a hand up against the wall. She was so close I could feel her through the cold metal of her scale gown and my silk. I put my hands around her waist and marveled at how good that felt.

But then she drew back, frowning. "Do you remember what I said to you about C'indrol?"

"I remember Valathea calling you that, but I don't–" I frowned. "Wait, you've mentioned that name before."

"I mentioned them last night," she said. "But I don't remember that life. Even though I remember saying I did–and that they knew you."

"No, before that," I said. "When you told me about the memories Suless pulled from you. One of them was someone named C'indrol."

She exhaled a ragged breath. "Valathea must have known me in that lifetime. Not just as Elana."

"I'm starting to feel like Valathea knows everyone." I pointed behind her, to the harp in the doorway. "Speaking of Valathea. I, uh . . ." I rubbed the back of my neck. "I was looking for you because I thought you might want to hear me play."

I don't know why the hell I felt so embarrassed, but there I was, blushing like an idiot.

Janel touched my cheek. "Indeed I would." Then, to my vast disappointment, she took a step back, out of my arms. "I spoke with Valathea after lunch." She turned around and walked over to the harp. I didn't know if she was actually interested in harps or just a prop to highlight the topic of reborn vané queens.

I straightened. "Oh?"

Janel ran a finger across the harp's neck, and I tried to not to think of the action as carnal. Janel's mouth quirked as she met my eyes. "Apparently, if I ever want to rekindle my relationship with Valathea–*and* Terindel–I have an open invitation."

I choked. "Oh wow. If you ever wanted to *kill* Teraeth without laying a finger on him–" Teraeth had been able to find the humor in the idea that Janel had once (again, in a past life) had a relationship with his father, Doc, but I didn't think he'd find that idea so funny in the present tense.

She laughed. "I thanked her for her extremely generous offer but politely declined. I'm not planning to have sex with either Teraeth's father or stepmother anytime soon. But she also told me–" Janel glanced down at the harp. "I thanked her for freeing you, and she looked at me oddly and said she'd had nothing to do with it. That I'd pried your soul out of Vol Karoth's body all by myself."

"Well, that is what I've always been told happened. Thaena certainly seems to think you're responsible." I smiled at her. "Have I said thank you? Because seriously. *Thank you.*"

"You're welcome." Janel looked troubled. "But have you ever given any thought to how? Elana Kandor wasn't a wizard. She wasn't even a witch. It's true she'd begged for Tya's protection to cross the Blight, but the favor of a goddess isn't the same–" She paused, her eyes far off, then shook her head. "I know enough about magic *now* to know I have no idea how I might have accomplished it back *then*. How did I manage it?"

"I don't–"

"I have a theory," she said. "I think *C'indrol* knew how. I think Elana remembered being C'indrol the same way I'm remembering being Elana. I just don't remember that life, and I'm desperately afraid that if I don't–" She crossed her arms over her chest and visibly shuddered.

I made a face as I pulled her into my arms. "I'm sorry."

She started to relax into my arms, but then stiffened and jerked away from me. Her eyes widened in horror.

"Janel? What is it?"

She stared past me, then visibly exhaled and relaxed. "I'm sorry. I looked over in the mirror and I didn't see you. I saw–" Janel shook her head, clearly shaken.

"Saw what?" I had a sinking feeling I already knew.

"A silhouette. Just a black outline."

My mouth dried.

"I'm sorry," Janel said. "We've been under a lot of strain. I suppose I shouldn't be surprised if my imagination gets the better of me after what happened with that morgage tribe."

"You really think you imagined it?" I said softly. I knew she hadn't. Maybe we were too far from the Korthaen Blight for Vol Karoth to manifest a psychic projection, but that didn't mean Vol Karoth and I weren't still linked. Maybe she'd sensed the connection.

She didn't answer.

"All right, that does it." I picked up the yet-to-be-renamed harp. "We're going to go back to my room, and I'm going to serenade you, and we're both going to forget how grim this all is. If just for the afternoon."

"There's something else I'd like to do too."

I raised an eyebrow. "Is that so?"

Janel put a hand on my arm. "I'll explain when we're somewhere more private."

I was hardly going to refuse.

I thought I already knew what Janel intended. And I was prepared to be an eager, willing, and entirely sober participant this time.

Except I'd guessed wrong.

Janel walked into my bedroom and sat down on a couch, throwing one leg up on the cushions while keeping the other on the floor. "When you and I first met in the Afterlife, the dragon Xaloma injured me. Badly injured me. You saved my life—not to mention healing yourself—by splitting Xaloma's heart between us."

"I did what now?" I blinked at her, because . . . yeah.

That sounded stupid. *Really* stupid. So sure. That probably happened.[1]

She gave me a rueful smile. "That was my reaction. I will admit it worked—we both survived." She shrugged. "Thurvishar tells me Xaloma is the dragon of death, the only dragon who lives in the Afterlife by preference. So I assume that means something. I suspect you and I share a connection because of it. Just as you and Vol Karoth share a connection."

"And you think that's good? Bad?"

"Suless once told me we never truly forget our past lives, that those memories stay with us in our souls even if we can't access them."

"Thurvishar just said something similar to me."

"I think it's time you and I *do* access them. And I think, if we do have this connection, that we may be uniquely suited to help each other. We don't have time to let this develop naturally."

I placed the harp at the foot of the bed before pulling a chair over

[1] At least he knows himself.

to her, spinning it around, and sitting down on it backward. “Okay. I suppose I see your point. You think this will help?”

She pursed her lips. “I’m not sure, but I want to know how Elana freed S’arric. I think we need that information. Just in case.”

I gave her a blank stare. I didn’t ask, “Just in case what?” I damn well knew.

I nodded. “Okay. Let’s do this.”

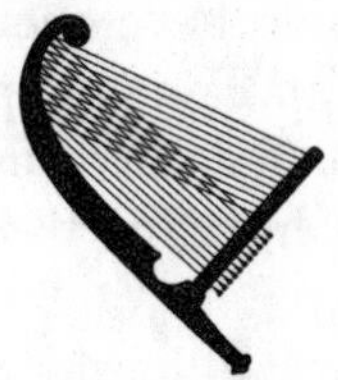

# 54: Hunting for Valathea

***(Grizzst's story)***

Grizzst wondered if this was some cosmic force's idea of humor. He briefly entertained the notion Valathea had gone into the mountains pursuing Rev'arric, which opened up the unfortunate possibility she'd been collateral damage in their fight. He hoped not. The Raenena Mountains were vast. Multiple dragons could spend centuries roaming its peaks and valleys without ever crossing paths. And that was true of a vané queen and a voras wizard as well.

Finding her would be luck as much as craft.

Fortune was with him, or rather the dreth. After checking a dozen settlements, presenting himself politely at their bunker entrances each time, he finally encountered one who'd seen a vané woman pass through. They'd entreated him not to follow her; she was clearly a fool. They'd told her a dragon was active in the area, but she hadn't heeded their warning.

Which dragon? Nobody was sure, but they'd all heard its roar. Nobody fancied venturing above ground for an identification.

So Grizzst would have to find out the hard way. At least he knew Valathea had survived. Or at least, she'd still been alive to trade with that particular dreth settlement.

A week later, he identified the dragon. Some were easier to spot than others. Sharanakal tended to create volcanic activity wherever he went and rarely traveled far from water. Baelosh liked to stay below the tree line, and Gorokai–well, the dreth wouldn't have recognized Gorokai as a dragon at all. There'd have been no mistaking Morios, and they'd have never heard Drehemia, who would have slipped through their world like an unseen plague. Rol'amar and Xaloma both would have brought stories of walking dead with their passing, if in radically different flavors. And, for obvious reasons, Rev'arric was no longer a candidate.

That left Aeyan'arric.

If Grizzst had been searching for anyone but Valathea–if Rev'arric's warning not to mention him hadn't echoed still through Grizzst's head–he might have gone back to fetch the wizard-turned-dragon. Rev'arric's ability to control dragons would have been handy. But it was too risky should they stumble across Valathea unexpectedly.

Grizzst stopped looking for Valathea and started tracking the dragon instead. Where he found one, he'd find the other.

It turned out to be both easier and harder than Grizzst had anticipated. Easier: he only had to look for the largest storm in the range and find Aeyan'arric at its heart. Harder: he didn't particularly feel like stumbling onto the dragon in the middle of a blizzard.

While he was searching for shelter, he heard a massive rumbling noise. He looked upward toward the mountains, the driving snow making sight difficult. Still, it was a distinctive sound.

"Aw, fuc—" He started casting, but it was too late.

The avalanche overtook him.

When Grizzst woke, he lay on the ground in a cave. He didn't feel particularly injured. He didn't even feel bruised, which should have been the least of his injuries after having tons of snow dropped on his head. Someone had rescued him, moved him, and healed him.

The air was comfortable instead of freezing. A large fire had been built in the center, smoke filtering out through a small chimney in the ceiling. Grizzst couldn't see the cave opening from his position.

Sitting next to the fire was the woman he'd been seeking.

Valathea looked like a flower bundled in furs, something fragile and delicate never meant to survive winter's chill. Her hair, soft as curling mist, had been woven in elaborate braids against her head, accentuating her heart-shaped face. She had a notebook open in her lap, where she'd been writing. She set the quill aside when he sat up.

"Thanks," Grizzst said. "I'd have been lunch for some lucky wolf pack next spring if you hadn't found me."

"This is a bad place to be caught outdoors, Grizzst," she told him. "Even for one such as yourself. I hope whatever you're seeking was worth it."

"I guess we'll see, since you're who I was—wait. How do you know my name?" He moved closer to the fire, where a kettle of something warm waited.

Her smile was kind. "Save god-kings, there's only one voras left in the whole world. So you must be Grizzst. Please, help yourself."

"How did you know I'd survived?" Her logic was sound, but Grizzst had thought he'd done a better job of avoiding attention. A bowl sat next to the kettle, so he ladled himself a serving. It looked like porridge, but he didn't care what it tasted like, as long as it was warm.

"N'ofero told me your name," Valathea admitted, naming the deceased leader of the voras Assembly. "He'd asked me to look at the ritual and give him my feedback, which I did. I assumed you'd be unaffected since you were holding the sword."

"N'ofero went to you?" Grizzst blinked. "You must be one hell of a wizard."

"He respected my opinion," Valathea corrected. "The world is less for his absence." She pulled a cloth square from her satchel, shaped it in her hands, and blew on it until it had the hardness and polish of pottery. She poured her own serving into the created bowl. "To what do I owe the honor of this visit? And how did you know where I'd be?"

"Oh, your husband said you were hunting dragons in the mountains."

"Hunting? No. Studying." Valathea held up her journal, filled with pages of neat, precise handwriting. "I keep hoping I'll find a way to reverse what was done. I feel . . . responsible."

Grizzst rubbed his eyes and set his bowl to the side. "Excuse me? That wasn't your fault."

"Oh, it was a little bit my fault," she said. "Do you remember much about politics? From the old days?"

"Well, I always remembered to vote, but . . ." Grizzst suddenly felt uncomfortable. "I didn't pay much attention, to be honest. I never ran for office or anything. I wasn't anyone important."

"And now you are very important," she said. "How the world changes. But you do remember the Preceptors, I assume?"

Grizzst frowned. "Multinational group, right? Their leader was, uh . . ." He bit his lip and squinted. "A'val, I think?"

Valathea smiled. "That's a name I haven't heard in a long time. *I* was leader of the Preceptors. And that meant, among our other duties, the choice as to whom would be made Guardians fell to us. To me. I approved every single one."

"Okay, wow. Uh, I had no idea . . ." Grizzst swallowed. No wonder Rev'arric had thought she wouldn't exactly be a fan. If she was the person who'd approved who became a Guardian, then presumably she was also the person who said who would *never* become a Guardian.

Namely, Rev'arric himself.

"So you can understand how I might feel some culpability."

"It wasn't one of the Eight who caused all this mess," Grizzst said. He made a point to not mention how he'd just woken that guilty party from a millennia of insanity and formed a pact with him. No need to go chasing trouble.

"No," Valathea said. "N'ofero believed the demons were responsible, but I knew better. Right from the start, I knew better." She looked away. "I should have recognized Rev'arric's ambitions much earlier. A friend even tried to warn me how jealous he was of his brother, S'arric, how Rev'arric hated that I hadn't cleared him to take part in the ritual. But I thought their own emotions were clouding their judgment."

"Why would you let him anywhere near the ritual if you–"

She made an inarticulate, exasperated noise. "Rev'arric invented the ritual! He *made* the Eight Guardians. I knew he was egotistical, but I thought his focus remained on defeating the demons. Why would anyone ever think he wanted to destroy–or at the very least supplant–what he had himself created?" She slumped, deflated, the anger draining away from her voice to a tired, worn trickle. "Did you ever meet him?"

"Rev'arric? I, uh . . . I saw him lecture a few times."

She smiles wryly. "I knew him much better than that. Not–" She responded to Grizzst's widening eyes. "Not like that. We were never friends, let alone lovers. But I like to think he respected me. Maybe I was a fool to think so. Rev'arric was brilliant, charming, and passionate. But also narcissistic, manipulative, and completely lacking remorse. Why would someone so convinced of his rightness ever need to feel doubt or guilt? And after all, he usually *was* right. But this time"–Valathea pressed her lips into a thin line–"Rev'arric had expected me to give him the role I instead gave to Argas. He never protested my decision either. Rev'arric ran the ritual perfectly: tied Argas to the proper concept. But I think that was the moment he started to think of all of the Preceptors–me especially–as his enemies. The moment he felt we'd betrayed him. The moment he started making his plans for the second iteration of the ritual, the one that went so very wrong."

She gestured toward what Grizzst had to assume was the cave opening. "I feel terrible about the people he pulled into that ritual, the ones who ended up like . . . that. I'm certain none of them expected to end up as monsters. I keep hoping I might discover some cure."

Grizzst started to explain about the Cornerstones, but then stopped himself. Because while he agreed with her, he didn't agree with *all* her statements. The conversations he'd had with some dragons had suggested their involvement hadn't been innocent, at least in a few cases. Did these godlike beings who'd betrayed their own families deserve to be cured? Maybe. Maybe not.

The only reason he'd fixed Rev'arric was because he'd had no other choice.

"I'm trying to resurrect the Eight Guardians," Grizzst finally said. "I thought . . . you might be able to help me."

She stared at him from other side of the flickering light, the campfire reflected in her large violet eyes. Valathea said nothing.

"Well, seven of the Guardians, anyway. I've been trying for centuries, but always running up against the same problem."

"Mortal matter's inability to contain that level of tenyé."

Grizzst tried his hardest not to let his disappointment show. That she immediately knew the issue meant she'd already given the matter thought. It meant she'd tried to solve the problem.

It meant she'd failed.

He pressed ahead as if she hadn't just subtly told him she couldn't help. "Someone told me you're the best when it comes to biological magics. I was hoping you might see something I have missed."

The queen sighed. "Even if I did, the discovery would be inconsequential. I have done enough research to know the seven Guardians slain at Vol Karoth's hands are beyond our touch. Their souls were cleaved from their bodies, yes, but those souls are . . . scattered. Discorporate. Stretched like a thin sheen of oil across the universal waters. How would you condense them back into something that could even be placed in a body?"

Grizzst shrugged. "Oh, I figured that out centuries ago."

Valathea blinked at him. "You did?"

"Sure. Souls don't want to be–what did you call it? Scattered? They want to be whole. Give them the excuse and they'll re-form. They'll heal. The universe wants it that way. The problem is without a body to house them, they never have enough time to kindle thought processes and just–" He made a fist with his fingers and then opened his hand suddenly.

"Perhaps in the Second World, where a physical body isn't required?"

"I've thought of that, but they weren't killed in the Second World. They were killed here in the First. I have no way to force their souls to cross the Veil. Besides, souls can't channel tenyé without a physical body to support the exchange. If it were that easy, the Guardians would have resurrected themselves."[1]

Queen Valathea finished her porridge and set the bowl aside. "That is a conundrum. But then, I suppose if there was easy solution, one of us would have come up with something centuries ago."

Grizzst swallowed the crushing disappointment. "Is there nothing you think can be done? There's–" He exhaled. "Vol Karoth's prison is failing."

Her violet eyes widened.

"That was supposed to last forever."

"It's not going to," Grizzst said. "We need the Eight back."

She seemed small and childlike, the shadows cast on the cave wall behind her very large. Grizzst felt like he was telling scary stories around

[1] Yes, I'm aware that this runs counter to what I reported happening to Kihrin in the Afterlife. Which I now believe is extremely significant.

a campfire. It was just that this particular scary story happened to be true.

Valathea didn't speak. She stared intently into the burning coals as if she might divine some answer there.

Finally, she said, "A few hundred years after the Cataclysm, some of my people's younger members became . . . discontent. They felt these new mortal voras posed a threat, too short-lived to remember or honor the old agreements between our groups. They believed that with voras knowledge lost, your people would degenerate."

Grizzst made a face. "They weren't wrong."

"Again, we should've listened better," Valathea said. "Been more sympathetic to the concerns of those younger than ourselves. Ironically, just as we vané were once younger than our voras parents. But we didn't and weren't, and so eventually, a large group left. They migrated to the summer lands we keep and declared it a sovereign nation."

Grizzst stamped down his impulse to tell her to get to the damn point. "I see," he lied.

She smiled. "I doubt that. I'm telling my tale very circuitously. Dreadfully boring, I imagine. But you see, within the Manol Jungle, there is a special tree. Special enough that it might be capable of containing a Guardian's tenyé. I know of no other living creature capable of doing so, or at least no other living creature capable of doing so that isn't already sentient. I recommend you start with Galava. She can form the bodies you need for the others." The queen paused. "Apologies. That was rude of me. I'm quite sure you've already thought of that."

"Don't worry about it." Grizzst straightened. "So if the Manol is now a separate nation . . ."

"There's some tension, but overall, we're on friendly terms. And Sovereign Khaevatz will help you. After all, she's Khaemezra's daughter."

Grizzst's eyes widened. Khaemezra might have been a Guardian, but she wasn't vané. Which meant the vané who'd left for the Manol had been open-minded indeed.

"I'll try that. Thank you."

Valathea nodded. "If you like, I'll be happy to open a gate for you and make introductions. Like my own nation, the Manol aren't necessarily friendly to strangers who show up unannounced."

"Again, that would be kind of you." Grizzst suddenly felt this might work out.

"With that said, have you considered . . . not . . . resurrecting the Eight?"

Grizzst startled. "What? Of all people, I assumed you'd want to see them brought back." Rev'arric would be just floored to find out Valathea shared his distaste for the idea.

She pursed her lips. “I haven’t quite decided.”

Grizzst hadn’t expected pushback from her. “We need them.”

“Perhaps,” she acknowledged, “but ask yourself a question. Seven of the Eight have been spread out across the universe for over a thousand years. If you coalesce them again, what will you be bringing back?”

## 55: A Window to Past Lives

***(Kihrin's story)***

The spell itself was almost annoyingly simple, built on what Janel had learned of enchantment magics from Suless and some creative guessing on my part. I have to say I think she had a point about us being linked, because I don't know that it would have been so easy with anyone else.

We let the spell take us, sinking down into a not-quite slumber while we plumbed down for hidden secrets and went deeper, *earlier.* Before we were us.

I dreamed of memories not my own. Some part of me knew, right from the beginning, these were Janel's memories. I hadn't really known how this would work. I suppose I'd thought I'd see my memories; she'd see hers. But no, it seemed we would share.

Her memories felt real, though. Fresh, bright, and sharp, full of edges. *Beautiful.*

***(Janel's memories)***

The morgage shelters are temporary, fugitive creations built against the ancient rubble, hooked over magic walls laced blue and gray. The silhouette of a city dead for millennia spreads out around her. Thick, powerful warriors prowl the streets, silent as they patrol the Dead City for intruders.

I watch the men work, secure in the knowledge they'd pay no attention to me. The Dry Mothers have declared me off limits, goschal–holy. I look down at the thin silk scarf wrapped around my ripe belly–the silk shiny and rare, shimmering with rainbow hues, so fine it looks like wind alone would rip the fabric. As far as I know, nothing will ever rip this fabric. I'm not goschal, but the veil most assuredly is.

"Mother Vamara would speak with you," a morgage man says. He looks young, barely free from his child-wraps, and probably aching to join the Quuros invasion in progress to prove his worth.

I glance at the tent where I've been sleeping, toward the harp resting against a magic-buttressed wall. I'm tempted to bring Valathea with me–the Dry Mothers love music, as it happens–but if they wanted performance, the messenger would have said so.

I nod and follow without saying a word.

Vamara is the most elusive of the Dry Mothers, old and vicious and feared at a level beyond what any morgage male could expect. I've only met her once. She sniffed in my direction and left, although she hadn't contradicted the other women when they'd welcomed me into the camp. Now she wants to see me.

As feared as Vamara is, I face the possibility that if she kills me, goschal or not, not a single morgage would utter a word of protest.

Some attempt has been made to re-create the homes the morgage lost when they'd been forced from their homes by Vol Karoth's waking. In Vamara's case, this meant stringing animal hides across a framework built from surviving pillars, so many it seems like a dark cave. My escort taps against the hole at the base, small enough on hands and knees. I'd have found the task annoying even if I weren't pregnant.

There's no help for it; I get down on my hands and knees and crawl.

When I emerge, I'm in darkness, and only gradually do my eyes adjust enough to see. A woman sits cross-legged before a collection of baskets and pottery, but I can barely make out her shape.

"I've been waiting for you," she says with a voice like white water and the deep, dark sea. The silk scarf wrapped around me glows in the darkness, throwing off the rainbow hues of its goddess. The shifting violet, red, and green light makes her skin color difficult to discern, but it's probably some shade of yellow, green, or gray. Most morgage are colored to match their unwelcoming and hostile homeland.

"I came as soon as your messenger arrived," I say.

She chuckles. "I don't mean today. I've been waiting longer than that." Vamara holds up a small vial containing pale liquid. "I'll honor your request. I'll order our people back. We'll leave the Green Lands. But you must do something." Without waiting for an answer she has to know can only end in a yes, the Dry Mother offers the vial. "You'll drink this, and you'll remember. And then you'll go to the Dead City's center and save the world."

I'm at a loss. Remember what, exactly? And going to the center of the Dead City–I had tried once, when I first arrived with Valathea. So many morgage had converged on me it was as if I'd been an entire army and not a single lone woman. But this is what I'd come for. The only reason I'd come.

I touch my forehead to the ground, setting my hands against the ground for balance. "I would be honored to–" Something warm and liquid touches my hands, and I jerk back. Free-flowing liquids are rare in the Blight and rarely safe when they exist. In the dim light, this liquid looks thick and black. As I trace it back to the toward the woman, I see it flows not from her but from the baskets behind her, from something behind them. A hand, outstretched on the rug, fingers curled in a final agony.

The Dry Mother sighs. "Oh, it would have been so much easier if you hadn't noticed that."

And then the Dry Mother . . . changes.

***NEVER MIND. WE'LL DO THIS THE HARD WAY.***

I gasp as a demon's voice screams in my mind. I scramble backward toward the entrance.

The demon is faster.

Her appearance is still feminine, the color lighter, and she has white hair instead of Vamara's bald pate. Her fingers end in lethal claws. Within eyeblinks, I find myself pushed up against a ruined wall, one set of claws at my neck, the other set held up, daggerlike, ready to plunge down into my belly.

***DON'T MOVE.***

There's no sound but my frantic heartbeat, my rapid, frightened breathing.

"You're a demon," I say, because I can think of nothing except to state the obvious.

In my defense, I'm terrified.

***AND YOU ARE ELANA KANDOR,*** the demon replies easily, shifting position so she is sitting on my lap, leg thrown to either side of mine. ***I HAVE SEARCHED FOR LIFETIMES TO FIND YOU.*** The clawed hand at my throat relaxes, moves up to caress a cheek. ***THEY'LL NEVER KNOW I'M NOT THEIR PRECIOUS DRY MOTHER. I'LL KEEP MY WORD. YOU CAN STILL SAVE YOUR PEOPLE. JUST DO ONE TINY LITTLE FAVOR FOR ME.***

The demon could kill me so easily. I choke back my fear, my desire to vomit, all my revulsion. "What?" I ask, my voice small. "What favor?"

The demon holds up the vial again. The liquid looks milky. ***YOUR LOVER KEEPS SCREWING UP MY PLANS, LITTLE IMP. SO YOU'RE GOING TO . . . FIX HIM . . . FOR ME. YOU JUST NEED TO REMEMBER HOW TO DO THAT.***

"My lover–" I blink, confused and uncertain. She couldn't mean Valathea. She'd said him. "Atrin–" I swallow a lump of grief and anger, a hot wash of bitterness. "Atrin's dead."

***NO, DEAR. NOT THAT LOVER. HE SERVED HIS PURPOSE. BUT WHEN YOUR OTHER LOVER FINALLY BREAKS FREE, HE'S GOING TO BE A PROBLEM FOR ME. UNLESS YOU SAVE HIM FIRST.***

I try to draw farther away from her, but my back is literally against the wall. The scarf's glow is the only light in the tent, enough to see the glint of blood on the demon's arms, the glitter in her eyes. She smells like sex and blood and rot. Her skin against my body is icy cold. "I don't understand," I whisper.

She holds the vial up to my lips, flexes the clawed fingers of the hand poised above my unborn child so I don't forget the consequences of rebellion.

***YOU WILL, LITTLE DEMON. YOU WILL.***

Tears stream down my face, but I drink. What else can I do? I'm not a wizard. I've never been a warrior. I can't defeat a demon with a song. The liquid is shockingly cold and tastes of bitter herbs. I feel it coat my throat, and the sensation is disturbingly soothing.

"I'm not a demon," I murmur as the ground tilts under me.

***OH?*** The demon finds that funny and laughs, a hundred cats yowling all at once. ***DO YOU KNOW, THEN, WHAT THE DIFFERENCE IS? THE DIFFERENCE BETWEEN THE THREE RACES THAT FLED TO THIS WORLD AND THE DEMONS WHO CHASED AFTER YOU WITH ENVY IN THEIR HEARTS?***

I don't know what she's talking about, of course. Three races? That means nothing to me.

Except suddenly, it means everything.

Voras for the land. Vordredd for the rock. Voramer for the sea. Three varieties of human, bespoke crafted to colonize a new world, no matter how inhospitable. And we naïvely thought ourselves so lucky when we found a home large enough for everyone. My heart stutters, slows its tempo, then begins to race to a new beat. An exquisite stab of pain shoots from the base of my skull all the way down my spine, and I convulse.

I dig my fingers into the rock under me, aware the demon has moved but uncertain where she's gone and in too much pain to care.

I pray this doesn't harm the baby.

***SHHHH. DON'T FIGHT IT. THE MORE YOU FIGHT, THE WORSE IT WILL HURT.***

Images start to flicker through my thoughts. Images that aren't my own and yet seem so familiar.

"What's the difference?" I whisper.

***WHAT?***

A low groan escapes me as another flare of pain burns through me. I clench my teeth, pull my knees up as far as they'll go. Everything hurts, but I hold on to that question like it's the rope to save me from drowning. "Between demons and . . . us. What's the difference?"

***OH, THAT.*** The demon reaches out and pets my hair as the mental rush overwhelms me. ***TIME.***

* * *

When I wake, I'm a new person.

I'm still Elana. Still six months pregnant with my dead husband's son. Still attempting the impossible–a peace treaty between our people and the morgage nation that they've zero reason to agree to.

But more than that. The memories are too much, so overflowing I feel like a cup trying to hold the ocean. I can only gulp mouthfuls, knowing it would take me centuries to swallow the sea. I am drunk on memory, drowned in my identities. It hasn't just been one or two. I've lived a dozen lives. But that first one lasted ten times longer than all the rest combined.

I don't see the demon; I don't look for her. Instead, I stagger from the tent, paying no mind to the morgage warriors and sand women around me. My tripping feet take me back to my tent, where I hoist Valathea over a shoulder and set out immediately toward Kharas Gulgoth's center. No one tries to stop me. I've become too familiar. They assume I know better now; after the time I've spent learning their ways, I'd never be stupid enough to try to enter the great hall again.

But it's different this time. Now I know what's inside those walls. Now I know *who* dwells there. And even though there's a demon loose somewhere in the morgage camp–I never did learn its name–who wants me to do this, I won't resist. Because I want this too. I want it more than anything. The longing is a fire scorching my souls.

As I step into the hall, I see him.

S'arric. Truthfully, I can't *see* him at all, because he's nothing but a silhouette. The light refuses to touch him. Yet I know it's him. And I know I'm the only hope he has–

### *(Kihrin's story)*

I screamed as the memory twisted in my mind. Fragments, shatters. Mirror shards of remembrance broke away and fell into the darkness. I felt a wrench in my souls as I stopped experiencing Janel's memory of another lifetime, a sharp, jarring loss of balance like taking a step down a stair that no longer exists. I was pulled, violently yanked into a horrifyingly familiar hungry blackness. I tried to untangle myself from Janel's mind, to force her away, to protect her, but it didn't work. We're were pulled in together.

We'd made a mistake. Vol Karoth could *feel* me–

No.

Vol Karoth could feel *us.*

# 56: The Manol Vané Queen

***(Grizzst's story)***

Valathea and Grizzst's arrival in the Manol caused a stir, but Valathea's presence offset the arrival of a "human." The vané here were different. Instead of being light-skinned like the vané who lived in the Kirpis, these were shades of night. It couldn't be natural–these vané would have been born in the Kirpis before they decided to split off.

Which made their skin and hair color a political statement.

They arrived on a platform attached to a giant tree branch, so far up only fog and birds stretched below them. The temperature soared murderously hot and humid. The scent of warm sunlight and flowers, fresh wood, and greenery surrounded them. The branch they stood upon led to a tree . . .

Well, Grizzst began to understand why the tree was special.

He had a difficult time grasping the scale. An entire city perched on its branches–and not a small city. In front of them a large island of graceful buildings waited, some built into the sides of the tree, others resting on special platforms like the world's most ornate tree house.

"This is the Mother of Trees," Valathea said as they began to walk forward. "She is the oldest living thing in the entire world."

"Well . . . ," Grizzst said, "probably not the oldest–"

"Oh, she was already here when we arrived."

Grizzst stopped, shocked. "I thought we–"

"Remade this world? No. Do you have any idea how many dimensions we searched through until we found a world we *didn't* have to remake? She was ancient, even then."

Grizzst looked around one more time and felt awe. He had only heard stories about the old days. He wasn't old enough to remember himself.

While he gawked, he forgot to pay attention to the main platform.

He missed the sovereign's entrance.[1]

[1] I'm unsure when the Manol vané stopped referring to their ruler by the gender-neutral title of *sovereign* and instead began using *king* and *queen,* but it's interesting to note that even among the vané, customs change.

"To what do we owe the honor of this visit, Your Majesty?"

Grizzst turned around and lost his breath.

The woman who stood before them was typically tall. Her skin was midnight and her hair a combination of bronzes and greens echoing the tree and canopy. Her face, her figure–both perfect. She held herself with a grace any god-queen might have envied. She wore a gown of gold and needed no crown.

"Oh please," Valathea said as she walked forward. "You know we only use the titles for outsiders." She held out her arms, and when Khaevatz walked over, she kissed her on each cheek. "I have brought you an interesting guest. This is Grizzst, the last voras wizard."

"How do I do . . . ?" Grizzst stammered and then blinked. "I mean, I'm honored."

"You are also impossible," Khaevatz pointed out. "I thought the voras all gone."

"Yes," Grizzst agreed. "I mean, no. I mean, I'm still here." He winced and cleared his throat. This wasn't the time to embarrass himself.

Valathea waved a hand. "I'm only here to drop him off and make introductions, Khaevatz. I do think you'll find what he has to say most interesting, however."

"Oh, I am already so certain that is true." Khaevatz reached over and quite casually took Grizzst's hand in hers. "Follow me and we shall talk. Have you eaten, Grizzst?"

"Ah yes," he confessed, trying to act like her touch hadn't set all his skin on fire. "If porridge counts."

"It most certainly does not. I have just finished preparing a meal, and I would love to share it with you."

Grizzst blinked. "You . . . you cooked? I thought you were, uh . . . ?" He looked around. Grizzst had seen guards and soldiers, but no one who looked like a servant.

Khaevatz smiled magnanimously. "Of course. I enjoy cooking. You will join me, I hope?"

"How could I refuse?" He allowed her to lead him farther into the tree.

"I hate to be rude, but are you always this friendly with total strangers?" Grizzst asked as the Manol ruler led him inside the palace. "I'm not complaining. Truthfully, I don't get out much. Too much research. It really takes up all my time–"

"Do you realize you are babbling, Grizzst?" Khaevatz sounded amused.

"Call me Gahan." The personal name left his lips before he could stop himself.

Khaevatz paused and turned to look at him. Her expression turned serious. “You do me a great honor, Gahan.”

“Well, I just, uh . . . it seemed, uh . . . like a good . . .” Grizzst shook his head. “What I mean to say is, I’d like borrow your tree.”

She blinked. “. . . which tree, exactly?”

Grizzst gestured around them. “This one. I want to summon a goddess–Galava, to be exact–and put her in this tree. Just for a little while.”

Khaevatz continued staring. “You’re serious?”

“As the Blight, Sovereign.”

Khaevatz sat down on a bench that looked like it hadn’t been carved as much as grown straight out of the tree itself. “That is quite a request.”

“Kay, why have you let a voras man into the palace?” The man who came into the room was as black-skinned as Khaevatz, but with dark hair and light green eyes.

Every bit as pretty, though.

“Mithraill.” Khaevatz rose to her feet again. “This is Grizzst. Grizzst, this is my consort, Mithraill. Darling, Grizzst is–”

“Yes, he’s a voras. I can see that. But why is he here?”

Grizzst straightened. “A pleasure.”

Mithraill raised an eyebrow. “I doubt that.”

“Queen Valathea brought him by. Grizzst thinks he can resurrect Galava.” Khaevatz pinched his arm. “So be nice.”

Mithraill looked more interested. “And you think this would work?”

“I’m not sure,” Khaevatz admitted. “He hasn’t finished explaining.”

“If my plan to bring Galava back works,” Grizzst said, “Galava should be able to bring the others back as well.”

Mithraill’s stare grew intense. “Really?”

Khaevatz patted her lover’s shoulder. “You see, just as my mother’s Khaemezra, my dearest Mithraill’s father is Mithros.”[2]

“You two are the children of Death and Destruction?” Grizzst said. “I bet your kids will be something else.”

Mithraill snickered. “If only it worked that way.” Then he paused. “You can really bring them back?”

“I’ve been trying for a long time. This is as close as I’ve come yet.” Grizzst looked at both of them, waiting for an answer. “You’ll need to evacuate the city, though. This isn’t without risk, and it would be better to be safe than sorry under the circumstances.”

“Risk?” Khaevatz cocked her head to the side. “What kind of risk?”

“Well . . . when I have tried this in the past, the vessels that didn’t work out . . . exploded.”

[2] Khaemezra being Thaena, and Mithros being Khored.

Khaevatz sighed. "Ah. What a shame we must refuse, then."

Grizzst berated himself for telling the truth. "This is our best chance to get your parents back!"

"I understand that," Khaevatz said, "but evacuating the city is impossible. We are in the middle of a war."

# 57: The Ritual Gone Wrong

***(Kihrin's memories)***

The sunlight is shining through the university great hall windows. The colors are wrong, though, washed out, faded. All the hues have been leached away, leaving only dull grays. The room should smell like warm leather and oranges, but even that smell has been purged, until all I have left is the knowledge of what should be, and how wrong the dull, numb air feels. From edges of my vision, I see reality itself flake off, peel away, the universe ending just outside my memory of this hall.

But like being trapped in a dream, I'm powerless to stop events. I feel Vol Karoth, but this doesn't feel like his condensed storm of hatred, despair, and hunger. This feels like someone reading from a sheet of paper, retelling a story. A rote recitation of a memorized script.

The tables and chairs have been pushed to the side, blockades set up down the hall to keep students from intruding at the wrong moment. In fact, the entire building has been emptied, faculty and students both given the day off. A wrong intrusion at the wrong moment will be worse than fatal.

I trace the pattern on the ground, bemused as I study the sigils. I don't quite follow all the markings, and it has been a while—centuries—since I last stood in a similar circle. It feels like looking at advanced mathematical formula before I've taken the right class. I *almost* understand it. Enough to recognize the calls to power, the binding to concepts, the same steps that took eight normal people and turned us into channels for something primal. Archetypes. This isn't the same ritual, however. This one will do something *more.*

If we're lucky, it'll be enough to finally defeat the demons.

I find myself wishing I could study my brother's notes. See exactly what he's trying to do. But that would mean admitting I'm interested and undo millennia's work. I've spent an eon pretending to be the pretty, stupid brother for the sake of Rev'arric's vanity.

I love my brother, but dear stars, is he ever insecure.

"You're not doing this by yourself, are you? Where's that no-good brother of yours?" I smile at the indignant tone in Argas's voice. Then again, he's never gotten along with Rev'arric. Usually, Argas keeps his disdain better hidden.

He's not alone. The rest of the my companions have arrived as well. Taja steps forward and gives me a quick hug, ruffling my hair. "Stop that," I mutter to her, which only makes her grin impishly. She obeys my orders on the battlefield and absolutely nowhere else.

"Argas has a point, though," Tya says. "Where is Rev'arric?" Her voice catches at the end of *Rev,* but she covers smoothly. Only someone who knows her well would realize she almost called my brother by his personal name.

Which means we *all* caught the slip. We may have started off as strangers, but we've been together for so long, we're better and worse than blood kin now. We love and hate each other, can hurt each other as only family and loved ones ever can. We try to keep all manner of secrets from each other and mostly fail. Everyone knows about Tya and Rev'arric, for example, and politely ignores how much Rol'amar looks like his father.

"He's preparing the others," I say. "They'll all be back in a moment."

Galava raises her head from where she's nestled against Ompher's side. "Where's everyone *else,* though? I expected to see Valathea."

"Valathea was called away by a last-minute Assembly meeting," Rev'arric says as he enters the room, with everyone else following. He looks tired, with drawn circles under his eyes. "She asked for this to be postponed, but it's quite impossible. And the rest of you must leave as well."

Thaena straightens. "What? Why?"

Khored crosses his arms over his chest and glares.

Rev'arric rolls his eyes toward the heavens. "Would you lot kindly consider the possibility your presence just possibly *might* affect what we're trying to do? There is an issue of sympathetic dissonance. Haven't you been paying attention at all?"

Khored's brother, Morios, snorts from behind Rev'arric. "We've got this handled. Go fight some demons or something."

Argas opens his mouth and starts to say something I know I'll regret. Argas is utterly loyal on the battlefield–I can and have entrusted him with my life–but in social situations? Hopeless. It doesn't help that my brother thinks Argas is an idiot and has never shied from expressing that opinion. They're not friends.

"It's fine," I say quickly. "We'll let you know as soon as the ritual's finished. You can bask in my radiance when this is over." That earns me the expected groans and rude gestures, because that particular joke has yet to grow old. At least not for me.

I find Aeyan'arric in the crowd behind her uncle and wink at her, but frown when she doesn't smile back. She looks tense, anxious. I remind myself what we're about to do is not without risk, and my daughter's smart enough to know it. Which reminds me of the other person who should be here and isn't.

Even with an emergency Assembly meeting, C'indrol would be here. This is their district, after all, and as a Preceptor, their right. Unfortunately, I can't–don't dare–ask why they're absent. Because C'indrol and I are a secret we *have* managed to keep. Even from the rest of the Guardians, *especially* from my brother. Taja suspects but doesn't care. Rev'arric would care a great deal.

Aeyan'arric doesn't even know. She thinks C'indrol's nothing more than an old family friend.

Ompher chuckles in a way that only shakes the ground a little. "Fine, fine. We'll go fight some demons or something." He points to his son, Baelosh. "Be good."

Baelosh gives his father a terse nod and a tight-lipped smile. He seems tense too.

I start to wonder if Revas has told them something I don't know. Is this ritual riskier than my brother has let on? I realize it's the first time we've tried this, but even so . . .

"Still want to be here," Argas grumbles, "in case something goes wrong."

"And yet you'll still leave," Rev'arric says.

"Looks like we're not getting our way." Khored turns to go.

"No one is," Taja says softly. "Not today." She gives me a sad look I feel in my souls just before she vanishes. Dread sweeps through me, matching the bitterness I suddenly taste in my throat.

Argas makes a face. "I hate it when she does that. Makes it sound like she can see the future. I swear she does it to just mess with me."

I know it's a sore point. A few of Taja's jokes have gone the wrong way over the years. Like the time she convinced Argas she could see the future, for instance.

Galava takes Argas's arm. "There now, it's fine. You know she's always like that." She turns back to us. "We'll see you all later." They vanish. The rest leave a second later.

I walk up to my brother. "What aren't you telling me?"

His eyes widen. "I've no idea what you mean."

I grab his arm and pull him toward me. "I mean, *what aren't you telling me*? Spit it out, or I walk."

He stares flatly at me for tense seconds, then sighs and surreptitiously glances around. "Valathea isn't here," he whispers, "because she thinks the ritual is happening two days from now. She's going to revoke my clearance tomorrow. She's shutting the project down."

"What?" The news is so unexpected, I can only stare. *"Why?"*

"She doesn't believe my findings. She wants her own people to look over my notes, analyze what I'm doing, debate it in the damn Assembly like a new trade agreement. It'll take *years.*" Rev'arric visibly grinds his teeth. "As if we have all the time in the world." My brother gives me a wary glance. "What we're doing is technically not illegal–if we do it today. If we do it now. Or else–" He shrugs.

So that's why C'indrol isn't here. Because they don't know this is happening.

"All right," I say. "Thanks for being honest. Let's do this."

Rev'arric looks surprised for a split second, then nods and turns toward the others. All Eight Guardians' relatives, to provide a sympathetic link to the universal forces we're trying to tap for a second time. He claps his hands. "Everyone to places! Let us begin."

I take the center point and help set up, although the sigils are already in place. I hear my brother's voice, chanting, but then it pauses unexpectedly.

"I'm sorry," Rev'arric whispers.

The warning comes too late. The sword is already sliding into my back, through my chest, bursting out the front in a splatter of gore. The blade feels like ice but does nothing to quench my sundered flesh's burning. My first reaction is dull shock, then incredulity that not only has my brother done this, he's done it with *intention.* He had to have crafted this sword especially for this task. A normal weapon wouldn't hurt me. My daughter cries out my name. I hear the horror in her voice and realize Revas must not have told her his plans.

Then my brother screams in pain, the horrified cries of eight other voices quickly distorted beyond recognition into something deep, guttural, elemental.

The light in me goes out; darkness takes its place. The sun tries to correct the imbalance.

The world turns white.

That bright flash is the sun manifesting its energy in a single ray. It punches through the atmosphere, slams to the ground centered on me. The area immediately around us survives miraculously intact, but beyond its boundaries, the world is fire. The explosion is so vast, it melts the countryside and then spreads out, a death wave covering half a continent.

But all I know is darkness. Darkness and *hunger.*

I pull the sword from my body and hurl it, as hard as I can, into the maelstrom. It's an act of impulse and anger. The moment the blade leaves me, I discover it took something of me with it, our natures twined.

Ah well. I'll have to hunt it down again.

Where my brother once stood, where all of them once stood, nine serpentine forms twist, warping, wrestling with massive distortions of tenyé, the guardian ritual gone horribly wrong. They're in pain, digging into themselves with distorting limbs as if the agony can be excised. When it can't, they run, crawl, crash through the walls or, in one case, dive through the actual doors. I can feel them–feel their minds, feel the insane fractal energy of their tenyé and their souls.

So these too are tools I'll reclaim later.

There are whispers around me. So many whispers. A circle of voices glow from the energy they've consumed to keep this hall intact, all whispering the same thing over and over, a chant or prayer.

*Vol Karoth. Vol Karoth. Vol Karoth.*

It's a title: King of Demons.

Voices break off the chanting, take nebulous form, and I realize that's exactly what they are: demons.

**FOR SO LONG, WE WATCHED,** they say. **WE WHISPERED, WE PLAYED ON YOUR BROTHER'S FEARS. ALL HAS COME TO THIS. THEY HAD THEIR AVATARS, AND NOW WE SHALL HAVE OURS TOO. THEY MADE GUARDIANS, BUT WE HAVE MADE A GOD. LEAD US, OUR KING. LEAD US TO VICTORY, VOL KAROTH.**

The demons did this? Somehow, yes. An act of espionage, to counter an escalation in weapons. We were arrogant fools to think they wouldn't fight back after we'd created the Guardians.

I can't find it in me to care. I don't even mind the name. Vol Karoth works as well as any other. I feel only . . . hatred. So much hatred. Enough hatred for everyone in the Twin Worlds. And enough hunger.

I laugh. I had wanted a better way to kill demons, hadn't I?

Well. I can do that.

I grab a monster and feast.

## 58: Herding Snakes

***(Grizzst's story)***

Khorvynis was one of the larger city-states that had sprouted up in the centuries after the deaths of the Eight, the rending of the voras, the dark slide into barbarity and despair. Grizzst had taken Rev'arric there to demonstrate what the god-kings had become.

And it was the nation with whom the Manol vané were at war.

Grizzst took the steps up to the main palace two at a time, ignoring the guards who were, at least for the moment, also ignoring him. When Grizzst reached the top, he encountered his first true obstacle: a group of honor guards defending a giant set of closed bronze doors (snakes in bas-relief, of course).

Grizzst scowled under his mask. "I'm here to see Ynis."

One of the guards looked at him and hissed.

"You spoke voral the last time I was here," Grizzst said. "I'll repeat myself: I'm here to see Ynis."

A guard's cobra-like hood flared out as he said, "Ynis doesn't want to see you."

Grizzst heard footsteps. Several more groups of soldiers approached, from the sides, from behind. Everyone had their weapons out. Grizzst wasn't familiar enough with thriss expressions to discern their mood, but he could make assumptions.

"I hate god-kings," Grizzst said. "They never learn."

The palace doors rang out like gongs as something hit them from the other side.

Once.

Twice.

On the third ring, the doors broke open.

A great snake, enormous and primeval, reared up in the room's center as Grizzst marched inside.

"Grizzzzzzzssssst," the snaked hissed.

Grizzst folded his arms over his chest and shook his head as though he was witnessing schoolboy antics. "Change back, Ynis. I'm not going to have this conversation while you don't even have arms. You look ridiculous."

The snake immediately shifted, flowed, and finally settled into a form not too dissimilar from the cobra-headed men who had waited for Grizzst outside. The clothes were nicer, and he wasn't wearing a weapon. Of course, he was a god-king. He was his own weapon.

"Really, Grizzst, do you have to be such a damn stick-in-the-mud? What have you done with my soldiers?"

"I'll give you three guesses. Hint: the answer rhymes with 'willed them.'" Grizzst walked forward into the throne room. "Next time, don't try to keep me out when we still have unfinished business."

"Next time, I'm going to rip your spine out through your heart!" Ynis shouted.

Grizzst wasn't offended. "You'll try, anyway."

Ynis hissed. "We have no business with each other."

"You still owe me from last time."

Ynis's tongue flicked from his mouth. "What? No, I don't. I *gave* you Chainbreaker!"

"Yeah, but then you tried to double-cross me. And please note I not only honored our original agreement, but I didn't even kill you." He tapped the sword at his waist. "Could have. Thus, you owe me."

Ynis eyed Urthaenriel with distaste. "I may have been a touch hasty. What did you have in mind?"

"Make peace with the vané."

Ynis narrowed his eyes. "Excuse me? They're the ones who started attacking my people! I'm not forgiving that."

"You can and you will. This war's personally inconvenient for me, so it stops. And I know you, Ynis. What did you *do*? They may have attacked first, but I damn well know it wasn't unprovoked."

Ynis hissed as he paced. "My people didn't do anything! We were minding our own business, fishing and hunting!"

"Where?"

Ynis hesitated.

"In the Manol. You sent your people to fish and hunt in the Manol." He shook his head. "I'm guessing you didn't bother to ask the vané first."

"What do they care? They never come out of their damn trees! Why should they begrudge us hunting in the swamps underneath them? It's ridiculous!" The god-king looked disgusted.

Grizzst wasn't in the mood to go into a lecture on how the vané felt about protecting their wilderness areas. "Let me guess: you went into the Manol because there were fewer demons there."

"I went into the Manol because I wouldn't be encroaching on the territory of another god-king," Ynis corrected. "Who knew they'd be so inhospitable?"

Grizzst rolled his eyes. "Yeah, who knew they'd defend their territory like that? If I can get them to stop fighting, will you stop too?"

Ynis paused. "Maybe. But we deserve access to those hunting grounds."

"That's not for me to decide. I'll get them to come to the bargaining table. You'd better make this right." He looked over his shoulder as he walked away. "Ynis, if you screw this up, when the fighting starts back up again, I'll be helping their side."

The god-king of snakes made a noise like a nest of vipers. "Damn you, Grizzst! Someday, I'm going to swallow you whole!"

Grizzst ignored him. One of these days, Ynis was going to pick the wrong fight, and when that happened, Grizzst would take great pleasure in ending him.[1]

By the time the peace treaty was finally signed, Grizzst wanted to kill everyone involved. Ynis had proved just as insufferable in conference with Sovereign Khaevatz as he was in private with Grizzst. Meanwhile, the vané didn't understand why Ynis and his people couldn't just *go away.*

Bringing both sides to the bargaining table took months, but eventually, finally, they reached an agreement. The thriss would be allowed inside the Manol's boundaries on a limited basis and with the understanding that they stay at ground level. More so, if they caused any damage to the Manol's trees, all bets were off.

It all seemed reasonable. Grizzst bet diamonds it wouldn't last a year. But that was fine as long as Sovereign Khaevatz let him use the Mother of Trees *now.*

After Ynis returned to his palace home in Khorvynis, Grizzst journeyed once more to the Mother of Trees and Khaevatz so he could finally finish resurrecting the Eight.

[1] And did, by all accounts.

# 59: Hidden Loves

***(Kihrin's story)***

I opened my eyes.

Janel and I stared at each other for an eternal second, our faces too shocked to express any other emotion. She still sat next to me on the couch, still held my hand. And we both . . . waited.

We didn't move. We barely breathed. Janel was waiting for the same thing I was: Vol Karoth. For the King of Demons to show up again. For him to follow our link back and bring annihilation with him. Shadows from the fish outside slipped across the floor, and all was a heavy quiet, weighted down by fear and dread.

Nothing happened.

I pulled Janel into my arms and held her tight against me.

Janel pulled away to stare at me, wide-eyed. "How can Vol Karoth be S'arric? *How?* You said Elana pulled S'arric out of Vol Karoth's body. That Vol Karoth was a separate being, but that's not . . ."

"That's not what we saw," I finished. I shifted in my seat, tried to slow my runaway heartbeat. "Khaemezra always made it sound like Vol Karoth was a demon possessing S'arric's body, but that can't be true. S'arric was corrupted, but there was no demon. So how can *both of us*—Vol Karoth and me—be S'arric?" I wrapped my arms around my stomach and studied the floor as I swore to myself I would not throw up, no matter how much I wanted to.

"I don't know," Janel whispered, "but I'm . . . C'indrol. Or rather, I *was* C'indrol. It worked."

I raised my head. "What? What worked?"

"I remembered what Xaltorath wanted me to forget." Janel scowled. "Last night—" She paused for a moment before continuing. "Xaltorath hadn't wanted me to remember C'indrol. She tried to erase the memories."

I straightened. "C'indrol and S'arric were having an affair."

"Kihrin, I'm fairly certain C'indrol and S'arric had a *child*." She stood up from the couch and paced, shuddering. "I've killed that child. Gods, Kihrin. *Aeyan'arric*."

"S'arric could've just been referring to the fact Aeyan'arric didn't know S'arric and C'indrol were lovers." As soon as the words left my mouth, I knew I didn't believe that. "I don't . . . I don't understand *why* it was a secret, but we probably thought we had good reasons. But let's talk about Xaltorath."

Janel whirled back to face me. "That was Xaltorath in the tent."

"I figured. But why did she want to help me?"

Janel raised an eyebrow. "Help you? Oh no. Don't you remember? 'When your other lover finally breaks free, he's going to be a problem for me.' This wasn't about helping anyone but herself. The whole point was weakening Vol Karoth. She used me because . . . well. C'indrol had both the motivation and knowledge to weaken Vol Karoth a lot."

"Why, though? Why would Xaltorath want to weaken Vol Karoth when the demons created him in the first place? Is it because Vol Karoth turned on them?"

Janel started to answer, then she laughed, in spite of herself. "Oh."

"What do you mean, 'Oh'?"

"You're thinking demons are organized again, aren't you? United. That they don't hate each other even more than they hate us."

I shut my eyes, rolled backward, and looked up toward where I could imagine fish swimming their merry away along with no idea what kind of chaos and churn was going on underneath them. The few times Janel had described demons to me–Kasmodeus, Xaltorath–they had indeed struck me as more like small bands or groups, with the strong controlling as many under them as possible. So Xaltorath might have plans the other demons probably didn't know about. The other demons might have plans Xaltorath didn't know about.

And I had a feeling none of the demons responsible for Vol Karoth had survived to see the sunset that day.

"Yeah, you're right. What was I thinking?" I sighed and refocused my attention on her. "What does the name *Xaltorath* mean, anyway?"

"Queen of Demons," she answered instantly.

I gave her a look. "You're fucking kidding, right?"

Janel just stared at me and slowly shook her head.

"Oh, well, that's . . . horrifying." I thought back to when my brother Darzin had sacrificed me to Xaltorath, who in turn had offered me an idyllic eternity spent in her bed. I hadn't thought the offer *serious* . . . It probably wasn't. The only romance ever cherished by Xaltorath started with the word *necro.*

I stood up and started to pace myself. We both seemed like we were about to duel as we circled each other. I had to think through this.

*I've spent an eon pretending to be the pretty, stupid brother for the sake of Rev'arric's vanity.*

S'arric hadn't been as dumb as his brother had thought. Too trusting yes, but not stupid.

"We know souls can be damaged," I said. "My souls were damaged when Tyentso ripped away a small section to gaesh me. That's why I couldn't remember my dreams. That's what made me vulnerable to demons later. But I fixed that damage using Xaloma's heart in the Afterlife. Souls can be damaged, but souls can also *heal*."

"Right," Janel agreed. "Yes. But that doesn't explain how you and Vol Karoth can both be S'arric. Unless . . ." Her face scrunched up in frustration. "Unless you both . . . What if Elana didn't free *all* of S'arric's soul? What if she only removed part of it? Not *freed* so much as . . . *separated*?"

"People take part of a soul when they're gaeshed, but nobody's ever mentioned those soul remnants becoming separate entities before. People would have noticed."

"A gaesh is a minute portion of someone's soul, the equivalent a little finger. No, a fingernail. I mean something much larger. How large–how small–can the souls be and still have the damage heal? Does it make a difference if the souls in question belong to a god? Might it be possible to end up with two *separate* souls?"

"We weren't gods," I muttered, but it was a semantic rebuttal, and Janel wisely ignored it. "But if Vol Karoth and I are entirely separate entities, why is he so damn eager to get his hands on me? Why would he even care?"

"Oh no," Janel said. "You might be separate, but only *you* would be whole. *You* have had five hundred years to heal, time probably spent in the Land of Peace basking in the tenyé of the Font of Souls, but Vol Karoth? Vol Karoth was frozen in time. Trapped. There's no way he's healed anything. He's broken, and he must know that." She sighed. "I still don't know what I did to free you. Even now, I don't remember. Xaltorath's buried it deep."

"Maybe Xaltorath's afraid you can reverse it and put me back."

Janel said, "That's never going to happen."

I sat down on the bed, elbows on my knees, leaned forward. "Ah, but think how many problems it would solve. No more figuring out what to wear in the morning. Wouldn't need to shave. Not to mention anything Xaltorath doesn't want to happen must be a good idea . . ."

"Kihrin, stop it." Her eyes widened with alarm.

I chuckled as I looked up at her. "I'm joking."

"It isn't funny."

I held my hand out to her. "Gallows humor, my love."

She froze, and I wondered what I'd said. Then I realized it was probably that word *love*. I felt a sense of dread settle in my stomach for a different reason than Vol Karoth. I pulled my hand back.

"C'indrol and S'arric might have been in love," Janel said, "but how long have you and I even known each other?" She worried at her lip, her expression troubled.

My breath was trapped in my chest. Because the answer was: not long at all. A couple of months at best. Completely out of proportion to her importance in my life. Common sense said I couldn't possibly be in love with her, and common sense could go jump in the Zaibur River.

"I'm not going to lie about how I feel," I finally said.

"Oh really?" Normally I'd have found a smile—any smile—on Janel's lips a welcome sight, but this was too mocking. All of it directed at me. "Then I'm curious: If you're so in love with me, why was the name you called out last night Teraeth's?"

*No.*

"I did what?" I felt my heartbeat race into a fluttery panic. Had I? Oh gods. I searched my memories, trying to pinpoint if I had in fact done that . . .

Janel studied my face, watched my reaction.

I let out my breath. "I didn't, did I?"

"No, but the fact you just gave serious consideration to the idea you might have *is* interesting, don't you think?"

I glared at her. "Not funny."

"Wasn't trying to be funny. I just don't think we should have this conversation without discussing the *other* person you're in love with. You have, after all, been in love with him a lot longer than you have with me." She paused a moment and then shrugged. "In this life, anyway."

"Can we not?" I growled.

She gave me that studied look again, and I realized what I hadn't done was deny her words. Deny her accusation about Teraeth. A sudden wave of dizziness swept over me, worse in its way than the memories of Vol Karoth.

"Very well. We'll not." The bed sank as she sat down next to me.

"Thank you." I felt picked raw by the tensions of the day. The last thing I wanted . . .

Did I have any clue what I wanted?

We just sat there for a few minutes, just watching the shadows move across the floor. The room became an uncomfortable space that I didn't know how to fill.

Janel reached out and picked up my hand. "I don't want to sleep tonight," she said. "I don't dare sleep tonight. Keep me awake."

I glanced at her, surprised. I looked down at her hand, ran my thumb over the back of it. She had beautifully shaped fingers, black as a starless night, calloused from sword fighting. "When you say keep you awake, any preferences on how you'd like me to do that?"

She laughed. "Something stimulating should work."

I half turned to her on the bed and reached over to cradle the back of her head with my hands. I kissed her forehead and then both her cheeks before she smiled, twisted her hand in my shirt, and pulled me in for a kiss on the mouth.

"Warning," I said when I took a moment to breathe. "I kick."

"That's fine. I bite."

"Gods, I hope so." I grinned when that pulled a laugh from her. I wrapped my arms around her body, pulled her against me, heady from the scent of her–metal and skin and flowers from the scented vané bathwaters. Her breathing quickened as I traced my fingers down her back and my heartbeat matched hers. The armor needed to go, on both of us.

"I wouldn't mind," Janel said, "finding out what sex with you is like when we're both sober enough to appreciate it."

Just the words sent sparks cascading through me. "Oh, I don't know. Just being this close to you is enough to leave me drunk." I lowered my head and skimmed the side of her neck, was rewarded by her gasp and the tremble that swept through her.

"You're terrible," Janel murmured.

"I'm honest," I whispered into her ear. "And you are music and songs and the light of a thousand stars. You are storm clouds and velvet skies and brilliant columns of fire. How can I not be drawn to you?"

Janel's breath grew ragged. She exhaled and drew back enough for me to see the heat in her eyes.

There was a knock at the door. From the other side, I heard Teraeth said, "Hey, Kihrin, you coming out for dinner?"

I glared at the door. *Gods damn it.* I should have thought this through. Of course Dolgariatz would also have dinner provided, and of course we'd be expected to attend.

"Teraeth, join us," Janel called out. She paid no attention at all to the betrayed look I gave her.

I fought down panic. Perhaps hiding under the bed was an option. Were we far enough south of the Blight for Thaena to grant my prayer if I asked to die of embarrassment?

Janel grabbed my wrist before I could do anything. "Don't you *dare* turn invisible," she whispered. Her grip would have done a dragon proud.

"Let go," I whispered.

*"No."*

I'd forgotten to lock the door, hadn't even checked to see if the door had a lock. And you'd think I'd have been more paranoid about that. Nothing stopped Teraeth from just walking right in.

So he did.

He had not come empty-handed, skillfully balancing a tray while he held the door open. He walked a few steps inside the door when his eyes flickered over to Janel, then back to me. No doubt he was noticing other details too: the tousled hair, our swollen lips.

Then a slow, broad smile spread over his face.

He looked *delighted.*

That hadn't been the reaction I'd been expecting. Nor had I been expecting what he carried on the tray–food.

"Well, then." Teraeth carried the tray over to the bed, setting it down on a side table. "You two look like you're about to start having fun. You have my permission to go right ahead. Pretend I'm not even here. It won't bother me at all."

"Teraeth!" I began to scold him, aware I was blushing to my toes. Then my gaze wandered to the food tray, and I blinked.

Three settings. Enough food for three people. Which meant he'd expected to find us together.

"Oh, you brought dinner. You wonderful, wonderful man." Janel scrambled over the bed to reach the tray.

"You knew Janel was in here, didn't you?"

Teraeth scoffed. "Of course I knew. I'm not an idiot. It was either your room or hers." Teraeth lay down on the bed, across from me, crossed one leg over the other, and rested on his elbow. He was all impudent grin and flashing emerald eyes. "It was a trick question earlier. We're not having a formal dinner, because nobody's around to attend one. Well, almost nobody. I think Thurvishar is busy interrogating Dolgariatz on pre–demonic invasion social customs of the vané. They'd both probably be available."

"Why isn't–" I stopped myself. "Never mind. I'm pretty sure I know." Doc and Valathea were finally reunited after a five-hundred-year forced separation, and my parents were . . . well, I wasn't sure. Aggressively ignoring each other or sharpening their knives. Maybe having angry sex. It could go any number of ways.

In any event, we weren't likely to see Doc and Valathea for days.

"Teraeth, I realize this is uncomfortable–"

Teraeth leaned over and placed a finger against my lips. "Shh. Don't make a fuss. We'll have dinner, then I'll leave, happy to know you two are happy."

Something tugged inside me, a pleasant burning spreading out across my lips. That simple touch had been purely carnal, even though I know he hadn't meant it that way.

Janel's brows knit together as she watched us. She played with the food on her plate for a moment before letting a roll drop from her fingers and forcing a smile on her face. "Honestly. What am I going to do with you two?"

Teraeth laughed as he stared fondly at her. "I could make suggestions if you like."

Her mouth twisted into a wry grin as she ate. Teraeth had brought us leftovers from lunch–all finger foods that could be eaten without too much bother. No doubt just in case he'd found us in a state less dressed than our present condition. Considerate of him.

Teraeth glanced in my direction and then looked again, longer. His expression turned to concern. "Kihrin?"

I shook my head and turned away, slid my legs over the edge of the bed and bent my head.

What *was* my problem? Shame? Guilt? Pride? I lied to myself every damn time I said I wasn't attracted to Teraeth. I'd been denying it for *years.* And it was more than attraction. I remembered the few days I'd been separated from him, when I'd left for Jorat to find Janel and he'd gone to sea. I remembered the emotions I'd felt when I thought he'd come back, the crushing disappointment when I realized it wasn't him. I thought about how infuriating he could be and how I didn't mind, because he was equally astonishing.

I thought of all Darzin's horrible tortured views of how a real man behaved–his messed-up conviction *masculine* was a synonym with *cruel.* How thoroughly he'd screwed up his own son by insisting Galen measure up to a standard that guaranteed a boy who should have been a poet would never be happy or at peace with himself. How I'd seen kids in the Lower Circle do just as thorough a job messing themselves up, so convinced their sexual attractions were weakness, they overcompensated with the violence Quur labeled as strength.

Was I really going to let the Capital's idiot views on what makes a man worthy control me? After all the things I'd done or those damn prophecies said I'd do, *that* was going to be the chain I kept? Nope, sorry, I reject all your views on women and slavery and who can use magic, but I'm totally down with the idea two souls can only love each other if they're born in bodies of the opposite sex?

I could hear Darzin laughing at me. And Janel just being disappointed.

I'm *honest,* right?

At least Teraeth was. He'd been honest enough to admit how he felt, refused to treat those feelings like a crime. That was a hell of a lot more than I could say.

And damn, I *knew* I wasn't a coward. Vol Karoth? Sure. I had good reason to be afraid of Vol Karoth. But I had no damn good reason at all to fear *this.*

"Kihrin?" I heard footsteps as Teraeth circled the bed. "I apologize. I didn't realize my visit would bother you *this* much. I'll leave you two–"

I stood up, grabbed him by the front of his robes, and kissed him.

He must have figured out what was going on, since he didn't stick a dozen daggers into me, which was his normal response to sharp, sudden movements in his direction. And if that kiss might have proved intent–some way to know I wasn't imagining how I felt–well, that kiss was perfect. It lasted forever; it was over in a second.

When we parted, he just stared at me in mute astonishment.

"I'm sorry," I told him. "I'm a fool, and I should've figured things out much earlier–"

Teraeth grabbed me and kissed me back. His fingers tangled in my hair with insistent urgency as I felt his warm lips, his tongue. I was sinking and floating upward all at once, the whole world dampened into silence. I breathed him in. His mouth smiled against mine just a moment before he bit down on my lower lip with a sharp, exquisite sting. I laughed but didn't stop.

Fabric rustled as a plate was set down. We both broke off the kiss to see Janel walking toward a window. She paid no attention to us, but instead tilted her head to the side as she stared out the glass. There was a small thump and then another. And another.

"Much as I hate to interrupt you two–" Janel pointed.

A white flash impacted the glass, too small to do any damage. More flashes followed, each causing a small, sharp thump.

Bones.

Small fish were slamming themselves against the glass. Except they weren't fish exactly. Rather, they were all sharp teeth and delicate skeletons. Even as they smashed themselves to shards, more dead fish swam up to take their place. Then more still, larger ones.

But still dead. Animated dead.

I felt cold. What a fool I'd been, to think Vol Karoth hadn't responded to what Janel and I had done. If he couldn't come himself, he could most certainly send a messenger in his place–Vol Karoth controlled the dragons too, didn't he? And Rol'amar, the undying dragon who animated the dead by mere proximity, was closest.

"What the hell?" Teraeth stared.

"Grab your things," I said. "We need to leave right now."

# 60: Resurrecting the Gods

***(Grizzst's story)***

It took three weeks to evacuate all the vané who lived near the Mother of Trees. During that time, Grizzst made preparations. Mithraill rarely visited, which suited both of them, but Khaevatz stopped by daily. She asked a lot of questions: about the process, how Grizzst had developed it, and still more about Grizzst himself.

He found himself entertaining the monarch while setting up his equipment. Even as high up as they were, sunlight couldn't reach them; they'd set up special lights strung among the branches, brilliant glowing flowers and shining leaves that gave off a perfume of ylang-ylang and sandalwood.

It was blazingly hot.

"There's not much to know about me," Grizzst insisted as he checked crystals. "I'm not that interesting."

Khaevatz smirked. She lounged on a couch carved to look like a honeycomb. "You've spent the last fifteen hundred years trying to raise seven beings of godlike power from the dead. That's at least a little interesting."

Grizzst rolled his eyes. It's not that he didn't believe her, but, well—he didn't believe her. He was at a loss to understand why someone like Khaevatz would ever find him "interesting."

"Godlike?" Grizzst said. "Just say *gods.*"

"They're not gods."

"You might as well call them gods." Grizzst laughed. "Looking forward to seeing the looks on their faces when they discover their religions."

The Manol vané sovereign gave him a slow blink. "Religions? They don't have religions."

"Now that's where you're wrong." Grizzst moved around the final components. Satisfied, he turned back to Khaevatz. "It didn't take long for the voras to . . . devolve. I mean, we lost so much knowledge when Karolaen was destroyed, and that was after what we lost evacuating Nythrawl. The god-kings—"

"We are well familiar with them. The god-kings are why we left the Kirpis," Khaevatz said. "The other vané would not see the danger. Just because most voras are short-lived now does not make them less dangerous. I believe underestimating the danger shall be the Kirpis's doom."[1]

"Yeah, maybe so," Grizzst agreed. "Anyway, my point is that people turned to gods, religions, cults almost immediately. Anyone who would protect them."

"Yes, I see that, but what does that have to do with the Guardians?"

"Oh, I founded religions for all of them."

Khaevatz stared. "You . . . you what? *What?*" She sat up from the couch.

Grizzst enjoyed seeing her completely lose that otherwise impenetrable composure. Not that he had anything against Khaevatz–just the opposite, really–but no comedian ever asked for a better straight man.

He grinned at her. "Among humans, gods are where the power is, so if I succeed in bringing them back, it'll be a lot easier if they come back to a waiting power base. So I started religions for everyone. Did it a while ago too, so that avalanche is out of my hands now. Some of them are becoming pretty darn popular."

"So my mother, Khaemezra . . . ?"

"Thaena," Grizzst said.

"Thaena–*Death*? You named her Death?"

"Sure," Grizzst said. "I figured it was best to keep it simple. So we have Thaena, Taja, Tya, Khored, Ompher, Argas, and Galava."

"Tya. Magic? Now I can see why you would describe my mother as Thaena, but there was never a guardian of 'magic.'"

"Oh, that's Ir'amar."[2]

Khaevatz blinked. "But that is . . . wrong. Irisia was tied to *ithon*."

Grizzst shrugged. "Sure, but that's a little difficult for most people to wrap their heads around, so . . . what does a mastery of self-possession, control, willpower, and agency bring? Magic. Just like I know Mithros isn't tied to actual destruction, he's tied to entropy. But again–keep it simple."

"And Eshimavari is . . . Taja?"

"Exactly. Huge with gamblers."

Khaevatz's mouth dropped open. "But she's still dead. And even if she wasn't, it does not work like that! The Guardians cannot give other people any advantages. For that matter, neither can the god-kings."

"I know that. You know that. Everyone else?" Grizzst shrugged.

[1] And so it was.

[2] You might know her better as Janel's mother, Irisia.

"They don't. Somebody prays to Taja for luck and has a good run at dice . . . Must have been Taja, right? And it's like that for most of them. And hey, once we bring back the Guardians, who knows? Maybe they'll even answer a prayer or two."

Khaevatz lay back down on the couch. After a few minutes, she began to chuckle. Then she laughed outright. "You are right. It will be priceless to see my mother's expression."

"That's the spirit," Grizzst told her. "And with any luck, you'll do so before dinner."

"Excuse me?" Khaevatz sat up again.

Grizzst gestured toward the equipment. "We're ready."

Khaevatz wouldn't leave. Even though Grizzst had warned she'd be in great danger if anything went wrong. She ordered everyone else out.

"If you're staying, you might as well help." Grizzst pointed toward a pale, transparent crystal on a table. "Toss me that, would you?"

"What is it?" She examined the stone. The crystal looked like pale smoky quartz, uncut and delicate. Khaevatz walked it over and set it in his hand. "Looks fragile."

He snorted. "It's not. This is Grimward. It's what I like to call a Cornerstone. I've been collecting them since Karolaen. Almost have the whole set. It's quite a bag of tricks."

"And what does Grimward do?"

Grizzst tipped the stone into a setting he'd created. "Today? It resurrects a goddess."

He watched as the stone glowed, trigging a succession of crystals that lit up brighter than the lamps Khaevatz had provided. That energy fed into the tree itself.

They both waited.

"Are we going to know if–"

"Shh." Grizzst held up a finger.

Nothing happened.

The leaves rustled, insects buzzed about flowers that somehow thrived in the darkness. Then a glow spread out from across the Mother of Trees, a phosphorescence covering the bark and gilding over each leaf. The glow pulsed and then sank into the wood itself.

"Galava?" Grizzst called out. "Galava, if you can hear me–"

"She can't," Khaevatz said. "That's not how trees work. They don't have ears. But there's another way." She walked to the platform's edge and placed both hands against the bark. "We learned how to do this a long time ago."

"Brilliant. Well, while you're . . . doing whatever you're doing . . . tell her we need her to make a body for herself and transfer into it."

Khaevatz nodded to him and then returned her attention to the tree. She concentrated. Nothing happened.

Khaevatz looked confused. "Wait, but–"

Grizzst sighed and plucked Grimward from its cradle. "It was too much to hope this time would be any different. But on the bright side, at least it didn't explode . . ."

A soft glow coalesced from the tree leaves and settled down onto the platform, forming a person-sized shape. That shape slowly solidified, became cohesive.

A woman formed, small and plump with blue-green skin, teal feather fins flowing down her head.

*Oh right,* Grizzst thought. Galava[3] had been voramer.

After a few minutes, the body became solid. Then it stopped glowing.

Galava opened her eyes.

She hadn't been wearing clothes at first, but the flowers reached up to cover her, the leaves wrapped around her, creating a living gown of flora.

Galava's eyes focused on them. "What . . . Where . . . ?"

"Galava," Grizzst said, "welcome back."

The Goddess of Life began weeping.

[3] Real name: Novalan.

# 61: The Sound of Bone

***(Kihrin's story)***

I'd debated removing the chain, but finally decided it was light enough to let me swim if necessary.

I desperately hoped it wouldn't be necessary.

I'd also grabbed the harp, even though it was awkward. Call me sentimental, but I wasn't willing to risk leaving it.

The skeletons slamming against the windows were larger now. Something cracked.

Everyone was running from their rooms, in various states of dress. Thurvishar and Dolgariatz had noticed the problem almost as soon as we had and so had gathered the others.

The skeletons continued to slam into the glass at an alarming rate. Not all the bones belonged to fish, but included crocodiles, snakes, and other associated lizards. For the moment, the glass held, but only because the glass was magically reinforced.

It couldn't hold forever. Dolgariatz had the few staff evacuate and urged the rest of us to do the same. We didn't need to be told.

"Where are my parents?" I said just before I spotted Therin all but dragging Khaeriel from her room.

Teraeth cursed, so I turned to see why.

He was staring wide-eyed out the window, at the large shape swimming in our direction. It vaguely resembled a crocodile, but it was too large—nearly fifty feet long. Moving fast.

"Run!" Janel screamed. That broke the spell as we stared out in shock.

Thurvishar would lag behind everyone, so I grabbed his arm. Behind us, glass shattered as something too massive to be blocked by the lake house's delicate walls (enchanted or otherwise) crashed into the building. A wall of water rushed into the break behind us.

My hand jerked back as Thurvishar stopped in place and turned around.

"Thurvishar, no!"

The wizard entwined his fingers and pushed outward, as if one could force back the water through assertive gestures. Silvery disks of overlapping symbols, notations, and glyphs moved around as if floating on an invisible pond—pushed backward and filled the hallway just as the water arrived. The visible web of energy hovered there, bulging.

"That won't hold it long," Thurvishar said. He started running again.

I followed him.

Thurvishar wasn't wrong. The giant dead crocodile hadn't been destroyed when it had rammed the house, and now it circled to try again. Its shadow crossed the hallway while I ran up the stairs leading back up to the surface.

As I crested the top, I heard shouting, orders . . . screaming. I turned around and saw why, while also confirming my worst fears.

Rol'amar—the dead dragon we'd stumbled across in the Korthaen Blight—had found me.

As if to underscore the point, Rol'amar stared directly at me.

Dolgariatz's solders were fighting it. Predictably, they weren't doing well. Arrows, even poisoned arrows, were worse than useless against such a creature. Worse, any soldiers who fell to the dragon animated and joined the fight against Dolgariatz's men. Our Manol vané host was now forced to defend his men against more of his own people.

I'm good with a sword, all right with magic, but not a single spell I knew could possibly do any good against a creature like that. I'd hurt Rol'amar once; I didn't think he'd be foolish enough to let me that close again.

So I ran.

"Teraeth!" Janel yelled. "Get Valathea out of here!" Without waiting to see if Teraeth would obey, Janel started smashing down the dead around her, rendering the threats harmless by virtue of reducing them to bone fragments too small to be effective. Sadly, it wasn't likely to work on Rol'amar himself.

Teraeth did obey, as it happened, and ran to the former Kirpis vané queen. Meanwhile, Doc stood by the house, concentrating, a look I knew well; he was using his Cornerstone, Chainbreaker, on the dragon.

Now, I don't know the full extent of Chainbreaker's powers, but I knew it largely involved illusions. Incredibly powerful illusions. And I'd seen Terindel use those illusions on a dragon.

But this time as Doc concentrated, that glowing blue-eyed draconic skull swiveled in his direction. The dragon lunged at him, seemingly immune to any attempt to distort his perceptions.

"Doc!" I shouted out my teacher's nickname as I ran to him, desperately afraid I was too late.

A rock wall sprang up from the ground before Doc, and Rol'amar's head slammed into it. At the same time, hurricane winds forced the dragon backward. A lightning bolt flashed down from the teal sky, striking the dragon's skull and sending bone fragments flying. A deafening boom rolled out over the lakeside. Everyone covered their ears and was temporarily deafened.

Rol'amar healed immediately.

"I don't think your necklace is working." I reached Doc's side of the wall.

"No kidding? I hadn't noticed." Doc scowled. "I'm not sure how the damn thing sees, but what I'm showing the dragon clearly isn't fooling it."

"It's here looking for me."

"Why would–" Doc stopped and took a second look at me. "Maybe so. Let's see if we can use that. You run!" Doc shouted out. "Khae, Geri, stop the dragon when it turns!"

I started running.

The dragon did indeed follow, ignoring more obvious targets to go stomping after me, shuddering the ground with each step. Explosions bellowed behind me as wizards took advantage of the opportunity to freely attack the monster.

I heard another lightning strike and the dragon's roar. I didn't dare look back. I could practically feel the creature at my back. I heard a second draconic bellow as Rol'amar stopped chasing.

Then I heard another scream: my mother's.

I turned back. She wasn't in any immediate danger, still by the tree line even as she summoned up winds to move the creature. No, the reason for her scream was the person hanging limp from Rol'amar's mouth, shaken, and then tossed to the ground.

My father Therin.

The whole world stopped.

Therin's broken body didn't move. There was no kidding myself about my father's fate, no possible confusion about his status. A large chunk of his back was torn away, his spine hanging like white thread, his body cut almost in two. Not fixable. Instantaneous.

My father was dead.

Even now, I have a hard time explaining what happened next. The world darkened. Not figuratively. Literally. The sun turned black, eclipsed in an instant even though the Three Sisters were nowhere in the sky. Shadows covered the lake.

My awareness condensed, focused, homed in on the dragon Rol'amar. My nephew. The dragon who'd just killed my father. I lifted my arms. I didn't notice the wind pick up and swirl dirt and torn leaves around me. I didn't notice how my eyes shifted color. They didn't turn black but *empty:* voids reflecting no light, darker than even a D'Lorus royal could desire.

I felt despair. I felt rage.

I pointed at the dragon; darkness spread over its body, a shadowy sickness sinking into bone and torn sinew, which flaked and blew away as ash.

Rol'amar reared back in panic, its broken, twisted wings flapping vainly in the air. He roared, as if that would stop his impending disintegration. The dragon didn't attack me, though. Looking back, that seemed odd, when he knew I had caused his suffering. The dragon ran.

It didn't make it.

As he floundered in the lake, the black miasma devouring his head, I felt . . . I felt the tenyé of the creature, the searing immensity of power dwarfing the strongest wizard, a soaring cacophony of godlike potential. That energy flowed back through me and vanished as Rol'amar said the first and only word I ever heard him utter.

"Yes."

Then the dragon was gone, as if he had never been.

I didn't want to stop. I could have kept burning, unmade it all, screamed out my pain until the cup of suffering had emptied out. Maybe that doesn't make sense. After all, what did I care about Therin D'Mon? I'd hardly known the man, and for the majority of that time, he'd refused to acknowledge his paternity. He'd been so ashamed to admit the circumstances of my birth, he'd gone along with my brother Darzin's hideous lies. But that talk we'd had. I'd just found my father. I'd just met him.

I couldn't bear to lose him.

The animated dead were already collapsing, reduced back to still corpses as their controller died. Someone was shouting my name. I heard the sound as if from a great distance, dimmed, rounded in shadow.

Finally, I blinked, swaying in place, and returned to my senses. The world grew brighter, in a fashion.

I collapsed to my knees, too numb to move or feel or think about what had just happened. I could only sit on the shore while I listened to wailing grief. My mother, I realized. It wasn't just anguished crying, no. She kept repeating a single sentence, over and over. Three little words. Three little words that stabbed into my heart because I knew exactly what they meant. What they *really* meant.

*I am sorry. I am sorry. I am sorry. I am sorry. I am sorry. I am sorry. I am sorry.*

No one else made any noise at all.

# 62: Back from the Dark

***(Grizzst's story)***

The rest was shockingly easy.

Once Galava recovered, she resurrected the others.

Grizzst didn't even have to use Grimward. Galava did it all by herself.

And in no time at all, seven gods–or at least seven beings of godlike power–stood on top of the Mother of Trees before Grizzst and Khaevatz. He probably should have had a banquet waiting.

He just hadn't really believed it would work

Also, it didn't feel like a celebration. The seven Guardians didn't look at him, they looked *through* him, connected with reality by the most tenuous of threads.

*Veils,* Grizzst thought to himself. *It's just like Rev'arric. It's just like Rev'arric all over again.*

He most sincerely, passionately hoped he wouldn't have to nursemaid seven godlike beings back to awareness again. Once was enough. He remembered Valathea's words and feared for their mental health. Rev'arric, at least, had only been a single entity. He hadn't been discorporated across the universe. Grizzst stepped back so Khaevatz could greet each of them in turn.

Ompher and Galava embraced and held each other. Argas sat there, blinking at nothing. Tya and Taja had an arm around each other, tears streaking Taja's face. Khored paced, resembling nothing so much as a caged hunting cat. Thaena looked off into the distance, shuddering.

And each of them looked numb, shocked, lost. They had the distant stares of people who had seen things that could never be unseen, things that would haunt them forever.

They didn't look like people who had been rescued or saved.

"Do you remember what happened while you were . . . gone?" The question slipped out before he had a chance to consider the wisdom of interrupting their recovery.

He never even saw Thaena move. One second, she faced away from him. The next, she'd wrapped her hand around his throat and shoved him up against the tree bark, rage twisting the skin around her mercurial silver eyes.

"Who are you?" Thaena asked. Her voice sounded like something from a nightmare. "What's happened here? Are you responsible for this?"

"I . . . saved . . . ," Grizzst tried to say. His words weren't intelligible. Frankly, what she was doing was only uncomfortable, maybe embarrassing, but at any moment, she'd turn this into something a lot more permanent.

"Kay, put him down," Taja said. "That's not S'arric."

"Mother, he's a friend!"

Thaena's fingers started to tighten. He felt a pull on his souls. Then she hesitated and finally released him. Grizzst saw her hands shaking as she turned back to the others. "Where is S'arric? What happened to him?" She glanced around with wide eyes, as if expecting the corrupted god to appear the moment his name was spoken.

"That monster's imprisoned," Grizzst managed to say, rubbing his throat. He trickled a wisp of healing through his fingers, let it wash over his damaged larynx. "N'ofero and the rest of the Assembly chained him up around thirteen hundred years ago. I've been trying to bring you lot back to life ever since."

"Where *is* N'ofero?" Khored said. "We should speak with him."

"Dead," Grizzst said. "Every voras you knew is dead."[1]

"That was the price the voras paid to fix Rev'arric's mistake." Khaevatz walked over to her mother and put a hand on the woman's shoulder. "They're mortal now. They age and grow old and die after a century at most."

A soft, hurt sound came from Tya, the only other voras present other than himself.

She'd lost almost everyone she'd ever known.

Thaena regarded Grizzst once more, her expression now thoughtful. He didn't think she'd try to immediately kill him again, but he couldn't be sure. He found her attention unnerving. "So you should be dead too," she told him.

"No," Grizzst said, backing away from the voramer woman. "I'm still the immortal sort of voras. It's just an exclusive club these days."

"Who are you again?" Tya frowned at him. "I don't remember you from the university."

"Uh . . . probably because I never graduated." He straightened. "My name's Grizzst. Magic systems engineer, grade two. I was working on the coast when everything went sideways. I just got lucky and survived."

[1] Not *every* voras. God-kings survived.

"Wait, so you're just a maintenance tech? And you put together . . . that?" Argas pointed toward the ritual kit Grizzst had used to resurrect Galava. Argas looked impressed. He gave Grizzst a lopsided grin. "Nice."

Grizzst straightened himself and focused on Thaena, since she was the main threat to life and limb.

"And you have brought us back," Thaena said softly, "and now your job is done."

"Hey, I've got a funny feeling I'm not going to like how you're about to repay me."

"Leave him alone," Galava admonished. "He's done more for us than anyone else."

"Oh, not just me. The sovereign here and Valathea had a lot to do with it too."

Sovereign Khaevatz gestured toward the Immortals and the tree in general. "Come. Let me summon back my people and make you all welcome. Banquets or solitude, as you desire. We are honored to have you walk among us once more."

## 63: Saying Goodbye

***(Kihrin's story)***

I sat on the ground staring out at nothing until I felt someone's hand on my shoulder. Teraeth, who must have come back at some time during the fighting, or just after.

"What . . . what happened?" Teraeth's voice was quiet, soft.

"Therin died—" I choked on the words. *My father died.*

"That's not what I mean."

"Oh. That." I swallowed, wishing it did anything to help the feeling of hopelessness and dread threatening to drown me. "I didn't really kill Rol'amar, you know. He'll be back."

"I am not at all sure that's true, Kihrin." Teraeth knelt next to me and threw an arm across my shoulders. "Were you the one who eclipsed the sun?" he asked quietly. Like he didn't want to startle me. Like that might not be safe.

Which was almost certainly true.

"Maybe. I'm not sure." I swallowed again. Everyone was just . . . staring. Staring at me or at my mother, with no idea what to do. And the look on Janel's face. It wasn't fear, which was a plus, but the guilt was almost worse. *She* knew why this had happened.

I leaned against Teraeth's shoulder. "It started happening in the Blight, you know. The first time we fought Rol'amar. I thought the Blight was twisting my healing into something else, but now that wasn't what was happening at all. This link between me and . . . between me and Vol Karoth. It's not one way." I looked up at Teraeth. "I still feel him."

"It's going to be okay," Teraeth lied.

"No. No, it won't. You can't get rid of him without also . . ." I coughed out a dark, bitter laugh. "Without also getting rid of me. The Eight must not have realized we were a package deal, but what can you do? I mean, maybe we should take those prophecies a little more seriously." My voice cracked. "I really am going to destroy the world, Teraeth. Unless you stop me."

"No." Teraeth shook his head. "No. Absolutely not. I don't believe that's true."

"You'll stop me, though, right? I know you can. Promise me you will."

Teraeth's eyes were glassy bright. Tears fell down his cheeks as he stared at me. Ridiculously, Teraeth was one of those people who cried beautifully. That seemed so ludicrously and perfectly appropriate. Of course.

"No," Teraeth whispered. "Not you. I'll stop Vol Karoth. I'll push a thousand swords through that bastard's heart. I'll make any sacrifice for any ritual that keeps him imprisoned. I'll carve my way through nations. But *don't* ask me to kill you. I'll kill Vol Karoth. I won't kill you."

My laughter was bitter and dark. "Don't you get it? *There's no difference.*"

"There is," Teraeth insisted. "There has to be." The look in his eyes started to turn desperate. "Janel–"

*"Thaena!"* Khaeriel's scream echoed over the lake waters. The raw pain in her voice stopped any other conversation.

Doc looked up from covering Therin's body with a robe. "No. Khaeriel, no. That's not going to work out the way you think–"

*"Thaena! I pray to you! Thaena, I need you!"* Then she screamed out once more, in a heartbroken, fractured voice. *"Grandmother!"*

And Thaena appeared.

If I thought it had been quiet before, that was nothing compared to the utter and total silence ushered in by the Goddess of Death herself. She hadn't come as Khaemezra, as an ancient, pale crone with quicksilver eyes, but in her full splendor. Ebony skin and hair floating around her head like strips of Tya's Veil. The white gown, the belt of skulls, but most of all the aura of dread made her identity perfectly clear.

Thaena examined the scene, gaze sliding past Teraeth and me, past Janel, before settling on Khaeriel. And the body just past her, next to Doc.

"I'm so sorry," Thaena said as she walked over and touched her granddaughter's hair. "What happened?"

Khaeriel turned her face into Thaena's skirts and sobbed. "Bring him back. Please bring him back. Return him. I will give you anything! *Anything!*"

Even though I wanted that too, I felt a sudden piercing conviction my mother was making a mistake. I suppose I could blame it on too many god-king tales at my other father Surdyeh's knee, but this wasn't a trade that ever ended well. Even in the Maevanos–the bawdy, Quuros version the Black Brotherhood hated–someone always gave up their soul. Someone had to die. Thaena always demanded her due. Teraeth's hand tightened around me, as if he was thinking the same.

Maybe he just knew his own mother better than I did.

"Anything?" Thaena's rocky voice turned as smooth as a dead sea. "There's only one thing I want."

"Khaeriel," Doc warned.

"Stay out of this," Thaena ordered before looking down again at her granddaughter, a crying wreck of a woman sobbing on the ground in front of her. "He was one of my favorites. I would be only too glad to give him back to you."

Khaeriel lifted her tear-streaked face. "If I perform the Ritual of Night, you mean."

"Yes. If you perform the Ritual of Night," Thaena agreed. "Call my name when you're ready, and we'll revisit this conversation, won't we, my dear?"

Khaeriel leaned back on her knees, pulled herself away from Thaena's gown. She wiped at her eyes. "Thank you."

Thaena hooked a finger under Khaeriel's chin. "You're one of my favorites too. In spite of recent . . . indiscretions."

Without waiting for Khaeriel to respond, Thaena straightened and gestured to the side. A large magical gate spun open in the air. The barrier roses meant nothing to her–the whole reason the Eight had originally opened the portal to take us to the vané capital in the first place.

"The Parliament of Flowers is a long journey, so in the interests of time, perhaps a quicker passage is more appropriate." Thaena gestured to the gate. "Consider it a demonstration of my goodwill."

I sucked in a lungful of air. It was easy enough to see how this would go. We'd travel to the Parliament of Flowers–whatever that was–and assuming we tore down Kelanis and put my mother in charge, she'd sacrifice herself to Return my father and re-imprison Vol Karoth.

Except . . .

Except I didn't think Vol Karoth would make it that easy. Vol Karoth wasn't going to stop reaching out to me. So if the plan had any chance to succeed, I had to leave.

And then there was Relos Var. Where was *he*?

I gently shrugged off Teraeth's arms and stood. "No."

Thaena blinked and looked over at me. "No?"

Teraeth stood. "Kihrin, what are you doing?"

I inhaled. I knew exactly what I had to do. I hated it, but I knew. "I understand that everyone has their tasks, but so do I. And I can't stay in the Manol."

Thurvishar nodded as he joined our group. "I agree. That would be for the best."

"What are you talking about?" Janel asked.

I made a face. "Janel, you can't think Rol'amar appearing here was an accident, can you? Vol Karoth sent him after me." I waved a hand.

"He's awake now, and I remember how crazy he made the Old Man even when Vol Karoth still slumbered. Now that Vol Karoth's awake, he's reclaiming his control over the dragons. He's going to have them *all* looking for me."

"Wait." Thaena held up a hand. "Rol'amar was here?" She eyed the damage around her, the dead, the many, many skeletons, fish, animals.

*"Was,"* Teraeth said. He turned back to me. "You can't leave." He pointed with his chin to Khaeriel, to Therin's corpse.

I swallowed, my throat painfully dry. "They're why I need to go. Once we're outside the Manol, Thurvishar can keep making gates for us. We'll keep moving, too quickly for the dragons to home in on me. Inside the Manol, inside the barrier roses, that won't be possible. You–" I gestured toward the group. "You do whatever you need to do. Whatever you feel is best. You know how I feel about the ritual, but I trust your judgment. Thurvishar and I are going to figure out what needs to happen after that." I paused, distraught as I turned to Thurvishar. "I mean, I shouldn't assume–"

"It's fine," Thurvishar said. "You read my mind. That's exactly what I think we should do."

I stepped toward Thaena, the woman I'd once known as Khaemezra. "If you'd be so kind as to open *two* gates, with the second one leading to–" I turned back to Thurvishar. "Where are we going?"

"It doesn't matter. Any place with a velvet district." He looked thoughtful. "Pick one at random."

I started to protest and then stopped myself. Thurvishar knew as well as I did Taja threw things my way. Random was best. Also, I couldn't bear the thought of going back to the Capital City.

There was an obvious answer. "Kishna-Farriga, then. If you'd open a gate to Kishna-Farriga, we'd be very grateful."

Thaena's gaze was sympathetic. Also worried. "I didn't realize Vol Karoth would affect you like this. Even with what happened with you and Tyentso back on the island, when you were drawn to Kharas Gulgoth, I never believed it would be this bad."

"How could you have known? How could anyone?"

Relos Var had known. *You shouldn't have brought him back. It was cruel.* I hadn't understood what Var had meant at the time, but now I saw the truth of it.

"Perhaps it's best you don't remain this close to the Blight." Thaena turned her mirror gaze to Teraeth. "Your task will be to restore Khaeriel to her throne. Make sure this happens as it needs to."

Teraeth swallowed and nodded.

Thaena motioned again, opened a second gate next to the first.

"I'll go with you," Janel offered, coming to me at last.

"No." I took her hands. "No. If Teraeth's staying, you know someone needs to keep him out of trouble. Protect him, please."

Janel narrowed her eyes. "I never should've told you how idorrá works."

I almost smiled. "That's true."

She grabbed me and kissed me. "Be careful, Monkey."

I let the nickname slide. It had always been a hopeless fight, anyway. "Are you kidding? Thurvishar and I are going barhopping. Worst thing that happens is someone tries to pick a fight with Thurvy and he turns them into a frog."

"'Thurvy'?" Thurvishar narrowed his eyes.

"As my nickname is 'Monkey,' I officially don't want to hear a word from you." I stepped back and faced Teraeth.

We stared at each other.

"Good luck," Teraeth said.

I had no idea what to say. Or, no, because that's not true. I had so many things I wanted to say I didn't know where to start. I wanted to tell him I would never have asked him to kill me if I didn't trust him implicitly. I wanted to tell him he deserved to live in a world where he was more than his mother's favorite knife. I wanted to tell him I'd come back, that Hell couldn't keep me away from him, that Thurvishar and I were going to find a way to make this right.

I wanted to tell him that last kiss had been amazing.

Teraeth nodded at my reaction–my lack of reaction–and turned away.

"Right," I whispered. "You too."

I took a deep breath and went to my mother. Khaeriel pulled herself to her feet and wrapped the tattered remains of her dignity back around herself. Except for the tear tracks running down her face, I'd have never guessed she'd just suffered a heartrending tragedy, that just minutes before she'd been on her knees crying and begging. She looked cool, collected, and numb.

Ah. So that's where I get that from.

I picked up her hands. "You'll get him back. I know you. There's no one more stubborn."

She nodded and squeezed my hands. "We shall be reunited soon." Khaeriel's gaze veered toward Doc for a moment. She started to say something else but stopped herself. Instead, she lifted her chin and said, "Fix this, Kihrin. *Please* find a way to fix this."

I faked a smile with all my might. "Believe me, if there's a way, I'm going to find it. Well, let's be real here; Thurvishar's going to find it. But I'm very motivated to guard his back while he does." I kissed my mother on the cheek. "Remember what I said about Talon. And watch out for your brother. He's watching out for you."

"I have no doubt at all." My mother stroked my hair once, then dropped her hand. She said to Thurvishar, "Take care of my son."

The D'Lorus wizard nodded solemnly. "Of course, Your Majesty." But to my surprise, Thurvishar then turned and addressed Doc. "Do you have a Gryphon Men ring?"

I didn't hide my surprise. There was no way–

"Sure," Doc admitted.[1] "You know what they are? You have one?"

Thurvishar nodded. "I can acquire one, yes. If we need to contact you for any reason, that's what I'll use."

Doc nodded. "I guess I'll start wearing mine, then."

Thurvishar motioned to me. "Shall we?"

"Might as well."

We walked through the gate to Kishna-Farriga, and Thaena shut the portal behind us.

[1] I can only assume Emperor Sandus gave him one.

# PART II

## Rituals of Darkness

# 64: The Snows of Kishna-Farriga

***(Kihrin's Story)***

I stepped through Thaena's gate onto the Kishna-Farrigan streets and knew I'd miscalculated. Made mistakes on so many levels, really, but the most immediate one was visceral, personal, and involved the weather.

It was snowing.

The Manol Jungle had boiled at a temperature excessive by Capital City standards. Dolgariatz's supplied clothing had been thin and designed to catch the breeze. Even the shanathá chain was so light, it had clearly been enchanted to ensure its wearer didn't die of heatstroke before they might die of sword stroke instead.

The chill cut through our clothing like we were wearing smoke.

The numbness echoed my feelings. I stood there for an eternity of heartbeats, perfectly still. I remembered my father's body, my mother's screams, the black ash flecks peeling away as I unmade Rol'amar. The look on everyone's face as they realized . . . well, I'm not sure. At the very least that my good intentions were meaningless. If the connection between Vol Karoth and me was growing stronger—as it seemed to be—then soon I'd be a hazard to everyone around me. Everything around me. A freed Vol Karoth had *darkened the sun.* And how would that work now? Would Vol Karoth slowly take me over? Would all that power, far too much for my body to contain, consume and destroy me? Would I become a second Vol Karoth so there would effectively be two?[1] I couldn't tell if my flesh prickled from the cold or my horror. Everything I feared most in the world, condensed into one sharp needle of possibility.

Thurvishar took my arm. "This way. You wait inside, and I'll go back to Shadrag Gor and fetch us both something more appropriate for this weather."

"Right," I managed to say. "Sure."

I knew a lot of spells to protect me from heat and fire, and not a single one to protect me from cold. Snow fell even as we stood there, lin-

[1] That's a horrifying thought. I have no idea if it's possible.

gering on my eyelashes, collecting like a film over my shoulders. While the cold did a blessedly good job of covering the scent of trash and gutted fish from the harbor, I would have rather kept that olfactory assault. Instead, the air smelled like salt, woodsmoke, and ice, the cold scraping my nostrils raw.

I'd never seen snow before, not even in Jorat; I just hid from it inside a toasty cellar tavern while I listened to Janel and her not-quite-so-trustworthy confidant Qown convince me to help them slay a dragon.[2] This stuff was pretty, but also uncomfortable.

I decided I didn't like it.

I didn't watch Thurvishar create his gate back to Shadrag Gor. I was . . . distracted.

Absently, as if thinking through fog, I wondered if the cold was natural or if Aeyan'arric had somehow beat us here. But everyone wore furs or warm wool coats. The snow was no surprise. Certainly no dragon-inspired panic. Demon inspired, maybe. A few buildings were burned shells not yet rebuilt, others merely singed. People were jumpy in a way that reminded me of Galen, never quite sure when Darzin would materialize, in the mood to teach him a "lesson."

My teeth began chattering, and I remembered Thurvishar had told me to wait inside. Inside what? Oh right. A tavern.

I'd seen little of Kishna-Farriga on my last visit, although I could tell you a great deal about the quality of their slave pits and sewers. The buildings weren't like the Capital's, where space was always at a premium. Back home, even the poorest quarter's walls were solid and thick, packed tight and layered high. In contrast, Kishna-Farriga spread out indulgently along hills ringing the harbor, each building rising up past its brethren like bleachers at a stadium.

My frosting breath and the numbing cold reminded me I was ill dressed to stay outside. I entered the tavern.

As commentary on Kishna-Farriga's metropolitan nature, my entrance only caused a minor stir. The large room brought to mind Joratese cellar houses, except above ground and made from wood. Still, it was a closed-in space, meant as shelter in a wide array of weather conditions. Great shutters lashed the windows closed. Fire roared from a hearth. Smoke from oil lamps filled the room with a sooty haze. The front room seemed unusually crowded for the hour, likely from merchants, clerks, and dock workers enjoying a break from the normal routine. The crowd seemed cheerful enough. The smell of food made my stomach rumble. With effort, I ignored it.

[2] The events that led to the destruction of Atrine, I'm afraid. To Janel's dismay, that was exactly what she had been trying to prevent.

Instead, I sat down in a chair as close to the hearth fire as possible, uncovered my harp (what *was* I going to call her? I still hadn't decided), and started to play.

Normal etiquette (or at least normal Capital City etiquette) demanded a musician check in with the public house owner before setting up shop, but nothing about my clothing suggested a normal musician. They'd probably cut some slack to a rich, eccentric vané living up to the racial reputation.

Also, I wasn't in the mood to ask permission.

So I played. I started with "The Ballad of Tirrin's Ride" and "The Song of Dawn." I also played the only two vané songs I knew, both of which were melancholy dirges. One was literally named "Valathea's Song" (which was why I'd learned to play it in the first place). As one might well imagine, it was a dire tragedy where everyone died and everything hurt.

I played it twice.

I normally would have sung too, but I didn't trust myself not to break into tears.

Finally, my aching fingers demanded I stop. It had been too long since I'd played the harp–my calluses were wrong. The bar fell silent and stayed that way for a vast, pregnant beat after I looked up.

The room broke out into applause. People shouted suggestions for what I assumed were local ballads, probably shanties. I ignored those and began packing away the harp. I couldn't keep calling her Valathea now that Valathea was a living person. Sorrow? Maybe Sorrow. That's what *Valathea* meant, after all.[3] The harp's curse had lost none of its potency. I'd gained the harp and, right on its heels, lost my father. Again.

A thickset man, pale by Quuros standards, walked up to me, cleaning his hands on his apron. "Want . . . life? In . . . tree . . . the . . ."

I blinked at him. He was trying to speak the vané language, voral. He was doing a terrible job at it. Still, I admired the effort. A Quuros tavern keep wouldn't have bothered. "I speak Guarem," I offered.

"Oh, thank the gods," the man said, visibly relaxing. "I asked if you want something to drink? On the house."

"I'd rather have something to eat, if you don't mind."

The man shrugged. "Sure, why not? I have steak pudding left if you want."

"Pudding–" I shook my head. I imagined the local idea of "pudding" and mine didn't resemble each other. Either that or the local cuisine was unbelievably foul. "Whatever you have. Thank you."

[3] Or, rather, that's what the word means now, but it's a more modern definition.

"Be right back. Also, you should pick that up before someone thinks you don't want it." He pointed to the ground.

Ords. I'd missed the crowd throwing money at my feet, and I almost laughed in dark humor. Would I have been complimented or scandalized if I had really been a vané lord?

Well, I needed the metal. I didn't have any local currency.

I bent down and picked up the coins, thinking three things. One, this wasn't how I'd expected my day to end. Second, that I already missed Teraeth and Janel like they were the air I needed to breathe. Lastly, that since time moved differently in the Lighthouse at Shadrag Gor, Thurvishar should have returned before I'd reached the end of that first song.

So something must have happened.

My mind raced with a thousand ugly possibilities. Relos Var knew about Shadrag Gor. Var wouldn't necessarily be polite if he ran into Thurvishar again. And if anything had happened, well, it was Shadrag Gor. Thurvishar could have been months dead, and I'd never know. I might be on my own.

I looked around. A few people were still giving me looks, ranging from wary to curious, but most had gone back to their drinks and chatter.

A group of people huddled around a table in the back, and they had a serious, focused intent I knew well. Gambling of some sort, although I wasn't close enough to tell the specific flavor. The game itself didn't matter, though, as long as luck was more important than skill.

"Thank you, Taja," I murmured.

I fingered the coins in my hand. Maybe it was enough to buy my way in.

# 65: THE PARLIAMENT OF FLOWERS

***(Teraeth's story)***

Teraeth had excellent focus. Which was handy, because at the moment, what he wanted to do and needed to do were very different things. He wanted to go after Kihrin. He wanted to scream. He wanted to kill, oh, anyone. Everyone.

He needed to keep calm and pay attention to his mother. Teraeth knew Thaena well enough to recognize her mood: smug. Oh, she was sincerely sorry to see Therin dead. She was probably even sincerely fond of Khaeriel and Therin. She'd honor the deal.

But she hadn't gotten her way yet. First, Khaeriel had to retake the Manol throne, and then and only then could she go through the ritual to make the vané people mortal, so they'd age like any other race. And maybe that would be enough. They'd imprison Vol Karoth again and this time, *this time,* they wouldn't waste the opportunity. They'd figure out how to destroy that abomination once and for all. For Kihrin's sake as well as the world's.

Teraeth watched as his father picked up Therin's corpse. Dolgariatz finished making arrangements with his people. Janel had her arms crossed under her breasts, her helplessness mirroring his own. Valathea took Khaeriel by the hand and led her to the open gate.

As the two women approached, Thaena tilted her head, and her expression shifted from satisfaction to shock. "Valathea?"

"What a pleasure to see you, Khaemezra," she said. "Thank you so much for your assistance."

Thaena's nostrils flared. "You're welcome." She met the vané woman's eyes.

Teraeth winced. That wasn't a fight Valathea could win. He'd seen his mother stare down dragons, god-kings, Relos Var.

Valathea held Thaena's stare without flinching, even as she gestured toward Teraeth. "I should compliment you on your son. He's lovely. You must be proud." She didn't make it sound like an insult.

Janel caught Teraeth's eye. She'd noticed the staring contest too. She raised an eyebrow at him, but all he could do was shrug.

He'd thought Valathea unimportant. Doc's wife and not much more.[1] Brought back by Khaeriel to bribe some favor from Doc himself.

But unimportant people didn't win staring contests with the Goddess of Death.

A flash of disbelief crossed Thaena's face. "I'm surprised to see you be so gracious."

"I can hardly be jealous," Valathea said. "Terindel thought I was dead. And truthfully, I may as well have been. I like to think you were looking after him for me."

Valathea sounded so . . . sweet. Genuine, warm, not even slightly cloying. So pleasantly agreeable and respectful in tone, Teraeth couldn't point to any single word as mockery or condescension. And yet . . .

Knives lurked in Valathea's words. Sharp, deadly edges. So well hidden he could see his mother struggle to find justification for complaint.

His father cleared his throat. "We should go."

"You'll get no argument from me," Teraeth said. He caught Janel's attention and gestured toward the gate.

"Where are we going?" Janel whispered.

"The Parliament of Flowers," he whispered back.

"The *what* of Flowers?"

"It's the legislature. I'll explain later." Teraeth eyed his mother and stepmother. The contest of wills between them hadn't quite finished.

Then Valathea smiled brightly and led Khaeriel through the gate, followed a few seconds later by Doc, carrying Therin's body.

As soon as Valathea left, a scowl settled onto Thaena's expression. Teraeth wondered if there might be jealousy after all—but not from Valathea's side. Kihrin had once insisted Doc and Thaena shared a venom between them reserved for failed romances, for soured love. If his mother still harbored feelings, however . . .

Well, Teraeth wouldn't want to be Valathea, that's for sure.

Dolgariatz followed and then Janel. As Teraeth started to take his turn, his mother caught his gaze. "My grandson won't give up his throne willingly."

His mouth quirked. "Does anyone?"

Teraeth felt his mother's will settle on him, and he flinched. This was the ugly side to being one of the Thaena's chosen, her angels, the side never mentioned in any recruitment pitch. To be a god's angel wasn't quite the same as a gaesh, but it meant being open to a god's will—for good or ill.

[1] You may take it as granted that Teraeth always refers to his father as Terindel. In the interest of consistency, I shall continue to refer to him as Doc except in cases where he's addressed in actual speech.

*You'll have to kill him.*

Teraeth swallowed and nodded. *Understood.*

*And if Khaeriel won't do what is needed, you know your task there too.*

Teraeth's eyes widened, and he glanced over at the gate Kihrin's mother had just walked through. "But, Mother–"

Thaena narrowed her eyes.

Pain arced through him. He shuddered and took a deep breath before bowing his head. *As you say.* Teraeth walked through the gate, and the Goddess of Death closed the portal behind him.

He wouldn't enjoy killing Khaeriel, but he would if it came to that. Teraeth could kill anyone, no matter how he felt about them, no matter how much they might mean to himself or others.[2]

It was, after all, the job his mother had created him for.

Teraeth approached Janel. He curled his fingers into a fist instead of putting an arm around her. She looked in a mood to burn anyone who touched her. Instead, he tilted his head and said, "Your mouth is open."

Yes. Much better. Fantastic.

Janel shut her mouth and glared.

He understood the gawking, though. The Parliament of Flowers was worth gawking at. Unlike the Mother of Trees, which sat in darkness broken by phosphorescence and mage-light, the parliament had been raised up above the tree line to glory in the sun's splendor.

The flowers grew better that way.

Flowers didn't cover *every* surface of the ornate building, but one might be forgiven for thinking they did. The building spiraled asymmetrically into lotus-like terraced petals, seemingly delicate but in fact enormously strong, lush with blooms. The scent of flowers mingled into a perfume that encompassed all flowers and none, heady sweet. Butterflies and bees and the sound of nearby birds hummed in the surrounding branches.

Teraeth watched Janel take it all in, and he couldn't help but smile. Up ahead, Dolgariatz and Valathea were speaking to the golden-skinned Kirpis vané who had greeted them.

If the parliament didn't grant their request for asylum, it would be short adventure.

"Teraeth," Janel said. "Something about that conversation between your mother and Valathea is bothering me . . ." She bit her lip and hesitated.

"Just say it," he told her.

"Well, if this was Jorat," Janel said, "I'd have thought Valathea was

2 How quickly he's forgotten the conversation he just had with Kihrin.

giving proper deference to Thaena's greater idorrá. But since it's not"—she tilted her head to the side—"it was the opposite, wasn't it?"

Teraeth almost looked back toward his mother, as if a thousand miles didn't separate them now. Kihrin had told him to ask Janel to explain idorrá. Teraeth wished he'd listened. The word clearly meant authority or prestige, which Thaena should have had in abundance.

Janel was right, though. Valathea had acted like a *queen.* A queen graciously thanking a subordinate for all her hard work. And Thaena hadn't corrected her.

"You know," he said, "all this time, I've known that the Eight Guardians were picked out, *chosen,* to represent the different races, but I've never once asked myself who did the choosing."

They both stared at Valathea, still talking to the vané reception. Teraeth couldn't help but notice she'd taken charge, when he'd have expected that honor to have fallen to one of the two deposed royals.

Of course, Doc and Khaeriel had both just lost someone dear to them. Maybe Valathea was trying to save them the effort of negotiating political arrangements before they'd recovered.

While Valathea spoke, vané guards approached Doc, who allowed them to remove the body.

As if she'd heard her name, Valathea walked straight over to Teraeth and Janel.

Or rather, just to Janel.

"Parliament has agreed to hear our case and provide amnesty until the final ruling. They'll allow us to use a safe house until then. We'd be well advised to retire to the main chamber until then. I expect King Kelanis will arrive shortly."

"And you want us surrounded by Founders when he does," Janel said.

"It would be prudent," Valathea agreed. "The easiest way for Kelanis to deal with the hearing is to never have it because we've all conveniently 'vanished.'"

Janel laughed. "This family does seem to prefer its politics served with a side of murder."

Teraeth frowned at the interplay between them. When had Janel and Valathea become friends? He was missing something. He hated that feeling. And he couldn't resort to his normal solution: asking his mother. He had a feeling "Who the fuck is Valathea?" wasn't an acceptable discussion topic even if Thaena had been around to ask.

Teraeth started to gesture for Janel to go first, realized she would, anyway, and aborted the movement. "Ready?"

Janel nodded and followed the vané contingent into the building.

# 66: The Voice of Heaven

***(Kihrin's story)***

I set down my cards. "And this is why I own all your metal."

The other gamblers groaned. The Doltari man on my left cursed something I didn't understand, likely a commentary on my ancestry or instructions on where I could put that winning hand. I grinned as I collected my ords and took a moment to finish off my meal.

Steak pudding turned out to be lightly spiced mutton hidden inside a bread wrapping and then simmered by the fire all day. I'd have liked it to have been spicier, but I wasn't going to complain.

I noticed no one was dealing out the next hand. Everyone at the table was giving the Doltari man next to me an uncomfortable look before turning their attention back to me.

Okay, so he also might have been accusing me of cheating.

I sighed as I licked my fingers clean. "Is this going to be trouble? I don't want trouble. I'm sure the nice tavern keep doesn't want trouble."

The Doltari man pushed his chair back from the table and stood. He was large and well muscled. Everyone at the table gave him the deference owed to the local big man, the one you made sure won more than he lost if you knew what was good for you.

Taja, I wasn't in the mood for this shit.

He growled something else I didn't understand before he pulled a knife. I blinked at him. Was he serious? I mean, I look pretty damn vané if I'm dressed for it, and by coincidence, I was dressed for it. Most Kishna-Farrigans knew what a vané looked like. Did he think he'd been lucky enough to play cards with the *one* vané who wasn't a thousand-year-old deadly wizard and duelist?

I mean, he *had,* but that's a hell of a thing to be right about. And I'm still damn good with a sword, which I happened to be wearing.

Before the gambler with the knife did anything stupid, I drew Dolgariatz's loaner sword, whipped it across his hand so he dropped the knife, and ended the motion with the sword point at the man's throat.

"I. Am. Not. In. The. Fucking. Mood." If the words wouldn't translate, the sword's meaning was universal. I held the blade on him while I tucked coins into my belt pouch with my free hand. It was time to leave.

The bar fell silent again, this time in a more judgmental way. Strangers stood to my back, and this man—whoever he was—might have friends in the crowd who'd object to how this had shaken out. Also, I didn't know the local laws on dueling, bar fights, or hell, just using a sword in public.

That's when I heard singing.

I might've been hearing the voice earlier, but the normal tavern sounds had drowned it out. I tilted my head as I listened.

"Do any of you hear that?"

A women who spoke Guarem blinked in confusion and shrugged. The door creaked open; someone entered from outside. A chair leg scraped against the wooden floor. I surmised at least one person had stood. Nobody seemed to have any idea what I was talking about, however.

The singing continued.

I sensed motion behind me. I moved to the side as a thick club missed my head. At the same time, the gambler saw his opening and tried to take it. Again, I don't know what he was thinking. He didn't even have a knife by then. I pricked him on the shoulder as a reminder that I was armed and he wasn't, then whipped my sword around and let the man attacking me from behind impale himself. The wood under our feet jumped as someone fell to their knees hard. At that point, I grabbed the strap on the harp's carrying case with one hand while keeping the sword out with the other, hoping to make any more would-be helpers pause as I backed my way to the door.

A man to my right pulled a crossbow up from under the table and started winding the crank.

"Shit," I muttered as I continued backing up. I'd probably still be in the room by the time that bastard finished. The Doltari man grabbed a poker from the hearth and started advancing with more confidence now that he held a weapon whose reach matched my own. I noticed the tavern keep who'd so graciously fed me was back behind the bar, looking frustrated.

But then someone screamed. The man who'd finished loading his crossbow fired his bolt, a ludicrously bad shot that hit the far wall. Or rather, it hit the rope tied to an iron peg on the far wall, which held up a heavy iron sconce above the main room, which promptly fell directly on top of the Doltari man's head. He went down like a netful of dead fish.

I paused. "Thanks, Taja."

I figured this was the perfect moment to stop backing up and run. I turned around and nearly slammed into Thurvishar, dressed in woolen D'Lorus black robes, holding a bundle over one arm.

"Are we done playing?" Thurvishar asked.

"Yes, we are," I agreed as I started to sheathe my sword. I grimaced, wiped the blade's edge on my thin silk shirt, and tried again. "Let's leave. There's something I need to do."

I didn't wait on him; I started to hurry out. I paused on the way as a faded piece of paper nailed to the wall next to the door caught my attention. I grabbed it and finished running out the door.

The cold hit me like a slap. It had still been daylight when we'd arrived in Kishna-Farriga, but now it was after dark. Snow had turned the brightly painted wooden buildings into a gray-and-white wonder, sparkling under the silver glow of mage-lights strung along the streets. The various god-king temples, cathedrals, and churches across the city had been limned in magical light, turning the city into a glory of rainbows by night. Honestly, one of the most beautiful sights I've ever seen.

Of course, it was also well below freezing, and the night air felt like I'd just jumped into the waters of a winter lake.[1]

Thurvishar offered me the bundle. "Hurry. Your new friends may be loath to part ways."

"Right. You take the harp." I traded and started walking toward the singing. I still heard the voice. I suppose I should have stopped to change clothes, but that singing . . . I unrolled the bundle as I walked. Thurvishar had given me a thick tunic, gloves, fur-lined boots, woolen kef, a down-lined coat, and a bundle of fur that was either a cloak or a skinned bear. I'd have bet anything the clothing was Yoran. "Also, what took you so long?"

"Why would you think I'd have clothing back at Shadrag Gor that would fit you?" Thurvishar made a vague gesture toward my build and height. I noticed he'd also reclaimed twin intaglio Gryphon Men rings that would allow him to talk directly to Empress Tyentso.[2] "That took time. And I'd assumed you'd warm yourself by the hearth and stay out of trouble!"

"Really? That's on you. I thought you knew me better than that." I didn't bother to undress, but instead just piled his clothing on top of my previous layers as we walked. The boots proved the most troublesome,

[1] Not that Kihrin has any idea what that's like. I myself tried it once, in Yor, on a dare from Darzin. It was strangely exhilarating.

[2] I didn't bring them with me originally, because we were afraid that if the vané discovered their true nature, they would interpret it as proof of a Quuros plot.

since I did have to remove the jeweled sandals first. I had to hand it to Thurvishar: they actually fit.

He rolled his eyes but didn't contradict me.

"Just out of curiosity . . . was it you or Taja who made that light sconce fall?"

"It wasn't *me,*" Thurvishar said. "I was going to trip him with the floorboards."

"Oh. Taja, then." I finished tapping my feet into the boots and wrapped the fur cloak around myself. Much better. "Come on, let's go. We need to hurry."

He frowned. "I don't hear anyone. I don't think they're chasing—" Then he stopped and stared at me, mouth falling open in shock. "Urthaenriel? You can't be hearing Urthaenriel. That's impossible."

I drew my sword. I hadn't said a word about Urthaenriel—Godslayer—or that I was hearing her voice in the air. But I'd been thinking it.

And of all the creatures in the world who can read minds, exactly none are friends.

Thurvishar's eyes widened as he realized his mistake.[3] He raised his hands in surrender. "Wait! Wait, just listen. I'm not a demon. I'm not Talon either. Or any other mimic."

"And exactly how would you prove that?" I said through gritted teeth.

"I've been able to read minds for as long as I can remember, Kihrin. It's my witch gift: the whole reason Gadrith didn't kill me when I was a child. Telepathy is too useful. It's almost impossible for me not to read someone's mind unless they're heavily shielded with talismans. You used to be, if you'll pardon the expression, an open book. Used to be. It's become more difficult." He tilted his head and studied me thoughtfully. "You really are hearing Urthaenriel." It wasn't a question; Thurvishar knew.

Of course. If he remembered being Simillion, the first Quuros emperor, then he'd held Urthaenriel himself once. He knew what she sounded like.

"Yeah."

"You know that's impossible, right?"

"You mean impossible like the way I have a link to the god of darkness and despair and just channeled his power to disintegrate a dragon?"

He made a face. "Point taken." But then Thurvishar glanced at my hands. "What was that you grabbed from the tavern, anyway?"

"Oh, this?" I held up the paper for a second before stuffing it into my coat. "My wanted poster. Fortunately, it's a terrible likeness, not to mention four years out of date."

[3] Because I had most definitely made one.

Thurvishar raised an eyebrow. "How much are they offering?"

"Quite a flattering sum. Something to remember if we need to collect heaps of metal in a hurry. Now, come on, then. Let's run–" I slid sideways on the ice, windmilled my arms, and managed to come to an undignified and precarious upright stance. I gestured. "Let's walk that way."

Thurvishar nodded and followed.

## 67: The King's Threat

***(Teraeth's story)***

Valathea had been right.

It didn't take King Kelanis long at all.

The vané monarch marched through the parliament doors and then stopped, looking backward with annoyance.

King Kelanis's soldiers hadn't come with him. Teraeth schooled his expression away from the smirk he so badly wanted to indulge; King Kelanis's soldiers *couldn't* come with him. This was the most enchanted spot in the entire Manol. The Founders controlled who was allowed here. He strongly suspected Janel had been given access because her appearance was so exotic she didn't immediately strike anyone as Quuros. He'd been allowed in because of his father.[1]

None of them had been allowed to keep their weapons.

King Kelanis recovered quickly. "Founders, we demand an explanation. You are harboring wanted criminals."

Valathea turned from the group she had been addressing. "We are not. There's no one present not involved with legal proceedings involving their status. But it's fortunate that you're here, Your Majesty, since those legal proceedings involve you as well."

Kelanis laughed lightly. "We wondered why our sister would go through all the effort to return to the Well of Spirals. We had thought she was showing family loyalty, but it seems she just wanted to hire a lawyer." His eyes slid to the side, where the sister in question sat still and quiet, drinking a glass of wine with an expression on her face a statue might envy.

"You left before we could be introduced, nephew," Valathea said, smiling. "It's such a pleasure to finally meet you. I must say you remind me of your father."

Teraeth raised his eyebrows. That last bit had *not* been a compliment.

But Kelanis took it that way. "Thank you. And what legal proceed-

[1] Teraeth doesn't do himself enough credit here. He *is* the king's uncle on his mother's side, never mind that he's the younger party by a factor of several centuries.

ing do you think should have our attention? Khaeriel died. Even if she stands here now, it changes nothing."

A tall razor blade of a vané dressed in silver, white, and soft gray answered. "Valathea has requested permission to argue for the overturning of the Law of Daynos. We've agreed to hear her arguments. If the state wishes to prepare a defense, we will naturally allow for that."

"Who's that?" Janel leaned over and whispered.

"Daynos," Teraeth replied.

"Oh."

King Kelanis looked like he'd tasted something poisonous. "We will require time."

"You have two weeks," Daynos said. "We will meet back here and hear arguments from both sides before the Founders make a ruling."

Kelanis looked like he wanted to protest. Instead, he turned and looked at everyone in the room. His gaze swept over Teraeth and Janel, paused momentarily, then continued on to Doc.

The flicker of confusion on Kelanis's face was so fast, Teraeth might have missed it if he hadn't been watching for the king's reaction. The brief glance back to Teraeth, whose name he knew, then back again to Doc.

Of course, if Teraeth had any doubt Kelanis had made the connection, it vanished as the king said to Khaeriel, "Terindel? Are you out of your *mind*? If you throw out the Law of Daynos, *he becomes king*."

"Your Majesty–" Daynos's voice was heavy with warning.

"If he had any interest in becoming king, yes. He does not. And if he changes his mind? He becomes king of the Kirpis vané, while I remain queen of the Manol vané. But as I have developed a renewed respect for the importance of righting old family wrongs, I would not begrudge him that." Khaeriel saluted her brother with her wineglass in a clearly mocking gesture. "Thank you for the lesson, little brother."

Daynos sighed, eyeing them like a parent prepared to step in to break up a fight.

"We have your son," Kelanis said.

Next to Teraeth, Janel straightened. Teraeth put a hand on her arm. "Wait."

Teraeth knew Kelanis was bluffing. There was zero chance Kelanis had somehow managed to send agents to Kishna-Farriga and capture Kihrin since they'd parted. Kelanis did *not* have Kihrin.

But was it possible Talon had somehow changed places with Kihrin at the prison? Teraeth thought back to the last day. How Kihrin had kissed him. How Kihrin had destroyed the dragon. No. That hadn't been a mimic.

It probably said something about Teraeth that the first event had seemed the more unreal.

Still, that Kelanis thought the threat would work seemed curious. Even if Kelanis had a mimic impersonating Kihrin, the Quarry warden would have informed him of their escape. And since two of those escapees stood present in the room . . . why would Kelanis think Khaeriel would ever believe her son remained in custody?

Khaeriel narrowed her eyes. "I do not believe you."

"Then we look forward to presenting our evidence," Kelanis growled, "but most especially our nephew's head."

He seemed . . . sincere. Kelanis was a good liar. A common trait in the family–arguably a required trait for rulers–but still, the venom, the anger, the repressed fury in his voice . . .

Kelanis wasn't lying. Or rather, Kelanis didn't *think* he was lying.

And Kihrin had encountered Talon at the Quarry. So what if Kelanis honestly thought he had Kihrin in custody?

"Oh, Talon," he whispered, "you crafty little bitch."

Janel leaned against Teraeth. "Do you think she did that on orders or improvisation? I don't know mimics except by reputation."

Teraeth blinked at her in surprise. He hadn't expected her to follow his train of thought. "Could be either, to be honest."

"Your Majesty," Valathea said, "even if she withdraws her request, this case will still be heard."

The king glared at her. "And nothing would please you more, we are sure. But the Law of Daynos exists for a reason. You are not going to convince the Founders to overturn it. Not in two weeks, not in two hundred years." He gestured toward Daynos. "We will return with our defense."

With that, he swept out of the room.

Teraeth sighed and settled back in his chair. "Well, that's done with, at least for now."

"So what happens next?" Janel looked over at him. "I'm not going to lie: I'd feel a lot more comfortable if we just had to kill something." She fidgeted. "I feel like leaving this building would be . . . unhealthy."

"And yet we'll have to. The Founders aren't going to let us camp out in the main hall. One assumes we'll have to retreat to that safe house. Let's hope it's secure."

Janel looked over to where Valathea, Khaeriel, and Doc clustered together, talking.

"Do you think there'll be assassins?"

"Oh yes," Teraeth said. "If I were Kelanis? I'd definitely send assassins. Although they won't be his best. Somehow, I suspect the Black Brotherhood won't be available."

# 68: The Temple of Vilfar

*Thurvishar said, "Now we're going to return to Senera."*

*Kihrin raised an eyebrow. "About time. I was starting to think you'd forgotten your girl–"*

*"Don't finish that sentence," Thurvishar growled.*

*Kihrin beamed. "Whatever you want. Please continue."*

### (Talea's story)

Rebel proved to be everything Talea had hoped.

She was some strange breed of wild dog Senera explained was called a *dhole,* whatever that was. Of far greater importance, she was adorable. Rebel reminded Talea of a dog crossed with a fox, all ginger coat and bushy black-tipped tail. She was social and gregarious and hated to be left by herself.[1] Rebel disliked the leash Senera used, but the wizard insisted. She said it wasn't to keep her dog under control as much as to assure people they met while traveling that Rebel was under control. Over the past ten cities, Talea and Rebel had become best friends.

Talea and Senera was still a work in progress.

Talea had rarely been outside the Capital City or various locations in Yor. The local buildings enthralled her, the way everything spread out. She loved the bright colors and ornate filigree in contrast to the Quuros capital's whitewashed streets and white stone walls. Talea had learned Kishna-Farriga wasn't technically one of the Doltari Free States but was used by almost all those independent and thoroughly autocratic city-states as a stopping point for their trade goods. It might have been more accurate to say Kishna-Farriga belonged to every god-king. Each had a temple there, brighter, more ostentatious, and more lavish than their neighbors'.

Except for Vilfar, God-Queen of Vengeance.

According to the Name of All Things, she was their next and hopefully last stop. Her temple sat in a giant pit at the edge of the main cemetery

[1] To be fair, this is also true of Talea.

and crematorium, a deep hole ringed by an impossibly long stair. The descent seemed custom designed to make devotees falling to their deaths a regular occurrence. The strong smell of roasting meat took on much more sinister connotations here. Above them, a rope network supported high awnings, twisted like overlapping flower petals, which kept snow from falling into the temple. Rows of cauldrons illuminated the temple floor, each burning merrily in unnatural chemical hues–bright green and blue. The thirty-foot-high black bronze statue of the temple's dedicated goddess, holding a sword in one hand and a hangman's noose in the other, towered over them.

Then the metallic rotten stench reached Talea's nose and she realized she'd assumed wrongly. The statue wasn't blackened bronze. It was just covered, head to toe, in layers and layers of blood, some dried and some wet enough to drip down to the altar underneath.

Talea fought the strong desire to roll her eyes. The blood seemed rather melodramatic, but she knew better than to say so out loud. Xivan wanted information from these people.

If Talea had anything to say about it, Xivan was going to get that information.

They didn't expect to find Suless here. They expected to find her in Bahl-Nimian, the city-state Vilfar controlled–but since they'd never been to Bahl-Nimian, their first stop was here.

Rebel didn't like the temple at all. The dhole held her head low as she sniffed around. Senera held down a hand to comfort the dog.

A red-robed devotee walked forward as the three women reached the bottom of the long spiraling pit. "Do you wish to make an offering to the goddess?"

"No," Xivan said. "I'm here to talk to her."

The priest took a step forward. "Of course. But we do ask for a nominal donation in order to maintain–"

"No," Senera interrupted. "We don't want an augury. We want Vilfar to show up. Here. Now. We have business with her."

Talea looked around the temple while the others spoke. Her initial impression hadn't changed since their arrival. The people praying here didn't fit any particular stereotype, but then revenge seldom paid attention to social class or station. Sacrificing animals to the goddess must have been encouraged, since goats and chickens waited in cages off to the side. Which explained the smell of roasting meat. Understandably, Rebel was far more agreeable to that aspect of religious services.

"I'm sorry, but you must know that's impossible."

When Talea looked up, the priest had thrown back his hood, revealing himself to be a middle-aged Doltari man, pale, but still nowhere near Senera's complexion.

"Nothing's impossible," Xivan said. She rested her hand on her sword's pommel.

Xivan didn't draw it, which was probably for the best. Vilfar wouldn't come within a hundred miles of this temple if she knew the visitors paying respects had brought Godslayer with them.

"Why is it impossible?" Talea asked. "Does Vilfar never visit this temple?"

The priest looked at Talea for the first time. "Well, no. The Holy Mother stays at her palace in Bahl-Nimian. She hasn't left in my lifetime."

Xivan tsked. "Fine. Then I assume you don't mind giving directions? We'll pay our respects in person."

Talea fought not to smile. Xivan was doing a horrible job of making such a visit sound respectful.

Then a deep, familiar voice said, "Talea?"

All three women turned. Two men had descended the stairs, both dressed for the weather. They were dark-skinned Quuros, but the one with the golden hair was even darker-skinned than his bald companion.

And Talea knew the bald man very well.

"Thurvishar!" She ran over to give him a hug. "You're here! What are you doing here? How are you? Who's your–" Then she stopped, blinking. The other man would've been extremely pretty if he didn't look so much like a D'Mon. "Wait."

He didn't just *look* like a D'Mon. She couldn't see his eyes in the odd temple light, but she knew they'd be blue.

The man in question shifted his position, still one foot on the stair. "Hello, Talea," he said. "You probably don't remember me . . ."

"You've met once before, but it was a few years ago," Thurvishar said.

"Oh. At that party.[2] You're a D'Mon." Talea tried, and utterly failed, to hide her loathing in that last sentence.

Kihrin didn't seem offended. "I'm doing my best to be bad at it."

"*What* are you doing here?" Senera demanded as Rebel darted forward as far as the leash would allow, sniffing the air.

Thurvishar gave the white-skinned Doltari witch a long look. "Hello, Senera."

"Don't make me repeat myself."

Thurvishar held out a hand for Rebel to sniff. "What are *you* doing here, Senera? Leaving offerings to god-kings really doesn't seem like your style."

"It's none of your business, High Lord," Senera snapped. "Now answer my question. What are you doing here?"

Thurvishar smiled, although perhaps that was because Rebel had begun licking his hand. "It's none of your–"

2 My Academy graduation party, to be precise.

"Rebel! Stop that! Come back here right now." Senera seemed aghast at her dog's approval of the D'Lorus wizard. "No. Not what are you doing in Kishna-Farriga. What are you doing *here*, in the temple of Vilfar? If this doesn't seem like my style, it sure as hell isn't yours. Why would you two even be here?"

"That's still none of your business," Thurvishar said pleasantly, but his eyes flicked over to Xivan.

Save for the brief greeting to Talea, Kihrin had stayed quiet during all this, but his attention also focused on Xivan. Senera looked at Kihrin, frowned, and followed the direction of his stare.

Xivan raised an eyebrow. "Do I have something on my face?"

"You're Xivan Kaen, aren't you?" Kihrin asked.

The duchess tilted her head. "I don't believe we've had the pleasure. You're Darzin's"–she scrunched up her face as she tried to remember the relationship–"son?"

"Brother," Kihrin corrected. "Although it doesn't matter. He's dead now."

The whole world tightened into focus around Kihrin D'Mon.

"What?" Talea said. "Darzin's dead? When did *that* happen? *How?*"

He glanced at her, looking embarrassed. "Oh, uh . . . I . . . killed him."

"Oh." Her voice was small and faint and indecipherable. The ground turned to quicksand under her feet; she couldn't stand.

Talea sat down on a temple bench, trying to make sense of her feelings.

Was she . . . happy? Should she feel happy? She was supposed to feel happy, wasn't she? For so long, all she'd wanted was to see Darzin D'Mon dead. She'd studied swordplay for nearly four years, hoping for the skill and opportunity to make that wish a reality.

Did it matter if someone else beat her to it?

She felt a cold nose press against her hand and realized Senera must have let Rebel go to her. Talea pulled the dog to her and pressed her face against Rebel's fur coat. A second later, Xivan put an arm around her.

Talea wiped away tears, glad beyond measure to feel Xivan's embrace. "Funny, isn't it? That I find this out at temple to the goddess of revenge?"

"Almost, yes," Xivan agreed.

Talea heard footsteps, and a soft growl from Rebel.

The footsteps stopped. "I'm sorry," Kihrin D'Mon said.

Talea looked up. "For killing Darzin? Don't be. You have no idea how glad I am he's dead."

He opened his mouth to say something, paused, and then closed it again. Instead, he focused his attention on Xivan. "I didn't know who

I'd find here, but I didn't expect it to be you. I'm guessing Relos Var gave you the sword so you could kill Suless?"

Xivan put a hand on Urthaenriel. She glanced at the attending priest, but he seemed focused on Senera and Thurvishar's conversation. Her gaze returned to Kihrin. "That's a surprisingly astute guess."

Kihrin shrugged. "Not really. Janel told me what happened. What Suless did to your husband. It's what I'd be doing in your position."

"You know Janel?" Talea asked.

Kihrin bit his lip and then smiled. "Yes." But the smile in his eyes darkened to match his laugh. "You know, if Relos Var had just asked, I'd have probably volunteered to help you kill her myself. Stealing the sword wasn't necessary."

Xivan raised her head. "But that would mean—oh. So *you're* Relos Var's brother."

Kihrin made a face. "Yeah. I suppose I am."

Xivan stood. "Then I assume you came here to reclaim what you think is yours. Are we going to have a problem?"

Talea blinked as she recognized the tension between the two. They both held themselves like swordsmen. Talea didn't think either of them would shy from a fight.

"Oh no. I don't want there to be a problem," Kihrin admitted. "Janel would hate it. She's fond of you."

Xivan smiled. "Good. I'm fond of her."

They were still staring at each other with grim determination when Thurvishar and Senera raised their voices.

"Protest all you want, High Lord," Senera said, "but I've read morgage romances with better attention to factual details."

"Is that so." Thurvishar's nostrils flared in anger. "Do you seriously expect me to believe if you collated a similar accounting, you would be completely unbiased? And what exactly did you find so inaccurate, if I may ask?"

"Seriously?"

"Yes, seriously! If you're going to besmirch the job I did, then I believe you're obligated to provide a formal critique."

Senera made a scoffing noise. "So do you mean to tell me a whore named Kame who died when Xaltorath first appeared in the Capital City really existed? Or . . . oh, I just loved this one . . . that entire scene told from Xaltorath's point of view? Do not claim you can read a demon's mind! Perhaps you started out with the intention of providing a factual account, but you must acknowledge that you stopped presenting facts in favor of crafted sensationalism."

"Wow," Kihrin said in a low voice. "Has *everyone* read that damn book?"

"What book?" Talea asked.

"It's hard to explain . . ." He studied the pair as they continued to argue. "Those two never courted, did they?"

Talea found her mouth was open. "Uh . . . I don't . . ." She glanced over at Kihrin. "I don't think Senera does that. With anyone."

"No. Thurvishar doesn't either. But you should have seen him lose his mind when he thought she'd been injured back in Atrine."[3]

"Really?" Talea started to grin. "That *is* interesting."

"Too bad the only thing Senera cares about is that dog," Xivan said dryly.

"Your Grace!" Talea scolded. "Be nice! You don't know that."

"Fine," Xivan acknowledged. "That dog *and* Relos Var."

"Wait, what was that?" Kihrin asked the question in a tone that carried to the arguing wizards.

Senera and Thurvishar both paused.

"What was what?" Thurvishar asked.

Kihrin shook his head. "Senera, go back to what you said about Thurvishar's lack of attention to detail."

Senera blinked at Kihrin, taken aback. "I said that Thurvishar's far too lax about following up on clearly unreliable narrative details or too prone to inventive fiction–"

"No, after that. When you mentioned the kraken." Kihrin looked grim.

"I said the idea Relos Var would summon up a Daughter of Laaka to chase down every ship leaving Kishna-Farriga should have been scrutinized with the greatest academic rigor, because there was no reason–"

Kihrin blinked and looked like he'd just been slapped. "Because Relos Var could have just asked you where I'd gone. Because you have the Name of All Things. He didn't need to summon a Daughter of Laaka to attack the ship."

"Right!" Senera rolled her eyes. "And you know what? *Lord Var asked me!* And my answer was a lot less messy than summoning up a dozen sea monsters to trail and attack a dozen ships." She glared at Thurvishar. "But did I see a footnote pointing out that narrative inaccuracy? No. No, I did not."[4]

Thurvishar ignored the barb. "But wait, if Relos Var didn't summon the kraken, who did?"

Kihrin looked simultaneously sick and angry. "Khaemezra. Veils, it had to have been Khaemezra." He made a fist with one hand and slammed it against his thigh.

[3] Fine. I suppose I can't claim it was just pragmatic concern.

[4] She . . . she has a point. Unfortunately.

Talea leaned toward Xivan. "Who's Khaemezra?"

"Thaena," Xivan said softly. "That's the Goddess of Death's true name."

"Oh." Talea cleared her throat. She knew Xivan wasn't exactly a fan of Thaena, mostly because the goddess was to blame for Xivan's present condition. If Thaena had been willing to Return Xivan, Relos Var wouldn't have brought her back as something stuck between life and death.

"But why?" Kihrin said. "Why would she do that?"

"You explained it yourself if I'm to believe Thurvishar's account," Senera reminded the D'Mon royal. "Her actions bought a quicker, untraceable passage. Or at least, Khaemezra thought it was untraceable. After all, she might be a goddess, but she's not omniscient, and she didn't know we had the Name of All Things until months later, when Janel told Teraeth. And then there's the part where Thaena wanted to make sure you kept thinking Relos Var was your enemy so you wouldn't listen to anything he had to say."

Kihrin looked up from biting the edge of his thumb to glare at her. "Relos Var *is* my enemy."

"Oh, boo-hoo, he took your fancy sword. Build a bridge and get over it. You and he are fighting for the same things."

"No," Kihrin said. "We're not. And even if we want the same result, he's proven he doesn't care what he has to do to get there. Who he has to kill, who has to die. Relos Var doesn't have friends or family, he has tools, something *you* might want to think about more often."

"So he's just like Khaemezra, then," Senera snapped. "At least now you know what I've been saying all along: Thaena is willing to do anything to get what she wants. What do lives matter to her?"

"What do lives matter to you?" Kihrin shot back. "Didn't you tell Qown physical bodies are just our prisons? Oh, and can we talk about how many thousands have died in Jorat because of you?"

"If you're going to start comparing my body counts against the Goddess of Death's murder tally," Senera said, "I'm reasonably sure she'll win. Come to think of it, so would you, *King of Demons*."

Kihrin flinched.

"That's enough." Xivan's tone was final.

An awkward silence settled over the group, the two men and three women all staring at each other.

Talea leaned toward Kihrin. "Thank you."

"For what?" Kihrin's expression tightened. "Oh. That. You're welcome." He bit his lip. "Do you want me to pass along any messages to Janel when I see her again?"

Talea's brown eyes sought out Xivan for a second, seeking permission, before she started to answer. "Oh yes, if you wouldn't mind—"

Talea stared at him. She found herself wondering if part of Kihrin's discomfort around her had less to do with her dead sister, Morea, than with Janel. Specifically, with Talea's history with Janel. "Wait, are you and Janel lovers?" She grinned at him. "You are, aren't you?"

"Well, I mean, uh–" He cleared his throat. "If I'm lucky."

Talea smiled warmly at the man. "If you hurt her–"

"If I hurt her, she'll rip off all my limbs long before you ever find out about it."

"Fair point."

Senera recovered Rebel's leash. "This was all heartwarming, not to mention immensely educational for everyone, but unless you intend to have this devolve into an infantile fight, I think we're done here." She stared at Kihrin pointedly. "Do you?"

Kihrin glanced at Xivan and sighed. "When you're done, can I have Urthaenriel back?"

Senera snorted. "Not happening."

Xivan's eyes narrowed at the witch. "That's not your decision." She nodded to Kihrin. "When I'm done, we'll talk."

Kihrin walked over to where Thurvishar had knelt to rub Rebel's stomach. "Let's get out of here."

The two men walked back up the stairs.

"Well, that was terrifying," Senera said after they'd gone.

"Oh, I don't know," Talea said. "They were nice. And I really appreciated finding out about Darzin."

Senera ignored her and instead said to Xivan, "He knew what you're wearing. He was somehow able to *track* Urthaenriel."

Xivan nodded once, tersely, her attention once more on the temple statue and the attendant priest of Vilfar. "Somehow, yes."

Senera started chewing on a knuckle. "That doesn't make any sense. He shouldn't be able to do that. *No one* should be able to do that. Gods can't do that." She made a vague gesture toward her Cornerstone. "Urthaenriel is the one item I can't use the Name of All Things to find."

"Maybe you're just not asking the right questions," Talea said.

Senera glared at her.

"The question I want to know is, just how do you *really* feel about Thurvishar?" Talea studied Senera carefully. Talea was positive she hadn't imagined the discomforted look that crossed Senera's face. Plus, the problem with having such pale skin is that it was almost impossible to hide blushing.[5]

"Come on," Xivan said. "Let's go. We'll answer riddles about royals and magic swords another time."

[5] Talea insists that question made Senera blush, but honestly, I can't imagine it.

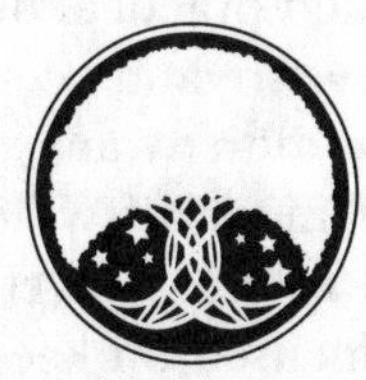

# 69: Seizing the Opportunity

***(Teraeth's story)***

Under normal circumstances, Teraeth would never have encouraged retreating to a parliament-sanctioned safe house. He would've assumed agents would follow them to the location, rendering its effectiveness moot from the start.

But under normal circumstances, they wouldn't have had Doc with them, whose Cornerstone, Chainbreaker, gave him the ability to create almost perfect illusions. Doc could only deceive someone if he was aware of them, however, while Teraeth's illusions, less powerful, didn't require such knowledge. Between them, it seemed unlikely Kelanis had managed to have them followed. The Founders had been generous with protections against divination too. Even Teraeth had to allow this seemed as secure as they were going to manage.

If the Mother of Trees possessed anything qualifying as a slum, they traveled there. It wasn't so much the poor area as the apathetic area–the place for people who just couldn't be bothered with the fantastic detail, illusion, and phantasmagoria for which the vané were so famous. These were the vané too absorbed by their particular obsessions–whatever those happened to be–to pay any attention to physical aesthetics.

Which was perfect.

The sunlight that had greeted their arrival faded quickly as they traveled below the canopy. The sky trees blocked out the sunlight, but they made up for it by channeling that light in the form of glowing, photosensitive sap down through the massive trunks. That light was then released in pinprick fans emerging from the bark so that the reflection from the flooded waters down below the branches looked like the night sky alight with a million stars. There were gardens too, deliberately tended using the sundew harvested from the Mother of Trees to grow all the flowers and plants upon which the vané depended.

The safe house rested right against the tree, part of a complex of dwellings denied fantastic views. There weren't a lot of windows, nor any balconies. A faint mildew odor suggested the roof had leaked at least once. The furniture looked practical but uninspiring. It did indeed seem like a place one could secure and keep that way.

Teraeth kept his focus. He didn't want to. He wanted to find a quiet room off by himself and scream for a few hours or, even better, find out if Janel was once again mad at him for yet another reason he couldn't discern. But he had to stay focused on keeping Khaeriel alive for long enough for her to die on his mother's terms.

Which was why, just as they were settling in to their temporary new home, he noticed something seemed off. Teraeth couldn't put his finger on exactly what. The rooms seemed adequately clean, but there was just something . . .

He'd learned to trust his instincts.

"Something's not right," he muttered to himself. He just needed to identify it.

He hadn't meant for anyone to hear, and he hadn't thought anyone had, but Khaeriel turned toward him. "And what might that be?"

Teraeth tried not to look as uncertain as he felt. "It's just that–" What bothered him about this situation? Was it a trap? How could it be? There's no way Kelanis could have known where they'd gone . . .

Oh.

"When you were still in power," Teraeth said, "did you have any agents inside parliament?"

"Of course I did," she said. "What kind of fool–" Khaeriel sighed. "Right. My brother's not that kind of fool either." She looked at a guard. "Gather all our people together inside the main room. I would speak with them."

"Yes, of course," the guard said.

Just as she started to turn away, that same guard pulled a dagger from her coat and plunged it into Khaeriel's back.

Teraeth's daggers leaped into his hands and across the assassin's throat in an eyeblink. But her blow had already landed.

It was not, however, a good hit. Good enough to puncture a lung, certainly, but not good enough to pierce the heart. Khaeriel didn't immediately drop from shock.

The vané queen in exile gasped and turned toward the would-be assassin. Khaeriel made a quick slashing motion with one arm. The assassin was already falling, but then began vomiting up a spidery mass of what looked like tangled thread.

"Khaeriel!" Teraeth put his daggers away and rushed to the woman's side.

She lowered herself into a chair, the horrible wheeze of her breathing suggesting she did indeed have a punctured lung.

Teraeth bent down and picked up the assassin's knife. He didn't think it would be poisoned, but only because there hadn't been an opportunity. This probably hadn't been an assassin specifically assigned to kill Khaeriel. More likely, she'd been a spy monitoring parliament activity who had taken advantage of an opening. He folded the blade in a piece of cloth just in case.

Khaeriel had put a hand to herself for healing as the door opened and Teraeth's father, Doc, came through, sword drawn.

Khaeriel waved her free hand, what was probably meant to mean something like, "I'm fine."

"Apparently, we brought our assassins with us. There's unlikely to be just the one," Teraeth said, gesturing toward the unusually still assassin. "We should check everyone parliament's sent with us."

"What's . . . wrong with her?" Doc cocked his head and frowned at the spidery, bloody thread mass the woman had coughed up. "Are you sure you're all right, Khaeriel?"

Khaeriel didn't waste breath on trying to answer right away. Finally, she gasped, taking in a deep breath and wincing as the act pulled at tender lung tissue. "I'm fine. I could heal this in my sleep, Terindel. And what's wrong with that one is I ripped out her nervous system."

The two men stared at her.

Teraeth looked back down at the dying body. He doubted the assassin had made her move without wearing talismans, which meant Khaeriel had simply *ignored* them. Like that was nothing particularly difficult. She'd done a thing that had absolutely required being able to overcome someone's magical resistances and had done so without any evident effort at all. It was hardly an impossible act, but it suggested Khaeriel's magical skills shouldn't be underestimated.

Teraeth felt a chill and reminded himself that if the time ever came to kill her, he'd need to make sure he did so before Khaeriel had time to react. He had no desire to end up on the floor without a nervous system.

"I'll go . . . get the others." Teraeth set the knife down. "You should check this for poison, just in case."

"Yes," Doc agreed. "That sounds like a fine idea."

Teraeth spared one last glance to the deposed queen. She was sitting very straight, concentrating, her expression almost placid. The faint light of the room's lanterns reflected gold against her hair and the metal of her eyes.

Teraeth left to gather the others.

# 70: The Lord of Little Houses

***(Kihrin's story)***

"So you and Senera–" I began as we walked away from the graveyard.

Thurvishar looked back at me. "No."

I must have failed to hide my smile. "No?"

"No, we're not having this conversation. There's nothing to have this conversation about. At best, Senera and I are academic rivals, but don't make the mistake of thinking there must be more to our relationship just because we're of the opposite sex." Thurvishar sounded thoroughly aggrieved.

I turned and started walking backward as we talked. "Oh no, I don't think there's more to it because of that. I think there's more to it because every time you look at her, the stars light up in your eyes. And every time she looks at you, she gets an expression on her face like you're a riddle she can't figure out."

"And which she finds intensely annoying. Hardly a good foundation for a relationship, even if I was interested in romance, which I am *not*."

"Are you so sure–" I saw the look in his eyes. "Right. Not talking about it." I returned to walking like a normal person. For a little bit. "So why did she keep calling you *High Lord*?"

Thurvishar took a deep breath. "While we've been gone, Empress Tyentso had my grandfather executed for treason."

I stopped in the middle of the road. "What?"

I'd never heard of a high lord being executed. Well, I suppose Pedron D'Mon would have been executed if my father hadn't killed the man first. But generally speaking, high lords never stood trial for their sins. They certainly weren't executed for them.

Thurvishar nodded. "And as I was still technically Lord Heir . . ."

"You're now High Lord of House D'Lorus," I finished.

"Yes." Thurvishar sighed. "You truly cannot even begin to imagine how little I care."

"You could care a little. I mean, think of all the good you could do if you reformed the Academy . . . ?"

"And how long I would live if I tried?" Thurvishar gave me a knowing look. "I've already played this game, Kihrin. I know how it ends."

We fell silent. I suppose Thurvishar must have discovered the happy news when he went back to Quur for supplies. For my part, I was thinking about Thaena and how she had lied to me. Manipulated me. Damn it, she'd summoned that kraken and then framed Relos Var for it, all to make *sure* I hated him. Which implied she had reason to think I might not.

I felt bitter bile linger in my throat. My feelings toward my brother hadn't needed coaching by Khaemezra. She'd just killed a lot of people for no good reason at all.

I wasn't sure exactly where we were going. I had no plan beyond "tag after Thurvishar," since he was the one with a plan to find Grizzst. I hadn't counted on hearing Urthaenriel's singing, let alone hearing her singing and then . . . walking away. Finding Urthaenriel was supposed to be impossible, which was the whole reason some Quuros emperor had gotten away with dumping the damn thing in the Arena grass without anyone noticing. But I could still hear her voice, calling out to me. Just like I could still—ever so faintly—feel Vol Karoth.

But then it all made sense. Because I was positive Urthaenriel was the sword Relos Var had used to murder S'arric, and—intentional or not—it still contained a bit of S'arric's soul. So the connection with me existed too.

The snow flitted down around us, beautiful and graceful if one didn't mind the cold. The air smelled less like the sea the farther we walked from the harbor, and the scent of woodsmoke fought the sharpness of ice. I found myself wishing Teraeth and Janel were here to see it, although I suspected if Janel never saw snow again it would be too soon. Still, Teraeth would like it . . .

Teraeth. I sighed to myself.

"You should have kissed him," Thurvishar said.

I stopped walking. "I'm sorry. What?"

Thurvishar stopped as well. "You should have kissed Teraeth. You should have told him how you feel."

I remembered our previous conversation about how Thurvishar could read minds. "Okay, first of all, that's rude. Second, I did kiss him. Earlier."

"And told him you love him?"

I choked. "I don't—" But for some reason, I couldn't finish the sentence. I felt my heart race as I became momentarily dizzy. I exhaled. "Oh? You wanted to talk more about Senera? Why didn't you just say so?"

He started to say something and then stopped. "Point taken."

"Where are we going?"

"Back to the harbor, actually." Thurvishar pointed in a direction I recognized as ocean because there were no lights that way. "We're looking for a tavern."

"Weren't we just in a tavern?"

"We need a tavern where everyone doesn't want to kill you. The god-king I'm looking for is new and unorthodox. His shrines are usually found in public areas like taverns, gambling halls, ale houses, and the like. Once we find one, we should be able to bribe a priest into introducing us to the Lord of Little Houses himself."

I eyed him as we walked. "The Lord of–? Just what does this god-king govern?" The title was vague enough to not be immediately obvious. Most of the time, a god's bailiwick was right there in the name.

"Oh, uh, well, you see . . . uh . . ." Thurvishar seemed to be searching for the right words.

"Thurvishar," I told him, "spit it out."

"Shit," he said, looking like he'd just eyed some of the same on his favorite shoes.

"It can't be that embarrassing–" I realized he hadn't been cursing in frustration, he'd been *answering* me. "Wait, what?"

"You must understand how territorial god-kings are. Even if a wizard understands the necessary spells, god-kings ruthlessly protect their monopolies. There's already a god of war, a goddess of love, a god of the harvest . . . ideally a god-king wants a sphere of control that will encourage constant sacrifices in his name. Anyone who tries to claim a sphere already taken will be quickly eliminated by their older and more powerful competitor."

I stopped walking and just stood there blinking at him. "The Lord of Little Houses is the god of . . . defecation?"

"It's kind of genius," Thurvishar said. "Think how many sailors and merchants are constantly arriving from foreign shores and running afoul of local food and drink. Then imagine someone sets up a shrine where you can go and, well, *go*." He made a vague gesture.

"Oh gods. Yeah, okay, I get the idea."

"The religion has spread with frightening speed, as I understand it."

"Sure, just like dysentery."

He ignored that. "Those titular 'little houses' are kept clean, safe, and comfortable. One can make donations to find relief from numerous digestive issues. Travelers arrive at new ports of call and demand their shrines come with them, because it's just so pleasant. And soon, he's worshipped all over Doltar, with the first shrine just opened in the Capital City of Quur. After all, no matter what one's normal religion, there are some needs, like food or air, which are universal. Not everyone worships the goddess of sex, but everybody poops."

I started laughing. I couldn't help myself.

This only seemed to encourage Thurvishar, or maybe he felt like he needed to defend himself. "The other god-kings tolerate the Lord of Little Houses because they've noticed cities with his shrines have a corresponding decrease in certain diseases. And public houses that allow shrines to be added to their establishments have a competitive advantage over those who don't. The result is that most taverns, dens, and brothels include a shrine. So the likelihood Grizzst doesn't use one on a regular basis is slim."

I managed to wrestle my laughter under control, because that actually sounded useful. "What if he's shielded himself from scrying?"

"What if he has?" Thurvishar countered. "It won't protect him from being physically viewed, and I've never known a god-king who hadn't figure out how to see what's happening at their altars."

"And we're right back to being gross."

"No argument. But if I'm right, then the Lord of Little Houses will be able to tell us where Grizzst is, because he'll have *seen* him. Given Grizzst's nature, it's impossible he wouldn't be remembered. There are very few living voras."

"Huh. Well, even if it doesn't work, I *could* stand to find a lavatory."

# 71: The Silk Farm

***(Teraeth's story)***

They couldn't trust the protection detail parliament had assigned them, which put them in an awkward position, as it meant their so-called safe house had been exposed before they'd even arrived. They were going to have to dismiss the guards, but as soon as said guards were out of sight, at least one would be promptly reporting their location to King Kelanis.

"Unfortunately," Valathea said, "any housing connected to a Founder—or known associate of yours, Khaeriel—is certainly monitored by Kelanis. It would only be prudent."

Janel had simply raised an eyebrow at Teraeth.

"Yes, fine," he said. "I know a place."

"Will it be secure?" Khaeriel asked. She looked ready to bend steel with her bare hands.

"Oh no," Teraeth said. "But no place really is. It is at least remote." He glanced around the room. "I'd say gather your things, but . . . none of us have anything."

They devised a different solution for the guards. Doc created contradictory illusions for each so that they'd report back alternate catastrophes that all resulted in the deaths of their charges. The hope was that Dolgariatz, who knew perfectly well Terindel carried Chainbreaker, would interpret this (correctly) as the group ditching their guards and going to ground.

Teraeth led them away from the main city, following a long staircase down the massive tree's trunk. They debouched to a balcony jutting out into the darkness. Broad avenues had been formed in the gaps between leaf structures shaped to resemble buildings, glowing with channeled sunlight. A group of vané busied themselves systematically dismantling one such structure, revealing masses of fine white fibers, fluffy clouds of silken thread.

"What is—" Janel started to ask, clearly confused.

"A silk farm," Valathea whispered. "If you look closely, you can see the ants." She pointed toward a leaf house's base, where small ants, each no larger than a fingertip, glued leaf edges to each other while still other ants filled the spaces in between with white fluff.

"I had no idea this was how silk was made," Janel murmured.

"Oh, it often isn't," Valathea said cheerfully. "There's also a special moth whose larval state creates a silken cocoon, but only a few vané use that method. It's a little more fiddly and a lot crueler."

"But more importantly," Teraeth explained, "silk farms are isolated, rarely receive visitors, and have regular shipments both coming and going." He gestured to catch the attention of the chapter house leader, overseeing the loading of a silk shipment. "Meahwa, right?"

The man stopped what he was doing and hurried over. "Hunter. We were warned you might have need of us. We are at your service." He gave Teraeth a short bow.

Teraeth nodded. "We're going to need maximum security. Nobody enters or leaves without authorization. And my friends and I will need living accommodations for the next several weeks."

"Of course." The man gave Janel an odd look but took Terindel's, Valathea's, and Khaeriel's presences in stride. "Easily accomplished. We'll put out a notice we've had an outbreak of kolyenro mold as an excuse. No one will question the quarantine."

"Excellent." Teraeth turned to the others. "Any concerns? Questions? Now's the time."

"Where are we staying?" Janel asked. She had no doubt noticed nothing looked like an actual building or suggested any residence.

"You're looking at it." Teraeth grinned as he pointed toward an ant house. Teraeth turned to the silk farmer. "We'll need perfume."

The man pulled a small glass vial from his pocket, tossing it to Teraeth. "I will make sure you all receive a bottle of your own."

"Thank you."

Janel looked at the others. "Perfume?"

Teraeth smiled as he opened the vial and applied a generous measure to the inside of his wrists, his neck, his ankles. "The ants are hostile to anyone who doesn't smell like the colony, and their bite is exquisitely painful. Another protective measure. Each silk farm perfume is just a little different from any other's." He passed the bottle to her.

"The walkway is safe," the silk farmer, Meahwa, added, "but do not enter a house without your perfume." He pointed toward the tree side of the balcony. "We keep a few houses in the back hollowed out as sleeping areas. Let me show you."

Teraeth had only been to the silk farm a few times, enough to remember the name of the Black Brotherhood member who ran it and its existence. He'd never actually stayed there.

Valathea seemed mildly interested, her manner that of someone visiting a museum she'd attended many times before. Doc looked bored and Janel concerned. Teraeth hoped she didn't have an insect phobia.

Khaeriel, though . . . Khaeriel's expression was cold and angry. One might be forgiven for thinking she contemplated tossing a torch into each ant house. Teraeth reminded himself Khaeriel had been assassinated by the Black Brotherhood. She would use them, but she wasn't required to look upon them fondly.

The "rooms" were small and undecorated unless unwound silk masses counted as decoration. Each was a small leaf flap that blended with its fellows. The silk inside had been shaped to form a bedroom and privy (the last magical, of course). The bed itself was simply a thicker, wider mass of silk, covered by a silken throw blanket.

"There's only three," Janel pointed out.

The farmer nodded. "It's rare we have more than a single person staying with us. We thought building three was more redundancy than we'd ever need."

"Valathea, you and Terindel should obviously have one to yourselves," Khaeriel said before turning to Teraeth and Janel. "But I admit I am not inclined to share. I hope that will not be a problem." Her tone of voice suggested it had *better* not be a problem.

Janel gave Teraeth a flat stare before turning back to Khaeriel. "Of course not, Your Majesty. That won't cause any difficulty."

Khaeriel studied them for a moment. Finally, she nodded. "Excellent. Teraeth, come see me after you have settled in. We have a few matters to discuss."

Teraeth blinked, then nodded. She knew his occupation. Anything she wanted to talk to him about would involve who needed a short end to their politically inconvenient life.

"Whatever you like."

# 72: The Names of Their Fathers

***(Kihrin's story)***

We randomly picked a tavern called the Four Winds, decorated with a wooden placard out front carved with a chrysanthemum flower–the Lord of Little Houses' symbol. The next part was embarrassingly easy.

We went to the lavatory.

The "little house" in question was an add-on to the main tavern. The main room included several comfortable-looking benches in case a line for the restroom formed, as well as an altar to the man himself and a priest on hand to deal with special cases. A running fountain sat before the altar, where people were encouraged to wash their hands before leaving. In at least a few cases, that might have been the closest thing some of these folks had come to an actual bath in months.

From the main room, a dozen small doors led to individual chambers, all comfortable, sweet smelling, and heated against the cold. I didn't think the private rooms connected to Kishna-Farriga's sewers–from the look of the toilet, it seemed more likely the waste was being destroyed.

In each room sat another small altar, where coins could be deposited should the user feel any sudden need for prayer. One wall was covered with a layer of slate, with pieces of chalk kept at the ready for the sharing of "profound" thoughts.

I had to admit, it was rather nice.

Use of a little house was free, but supplicants were encouraged to pray, and I assumed more complicated digestive issues required a monetary donation. If the tavern owner paid a stipend to host the mini-temple (which I could easily see being the case), then I had to imagine the Lord of Little Houses and his priests were sitting on a sizable stack of metal.

After paying my respects, as it were, both Thurvishar and I approached the acolyte on duty, who smiled at us and bowed with arms crossed over each other.

"How may I make you more comfortable?"

Thurvishar cleared his throat to suggest absolutely nothing about this would make him comfortable. "We'd like to speak with Lord Khital himself."

That smile froze. "Oh, I'm afraid that's quite impossible."

I sighed and stretched, working through the crick in my neck. "How big a donation do you need?"

"It's not just a matter of–" The priest paused and looked us over again. "How big a donation can you give?"

Thurvishar reached into his fur-lined coat, brought out a small pouch, and slowly overturned the contents into a fountain. A small rain of diamonds fell from his hand.

Rather, they looked like diamonds, and given Thurvishar had planned for this, they were probably genuine.[1] It's good to be a Quuros high lord.

"Oh, I see," the man said. "That's different."

I grinned at him, then sat down on a bench, uncovered Sorrow, and started to play.

I figured I might as well pass the time while the priest set up the interview. Funnily enough, the people passing into the little houses from the tavern didn't seem to find my presence unusual, although a few people thanked the priest for that extra touch.

I had a few tips thrown my way too.

While I played and Thurvishar waited patiently, the priest went to the altar. He closed his eyes. He chanted softly. He lit incense.

And finally, he walked back to us.

"One of you," the priest said, "may meet with my lord and present your case. Just one."

Thurvishar turned to me.

"Oh no," I said. "I don't know the man we're trying to find. You do. You'll be able to describe him."

Thurvishar sighed. "Very well." He gestured toward the doors. "In one of those?"

"The middle one," the priest replied, "but you must be sanctified first." He opened up a low cabinet set against one wall and pulled out a thin cloth robe.

"Seriously?" I raised an eyebrow.

"Oh yes," the priest said. "Nothing but yourself and your modesty." He held out the robe to Thurvishar. "You may choose to change in one of the private rooms if you so desire–not the middle room–and may then give your belongings to me for safekeeping. Or to your friend. Whichever you prefer."

Thurvishar looked annoyed, but he took the robe from the priest's

[1] They were. One can't afford to be cheap when bribing a god-king.

hand and walked into a free room. A short time later, he walked back out again, and handed his clothing and shoes to me. On top of the pile sat the two intaglio ruby rings he'd brought with him.

He nodded to the pile. "If I don't come back out in a reasonable time, you know what to do."

I nodded while I hoped my idea about what to do matched his. Because my idea would be to call in the gods and the empress of Quur, not necessarily in that order. I had a fleeting, wistful regret Senera and Xivan weren't our allies. Urthaenriel would have been so useful if anything went wrong.

Thurvishar walked into the indicated cell and closed the door behind him.

I sat back down, smiling thinly at the attending priest. The man gave me a nervous nod in return and then went back to dealing with customers, or worshippers, or whatever they were. No one seemed particularly keen to discuss their constipation or whatever loudly, so a lot of emphatic whispering occurred.

I played a few more songs before my fingertips protested. So then I put away Sorrow and sat there with Thurvishar's clothes in my lap. Because I was bored, I picked up one of the intaglio rings and looked at it. Not the ring that was my size–that one had in fact been made for me, which is why Thurvishar wore it on his pinkie finger. No, the second ring. The one that had belonged to Thurvishar's father, Emperor Sandus.

It looked like all the others. Just like the one my adoptive father, Surdyeh, had owned. They all had a curious identical sameness to them, the uniformity that made me certain magic had been used to create them.

Then I looked inside the ring band and found something different. Inscribed writing, written in something other than Guarem. This was all angles and hard edges, a script that seemed tailored for carving onto stone or inscribing into metal.

But it was a language I could read, anyway, the knowledge of it returning in a flash of understanding.

It was a name. Sandus's name. Although that was a guess, since the voras custom had always been to form a contraction of the familiar name and surname.

"Hell," I whispered. "The children will not know the names of their fathers."

"What was that?" Thurvishar asked.

I hadn't heard him return, and I looked up in surprise. He seemed fine. Same robe, same vaguely embarrassed expression. He pointed toward the pile.

"Did you find out what we need?" I asked as I handed him his clothing back.

"Yes," he said. "I have a city. Not more than that, but if we hurry, we might be able to find him before he moves on."

I picked up the harp. "That's great."

Thurvishar gave me a slightly concerned look before he left to change. When he returned, the look hadn't significantly faded.

"Let's go outside," I suggested.

"It's cold outside," he said.

"Not outside into the snow. Outside into the tavern. It looked friendly enough."

Thurvishar again studied me, then nodded. We found a space at the bar, and I ordered the strongest drink they had, which turned out to be an anise-flavored milky substance called sejin, which was served warm. I bought a bottle with the coins I'd won from earlier and poured us both a cup. I didn't touch mine.

"What's wrong?" he said. "You've closed yourself off. Why are you blocking me?"

"Did you ever look inside that ring of your father's?"

Thurvishar glanced down at his hands. "Of course. It has an inscription, but I haven't been able to—" He looked back up. "You know what it says, don't you?"

"It's your father's name," I told him. "Your father's *real* name."

"What? I know my father's real name." Thurvishar's expression grew worried. "If you're about to tell me that Sandus wasn't my real father . . ."

"No, no," I said quickly. "Your father was Sandus. Not at all in question. Although to be fair, I am only assuming that name inside the ring is your father's. It's just that the voras custom . . ."

"Spit it out, would you?"

"*For Sand'arric,*" I told him. "That's what it says. The ring is inscribed in a very old voras alphabet that says, 'For Sand'arric.' You weren't able to translate it?"

The look on his face said no.

Thurvishar wasn't stupid. I watched as all the pieces fell together for him. He reached for his drink with shaking fingers.

"Remember when you, Qown, and I were under Lake Jorat," I said, "and Qown mentioned how he'd learned Relos Var had never moved against Gadrith because Gadrith owned something important to him? Something Gadrith was using as leverage? And we all assumed it was an artifact or blackmail evidence?"

"But it was me," Thurvishar said numbly. "Gadrith was using me." He drank a large swallow and made a face.

"It would fit." I sipped at my glass. It wasn't half-bad, assuming one liked licorice. Best of all, I suspected it was strong enough to knock out a water buffalo. And hell, I needed a drink too. "I always assumed my brother couldn't have children because, you know, *dragon,* but, uh, maybe not. If your father, Sandus, was his son . . ."

Thurvishar made a noise deep in the back of his throat and topped off his glass.

"If you're Relos Var's grandson," I continued, "it would explain why he put up with Gadrith, who had your gaesh. It also explains why Gadrith didn't kill you. Why he kept you around instead of eating you. Even if you'd never learned a single spell, you'd have been leverage."

Thurvishar snorted. "Be realistic, Kihrin. This is Relos Var. If I'd never learned a single spell, he wouldn't have cared."

I winced. "Far be it from me to defend the man, but I don't think that's true."

He gave me an incredulous stare. "He *murdered* you."

I shrugged and finished off my glass before pouring another one. "People are complicated. Maybe if Relos Var had *needed* to kill Gadrith, he'd have done so, and damn the consequences. It's also possible that he loved your father and by extension loves you. But it's certainly interesting to note how he's left you completely alone, isn't it? He never tried to recruit you. No offers to join his righteous crusade. I don't know what that means."[2] I frowned at the ring back on his finger. "Can I see that?"

Thurvishar took it off as though it was red hot and slid it across the table.

I looked at the inscription again. Although legible, it wasn't neatly inscribed. And my brother was meticulous. His lettering would be perfect. "Relos Var didn't write this. Although whoever did was voras. That script hasn't been in use for millennia." I pushed the ring toward him. "Give me the other one. That way we each have one if we're separated."

"Good idea." He tossed me the ring, which I turned invisible the moment it was on my finger. "Do you think Sandus knew?" Thurvishar mused before downing another glass. He didn't seem to be a fan of the taste and so was drinking it as quickly as possible.

"I don't know," I answered. "But whoever made this knew. And whoever made this is also behind the Gryphon Men, which means whoever made this is the one responsible for me ending up with Surdyeh in the Lower Circle." I snorted. "Not Relos Var. I mean, let's be real here. Can you honestly see Relos Var putting me—putting *anyone*—in a brothel for

[2] I don't either. I still don't know.

safekeeping? Shit, he'd have done this properly. I *would* have grown up on a farm in Eamithon."

"Huh." He poured himself another glass.

I slammed my hand on the bar several times to catch the innkeeper's attention. "My friend, do you have rooms for let?"

He looked at me like I was speaking another language. I sighed to myself as I remembered I'd spoken to the other tavern keep the first time. So I was speaking another language.

The second man ushered over the first, who spoke Guarem. "Want another bottle?"

"Do you have rooms for the night?" I pushed money forward.

I didn't plan on getting pass-out drunk–not in a place where we barely understood the language, had no friends, and there was a huge bounty on my head–but I didn't think we were in any condition to safely open magic portals either. That meant staying there for the night.

"Uh, yes, we have an open room in the back for sailors who don't want to walk back to their ship. Two pira a night each. There are footlockers for your valuables." He gave the harp, which clearly wouldn't fit in any size footlocker, an uneasy eye.

I counted out the remainder of my money and pushed over the entire pile. "Good. We'll take the whole room. Oh, and now that you mention it, yeah. Another bottle of that sejin."

When the man left, I turned back to Thurvishar.

He topped off both our glasses. "He must have known."

"If Sandus thought you were dead, you can't be upset he never told you about your grandfather," I pointed out. "It does pretty strongly imply he wasn't working with Relos Var. Because I just can't imagine Var wouldn't have said anything to Sandus about you if they were on speaking terms."

"True." Thurvishar looked a bit glassy-eyed. "Even if Sandus knew the man was his father, it didn't mean he liked him."

"No. No, it didn't." I felt that right in my chest, an aching burn as I remembered Surdyeh and Therin. I'd been starting to like Therin there at the end.

Apparently, he'd been proud of me. Go figure.

"We'll get him back," Thurvishar said, who was either pretty good at mind reading even when I was shutting him out or I was more drunk than I realized. "Thaena said she'd Return him."

"Yeah, she did." I made a face. "But I don't trust Thaena anymore. Apparently, I never could."

Thurvishar sipped at his glass. "No, I suppose not." He looked at the milky liquor. "You know, after half a bottle, this starts to grow on you."

I refilled my glass. "I bet by the time we're finished, we'll think this is the best stuff ever." I studied him sideways. "So where are we going next?"

"Bahl-Nimian," Thurvishar replied. "It's toward the mountains."

"Is it nice?"

Thurvishar laughed. "Oh no. It's exactly the opposite of nice."

# 73: Bahl-Nimian

***(Senera's Story)***

In the end, Senera used the Name of All Things to discover how to travel to Bahl-Nimian, because while the priests of Vilfar did indeed give excellent directions, they weren't explicit enough to allow Senera to open a gate. Indeed, even with the Cornerstone, it was difficult to ask a question in such a way that the answer would be meaningful enough for a magical portal.

In the end, Senera cheated. She purchased sandals from a priest who swore they'd been made in the mother city. Using that link to its origin, she then successfully opened a portal. True, the portal opened up in the middle of a cobbler's shop, but the cobbler's assistant had only fainted. He would be fine once he had a chance to rest.

It was still nighttime when they left the shop. The city of Bahl-Nimian was a cramped and claustrophobic metropolis. Although lamps lit the thoroughfare upon which they stood, they weren't mage-light. Rather, the lamps ran on oil, producing an ugly smoke. Grease and graffiti stained the walls. While most of the city was carved from stone, no great artistry or care had been taken with its construction. Later additions, usually made from wood, were slapped over crumbling rock in unskilled repair. The entire place reminded Senera of a pirates' den, a criminal sanctuary.

Senera found herself wishing they'd spent the night back in Kishna-Farriga.

"This isn't quite what I expected," said Talea as she eyed the beggars on the road. They seemed genuine, with most missing at least one limb.

"This is revenge embraced as a way of life," Senera replied. She made an effort not to look at Xivan, who pointedly didn't look at her.

Rebel began growling softly at a group of men looking in their direction. All five men paused when they noticed the dog, and then began fingering daggers at their waist.

"I wouldn't," Senera told them. "She may look small, but she can bite through iron."

They scoffed, but then noticed both Xivan and Talea wore swords. All five men seemed far less interested in introductions.

"I assume they have something here that resembles an inn?" Xivan asked.

Senera arched an eyebrow as she looked over at the woman. "I haven't been here before either. One does assume." She bent down and began to pet Rebel in order to calm her.

"Why don't we find a place to stay the night," Talea suggested, "and in the morning, we can go find this temple and speak with Vilfar."

Senera resisted the temptation to pull the Name of All Things from her bodice and ask it if a single sorry inn in this entire city existed where they might safely spend the night without being robbed, murdered, or subjected to other indignities. Unfortunately, this ventured too far into the realm of opinion for the artifact to give her a useful answer.

So instead, Senera utilized the time-honored technique of handing a coin to a beggar, with instructions for the woman to lead them to a hostel and the promise of an additional coin if Senera liked the look of the place when they arrived. This seemed to work. Or at least, the woman–whose name was Molas–led them away from the area of the city in which they'd originally arrived and into a much nicer section of town.

Molas seemed eager to attach herself, and it wasn't worth shooing her away. In fact, a local guide might prove convenient. So she gave Molas her extra coin, with the promise of more to come in the following days if the woman proved her worth.

"Surely, we can give her more," Talea said.

"I didn't bring an infinite amount of the local currency with me," Senera replied. "Besides, if I gave her a large amount in a lump sum, we'll never see her again. Which defeats the point of paying for her help."

"I believe what my dear Talea is trying to say is why can't we help them all?" Xivan's expression was affectionate and wry. "And while I do appreciate the sentiment, let's remain focused."

Talea bit her lip, looked down at the ground, and said nothing.

Senera felt a pang of . . . something. Guilt? Talea reminded her of the damn dog. Of the way Rebel would look up at her with sad eyes as if to remind her there were good things in the world, and those things could be hurt.

And were worth protecting.

Senera pushed past Talea and Xivan both, entered the inn, and bought them all rooms. The only matter that even resembled a difficulty was the innkeeper's half-hearted attempt to keep Rebel outside. She dealt with that by paying extra to cover any potential damage.

Now in a slightly less slummy part of town, Senera realized their original arrival point's claustrophobic air hadn't been coincidence. Bahl-Nimian sat in a giant cleft of rose-colored sandstone. Most buildings had been dug directly into the rock face, with later buildings added as the town grew. The entrance to the town was probably something small and defensible. She could only speculate on where the residents got their water or what they did with their sewage.

The rooms were a pleasant surprise: neat, well maintained, and reasonably clean. The local bed style seemed to be an elevated piece of carved wood, slanted at an angle, so a sleeper's head was kept higher than their feet. They were provided with thick wool blankets as well, because although Bahl-Nimian was in a desert, the night air was cold.

They ate dinner, went to bed early, and vowed to start their hunt again in the morning. The whole time, Senera felt a nagging sense of unease.

Senera didn't want to be here. She didn't want to help Xivan on some idiot quest for revenge. But no, she was babysitting a pair of hopeless fools, because Relos Var wanted Suless dead and because Xivan was his chosen weapon for the task. Senera understood that part; few people in the whole world possessed a better motivation to hunt down Suless than Xivan Kaen. But it didn't mean Relos Var had Xivan Kaen's loyalty, and it bothered Senera that Var didn't seem to care. It implied that Var didn't intend on keeping Xivan Kaen around for very long after the job was done.

Senera tried not to think about it.

# 74: Who They Used to Be

***(Teraeth's story)***

When Teraeth followed Janel into the ant house, he found her standing in the middle of the room, looking at nothing. They owned nothing to unpack. They had nothing with them but the clothes they'd been wearing when Rol'amar struck. Teraeth would, in fact, have to arrange for the Brotherhood to provide all such sundry supplies for them, from clothing to soap. Janel didn't say a word.

This didn't bode well.

"I didn't ask Khaeriel to put us in the same room," he protested.

She frowned, looking surprised as she turned to face him. "I never suggested you had."

"Then why are you looking at me like I murdered your favorite horse."

Janel gave him an even look. "You can't guess why I'm not in a fantastic mood? Hint: it's not because of you."

He sighed and sat down on the bed. "Kihrin."

"Kihrin," she agreed. "The others seem content to pretend nothing happened back there, that none of us saw what we *all saw*."

"Maybe they didn't know what it means." He exhaled slowly. "In point of fact, I don't know what it means."

Janel seemed taut and drawn, every muscle tensed. "This is my fault."

"I doubt that's true," Teraeth said.

She made a scoffing noise and rolled her eyes. "Why can't you simply take me at my word for once?"

"Veils, Janel. We don't have time for self-pity–"

She moved damn fast when she meant to. She was suddenly only a few inches from him, leaning over with her face next to his. "No, damn it. Listen to me. This. Is. My. Fault. I don't mean in a 'whoops, I tripped and broke my favorite crystal glass' kind of way. I mean I'm responsible for this. Elana Kandor didn't free S'arric's soul the way everyone assumes. That's why this is happening." Her eyes were hot and wet, on the verge of murderous, angry tears.

It would have been easy to tell her she was wrong. Teraeth forced himself not to. "Would you mind explaining what you mean, then?"

"I'm starting to remember my past lives." She made a face.

He swallowed an angry knot. "I suspected that was happening from the way our relationship has taken such a delightful turn for the worse in the past month."

She ignored that. "I'm starting to remember what I did. I didn't free S'arric. If I had, that would've meant he and Vol Karoth were separate entities, but they aren't. It's more like—" She straightened, turned away from him and then back as she struggled to find the words. "It's like Vol Karoth was the rot eating away at a tree, the cancer taking it over. So I cut away the healthy parts of the tree—branches and leaves—transplanting them so they could put down new roots and grow into another separate tree. Kihrin isn't S'arric. Kihrin is more akin to a *cutting* taken from S'arric. But the first tree still exists. I couldn't destroy it."

"Wait." Teraeth shook his head. "You're saying that Kihrin's souls are just . . . pieces? Half of what they should be?"

She made an angry, frustrated hand flip. "S'arric's soul is. Not Kihrin's. And less than half. What was left of his soul barely qualified at all. Mostly upper soul, a few tattered wisps of lower soul."

"No. I'm sorry, Janel, but Kihrin's been gaeshed. You can't gaesh a broken soul. That's why you can't gaesh someone who was already gaeshed."

She rolled her eyes. "*Listen* to me. The transplanted cutting grew into a new tree, Teraeth. It took about five hundred years, but the missing sections healed. Vol Karoth's souls are damaged and incomplete. Kihrin's are *not.* And Elana did something. Strengthened Kihrin's souls somehow so he could survive the trauma of what she—what I—did to him. I did the same thing to his soul that I did to yours."

That last statement caught him completely off guard. "What? That can't be right. Elana didn't even know any magic. She shouldn't have been able to—" He paused.

She shouldn't have been able to free S'arric the way she had. Teraeth had heard that story so many times, he'd never questioned it, not even after he remembered being Atrin Kandor. He'd never questioned how Elana had done it. Deep down, he'd assumed Valathea had somehow been involved or Tya had been responsible. He hadn't believed Elana had done it alone.

But if Elana had—if the Elana he had known, who most certainly had not been a wizard—had performed a magical feat of that magnitude without the aid of goddess or wizard, there was only one way it was possible. Only one way he could think of.

"*Elana* was remembering a past life too. That's how she knew how to do this."

She closed her eyes. "Yes."

"A past life where you knew S'arric." He sat down on the faux bed. Of course. It made so much sense. It certainly explained–

She whispered, "Yes."

Being around Kihrin and Janel was like watching two lodestones draw to each other. The pull was irresistible and immediate. And of course, the thing about magnets was they only worked in pairs. Trying to force the issue with three lodestones just made a mess.

He'd never stood a chance, had he?

"The more I remember, the more I hate being able to remember," Janel said. "It feels like another person taking over my mind. Someone else's thoughts intruding on my own. I'm not . . . those people anymore. You don't know how–"

"I don't know how . . . what?"

She put a hand against the silken wall, turned away from him. She had tears running down her cheeks she didn't want him to see. "You don't know how I envy you and Kihrin."

He could only stare. Of all the things he'd thought she'd confess, he'd never once imagined those words. "What? Why would you envy us? That's ridiculous!"

Janel wiped her eyes as she turned back toward him angrily. "Is it? What you have between you is real. That friendship, that love, is *real.* The two of you earned it together. You don't have to question if you're feeling it because it's genuine or because some phantasm from another life is intruding on your own. Whereas the love I feel for Kihrin, the love I feel for you, will always be tainted by the love my other lives felt for S'arric and Atrin. You love me because of guilt, and he loves me because S'arric loved C'indrol, but I haven't earned either emotion."

He had no idea what to say. Teraeth could only sit there, shocked to his core, quite unable to comprehend.

But then part of what Janel said struck home like sword blows. "What? The love your other life felt for Atrin? Elana didn't *love* Atrin."

Janel looked at him oddly. "You don't think she did? Why would I–Elana–have strengthened Atrin's souls otherwise? I'm the reason you're remembering your past life too, you know, but I have to say if I could go back in time, I'd kick Elana's ass for doing it."

"If that's true, then I don't know what your motive was, but it wasn't love. Not after what Atrin did to her."

Janel stared at him and scoffed under her breath. "After what Atrin did to her. Do you understand what Atrin did?"

He bit back on the impulse to snap at her. "I was there, so I'd think so, yes. Elana didn't marry Atrin willingly."

"Are you so sure?"

He blinked. "I *bought* you. I didn't ask your permission first. I'd barely even spoken to you before our wedding night, and we didn't do a lot of talking then either, as I recall."

"So? Do you think it would've been different with another husband? Just because Atrin Kandor's motives were suspect doesn't mean Elana was automatically his *victim*. Because surely Elana was miserable being swept away from her horrible, abusive family by the emperor of Quur. The peasant girl whisked away by the handsome king, like something out of a god-king tale." She raised an eyebrow. "Oh no. Such cruelty. How dare you."

Teraeth stood up, mostly because what she was saying so unnerved him that he felt like he might need to be near an exit. "Kandor was a monster."

She regarded him coolly. "Kandor freed Jorat from Khorsal. He did so in a way that allowed the native Joratese to maintain their culture, dignity, and identity. He may not have been a good ruler, but he was undeniably a great one. And if he hadn't married Elana, she wouldn't have had the authority to negotiate with the Dry Mothers, she wouldn't have been in a position to free S'arric, and I doubt either Kihrin or I would be here now." Janel paused. "Well, Janel and Kihrin might exist, but their bodies would house a different pair of souls."

Teraeth slowly shook his head, searching for some flaw in her reasoning, her logic. "But what he did to the vané . . ."

"Was a mistake. You did make them, you know."

"That was a pretty big mistake."

"You ruled a pretty big country, didn't you? I'm not saying you were perfect. You were arrogant, conceited, insufferable"–she rolled her eyes up to the ceiling and laughed–"also very, very good in bed."

"That last part hasn't changed."

She studied him. "Don't kid yourself, Teraeth. None of it's changed. You've gone from professional mass murder to custom one-off jobs. It's just a question of scale."

Teraeth's mouth twisted. "*Now* you're mocking me."

"Kihrin's not here. Someone has to pick up the slack." She drew in a deep breath. "I'm . . . sorry. I shouldn't have said any of that."

Teraeth wasn't about to disagree. "I refuse to be Atrin Kandor. I don't want to be anything like him. He nearly doomed the whole world. If he hadn't invaded the Kirpis, because . . . I don't know. Because I wanted my soldiers to have better armor? Terindel might have done the right thing, but the fucking vané king was so incensed at me–at my mere involvement with the Ritual of Night–that he refused to cooperate."[1]

[1] It clearly hasn't come up often, but evidently, the Eight Immortals really did expect the

A strange look crossed Janel's face. "Who told you that?"

"My mother! And she was there. I just . . . I just want to be my own person. I don't want to constantly keep defining myself by what Kandor did or didn't do! By his powers, by my shitty judgment–"

"So you do understand."

Teraeth stopped. He rubbed his hand across his face as he stared at her. "I suppose I do," he finally said. "I suppose I do at that."

The room fell into silence. He didn't know what to say to her, and the feeling seemed mutual. Two magnets, after all, but too alike to pull together. The harder he pushed, the more resistance he felt.

Teraeth pointed toward the door. "I should go find out what Khaeriel wants."

She nodded without speaking and watched as he left.

Teraeth found Khaeriel in her room. The woman had wasted little time decorating, so it no longer resembled a hollowed-out mass of silk. Delicate floral tapestries and watered fabrics covered the walls, making it seem like a luxurious tent. Teraeth wasn't sure if she'd used illusions or had literally transformed the silken material. Perhaps it didn't matter.

She sat on a chair, hands in her lap, staring at a wall.

Teraeth cleared his throat. "You wished to speak with me?"

The deposed queen glanced over. "Sit down, Teraeth."

He did, glad she'd created more than one chair.

"We have two weeks to secure a two-thirds majority of Founders who support our case. If we fail . . ." Her mouth twitched. "Well."

"If we fail, the parliament's amnesty is over, and we'll all be arrested."

"Exactly," Khaeriel agreed. "Although I doubt you would come to any permanent harm." She didn't clarify the perfectly obvious: that she would come to a great deal of harm.

But then, she was going to die no matter how this played out.

Teraeth leaned back in the chair and examined his knuckles. "I admit I'm curious about your enthusiasm to see this done, given what will happen to you when you perform the ritual."

She lifted her chin. "I didn't realize you knew about that."

"As it happens, I was there the last time it was performed. I saw a whole room full of very nice dreth elders die spectacularly."

She frowned at him, because she knew he wasn't that old.

"I'm not lying to you," Teraeth said. "I'm remembering a past life. Your son isn't the only one the gods reincarnated."

---

emperor of Quur to be the person organizing the Ritual of Night back then. So yes, that was likely something of a diplomatic disaster considering the previous relationship between Atrin Kandor and King Terindel.

Khaeriel tapped her fingers against the arm of the chair. "How close *are* you to my son?"

Teraeth wished he understood her motives. It would make this so much easier. He had a terrible suspicion she was planning something. That she'd thought of some clever scheme to escape her current predicament. He'd tell her the truth: that he was desperately, ridiculously in love with her son and had been since *before* he was born.

"We're friends," Teraeth answered.

An amused expression stole over her features. "A good enough 'friend' to consent to an arranged marriage with him?"

Teraeth blinked.

She smirked. "Would that be so terrible? You clearly like him. I suspect he likes you. And since you are Terindel's only living child, a match between the two of you would result in reuniting the vané royal lines. That would be a reassuring idea to the Founders who might otherwise hesitate to overturn the Law of Daynos for fear of returning to the days that led to civil war. A political marriage between the two of you seems an obvious solution to a great many problems."

Teraeth felt his throat go dry. That "solution" had never occurred to him, in large part because his father was, well, Doc, which made the likelihood of him ever inheriting a title something less than zero. And as much as he'd be the most extraordinary liar to claim he had no interest in marrying Kihrin . . .

But he had to say something. "A same-sex marriage is hardly a scandal to our people, I know. You and Miyane being a prime example. And yet–"

Khaeriel's expression turned disdainful. "Go on."

"My point is there's usually an expectation of progeny–" Teraeth paused, then exhaled, and again felt a fool. Damn it. "You know about voramer."

"Young man," she told him, "if this business with the Stone of Shackles had never occurred, you would be my *uncle.* And your older sister, my mother, never hid her nature. Her marriage to my father was conditional on the magical guarantee neither myself nor my brother would inherit her voramer qualities. So yes, I am well aware this would only be a same-sex marriage in the short term."

Teraeth kept his face blank. He had no intention of allowing the voramer transition to happen to him. He had nothing against the idea of being female; but he had nothing against the idea of staying male either. He enjoyed being a man. Why would he change that? If they wanted an heir that badly, they could damn well use the Well of Spirals to make one.

She must have suspected what he was feeling. "I know this must be difficult for you."

"With all respect, Your Majesty, you don't know me."

Khaeriel inclined her head. "As you say. But I see no reason for you to deny yourself what you already want. In the meantime, we have two weeks and a lot of people to convince to do the right thing. I assume I can count on your cooperation in persuading them?"

Meaning, Teraeth knew, his cooperation in making sure the right people went to his mother's realm early.

He bowed. "Of course, Your Majesty. I live to serve."

# 75: The Temple of Vilfar

***(Senera's story)***

The next morning, they ate a bland meal of bread and sausages, before Molas led them to the temple of Vilfar. They wouldn't have needed the guide. The temple was the most ostentatious building in the entire city, the highest up, it was impossible to miss.

Gaining an audience with Vilfar proved to be a different matter. A line of petitioners ran out the door, down the main steps, and several blocks past the temple grounds. Every person in that line had the cold, hateful stare of someone with a grudge, a reason to nurse it, and an unwillingness to let go.

Xivan could've been standing in that line. Looking at the duchess's expression as she traced the assembled crowd, Senera could tell the same thought had occurred to Xivan too. Her eyes narrowed, and her jaw flexed inside her mouth. Her hand strayed toward the pommel of her sword. Then the woman squared her shoulders and turned back toward the temple.

"Well," she said. "How do we skip the line? That's the question. I don't know about you, but I don't feel like waiting here for a month just to have Vilfar lie to my face and tell me she has no idea where Suless is."

"You don't really think Vilfar would–"

Xivan gave Talea a look.

Talea closed her mouth.

Senera fought not to smile. "I think we'll do it the same way we'd get to the front of any other kind of line–we bribe the doorman."

The temple of Vilfar's interior repeated the theme established in Kishna-Farriga. True, it wasn't buried in a pit in the ground and it was much more elaborate, catering to a far broader range of worshipper, but it had the same basics. A giant blood-covered statue presided over a vast array of offering bowls, priests, and the various animals who would be sacrificed to appease Vilfar's apparent thirst for blood.

Senera ignored the normal priests. Her target was particular–the priest whose robes were finer, manner stiffer, and nose held higher, too important to talk to the common rabble.

He or she wouldn't be the head priest, but they'd be someone who wanted to be the head priest. Someone with ambitions. Someone so interested in putting themselves into their goddess's good graces that they were willing to take a risk. And even then, the *who* didn't matter nearly as much as the *where:* within earshot of the goddess's altar.

She found her mark and approached. "Would you be so kind as to inquire with your lady if she would have any interest in buying a Cornerstone?"

The priest blinked. He looked like a local, but if any local Doltari had ever been as pale as Senera–which she doubted–generations with Vilfar and the dark-skinned Marakori she'd brought with her had changed that. So he was fair-haired and tan and handsome enough if one liked that sort of thing.

"A what?" He seemed confused. "You're selling part of a house?"

Senera resisted the strong urge to roll her eyes. "No," Senera said gently. "A Cornerstone. One of the Eight Cornerstones. In particular, I'm talking about Warmonger, which is a hematite stone around so big and–"

The ground shook.

Senera heard screams and then the curious sound of many knees all hitting the ground at once. She looked back at Xivan and Talea. The three of them were the only people standing.

Vilfar's statue pointed a single grisly finger in Senera's direction. "Bring her to the private chambers." The statue's voice boomed and echoed loudly through the giant hall.

Rebel made a low growling sound, and Senera shushed her.

A priest stood and ran over to Senera, bowing. "If you'll follow me?" Without waiting to see if they would, he walked into the inner sanctum. As they followed the priest, Senera felt the eyes of the entire temple on them, every single person watching them go.

The god-queen Vilfar's private chambers were significantly less ghoulish than the blood-filled temple outside, but no less melodramatic. The red-and-black color scheme played backdrop to bronze statuary showing acts of vengeance in progress, whether slow torture or violent surprise murders. The goddess herself reclined on a velvet couch, eating from a silver platter.

Vilfar's hair was glossy black, cut short and practical but with great precision. Her skin color was a lovely deep tan. Unexpectedly, her eyes were solid black. Senera found herself wondering if Vilfar might have originally been a member of House D'Lorus.

Vilfar didn't rise from her couch. "Did I hear that correctly? Are you claiming to have a Cornerstone?"

Senera stepped forward. This next part might prove tricky. No matter that Xivan carried Urthaenriel, Vilfar was still a wizard savvy enough to have learned the map of godhood. She was nothing to be taken trivially.

"I do, Your Holiness," replied Senera. She bowed her head low. "But first I must beg your forgiveness. You see, I'm not selling said Cornerstone, but I needed this audience. Goddesses are rarely in the practice of taking meetings with people they don't know."

Vilfar's nostrils flared. "Indeed. But we are in the business of killing people who waste our time."

Senera immediately liked her.

"We're not doing that," said Xivan. "I need your help."

Vilfar turned her attention to Xivan for the first time. "Your body temperature is wrong. You can't be alive, but my every sense . . ." She raised herself up a little from the couch. "I can't tell anything else about you. Why is that?"[1]

"My name is Xivan Kaen," replied Xivan, ignoring the question, "and I'm here to kill Suless."

Senera sighed. She'd really just done that, hadn't she?

Recognition swept over Vilfar's expression. "And you thought to look for the goddess of betrayal . . . here?" She smiled to make sure none of them missed the joke; looking for the goddess of betrayal in the temple of the goddess of vengeance.

"Yes, because we know she's here," Senera said. "I *do* have a Cornerstone: the Name of All Things, which was given to me by my husband, Relos Var."

This was a gamble. A gamble that Vilfar knew who Relos Var was. A gamble that Vilfar would respect the name enough to realize she shouldn't murder them without risking his wrath. And the gamble that Vilfar would believe Senera was Relos Var's wife, technically true even if it had never come close to being practiced in reality.[2]

But the way Vilfar's eyes narrowed suggested one of those gambles had paid off. "And what has that bitch done this time?"

"She has my husband, my son, and my grandchild." Xivan stood there with an expression to burn the heavens.

Vilfar, Goddess of Vengeance, didn't look surprised.

During this discussion, Talea seemed to have decided she wasn't needed. And so, Talea had gone over and spent the time distracting Rebel, mostly with belly rubs. With this announcement, however, Talea stood, took Rebel's leash in hand, and went back over to Xivan. She placed a comforting hand on the older woman's shoulder.

[1] Her inability to divine any information about Xivan was obviously due to Urthaenriel.

[2] For which I find myself extremely grateful.

"I cannot . . ." Vilfar seemed to be trying to search for the right words. "She *is* here, but I would never give that hag shelter. Since you have the Name of All Things, you can verify that."

"If you haven't given her shelter, then you won't mind handing her over." Senera smiled and hoped this meant the job would be easy, almost over.

The apologetic look in Vilfar's eyes killed that hope quickly.

"I haven't given her shelter," Vilfar clarified, "but someone else has." The goddess paused. "I don't suppose you were serious earlier when you said you were willing to sell Warmonger?"

Senera held out her hands. "It's not mine to sell. But I doubt my husband ever would. Something about it being too dangerous to be allowed out in the world."

"What does it do?" whispered Talea.

If Talea had asked the question of Senera, it was Vilfar who answered. "Oh, exactly what the name says. I suppose you might say population control. But if you ever want to start a war and make sure your people are absolutely behind it, there's no better thing for it. Nemesan had the stone, and it took Quur and Kirpis combined over a hundred years to defeat him."

"Oh." Talea swallowed.

"Who's given Suless shelter?" Xivan was focused on one thing only.

Vilfar scowled. "A new neighbor who's settled in my lands. An unappreciated new neighbor. I would've thought Suless went to her death, but if you say she's still alive, she must have found a way to placate him. That's where you'll find her. I'd help but"—the goddess shrugged—"I don't like picking fights I can't win. It's bad for business."

The three women looked at each other. Then Senera sighed. "And who is this intruder, that you can't deal with them?"

Vilfar smiled. "Oh, he's quite out of my league. It's Baelosh."

Senera groaned. Vilfar nodded sympathetically.

"Who's Baelosh?" Talea asked.

"Baelosh," Senera answered, "is a dragon."

"That went rather well," Talea said after they'd left with nothing but a map indicating Baelosh's last known location.

They'd had to push a few people out of the way to leave the temple too. Word had spread the goddess herself had spoken to these three, so as soon as they left her chambers the women found themselves surrounded by hopefuls trying to speak with them, look at them, or just touch them. Senera had been forced to resort to some minor, harmless, but threatening-looking magics to convince the worshippers to go somewhere else for their divine blessings.

Senera gave her a look. "That's only because you have no idea who Baelosh is."

"We'll deal with him," Xivan replied. "We know she's here. Soon we shall have her." The irritation on her face suggested she wasn't feeling the confidence she was preaching, however. "What can you tell us about Baelosh?"

Senera shooed a group of vagrants from their position against a carved rose sandstone wall. It seemed safer to have their backs up against something. A vendor on the corner sold sliced fruit dipped in spices and roasted meat wrapped in something that looked like sag. Senera's stomach rumbled at the smell, but she ignored it for the moment.

Senera spread the map out on the stone floor with one hand. "So this is where we are now." She traced a finger along the line on the map. "And this is the main road that leads west and ultimately heads to Kishna-Farriga." She tapped the large red circle. "So somewhere in all of this is where we'll find Baelosh."

"I still don't understand how we're supposed to kill a dragon," Talea said.

"We're not here to kill him. We're here to convince him to give up Suless." Xivan looked over at Senera. "Right?"

"That's the theory." The wizard rubbed a finger against the bridge of her nose. "Baelosh is infamous. Admittedly, that's mostly because of his encounter with the first emperor of Quur, but he deserves his reputation. He's associated with jungle and wilderness. As if nature itself was a dragon. Areas where he nests tend to be lush, verdant regions. Probably why Vilfar hadn't previously made a serious effort to drive him off."

"Does he have any vulnerabilities?" Xivan asked.

Senera shrugged. "The obvious: fire."

"Oh," Talea said, "it's a real shame Janel's not here. She's good at that."

Senera snorted. Yes, Janel would be quite handy. Except Janel would be too busy trying to kill Senera first. They hadn't parted on the best terms.[3] "I strongly recommend against trying to fight him. The stories depict him as one of the saner dragons and thus capable of casting spells, he regurgitates this caustic—" She shook her head. "Basically, Baelosh will kill you, melt you, and then turn you into wonderfully useful fertilizer for all the plants he'll grow from your corpse."

"So how do we deal with him?" The determined look on Xivan's face left little doubt walking away was not an option.

"Well, not by playing fair, that's for certain." Senera eyed the ven-

[3] That wouldn't have anything to do with the fact Senera tricked Janel and Kihrin into waking up Vol Karoth, would it? Hmm?

dor's selection of meat. Its provenance seemed uncertain. Rat? Probably. "Oh, I never thought I'd miss Yoran food."

Talea nodded. "I miss Khorveshan food."

Xivan patted her on the shoulder. "When this is all finished, we'll go back there. You'll be able to have anything you'd like."

The look Talea gave Xivan in return was so adoring, Senera felt certain the woman had been taking lessons from Rebel.

"If we're going to convince Baelosh to leave," Senera said, "we'll have to do something a little bit more significant than asking nicely."

Xivan shifted on her feet. "I don't suppose he cares for money?"

"Possibly? The main story about Baelosh involves his encounter with Emperor Simillion, who stole a necklace of star tears from the dragon's hoard. From this, one might assume he actually does collect wealth, or at least jewels. But there are other stories where Baelosh seems to collect riddles or poetry . . ."

"That's less than helpful," Xivan said.

"I can ask the Name of All Things," Senera admitted, "but one has to be careful about wording. It can't tell us if Baelosh *will* accept metal or gems as a bribe, only if he has in the past. That isn't necessarily an accurate predictor of future behavior."

"Pity we can't just ask someone who knows him," Talea mourned.

"He's Ompher and Galava's son, but I somehow doubt either would be willing to help. And anyone else is thousands of years dead–" Senera let her statement fall away as she realized the obvious answer. "Right. The one who got away."

"You're in serious danger of starting to sound like a wizard," Xivan warned. "Meaning, we speak the same language, yet I have no idea what you're saying."

"I'm talking about the person most famous for his interactions with Baelosh. We could just ask him."

Talea and Xivan shared a look.

"Are you . . . still talking about Emperor Simillion?" Talea asked.

"Yes," Senera admitted, "but you know him better as Thurvishar D'Lorus."[4]

[4] I'll admit to being surprised she knew this information. I must assume Relos Var had her check on all our past lives at one point or another.

# 76: The Definition of Talk

***(Teraeth's story)***

When Teraeth returned to the silk farm a week later, he found Khaeriel waiting for him. His first reaction was irritation, because Khaeriel was waiting out in the open. Theoretically, anyone could have seen her. Then he realized his father, Doc, was waiting there as well.[1] His father rested against the railing, looking out into the thick dark of the Manol Jungle. If Teraeth hadn't known better, he might have assumed his father wasn't paying any attention. But he did know better, and he knew Doc watched his every move. The only thing he didn't know was if Doc's presence indicated Khaeriel didn't trust him or if Doc didn't trust her.

The evening was lovely. Silk ants pursuing their daily routines created a pleasant drone that played counterpoint to birdcalls. Something about the silk itself had a strangely fishy odor, which Teraeth only noticed at times like this, when he returned from a mission.

Khaeriel herself might as well have been a statue. She wasn't dressed in anything regal. Just a very basic silk gown they'd been able to smuggle back into the farm using some flimsy excuse. Teraeth had to admit she made the damn thing seem like the finest court dress.

"How was your trip?" Khaeriel asked with a deceptively mild voice.

Teraeth drew up short. "The trip" had gone well indeed. There'd been a small amount of resistance from his target but nothing he hadn't been able to handle.

None of which explained why Khaeriel was this furious.

"Everything's fine," Teraeth responded. "What seems to be the matter?"

Khaeriel looked to the side. "Terindel, would you mind clearing the room?"

And the scene around them changed. This was, of course, why Khaeriel had asked Doc to be there in the first place. Because if nothing else, Chainbreaker was a remarkably handy way to ensure privacy.

[1] I suspect Terindel wasn't using Chainbreaker to cloak their location but was using Chainbreaker on Teraeth—presumably while he and Khaeriel sat someplace more discreet.

The scene that Doc conjured using the stone was nothing inventive. The platform stood empty, the silk houses removed. A throne room took their place. Strings of lights and floating charms filled the area with a soft glow. Flowers bloomed profusely from boxes that hadn't been there a moment ago. And of course, there was a throne. Doc had made it look like a living thing, crafted from flowers, branches, and green leaves. Teraeth decided that it must have been a real throne, a real scene that must have once existed, because Khaeriel spared Doc one brief shocked glance before she turned to Teraeth.

"One of the messengers has informed me that Vayldeba is dead," Khaeriel said. She didn't bother to hide the iron in her voice. "What on this earth possessed you to think that was a good idea?"

Teraeth blinked. He suspected Khaeriel was upset with him about something, but he hadn't thought it would be about *that*.

"Excuse me? You asked me to do that."

Khaeriel cocked her head and examined him in the same way a hawk might look at a mouse. He fought the temptation to reach for his knives. "No," she said, "I asked you to do no such thing. What I asked you to do was talk to the man, find out what was needed to turn his vote, and make that thing happen. I did not ask you to kill him."

Teraeth laughed. "When people ask me to 'talk' to someone, what they mean is kill them."

Off at the side of the platform, Doc sighed.

Teraeth spared his father the briefest glance before returning his attention back to Khaeriel. "If you had meant for the man to live, you should have sent a diplomat."

Khaeriel rubbed her temples and seemed to be in physical pain. "I cannot believe . . ." She inhaled deeply and steadied herself. "Teraeth," she began, "if you ever plan to be a good ruler, it is rather essential you learn to actually talk to people. You cannot kill *everyone* who disagrees with you, no matter how tempting the idea might be."

Teraeth managed, barely, not to let out an exasperated sigh himself. "With all respect, Your Majesty, I have no desire or intention to rule anything, least of all the vané people."

Khaeriel just stared at him, as though he had said something in a language she didn't understand. "What was that?"

Teraeth ran a frustrated hand through his hair. "I don't know how to make it clearer. I don't want the throne. I have no desire to rule. And frankly, since doing so requires one or both of you to die, I shouldn't think you'd want me to either."

Silence filled the imaginary antechamber.

Khaeriel drummed her fingers against the throne's branches. She gave Doc a look of stunned amazement. Finally, she shook her head.

"Fine. I suppose that is a matter to discuss at a later date. For now, let us confine our discussion to the fate of Vayldeba. Because I want you to understand what you did and why it is a problem."

"He was going to vote against you, wasn't he?"

"That was a distinct possibility. It was not a certainty. I had hoped we might be able to sway his opinion. Now he has no opinion. And worse, I know nothing about the opinions, goals, or ambitions of his replacement. Will the new representative be better? Will they be significantly worse? We have no way to know and not enough time to find out."

Teraeth felt the barest trickle of something like to dread wrap its way around his lower intestine and squeeze. The part of him that always had and always would hate failure clamored for attention.

"I see," Teraeth said.

"Because of his death, our job is made more difficult. Please do me the honor of not assuming I speak in innuendo or metaphor. When I give you an order, I am giving you an order. I am not afraid of telling you to kill someone if that is what I want you to do." Khaeriel inhaled deeply and stared off into the distance for a moment. "Understand, Teraeth. This failure is mine. I should have made certain you understood me. I should not have assumed you did."

Teraeth swallowed. "Thank you, Your Majesty. That is very gracious. However, I believe we both know that the fault is mine."

Her gaze was molten gold, scalding. "Then it will not happen again."

"No, Your Majesty."

Khaeriel stood up from the throne and looked in Doc's direction. "Would you be so kind as to make me a door?"

Doc waved a hand, a thoroughly unnecessary gesture, and the door appeared in midair. Without waiting on either of the other two, Khaeriel left. The door closed before Teraeth could step through.

Teraeth turned to his father.

Doc lowered his foot from where it had been resting against the railing. He crossed his arms over his chest. "I thought we might talk."

"Do we have anything to say to each other?" Teraeth resisted the urge to fidget, or pace, or start sharpening weapons. He wasn't at all comfortable being in the same space with this man. But he was damned if he was going to let it show.

Doc studied his son. "When did she tell you I was your father? Before or after you remembered being Kandor?"

Teraeth looked upward toward the height of the tree canopy and sighed. "Is that really what we should be focusing on right now?"

"Before? Or after?"

Teraeth stared at the other man. "I–" Teraeth spun on his heels. He wondered if it would work if he ran. Would Terindel stop him? Would he go right over the edge of one of these balconies? Plummeting to his death was starting to sound quite appealing.

Teraeth turned back around. "We don't have to talk like this. Take down the illusion and we'll go have a drink or something."

Instead, the room vanished around them. A sea of blank white stared at Teraeth in every direction. Doc and he both stood in endless glowing void.

"That's not better, you know. Stop this."

Doc ignored him. "Before or after? Simple question. Did you grow up thinking you're the son of Terindel the Black, the traitor who slew the entire Kirpis Star Court, nearly damned the vané through his hubris, or did you grow up knowing you'd been reincarnated as the son of your mortal enemy, the man you forced to flee his homeland along with his people?"

Teraeth's throat went dry. His father waited for an answer. "It was that first one," Teraeth finally said. "I didn't start remembering my past life until I was a teenager."

Slowly, the color started to come back into the world. Form and texture began to leak back in around them.

"Of all the reasons I occasionally curse your mother's name," Doc said, "I think the worst is that she gave me a son as the punch line to a joke."

Teraeth flinched.

He hadn't expected that to hurt as much as it did, but the words were numb and cold and very sharp. He couldn't say his father was wrong, could he? Not when the irony twisted so tight around their screwed-up, multilayered relationship, any chance they might have had to mean something to each other had long since been choked to death. Perfectly garroted. Assassinated.

Teraeth's hands slowly clenched into fists.

"I'm not Kandor," he finally said.

"Bullshit."

"No, it's not. You think he didn't die neck-deep in regret? Do you think he died proud of himself, thinking he had lived a life worth living?"

"You were the greatest emperor Quur's ever known."

"And if that's not an indictment of Quur, I don't what is. Kandor was a miserable bastard who should have been a potter. And when I remembered, when I finally remembered who I'd been—" Teraeth scowled and looked away. "I never tried to relearn his magic, you know. I could've. I remember the spells, but I've never practiced a single one. I learned new spells. My own spells. My own skills. I don't want to be the person that people bow down before. Who only sees people as casualty numbers in a report. As something to be conquered or won."

"So you've gone from being a wizard to being an assassin. I don't see much improvement," Doc said.

It was too close to what Janel had said. And Teraeth could not, would not, let it stand. "I kill evil men," Teraeth said. "I kill people who deserve their fate."

"No," Doc said, "you kill people your mother has told you to kill. And because you don't trust yourself to know the difference, you believe Khaemezra when she tells you they deserved it. So let me ask you this: Who gave Khaemezra the right to decide who lives and who dies?"

Teraeth blinked. "Are you serious? Who gave her the right? She's the Goddess of Death!"

"No!" Doc said. "No, *she's not*. She is not a goddess. *None of the Eight are gods*. She is an all-too-fallible woman who has been tied to a cosmic force. Yes, that force is death, but nobody told her she was responsible for judging the dead or making sure anyone stays that way. Nobody told her she had to police death. Nobody demanded she should only Return the special chosen favorites she thinks are worthy. Nobody–*nobody*–gave her any kind of moral responsibility for punishing the wicked as defined by Khaemezra. She's taken that on all by herself."

Teraeth felt something twist inside him, an emotion he couldn't name tugging at his chest. "She's protecting us," he finally said.

"That's what she says," Doc said, "but I want you, *my son,* to think about this: you may have tried to distance yourself from what you were as Kandor, but you're still taking orders from someone who sees people as numbers in a report. If Thaena and Kandor didn't get along, it's only because they were too much alike."

"If you hate her so much, why did you *sleep with her*?"

"Because Elana died in childbirth."

Teraeth could only stare at his father, mouth open in shock.

"What?"

Doc shook his head and threw up a hand. "Elana and I met on the edge of the Manol Jungle. She was coming back from Kharas Gulgoth, from the middle of the Korthaen Blight. I was trying to escape . . . everyone. As far as I knew, my daughter was dead and my wife might as well have been. And here was this brave, beautiful girl, pregnant with the child of the man I hated, but that was hardly her fault, was it? As much as I loathed Kandor, as much as I'd wished my sword could have been the one to kill him, I couldn't take it out on her. I guess I'd finally reached my limit."

"Weren't there . . . I don't understand. Weren't there–" Teraeth stumbled over his own words. He knew perfectly well there wouldn't have been any healers in Khorvesh. He'd conscripted them all. There might've been a few witches who escaped Kandor's attention, but every legal healer in the region was dead on the floor of the Manol Jungle by that point.

"I was in a brand-new body," Terindel continued. "I couldn't cast any spells–and there were complications during the birth. She delivered a healthy son and then bled out right in front of me. I just couldn't take it. I couldn't stand to be witness to one more tragedy, one more life cut short in the story where everyone else I cared about had already died. So . . . so I *prayed*. I prayed to Thaena and offered my life for Elana's. I mean, why not? What was my life worth by then?"

"You didn't even know her," Teraeth said. "She was just a . . . human. Nobody to you."

"Yes," he agreed. "Absolutely nobody. What was the life of a woman who'd at best live another sixty years compared to my immortal life span." Doc started laughing. "But it was too much. Just . . . too much. Thaena accepted my offer. She just didn't take payment in the way I expected."

Teraeth grimaced. Somehow that was even worse than he'd imagined when he'd grown up assuming he was conceived through necromancy.

"After that, we were on-again, off-again for a few centuries." His smile was self-deprecating and cruel. "I don't think she ever forgave me for not falling in love with her. Boy, did she ever teach me." He gestured toward Teraeth.

"Right." Teraeth found himself grinding his teeth and forced himself to relax. "Thank you," he finally said.

"For what?"

"For Elana. Thank you." Teraeth shut his eyes, fighting the dull ache of it all. "I don't think Janel remembers that part."

Teraeth immediately opened his eyes again as he realized his mistake. "I meant to say–"

Doc raised a hand. "Valathea told me. I'm not getting anywhere near Janel or that situation for so many reasons, I could open up my own store and sell wisdom."[2]

Teraeth hesitated. "Then thank you for that as well."

"It's bad enough I might one day have to explain to Qoran that my son is getting involved with his daughter."

"I don't think they're on speaking terms." Teraeth almost asked Doc if Khaeriel had approached him about that arranged marriage, but he thought better of it. Doc might agree with her about it being a good idea. No matter how much Teraeth wanted it, he didn't want it like that.

"Neither are we."

[2] One assumes Valathea had not checked with her husband before making her rather generous offer to Janel back at the lake house.

They both stood there, letting the silence lap around them.

"If it's any consolation," Doc said, "I'd have made the same mistake."

Teraeth wasn't sure exactly which mistake Doc was referring to. A lot of possibilities had been left on the table. "Oh?"

"I'd have assumed Khaeriel wanted me to kill Vayldeba too." His father shrugged amiably. "And although far be it from me to contradict my niece, I happen to think there's at least one person we'd be much better off just getting out of the way right now before we have to face him in parliament."

Teraeth found himself starting to smile. "Is that so? And who might that be?"

"Oh, don't be coy. Don't tell me your mother hasn't already given you the assignment."

"Just to be perfectly clear, though–"

"Kelanis," Doc said. "You should assassinate the king."

# 77: Chance Encounters

***(Kihrin's story)***

"So you've been to Bahl-Nimian?" I asked Thurvishar the next morning over breakfast. Fortunately for both of us, Kishna-Farriga offered a wide range of food options, including some surprisingly well-done Quuros cuisine.

"No," Thurvishar admitted, "but it doesn't matter. After breakfast, we'll return to the temple of Vilfar. Someone there's been to the city and will give me the directions we need."

I grinned at him. "Will this kind of volunteer be aware they're giving you said directions?"

He just chuckled and tore a strip off his sag bread. "I'm curious about something. Yesterday, back at the temple, when we ran across Senera and the others, I was legitimately surprised you didn't try to force Xivan to give Urthaenriel back. I realize we were outnumbered and they did have Urthaenriel to use, but I had expected you'd at least make the attempt."

"Ah," I said. "That's because I've finally figured out what Urthaenriel is. And if I fought the duchess for it, she might have figured it out too. I couldn't take that chance."

For the first time that morning, Thurvishar looked confused. "I don't understand. It's completely obvious what Urthaenriel is. It's right there in one of its more popular names: *Godslayer.*"

I slowly shook my head. "No. That's a side effect. It's not why the sword exists." I leaned forward across the table and lowered my voice. "The question I have been asking myself for some time now is this: Was Vol Karoth's creation an accident? And I think the answer is no. I think Relos Var–Rev'arric–did what he meant to do. The mistake he hadn't counted on was what happened to everyone *else* involved in the ritual. Vol Karoth? That part went off perfectly."

Thurvishar cocked his head. "But . . . how does that tie into Urthaenriel?"

"Think about it. Some of the earliest stories I've ever heard about Vol Karoth consistently claim Urthaenriel was used to defeat him. But that doesn't make any sense. Urthaenriel is antithetical to magic, and so is Vol Karoth. Vol Karoth should be the one being in the universe Urthaenriel isn't effective against. So I've been trying to think of how both could be true. And since I seem to have this . . . connection . . . with Urthaenriel as well as with Vol Karoth, a potential solution became obvious. I think Urthaenriel is Vol Karoth's *gaesh*."

Thurvishar's eyes widened. He too began whispering. "What? But how would that even be possible? Vol Karoth was created at the same time as the Stone of Shackles."

I shrugged. "So? We've been assuming gaeshing is impossible without the Stone of Shackles, but we don't actually know that, do we? What if it's not? What if the only reason everyone uses the Cornerstone is because that makes it much easier? If I'm right, Urthaenriel was created independently, which is why it wasn't destroyed when I shattered the Stone of Shackles. The sword contains a sliver of Vol Karoth's soul, which means whoever is holding it can *control Vol Karoth*."[1]

Thurvishar just stared at me.

"He would have . . . I mean, he couldn't just . . . What if . . ." His eyes unfocused as he dealt with the repercussions of what I'd just told him. He looked out at nothing, rubbing his lower lip. "So if the sword contains a sliver of his soul, then that means it also contains a sliver of yours–" Thurvishar gave me a significant look.

I made a face. "I don't know. The sword and I have a connection, just as Vol Karoth and I seem to have a connection. That's why I can hear the damn thing even when I'm not holding it. The first time I picked up Urthaenriel back at the Culling Fields, something in that sword woke up and recognized me. I guarantee you no one will ever be able to hide its location from me again. But I don't know if that gaesh works on me. I'm a different soul now. I'm not S'arric anymore. But you understand my dilemma, right? What if I'm wrong? Standing in front of Senera and the Duchess of Yor wouldn't be the right time to find out."

"But why?" Thurvishar clarified himself immediately. "I mean, why would Relos Var create something like that? What purpose does it serve?" He pondered that for a second before adding, "Killing the rest of the Eight Immortals, I suppose."

"No, if that was his motivation, Relos Var would be going on an Eight Immortals killing spree right now. He wouldn't have given the sword to Xivan Kaen. It's something else. I just haven't figured out what yet." I tapped my finger on the wooden table. "And where *is* Relos Var, anyway? We saw Senera, but where's her master? It's not like I can just

[1] While Kihrin's theories often prove nothing more than interesting conjecture, so far I've seen nothing to indicate this one isn't correct.

shrug and say, 'Oh well, he's probably just been at home taking it easy, working on his wood carving skills. Maybe he's taken up knitting?'"

Thurvishar scowled. "I've been trying so very hard not to think about that. Not to think about him."

I could only feel sympathy for the man. He'd grown up his whole life thinking all his family were dead, and unlike me, he hadn't been adopted by people who loved him. It had to be tough to realize his only living family was Relos Var.

Of course, that set me to thinking about my own father and that situation. Before I knew it, we were both sitting at the table, staring out at nothing, eating the rest of our breakfast in mute, mournful silence.

Finally, I slapped my hand on the table, stood, and picked up my harp. "Come on. Let's go find that friendly volunteer so we can tour the lovely city of Bahl-Nimian."

We stepped through Thurvishar's gate into a small cul-de-sac of red stone walls without a sky. Even though it was daytime, the dim light made it feel otherwise. The odor, on the other hand, suggested a city of people with questionable bathing habits housed too tightly together, probably along with their livestock.

Graffiti and lewd messages covered the stone wall for almost the entire length that I could see. Most of the graffiti seemed dedicated to curses. I felt a little sad Tyentso wasn't here to see them. She was a great connoisseur of foul language and would absolutely have appreciated it.

"Are we sure we're in the right place?" I looked to Thurvishar.

"Yes?" His expression seemed equally dubious.

Then I heard the singing. "Oh, for fuck's sake," I said. "Are you joking? Taja, this isn't funny."

Thurvishar stopped and turned back to face me. "What's wrong?"

"They're here." I stabbed a finger downward for emphasis. "What the ever icy hell, Thurvishar? I can *still* hear Urthaenriel. Godslayer's here in Bahl-Nimian. *Right now.*"

Thurvishar's eyes widened. "That's not possible."

I was frankly amazed by his ability to say those words with a straight face. "Seriously?"

"Okay," he acknowledged. "Possible. Just highly improbable." Then he grimaced. "I should have realized—when we saw Senera, Talea, and Xivan in Kishna-Farriga, they were at a temple of Vilfar. And Bahl-Nimian is Vilfar's sacred city. So whatever they're doing, it probably involves dealing with the god-queen herself."

"So the highly improbable bit is that Grizzst picked *this* city for his whoring. Gotcha. Fine. Shouldn't be an issue. Since I can hear Urthaenriel, it should also be easy to *avoid* Urthaenriel."

"Right. So we shall ask around for the velvet houses, find Grizzst, and then be on our way before Senera, Xivan, or Talea is the wiser." Thurvishar began walking toward the mouth of the cul-de-sac.

I followed. "Sounds foolproof."

I tried to ask around, realized that was complicated by the fact I didn't speak the local language, and ended up passing off that duty to Thurvishar. He didn't speak the language either, but it turns out being able to read minds is just amazingly handy under such circumstances. We had a few close calls along the way, when Urthaenriel's song clearly became louder, thus indicating Xivan had strayed uncomfortably close. We had to duck around some buildings and even backtrack once, before we finally ended up at a brothel. It wasn't the one Thurvishar had been looking for, but it was *a* brothel. (I refuse to call it a velvet house. It wasn't that nice.)

I scoffed under my breath the moment I entered. *Squalid,* I think, would be the appropriate word. This wasn't one of the buildings carved into the bedrock–those seemed well maintained. This was built in an interior space, and its stability was questionable. If this was an establishment that tendered a great deal of traffic, the owners clearly didn't believe in investing it back into the business. I suspected the building did as much business in drugs as whores.

A thin, sickly-looking man came out and said something. I have no idea what, but I could fill in the gaps. *What do you want? Women? Men? What sort? We have everything! No tastes too exotic! All very sexy!*

Maybe the people he'd offer up were being treated fairly. This might be the one town in the whole world where someone might hesitate to take advantage of prostitutes. Somehow I had my doubts.

I turned to Thurvishar. "I don't speak the local language, so this is on you."

He made a face. "Does it have to be?"[2]

"Oh, you're Quur?" the man said. The accent was terrible, but the fact I could understand him at all was a miracle in itself.

"Oh good, he speaks a little Guarem." Thurvishar shoved me forward. "He's all yours."

I gave Thurvishar a hurt look, but he was having none of it. So instead, I walked over to the brothel owner and slipped a few ords into the man's hand. He was a pro–that metal vanished like it had never been there at all, but his smile widened.

"Yes, we're Quuros," I told him. "We're looking for a particular someone–"

"We have everything!" His smile was as wide as it was fake.

[2] It's often quite horrifying to know what people are thinking. This was an excellent example.

"No, we're not here for whores," I said. "This man is special–"

His expression fell into something tired and a bit bored. "Give me his look. Twenty-five ord for thirty-second start." He made a running motion with his fingers. "Fifty for surprise visit." This time he ran a finger across his throat, with his tongue hanging out. "You damage house, you pay extra."

I stared at him.

He sighed. "This *Bahl-Nimian,*" he said, as if that explained all I might need to know about why a brothel owner was so inured to the idea of letting people in his clients' rooms, he had a standard rate for the service.

"Right. Um–wait–" I looked back toward Thurvishar. "What does he look like–"

Urthaenriel's song rang out loud and clear.

Simultaneously, the door to the brothel opened. Xivan Kaen stepped into the room, followed by Senera and Talea.

"There you are," Senera said. "I was starting to think you were avoiding us."

# 78: Fatal Improvisations

***(Teraeth's story)***

The problem with assassinations is that they rely as much on blind luck as careful planning and meticulous execution. A hapless fool might get lucky, while an expert assassin who had spent years carefully monitoring and planning their strike might find their target unexpectedly changing plans, sitting in the wrong spot, choosing the steak instead of their normal evening oysters.

Of course, the hapless fool was usually found and killed quickly after their unexpected success, while the expert had a backup plan and an escape route in case of complications.

Since Teraeth had neither a backup plan nor an escape route and was basically making this up as he went, he was uncomfortably aware of which category he fell into at that moment.

"Come on, Taja," he muttered under his breath. "You like Kihrin, right? He'll vouch for me."

Teraeth had passed by the entrance to the palace a dozen times, always using a different disguise, which would mean nothing if he chose to wander too close to wards designed to strip away exactly the sort of illusion he was using. Teraeth wasn't trying to make it inside the palace, however. He was observing.

The vané royal palace wasn't located on the branches of the Mother of Trees, as the rest of the capital was. Instead, it nestled into the tree itself. It had no windows. No way for any ne'er-do-well or miscreant to find their way inside except to pass through the same set of doors everyone used, from king to merchant. That passage into the palace was arguably the most heavily warded doorway in the entire world.[1] Inside, illusions created the appearance of windows, of wide and sweeping views of the phosphorescent forests. Magic kept the air fresh. Magic took care of the sanitation. There was a Gatestone, but it was even more heavily warded and guarded than the front door. The palace itself had been—not carved—but trained into the tree, a kind of massive negative

[1] The Parliament of Flowers would be another such spot.

topiary. Rumor had it that even the ants, bugs, and various vermin sheltering in the tree herself acted as active guards. The palace was luxurious, beautiful, and mind-numbingly secure.

The Manol royal palace had never fallen to attack in the entire history of the vané, not even when Terindel had waged his war against Khaevatz. The only successful assassination ever carried out within its walls had been Miyathreall's assassination of Khaeriel, and technically speaking, Miyathreall hadn't survived it.

Everyone knew attempting an assassination within the palace walls was suicide. But Teraeth was of the opinion that worked to his advantage. When people think they're vulnerable is exactly when people gird their loins, board up all the windows, and take sensible precautions. And conversely, when people *know* they're completely safe . . .

Well. That's when security is sacrificed in the name of convenience. That's when matters are allowed to get a little sloppy. Sure, Kelanis logically knew the Black Brotherhood would not be happy with him—he'd broken his word to Thaena, after all—but that had to be fighting with the emotional certainty no one would ever, could ever reach him.

To make matters worse for Kelanis and better for Teraeth, there was the rather inconvenient matter of royal blood. Most of the magical defenses of the palace were designed to allow access to a cleared group of staff and the royal family itself. Khaeriel, ironically, might still be perfectly capable of entering the palace grounds because she now inhabited the body of Queen Miyane's sister. Teraeth, meanwhile, was the half brother of Kelanis and Khaeriel's mother, Khaevatz, which meant that he was technically a member of the royal family, regardless of whether or not his father still counted.

If Kelanis was smart—and he did seem to be smart—that would virtually guarantee the need to come up with new security arrangements, something that didn't depend on bloodlines. Except, of course, that unpredictable, last-minute changes in procedure and schedule were just the sort of thing that encouraged mistakes and made Teraeth's job much easier. The vané were no more immune to bureaucratic errors than anyone else.

Teraeth watched the comings and goings of the palace retinue, retainers, and guests for a while longer. Then he gave the palace a wink on his last pass and headed back to the silk farm.

Normally, Teraeth liked to have more time. Significantly more time. He didn't enjoy making it up as he went. But at least there was a Black Brotherhood chapter house; the silk farm proved every sort of useful.

He avoided Khaeriel while he made the preparations. The supplies he needed were easy to obtain, but he'd didn't want any of it traced back to the safe house. Unfortunately, Kelanis had every bit as much motive to see Khaeriel and Doc done away with as the reverse.

Teraeth had finished his last preparations, which included a well-deserved bath, and dressed for the job. Which was when he discovered he'd lost his necklace.

Technically, this wasn't important. Technically. However, in reality, even if he didn't always wear it (especially not on jobs), he fastidiously made certain he knew where it was at all times. And when he did wear it, Teraeth often used it as a talisman, which made it extremely important to keep it from falling into unfriendly hands. That necklace was his most cherished possession.

He searched the entirety of the washroom (normally for washing silk fibers, converted into something more standardly utilitarian for the safe house's new guests) but couldn't find the pendant anywhere. And he knew he'd been wearing it when he came inside.

Doc? Maybe. Certainly Doc could have easily made it inside the washroom without anyone noticing. He was even better at moving around quietly than Kihrin, although in Doc's case, he did have to know you were there. Still, Teraeth couldn't imagine who else could have taken the necklace.

He walked outside to find Doc, when he saw Janel leaning against one of the ant houses, one arm crossed over her chest, the second arm held out, spinning his necklace on her index finger.

Teraeth stopped. "Where did you find that?"

Janel stopped spinning the necklace, holding it up to look at the black arrowhead that formed the main pendant. "This was the arrow that killed Atrin Kandor, wasn't it? The actual arrowhead."

Teraeth cleared his throat. "Yes."

She raised an eyebrow. "Has anyone ever told you how remarkably unhealthy keeping something like this around as a memento is? Although I believe the expression Kihrin would use would be: 'That's fucked up.'"

Teraeth held out his hand. "Give it to me."

She closed her fingers around the necklace. "Of course. After you agree that I'm coming with you."

Teraeth's eyes widened. "Excuse me?"

Janel pushed herself away from the ant house and walked over to him. She had a way of swaying her hips that made him . . .

Teraeth reminded himself to focus.

She stopped before him and held up the necklace. "I know where you're going," Janel said, "and I want to come along."

Teraeth cleared his throat. "Much as I'd like to think you meant that as an invitation to the bedroom—"

"I'm serious."

Teraeth had his doubts but was equally sure he'd regret saying so. "All right. You're serious. Why do you want to come along?"

She crossed her arms over her chest, tucking his necklace out of sight. "Because. I don't like Kelanis. I'd like to see him dead. And I'd like to confirm he does not, in fact, have Kihrin."

He hesitated. "This isn't . . . This isn't like being on the field of battle. I'm not saying you can't do it, just that it's not the sort of thing I'd ever expect you to *want* to do."

"Oh, I'm not going to assassinate anyone," Janel said. "Do you honestly think I'd be able to get anywhere near Kelanis? No. But I do know a few tricks that might prove useful. I can be a distraction. I'm very good at distraction."

"You distract me constantly, but I don't think that's what you meant."

"No, I meant we're on a tree and I excel at making things burn."

A small worm of possibility began to thread its way up the back of Teraeth's spine. He frowned at her. "We'd never pass you off as a vané. Any illusions would be stripped away as soon as you entered the palace, unless we used Chainbreaker. And if we did that, we might as well bring Doc along for the rest of the assassination and make it a party."

"Which we both know is not a good idea," Janel said. "I can't recommend we let either Doc or Khaeriel anywhere near there. It just seems like asking for trouble."

"Right, so . . ."

"Teraeth," Janel said gently, "if illusions won't work, how are *you* planning on breaking in?"

Teraeth started to tell her that didn't matter. He stopped himself. "My way was going to be a little . . . messy."

She gave him an incredulous stare. "You thought I'd be put off by violence? Have you met me?"

"Not that kind of messy. But once past the main entrance, illusions will work again, so from that point forward, I'll be golden." He chewed on his lip as he considered her. "I'm not that good with voices, you realize, so I don't suggest you talk to anyone once we're inside."

The corner of her lips rose. "I think I can manage."

"I've seen no evidence that's true."

"Said the snake to the serpent," Janel replied.

He laughed. He couldn't help himself. "Fine, but I would plead for your help in one small area."

"Yes?" She looked ever so slightly wary.

"Teach me about idorrá and thudajé," Teraeth said. "We somehow never got around to talking about that in the Afterlife."

"No, I suppose we never did." Janel visibly relaxed. "I should have done that weeks ago."

Teraeth held out his hand. "The necklace, if you don't mind."

She looked him in the eyes, lifted up the necklace, and then quite deliberately fastened it around her own neck, so the arrow point fell just above her cleavage. "I'll just keep this safe for you."

Teraeth was surprised to realize that idea didn't especially bother him, although it did make him want to delay going out in favor of admiring her wearing that necklace and nothing else. "All right," he said, smiling. "You do that."

# 79: The First Question

***(Kihrin's story)***

We ended up in a tavern.[1] To my surprise, it was even a nice tavern, but then, apparently, the women had hired a "guide" (one of the city's many beggars to judge from her smell) to take them to a nicer part of town and keep them from any costly missteps. So this was a building built into the cliff side, a wide, warm area with little arched alcoves of red sandstone lined with pillows and rugs where one might comfortably lounge with friends with some modicum of privacy. One of the women paid for a meal for their guide, which was presumably handed out elsewhere, and rented an alcove for the rest of us.

"So why were you looking for us again?" I asked after we'd settled in and ordered several platters of the local specialty. "I'd assumed you wanted to put us as far behind you as possible."

"I'd like to offer you a trade," Senera said. Then she corrected herself and pointed to Thurvishar. "Actually, I'd like to offer *you* a trade."

"Vilfar was helpful to a point," Xivan said. "Unfortunately, that point is where Suless has claimed sanctuary with the dragon Baelosh."

"Ah," Thurvishar said.

I nudged him. "Looks like it's your turn to take care of a dragon." I pantomimed being handed a note. "Oh wait, I've just been told we're terribly busy and also aren't that gullible." I gave Senera an arch look. "You seriously think we're going to fall for this con *twice*?"

"This isn't–" Senera started to protest, then she sighed. "Right. Of course you'd think that."

"What is he talking about?" Xivan asked.

"Oh, did Senera forget to tell you how she and Relos Var exploited the whole 'oh look, there's a dragon about to attack and you're the only one who can save us' routine to betray *everyone*? Most especially us?"

[1] The velvet house owner offered to "rent" us a room, claiming he had a bed large enough to fit all of us. Needless to say, none of us were interested in taking him up on his noble gesture. Kihrin also believed it was less a possibility than a certainty that he would spy on us, and while we could have taken steps . . . it just wasn't worth it.

I tilted my head in Xivan's direction. "Don't get me wrong. You seem sincere, but so was Janel. You shouldn't trust Senera."

Talea threw Senera a scandalized look. Xivan looked displeased.

Senera growled, "I'll explain it all later."

"I'm sure you have a fine selection of excuses to choose from," I said, "but it doesn't change the fact that there's absolutely no way we're helping you."

"What are you offering in trade?" Thurvishar asked in a soft voice.

"Thurvishar, no." I shook my head at him.

"A question," Senera told him. "You can ask any question you like, and I'll give you an answer using the Name of All Things." She paused. "Within reason. I'm not going to ask a question that would result in my death or incapacitation. You know how this works."

Thurvishar sucked on his teeth while he narrowed his eyes and studied the woman. "Three questions. And I'll use magic to confirm the question we give you is the question you actually ask."

I stared at the wizard. "Thurvishar, no!"

He shushed me. "It's fine, Kihrin. I've got this."

"You so do *not* have this," I snapped back, but he ignored me. "I swear to the Veils, I will do this without you." Unfortunately, I had a dilemma: he hadn't told me what Grizzst looked like, so technically speaking, I couldn't do this without him. Which he knew.

"Two questions," Senera offered back. "And I'll say the question out loud so you know I'm not deceiving you–there's no need to read my mind, which I know perfectly well is what you mean when you say you'll 'use magic.'"

Thurvishar pondered that. "I ask the questions first. Before we leave with you to take care of Baelosh."

"And then you simply abandon us? Not a chance. Help us first, then you can ask your questions." She leaned forward and rested her elbows on the table as she studied him.

"Who betrayed *who* back at Atrine?" Thurvishar countered. "One question now, one question after we've helped you deal with Baelosh. You'll repeat the question out loud before you write out the answer."

Senera didn't hesitate. "Deal."

I slumped against the rock face. "Thurvishar, what are you doing?"

"Trust me," Thurvishar said.

Senera looked pretty damn pleased with herself. Thurvishar had more than taken the bait of whatever trap she had in mind. Even if we only needed the one question to find out exactly where Grizzst was, I just knew Thurvishar would insist on following through on his end of the bargain.

"Do you want to do this now or wait until after we eat?" Senera asked.

"Oh, could we eat first?" Talea said. "I'm famished."

Xivan shrugged and stood. "I'm feeling hungry myself. I'll be back in a bit." She unbuckled Urthaenriel and handed the sword, scabbard and all, to Talea, who took it and wrapped it around her own waist without a word spoken. Xivan's eyes never left me; she clearly understood who would be the most likely to cause a problem during such an exchange.

Everyone fell silent as she left. We all knew what her announcement meant: Xivan's "food" was inevitably human, or more specifically, human souls. According to Janel, though, she tended to confine her appetites to the more unsavory examples of human behavior.

I suppose Bahl-Nimian must have seemed like a banquet.

That quieted conversation until the food arrived, which turned out to be trays of roasted meats, vegetables, and something I suspected was cactus chopped extremely fine, mixed with hot spices, and meant to be eaten with a spongy flatbread that managed to be nothing like Quuros sag. I could see the ancestry–see how this had probably evolved from something Vilfar and her followers had brought with her when they'd moved south. And in the centuries since, it had changed and shifted until it became what we were eating–which was both spicy and good.

After the four of us had finished and the plates were cleared away, Senera pulled a small journal out of her satchel. "So what's your question? Or do you need a little time to think it over?" She pulled the Name of All Things out of her bodice, an ink stick from her belt, and the brush from her hair, where she'd been using it as a hairpin. With that linchpin freed, her blond hair fell over her face like a delicate silk curtain settling into place.

"Oh, there's no need to wait," Thurvishar said. "I know exactly what I want to ask."

I thought that meant he was going to ask about Grizzst first. Nope.

"Well?" Senera began pouring water into the stone's well as she ground the ink with a noise like polishing the edge of a sword.

"Ask this: What's the one piece of information that Relos Var most doesn't want Senera Var to know?"

Senera froze. Slowly, her mouth dropped open as she stared at the wizard across from her.

"Oh wow," Talea said and sank back into her pillow.

"You manipulative bastard," Senera said.[2]

I had to laugh. "Runs in the family, I suppose."[3]

[2] That's the snowstorm calling a piece of paper white.

[3] I suppose it does. Damn it.

They both ignored me. Senera's expression was a picture of furious outrage, and Thurvishar looked, well, smug. "You can't be serious," she hissed.

"We had a deal, Senera." He smiled. "I'll make it easy; you don't even have to tell me what the answer is. I wouldn't want to trick you into accidentally betraying your master's secrets, after all."

I bit my lip. Because . . . yeah. *Accidentally* betraying Relos Var clearly wasn't what Thurvishar had in mind.

"You should have saved your question for something important," Senera said, "instead of a question with no answer. He gave me the Name of All Things, idiot. He's clearly not hiding any secrets from me."

Thurvishar waved a magnanimous hand toward the stone. "Then ask and see."

Only then did Senera break eye contact with Thurvishar and stare down at the stone. She picked up the ink stick and finished grinding out the ink, while the rest of us watched in pregnant silence. Rebel must have sensed Senera's distress, because the dog nudged up next to her mistress and set her head on Senera's lap.

Finally, Senera picked up the brush.

"Out loud," Thurvishar reminded her.

"Oh for fuck's–" Senera inhaled deeply. "What's the one piece of information that Relos Var most doesn't want me to know?"

For a second, nothing happened. Senera started to smile, no doubt thinking that proved her right. Then her hand yanked down and started to write on the page. I didn't see what she wrote–the angle was wrong. Whatever it was, though, it was not "nothing"–I watched as what little color ever existed in that milk-pale face vanished, leaving her as white as the paper she used. Senera stared at the journal page for a second longer, then ripped the page out, crumpled it, and tossed it into the air, where it burst into flames and vanished.

"Yes, Senera, I see what you mean. Relos Var has clearly kept no secrets from you," Thurvishar said.

"Wretch," she spat. "Fine, if that's how you want to do this, let's do this." She picked the brush again. "What's the one secret that Thurvishar–"

"Um, wait," I said.

Worry, and then undisguised fear, quickly made their way across Thurvishar's face. "No, don't ask that. Senera, please!"

She stared at him hatefully. "What's the one secret that Thurvishar D'Lorus most doesn't want me to know?" And again, she began to write.

Thurvishar sighed and looked away.

When she finished, which admittedly didn't take nearly as long as when she'd written out Relos Var's secret, she read the result and then raised her gray eyes to stare at Thurvishar. She said nothing at all. To be honest, I thought she just looked confused.

Senera closed the journal, tucked it back into her satchel, and looked at the wall. She picked up a cloth and mechanically began to clean the Name of All Things before tucking it back into her bodice. She didn't do a very good job of it. Black ink spilled, staining her blouse.

Senera didn't notice.

"Well?" Talea said. "What was it? I'm really curious." She smiled and winked at Thurvishar, trying to make light of it. Neither Senera nor Thurvishar were smiling.

"How long?" Senera asked suddenly, looking up at Thurvishar.

"Oh . . . years," he admitted.

*"Years?"* She sounded equal parts incredulous and furious.

Thurvishar turned up his hands and shrugged.

Senera grabbed the rest of her supplies and stood, dislodging Rebel, who gave an annoyed whine of protest. "I'll pay the tavern keeper for the meal. Xivan will be back soon. You should wait for her, Talea. I'll meet you and Xivan back at the inn. You two—" She pointed at Thurvishar and myself without ever actually managing to look at Thurvishar. "You should find someplace close to sleep. It's a safer part of town than where we met. I'll find you in the morning, and we can make plans on how to deal with Baelosh."

She picked up Rebel's leash and left, presumably to pay the bill.

After Senera had gone, we sat there, now down to just three.

After a moment of silence, Talea threw up her arms. "What just happened?"

"Pretty sure Senera just learned not to ask questions unless she's prepared to hear the answer." I nudged Thurvishar with my elbow. "What did the first message say?"

Thurvishar was still staring at the doorway Senera had just vacated. Then he realized I'd asked him a question. "What makes you think I'd know?"

I raised an eyebrow. "I caught the wording on what you promised even if Senera didn't. You never said you *wouldn't* read her mind."

"Ah." He picked up his drink and sipped it. "I suppose that's true. Anyway, it didn't say a thing that you or I didn't already know. Relos Var doesn't intend to topple the Eight Immortals; he intends to replace them. With himself."

Talea tilted her head. "I thought he wanted to overthrow Quur. Wasn't that why he was supporting Duke Kaen?"

"He couldn't give two chalices about Quur, dear Talea," Thurvishar told her gently. "Relos Var has much grander plans than that."

"But I bet he's always sold Senera on the idea they were freeing humanity from divine tyranny, hasn't he?" I added. "And to find out that he's no better . . . that in fact he always just intended to put himself in charge . . . that has to sting."

"Exactly. But she does his dirtiest dirty work. She deserves to know the truth."

"What did the second note say?" Talea asked Thurvishar.

A cloud cast a shadow over the wizard's face. "I'd rather not, if you don't mind," Thurvishar said. "I believe I've already suffered enough humiliation for one evening."

She rose to her feet. "I'll just go find Xivan."

I didn't ask, because I was pretty sure I already knew. Now, I might have been wrong. Maybe Thurvishar secretly had a hidden love child or worked for the Devoran priests or . . . I don't know . . . any number of things that he wouldn't want known. But I was reasonably certain that Senera had left so shocked and troubled because Thurvishar's secret had been so personal and had, against all her expectations, involved herself.

I was pretty sure the message had probably been short and simple. Three little words would have done the trick. Something like: *He loves you.*

Which, if that was the case, made her reaction interesting indeed.

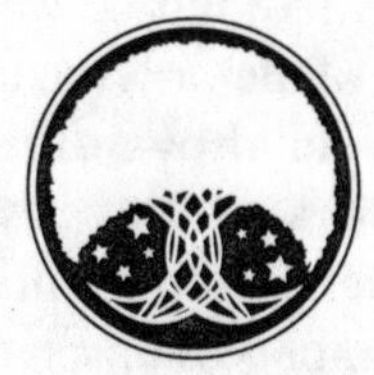

# 80: Kingkiller

***(Teraeth's story)***

The vané man pulled a small wagon led by two large, gentle-looking lizards up to the front doors of the palace. "Delivery." He motioned back to the wagon, which contained several large barrels.

"Not your normal time, is it?" The guard frowned.

The deliveryman shrugged. "They've been changing up all the schedules. I don't question it. I just bring it over." He handed the guard a set of papers.

The guard looked them over. "This all seems in order. We'll need to open the barrels to check."

The deliveryman pulled out a crowbar, clearly expecting that command. "Sure enough."

It took a few moments to open each barrel and confirm the contents: wine. Each time, the soldier dipped a crystal and inspected the result, checking for additives, poisons, or alterations. Satisfied that the barrels contained exactly what was promised, they tapped the lids back down again.

"We'll take it from here." The guard did something with an amulet around his neck, and several large insects–not actual insects but magical constructs made to look like insects–ambled forward. "Unload that into the secure storeroom. Be careful. Do not spill the barrels." The automatons went to work while the guard signed the paperwork and handed it back.

"A pleasure as always," the deliveryman said as he drove away.

The insects made a discreet single-file line as they carried the barrels into the palace. None of the normal guests and staff coming and going paid any attention to them.

The guards went back to their jobs.

The constructs dropped off the barrels, shut and locked the secure door, and went back to their normal posts.

One of the lids on a barrel pushed up and off. Teraeth carefully unfolded himself and climbed out. He dragged a sealed waxed cloth package with him, which included clothes, jewelry, and a wine goblet.

Hiding in the food was a time-honored way of sneaking into any castle, but no one did it with barrels of ale or wine for the obvious reason: they'd drown. Even a voramer would drown–they worked best underwater, not under alcohol. And so the security on such barrels mostly centered around making sure the contents weren't poisoned or contaminated, not making sure no one had crammed themselves into the bottom.

Teraeth hadn't drowned, not because he was half-voramer, but because a certain Joratese woman knew a terribly convenient glyph for air. He created a small mage-light no brighter than a small candle and set it on a nearby shelf. The storeroom was one of many in the castle, large and cool and dark, filled to the brim with barrels and rows upon rows of all manner of alcohol, but also bins of vegetables, herbs, and dried fruits, which might be needed on any given night.

He tapped three times on the lid of another barrel before prying open the lid. A few seconds later, Janel raised her hands to the edge and lifted herself up and out. She was as naked as he, wine dripping from her body and the sealed waxed package that contained her clothing. As soon as she was free from the barrel, he tapped the lids back on both barrels and used a quick cleanup spell to eliminate the wine they'd spilled. No doubt the next person to come open these barrels would be filing a strongly worded complaint with the vintner about their fill levels.

Of course, that didn't do a thing about the new drops of wine they were dripping from themselves with every second. The single mage-light limned Janel's body with a diffuse golden glow. He didn't even pretend he wasn't staring.

She noticed, paused, and returned the favor, eyes lingering like touches across his skin. Then Janel looked around.

"How well hidden are the rows in the back?" Janel began walking among the wine racks and stacked boxes.

Teraeth watched her for a moment and then cleaned up the wine from himself and the floor and grabbed that single mage-light from its resting place. By the time he caught up with her, she'd created her own light, which she tucked to the side as she pushed a large wooden box back a foot or so from the crate it sat atop, forming a chair. She hopped up onto the ledge and sat down. In the mage-glow, she looked like a statue of a goddess. There was no mistaking her intent.

Teraeth looked back toward the door. In the dim light, an open door would be like the dawning of a new day. Anyone entering would need time for their eyes to adjust. More than enough time to spin an illusion to hide themselves.

This wasn't exactly the smartest thing he'd ever done, although it was still miles above the stupidest, which was and hopefully always would be "March into the Manol with a full army in the middle of summer."

He felt a sense of desperate need for her, a yearning he found wasn't mysterious at all. She must have been thinking along similar lines, because as soon as he reached her–

*Kihrin cleared his throat.*

*Thurvishar stopped. "Oh. Right. I suppose you wouldn't want to hear this, would you? And to be honest, it's quite a bit more graphic than the descriptions with your parents, so I'm perfectly happy to skip it."*

*"Is it now?" Kihrin raised an eyebrow. "May I see those?"*

*"No destroying pages," Thurvishar chided.*

*"Wouldn't dream of it." As Thurvishar handed over the pages, Kihrin looked them over briefly, nodding to himself. Then he rolled the pages into a tube and tucked them into his agolé. "I'll just keep this for later, why don't I? You don't really need them for your chronicle, anyway. Just a lot of unnecessary description."*

*"Kihrin–"*

*He raised a hand to forestall any further complaints. "Let me have this, Thurvishar."*

*"Fine," Thurvishar said. "Saves me from having to read it out loud."*

When Teraeth and Janel finished, they both dressed in the finery they'd brought with them. Teraeth wove their illusions. The wonderful thing about most vané is how rarely they wore talismans or any kind of defense against phantasms. Most vané *wanted* to be fooled, wanted to revel in a thousand impossible sights. For those who didn't–a few special guards–they had real court clothing for them both, including makeup and wigs.

Once they were cleaned and properly disguised, he no longer worried about who might come into the storeroom. It would hardly be the first time a pair of vané had slipped away for rough sex against the wine racks.

Teraeth winked at her and pretended to be drunk. He didn't stagger. Vané never staggered, drunk or otherwise. They lingered beautifully, glassy-eyed and elegant.

"How do I look?" she asked, straightening her clothes.

He smoothed her hair. "Freshly fucked." Teraeth sniffed the air near her. "Which is entirely appropriate. It's been a long time since I've been here–"

"Wait, you've been here before?"

"My mother brought me here once. Everyone gave me the sort of delighted neglect vané always give our children. We have no idea what to do with them except to dress them up in cute outfits and suggest they come back in thirty years." Teraeth's impression then had been a never-ending swirling dance of sybaritic grandeur and intoxicating dissipation.

The court was more popular with the Kirpis vané than the Manol vané, but sooner or later, every vané danced on these hallowed floors for the pleasure of their king. "Anyway, my point is that we'll blend. Let's go visit the party."

"How do you know there's a party?"

He took her arm. "There's always a party. But don't worry, I've never heard of the king actually attending."

"Oh good, because I'd hate for this whole thing to be spoiled because he simply *recognized* us."

"Not a problem. Just act like a stupid, drunk teenage girl instead of your normal state of being an inferno somehow trapped in a human body. He'll never recognize you."

She raised an eyebrow. "You do realize we're only twenty. Technically speaking, we were stupid teenagers *last year*."

"Then this shouldn't be that hard."

The main ballroom was every bit as wondrous as one might expect. Janel probably wasn't faking the look of awe that came over her face. The entire room was heavily enchanted, but since this had been a Manol palace long before the Kirpis moved in, almost none of it came in the form of illusions. Rather, the walls had been shaped into a thousand fantastical forms–trees and flowers and every kind of jungle denizen. Fireflies flitted about providing light. Still more lights were woven into the carved surfaces. The floor itself was mirror smooth, so one might become a bit dizzy if not careful.

Teraeth saw Queen Miyane first, laughing delightedly at some joke or witty barb cast for her amusement. Miyane was young by vané standards and, like her late sister, was half-Manol and half-Kirpis, products of the short-lived fad of symbolically uniting the two nations after the disastrous civil war. That was probably why the two sisters had caught the eyes of the royal family in the first place.

She seemed to be enjoying the party. And King Kelanis had given her Kihrin's star tears.

Janel had clearly noticed too. "Oh, that–"

"Shhh," he told her. "Ignore that for the moment. We'll deal with it later." He began wandering about the room with Janel at his side, pretending he knew people who didn't want to admit they didn't remember him.

He heard applause and felt Janel stiffen next to him. He turned his head, dreading and knowing exactly what he was going to see.

King Kelanis had decided to attend the party after all.

# 81: In Search of Dragons

***(Talea's story)***

Apparently, Baelosh's lair was a week's ride from Bahl-Nimian and quite a bit longer than that if walking. Talea wouldn't have minded the walking so much, but she knew Xivan wouldn't have the patience for it. The only difficulty as far as Talea saw the matter was that she had never ridden a horse before.

Horses were strange and terrifying creatures. Janel had loved to go on about their qualities at absurd length, but Talea had never understood the appeal. She'd been pleased to discover Kihrin had nearly the same impression of them, but then realized it was just that he had the same impression of these *particular* horses. Apparently, they were inferior to the Quuros variety, and he even went so far as to suggest they take a quick trip back to Quur to retrieve "proper" horses. Talea didn't care; all horses seemed equally capable of dumping her on her head.

Xivan was rather bemused to discover she'd neglected Talea's education this way, and quickly promised she'd give lessons. And after that, it wasn't like Talea could say no, was it?

Kihrin vanished for a few hours, leaving his harp behind. When he'd returned, his clothing was a bit more rumpled, he looked like he'd gotten into at least one fistfight, and he had a lot more metal—enough coin to easily buy all the supplies they needed.[1] Once that was done, they made a quick exit from Bahl-Nimian.

Well. They tried.

There was only one entrance or exit from Bahl-Nimian. This came in the form of a narrow cleft in the rock face that could only be navigated single file. In turn, this resulted in some interesting logistical difficulties, which made necessary a system of flags and two full-time watchmen stationed at each end of the canyon whose only job was to signal to each other when the way was clear. So there was a line on either side of merchants, travelers, petitioners, and all the other unsavory characters who might ever need to travel to a place like Bahl-Nimian, each waiting their

[1] He'd gone gambling.

turn with varying degrees of patience. Tempers often flared, which Talea had to imagine resulted in later visits to petition the Lady of Vengeance.

By the time they made it out of the city, it was dark, but no one seemed keen to turn around and go back inside to find an inn. Thurvishar summoned lights so the horses (which they walked) wouldn't trip in the dark. With that precaution taken, they traveled for several hours before making camp for the night and giving the rather confused horses a brushing and their evening meal.

Rebel loved the horses, would make a nuisance of herself tangling herself in their legs, and generally seemed just thrilled at this turn of events. She seemed equally thrilled at the opportunity to make the acquaintance of each of her new traveling companions and petition them for belly rubs.

Xivan carefully walked Talea through the process of caring for the horses, which in Talea's case was a somewhat anxious chestnut gelding named Fidget. Talea wasn't at all sure about this whole process, which was smelly and annoying. Fidget twice tried to bite her, although the gelding settled down a bit after being brushed, which he evidently enjoyed.

Senera still wasn't talking to Thurvishar, but she *watched* him. Usually out of the corner of her eye, when he was looking elsewhere, and then pulling her gaze away with an angry shake of her head when she realized what she was doing.

Talea decided it was probably best not to let Senera know she'd noticed.

"Are you going to play for us?" Talea asked Kihrin that evening, because why bring a harp along if it was never used.

"Sure, there's no reason–"

"I wouldn't," Thurvishar said.

Kihrin looked at him strangely, as if debating whether to be insulted or not.

"*All* dragons like music," Senera had explained then. "Let's not have Baelosh find us before we can find him."

The harp stayed in its case.

The next morning brought more caring for the horses, until Talea was starting to wonder if people who kept horses were ever allowed to do anything else. She supposed she understood now why this was considered a full-time job. And then came the actual riding of said horses, which felt like half a sex act that managed to skip all the fun parts.

Talea was quite certain she was going to hugely regret everything in her life come evening.

At one point while they rode, Talea noticed Xivan pull her horse up next to Kihrin, and whispers of their conversation drifted back on the air toward her.

"What's going on with those two?" Xivan asked, pointing up ahead with her chin toward where Senera and Thurvishar had managed to be riding right next to each other while pointedly ignoring this fact.

"Ah. I believe certain truths came to light after you left. Senera's still trying to decide just how she feels about the matter." Kihrin visibly shrugged. "Any more than that really isn't any of my business."

"Huh. So what I heard before I left . . . Did Senera really betray you?"

Talea thought that was an excellent question. It was her opinion that a person who would betray one ally would sooner or later betray others, and she liked Senera. It would be rather disappointing to discover disloyalty formed a foundational piece of the woman's character.

"I'm not sure what she did counts as betrayal. It's not like she made any secret about where her loyalties lie. But we assumed she was telling us the truth, and it turns out that was foolish of us. We really should have known better."

"So it was enemy subterfuge?" Talea interrupted, then swallowed when Kihrin looked back at her in surprise. "I mean, I couldn't help but hear."

Kihrin snorted. "Yes, I suppose it was. But honestly"–he addressed that comment back to Xivan–"the way Janel talks about you, I never would have thought you were the sort of person to have any misconceptions about Relos Var's nature."

Xivan glanced down at Urthaenriel at her waist, then back at Talea. Their eyes met. "No. No delusions at all. Although Relos Var has always played fairly with me."

Kihrin laughed in a rather nasty way. "My brother is smart enough to save his lies and betrayals for special occasions."

"That doesn't mean you're better," Talea said. "You're a D'Mon, after all. I know what D'Mons are like."

He half turned in the saddle. "I'm not a D'Mon by choice, you realize. After all, I–" At that moment, his own horse, a mare named Wander, tried once more to go off the road to nibble on tasty cactus flowers. Since Kihrin was distracted, this time she actually succeeded. Talea started to laugh–

–which was when Fidget decided this was a fine idea and followed right behind Wander. That forced Xivan to rescue both of them, and by the time everyone was back on the road, the topic of conversation seemed frustratingly closed.

The countryside outside Bahl-Nimian was bleak, surprisingly hot during the day, equally cold at night. The dry land was full of plants, but they were all prickly things one Should Not Touch. There was a kind of beauty to the landscape even so, to the way the cactus would occasionally flower and the way the wind eroded the edges of the sandstone cliffs, creating layers of color, all rose, red, orange, and yellow. It didn't seem like the sort of place pale people might hail from, but then just because most Quuros–Talea included–had grown up thinking that all Doltari were white-skinned didn't make it true. Talea had also always thought Doltar was a single country, not a collection of city-states who were at best loosely aligned and more realistically in a constant state of warfare.[2] The area on the other side of the mountain range to their south was evidently colder and wetter, so she imagined that was probably much closer to Senera's ancestral homeland.

Talea was indeed miserable by the time they made camp and even more so because Xivan wouldn't let her skip taking care of the horses. At least Fidget seemed to take a little pity on her and only tried to bite her once, but then he seemed tired too. After Talea finished, Senera offered to help heal her soreness, which Talea gratefully accepted.

Really, Senera couldn't be as bad as Kihrin claimed.

Talea tried to ignore the way Kihrin was staring at her, but finally she sighed and sat down next to him. "Can I help you?" she asked.

Even by the firelight, she could see his blush. "Ah, I'm sorry. I thought I was being at least a little discreet."

"Not really. I thought you were in a relationship with Janel?" She usually found it best to address this sort of thing quickly.

"Oh, I am. It's not that." Kihrin shook his head. "I was just–" He made a face. "I was just thinking how proud Morea would be."

Talea felt his words like a punch, although she knew he'd meant no malice. "I suppose she might. I don't really think about it."

"I shouldn't talk about her. Truthfully, I didn't know her for long." He smiled sadly. "But don't worry. I'm not making a play for you. And Janel's told me that–what's the expression?–you run with mares."

"True," Talea lied. Theoretically, she ran with the whole herd, the same as Janel did, but hadn't indulged in running with any men in a rather long time. And certainly wasn't about to start now. Men were just so exhausting.

Kihrin picked up pebbles and started tossing them into the evening fire. "So how long have you and Xivan been an item, anyway?"

Talea's eyes widened. "Uh, we're not?"

"Really?" He looked sideways at her. "I'd assumed you were. I've seen the way you look at her." Then he sighed. "Oh. I'm sorry. I shouldn't have said anything."

Talea felt the blood rising to her cheeks. "I have no idea what you're talking about," she lied again, not so skillfully that time. She scrambled

[2] If you were ever curious what the city-states of Zaibur in what is now Marakor used to be like, now you know.

to her feet. "Excuse me, I have to . . . something with the horses." She left quickly.

As it turned out, Xivan actually did need her to help, with cooking instead of horses, so that distracted her from extremely annoying royals and their extremely stupid comments. Senera could have cooked as well, and she made several very disparaging comments about the fact that neither of the two men could. Which Thurvishar tolerated and Kihrin ignored.

"What are we doing about Baelosh?" Xivan finally asked. She'd made a meal she hadn't eaten herself, and she watched patiently while the others did, but it seemed her tolerance had finally come to an end.

"If it's all right with you, I'd prefer it not involve killing myself in order to give Baelosh a chance to 'finish the job,'" Thurvishar said. Rebel was currently lying down against his leg, which Senera seemed to be tolerating. Probably because forcing Rebel to move would have revealed that her dog's "betrayal" was bothering her.

Senera snorted.

Thurvishar regarded her calmly. "You think I'm being unreasonable, I suppose?"

She lifted her chin. "Completely. Inconsiderate and rude. Honestly, you're so selfish sometimes." The corner of her mouth lifted.

Talea was all but holding her breath. She was fairly certain this was the first time Senera had directly spoken to Thurvishar since the night before. Talea realized Kihrin seemed equally enraptured.

Thurvishar tilted his head. "Guilty as charged."

Senera coughed and repositioned herself by the fire. Her voice took on a more serious tone as she continued staring at the other wizard. "All joking aside, you've actually fought Baelosh. That makes you our only expert."

"Who told you that, by the way? The Name of All Things?" Thurvishar asked.

"Yes." Her mouth twisted. "Relos Var asked me to find out the past lives of a number of people. You were on that list."[3]

"I see. Apologies for the interruption. Please continue."

"Well, Baelosh and Simillion had a legendary feud. I have to imagine that he still wants to kill you, and the fact that you're reincarnated wouldn't stop him. So you'd make excellent bait."

Kihrin leaned forward. "Yes, but the problem with bait is that the fish tend to swallow it before they find out there's a hook attached."

Senera shrugged. "Much as neither of you want to believe me, Relos Var cares what happens to you. He'd be incredibly upset with me if I allowed either of you to come to harm."

[3] Nice to have that confirmed.

Kihrin started to say something and then bit down on whatever it was. Instead, he asked, "Where is Relos Var, anyway?"

"I couldn't say," Senera replied smoothly. "It's not like he checks in with me."

Xivan said, "I don't care where Relos Var is right now. I care where Baelosh is and how we might convince Baelosh to stop protecting Suless."

"Oh, that part is quite simple," Thurvishar replied. "We just need to give him a reason to think what he wants has gone somewhere else."

"Isn't it a shame that simple things are often so difficult," Talea said.

"But what does he want?" Senera asked. "What will he chase if given the motivation?"

Thurvishar seemed surprised. "You haven't–?" He waved a hand. "Never mind. He loves tsali stones most of all, but any gem will do. Green gems in particular, but you may have noticed he won't shy from diamonds or other priceless jewels. But not pearls, not amber."

"So it's just what you said, isn't it?" Talea said to Senera. "You were right all along."

Senera's mouth twisted.

"At least we have confirmation of what you suspected," Xivan told her, "before we actually have to face Baelosh."

Senera nodded. "True. Let me check a few things." She began setting up her scribing setting–paper, brush, ink, and inkstone–and was effectively dead to the rest of them while doing so.

"So bribing Baelosh to give Suless up is an acceptable solution?" Kihrin asked Xivan. "Although we don't know how Suless convinced Baelosh to help her in the first place. We might have a problem if they're old friends."

"Suless doesn't have friends," Xivan answered.

"Aha!" Senera looked up from writing. "Perfect. I have the location of the D'Molo emerald mines in the Dragonspires. Richest strike anyone has found in three centuries. That should convince Baelosh to go elsewhere."

"Great, that sounds–wait." Kihrin paused and frowned.

"How many people live or work near those mines?" Thurvishar asked.

"Oh, I don't know. Twenty thousand or so?" She rolled her eyes as both men gave her shocked looks. "He's a *dragon*. Baelosh is going to kill people no matter what we do. Short of killing the damn creature, which we can't do, there's no solution to this problem where people don't die, including doing *nothing at all*. At least this way, most of the people killed will be Quuros."

"And I refuse to embrace the loss of any human life as the more acceptable solution," Thurvishar replied. He studied the wizard. "If I opened a gate, could you keep it open for five minutes?"

"Oh please. I could keep a gate open for a lot longer than that. I could enchant you a Gatestone if necessary." She tilted her head. "Why?"

"Because I know where Baelosh's Cornerstone is. Which means we don't have to tolerate twenty thousand deaths as an acceptable loss. Because you're wrong; we *can* kill Baelosh." Thurvishar pointed to Xivan. "We have Urthaenriel. One gate spell and we'll have everything we need."

Kihrin's eyes widened. "You want us to go back to the Blight."

"Not you," Thurvishar said quickly. "You'll stay here. But if we open it from this side, we shouldn't have to worry about chaos storms."

"You're assuming Bevrosa's still there," Kihrin pointed out.

"You're assuming Bevrosa's still alive," Thurvishar said.

Kihrin fell silent.

"Who's Bevrosa?" Talea asked.

"A very brave woman," Kihrin answered. Then, apparently realizing that was at best half an answer, he added. "A morgage leader, who as of a week ago, was the holder of Wildheart. And Thurvishar's right; she's probably dead."

The name Wildheart didn't mean anything to Talea, but Senera's eyes widened. "You were serious about killing Baelosh."

"You said that short of killing him, there's no solution where innocent people don't die. Fine. Let's kill him."

"Possible, but not probable!" Senera protested.

"No," Xivan said.

Both Senera and Thurvishar pulled up short. There was a beat of silence as the others looked at each other.

"No what?" Senera asked. "No, it's not possible?"

"No, we're not going to kill Baelosh," Xivan said. "Going after Suless is dangerous enough without trying to take down a creature that normally requires an army. This isn't what I'm here to do, and I won't risk any of us doing it. We're here for Suless, not Baelosh. That's final."

Talea beamed at Xivan even as Senera and Thurvishar started to loudly protest.

"Can Wildheart be used to control Baelosh?" Kihrin's voice somehow cut through all their chatter even though he'd spoken quite softly.

Everyone looked at Senera.

She raised her hands. "How would I know?" She immediately made a face as she realized what she'd just said.

Senera grumbled and reached for the Name of All Things.

Recovering Wildheart ended up being a logistical juggling act. Senera could open (and keep open) the necessary gate, but Senera couldn't reclaim the stone, because apparently the owner of a Cornerstone couldn't use a second one. Xivan couldn't even pick up the stone because of Urthaenriel. Senera suggested Talea hold Wildheart, but Talea refused, because she too periodically needed to hold Urthaenriel. Kihrin wasn't stepping a single foot anywhere near the Blight and in fact preferred to be several miles away when the portal was opened.

That left Thurvishar to reclaim Wildheart, assuming Bevrosa had indeed given her life to ensure the rest of her tribe escaped Vol Karoth.

Which turned out to be the case.

Thurvishar came back with the green gem in his hand and a grim expression on his face. Talea went over to him and put a hand on his arm. "Was it bad?"

Thurvishar made a face. "Based on what I saw, I think some of them got away. But clearly not everyone."

Senera collapsed the gate, scowling. "Great, morgage escaped. Can we move on now?"

Thurvishar stopped and then turned to face her. "Those people's ancestors volunteered to keep watch over a monster so toxic, he distorts the very land around them. They did this even though the Korthaen Blight is an alkaline desert and they were *a water-based race*. They have done this job with faithful and loyal dedication for over a thousand years. And their reward for this? Now they're about to be a dispossessed people with no homeland, no one who will ever be willing to take them in–because they're *morgage*–and a whole group of them just sacrificed most of their people to allow my friends and me to escape. Perhaps, just perhaps, show them a modicum of respect. They've earned it." He stalked past her, heading toward the horses.

Talea bit her lip. She'd rarely seen Thurvishar quite so angry before.

Senera seemed quite taken aback. "Noted."

# 82: A Counterfeit of Royalty, II

***(Teraeth's story)***

Teraeth put his hands on Janel's waist to keep her from running. Not that he could have stopped her, but it reminded her to stay still. Running would only draw people's attention, and they might wonder why a vané felt the need.

"Everything's going to be fine," Teraeth whispered. "In fact, this makes our job much easier."

Janel glanced up at him. "And how do you figure that's true?"

"Look around, my love," he said, grinning. "Look around."

Because even more so than before, every eye was on the silver-strewn green tree throne of vané royalty. Since King Kelanis so rarely came to these events, his presence monopolized all conversation. Everyone wondered why he had chosen to attend that night's festivities or if this had anything to do with the reappearance of Khaeriel. Or if indeed Khaeriel had resurfaced at all. How could it be, when everyone knew she had died?

What people might have saved for quiet whispers in private became open and preferred topics of conversation. And since every eye was on Kelanis, those same eyes were not on Teraeth or Janel.

"So what do we do?"

"Dance," he said. "Eat. Enjoy ourselves. Stay in the back and wait for the right moment to slip away." The music started up again, and he picked up her hand. "May I teach you this dance?"

Janel laughed. "Yes, thank you."

Everything was going well. No one had recognized either Teraeth or Janel. No one had raised any alarms. And eventually, King Kelanis bade his farewells and retired for the evening. Queen Miyane wasn't done with her dancing and didn't join him. Which was fine by Teraeth. He wanted Kelanis alone.

When the time came, Janel threw a beautifully staged tantrum that amounted to screaming, "I cannot believe you did this to me!" before flouncing from the ballroom. Teraeth received a lot of sympathetic looks, but no one seemed to find it particularly odd when he followed her. Even if he was following her into the royal wing of the palace.

When he "finally" caught up with Janel, she was waiting by the guards at the door to the royal family's private chambers. He started to say something and then noticed the guards were just standing there, staring out at nothing, unresponsive. He'd been prepared to use an illusion to get past them or even if necessary knock them unconscious, but they didn't seem to even be aware that he was there.

"What?"

"Go on," Janel said, pointing toward the door. "My spell won't last forever. They're in a daze right now. Just for a few minutes. When they snap out of it, they won't realize any time has passed at all."

Teraeth blinked. "You enchanted them? You know how to *enchant*? Where did you learn how to do that?"

People often meant many different things when they talked about enchantment, but when they talked about people, they were, generally speaking, talking about some form of mind control.

And controlling minds was hellishly difficult. Then again, so was splitting off parts of a god's soul, and she'd somehow managed that too.

Janel shrugged. "Go on already. If you need help, you know the signal. I'll come find you."

"If I send the signal, go find my father, and you both can come find me."

She winked at him.

Teraeth opened the door and slipped into the room beyond. If there were any wards, he either triggered them silently or didn't trigger them at all; there was no time to check.

The royal chambers of the palace were quite large, as one might expect, and they weren't exactly devoid of people. There were servants, there were soldiers, there were various experts who for one reason or another were expected to be easily available. Teraeth had to silently slide past all of them, unseen, while he searched for the one particular vané he most wanted to find that evening.

After looking in Kelanis's bedroom, the dining room, and one of the sitting rooms, Teraeth finally found something interesting when he reached the library. He really should have known; King Kelanis was a man who really liked his library.

Except . . . whatever had been going on there had nothing to do with books.

Besides the graceful sweep of bookcases, the lovingly carved tables, the low comfortable chairs, the many plants and flowers, someone had placed a much-less-comfortable-looking iron chair in the middle of the room. The arms of the chair had been equipped with shackles, now opened. Another set of shackles, joined together by a thick length of chain, lay discarded on the floor.

Teraeth bent down and picked up the restraint. It was still locked. He heard a noise from behind one of the couches.

As he started to investigate, King Kelanis stood from whatever he'd been doing on the ground. "You startled us. We did not hear you enter."

"Oh?" Teraeth gave himself a bit of a sway as he stood there. "Oh, Your Majesty." He allowed himself a slow, wide smile. He'd had enough practice to fake "extremely stewed." "I thought this was one of the bedrooms."

"They are not here," Kelanis said, frowning. "Go back to the ballroom. You should not be here."

Teraeth knew something was wrong. Kelanis wasn't an idiot. He should have been shouting for all the guards, if not outright attacking Teraeth. And what had he been doing behind the couch? So he kept the charade going for a bit longer.

"But wait–" Teraeth dropped the shackles and shambled toward the king. "I wanted to–I'm almost sure–there was something–"

"Tell us tomorrow," the king said. "We are busy–"

"Are we? What are we doing? Is it fun?" Teraeth stepped around the side of the couch–

–to where King Kelanis's corpse lay on the floor in a puddle of blood. A significant chunk of his skull was missing.

There was a moment of stillness. Just a split second, as Teraeth took in the sight, realized what it meant, and knew that everything had just gone terribly wrong.

Then Talon attacked.

# 83: The Monastery of Sherna-Veng

***(Talea's story)***

After they collected Kihrin, they continued traveling. By the third day, they started to see the effects of Baelosh's presence on the surrounding land. They'd continued traveling down the main road, working their way out of the maze of winding canyons. Then, without warning, the desert turned into inexplicably lush greenery. A winding, overreaching perfusion of plants, vines, flowers, and trees that had no business growing in this hot, dry climate spread out over the landscape.

Sometimes, Talea noticed signs of civilization buried in these profusions of flora. The spokes of a wagon wheel. Planks from a cart. The shape of a wall nearly buried under morning glories, but suggesting the original, ruined building. She never saw a body or bones, but she had a feeling they were under there too. The land was very quiet, with no sound of birds or animals, just the rustling of leaves and the sweet smell of honeysuckle.

It occurred to Talea that they might wind up testing whether or not Wildheart could really control Baelosh quicker than they'd intended if the dragon chose to go after them on the road.

As if the fates had heard that thought, Fidget had an attack of nerves and began whinnying, ears back. Xivan's horse, Noisy Boy, even went so far as to start to rear before she brought him back under control. Kihrin's horse, Wander, seemed about a second from bolting.

Thurvishar reached out and grabbed the reins for Fidget and Wander.

A winged, serpentine shadow flew out over the land.

"Is that–?" Senera shielded her eyes from the sun as she tried to see while simultaneously trying to keep her horse, Thirsty, from bolting.

Thurvishar replied, "That's not Baelosh."

"No," Kihrin replied, his voice strained. "That's Sharanakal. That's the Old Man. We need to hide."

Senera's eyes widened. "Hide *where*?" She glanced around. There were no buildings, no cliffs, no shelter anywhere save the trees Baelosh had created.

"Tree line," Kihrin ordered. "Right now. Thurvishar, keep us alive."

Thurvishar somehow ordered his horse–the only one who wasn't panicking–toward the trees, with the necessary side effect of bringing Talea's and Kihrin's horses with him, and also Talea and Kihrin. Halfway there, Talea nearly fell off her horse as Kihrin simply vanished.

Her heart was hammering at her ribs. She imagined it must not have been too dissimilar to what a rabbit must feel when the shadow of a hawk crosses the ground.

Since she didn't have to steer (or to be more precise really couldn't steer), Talea shaded her eyes and looked up. She'd only ever seen one dragon before–Aeyan'arric–and she found herself curious what the others looked like.

Terrifying. The dragon looked very dark, although Talea wasn't entirely certain if it was dark or it just appeared that way because she was seeing it silhouetted against the sun. Glowing cracks outlined its form. The dragon soared up above, neck twisting from side to side as the creature hunted.

"Vol Karoth must have given Sharanakal the good news: I'm still alive," Kihrin said.

Talea looked over at Kihrin's horse, Wander. The horse was still there, still saddled, still packed with supplies and a strapped-down lap harp. She still couldn't see Kihrin himself.

As soon as they rode under the trees, they stopped their horses. Thurvishar raised Wildheart. He grew no new trees, but the branches overhead became so thick and full of green, it was impossible for the horses to see the sky.

They didn't completely calm. Even without being able to see, some sixth sense whispered of unnatural danger nearby. The scent of hot metal filled the air.

"Stay invisible," Thurvishar said.

"You think I need to be told that?" Kihrin replied.

As far as Talea could tell, he was still riding Wander's back.

"Why is Sharanakal looking for you?" Senera asked. "I thought you'd fooled him into thinking you died in that volcanic eruption?"

"How do you know–?" Kihrin asked. "Thurvishar, I hate that godsdamned book."

"One dragon is bad enough," Xivan said. "No one said anything about two dragons."

"We are in no way prepared to deal with Sharanakal," Senera said, stating the obvious.

"Oh, well, that's fine," Talea said. "We're not really prepared to deal with Baelosh."

Thurvishar cleared his throat. "Let's see if we can find a better route.

Something with more hiding spots in case he comes back. According to the map, there should be some sort of settlement to our east. I'm sure it hasn't escaped Baelosh's attention, but it should have more cover."

Kihrin turned visible and started to get off the horse.

"Don't dismount," Thurvishar warned. He pointed down to the hooves of the horses, where tiny green vines and shoots were straining to wrap around equine hooves. They were not succeeding, but it wasn't entirely clear what was stopping them.

Talea suspected Thurvishar was the one stopping them. She could see the yellow-green stone in his hand.

"Got it," Kihrin said. "Staying on the horse." He leaned against the pommel of his saddle. "Just out of curiosity, what's Sharanakal's Cornerstone?"

Thurvishar frowned. "I'm not entirely sure—"

"Worldhearth," Senera said.

"You mean Qown's Cornerstone?" Kihrin looks surprised. "The one he's using to spy on people?"

"The same," she said, chewing on her lip. "And no, I'm not telling you where Qown is. You'd both try to go rescue him and get yourselves killed."

Thurvishar looked rather indignant, and Kihrin laughed.

"Didn't that map show a village near here?" Talea asked.

Senera frowned at her. "Don't encourage them."

"I don't think that's a village," Thurvishar said. "Someplace called Sherna-Veng? It's a different symbol. Not a village, town, or city. I'm honestly not sure what it is."

"Whatever it is, the dragons may not have destroyed it." Talea turned to Xivan for support. "And if we want to stay under cover, a building is a great way to do it."

Xivan pursed her lips. "I would be curious if this business with a second dragon showing up is news or not. Let's go see."

"Fine." Senera led her horse back onto the road.

Talea's optimism was dashed all too quickly. By the time they reached the location the map had indicated, they'd already seen the plumes of smoke in the sky for several hours. Which Talea thought had a rather interesting implication, namely that Baelosh probably wasn't responsible. *He* wouldn't have caused any burning.

The "settlement" turned out to be another red sandstone cliff-carved building that resembled a temple. Shallow stone steps led up to broad columned avenue, an inset courtyard, and more steps leading up to a massive set of front doors.

There were corpses everywhere.

Thurvishar dismounted first, but everyone else quickly followed.

"The dragons didn't attack here," Kihrin said. He had an ugly expression on his face as he looked down at the bloody work before him.

"Rebel, sit," Senera ordered.

Talea began walking around the area, looking at the ground, at the bodies. They were all at least a day old. The flies had been busy, and the smell of death–which to Talea had always been and would always be the odor of blood, rot, and shit–attacked the back of her throat with every breath. There were no children, thankfully, just men and women of various ages, all with shaved heads and all wearing simple broadcloth tunics of the same dyed homespun. Priests, perhaps, of some monastic order.

She didn't see a single body that hadn't died with a weapon close at hand. Most of the bodies had visible weapon wounds, some from the front, but many more from the back. Throats had been slit; the survivors had fought to the death. Yet despite the similarity of wounds, most of the people had died with an expression of horror on their faces that implied something other than anger had been their last emotion.

"They slew each other?" Talea turned to Xivan for confirmation. "But they all look so scared."

Xivan nodded as she looked around. "Terrified."

"Xivan?" Kihrin called from one of the buildings. "I don't think you should see–" He paused at the doorway, his lips pressed together. He rubbed his forehead. "I'm sorry, but I found them."

Xivan froze. Her eyes widened for a second with panic and shock, then she rushed past Kihrin.

Talea followed her liege into the building, which had a large main chapel area and various passages that branched off into living areas, workrooms, training rooms. The place must have been quite a sanctuary once. Before all the murder.

Kihrin led them both into the back. A woman slumped over a wide table, the front of her tunic first soaked and then dried red with her death's blood. More blood stained the floor, but from a different source:

Azhen and Exidhar Kaen both hung from ropes hanged into the walls and ceiling.

Both were dead.

They'd been tortured, although even prior to that, they'd clearly been mistreated. Both men had clearly suffered from malnourishment before their deaths. They'd probably been forced to suffer all manner of indignities. Talea had never looked highly upon either of them, but she couldn't help but feel the pain of this in her heart, a savage twisting of spiritual knives. Like the woman in the room–the bodies outside–both men had died with expressions of abject terror on their faces.

A small, nearly inaudible gasp came from Xivan as she stared at them. She sank to her knees in front of their bodies, glassy-eyed and staring. Talea went to her immediately and put a hand on her shoulder. Xivan clutched her hand to her chest and bent over it.

"Where's the baby?" Senera asked, arms folded over her chest as she examined the room. She sounded utterly indifferent to the fate of Xivan's dead husband and son, which was probably the truth of the matter.

"What did you just say?" Xivan looked up.

"Your granddaughter," Senera clarified. "Where is she? And where's her mother, Veixizhau? I don't see their bodies here."

"Suless doesn't kill baby girls," Kihrin reminded Senera. "She turns them into witch mothers, remember? She wouldn't kill the kid. She'd use her."

"Gods! That bitch." Xivan closed her eyes, still on her knees. "That bitch left this for me to find!" She gestured toward the bodies.

"Yes," Thurvishar said. "That does seems the logical conclusion." He shuddered and turned his head away.

"I've seen people die like this before," Kihrin said.

Talea didn't think Xivan heard him. He said the words so softly.

"What was that?"

Kihrin's attention was focused on Thurvishar, who sighed and nodded. "Yes, I have too."

"Mind explaining it for the rest of us?" Senera said.

Xivan looked like she was about to pick up each man by their collars and shake them.

Thurvishar turned to Senera and Xivan. "My adoptive father would leave people with this sort of expression when he pulled their souls from their bodies to make tsali. Your family didn't die of blood loss. They died of soul loss."

Talea said, "The whole monastery looks like that."

Thurvishar nodded. "Yes. She must have done this to everyone here." He looked uncomfortable, ill. "Baelosh collects tsali. I imagine this is the payment she used to gain his protection."

None of them said anything. The silence was heavy and thick, floating through the room like a cloying fume.

Xivan rose to her feet. Her expression was stony. "Let's go find my granddaughter."

# 84: THE KING'S TRAP

***(Teraeth's story)***

"Oh, ducky," Talon said, grinning. "I've missed you so much."

Teraeth dove to the carpet to avoid a tentacle hitting the ground next to him like a spear, sending shards of wood up into the air. More tentacles followed, forcing him to spend the next seconds in a desperate attempt to dodge them all.

*This* time, it wasn't all an illusion. *This* time, he was really fighting her.

Teraeth drew his knives and deflected each tentacle as they struck. He managed to even slice a few wounds into the mimic's flesh, but he knew exactly how little good it did in the long run. Teraeth didn't have the spike that could paralyze her either. Stupid King Kelanis–

Wait. Stupid King Kelanis had confiscated it when he'd had them all put under arrest.

Where would Kelanis have kept it? Was it possible the spike was actually in the same room?

Talon scowled and flowed to the side, re-forming in time to block Teraeth's path from reaching the larger desk. "Looking for something?"

Teraeth feinted, then slid across the wooden floor on one of the carpets and managed to duck under one of Talon's arms. If he could manage to get out of her line of sight for even a second, he could spin an illusion to fool her. Unfortunately, Talon knew that and wasn't letting Teraeth out of her sight.

Teraeth crouched on the carpet, a dagger in each hand. He grimaced as the fabric of his sleeve rubbed against the thin, bleeding cut there.

"Talon, we're not enemies." Teraeth paused as he realized what he'd just said. "Fine. We are enemies, but we don't have to be enemies *right now*. Frankly, you've done me a favor by killing the king." He gestured toward the corpse without taking his eyes from the mimic.

Talon smirked. "If only I had."

Teraeth cocked his head. "Excuse me?"

"That's not the king," Talon explained. "I thought he was, but, uh, no, sorry. Brains don't lie. That's a double."

"You mean that was never the real king? Where is he, then?"

The doors to the library didn't exactly slam open. It was more like the entire outward-facing wall of the library simply vanished. And in the gap thus formed was a small army of vané royal guard, several wizards, and King Kelanis himself.

Presumably the real one this time.

"I have been wondering when someone was going to make an attempt," Kelanis said. "You made it farther than I expected, to be perfectly honest. And I have no idea how a mimic managed to sneak past our wards." He turned to the others.

"Kill them," the king ordered and then walked away.

Teraeth looked over at Talon. "Truce?"

The mimic nodded. "Truce."

Talon spun up a barrier just as the first wizards began their attack. Teraeth jumped behind the couch that had previously concealed the body of the king's double. He turned himself invisible while weaving an illusion of himself scrambling to the other side of the room.

The wizards, meanwhile, had started off their attack by the time-honored but simple expedient of summoning a giant ball of lightning in the center of the room. A good start, Teraeth thought, for dealing with a mimic. If one could manage to short out the nervous system, it would probably be every bit as effective as the silver spike. Unfortunately, a giant ball of lightning was equally good at dealing with every other kind of nervous system–including his own.

Teraeth ducked under an arc of electricity as it tore an ugly gash across the bookcases. Teraeth levitated–a spell he usually used for making his way across nightingale floors–taking a few painful but no longer lethal shocks in the process. Teraeth spun the effect of being fully grounded on the phantasm of himself. He wasn't sure if it was really going to fool the wizards, but it was always possible that they were too busy casting spells to take the time to pierce the illusion.

If so, then what they saw was Teraeth take a direct strike from the lightning and begin to convulse, his body temporarily locked rigid by the electricity.

The lightning bounced against Talon's barrier. She'd evidently been expecting something like that and had taken appropriate precautions.

While Talon leaped at one of the royal guards, Teraeth came up behind the wizard controlling the lightning and put a knife through her throat. The mage next to her didn't have time to react before he too was dying. Teraeth didn't wait for their compatriots to put two and two together and start laying down spells capable of breaking his illusions. More guards would be on their way, and more wizards, and since this was the Manol, a great many of them would be both.

Teraeth reached to his neck, pulled away the glass orb that hung on a thread there, and crushed it underfoot.

Teraeth rather suspected Janel wouldn't stop to go get Terindel, but she could at least create a diversion. She was, as she had pointed out, good at fire, and this was a tree.

He ran.

Teraeth heard shouting behind him. Teraeth wasn't sure if that indicated that they'd caught Talon or they'd lost her. He wasn't about to stop to check. He sprinted down the main hallway, heading toward the private kitchen. He absolutely didn't expect to find an exit, but it accessed some of the servants' passages, which meant there was at least a chance that he might slip by invisibly before anyone noticed.

A tentacle reached out, grabbed his waist, and caught him before could trip.

He sliced down with the knife, but another tentacle had already pinned him, pulling him into a side room.

Kihrin pushed him against the inside door. "Shh," he said. "Quiet."

Not Kihrin, of course. Teraeth knew better; Kihrin was with Thurvishar, chasing down alternatives. Also, the actual Kihrin didn't have tentacles.

Any impulse to begin slicing with knives was undercut by the sound of running feet. Before he could respond, Talon reached out and pressed against a carved knot on the wall. A panel opened, leading into darkness.

"Come on, ducky," Talon said. "If you want to get out of this alive, you'd better follow me."

# 85: A Riddle for Baelosh

***(Kihrin's story)***

I found Thurvishar the morning after we'd finished burning the bodies and left the monastery.[1] "What are we doing here?" I asked rhetorically. Mostly.

He was crouched down, staring at that yellow-green stone. I thought he was ignoring me and then realized why. He was magically warping a gold coin, spinning off fine filaments of metal, which he was weaving into a mesh net so he could drop the stone into it and wear it around his neck. He finished and did so, hanging the result off a piece of wire he'd shaped into a loop. "Keeping our word. If it's any consolation, I suspect we'd be in just as much danger exploring brothels. Hopefully, we have to do less slumming through the worst parts of Bahl-Nimian this way." Thurvishar put the Cornerstone around his neck.

My attention was now focused on Wildheart. "I've always heard that it's impossible to steal a Cornerstone, but I don't see how that could possibly be true."

"Try it." He pointed to the necklace.

I reached for the hook on the back of the wire. And then felt my hand fall way. I frowned and tried again. This time, I actually managed to touch the metal wire before I stopped. I paused. "Oh."

I'd once tried to remove the Stone of Shackles from my own neck, under duress, to hand over to Thurvishar. I hadn't been able to. This felt the same.

"And if, for example, Senera dropped the Name of All Things accidentally, she might very well find that it had mysteriously appeared back on her person."

[1] It is interesting to note that local Bahl-Nimian funerary customs involve fire, which makes them quite similar to Marakori and Joratese funeral rites. Of course, these days, there's little chance of an unburned body becoming home to a demon. Why bother when the demon can show up directly?

"So how's it feel? My Cornerstone was sort of . . . passive . . . in a lot of ways. I never had to actively control it."[2]

"Disturbingly nice. I'd be lying if I said I wasn't enjoying it." Thurvishar made a face. "I can see why people don't want to give these up, which I may have to do. This may not work on Baelosh the way we think. Or if it does . . . I'm honestly not sure how effective a gaesh will be separated by the sort of distance we're talking about. Even if we can send Baelosh away, can we keep him away?"

"What happens if we give a dragon their own Cornerstone? I mean, that basically makes him unkillable, right?"

"Does it? I'm not so certain." Thurvishar sighed, dusted himself off, and stood. "I think it might have the opposite effect unless they go to great lengths to hide the Cornerstone. And hope Senera never has reason to ask where it's hidden."

I chuckled, but it was dry and distant and a bit hollow. Truthfully, I was feeling a sense of ennui I couldn't quite explain. I don't think it was just because we were less than a day away from a place where we might well have to fight one of the most dangerous creatures in the whole world. I suppose I was just being given a bit too much time with my own thoughts, and these days, those tended to hover around my hopes and my fears and the very real possibility that the latter would keep me from ever obtaining the former.

Vol Karoth waited for me, and no matter how much faith the others were putting in the Ritual of Night, I knew in my soul that this time it wouldn't be enough to stop him.

Honestly, dragons seemed like such a minor problem by comparison.

We knew we were in Baelosh's territory long before we saw Baelosh himself. The desert had given way entirely, replaced by verdant growth that belonged to no single climate and that was all in theory entirely alien to their present surroundings. This wasn't just jungle, or rain forest, or woods, but all of them, all mingled together in impossible combinations. And in all cases, there was a kind of predatory violence to the plant life. Any animals who made the mistake of crossing into that land never left again.

I didn't have to ask where Baelosh kept his hoard. It was all around us–gems hanging from tree branches, sparkling from the cups of wild orchid flowers, embedded in bark, and tossed around the ground like the most valuable and shining of pebbles. The trees wore necklaces, the

[2] Please note that Kihrin never tried experimenting. I'm of the opinion that most of the Cornerstones have both active and passive abilities.

vines showed off their rings. The part of me that remembered being a thief named Rook desperately wanted to help myself to handfuls, but I pushed back against the temptation; I suspected Baelosh would somehow know if we'd stolen from his hoard.

The worst part was that so many of the gems were not gems. They were tsali stones, slowly leaking away the tenyé of the souls they held trapped, until eventually the tsali gem would be a hollow, empty shell. The trapped souls here would never go to the Afterlife. They would never be reincarnated. They would simply *fade*.

Senera stopped complaining about the wisdom of retrieving Wildheart as it became increasingly obvious that none of us would have survived a hundred feet into Baelosh's territory without it. Only Thurvishar's direct intervention using the Cornerstone kept us safe from animated vines, poisoned thorns, and aggressive spore clouds. Which made me more than a little nervous about the idea of trading away Wildheart in order to convince Baelosh to give up Suless.

Even knowing we were in the dragon's territory, we had no warning at all when he struck.

The trees near us gave the briefest shiver, and then a giant shape rose up from the underbrush and vines. Or rather, the vines and underbrush rose up and revealed that it had never been simple plant matter at all.

**"Visitors? It's been a long time since I've had visitors,"** Baelosh said. **"And now I have so many. So what have *you* come to offer me?"**

The dragon was massive and green, and although he was not quite the same as Morios–not made from plants the same way Morios was made from swords–flowers grew from the cracks in his scales, and lichen had made a home along his stomach and the underside of his forearms. Indeed, even as Baelosh dislodged plants and trees from the ground, more were growing to take their place, an endless regeneration of ridiculous flora. The dragon's eyes were bright, glittering green–the same color, I noticed, as his matching Cornerstone.

If the horses didn't freak out, it was only because we'd stopped that morning to give Senera and Thurvishar a chance to cast spells to stop the animals from seeing either dragons or the surrounding plant life. We'd all agreed that this was prudent, given the likelihood that, one, there would definitely be more dragon encounters, and two, Baelosh's plants would probably kill the horses if they bolted away from Thurvishar's ability to protect them.

So the horses just stood there, clearly a little curious why we'd stopped and even more curious if any of us planned to feed them.

Rebel didn't bark,[3] but the way her head went down suggested she both could see Baelosh and wasn't at all happy about it.

Thurvishar dismounted his horse and walked forward. "Greetings, Baelosh. Yes, we have a gift for you." He pulled a bag from his belt and overturned it into his hand, revealing green stones that I suspected were probably emeralds. They weren't tsalis.

I had no idea where Thurvishar had gotten a handful of emeralds from, mind you, but I didn't think they'd be fake. It was too easy to check.[4]

"There's more for you, Baelosh," Thurvishar added, "but only if you win my contest."

Senera looked over at him and mouthed the word, "Contest?"

Baelosh's eyes narrowed. **"Contest? What sort of contest?"**

"A riddle contest, of course," Thurvishar said. "I believe that's traditional, yes? If you win, I'll give you the rest of the gems, and if I win, then all I ask is you hand over Suless and everyone she has with her."

**"Who?"**

Thurvishar cocked his head. "You know who I mean. You know who Suless is."

The dragon didn't immediately answer. Then Baelosh asked, **"How many gems?"**

"I have five more bags full."

The dragon pulled himself up to full height. **"Then begin."**

Thurvishar had clearly prepared for this. "I live in a house where all who enter it are blind and all who pass out its doors can see. Where do I live?"

The dragon's nostrils flared. **"A school. Was this meant to be a difficult contest?"** The dragon cocked his head. **"While traveling to Karolaen, I met a woman. The woman had eight children, and the eight children carried eight snakes, and each snake clutched a mouse. How many traveled to Karolaen?"**

"Just the one, yourself," Thurvishar said. "That which you used to gain me becomes useless once you hold me. Once you possess me, only dull violence will make you lose me. What am I?"

**"Why that's–"** The dragon paused. **"That's Urthaenriel, but I've heard that riddle before."** Baelosh leaned forward, eyes narrowed. The dragon reached forward until his nose almost touched the front of Thurvishar's horse, Dust Dancer.

The horse blew air out its nose.

3 Dholes don't bark, one of the features that distinguishes them from other canines.

4 Among its many other abilities, Wildheart can apparently absolutely wreck economies.

I leaned over toward Talea. "We might want to be ready to run." I couldn't see Suless, anyway–I had no idea where Baelosh might have hidden her. Truthfully, she might have been watching even at that very moment, but it certainly wasn't in her best interests to reveal herself.

I slipped my vision past the Veil and started searching, anyway. Everything around us not dragon would be plant–living humans should stand out like blood against snow.

**"I know you,"** Baelosh said. **"I've met you before."**

"Not in this lifetime," Thurvishar said.

"Thurvishar–" Senera's voice was thick with warning.

The dragon tilted his head so he could stare at Thurvishar with one eye (there was simply no way he could focus both eyes at that distance). **"Simillion?"**

"Thurvishar," the wizard corrected.

I exhaled. Much as I didn't want Thurvishar to come to harm, I had been rather worried that the dragon would immediately home in on the fact that Thurvishar carried Wildheart, or even worse, that I was standing right behind him. But no, just as Senera had predicted, Baelosh was much more interested in the one who got away.

There. I saw a bright flash of tenyé resonating behind Baelosh. It was hard to see because the dragon distorted everything around him. Had Suless been a normal human woman, I'm sure I'd never have noticed. But she wasn't, so I did. That tenyé flare had to be a spell.

"Found her," I said. "She's trying something–"

Baelosh pulled back his long neck. **"Simillion!"** He sounded gleeful.

Thurvishar's lips pressed together. "You agreed to the rules."

"Thurvishar," I whispered, "she's about five hundred feet behind him. Look, why don't–"

What I did next was tricky, and I wasn't sure if it would work, but I thought at Thurvishar as hard as I could. *Come on, Thurvy. You're not going to win with a classic riddle. It needs to be something he can't answer because he doesn't understand the context. Use context against him.*

Thurvishar blinked at me and then turned back to the dragon. He pursed his lips, exhaled slowly, and then said, "I am a table with twelve settings for a feast that never ends. Many serve me, but only those uninvited can ever rule me. Who am I?"[5]

Baelosh blinked. **"What?"**

"Is that your answer?"

I saw Suless's tenyé move. She must have had some idea what was happening–and was beginning to flee. But there was no chance to get to her while Baelosh was in the way.

[5] Any native Quuros would have been able to answer this one in seconds, of course.

Baelosh's lip curled. **"No. Give me a minute."** The dragon stood very still, eyes almost closed, concentrating intensely. Nothing in the overgrown foliage made a sound, except perhaps for the wind rustling through tree leaves and a faint whistling. It was all I could do to stand still. The others didn't realize what was happening with Suless. That she was just seconds from getting away.

The whistling grew louder. The ground began to shake.

"What?" As everyone else searched around us, I looked up.

Just in time to see Sharanakal slam into Baelosh.[6]

I ducked as half a tree crashed into the ground next to me. The earth erupted up ahead, sending a wall of red-hot lava soaring up into the air. A blast wave of heat collided with us as the nearby plants went up in flames.

The horses hadn't been enchanted not to see *fire*. They reacted quite predictably: by running. Except for Thurvishar's horse, who seemed seconds from attacking the fire and giving it a piece of his mind.[7]

I was hanging on for dear life as my horse ran and tried to dodge around the churning earth and flying plant matter. "The other side!" I screamed. "Suless is on the other side!"

Xivan nodded in my direction, wheeled her horse around, and began galloping—in between the two dragons.

"Shit." I moved to follow her. I think the only reason I was successful was because my horse was so panicked, he had no idea where "safe" was anymore. In between two dragons? Sure, why not. The others were galloping too, trying to stay together. I heard Senera's voice, knew she was casting a spell. Thurvishar's voice joined hers a second later.

A huge section of land up behind us melted as Sharanakal breathed superhot ash and fire in a line, presumably the culmination of some long-standing feud with Baelosh. The good news was that I didn't think either of the dragons had any idea I was nearby.

The bad news was that didn't make me safe.

As the dragons fought above us, soon running toward Suless meant running away from the fight, and this made the horses considerably more cooperative. I couldn't fault their instinct to escape fire.

"Suless!" Xivan screamed.

I saw the old woman ahead of us, leading a young woman holding a package—almost certainly a baby—out of a hillside cave. Xivan headed in their direction at once, with the rest of us close behind.

As Suless tried to flee, a crack opened up in the ground ahead of her,

[6] Baelosh and Sharanakal are half brothers, sons of Ompher. One assumes this has not stopped them from passionately hating each other.

[7] I didn't even *do* anything to that horse. Dust Dancer was just like that.

and a giant welling of lava came pouring out, blocking her path. The young woman with her screamed. The baby began to wail.

Suless gestured. A giant pool of the magma rose up in the air and crashed down straight at Xivan. The woman simply swung out Godslayer in front of her. The magma split, sizzled, and fell to each side of her, leaving Xivan unharmed. Several more spells followed that one in rapid succession, but Xivan either parried them with Urthaenriel or they were blocked by one of the wizards, Thurvishar or Senera.

A gigantic roar caught my attention. I looked around in time to see the Old Man–Sharanakal–take a bite from Baelosh's side. Baelosh twisted around and opened his mouth, spitting out a stream of green sap-like material moving at terrific speeds.

I didn't think it was going to do much against the fire dragon, honestly, but then I realized that wasn't the problem. Suless cackled as she pulled up a huge chunk of ground, deflecting the draconic blast and sending it streaming in a new direction. Straight at us.

"Duck!" I screamed.

The horses didn't see the danger. The horses *couldn't* see the danger. Thin sticky ribbons of toxic green sap rained down in front of us, sending up clouds of spores as they impacted the earth.

Most of us managed to pull our horses up in time, to change course. But not Xivan.

And not Talea.

I didn't see what happened to their horses, although it seemed a pretty safe assumption that they hadn't survived being in the path of that deadly blast. I heard a scream from another direction. I turned back in time to see that Thurvishar hadn't used Wildheart to save Xivan and Talea, because he'd been using the stone to save Veixizhau and her baby. Senera scooped the baby up into her arms while Thurvishar grabbed the mother.

Baelosh's breath continued in a straight line, right across the Old Man and over Suless's path. I didn't hear her scream, but I made assumptions.

For a terrifying split second, I thought the same fate must have befallen Xivan and Talea, but then Xivan came staggering out of the spore cloud. Tiny shoots of greenery kept trying to gain purchase in her dead flesh and failed, withering almost immediately–likely because of Urthaenriel. Talea, however, wasn't so lucky. Half her side was nothing but a mass of flowers.

Beautiful–and fatal.

"This way!" I screamed and pointed toward the lee of a cliff that seemed far enough from the battle to offer at least the illusion of protection from the dragons. Senera and Thurvishar reached the spot first, bringing the living mother and child with them. The two wizards immediately began setting up wards and protections, what magical defenses they could devise to keep from being caught in any more stray collateral damage from the dragon battle.

"Don't stop for us," Xivan ordered me. "I have her."

"No! Give her Urthaenriel!" I screamed at Xivan. I jumped off the horse (*dismounting* was the wrong word for it) and ran over to the two women. "It'll slow the spread."

Xivan pulled the sword out and lay the blade against Talea so the length of it was pressed against her. Urthaenriel had no real complaint about this, although I could tell that the sword knew I was right there. I ignored the sword's whispers suggesting I should reclaim her.

As we ran toward the magical shelter, I heard a mighty screech behind me. I turned to see the ball of twisting plants and fire separate. Baelosh–a very singed and burned-looking Baelosh–flew up into the air, heading north with all the speed of a lightning flash.

Sharanakal followed. That quickly, they were gone.

Xivan placed Talea down on the ground, setting Urthaenriel to the side in the process. Her lieutenant didn't look great. Several of the wounds in Talea's side had turned an ugly dark green, and veins of that color were spiking off the wounds like spreading rot. Urthaenriel *had* helped, but much of the damage was already done.

Veixizhau stood immediately and rushed over to Xivan.

"My lady! Please, you don't know–"

Xivan stood up and put her hands on the woman's cheeks. "Shhh."

Veixizhau closed her mouth.

Xivan turned back to Talea and didn't say another word to her daughter-in-law.

Much as it killed me to do it, I picked up Urthaenriel and handed the sword back to Xivan. "You dropped this."

I don't think Xivan even realized what I'd just done. She was too much in shock about what had just happened to her lieutenant to pay any attention to the fact that I'd picked up Godslayer and simply given it back to her.

To be fair, I wouldn't realize until later that Xivan had given me an order while holding the sword, and I'd refused it. That neatly eviscerated my worry that Vol Karoth's gaesh was also *my* gaesh.

I forced myself to focus on healing, but ran into a problem immediately. Any tenyé I poured into Talea was going to feed the spreading floral infection as well, make it worse. And so much of her was already infected . . . if I tried amputating limbs, I was going to kill her outright.

I had no idea what to do. Maybe Thurvishar could use Wildheart? "Thurvishar, can you–"

Talea opened her eyes. "I'm sorry," Talea whispered. She was very pale, and her voice was very soft. She wasn't looking at me. Her attention was fixed on Xivan.

"Shut up," Xivan said. "Don't apologize. This isn't your fault."

Thurvishar started to say something, but Senera put a hand on his chest and shook her head. He stopped.

"I just wanted you–" Talea started coughing, wincing. "There's something I need to tell you–"

"What is it?" Xivan bent down close. She pulled the agolé off her shoulders and used it to cover Talea's body, tucking the fabric around the other woman like it was a blanket.

Talea's gaze flickered over to me, and I felt my heart tighten in my chest. Then Talea looked up at Xivan, reached up with her good hand to touch the woman's face. "I love you, Xivan. I love you so much. I'm sorry. I should have said something."

Xivan's mouth dropped open. "You–what?"

Talea smiled weakly. "I'm sorry."

"You–" Xivan didn't even try to conceal her shock. "Talea, I'm *dead.* I'm not . . . You can't *love* me. That's impossible."

"Don't care," Talea said. "I've been in love with you for years."

Thurvishar made a low noise and turned away.

Xivan started to cry. She couldn't cry–no tears came from her eyes–but I saw her throat work and a deep guttural sob come from her chest. "Damn it, why didn't you say anything?" she whispered.

Senera rolled her eyes as she called Rebel back over to stand next to her.

Talea's hand lingered on the side of Xivan's face. "You had Azhen. You had your family. You didn't need me."

"Need doesn't have anything to do with it! He had fifty wives! He didn't get to say a damn thing about who I love. Of course I love you. What idiot wouldn't love you?" Xivan looked fond and furious simultaneously.

Talea started smiling. "I can die happy, knowing that."

"I don't want you to die at all!"

Talea's hand dropped back to her chest. "It's okay. It doesn't even hurt anymore."

Senera crossed her arms over her chest as she let out an exasperated sigh. "It doesn't hurt anymore because Thurvishar's already healed you, Talea. You're going to be *fine.*"

Thurvishar cleared his throat and nodded in agreement.

The stillness was so total, it was as if time itself had stopped.

I covered my mouth as I fought back laughter. Xivan and Talea both just turned their heads and stared blankly at the two wizards.

No one said a word. Xivan pulled the cloth away from Talea so we could all see that her flesh was fine. No wounds. No spreading green poison. No flowers. An uncomfortable, comedic silence settled over us. Bird cries sounded in the distance as some bright hawk realized there was no longer a dragon in the vicinity and it was safe to hunt for rabbits again.

*"Well."* I stood up. "You two have a lot to talk about, and Senera needs to answer a question for Thurvishar and me as payment for a job well done, so why don't the three of us leave you two alone?"

I turned around and grinned at Senera and Thurvishar. "Nicely done, both of you." Thurvishar might have healed Talea, but Senera was the one who'd made sure Talea'd had enough time to confess her feelings. Which was–from Senera, anyway–almost shockingly romantic.

Senera returned my expression with a haughty shrug, but didn't do nearly a good enough job of hiding her smile.[8]

Thurvishar smiled happily before schooling his expression into something more serious. "Why don't we talk? And then perhaps see if we can find Suless's body in this mess."

[8] You don't suppose we're actually starting to sway her, do you?

# 86: The Death of Suless

***(Senera's story)***

Senera suspected that Baelosh was, at least temporarily, dead. At the very least, he was so distracted by his chase with Sharanakal that any ability to hold together the various magically supported gardens had begun to fade. Flowers were beginning to shrink; vines had begun to whither. The plants themselves no longer reached out to wrap around ankles and pierce skin. The barrier that she and Thurvishar had hastily constructed became unnecessary.

They found Suless's body without much difficulty. She lay half merged with the soil of a hillside, the vines and flowers briefly born of her body already dying.

She'd died screaming. Kihrin sliced the old woman's body free from the dead vines and plants holding it fast, and they carried the corpse back to the others. Veixizhau began crying as soon as she saw it.

"You can't be sad she's dead," Kihrin said, kneeling down to comfort the woman.

"That's not sadness," Senera said as she passed them. "Those are tears of hate."

Senera sat down on the ground a few hundred feet from where they'd left Xivan and Talea and pulled out her supplies. Before she could say anything, Thurvishar sat down across from her. He felt too close, which was stupid, because he wasn't touching her. Thurvishar had never once in all the years that she'd known him ever tried to touch her. He wasn't even within a few feet of her. And yet, she felt his presence in a way she found rather . . . disquieting.

Mostly because she didn't mind his proximity at all.

Sitting next to Thurvishar was like setting the wards, like every time they'd worked magic together—quick, efficient, pleasingly comfortable. He respected her skills and abilities. He neither coddled her nor condescended. They worked *well* together.

"I should warn you that if your second question is in any way personal, I'm not answering it," Senera said.

Thurvishar blinked in surprise. "That's fine. It won't be."

"Good." She distracted herself from looking at him by starting to grind the ink. "It wouldn't work between us."

He didn't answer, so she glanced up. That blasted D'Lorus wizard was just watching her with those big black eyes and that face that might as well have been carved from stone. She could never tell what he was thinking. Whereas the reverse . . .

"It wouldn't work," she continued, returning her eyes down to the stone. "I don't . . . do . . . romance."

"You mean sex," Thurvishar corrected.

She glared. "I mean love."

The corner of Thurvishar's mouth quirked as though he found her answer amusing. He snapped his fingers, and Rebel–Rebel!–trotted over and put her head on Thurvishar's knee, as quick and obedient as though he were the one who'd raised her from a puppy and not Senera. "I don't believe you. I think you're perfectly capable of love. You just think love makes you vulnerable."

"A dog isn't the same as a man," she said.

"It's an emotional connection, thus proving that you are in fact perfectly capable of making emotional connections." He sounded tired, drained, and very much done with that particular argument, as if they'd brought it up with each other on several occasions instead of this, this first time. "Plus there is the small matter of how you're completely wrong about what I want from you or why."

"It's perfectly obvious," Senera said. "Turn me to your side and you weaken Relos Var."

"Do you honestly think the Name of All Things would have told you what it did if my only goal was to weaken Relos Var?" Thurvishar leaned forward, put his elbows on his knees. "I'm not interested in you because of Relos Var. And in point of fact, if you believe Relos Var is right, I think you should stay by his side and help him to the best of your ability. The last thing I would want is for you to betray him or turn against him or any variation of that theme for no other reason than because of a romantic interest. How petty and droll would that be? How cliché and small."

She stared at him.

Thurvishar continued, "When you finally turn against him, Senera, I want it to be for one reason and one reason only: because you've realized he's wrong."

"He's *not* wrong," she snapped.

"Is that so?" Thurvishar smiled. "I think we just barely escaped two dramatic examples of just how wrong Relos Var can be."

"You're confusing an error with a basic flaw in reasoning. And there is no flaw. He's right; the gods are–" She paused. Senera had been about to give her normal answer. How the gods are unworthy of the power they wield. How people should rule themselves.

"Go on," Thurvishar said. "Please. Tell me how he doesn't crave power the way the gods do, how he doesn't think he's the *only one* worthy to wield it. Tell me how he's better than that."

"If that were true, he'd have never given me a Cornerstone," Senera said.

"He gave you a Cornerstone because he wants the benefit of something he can't use himself," Thurvishar said. "You're a useful tool and nothing more than that."

"He's never made any secret of that." Even as she said the words, Senera wondered why they hurt so much. Thurvishar wasn't saying anything she didn't already know, yet somehow the sum of his statements were dull-edged daggers she felt deep under her sternum.

She'd always been resigned to this reality. It was the price she had long since accepted she was willing to pay in exchange for making the world a better place. A place without tyranny, a place without gods.

Except . . .

She looked away. "Ask your question, damn it. We made a deal."

Thurvishar sighed. "Where can I find Grizzst?"

Senera blinked. "Grizzst? But why?" She held up a hand. "Never mind. I don't need to know, and you don't need to tell me." She picked up a brushful of ink and wrote out the answer. "Back in Bahl-Nimian," she said. "At the House of Spring Rains." She paused and stared at the answer. "A brothel?"

"Probably. Knowing him." Thurvishar studied her. "And I know you want to ask, so go ahead. I give you permission."

She pressed her lips into a thin line for a moment before responding. "Simillion shared his bed with *goddesses*. Caless. Dana. Why on earth would you ever–" Senera shook her head. "Regardless of how I feel about the matter, why would the man who has had women like that–who remembers those experiences–have any interest in someone like me?"

"Ah," Thurvishar said. "You really can't imagine anyone would want you for anything that doesn't have a purpose, a use, can you? As anything but a tool, whether that's for sexual gratification or conquering the world."

Senera didn't answer.

"Perhaps," Thurvishar said, "just perhaps, you might ponder the possibility that how I feel with you doesn't have anything to do with what you look like, or how you would perform in bed, or what you can *do* for me. It must be something else. Something more ephemeral than sex, beauty, or your skill at magic. For someone who likes to say the physical body is a cage, I'm really rather surprised you've taken so long to figure this out."

She scowled at him. "And I'm rather surprised you're being so ridiculously sentimental. I've done terrible, terrible things. Willingly. Understanding exactly what I was doing. I am not a good person. In no way am I a good person."

Thurvishar laughed, just once, as he stood.

"That wasn't funny," she told him as she gathered up her scribing supplies.

"Not only was it not funny," he agreed, "it was absolutely tragic. And you're right; you're not a good person."

She blinked at his answer. Senera had expected him to debate her on that point, to try to convince her that she could somehow be redeemed. She'd been prepared to pull out a very long list of sins as proof of how very wrong he was.

"But you could be," Thurvishar continued, "if you wanted. And there is a part of you–not a small part either–that really does want to be a good person. You *want* to do the right thing, Senera. You want to help make the world a better place. You *like it*."

"I've never claimed otherwise. The difference is that I think I *am* doing the right thing."

"Do you really? I have my doubts. I think my grandfather's convinced you that the only way to do good is to sacrifice all of yourself–your morals, your heart, your soul–and *that's* the lie. He told you that your physical form was unimportant and then made you sacrifice everything else on his altar."

"Your grandfather? Who–" But then Senera realized who he had to mean, and it seemed so completely obvious, she was astonished she hadn't noticed the connection earlier. They looked nothing like each other, but even so, Senera couldn't help but feel she could recognize the resemblance between the two wizards. She thought of every time Relos Var had refused to take action against Gadrith and how frustrated that had always made her. Because Var should have destroyed Gadrith. A thousand times, he should have. And never had.

But now she understood the nature of Gadrith's hostage, why Relos Var had put up with the necromancer.

She was so caught off guard, she actually closed her eyes. *Relos, you damn hypocrite.* How many conversations had she had with Relos Var on the trivialness of bloodlines, of the unimportance of inheritance? And yet, he hadn't treated his own bloodline as optional, had he? Had Relos Var been the one to teach his son–Thurvishar's father, Sandus–magic?

Had Relos Var set Sandus on the path to becoming the Quuros emperor? Or was that just a *remarkable* coincidence?[1]

She didn't consider the idea that Thurvishar might have lied for more than a fleeting second. He knew this was far too easy for her to confirm, and oh yes, she most definitely would confirm it. But she already knew what the Name of All Things would tell her. Thurvishar was Relos Var's grandson.

"We'll see each other again," Thurvishar said pleasantly. "I'm very much looking forward to it." He started to walk away, toward the end of the cliff area where Kihrin was leaning against a rock waiting for them.

Senera felt her hands moving toward her satchel as if of their own volition. "Wait."

Thurvishar paused.

Senera pulled a bound book out of her pack and handed it to him. "Here."

Thurvishar looked at the book, then looked at her. The question was clear.

"It's everything that led up to Atrine." She made a face. "You're not the only one who can collate transcripts, you know. It's just that mine are *accurate*."

"I look forward to reading it, then." Their eyes met, just briefly, and broke contact, just as quickly. Thurvishar's fingers brushed over the spine of the book. "I assume you'll want my thoughts on this?"

"And cite your sources this time," Senera said.

"Wouldn't dream of doing otherwise," he answered.

She should have let it go at that. Instead, she found herself exclaiming in a rush, "I can't be on your side. Please try to understand–I *can't* support the Eight the way you do."

Thurvishar smiled wickedly. "Who said anything about me being on the Eight's side?"

Senera paused and then shut her mouth, which had dropped open.

"I'll let you in on a secret, Senera. I'm not on their side." His gaze flicked over toward where Kihrin waited. "I'm on *his* side. And on the side of a lot of people who don't have any say in what's going on in this war between gods, dragons, and demons but who can and will most certainly die because of it. I don't see how four thousand years of not solving anything qualifies the Eight Immortals to be experts on fixing this, any more than I expect the man who caused this whole mess to do the right thing. They messed this up, for all of us. I have no intention of blindly following either Relos Var or the Eight's lead." Thur-

[1] Not coincidental, no, but also nothing Relos Var can directly claim responsibility for either. I believe that particular sin must be laid at Grizzst's feet.

vishar smiled. "I've done that already in another lifetime. I know where it leads. This time, I'm doing things my way."

Senera found herself unable to speak, mute with surprise. Wondering if she was being lied to.

Knowing she wasn't.

The bastard actually winked at her. Then she watched as Thurvishar walked over to Kihrin, opened another gate, and left, presumably back to Bahl-Nimian.

They were on their own now.

Senera watched the empty space where the two men had been for a few seconds longer and then turned around and returned to the rest of the women.[2]

[2] I rather liked Dust Dancer, even if he was a distressingly fragile, colicky creature who didn't have the sense of self-preservation the gods gave rhinoceroses. May his next owner give him green fields and plenty of carrots.

# 87: The Tree Tunnels

***(Teraeth's story)***

The passage led deep into the tree. Where, exactly, was a mystery to Teraeth, but not, it seemed, to Talon.

"How do you even know about this place?" Teraeth asked as they traveled. The passage was narrow and, like most construction inside the Mother of Trees, seemed less carved than a space where the tree had simply decided not to grow. The passage was lit by veins of sundew that filtered down, the stuff no doubt eventually reaching its final destination of various gardens and wilderness areas at the roots of the massive tree.

"We can't stop," Talon warned. "I learned about it from the charming Laudvyis–the king's double I killed back there. So as soon as Kelanis stops and realizes I had time for a snack, he'll think to look here."

Teraeth growled. "Okay, different question: How did you get past the wards?"

Talon began laughing.

"No, really, I'd like to know," Teraeth said. "Because as far as I know, the palace is supposed to be completely warded against mimics. How did you even get in here? Also, could you please stop looking like Kihrin?"

Despite her warning that they needed to keep moving, Talon stopped and turned back to face Teraeth. "I thought you liked Kihrin."

"I do," Teraeth said, "which is exactly why I don't want you taking his form."

She shrugged and changed her shape, this time choosing to look like Miyathreall. That was a *slight* improvement. "Better?"

"Not really. Now about how you got here?"

Talon grinned. "You've been lied to, my handsome boy. The palace isn't warded against mimics at all."

He frowned. "But, uh–"

"It's warded against the souls of the twelve vané who *became* mimics." She glanced backward as she started walking again, this time up the stairs. "Did you know there are only twelve? And the vané know exactly who they are. Well, they used to know, anyway."

Teraeth's eyes widened. "But yours isn't the same soul."

"Why no, it isn't, is it? My souls belongs to a former Quuros slave girl, and thus, there isn't a single ward anywhere in the palace that's set up to stop me. I can easily fool the wards meant to weed out anyone without royal blood in their veins. The only thing I wouldn't be able to fool would be that soul ward, except again, it's not set to detect me. Lucky me." She grinned.

"So you just snuck in." Teraeth shook his head. He was actually sad that it hadn't worked.

"Oh, I didn't have to sneak. They invited me in, under armed escort, no less."

Teraeth rolled his eyes, thinking back to the prison chair and the shackles in the library. "You're why Kelanis thought he had Kihrin. We'd wondered if that might be the case."

"Aren't you clever." Talon stopped once more and turned around. "I want your word that you'll let me go."

"Excuse me? You're a mimic. Your word isn't any good. Why would I think you'd believe mine?" Teraeth looked around the luminous passageway. He had no idea how to get back to the rest of the palace, let alone the party, where he suspected Janel was already causing a bit of a fuss.

This was not an ideal location in which to be stuck with the mimic.

"Kihrin trusts you." The mimic looked him up and down, slowly. A calculating gleam came into her eyes. "I want your word that if I help you get out of this, you won't try to kill me, capture me, paralyze me, or any of the like."

In the silence that followed, Teraeth liked to imagine he could hear the tree herself. The scrabble of insects. The drill of tiny occupying feet. Distantly, the sound of one of the doors being thrown open and men begin to pour into the secret passage.

Teraeth chuckled. "You're a survivor, you know that?" He could almost respect it.

Talon smirked at him and ran a hand down the front of his chest. Teraeth didn't try to stop her. There seemed little point; she could simply grow a new hand if she wanted to make the effort. At least she didn't look like Kihrin at the time; he considered that a win.

"So we have a deal?" she asked.

Teraeth nodded. "We have a deal."

They came out of the tunnel into one of the upper passages of the palace. Talon quickly changed her form to look like one of the servants; Teraeth set up illusions to do the same.

Everything, all around them, was chaos.

Janel must've started setting fires. She might have been doing more—the vané were, after all, very good at putting out fires, but still seemed to be running around in a blind panic. Teraeth had no time to question it. He could simply take advantage of the mayhem in order to blend with the crowds who were all rapidly trying to evacuate.

Halfway through the main hall, Teraeth spotted Janel. She gave no outward sign that she was the one causing the fires. She never moved her fingers, she never said any words, and indeed she seemed to be in tears. But Teraeth knew her well enough to realize that was all a ruse.

Talon and he caught up with her, and Teraeth took Janel's arm.

"Are you all right?" he said with all the care of a worried lover. "I've been looking for you all evening."

"I—" Janel doubled over in pain.

Teraeth blinked. This didn't seem staged, and he didn't understand the point of it. She seemed to be in genuine distress.

He bent down over. "Janel," he whispered, "what's going on? What's wrong?"

Janel collapsed.

He picked her up immediately and motioned for Talon to follow him to the exit. At some point on the journey, he turned around and realized that Talon had somehow managed to change her form until she looked like one of the better known members of the royal court.

"Come, then," Talon ordered imperiously. "We'll take her back to my estates and find out what is the matter. Probably just all the excitement caused an attack of nerves."

"Yes," Teraeth managed to stammer.

The fires stopped without Janel to continue them, but the damage had already been done. No one wanted to stay at the palace, which meant they had all the cover they might possibly want for their escape. It also meant no one noticed when the illusions on Teraeth and Janel fell away.

They fled out into the night while Janel shuddered in Teraeth's arms.

# 88: Every Brothel in the World

***(Kihrin's story)***

I paused and shifted the harp case on my back as we prepared to enter the House of Spring Rains. Much as I was glad to have the harp again, I really needed someplace to stash the instrument so I could travel with something much, much smaller. A flute, perhaps. "So I'm curious. Are we still not talking about Senera?"

Thurvishar glared at me.

I grinned. "She seemed awfully flustered there at the end for someone who you could never possibly be interested in or have a romantic relationship with."

Thurvishar paused. "I'll admit that did go somewhat differently from what I'd expected. I just assumed she would never . . . I mean . . ." The most spectacularly idiotic smile I'd ever seen decided that would be the perfect time to take up a position on Thurvishar's face.[1]

I slapped him lightly on the chest. "Come on," I said, "let's find us a wizard."

Since it hadn't been particularly light outside the brothel, it took no time at all for my eyes to adjust to the interior. This was a nicer establishment than the one that we had first entered upon finding ourselves in Bahl-Nimian, but only marginally. I suspected Bahl-Nimian just didn't understand or see the need for high-class, well-maintained facilities for its sex trade. Sex was something seedy here and was treated as such. Tiny little shops tucked out of the way where they could be ignored or people could pretend they didn't exist.

But I bet the sword and poison shops were immaculate.

A woman ran this particular brothel, almost as pale as Senera, with bright blue eyes and an easy smile. I held up my hands in a gesture of peace. "Do you speak Guarem?"

She responded with something that made me think the answer was no.

I clapped a hand on Thurvishar's shoulder. "You're not ducking out of this one."

[1] An outlandish fabrication. I do not ever smile "idiotically."

"Yes, I can see that." Thurvishar put a bright smile on his face and walked forward. He initially wasn't even trying to speak the same language as the woman. However, as he said things in Guarem and she responded in whatever she was speaking,[2] I realized that her language had a whole lot of loan words from Guarem, and I could almost but not quite follow the meaning. Sometimes.

After a bit of haggling and a whole lot of what was often hilarious pantomime, a great deal of money changed hands. She was grinning at the end, and why not?

She led us to another door, which led to a bar. Or rather it led to a place where one could, if one was so inclined, drink oneself senseless before or after indulging other appetites. It was as clean as the rest of the velvet house, meaning no place I'd ever want to actually drink–or do anything else, for that matter, including spill blood.

Thurvishar spotted our target right away.

I'm not sure what I'd been expecting. He wasn't particularly imposing, although he was taller than the average Quuros, with curly black hair. He didn't quite possess Relos Var's excruciatingly well-crafted normalness, but I wouldn't have glanced twice at him on the street either.

"Gahan!" the woman screamed, followed by what I assumed meant something along the lines of "People to see you."

The wizard raised his head and blinked. I'd been wrong on one detail; his eyes were *extraordinary*. Amber gold and glittering.

He was also very drunk. He didn't so much look at us as look through us, a distant stare that spoke not only of deep and serious inebriation but of naked grief.

"Might we speak to you in private?" Thurvishar asked.

"Fuck off," the man said succinctly and put his head down in his arms. As he did, something flashed red, and my focus centered on his hands.

He was wearing a Gryphon Men ring. Just like the one my adoptive father, Surdyeh, had carried. Just like the one Thurvishar's father, Sandus, had carried–that Thurvishar wore now–inscribed with his father's real name on the inside. Just like the one I wore.

Sure, maybe there are intaglio ruby rings out there that *aren't* magical communication devices, but I haven't found one yet.

And it was the mark of membership to a secret cabal whose goals were still a bit fuzzy to me, but I knew one thing: Surdyeh had likely raised me in the back of a velvet house on their orders. That meant on Emperor Sandus's orders.

And I'd always wondered if Sandus had been working with someone else, or worse, *for* someone else.

[2] Kapak.

The anger I felt rise in response caught me off guard. On some deep visceral level, I knew that Sandus hadn't really been responsible for Surdyeh's death, but . . . [3]

But Sandus had been my father's *friend.* And he'd repaid that friendship by hiding me away in the Lower Circle so I could be raised in the slums of the Capital. Sandus was a poor target for my anger, but Grizzst? Sitting right here, telling me to fuck off.

"Nice ring," I said flatly.

Thurvishar's quick hiss of breath told me he'd finally noticed.

Grizzst wiped a hand across his bleary eyes. "Yeah," he said. "I stole it from a baby. Now piss off before you make me angry. You're interrupting my drinking time."

I reminded myself that this was a deadly wizard who could probably turn us both to a fine sludge even if he was too drunk to stand. Beating the crap out of him wasn't practical, no matter how much I wanted to.

And, oh Veils, how I wanted to.

I set my hand down on the table in front of him. "Ask me if I care," I said, "*Grizzst.*"

Thurvishar looked around as if he was worried who might have heard me say the name. He also seemed a bit surprised by my anger. I suppose he just hadn't put together exactly what Grizzst wearing a Gryphon Men ring meant. Or what it meant to me.

Grizzst turned to face me, looked me up and down, and started to say something. (I assumed it would contain his favorite four-letter word.) Then he recognized me. I saw the moment he did, the look in his eyes as he figured out just who was staring down at him. He cursed under his breath and stood, knocking over his chair in the process.

"Yeah, fine," he muttered. "Somewhere private."

He led us through a battered door into a chamber that appeared to be used for all sorts of purposes and never cleaned. He rubbed his eyes, leaned against the wall, and then immediately wiped his hand as he came into contact with something unpleasant. He swayed in place, gazing unsteadily at the two of us. "What do you want?"

"Let's start with sobering you up," Thurvishar suggested. He held none of my anger. Indeed, he was gazing at Grizzst with quite a bit of affection.

"Kid, I haven't been sober in twenty years," he growled. "And that was just for a special occasion–"

[3] It is true that a great many events were set in motion when Sandus asked High General Qoran Milligreest to replace Surdyeh's broken harp with Valathea (in harp form), but considering the other coincidences surrounding those events, I feel Xaltorath also needs some blame here. And maybe Taja too.

The bastard actually looked in my direction.

"Yeah, okay," I said. "Thurvishar, open a gate. Let's not have this conversation *here*."

Grizzst straightened. "Good idea. Avoids any colloidal . . . collaterval . . . collat–" He paused. "No sense wrecking the place."

I crossed my arms over chest and gave the man a thin smile. At least *he* realized how this was going to go.

Thurvishar shot us both a worried look, but he opened the gate. The destination on the other side appeared to be someone's messy study or library, which was somehow even more in need of cleaning than the room we were in. Impressive. I honestly hadn't thought that possible.

Grizzst focused on the gate, the room beyond it, and then he drew back in shock. "What the hell?"

"I thought we might want to go someplace where you'd feel more comfortable," Thurvishar explained. "I promise I'll explain how I know that later. Just not here."

Grizzst blinked. "You'd better, or I'm turning you into a goldfish and feeding you to the giant carp that lives in my lake. Fuck." He sighed and passed a hand over himself. He immediately shivered and looked bright-eyed and sober. He did something–probably cast a few spells–and then marched through the opening.

I caught Thurvishar's eye, shrugged, and then followed.

# 89: The Hideous Truth

***(Senera's story)***

When Senera returned, she first encountered Veixizhau mutilating Suless's body. She'd stabbed out the old woman's eyes and was in the process of cutting off her fingers.

"Is that necessary?" Senera asked. No sooner had the words left her mouth than she felt like a fool. This woman had almost certainly seen the massacre of that entire monastery, including her husband and father-in-law. She'd probably witnessed those events thinking she and her child would be next.

In her place, Senera would probably have dismembered the corpse and burned every bit of it, piece by piece, into ash. Yes, it was necessary.

"She died too quickly," Veixizhau said bitterly. Her eyes were wide as she set down the knife and picked up her baby, who had started to fuss.

"I know it must seem—" Senera paused.

Veixizhau didn't mean that Suless should have died slowly, that it should have been more torturous. She meant Suless had died too quickly. And far too easily. Suless had been a god-queen. Why hadn't she blocked Baelosh's attack?

Xivan and Talea were still wrapped up in each other. Talea lay in Xivan's lap, and the two were whispering in hushed tones. Senera decided not to disturb them. There were no sense calling a false alarm if it turned out that all was as it seemed.

Senera sat down next to Veixizhau, ignored the bloody dismembered fingers and the corpse, and unpacked her Cornerstone. The question was the easiest thing in the world. Was Suless dead?

And the answer was *no*.

Senera felt a chill. Was that really Suless's body? She hadn't meant to ask the question of the stone, but realized she had as her fingers began to write.

*Yes.*

Senera set down her brush, pushed the inkstone away from her. "If that's her body," Senera said out loud, "why does the Name of All

Things think she's still alive?" Senera stopped herself. She hadn't asked if Suless was still alive. She asked if Suless was dead. That was not the same question.

She met Veixizhau's eyes. "What do you know? Xivan's too preoccupied right now to pay attention to you, but as soon as that changes, she may not be in a forgiving mood."

Veixizhau shook her head. "I don't know. I really don't know. She was . . . Suless liked to gloat when everything was going her way, and that's how she was acting at the end. Like everything was going according to her plans. She knew you were coming after her. She just didn't care."

Senera pulled the inkstone back over to her. "What was Suless's plan for surviving Xivan's arrival?"

*She planned to transfer her souls to a witch mother.*

Senera blinked. Transferring souls from one body to another was possible, but incredibly difficult, which was why it typically only happened with the help of an artifact like the Stone of Shackles. "Did she transfer her souls to a witch mother?"

*Yes.*

Senera looked up at Veixizhau, who shook her head. "I don't know! All the witch mothers are dead. Except . . . Oh no." She looked back at Talea and Xivan with horrified eyes, clutching the baby to her tightly.

Senera didn't have time to slowly drag the answers from the traumatized woman. "Who are Suless's witch mothers?" Senera asked.

To her surprise, only a single name resulted.

*Janel Theranon.*

"Oh fuck," Senera said.

Senera gave serious consideration to the idea of not telling Xivan the truth, but short of killing Veixizhau to keep the secret, there seemed little point. Xivan would figure out what really happened eventually.

The surviving horses had gathered in a tight cluster, not quite certain of exactly what had happened, but glad to have survived it. Other than their nervous reassurances to each other, little sound echoed through the lush valley. The air was thick with the smell of rot and sulfur as Senera walked back to Xivan and Talea. Talea had been crying; they both were still busy mooning over each other. Xivan was stroking Talea's hair. It all made Senera deeply uncomfortable.

Senera sighed and crossed her arms over her chest. "Suless isn't dead."

Xivan looked up. "What?"

Talea sat up. "But no—you said you found her body!"

Senera nodded and made a frustrated gesture behind her. "Yes, her body is dead. Her souls are hiding out somewhere else. And she finally managed to figure out a hiding spot where we can't reach her. So . . . you've found your granddaughter at least. That's honestly better than it could have gone. I'll take you both back."

Xivan stood up. "I'm not giving up. If Suless is still alive, my work here isn't done."

Senera rubbed her eyes. "I already asked the Name of All Things. Suless is at the Mother of Trees in the Manol Jungle. She might as well be on one of the moons; I can't take you there."

"Why not?" Talea asked.

Senera waved a hand. "One cannot simply open a gate into the Manol. It is protected by a web of defenses that prevent exactly such a thing. Suless didn't teleport there; she just transported her souls. We don't have that advantage. Thus, we can't follow her."

"The Mother of Trees?" Xivan tilted her head. "Why would Suless go to the Mother of Trees."

"Oh, I don't think it was intentional," Senera said. "But seriously, we should go. I have no idea how long it will before Sharanakal or Baelosh or both return, but we don't want to be here."

"We're not leaving yet," Talea said. She walked over to a wilting bush and started plucking gems from the leaves. "So you might as well explain exactly what Suless has done. If she transported just her souls, that means she transported them *to* something. What? Or who?"

Senera stared.

Every time she made the mistake of thinking Talea was simple, the woman pulled something like this. "What are you doing?" Senera asked, choosing instead to target Talea's odd jewel harvest.

"Thurvishar said these were tsalis–souls trapped in stone," Talea explained. "We're not just *leaving* them." She paused. "It might go faster if you helped, though."

Senera scoffed and turned back to face Xivan. "There's an impenetrable barrier around the Manol Jungle. No one breaks it short of one of the Eight Immortals. Suless anticipated that we'd successfully reach her. She planned for it. So she had a prepared body waiting. Baelosh didn't kill her; she had already moved her souls into the prepared body and let her old body die."

"A prepared body?" Xivan scowled. "A witch mother? But we didn't let her keep any–" All expression fled her face, then a furious anger moved in to fill the void. "When were you going to tell me Janel was in danger?"

"Oh, Your Grace . . ." Senera sighed. "Janel isn't in danger. Janel's already dead."

"Is she?" Talea said. "Have you checked?"

"I don't need to check!" Senera protested. "She's gone. Suless wouldn't have taken her over in a gentle, kind way that allows for us to recover her. When Suless did this, she annihilated Janel's soul—and now she's set up shop. Your friend is dead."

"She's your friend too," Talea whispered.

"No, she's not," Senera said emphatically. "We never liked each other. She'll never forgive me for what I've done to her, which I can hardly blame her for. The only reason I ever helped her was because—" Senera paused. The only reason she had ever helped Janel was because Relos Var had asked her to. Because Janel was important to Relos Var's plans. An importance that probably hadn't changed.

So Suless not only wasn't dead but Janel was.

Relos Var would not be pleased to discover that Suless had once again meddled with his plans. Despite what Thurvishar thought, Senera was loyal to Relos Var. She *was.* She would, absolutely would, make sure his will was done.

"You're being either disingenuous or naïve, Senera," Xivan said. "You know perfectly well Janel isn't a normal person. She's been possessed before. I rather doubt Suless would be able to destroy a soul Xaltorath could not."

Senera paused. "That's . . . that's actually a good point."

"So check," Xivan said.

Senera did.

"Ha!" Talea said, pointing down at the word *yes* scratched into the ground. "I knew it!"

Senera stood to her feet. "I think you're still forgetting that the same logistical difficulties that applied to Suless absolutely apply to us. We can't just open a gate to Janel's location. There is a magical ward that blocks our way."

Xivan shrugged and pulled Urthaenriel free from its scabbard. "Then we'll break it."

Senera rolled her eyes. "It doesn't work like that." Her eyes narrowed as she looked at the black sword. "Wait. Maybe it could." The wizard looked thoughtful. "I suppose it couldn't hurt to try an experiment."

Talea grinned. "Help me gather up all these tsalis. Then I'll grab our supplies."

# 90: A Useless Wizard

***(Kihrin's story)***

It may sound strange coming from someone who grew up in a less-than--ideal part of town, but the Shattered Veil Club had always placed a high importance on keeping the place clean. Sure, mostly that was for business reasons, but even so. Ola had absolutely no tolerance for dirt, and Surdyeh liked everything to be in its place so he wouldn't accidentally trip over it.

What I'm saying is that Grizzst's workshop was a god-awful mess. The clutter offended me on a visceral level. I assume that there were tables, and probably some sort of floor, but it's not like I could actually see them. I had to take it on faith that under great, giant stacks of books, papers, and weird junk, there was in fact the foundations of a house.

And given the way Grizzst pushed a huge stack of papers over and sat down on one of the benches, I also took it on faith that this was *his* house.

I set the harp down in a corner. "Seriously, what kind of person looks at a newborn baby and says, 'I know just the place to hide him. Let's raise him in a brothel'?"

The wizard squinted at me. "You turned out fine."

Thurvishar blinked. "Wait, what? What is he talking about?"

"He's the leader of the Gryphon Men, Thurvishar. Your father worked for him. *My* father Surdyeh worked for him. This is the bastard who was pulling all those strings. Why?" I stared him down. "What was the point of it all? The prophecies?"

Grizzst narrowed his eyes at both of us. "Where the fuck are you getting your information? I'll own up to Surdyeh, but Gadrith D'Lorus absolutely did *not* work for me."

Thurvishar sighed. "In my past life, I was Simillion. In *this* life, I was Cimillion. I hope you can appreciate the irony of my father Sandus naming me after myself."[1]

[1] Obviously, Gadrith wouldn't have kept the name Sandus and Dyana named me, would he? For many, many reasons, I have elected not to return to using it.

Grizzst *stared,* the shock to his system far worse than me showing up on his doorstep. Even worse than finding out the hero he'd so famously trained had been reincarnated.

"Shit. So that's how you knew about my workshop."

"Gahan, do you really expect me to believe you had no idea?" Thurvishar didn't look angry exactly. Just . . . disappointed.

"Sandus was my *apprentice,* kid. If I'd known where you were, I'd have told him. I'm not a fucking monster." Grizzst turned his head and began scanning the stacks around himself until he finally extricated a flagon and dumped its contents out on the floor. His expression tightened. "Surdyeh was my student too. Sorry about both of them. They were good men."

I suddenly felt dizzy. This was . . . not what I'd expected. I'd have said that this was like finding family you never knew about, but I'd already *done* that, and this was somehow worse.

Thurvishar looked equally flustered. We'd both lost the trail of our purpose for being there.

Grizzst did something over his mug, and it filled with liquid. I wondered if it was water or something more intoxicating, and if the latter, why he'd been hanging out in a bar at a brothel in the first place. He leaned back against a stack of books. "All right. Spit it out. You didn't show up for no reason."

"We, uh . . ." Thurvishar started over. "We wanted your help figuring out how to stop Vol Karoth without using the Ritual of Night."

Grizzst shrugged. "Then you've come a long way for nothing. Fuck if I know."

"Well, then . . ." I glared at him. "Wait, why? Why any of this? Why Sandus and Surdyeh and all the rest of your strange little prophecy-hunting club? You must have been chasing some kind of point, right?"

He shrugged. "Mostly just pissing in Relos Var's tea, to be honest."

"You're lying."

Grizzst ignored me and made a shooing motion with his fingers. "Now run along, you two. You interrupted a twenty-year binge, and I have some catching up to do."

"By all the gods," Thurvishar murmured. He scrubbed a hand over his face.

"Let's go," I said. "Let's just go. This was a mistake. Now I understand why the Eight Immortals didn't ask this slug for help. Would you have if you were in their place?"

"No, probably not." Clearly disgusted, Thurvishar opened up a new gate, this time back to what I suspected was Kishna-Farriga.

I couldn't believe that this whole trip was ending so quickly and in complete, abject failure. We'd hardly even had a chance to explain. No, scratch that. There had been no explanation at all. But here we were being ushered out, because the man that even Thurvishar had admitted was usually a drunken wretch had managed to become even more especially useless than normal about it. Consulting the wise wizard living up in the mountains this was *not.*

I was about ready to step through the gate, when I stopped.

"I would rather not keep this open forever," Thurvishar cautioned me. "One does become exhausted."

"Close it," I said absently. I turned back and regarded the House D'Lorus wizard. "Who fixed the broken warding crystal?"

Behind Thurvishar, still sitting on that bench, Grizzst raised his head and met my stare.

"I'm sorry?" Thurvishar said.

"Who repaired the warding crystal? I said it myself; the Eight *didn't* ask this slug for help."

"Hey, watch it with the slug comments. I've always consider myself more of a frog. Maybe a toad."

I ignored Grizzst as I chewed on my lower lip for a minute, eyes distant. "I shattered the damn thing. Now if Thaena wants to redo the Ritual of Night and charge it up again, that's all well and good, but there has to be something to recharge, doesn't there? So who made a new warding crystal?" I pointed at Grizzst. "If he's been on a drinking binge for the last two decades, he didn't do it, so who did?"

Thurvishar stared blankly at me. "Argas? I mean, he's the god of invention."

Grizzst didn't quite manage to stop himself from snorting.

"No," I said, shaking my head. "Not Argas. I mean, no offense, he's a great guy. Good at taking orders. *Really* loyal. Will absolutely watch your back or get you home after a night of barhopping, but I'm pretty sure I've known hunting drakes with more capacity for original thought. Unless the voras left behind very specific instructions telling Argas exactly what to do to repair the crystals, I have a hard time believing that he would be capable of fixing that damage by himself. So who did?"

Thurvishar ran a hand over his bald pate and sighed. "I see your point. Honestly, I've wondered why Relos Var hasn't been trying to stop us."

"He went through all that effort to shatter the warding crystal, and now he just lets us *fix* it? That doesn't make sense, does it?"

Thurvishar frowned. "He wants the vané to be mortal?"

"Does he? Why? What would that buy him? I'd bet good metal and a lot of it that Relos Var knew breaking the eighth crystal wouldn't be enough to actually free Vol Karoth. Wake him, sure. But not *free* him. So what comes next? What would be the smart thing to do? After all, we both know Relos Var is very, very smart. You're very, very smart, Thurvishar. What would *you* do?"

Thurvishar exhaled. "I'd trick my enemies–the people who would be trying to stop me–into doing it themselves."

"Right. That. Think you could reach Khorsal's palace again?"

He nodded. "Oh yes. I know the way."

# 91: Sisterhood

***(Senera's story)***

They traveled back to Senera's cottage, while Senera consulted various books, scribbled in a journal, and muttered a great deal under her breath. She didn't technically need to research, but it gave Xivan time to deal with Veixizhau and her infant daughter, Nexara. Of the two, only Nexara was in a healthy state. Veixizhau was going to need a lot of time in quiet places where gentle people served her equally gentle broths.

Senera hoped Xivan took up her suggestion of sending the mother and child to the Vishai. They were very good at that sort of thing. She knew from personal experience.

Talea spent a lot of time supporting Xivan, of which Senera also approved. Xivan struck her as one of those people who thought she was invulnerable and would continue to think that right up until the point she suffered a severe mental collapse. Especially since Xivan's lack of need to eat, drink, or sleep might easily fool her into thinking she had a lack of every kind of need, which was absolutely not true.

When Senera was finally ready, she called the others back. "I believe I've figured out how we can quickly reach Janel." She paused. "There are a few issues, however."

Xivan raised an eyebrow at her and waited.

Senera forced herself not to fidget. Xivan had always done the mother thing very well, a skill only sharpened with the addition of several dozen women who followed her every order. Sometimes even Senera felt the power of that disapproving stare.

"The main issue is that if it works, the vané are almost certainly going to want to kill us. Me, at the very least. The barrier roses have been one of their primary defenses against invasion for millennia. They won't be happy about the idea that anyone–least of all a trio of Quuros–have figured out how to negate them."

Talea shrugged. "We're only going to do it one time. They never have to know."

Senera bit her lip. "Talea . . ." She took a deep breath and started over. "Talea, if you ran a country that was surrounded by a gigantic, extremely effective magical wall and someone just . . . walked . . . through it, wouldn't you try to find out how they had done it? Wouldn't you do just about anything to find out how they had done it? After all, it's not just your life we're talking about here. You have people to protect."

Talea frowned. "I see your point."

"Are we still doing this?" The other two women gave her precisely the same flat stares she'd been expecting. Senera sighed and waved a hand. "Fine. I had to ask. All right, come over here." She picked up a small potted plant.

"What is that for?" Xivan asked, looking understandably confused.

Senera grinned. "I'm glad you asked. This is how we're going to take down the single greatest magical protection possessed by any nation in the world."

"With gardening?" The amusement in Xivan's voice fought with her skepticism.

"Oh yes," Senera said. "With gardening. If nothing else, I like to think the vané will appreciate our style."

Senera wove the elements of the gate again, this time to a point in Doltar that was as close to the Manol Jungle as she personally had ever been. As close as she would probably be able to go while the protective wards were still in place, anyway.

She left Rebel behind this time. She hated doing it, but she couldn't in good conscience justify bringing the dhole. At least if the worst happened and Senera didn't come back, she wouldn't have to worry about Rebel being trapped inside the cottage; her dog was perfectly capable of tearing the doors off their hinges.

They came out of the gate in a warm, humid landscape that might fool one into thinking this was the Manol Jungle if one had never seen a sky tree. This was a lesser rain forest, and from here, one couldn't actually see the giant canopy line of the larger jungle. It was lush and green and filled with every sort of living plant. The floor was so covered with fallen trees, roots, plants, flowers, and detritus that one was basically assured of standing on something living, rather than standing on actual soil. It seemed like the sort of place Baelosh would have liked.

"Why were you ever down here?" Xivan asked.

"There are a few herbs that only grow in this region," Senera explained. "Relos Var brought me here so I could collect them."

That explanation given, Senera looked for a spot to set down her potted plant. "Be careful of snakes and spiders, by the way. The sigils I gave you will protect from bug bites, but there are other creatures down here besides those."

Talea looked around rather nervously, and her hand inched toward her sword as if that would somehow do any good at all.

Senera concentrated on the plant in front of her. "You see," she explained, "we can't actually get anywhere near a barrier rose. They're not like a net that encircles the Manol. It's more like a series of lanterns, with the light of each lantern overlapping. And anywhere that light reaches, one cannot open a gate. Unfortunately, those lanterns tend to be intelligently placed in the middle of vané cities—sensibly fortified locations that we probably couldn't get within a hundred miles of without being spotted and filled with black vané arrows."

"But obviously, you have a way to deal with it."

"No, actually you do," Senera said to Xivan. "As you said, you're going to use Urthaenriel."

Xivan tilted her head. "Should I point out that Atrin Kandor tried invading the Manol with Urthaenriel and it did him no good?"

"I've always felt Atrin Kandor suffered from a distinct lack of imagination,"[1] Senera said. "Atrin was clever, mind you, but demonstrated a tendency to brute force his way through problems. This needs something a bit subtler."

Senera began painting sigils on the bottom of the plant's pot, and almost immediately, the plant began to bloom.

"Oh, it's a rosebush," Talea said.

"Not just a rosebush," Senera explained. "The very same variety of roses they use to make their fabled barriers from. It's just this version isn't magical. Or, should I say, didn't used to be magical? That's about to change."

"So wait, you're going to enchant this to be a barrier rose?" Talea put her hands on her hips. "How is making another barrier rose going to help us?"

"Wait and see," Senera said. "This had better work, because if the first part is successful but the second part fails, we're walking home."[2]

Xivan crossed her arms over her chest and watched.

Senera thought the principle was simple enough. She needed to have access to one of the barrier roses in order for this to work, but she couldn't get access until she was much farther inside the country than she would ever be allowed to get without first taking down the barrier roses.

She smiled, thinking of the Quuros Academy wizards who had been stopped by this very problem. They could all eat a block of mud.

[1] I'm honestly not sure if Teraeth would be offended or not by that statement. He might agree that was a fair criticism.

[2] While humorous, I'm sure Senera would have just destroyed the rosebush.

When she was finished, Senera straightened and tried to open a gate back to the cottage.

She couldn't. The gate refused to open.

"Step one is complete," Senera announced. "Now for step two. Xivan, would you be so kind as to draw Urthaenriel and stab the rosebush with it? And don't take it out again. Just keep holding your sword inside the rosebush."

Xivan looked skeptical, but she stood up and did as Senera asked. Parts of the rosebush wilted in response, but since the majority of the rosebush had existed quite happily for some time without the aid of any magic at all, it continued to exist without it in the presence of Godslayer.

"And how long am I supposed to do this for?" Xivan asked.

"An hour. Maybe two. It occurs to me that we should have packed a lunch."

Xivan narrowed her eyes at Senera. "Is this some kind of prank?"

"Xivan, this is Senera we're talking about," Talea reminded her. "She doesn't have a sense of humor."

"Thank you . . . I think," Senera said. "It's not a prank. Urthaenriel is draining the magic from that enchantment. Now normally, that would be as far as it went, but despite what I said earlier, the barrier roses that protect the jungle are a kind of net. If one part of the net fails, the weave is tight enough for the other roses to take over, to cover the gap, which they will try to do. They are, even as we speak, directing their energy toward this disenchanted barrier rose to make sure the barrier stays strong."

Xivan motioned with her free hand. "And . . ."

"And that energy is not infinite," Senera explained. "Eventually, the rest of the roses will be so weakened trying to maintain this one–which cannot be maintained because Urthaenriel is constantly draining it–that they will all simultaneously fail. The whole damn net will just . . . disintegrate." She put her hands together and then moved them apart, wriggling her fingers as she did.

"You're enjoying this, aren't you?" Talea said.

"I might be, yes," Senera admitted. "Normally, the method we're using would be impossible and beyond the reach of even most Quuros wizards, but Urthaenriel is just so very useful, isn't it?" She joined Talea on the log. "Now while Xivan is busy, I'm going to take a bit of time to see if I can't figure out exactly who we'll be facing when we do go to confront Suless and just what we can do to make sure Janel comes out of the situation alive." She waved her brush. "If that is the right word."

"Thank you," Talea told her. "I really appreciate it. I'm just sure Janel will too."

"Whether she will or not remains to be seen, but you'd never let me hear the end of it otherwise." Senera set up her writing supplies and started to work.

***(Janel's story)***

Janel woke to ice and cold.

She wasn't in the Afterlife, the dark, crawling, fetid woods that she had grown up roaming. This was another place, familiar, even less welcome.

She stood on top of a glass pyramid in the icy, frozen wastes of the Yoran mountains. The clouds thundered below her in the valleys, wrapping blizzard gusts through the narrow canyons. The icy winds scoured the high peaks, while ice crystals glittered like diamonds across the top of the truncated pyramid. Janel didn't feel the cold at all.

Hyenas laughed and called to each other in the distance. Then one laugh from much closer.

Janel turned toward the sound.

Suless sat on her throne. Unlike all the other times she had ever seen the god-queen, this Suless was young. She had brown skin and orange-red eyes, while her dark hair was streaked with white from artifice rather than age. She was rather shockingly pretty, although her eyes still looked hard and the twist in her mouth could only be described as cruel.

"Hello, little lion," Suless said.

"What am I doing here?" Janel looked around. She didn't think this was real. That didn't mean she could see any obvious way to escape. "Suless, what trickery is this?"

Suless stood. "Normally, I'd have killed you already. That is tradition. But you're a special case."

Janel reached for her sword, only to realize she didn't have it. She was dressed in little better than a thin chemise, with no armor, no weapons. Janel clenched her fist and summoned fire.

Suless snapped her fingers. Instantly, Janel found herself dragged backward, wrists and ankles bound in thick manacles of ice, to a frozen wall that hadn't been there a moment before. Janel fought down panic. Even with all her strength, she couldn't pull herself free. "Suless! Stop this!"

"No, I don't think so." Suless walked over to her. "Your little friend Xivan's been proving an inconvenience, and I've decided I'm done with it."

Janel momentarily stopped struggling. "And you think I'm going to help with that? I have news for you, old woman–Xivan isn't going to stop trying to kill you no matter how many hostages you take. You're only going to strengthen her resolve."

Suless laughed. No, Suless cackled. She might have looked young, but she still laughed to make a child's hairs stand on end. "Oh no," Suless said. "You're not a hostage. In fact, our positions have been reversed, little lion. Once, I taught you. Now, you're going to return the favor."

Janel frowned. "What could I possibly teach you that you don't already know?"

"Well." Suless reached over to the edge of her throne and broke off an icicle. "It occurred me while I was trying to evade that bitch Xivan that there was hardly anyplace in the world I could go where she couldn't follow. The Manol? Safe in the short term, but eventually she'll find a way inside. And while I've never much cared for friends, in this one instance, that's an inconvenience. I'm running out of safe havens. So what to do?"

"Give up and die?" Janel suggested. She tried heating up her hands to melt the restraints. It didn't work. The thick bands looked like ice, but they were clearly made of something far more permanent.

"Hilarious," Suless said. "But then I remembered that there is one place in all the Twin Worlds where Xivan can't follow me. The Afterlife."

"Perfect. I'll help send you there," Janel spat.

"You go there every night, my dear. You go there and return at will. And you and I both know it's not because of Xaltorath."

Janel didn't respond. She didn't know that, although she'd been starting to suspect. This was one of the things that Xaltorath didn't seem to want her to remember. "You think I can teach you? I can't."

Suless walked up to her. "You can, daughter. You weren't cursed by demons. You weren't infected by Xaltorath, no matter what she wanted you to think. You made *yourself* this way. Did you think you could hide the truth from me? I know you better than you know yourself. You turned yourself into a demon. And somewhere inside your souls, you remember how you did it. You're going to teach me."

"I can't," Janel said.

"Then let's jog that memory together, shall we?" Suless stabbed the icicle through Janel's shoulder, and began to twist.

# 92: Return to Khorsal's Palace

***(Kihrin's story)***

It's difficult to explain the sense of haste and dread that quickened our every step and made us rush to draw the right glyphs, prepare the right spells. We barely paid any attention to Grizzst. It didn't matter that just moments before he'd been the whole reason we'd come to . . . wherever his workshop was located.[1]

Both Thurvishar and I were feverishly aware that at any time our friends in the Manol might actually succeed at what they were doing. My mother might cast the Ritual of Night. Or Kelanis might be persuaded to do so. Someone. When that happened, then whatever terrible trap Relos Var had planned would snap shut on the whole world.

Unless Thurvishar and I managed to get there first.

Thurvishar opened the gate, and we stepped through into the water. This time, our surroundings were slightly different. Since Thurvishar knew the place, we didn't have to swim around until we found it. And this time, it was Thurvishar who parted the water so we were once again able to breathe air and walk on the (still) extremely muddy lake bottom. The air still stank of decay and rotting fish, old water and damp metal. I created lights, which reflected against the curtains of held-back water until they looked like black rippling mirrors.

There was no sign of our previous trip to this same location, the night when I was tricked into waking up Vol Karoth. No crystal fragments remained, no signs of the admittedly brief fight chronicled those other events.

And the warding crystal sat on top of the spire behind Khorsal's throne, whole, looking like it had never been broken at all. It lacked the beam of light that had previously streamed toward Vol Karoth's prison, but someone had indeed replaced the crystal.

Both of us stood there and stared at the damn thing.

"How sad is it that I find myself wishing Senera were here?" I said.

[1] Rainbow Lake, right next to the main Vishai temple. It occurs to me in hindsight perhaps we should have paid more attention to that fact.

"Not sad at all," Thurvishar said glumly. "The Name of All Things would be extremely useful." He walked up to the throne and hopped up on the hard gold seat to get a better look at the crystal. "There are only two real possibilities," he said. "Either the gods replaced this crystal, in which case it will do basically what it's supposed to do, or someone else replaced the crystal, in which case it won't."

"We could always just, I don't know, ask the Immortals." I contemplated the possibility of flipping a coin for the answer. It wasn't quite as ludicrous as it might sound, all things considered.

"Neither of us follow Argas," he said, "so there's an excellent chance that he just wouldn't show up. And would Taja or Tya know the answer?"

I made a face. "No, but they might be able to tell what it does do. If it does what it's supposed to do."

"Possibly." He shrugged. "Tya? Are you listening? Can you come to me?"

We both waited for several seconds.

"Taja? I need you . . ." I looked around, as if she might walk through the curtain of water with a picnic basket and the solutions to all our problems.

No one made any appearances.

"Okay, hold on," I said, climbing the stairs. "Make a space for me. I'm going to try something."

"And that something would be?"

"Don't you trust me?" I winked at him.

"I . . . I just think a second opinion might be useful," he replied. "I do know more about magical theory than you do."

"Very well. I'm going to turn the crystal invisible." I motioned for him to jump off the throne so I could take his place.

"Invisible? What good is that going to do?" He frowned deeply at me. Thurvishar probably wondered if all the pressure was going to my head.

"When I broke this thing last time," I explained gently, "there were a lot of things inside it. It was hollow, and it was just filled with junk. I don't know what any of those items did, but my point is that it was not a solid piece of crystal. So let's see if that's still true and, if it is still true, what we can tell about the interior."

He blinked and slowly lowered himself down from the throne. "I see. That . . . yes, that might indeed be useful for analysis."

"Thank you." I concentrated on shifting my vision past the First Veil and seeing what there was to see.

It wasn't glass or quartz, but some sort of diamond. And once I understood what the basic material was, I could then work on making that basic material transparent. Slowly, the crystal faded from view.

Its contents did not, and the first thing we saw was the slow, graceful swirl of one of Senera's sigils. A whole lot of Senera's sigils.

"Son of a bitch," I said, "maybe I'm glad Senera's not here after all."

"What do you think those do?" Thurvishar asked.

"Well, Senera wasn't terribly interested in stopping the Ritual of Night. Relos Var hasn't been any kind of thorn in our sides. So I'm going to guess whatever it does is something that they will want and the gods will not." I studied the interior. It was not the same as the original crystal I'd shattered. That had been filled with more crystals and odd little coiled pieces and springs. This was just layers and layers of sigils.

"Unfortunately, we're faced with something of a quandary," Thurvishar said. "After all, she may well have trapped the crystal to do something if it's shattered instead of being empowered."

"Probably," I said, "so I'd really appreciate it if you did your best to keep me alive." I pulled my sword from my scabbard.

"What?" Thurvishar's eyes widened. "Wait, we don't know what that–don't!"

But it was too late. I was already bringing my sword down to shatter the crystal a second time.

The sword bounced right off a shimmering rainbow force field that seemingly sprang up out of nowhere.

Grizzst said, "Sorry, kids. I can't let you do that."

I turned around to see the wizard, who was completely sober and equally annoyed.

I pointed back at the crystal. "It's trapped."

Grizzst nodded. "I *know*. That was kind of the whole point." He gestured, and the intaglio ring sailed right off Thurvishar's finger and landed in the palm of the other wizard's hand. He closed his fingers over it.

I felt my stomach sink. "You're working with Relos Var."

The wizard nodded. "Hell yes, I'm working with Relos Var. Have been the whole time."

# 93: An Unexpected Visit

***(Teraeth's story)***

Teraeth woke when Janel threw off the covers and got out of bed. He'd been sitting in a chair by her bedside all night, although at some point during the evening, she'd stopped with whatever seizure had grabbed her and transitioned into what could only be described as normal sleep. Or what would have been normal sleep if it had involved anyone else. The fact that she was visibly sleeping, chest rising and falling, was troubling.

Khaeriel had examined Janel and pronounced her perfectly fine, completely free from any physical illnesses, poisons, or defects. Unfortunately, having Khaeriel examine Janel had meant subjecting himself to Khaeriel's questions about just what he'd been doing and why.

That conversation hadn't gone well at all, and it was far from over.

Worse, Khaeriel threw a spell over Talon the moment she saw the mimic again, and while Teraeth might not have minded that so much under normal circumstances, it made him feel uncomfortable this time. Mostly because he had given the monster his word, and to his vast surprise, that apparently meant something to him.

All of which was a problem for another time, trumped as it was by the much more pleasant realization that Janel was awake and fine. He smiled as he went to her. "Janel, thank the gods, I'd been worried–" He touched her shoulder.

She pulled away from him as her eyes flared. "Don't touch me." Her expression was malignant.

Teraeth pulled his hand back. "I don't understand. What happened?"

"I have no idea," she said at last. She looked down at herself, noted the pile of clothing that had been folded off to the side, and began to dress herself. "Get out of my room," she said.

Teraeth frowned. Even when Janel was very, very angry with him, she usually managed a more congenial tone than that. "It's not just your room," he reminded her.

She threw him a disgusted glance. "I'm tired of sharing it. A woman needs her space. Leave."

Teraeth opened his mouth to say something, but he honestly had no idea what to say. She was tired of sharing it? He thought they had patched things up, to put it lightly. What exactly had happened while he was sneaking off on his own at the palace? "It won't be for much longer," he finally managed to say. "Just a few more days until parliament reconvenes and the trial begins."

She nodded, eyes scanning the room as if she was seeing it for the first time. "Fine."

Janel didn't say another word to him as she finished dressing. Shocked by her unexpected behavior, Teraeth decided it might be better if he waited outside. When he exited, Doc, Valathea, and Khaeriel waited for him. Khaeriel had Talon trapped in a column of spinning air in the center of the rows of silk-farm houses, where several cleared plots had created a central courtyard. Teraeth assumed someone had cloaked them in an illusion. Probably Terindel, who liked using illusions even when he wasn't using Chainbreaker.

He looked at Talon, who was in her Lyrilyn form, and then back at the ant house where he'd left Janel. If he hadn't known better, Teraeth would have genuinely wondered if they'd accidentally brought two mimics back with them when they'd escaped from the palace.

"Janel will be along in a minute," Teraeth said.

"Could you please talk some sense into them?" Talon asked him. "You did promise that you wouldn't hurt me."

"He promised," Khaeriel pointed out. "I did not promise. And I am not happy with you right now. Not happy at all."

The door to the ant house opened, and Janel exited. She paused, staring at the gathered crowd as if they were all strangers. Teraeth motioned her over, but she ignored him.

"I would also like to discuss your attempt to kill my brother," Khaeriel said to Teraeth, "and what idiocy possessed you to try to do that."

"Oh, that idiot would be me," Doc said.

Teraeth would have smiled at his father if he hadn't been worrying at his lip over whatever was going on with Janel. Teraeth hadn't been sure the man would own up to the fact this had all been his idea.

Khaeriel glared at him. "I expected better of you."

Doc shrugged. "It was worth a shot. And you have to admit, we came pretty close."

"If only body doubles counted," Valathea reminded him. "And if only Kelanis wasn't almost guaranteed to bring this up again in front of parliament."

"I was disguised," Teraeth offered. "And the mimic will probably throw him off."

Doc frowned at Talon. "How did you get inside the palace, anyway?"

"Pardon?" She smiled at him.

"How did you get inside the palace. The wards are designed to stop the mimics–" He paused and then shook his head. "Never mind. I figured it out. The Stone of Shackles."

"Right," Teraeth said. "Took me a little while to realize too. Now that being the case, I really think we should use that to–"

But he never had a chance to finish his sentence.

A gate–an actual magical gate in the middle of the damn Manol–opened on the balcony, just a few feet away from Terindel. Before anyone had a chance to fully digest this information, let alone react to it, three women emerged from the portal: two Khorveshan women (one holding a glass bottle and the other a black sword) and a white-skinned woman with pale hair. They were all covered in what looked like tattoos–swirling black marks on their faces and hands. The woman with the bottle smashed it down against the balcony, releasing a giant cloud of white smoke. At the same time, the white-haired woman gestured and encased Talon–already trapped by Khaeriel–in a glowing green field of energy.[1] The last woman, holding the sword, lowered the edge of it to Doc's neck.

She looked over at Khaeriel. "Move and he dies." The warning had been spoken in Guarem.

The moment that sword touched Teraeth's father, all illusions surrounding them at the silk farm disappeared. The illusions that Doc had been maintaining vanished as though they'd never been. Teraeth eyed that sword, harboring a nasty suspicion about just what they were facing.

It was the wrong color, but Urthaenriel was a shape-changer too.

Khaeriel wouldn't be able to handle that, but Teraeth knew what to do. Urthaenriel would protect its wearer from magic, but not from something as mundane as a blade. He sprang into action immediately, skillfully stepping up behind the woman, quickly sliding a dagger under her rib cage, into her heart. The same motion carried a second dagger across the woman's throat.

He had just enough time to notice that she didn't react to his attack, didn't start bleeding from any of the wounds, and most infuriatingly, didn't go into shock and *die*. Then the white billowing gas reached him and cut off his vision.

He started choking. Teraeth's eyes burned and tears sprang up. He wasn't the only one having this reaction; he heard coughing from other people on the balcony, including his father. That was the only comfort to be

[1] She used my spell. That was *my* spell for dealing with mimics.

had in the situation, since it meant the attacker hadn't shoved Urthaenriel forward in response to Teraeth's actions. At least for the moment.

Gods, he *hated* undead.

Teraeth sheathed one of his knives, sliced the edge of the other against his lower arm, and wiped away the welling blood. Of course, trying to draw that damn sigil while he was in pain and blind was a bit of a challenge, but he didn't have many other options.

Then everything exploded.

*Exploded* was the wrong word. This was applying a flame to pure alcohol. A giant flash of heat filled the air and burned away the cloud of gas in its wake. Teraeth's eyes were still full of tears, but at least the situation wasn't growing worse. He finished drawing the glyph on the back of one hand, just in case someone brought back the smoke, and pulled out more knives.

Khaeriel was on the floor unconscious, although Teraeth suspected that it had less to do with the fire than with something the white-haired wizard had done. And said woman was trying to find the source of the fire, which Teraeth was curious about himself.

Teraeth noticed Valathea, standing over by one of the railings and looking quite serene and untroubled. The white-haired woman must have seen her too, because she scowled and drew back her hand, probably to cast some spell.

Valathea pointed to the woman's feet with the same sort of manner one might use to point out someone was about to step in a puddle.

A tangle of greenery, pretty red flowers and sharp thorns grew out of the platform under the woman's feet, shifting and moving like a living snake instead of a plant. As the woman looked down at this, the thorns sprang forward, piercing her leg like an attack of needles.

The woman's eyes rolled back in her head, and she collapsed to the ground. The force field trapping Talon vanished.

The bare-handed woman—the one who had smashed the bottle and released the white smoke—ran up to Janel and touched her on the shoulder. Nothing seemed to happen, but Janel's reaction was immediate; she pushed hard against the other woman, sending her flying back and through one of the nearby ant structures. She then started screaming at the swarm of ants, which immediately began biting the very unwelcome intruder.

"Talea!" Talon shouted and ran to the woman.

Doc, meanwhile, had seemed only slightly bothered by the smoke, even though he also had tears streaming down his cheeks. When Talon called out that name, the undead woman couldn't help but look to the side for a split second.

Doc smiled at the woman holding the sword to him and then moved—very quickly—batting the blade out of the way as he stepped back and pulled out his own sword. She recovered right away and swung downward, missing him by a matter of inches.

But not missing the necklace supporting Chainbreaker, which broke and fell to the ground.

"Not bad," Doc said as he moved his sword in line. "You've studied with the Terrini school."

The woman raised an eyebrow. "You're familiar with it?" Teraeth had either missed her vocal cords or she didn't really need them.

"I should be; I founded it. I doubt there's a sword move you know that I didn't invent, and believe me, I can beat myself."

She choked back a laugh. "Shouldn't you be in private for that?"

Doc sighed. "That's not what I meant." Doc lunged forward with his sword, a move she easily blocked.

Teraeth looked around. The white-haired woman was unconscious, and Talon—Talon!—was helping the other woman stand, trying to shoo ants away. Janel was . . . Janel was gone. He couldn't see her anywhere.

While he was searching, the ground under the swordswoman's feet vanished.

Doc clearly hadn't expected this. His eyes went wide as she fell past him. She made a wild grab for the ledge, so she was hanging on with one hand and still holding Urthaenriel with the other.

Doc gave his wife a rather reproachful stare. "Did you have to do that? We were just starting."

Valathea crossed her arms over her chest. "Yes, I did have to do that. She's holding Godslayer." She looked over at the unconscious pale woman. "Who are these people?"

"I don't know," Teraeth said. "Talon? Mind explaining?"

"Oh, uh . . ." Talon turned to the woman she was helping—Talea—with an embarrassed expression. "Lucky guess? We've never met before. Ever."[2]

Doc looked down at the hole in the balcony wood, the woman holding on. She looked alive enough if one ignored the milky eyes, the clearly slit throat. "If you drop the sword, you could probably pull yourself up."

"Not going to happen," she growled.

"It's a long way down," Doc pointed out. "The fall is guaranteed to kill you."

[2] Technically true. I never allowed Talon to have contact with Talea for fear Talon would try something rash. Especially since Talon had murdered and then consumed Talea's twin sister, Morea. I feared Talon would try to complete the set. But mimics often have difficulty separating their own memories from those of their victims, so I suspect Talon was having just such a problem at that moment.

"So? I've been dead for years." The woman started pulling herself up, using the sword as leverage. "And we're not here after any of you. We're here because Janel's been possessed by the witch-queen Suless."

Talea was still busy trying to remove ants, but she raised up a hand to show that another one of the strange ornate glyphs was drawn there. "Exorcism sigil," she volunteered.

Doc and Valathea glanced at each other.

Teraeth heard the words like an ocean wave slamming down on him. He remembered Janel's seizure the night before, her inexplicable shift in personality on waking. How she had actually *slept.* The way she'd referred to herself as a woman.

Almost as if she were a different person.

"You people really should have started with that," Teraeth said. "Pull her up."

# 94: Assumed Loyalties

***(Kihrin's story)***

The wizard held a slender wand in his hand. My first thought was that it looked a lot like the Scepter of Quur, and then I remember Grizzst was supposed to be the man who'd created the Crown and Scepter of Quur.

What were the odds he hadn't made himself a spare set? And Tyentso had been able to do all sorts of things with hers. Magical barriers were just part of it. Its other powers were far more deadly.

I looked down at the sword in my hand and sighed. That was going to do me a whole lot of good. I might as well have been armed with a kitten.

"Why?" Thurvishar sounded appropriately horrified. "By the Veils, Gahan. Why?"

Grizzst ignored him and stared at me. "You were really going to just . . . smash it? Seriously? Your brother told me you were stupid, but I didn't actually believe him. I always thought that was just sour grapes. Yet here you are."

I sheathed my sword and leaned against the throne. "The crystal wasn't powered," I reminded him. "The worst it could do is fire off whatever booby trap Senera put inside, because if triggering the glyph was enough to do anything on a Vol Karoth scale of effectiveness, Relos Var and Senera would have done it themselves and not waited for me."

Grizzst narrowed his eyes at me.

"Oh right. Turns out I actually did put some thought into it." I smiled. "You didn't believe my brother *at all*? Whatever gave you the idea his word might not be trustworthy?"

I'm honestly not sure why I wasn't angrier. I definitely had been earlier. I'd lost my temper many a time in similar situations. I think I was just . . . done. Done with all of it. Done with the betrayals and the lies and the many, many traps.

So sure, Grizzst had turned out to be working with Relos Var. Why not?

I didn't know what we were going to do about it, but I was reasonably sure that losing my temper at him wouldn't buy me into any game worth playing.

"How could you believe that helping Relos Var is the right thing to do?" Thurvishar was still shaking with anger and indignation. "How could you possibly be that stupid?"

This was a hell of a lot more personal for him than it was for me. I'd never known this jerk as anything more than a legend, but Thurvishar had history here. Or I guess Simillion did, but it was a bit like my relationship with Relos Var. The past lives were bleeding over.

"It's a long story, kid," Grizzst told Thurvishar. "The two of us had a deal. I'm honoring my side of it."

"What's it going to do?" I asked. "When they cast the Ritual of Night and charge up the crystal, what's going to happen?"

Grizzst cast a spell that pushed aside the muck and dirt of centuries and sat down on the pedestal of a gold horse. "Fuck," he said. "Isn't this just a fantastic clusterfuck of fun?"

"Nice to know we agree on some things, anyway."

"Gahan!" Thurvishar screamed. "What. The. Fuck?"

Grizzst looked over at Thurvishar and sighed. "You know how long I've been trying to deal with Vol Karoth. You know how long it took me to bring back the Eight."

"Then why are you working with the man who's trying to undo it all?" Thurvishar said. His expression was equal parts anguished and furious.

"What's it going to do?" I asked one more time.

"Well, I tell you what it's not going to do—it's not going to strip the immortality from the vané, that's what."

"Gahan!"

Grizzst sighed. "I swapped out the ritual a few centuries back. Instead of affecting the vané, this version taps each of the Eight—except for Vol Karoth, of course—a second time, weakens them a little, and sends that energy channeled through this one crystal back to the other seven. Except it'll be more tenyé than those wards were ever designed to handle, so it'll shatter each of them, all at once."

"That will free Vol Karoth," Thurvishar said. "Free him completely."

Grizzst pressed his lips together and nodded. "Mmm-hmm."

Thurvishar stared at him. "Why? Damn it, Gahan, I always knew you were self-destructive, but when did you decide to take the whole world with you?"

At that, Grizzst shook his head. "Oh, just the opposite, kid. You can't destroy Vol Karoth while he's imprisoned. We're safe from him, but he's also perfectly safe from us. Which is a problem, because we need Vol Karoth."

I tilted my head. "*Need* him? Vol Karoth's a mistake."

"Naw. He's exactly what Relos Var meant to make."

Thurvishar and I shared a glance. That perfectly mirrored my own theory about the ritual that had created Vol Karoth, but it was interesting to hear it coming from the mouth of the so-called greatest wizard in the world.

I chewed on my lip as if thinking something over. "So what's Vol Karoth supposed to do?" I asked Grizzst. "What was he made for?"

Grizzst looked annoyed. He made a face as he reached some sort of decision and stood. "I can't just kill you two."

"We're so relieved," Thurvishar said bitterly.

"Afraid we'll tell Thaena?" Even as I said the words, I was concentrating on the intaglio ring. It was possible that Grizzst had some sort of master control, in which case as soon as I used the ring, I'd give myself away, but I didn't think that was so. Sandus had made the rings and had given Grizzst one for the same reason he'd given Doc one: so they could keep in touch if needed. No one was wearing *Sandus's* ring—which meant no one could stop me from bouncing my message off it back to Doc.

*You need to stop them from performing the Ritual of Night. Do whatever it takes.*

*Kihrin, are you all right? What's going on?*

*It's a trap. The ritual's trapped. It's going to free Vol Karoth, not seal him away. Do not, under any circumstances, let them power the crystal.*

A moment of hesitation. *I'll do what I can.*

Grizzst chuckled and pointed a finger at me, like he was giving a point to a student in class. "Can't let you go back and warn your friends before they've completed their work either. So I might as well show you why I decided helping Relos Var was the lesser evil."

The wizard opened a gate into void.

# 95: The Hyena Queen

***(Teraeth's story)***

"Do you have any proof of any of this?" Doc said as he handed tea to the three women.

Valathea had insisted on the tea, right after a rather grumpy Khaeriel fixed Talea's ant bites.

Senera rubbed a hand over her face. "Do you seriously think we would have come up with a story this ridiculous and invaded the Manol with *three whole people* if it wasn't true?"

"Strange as this may seem coming from me, I believe them," Teraeth said. "Although I can't help but notice that your sigil didn't work."

Xivan scowled. "Yes, that is a problem." She rubbed at her throat where Valathea had closed the wound. Now that she'd put Urthaenriel away, she looked like a living, breathing woman again, but that just made the injuries all the more gruesome.

"I didn't say it *would* work," Senera protested. "I said it *might*. As happens, it didn't. We're going to have to think of something else."

"How does one evict a goddess?" Talea asked. "Oh, this tea is very good. Thank you."

"Of course, dear." Valathea sighed. "As much as we need to discuss our options, we really can't stay here. This is a bit of a mess, I'm afraid."

Teraeth thought she had a fine gift for understatement. Khaeriel might have had her feelings a bit hurt by being one of the first people taken out of the fight, but it was a sort of compliment; Senera had simply decided that she was the second most dangerous person there, with the most dangerous being Doc.

*He* was sitting off to the side, ruefully examining Chainbreaker's broken necklace. "I suppose it was only a matter of time before it lived up to the name. Although five hundred years is a pretty good run."

"We'll fix it," Valathea promised.

Khaeriel had passed on re-imprisoning Talon, at least for the moment, mostly because Talon had once again decided to behave unpredictably and hadn't run when she'd had the chance. She'd claimed, once again, to still be loyal to Khaeriel.

Teraeth was starting to admire Talon's ability to convince people she was too useful to destroy.

"Very well," Senera said. "I propose a temporary truce while we find and deal with Suless."

"You work for *Relos Var,*" Teraeth pointed out.

"That's exactly why I'm inclined to accept her offer," Khaeriel said.

Teraeth snorted. "What? Relos Var's the one who betrayed us at Atrine. Relos Var is the reason Vol Karoth is awake right now and literally the reason we're being forced to perform the Ritual of Night."

Khaeriel waved a hand. "Oh, surely you're mistaken about that."

"I'm really not, Your Majesty."

"Does it really matter whose side we're on?" Talea asked. "We all want to help Janel. Or at least none of us want Suless to get away."

Xivan considered the others. "Regardless of how you feel about that wizard, *we* are not here as your enemies."

An alarm bell began to sound from the front of the farm.

"You've had everyone evacuate?" Valathea asked Teraeth.

He nodded. "Everyone but a few watchers. So we can assume the worst."

The worst, of course, was that Suless hadn't just run off in Janel's body–she'd run off in Janel's body and then promptly sold out everyone to the authorities. Which apparently was exactly her style. They were less sure of what story she'd told them or if she even understood the nature of the current political climate, but Senera had reassured them that Suless would have no trouble coming up with an appropriately enraging story.

Besides those few lookouts, everyone else–Teraeth, Khaeriel, Valathea, Doc, Talon, Senera, Xivan, and Talea–had stayed because, unlike the workers, they couldn't be seen on the streets. Illusions could cover the whole group, but it seemed easier to remain, hash out their plans, and only vacate if their current location turned out to be known. No sense leaving a perfectly good safe house unless it proved necessary.

Unfortunately, it was proving necessary.

The three Quuros women had the additional difficulty that, although they weren't wanted, they most certainly were identifiable as trespassers. Additionally, none of them had any idea how quickly the vané would fix the damage to the barrier roses, so if they tried to use a gate to leave, there was every possibility they wouldn't be able to return. That made opening a gate and just leaving the Manol an impractical solution as well. If the timing didn't work out in their favor, the vané might very well find themselves stuck outside the Manol Jungle with no way to get back to the parliament building before deliberations commenced. In which case, Kelanis wouldn't *need* to kill them.

"Darling," Valathea said to Doc, "would you mind helping me with this one?"

Teraeth didn't see exactly what his father did, but the royal guards poured down the thoroughfares of the farm, they ran around, chased phantoms, and shouted a lot of orders about how "they" were getting away. One by one, they proceeded to fall to poisoned thorns created by Valathea or by holes in the platform that opened and then closed again quickly enough to trap the struggling soldiers in a wooden embrace. They didn't want to kill the soldiers if they could help it–that sort of thing would only be a strike against them by the time they came back to parliament. Valathea was spectacularly skilled at this.

Xivan turned to Senera. "Let's go after Khaeriel and Terindel first, you said. They're the biggest dangers, you said."

Senera scowled. "How was I supposed to know? The Name of All Things can't see past its own creation. That's millennia worth of blind spots. Nobody told me King Terindel's wife was the dangerous one."

Valathea beamed at her.

Teraeth sighed. "I hate to interrupt this analysis of why your attack strategies failed, but we can't stay here. More guards will be on their way, so as Valathea suggested, this safe house is officially no longer safe."

"So where do we go next?" Khaeriel seemed less than thrilled about the current course of events.

"I know how we can find a place to hide," Talon offered.

Teraeth said, "Does this plan entail you picking a person at random, following them home, murdering them, and then stealing their house?"

"Oh, so you've done this before. I knew I liked you."

"I might know a place," Valathea offered. She inclined her head toward Doc. "Lefoarnan's?"

Doc made a face. "It's been five hundred years. I'm sure they're not still–"

"No, no," Teraeth interrupted before he could stop himself. "Let's find someplace else." As soon as he said the words, he knew he'd given himself away. After all, why react so poorly at the thought of going to a place that didn't exist?

Valathea raised an eyebrow. "So it's still in operation."

"Lefoarnan's?" Khaeriel pursed her lips. "I hadn't thought of that. Risky, though. So many people are always coming and going." She paused. "I suppose we could wear masks."

Teraeth covered half his face with a hand. He had never wanted to not do a thing so badly in his entire life. "So this is what it feels like to be Kihrin. I've always wondered."

"Would someone mind explaining to the people who've never lived here?" Xivan asked mildly.

Talon was only too eager to be the person providing context. "Lefoarnan's is a velvet house."

"Oh, don't be silly, dear," Valathea scolded. "We don't have velvet houses in the Manol. Lefoarnan's is a sex club."

Senera's eyes narrowed. "You're joking."

"Oh. Oh, how I wish they were." Teraeth eyed his father. "I suppose if I never left my room, I might survive this with my sanity intact. Maybe."

The horrible part of it all was that Teraeth *loved* Lefoarnan's. He would have been thrilled at the opportunity to show Kihrin or Janel—or best still, Kihrin *and* Janel—the resort's many amenities. And here he was, going to Lefoarnan's with absolutely no one that he might otherwise enjoy being at Lefoarnan's *with*.

He sighed. At least this would keep him focused.

Lefoarnan's wasn't even really a sex club when one got right down to it. Yes, there definitely were parts of the resort where that was an easily accessible option, but other buildings were dedicated to elaborate baths (perhaps a bit of sex also occurred there), massage parlors (there as well), a spectacularly elaborate garden (yes, fine, there too), theaters (yes), dining venues, sports arenas, gaming rooms, music halls, and a museum. If one wanted, it was possible to spend quite a bit of time at Lefoarnan's without ever seeing anyone nude at all.

But seriously, what was the fun of that?

Teraeth would have been extremely grumpy about the whole thing, except he found himself too worried sick about Janel to care. Senera had used her Cornerstone and come back with the extremely unsettling information that Suless, and thus Janel, was now to be found at the palace.

She'd evidently run straight to King Kelanis.

"Oh, he's going to regret that," Talea said.

Teraeth, Senera, Talea, and Xivan had all gathered together in the common area of their suite to talk. Teraeth would have liked to have included Doc, Valathea, and Khaeriel, but they were preparing for the trial. They couldn't let anything distract them from the upcoming parliament hearing, which Teraeth understood, even if he didn't like it.

Teraeth didn't know where Talon had gone, but none of the others seemed particularly concerned, so he didn't ask.

"I don't care if he regrets it or not," Teraeth said. "I just want Janel back."

"We all want her back—" An odd look crossed Senera's features, and she looked around as if checking to see if anyone had noticed her do something embarrassing.[1] She shook her head. "You know, the sooner this is all over with, the sooner I can go home. I was ordered to help kill a god-queen, not rescue a Quuros revolutionary."

Teraeth's lips curled up as he watched her. Senera was, as he saw it, an interesting opportunity. He knew what she'd done at Atrine, and he knew who she worked for. He'd been quite serious about the idea that he couldn't trust her. But even with that said, he could still learn quite a bit from her.

And people hesitated when they thought they were being forced to make a move against friends. *He* wouldn't, but Senera might.[2]

They'd ended up setting up shop in a collection of cottages that Lefoarnan's kept on its sprawling estate, although in this case "cottages" meant a collection of hanging buildings linked together by delicate enclosed staircases and surrounded by artful arrays of flowers. All completely safe, but with spectacular views and the general assumption that the people staying there might well be too occupied with each other to enjoy the rest of Lefoarnan's pleasures. They'd been told they could stay as long as they liked–or at least as long as it took for the front desk clerk to realize they'd been paid in nothing more than Chainbreaker's illusions.

While technically there was nothing stopping Teraeth from donning an illusion and playing, he found himself remarkably disinclined to take advantage of the opportunity. Because the very real possibility of accidentally running into his father while both of them were cloaked in illusions and unable to recognize each other was the stuff of nightmares, tragedies, and the blackest comedies. Technically, the vané had no incest taboo. *Technically*. The reality was a different matter. And he was starting to feel nearly the same about Valathea. Khaeriel? Incredibly awkward, especially if Kihrin ever found out. Either Xivan or Talea were both lovely, but also clearly so involved with each other they had no interest in anyone else. Senera was a nonstarter. Talon had vanished; when Teraeth informed Khaeriel, he was informed she'd been sent on a mission, and he didn't need to know the details.[3]

"Kelanis doesn't know Suless like we do," Xivan pointed out. She was sitting on a wide couch with Talea's head in her lap, stroking the other woman's hair. The ant bites had long since been healed, and both women seemed to be enjoying their stay. "Is there any way we can sneak

1 Yes, Senera. You just admitted you might–*might*–like Janel.

2 I have my doubts.

3 Is it interesting or sad that Teraeth assumed he would run into one of his other conspirators while using the facilities? He has a low opinion of either Taja or her sense of humor.

into the palace? Although I'm not sure what we'd do even if that were possible, considering the sigil didn't work."

Senera glanced up from the table where she had spread out numerous papers, the Name of All Things, and all her drawing supplies. "It would have worked if Suless was a demon. We need to come up with a plan B."

"There's always plan C," Xivan said.

Talea made a face. "What's plan C again?"

"We kill Janel." Xivan didn't sound like she was joking.

Teraeth gave the idea serious consideration for a few seconds. Killing Janel might well work, in that Thaena could then Return her with Janel's soul and without Suless's. The problem was that he couldn't count on Thaena to do it. Now that Senera had explained how Janel had been consecrated (if unwillingly) to Suless at one point, Teraeth had a nasty suspicion that Suless would claim Janel as one of her angels. That was territory that even one of the Eight Immortals might hesitate to break, no matter how much Teraeth wished it otherwise. And Thaena might be too busy to get to Janel before Xaltorath did.

"No," he finally said. "Too many uncertainties. I'm for it if we have no other choice, but I'd rather we try to find a different solution."

Talea threw him a disappointed look, which Teraeth was certain involved his willingness to entertain the idea at all rather than his rejection of it.

"And anyway," Teraeth added, "after the assassination attempt on the king, security is so tight, I'm pretty sure they're giving full-body searches to the butterflies." He shifted in his seat, threw one leg over the arm of the chair. "I'll be damned if I'm giving up this easily."

"It's a real shame someone can't just go to the Afterlife and lead Janel back to her body," Talea said. "I mean, she can cross the Second Veil on her own, right? She'd be like—"

"Like a demon possessing a body." Teraeth raised himself up and turned to Senera. "I can go to the Afterlife—"

"You mean commit suicide," she corrected.

Teraeth rolled his eyes. "Yes, fine. But I can't navigate while I'm there. I don't have a way to orient my position in the Afterlife to Suless's location in the Living World, assuming I could even locate Janel." He chewed on his lip. "The Afterlife's a big place."

"What about what Relos Var did to me?" Xivan suggested.

Teraeth paused. "As I wasn't there, mind explaining?"

Senera's gaze turned contemplative as she began chewing on the back of her calligraphy brush. "The closest we can come to resurrecting someone right now—because of Thaena"—at this, she gave Teraeth a dirty look—"is set out a magical beacon a soul can home in on, then grab that soul and stuff it back into its native body. But since the body is dead, the link is . . . artificial. Weak. So you end up with someone like Xivan. No offense."

"None taken."

Teraeth swung both feet down, stood, and began to pace. He felt manic, full of energy. He desperately wanted to do something, and none of his usual outlets were available at the moment. "That might work. What form does this beacon take? How long does it take to work? What do you need to make it happen?"

"I can make it as a sigil," Senera said. "I have the necessary supplies already, and as for how long . . . it's different for everyone. Janel's physical body will need to be in relative proximity to the sigil for at least a few hours. If it were any other soul, I'd then need to do all sorts of things to pull it to this side of the Veil, but Talea's right. Janel can handle that part on her own."

"But we're right back to the problem of being unable to break into the palace," Xivan said. "We can't get close enough to her."

Teraeth started laughing. Of course. "The hearing," he said. "We can do it at the hearing."

Xivan frowned. "We can't be sure she'll attend."

"No." Senera pointed to Teraeth with her brush. "He's right. Suless thrives on discord, betrayal, and malice. A hearing like this? With a background of sibling murder, palace coups, and arguing for the fate of the entire vané people? Expecting Suless to stay away would be like asking Rebel to resist a juicy steak. There's no way she won't attend unless she's Kelanis's prisoner." She thought that over for a moment before shaking her head. "Which I doubt."

Teraeth tapped one foot on the ground, nervous energy leaking out. "This sigil, does it have to be carved or written on anything in particular?"

"Any material I can mark on will work. Normal paper is the easiest. I can complete all but one part of the sigil and then someone–me, you, someone else–only has to draw a single line before it will start calling. Then we wait."

"Good. Then that sounds like a plan."

"And if she doesn't show up for the hearing?" Talea asked.

Teraeth wished she wouldn't ask questions when she already knew perfectly well what the answer was. "Then we go to plan C."

# 96: The Wound in the World

***(Kihrin's story)***

I followed the wizard. I didn't really feel like it was optional, and I wasn't eager to see what he could probably do to enforce our cooperation. If he'd meant to kill us . . .

Well, he was Grizzst. If he meant to kill us, we'd be dead. And that whole business about Thaena was cute and all, but I was well aware there were ways to "kill" a person that didn't send their soul to the Afterlife.

I forgot all of that the moment we stepped through the gate.

Grizzst had summoned up another one of his rainbow fields of energy, much like the field surrounding the Arena back in the Capital. "Don't leave the circle," he told us. "You wouldn't last more than a second or two."

All around us was . . . ice.

That doesn't really do the scene justice.

Imagine a world covered in ice, but where what little light met the surface was red, so everything looked like it had been crafted from glaciers of blood. The smell of cold was crisp and so sharp as to be physically painful, a sign of a cold so deep, it was outside anything I had ever experienced before. This was the cold of lands that had never seen a spring, would never know the sun's warmth, had never, ever thawed. These were lands that would take all the warmth they could steal from every living thing and leave behind only tombs and snow.

And ahead of us in this land of immense and ponderous red winter, lay a chasm.

I had no idea how deep it was. It was a crack splitting the land, and as I watched, pieces of that land–bits of glacier, boulder, bedrock–broke away and fell down into that giant ravine.

"It's *the* Chasm," Thurvishar said. His eyes were wide with horror.

I blinked at him, then looked back at the scene. I realized it did look like the Chasm–a huge fissure that split the Afterlife and that seemed to be slowly advancing, expanding . . .

"This is the Nythrawl Wound," Grizzst explained. He grimaced and wiped at his mouth. "It's the point where the demons broke into the Living World from the Afterlife, just like the Chasm in the Afterlife is the point where they broke into our universe from theirs." He glanced back at us. "It's growing, you see. And it's never going to stop."

I felt a dull ache deep inside me. "It's stealing heat."

"Oh, not just heat. Everything. Energy of all kinds. Matter too. That other universe is apparently a cold one, and this is a rip in the very fabric of reality. Our universe is slowly falling into theirs." Grizzst shook his head. "Not even the demons want to live in their universe. I'm not sure anything can."

"When did this start?" Thurvishar turned back to Grizzst, tearing his gaze away from the Wound.

"As soon as the demons arrived," Grizzst said. "We just didn't understand the danger. And even later on, we thought the demons were the problem and not just a symptom. We thought that even when this"–he gestured toward the Wound–"got so bad, it forced us all to desert Nythrawl and go to the other continents. We fought the demons, tried to do something about them, fucked that up good. All the while, this disaster has been growing and will keep growing until it probably destroys the whole damn universe. Although we'll be long gone by the time that happens."

I felt the cold even through his magical barrier. The red light gave everything a horrible cast that seemed to highlight the danger of his warning.

I took a deep breath, regretted it immediately as the cold stabbed daggers into my lungs. "And Vol Karoth?"

"Relos Var eventually explained it to me. It's messed up, but . . ." The wizard shrugged. "Practical. Very practical. We're pretty sure the Wound can only be closed from the other side, and it's going to require an enormous amount of energy to do it. So Var had to create something capable of holding that much energy. Something capable of the kind of precision control necessary to use it the right way."

I closed my eyes and felt sick.

"I bet it never occurred to the fucking bastard to just ask me to help."

Grizzst snorted. "Would you have said yes?"

I rolled my eyes at him. "We'll never know, will we?"

"And I assume Vol Karoth would stay on the other side of the Wound once it's closed," Thurvishar said.

Our eyes met. I could tell he was every bit as horrified as I was.

"Yeah, that's the plan. A plan that can't move forward until he's fucking well freed, can it?"

Thurvishar shouted, "Are you kidding me? It's a stupid plan!"

I heard a noise off in the distance, something other than the grinding of ice calving off the glaciers and falling down into the Wound. I tried to listen to it, to understand it, took a step in that direction.

I stopped myself as I realized what I was hearing: a droning sound, almost like a croon.

"We need to leave right now," I said.

I could feel the pull of it. And I damn well knew that could only mean one thing.

Unfortunately, this time, I had far less warning than back in the Blight.

Vol Karoth appeared just outside Grizzst's field.

The barrier must have provided some protection, which is the only reason I can come up with for why Grizzst didn't die instantly. Time stretched out. I could feel Vol Karoth's mind trying to sync with mine.

*Come back. Join me.*

Grizzst started moving his fingers, no doubt the beginning of a gate spell we could use to escape, but I knew he'd never complete it in time.

I stepped in front of Grizzst and pressed my hand against the wall of energy. It felt like pressing my hand against a wall of ice, but I *wanted* to push through into what lay beyond. I *wanted* to do exactly what Vol Karoth asked and go to him.

I resisted that urge with everything in me.

"Go back home!" I screamed. "I'm *busy*!"

I felt the time differences between us insert themselves. There was a beat of hesitation from Vol Karoth, a pause. *Confusion.*

He vanished.

All was quiet, save for the sound of our breathing and the cracking of the world falling away into nothing. All three of us just stood there like we'd never seen the end of the world before.

"Did you just send Vol Karoth to his room like he was a gods-damn four-year-old?" Grizzst asked.

"Uh . . ." I was speechless.

"Yes," Thurvishar answered. "Definitely yes. He did that, yes."

"Right," Grizzst said. "That's what I thought too."

I stared out at the rest of frozen Nythrawl, but all I could think about was the words of the Old Man, Sharanakal, so many years before: *You are Vol Karoth's Cornerstone.*

I was increasingly convinced that he hadn't been speaking in metaphor.

Grizzst shook his head as he finished casting the spell. "Come on, you two. Evidently, we really do need to talk."

# 97: The Law of Daynos

***(Teraeth's story)***

The first day of the hearing, the entire group gathered together and finally left the resort. Teraeth had to admit he enjoyed the looks on everyone's faces when the whole party just materialized, seemingly teleporting to the location in exactly the way no one typically could. Unfortunately, that was the only reason he had to smile. After two weeks of cajoling, threatening, bribing, and in several cases, killing, Khaeriel had been forced to admit an uncomfortable truth:

They didn't have enough votes.

"You know it is possible that I might actually sway people, don't you?" Valathea said. "Isn't that the entire reason you restored me?"

Khaeriel's nostrils flared. "I wanted to be certain."

"Nothing in life is, my dear."

Khaeriel scowled in reply and said nothing more. Teraeth couldn't help but feel some sympathy. She had to be under pressures that he could only pretend to understand. If the day turned out well for her–

If the day turned out well for her, Khaeriel might still be dead by the end of it. If she succeeded in winning back the throne, her reward would be her own death enacting the Ritual of Night.

So with those cheerful thoughts in mind, Teraeth himself, along with Xivan, Talea, and Senera, was relegated to the upper-level viewing stands. They were unsurprisingly packed to capacity.

The outcome of this decision would have major ramifications for the entire nation, and everyone knew it. They just didn't know *how* major.

Everyone stood as the king and queen entered, but Teraeth's eyes were for exactly one person, who followed close behind the royal couple: Janel.

She wore a revealing gown of icy-blue silk. It was the sort of thing that Janel would never, ever normally wear simply because it was so impractical for fighting, never mind the color. White crystals studded the hem of the gown, sparkling in the hall's light. They'd put something in her hair to change its normal red sheen to blue and threaded it with silver. Gems–almost certainly diamonds–sparkled from around her neck.

He felt Xivan shift next to him, and he reached out and put out a hand. "Not yet. We have a plan. Follow the plan."

She ground her teeth and sat down again. "She's right *there.*"

"She's right there being protected by the finest archers in the world," Teraeth pointed out, "and believe me when I say that lovely sword you're wearing won't do much good against vané arrows."

"What's the queen's problem with–" Talea stopped and then exhaled. "What's their queen's problem with *our* queen." She pointed down to where Queen Miyane was staring swords, knives, and every kind of deadly weapon at Queen Khaeriel before ignoring her completely and sitting down by Kelanis's side.

"Oh," Teraeth said. "They used to be married."[1]

Talea glanced sideways. "Really?"

"Shh, it's starting."

Daynos came to the center of the room. Teraeth saw Valathea and a number of other Founders waiting in the wings, but it was really only Valathea he was interested in. She held a small group of papers together. One of those pieces of paper included a very, very small sigil drawn in the corner. It was easy. Literally all Valathea had to do was her normal job. She'd be close enough to Janel that the sigil would be within the required distance all day long–more than enough time for the beacon to do its work. Next to Valathea, Teraeth's father suddenly drew in his breath sharply, his eyes unfocused and distant. He put his hand on his wife's arm, pulled her to the side, and whispered something to her.

Teraeth frowned. Doc looked upset, and by the time he was done talking to his wife, Valathea looked even more upset. She shook her head as if to deny or refute something.

Daynos began to speak. "Together we have assembled to contemplate the ways of our people and the rules of our nation. Given the scope, complexity, and ramifications of today's decision, all Founders have joined us–"

"That's not true," Doc called out. His voice easily carried to every corner of the hall.

Arguably, it shouldn't have. The Assembly hall was designed to acoustically carry voices in the center to all the onlooker seats and muffle noises made in those same seats. Magic helped seal the effect.

His voice *still* carried to every corner.

[1] That's a grotesque oversimplification of the situation. Not only had they previously been married (a marriage, I must point out, that would return to being legally valid if Khaeriel succeeded in overturning the Law of Daynos), but Khaeriel is currently in Miyane's sister's body, thanks to the soul-swap that occurred when Khaeriel was assassinated, turning that marriage unintentionally incestuous. Messy.

A clamor broke out immediately.

Teraeth rose to his feet along with everyone else. "What is he doing?" Teraeth said. "This *wasn't* part of the plan."

"Quiet!" Daynos said. He turned to Doc. "Terindel, you have not been given permission to speak."

Doc shrugged. "It's still not true. You don't have all the Founders here. May I come to the center?"

Daynos gave the man a mighty frowning, before nodding once.

Doc hopped over the low barrier and walked to the middle of the room. As he arrived, he was suddenly holding a small bag that he hadn't been holding a moment before. Without prelude or explanation, he upended the contents of the bag on one of the tables.

Gemstones bounced against the carved wood. At least a hundred, possibly more, all glittering with blue or violet flashes of color.

Every single one of them was a star tear diamond.

It took a moment for Teraeth to understand. The number of star tears that had just spilled out on that table was worth so much money, it beggared all understanding. *Priceless* was the only descriptor with any meaning. But in the context Doc had presented here—as though these star tears were themselves somehow missing Founders . . .

Teraeth felt his gut twist. He'd grown up on stories of his father and his many crimes—the worst of which by far was the fearfully whispered story that Terindel had slain the entire Kirpis vané court when he'd usurped the throne from his brother.[2] Rather than allow those souls to pass on, he'd cruelly kept them as tsalis, hidden away forever. Teraeth had always dismissed this tale as too sensational to possibly be true.

And yet . . .

"The Star Court," Doc said. "The tsali stones containing the souls of one hundred and fifty Founders. Do with them what you will, but I assume you'll want to take them to the Well of Spirals before we begin to hear arguments."

He walked out of the hall.

Teraeth said, "Now that's a complication."

Xivan started heading for the doors well before the rest of the crowd realized nothing else interesting was going to happen that day and they should probably all go home. And Teraeth almost thought that she was simply ahead of the game before the expression on her face registered.

No, that's not what was happening here.

2 Please note that it was Kelindel who usurped Terindel's throne, not the other way around, and it happened some time after the Star Court incident. It does appear that Terindel murdered his entire court, however.

Xivan was going to plan C.

"Damn it," Teraeth cursed and sprang up from the bench to chase after her. He practically leaped over two rows in his haste to reach the door before she did. Xivan paused, her expression murderous.

"We have a plan," he repeated.

"The plan failed," Xivan spat. "Your father just tore the plan into little, tiny pieces and scattered them all over the parliament hall floor."

"We can wait a day!" Teraeth said. He saw a flash of confusion cross her features and raised a hand. "Do you even understand what just happened back there?"

Senera and Talea caught up to them.

"Everyone seems to think Terindel just screwed himself over, as near as I can tell," Senera said. "He's apparently infamous for having murdered his entire royal court and trapping their souls. Why he would think restoring them is a good idea is frankly beyond me. They're not going to vote in his favor."

Teraeth drew himself up. "We'll ask him. I know my father well enough to know that he wouldn't do something like this to make our situation *worse*. He must have some kind of plan."

"Get out of my way," Xivan growled. "She's going to be leaving any second now."

"Xivan, wait until they reconvene," Teraeth said. "This isn't your only chance. You think I don't want the woman I love back?"

Xivan paused and studied him for a moment, confused. "But I thought Kihrin–"

"Whatever. The woman Kihrin and I *both* love."

She looked past him toward the door, looking like all her hopes and desires lay just on the other side of it. Then she seemed to deflate. "Fine."

Teraeth studied her a second, decided that she truly seemed to be serious about allowing matters to lie for the moment, and then opened the door for them both.

Janel–no, Suless–stood on the other side of the door with two dozen archers behind her.

"I didn't think you lot were ever going to leave."

Teraeth felt a moment's flash of both panic and exhilaration. She was *here*. Suless had come to them. He almost glanced at Senera, but then looked away quickly. He could only hope she had the same thought he did, because he had no way to communicate it to her without giving the whole thing away.

Xivan's eyes went wide, and she started reaching for her sword. Talea followed suit, while Senera looked around as if to check for witnesses.

"Stand down!" Teraeth ordered. "Right now!"

Suless watched Xivan's reaction and just smirked. "I thought you and I might have a little talk, Xivan."

"The only conversation I want to have with you involves this blade," Xivan spat.

Suless didn't seem to take it personally. "Oh, I don't think that's true." She reached down the cleavage of her dress and pulled out a small star tear diamond. "Or you might not recover this."

"Xivan," Senera warned. "We need to go back inside. Right now."[3] She clasped an art journal to her chest as though it might somehow prove a shield.

Behind them, a number of vané started to use that exit, saw the soldiers, and then decided that perhaps the lines elsewhere were shorter. Senera let the door close behind her, where it banged shut with an ominously loud noise.

"Those star tears suddenly aren't so rare anymore," Teraeth said. "You can't possibly think Xivan can be bribed?"

The woman who was not, *not* Janel flashed a feral grin at him. "Oh no. Just like the souls that your father just dumped out on the table in there, *this* is a tsali. Turns out that Xivan's dear husband, Azhen Kaen, is an old soul. I know, you're wondering how I brought him with me. Trust me, it was easy enough if you're as good at magic as I am."

Talea did put her arms out to keep Xivan from moving forward.

"With it, you could restore your husband," Suless explained. "He'd be no more truly alive than you are, but there's a sort of symmetry to that, I suppose. All for the quite reasonable price of you and your friends walking away from here and never bothering me again." Suless paused. "Oh, my apologies. I guess I do think Xivan can be bribed."

The hallway wasn't quiet. Teraeth could hear the sound of the archers' bowstrings creaking, the murmur of the vané crowds leaving the parliament building and debating what had just happened and its significance. No doubt a great many stories were being told to younger vané about exactly what the Star Court was and how it had come to be.

But no one in *this* hallway said a word.

"You should leave," Talea said to Suless, "while you still can."

Suless gave the warrior a disgusted look. "I remember you. You're nobody." She smiled. "Oh wait, that's not true, is it? You're like Senera's puppy. Except Xivan's the one who holds your leash. Do you think little Rebel's going to make any great difference in the world? No. She's there to look pretty and wag her tail when she's pet."

Talea raised her chin. "I don't like you."

[3] A reasonable reaction. The soldiers were not cleared to follow them inside.

Suless scoffed. "I'll somehow find a way to live with myself." She looked past Talea to Senera. "Ready to come back to me, daughter? You're one of mine, after all."

"Fuck you," Senera said.

Suless shrugged and turned back to Xivan. "Last chance before I send your husband's soul into the void, where he will spend eternity screaming."

Xivan's expression was set in stone. "You're a fool to think I would agree to anything you want."

"Ah, but this is far more about what *you* want," Suless crooned. "Don't you want your husband back? Or do you not care now that you've found your cute little piece of tail here."

Xivan seemed to take a moment to collect herself. "You currently hold a great many things that do not belong to you," Xivan finally said, "and none of those thefts are crimes I can or will forgive."

"This could have been easy," Suless said. "But you of all people should know just how nasty I can be when provoked. Nothing is beyond my hate." She reached behind her, and this time when her hand came up, she held Teraeth's arrowhead necklace.

Teraeth forced himself not to react.

"So who gave this to my daughter Janel, I wonder?" Suless let the necklace swing on her finger. "It's not her normal style, and it seems to me to be the sort of thing that has sentimental rather than material value." She ran a finger over one of the beads. "Someone's been using it as a talisman. I wonder if I used it as a focus for *my* magic, who will feel the pain?" She grinned that feral, nasty smile at Teraeth.

Teraeth met her gaze calmly. He *had* been using it as a talisman, which meant Suless knew perfectly well who it belonged to; their auras matched. And this wasn't anything that Suless needed to do. It didn't support her cause. Suless had no reason to think Teraeth was anyone important to Xivan. Suless was doing this for precisely one reason: because she could.

"It's not a gaesh," he said. "You can use it to hurt me, but you can't control me."

"But what if I only want to hurt you?" Suless closed her fist around the arrow.

He felt the pain like she'd shoved it straight into his heart. Teraeth inhaled sharply and ground his teeth. Then it increased. He made fists at his sides and stood there, while the pain rolled through him like waves crashing against the shore. "Is that all you have?" he said, forcing a strained laugh through his throat. "That tickles."

Suless growled at him and closed her hand so tight around the arrow, blood dripped down from her closed fist. The pain flashed purple and red at the periphery of his vision, so great now that he was starting to lose sensation as nerve endings decided to simply quit working.

Then, abruptly, the pain stopped.

He almost collapsed but caught himself, only staggering slightly instead.

Suless had an indecipherable expression on her face. She looked around as if expecting someone to arrive any minute. "Don't say I never showed you mercy." Suless walked away first, with the archers covering her retreat.

When she was gone, they all remembered how to breathe again.

Senera slapped Teraeth's arm. "Idiot! She would have killed you."

"I was buying you time," he told her through clenched teeth. "Tell me you redrew the sigil."

She rolled her eyes and turned the journal around so he could see the marks on the page. "I didn't have to. I made a second one while we were waiting for everything to start."

"It didn't work," Talea said, sounding heartbroken. "Damn it. It didn't work!"

"We may not have given it enough time," Xivan said. "She wasn't here for very long."

Teraeth couldn't fault her reasoning. "Nice job on the acting, by the way."

"Acting?" Xivan raised an eyebrow at him.

He paused. No, it probably hadn't been acting at all. "Never mind."

Senera raised an eyebrow at him as she passed. "You know, for someone who claims he just follows orders, you give them pretty well."

He scowled. "We're just starting to get along, Senera. There's no reason to be nasty. Let's catch up with the others. I want to have some words with my father."

The others hadn't waited for them, which meant it had taken Teraeth and Senera working together to sneak their way back past any patrols. When they finally returned, they arrived to chaos and fury, to put it lightly.

"What. Was. That?" Khaeriel was asking. "The Star Court is real? *You had it this whole time?*"

Doc paused as Teraeth, Xivan, Senera, and Talea entered the room. Teraeth had the feeling that his father immediately changed whatever answer he had been about to give. He also suspected his father would have preferred to speak with Khaeriel in private, but Khaeriel clearly hadn't seemed inclined to wait that long. He was honestly surprised his father didn't force a private setting using Chainbreaker.

Then Teraeth realized there was no way to know if he had.

"I found you the votes, Khaeriel," Doc said. "I thought that's what you wanted."

"Found me the votes?" Her mouth dropped open in outrage. "One hundred and fifty people that you murdered aren't going to vote to overturn the Law of Daynos!"

"They will. Now, we both agreed to this plan, Khaeriel. I'm not stopping now, so don't mess with the plan." Doc crossed his arms over his chest in a way that suggested there would be no more said on the matter.

Teraeth frowned. There was no reason for Doc to have kept this a secret, no reason for him to have pulled a last-minute improvisation. So why had he?

"Excuse me?" Talea held up a hand. "If those are tsali stones, why do they look like star tears?"

Valathea turned in her direction. "Oh, that's because they are star tears. Any star tear you've ever seen either currently holds or once held the souls of one of this world's original settlers. The first generation who were born . . . somewhere else. My tsali stone would look very similar."

Talea made a small, "Oh."

Khaeriel rubbed her eyes, clearly still upset. "Can you be sure they'll vote in our interests?"

"I'm more sure of them than I am of anyone else," Doc admitted.

"Why?" Teraeth asked. "Every story about the Star Court says you murdered the lot of them. Why would you think they'd vote for you?"

Doc gave him an irritated glance. "They'll do what I ask. That's all you need to know."

Teraeth shook his head. "You screwed up our chance to get Janel back with your little stunt back there. We deserve—"

"No," Doc said. "You don't *deserve* anything. I'm sorry about Janel, but I have every faith you'll find a way. This is more important than one person."

He vanished.

"Son of a bitch," Xivan muttered.

"I see my husband's going to be very difficult to pin down when he doesn't feel like having an argument. I'm as surprised by this as any of you. I'll talk to him." Without waiting for anyone to respond, Valathea swept out of the room.

Teraeth turned to Khaeriel, but she simply raised a hand, shook her head, and left.

The room fell silent. "Fuck!" Teraeth finally screamed in pure aggravation.

Senera sat down in one of the chairs and turned the page in the art book. "I don't know, Teraeth. I'm not entirely sure he did ruin our chance to recover Janel."

He turned on her. "Oh? Is she here and I just missed it?" He turned and looked around. "Funny, I don't see her here anywhere."

She kicked up her feet. "Yes, I understand you're frustrated, in every possible sense of the term, but you did notice Suless's expression when she left, didn't you?"

Teraeth stopped. "What do you mean?"

Senera looked up at him from whatever sketch she'd started. "I mean, maybe you convinced her to stay close to us for long enough. When Suless left, she looked like she'd seen a ghost."

# 98: No Trust for Wizards

***(Kihrin's story)***

Grizzst broke out the booze immediately.

"Why visit all the brothels if you have this much alcohol here already?" Thurvishar asked.

We'd gone downstairs into the workshop, partly because there was no room up in the library, but mostly because Thurvishar had insisted. I saw his point; there was too much chance of spilling something on important papers, and nobody wanted to see Thurvishar lose his temper about that. Personally, I had zero interest in getting drunk but a lot of interest in plying Grizzst with enough alcohol to get him to tell us something useful.

Like how to stop Relos Var's plans.

Grizzst paused in the middle of pouring several fingers of brandy. "Are you joking? Brothels are great." He handed me a rather large glass, which I turned into something nonalcoholic as soon as his back was turned.

Don't get me wrong; I wanted a drink. After that encounter with Vol Karoth? Oh yeah. But fate of the whole world and all that. This didn't seem like the time.

I set the drink down and put my head in my hands.

"I always wondered why the weather patterns were wrong," Thurvishar said.

I pulled my head up and stared at him. "What are you babbling about?"

He made a vague gesture. "The currents are all wrong. Nythrawl's throwing it all off. Never mind. It's not really important right now."[1]

I spun around on the bench to face Grizzst, who seemed to have forgotten that he was keeping us prisoner and was making a

[1] The weather patterns in eastern Quur (what I suppose is more accurately western Quur if one remembers that Quur is actually on the southern continent) are quite wrong from what I feel they should be, and it all makes sense if there's a cold current happening in the wrong place because of Nythrawl.

really excellent attempt at finishing off the bottle he'd opened. "Can Urthaenriel be used to control Vol Karoth? Is that what you did the first time?"

His glassy gold eyes focused on me. "Yes. Yes, that's it exactly. I used the sword to keep him in place so the Assembly could do the ritual the first time."

"Right." The room fell into silence again for a few minutes. "I didn't think his influence was quite that"–I spread my hands–"large."

"You know, if I had a coin for every time a woman's said that to me . . . ," Grizzst mused.

Thurvishar and I both stopped, turned to stare at him, and then turned back to each other.[2]

"We may have to admit the possibility that Vol Karoth hasn't been appearing outside the Blight because he simply hasn't cared to," Thurvishar said.[3]

"Oh, that's just . . . terrifying." I picked up my glass and took another sip. "You know, this is pretty good." I'd only changed the alcohol, not the taste.

"Should be," Grizzst said. "It's old enough to be your grandfather." The wizard pulled the circlet off his head, slammed the wand down on the table next to him. "Let's go back to the part where you gave Vol Karoth an order and he fucking obeyed it."

I glared at him. "Did you not bother to find out just who you were setting up to be raised in that brothel? I'm Relos Var's *brother,* remember? What did you think that meant?"

"I didn't think it meant . . . that." The wizard looked deep in thought. "I'm trying to decide if this is a good thing or not."

"If you figure it out, let me know."

Thurvishar sighed and walked over to Grizzst, then heaved himself up onto the worktable itself and sat down on it. "Gahan, Gahan, Gahan. Damn it, Gahan. What are you doing? You're going to let the last immortal race be cast down and lose all that accumulated knowledge for what? So you can free Vol Karoth? There are better ways. Ways that don't . . . My grandfather's an idiot."

"Relos Var is very much not an idiot." Grizzst scoffed. "And weren't you listening? I told you that isn't what the ritual is going to do. The vané people will be fine. I changed the ritual so it will actually do something instead. Nobody is going to lose their immortality."

"If there is one thing I know about Relos Var," Thurvishar said, "it's

[2] It's really best not to encourage Grizzst sometimes.

[3] Had I known some mysterious entity was destroying demons who stayed in one place for too long, I'd have made this statement with more confidence.

that whatever deal you think you're getting from him will always turn out to be a lie. And I don't feel like playing along with his games. Aren't you tired of letting that bastard set the rules?"

Grizzst shook his head. "I wish it were that easy. Nothing moves forward without Vol Karoth being freed. And the Eight–oh, how I do regret that bit of genius on my part–the Eight will never allow that. They're going to fight to the last inch to keep that from happening."

"Well, sure, because millions of people will die," I pointed out.

"Because they're scared. And if we don't do this, everyone dies!" Grizzst slammed his hand against the table.

Thurvishar put out his hand to stop the wand from rolling off the edge. "No, if you don't do this, we'll have to find another way. It's a false dichotomy to claim that your way is the only other option." He spread his arms. "The universe is not black and white."

Grizzst narrowed his eyes. "You're not nearly drunk enough if you can say dichoto . . . diko . . ." He made a face. "What you said."

"Oh, I'm quite drunk," Thurvishar said. "You'll just have to take my word for it."

"Look–" Grizzst looked to the side, chewed on the inside of his mouth, and grumbled a few curse words. "If I had another way, I'd take it. But breaking that prison requires a tremendous amount of tenyé, and I don't have it. I don't have a convenient religion I can direct at the issue. The Eight can do it, but won't, so I'm tricking them into doing it, anyway. If C'indrol had bothered explaining how their damn theories actually worked, I might have been able to fix up something, but everything I've ever learned from their notes I've had to reverse engineer. Pisses me off. Fucking Rev'arric."

I straightened. "What was that?"

"I said I need a way to create enough energy–"

"No." I moved to a closer bench. "You said the name C'indrol. Did you know a lot of people named that? Was that a common voras name?"

Grizzst scowled. "Probably among any members of the Indrol family, I imagine. They were researchers, specialized in ousology–souls and energy transfer between the Twin Worlds. Unfortunately, since they lived in Karolaen, they died during the great cataclysm. I found some of their notes, but–" He shook his head. "You find any more, let me know. I'll tip you extra."

"What if I just brought you C'indrol?"

Grizzst stared at me in disbelief. "C'indrol's dead. Very dead."

"C'indrol was *reincarnated*. And we know her. If you're saying that C'indrol might know how to pull together enough energy without having to sacrifice an entire race's immortality, then why don't we ask who she is now, in this life?"

He stared at me for a long beat, then shook his head as if to clear the fog. "Wait. Okay. Even if that were true–which I will allow is possible–she wouldn't remember that past life, and no one–not me, not Rev'arric, not any of the Eight–have figured out how to soul imprint past lives once someone has been reincarnated, reborn from birth, and not just resurrected."

Thurvishar straightened. "That's not true."

"Who would have thought Gadrith was such a prodigy?" I told Thurvishar. "But even without Gadrith, C'indrol definitely knew how. I mean, I'm pretty sure they're the reason I'm remembering being S'arric. Same with Teraeth."

Grizzst just stared at both of us. "You're joking, right? This is a joke? You can't be–" He rubbed his forehead.

I held out my hands. "Seems to me that my brother's way isn't the only way, and if you insist on pretending it is . . ."

"What are you going to do, Gahan?" Thurvishar said. "Keep with Relos Var's plan, which will kill thousands, if not millions? Or try something new?"

"Seems to me that if our way doesn't work," I commented, "there are other sources of tenyé in the universe to charge that crystal. Why not try our way first, before you default to worst-case solutions?"

Grizzst ran both hands through his hair. "I shouldn't have started drinking."

"Sober yourself up," Thurvishar said, "if that will help. But you know we're right."

Grizzst rubbed his eyes. "Yeah, I do." He stood. "Come on, then. Let's go disable my little toy before the vané complete that ritual and set Vol Karoth free."

So we returned to the bottom of Lake Jorat.

As we stepped out of the magical gate and found ourselves once more swimming in a whole lot of water, Grizzst made a gesture, and a lever behind one of the statues flipped. There was a terrific boom, and giant metal walls slowly began to rise out of the ground around the throne area. Once they reached a height of forty feet or so, each side began to iris out a metal ceiling, which fit together in the center. Water drained out of the room.

I turned to Grizzst. "That was here *the whole time*?"

He shrugged. "I've spent a lot of time here over the centuries. You think I wanted to work on the warding crystal while underwater? No, thank you."

"I wish I'd known about it, that's all." I sat down on one of the stairs that were almost clean from the last visit to this same spot.

"I assume you know how to disable that safely," Thurvishar said.

"It'll be a tiny bit tricky," Grizzst admitted, "since I've spelled the fuck out of it. I'm not saying this thing is any Urthaenriel, but I wouldn't try to destroy it using your typical magic spell, that's all." He climbed up on top of the throne and started looking at the crystal.

I looked over at Thurvishar. I suspected we were having the same thought: that if Grizzst wanted to lie to us and tell us that the crystal had been turned off, we weren't terribly likely to have a way of verifying it. At least not without breaking the crystal.

Thurvishar moved his robe sleeve and showed me where he'd been hiding the wand Grizzst had left on the table. I looked away quickly. Surely, if anything qualified as "not your typical magical spell," it would be that.

We didn't say anything, just watched the man work. After a bit, Grizzst stepped back and nodded to himself. "That's the first bit. Sorry, kids, but we're going to be here for a little while. Just make yourself comfortable."

"Or better still, don't." Relos Var walked through one of the walls and closed the opening behind him.

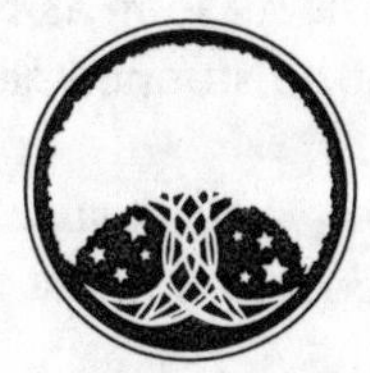

# 99: The Rules of the Game

***(Teraeth's story)***

As predicted, it didn't take long at all for the Star Court to be given new bodies, or rather, copies of their old ones. Teraeth had never heard of any tsalis that old being recovered before. Tsalis leaked tenyé as they aged. After no more than a few centuries there wasn't enough left to maintain the soul itself. It was a horrible and painfully slow way to end one's existence, which is why tsalis were either returned to the Well of Spirals or destroyed, allowing the souls in question to return to the Afterlife, the Land of Peace, and eventual reincarnation.

Except these tsalis–and even Teraeth hadn't understood that star tears were a very specific kind of tsali[1]–hadn't suffered any deterioration whatsoever. Nor had any perception of time passed for them.

It must have been one hell of an attack of culture shock. One minute, most of the Kirpis vané now being reintroduced into the world had been the privileged elite of one of the greatest nations in the world. The next, they had woken to find the Kirpis had been lost, the man who'd ordered their execution was no longer either king or Kirpis, and they were now permanently sharing a country with the same upstart children who had once fled their nation in protest.

Teraeth found himself extremely glad most people didn't know he'd been Atrin Kandor in a previous life.

When King Kelanis arrived that day, Teraeth couldn't help but notice Suless stood by his side, wearing Teraeth's arrowhead necklace around her neck. Queen Miyane was there, but impossibly seemed to be acting as Suless's lady-in-waiting.

"Oh, Suless moved fast," Talea said.

Senera scoffed. "I'm shocked Miyane isn't either in a jail cell or no longer in the Living World. Suless is very good at inciting paranoia."

"That might still happen," Teraeth said. "Her sister was a Black

[1] It can be assumed that Thaena was aware, however. For this reason, I believe it's likely–even certain–that whichever souls had once been in Kihrin's star tear necklace have long since been sent on to the Afterlife. Vacated star tears still have extraordinary magical uses.

Brotherhood assassin, after all. As soon as Kelanis decided not to honor his promise to Thaena, I bet he stopped sleeping in the same room as his wife."

"Valathea still has the sigil, doesn't she?" Xivan leaned forward, put her elbows on her knees. She looked like a wolf eyeing its prey.

"She does," Teraeth said.

"Good."

Valathea stood and walked forward where the judge sat.

"Hear my words, for I will tell no lies," Valathea said, bowing. "The Law of Daynos is an obsolete hanger-on of a system that no longer has any meaning in our world. This well-intentioned but impractical law seemed like wisdom when the idea of souls was new to us, when we were still coming to grips with magic and what magic meant to us as a culture and people. Now we know that souls are not intangible, not fugitive–and not diminished, not even by death. Why would we insist that someone who has the same souls, the same personality, the same strength of character should be denied the privilege and benefits of their own identity? The time has come for us to acknowledge that we are ready to move beyond a law that claims we are only as important as the flesh and blood of our birth. Thank you."

She sat back down in her chair.

Daynos gave her a single nod and then stood himself. He flexed his shoulders, held his hands out. "Hear my words, for I will tell no lies," Daynos said. "We vané have never been much for rules. Our laws are few, but because they are few, we are obligated to be scrupulous in their execution. The Law of Daynos protects us from anarchy, for as you know, there is nothing to stop us from resurrecting a long-dead ruler and insisting their claim more legitimate than that of the monarch on the throne. Were someone to resurrect Queen Terrin, none of us could deny her obvious merit, but should someone who has been dead for over four thousand years be allowed to simply reclaim her throne and rule us once more? The Law of Daynos allows us to have orderly successions and inheritance, and more so, it protects those who are resurrected or reborn from being held responsible for the crimes of previous lives. The slate of our lives is wiped free so that we may begin again. This is a system that we have used for thousands of years. To change it now for the sake of expediency undermines everything we represent. Thank you."

The judge, Megrea, nodded and waved to Valathea. "You may discuss the matter."

"Thank you," Valathea said as she stood. She walked over to the center, facing Daynos, who stood as well. "You say the Law of Daynos protects us from anarchy, but I say that we already are inconsistent and mercurial in its application. Have I not broken the Law of Daynos?

Have not the Founders in this room broken the Law of Daynos?" She turned to face them. "Have we not *all* been brought back from tsali that had lain dormant for centuries if not millennia? And yet we were all embraced as Founders. We were all given that respect, that honor, because no matter that our bodies are fresh and new, all of us recognized one undeniable truth: that we are . . ." She stopped, smiled. "Really, really damn old."

Teraeth's eyes widened. "Oh, now I see why Terindel was so sure they'd vote his way. Self-interest."

"Are they . . . going to go on like this all day?" Talea asked.

He nodded. "Pretty much."

"Well, then." Talea leaned back in her seat. "I suppose we don't need to worry about whether or not she'll be exposed to the sigil for long enough."

Down on the parliament floor, the judge, Megrea, watched Valathea as she finished her speech. "Was there a question in that?"

Valathea laughed. "Pardon." She smiled warmly at Daynos. "Have you ever been to the Well of Spirals for a new body?"

Daynos chuckled. "Of course."

"So why is the tsali you transferred yourself into before your soul was placed in a new body different from a tsali that's sat on a shelf for five hundred years?"

Daynos raised an eyebrow. "It isn't. You seem to be under the mistaken impression that we don't differentiate between someone who has died and been resurrected and someone who simply stayed for a long time inside a tsali, but we do and always have. You and the other Founders still have your titles because the Law of Daynos doesn't apply to you. You didn't die."

Valathea pointed. "Khaeriel and Terindel didn't die either."

"But they did," Daynos pointed out. "In both cases, we had their corpses. They clearly *did* die."

"Ooooh," Valathea said, "then I believe we must first define what 'death' is."

Daynos held up his hands. "Is it not obviously a cessation of body and brain function?"

"No, it is not obvious at all. Especially since when you projected into a tsali, you left behind a body bereft of pulse, inanimate and nonfunctional, which under any other circumstances would have been considered a corpse. And yet we do not define that as death. Why is that?"

"Well, because my souls didn't cross the—" Daynos fell silent.

Valathea smiled triumphantly as she held up a finger. "Because your souls didn't cross the Second Veil." She paused. "That is what you were going to say, is it not?"

Daynos tilted his head. "It was."

"I like that definition," Valathea said. "It is simple and elegant. *Death* is crossing the Second Veil. Return or resurrection is coming back in the same body–one would hope healed–that you originally left in."

Teraeth began to see where this was going.

Daynos shook his head. "But there are entities that do freely cross the Second Veil. Demons. Gods. Are we to say that demons 'die' every time they go back to Hell?"

"Well, I don't know. Are there any demons in line for the throne?"

Laughter broke out. Megrea cleared her throat and gave Valathea an admonishing look.

"Apologies," Valathea said. "But truly, I think we can make exceptions for demons and gods. They are a reasonably small community that rarely interacts with the vané. For the rest of us, though, I would like us to move forward with this definition of death. Is that acceptable to you?"

Daynos seemed to chew over that. Finally, he sighed. "Yes, it is."

"Excellent. So right away, honestly without invalidating the Law of Daynos, we have established that neither Terindel nor Khaeriel ever actually *died*."

"No, we don't know that!" Daynos complained. "Are we expected to take their words for it when they have every reason to prevaricate?"

Megrea said, "Daynos–"

Daynos tilted his head in Megrea's direction. "Apologies." He looked back at Valathea. "You cannot expect me to simply take your word for it."

"No, of course not," Valathea agreed. "Terindel, would you mind stepping into the center?"

Daynos narrowed his eyes, but made no other protest.

Teraeth's father crossed over from the side of the room to the center.

"Now please repeat after me," Valathea said to Doc. "Hear my words, for I will tell no lies.

"Hear my words, for I will tell no lies," Doc repeated.

Talea leaned over to Senera. "Why do they keep using that phrase?"

"Truth spell," Teraeth answered. "It's considered all but impossible to lie while under its effects."

"Excellent," Valathea said. "Did you own for a time a necklace known as the Stone of Shackles?"

"I did," Doc responded.

"Would you explain for Daynos's benefit what the main defensive function of the Stone of Shackles is?"

"It switches your souls with that of your killer," Doc explained. "So that even though they've just murdered you, they are the one who actually dies, not you."

"So when you were killed by Mithraill, you never entered the Afterlife? You never crossed the Second Veil?"

Doc shook his head. "No. I was instantly in his body." He paused. "My body. It's been my body for over five hundred years."

Valathea looked at Daynos expectantly as if to say, "See?"

"Where did you acquire this Stone of Shackles?" Daynos asked.

"A wizard named Grizzst gave it to me in return for a favor."

"And we all know who Grizzst is," Valathea said. "Now if you–"

"Why did you create the Star Court?" Daynos asked.

Doc stared flatly. "I won't answer that question."

The judge, Megrea, turned to regard Daynos with surprise. "Is that question relevant?"

"It might be," Daynos said.

She studied the Founder for a long, expectant pause. "You're foraging," she finally announced. "Convince me how it is relevant, and I may change my mind. Terindel, you may sit down."

Doc exhaled and went back to his seat.

Valathea once again turned to Daynos. "So do you recognize that Terindel did not actually die? And will you recognize that Khaeriel was also wearing the Stone of Shackles when she was attacked and did not die as well?" She gestured. "We can call her over here as well."

Daynos held up a hand. "Not necessary. Very well. I acknowledge the validity of your point. So it would seem to me that there is no need to overturn the Law of Daynos. After all, it does not even apply to our two main claimants."

The crowd broke out into applause.

Teraeth let out a dark chuckle. "Well, at least one thing's gone right."

"Hold!" Valathea said, raising her hand. "We are not done here. No, I am sorry Daynos, but the law itself is still very much under debate, for now that I have proven it does not apply to those who have not died, I intend to prove that it should not apply to those who have."

Teraeth tilted his head.

"Didn't we just win?" Xivan asked. "Why is she still arguing a case we've won?"

"I do not know," Teraeth admitted, "but I don't like it."

"They're up to something," Senera said, summarizing Teraeth's own sentiments perfectly.

Daynos laughed at Valathea's statement. "Very well. If you insist."

"I would like to call another witness," Valathea said.

Megrea nodded. "Very well."

"Teraeth, please come to the center." Valathea waved at him.

Teraeth felt his stomach tighten. Valathea hadn't said a word to him about calling him as any kind of witness. This was new. This was also not part of the plan.

He *really* didn't like it.

Teraeth glanced briefly at the three women with him. "Keep an eye on Janel."

Senera gave him a single terse nod.

The hall was a low murmur of chatter as he made his way down to the center of the room.

"Repeat after me—"

"Hear my words, for I will tell no lies," Teraeth growled, scowling. Everyone was looking at him. Listening to him. He hated that.

Valathea smiled. "Perfect. Now, Teraeth, who is your mother? By her common name and title, please."

Teraeth sighed. Oh. "Thaena, Goddess of Death."

He couldn't actually hear the grumble of the crowd because of the acoustics, but he could imagine it well enough.

"Thaena, Goddess of Death herself. So you must have more than a passing familiarity with the Afterlife, yes?"

Teraeth looked sideways. Daynos was looking at him like Teraeth was made of poison. Teraeth found himself wondering just how much he resembled his sister Khaevatz and how Khaevatz and Daynos had felt about each other.

"Answer the question," Megrea said.

"Yes," Teraeth said. "I am quite familiar with the Afterlife."

"And how many times have you died in the past two years? Just a rough estimate is fine."

Teraeth resisted the temptation to roll his eyes. "I don't know . . . forty times?"

"Forty? Oh my. Well. I'm going to assume these deaths are not . . . accidental. Is that correct?"

"There's a ritual sacred to Thaena that requires me to kill myself."

Valathea just raised her eyebrows at Daynos.

"On purpose?" Daynos seemed momentarily stunned. He shook his head. "And how are you coming back to life?"

Teraeth raised an eyebrow. "My. Mother. Is. Thaena. I'm one of her servitors. I believe the common word for it is *angel*."

"Indeed," Valathea said. "Are we to believe that this young man is stripped of all obligations, rank, titles, and *sins* every time he dies? Never mind the common sense that says he is here, whole and hale and clearly his own person—if he practiced a less-than-savory occupation, he would always have a ready pardon for all manner of crimes simply by conducting this holy rite in his mother's name."

Teraeth's eyes narrowed. *If you bring up the Black Brotherhood, I swear I'm knifing you right now.*

"Well, that hardly seems . . ." But Daynos's voice trailed off, and he looked thoughtful.

"The Law of Daynos was designed to prevent someone from being resurrected decades, even centuries later and demanding a return of assets that had already passed on to heirs, but I am over fourteen thousand years old, and I can count the number of times I've seen the opportunity for such a situation on my hands."

"Am I still needed here?" Teraeth asked.

"Oh? So sorry, my dear. You can go."

Teraeth stalked back to his seat. "What the hell is her game?"

Valathea continued, "Most people either petition to have someone Returned immediately, while their grief is still fresh and strong, or they let the dead do what the dead are meant to do—move on to the Land of Peace and their next life. So I sincerely ask you, Daynos, who does this law serve?"

Daynos made a face. "I think . . . I think you make a good point."

Megrea stood. "Let us begin deliberations. You will be alerted once the Founders have made a decision. Your Majesty—" Her voice faltered.

King Kelanis and Janel were both gone.

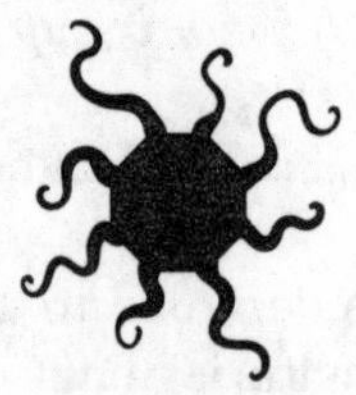

## 100: The Demon Queen

***(Janel's story)***

Janel wasn't sure how long she'd been in the box.

It wasn't a normal box. It appeared as a tunnel made of black ice. It had no exit, just a series of looping, meandering paths that branched off and around and back into each other. It was a maze, and she had no idea how she'd gotten there.

But the pattern was always the same. She'd find herself on top of that glass pyramid, being tortured by Suless repeatedly. Then she'd find herself in the box. She was reasonably certain none of it was real. The more she looked at the walls of her magical prison, the more she became convinced that they were only a metaphor for ice. This was something else.

A gem, perhaps.

She tried to discover a way out, but the walls had been strengthened against every attack she could devise. This had been built, carefully and deliberately, precisely to imprison a soul, upper and lower, and keep it locked in place. Suless had done this to her, to keep her out of the way while Suless used Janel's body. And then, when Suless had time, she would once more try to pry the secret to becoming a demon from Janel.

To travel between the Twin Worlds at will, to be able to make a body for herself at will. No one would ever capture Suless again.

Janel found herself wishing she actually *was* a demon. She'd be able to escape. Unfortunately, the price for that escape would be the possibility that Suless would gain access to that knowledge too. It was a bit of a quandary.

In the end, she decided there was no help for it. Every time Suless tortured her, she lost a little more of her lower soul, her tenyé power—if she didn't do something soon, she'd soon end up in a position where she couldn't do anything at all.

She stopped trying to find an end to the maze and instead sat down and concentrated on what she could do in this monotonous landscape. What were the laws she had to work with? Was there anything that might resemble a loophole to be found within them?

After an unknowable amount of time, Janel realized that her body was . . . discretionary. Fungible. Malleable. She could pick apart the pieces of herself, examine them from every side, and recombine herself. As she did this, she began to realize that certain pieces were . . . not missing, exactly. No, not missing. But suppressed, cordoned off. Bits of her pulled off, wrapped up in string, and tucked away somewhere else, connected but never touching the rest of her. She began to pluck at the string and then began using that string to map out the fullness of the maze.

With the string pulled away, she once more had access to all of herself.

She'd lived five whole lives before the first time Xaltorath had found her. The first very long, and the following lives very short. The genders had varied. In between those breaks, she'd gone to the Land of Peace, which had not in those early days been so much a cordoned area under a goddess's control, but simply the lands closest to the spring where all souls eventually went to be reborn. Each time she'd been there, she'd eventually grown bored enough to want to start over.

Then Xaltorath found her. On two separate occasions, and each time just as Janel had started remembering her previous lives, Xaltorath had ripped off another piece of her and tied it up with metaphoric string. Not a gaesh, not technically. Her souls were still all in the right place.

Then came Elana, when Xaltorath had found her a third time and had, instead of adding string, ripped the bindings all away so she remembered everything.

And what she had done had been to excise S'arric from Vol Karoth. She'd accepted her death afterward, content that at least she'd be with him, but Doc—passionately obstinate Doc—hadn't let her die. So she'd stayed alive awhile longer, fifty years or so, give or take, and at least tried to make a little bit of a difference in the world. If she'd remembered what she'd done to S'arric, the way of it, maybe she'd have taken a different route—but she hadn't. Xaltorath had stopped by to visit once more. Eventually, Elena died, this time of old age instead of childbirth. She stayed in the Land of Peace a long time after that, because S'arric was there, still recovering.

Atrin, of all people, had been helping him.

And then the Eight Guardians had shown up, asking for volunteers. When S'arric's was the first hand raised, how could hers not be the second? She hadn't expected Atrin's to be the third, but it was, and there'd been some consolation to that. She'd looked forward to a new start.

So she let herself be reborn, not remembering a thing. What she hadn't counted on was Xaltorath. That Xaltorath would want to enforce her ignorance, wipe her memories each time the walls would start to break down.

Xaltorath, Janel realized, was scared of her.

Around the time she came to this conclusion, she noticed the light. It was bright and large and close. It shimmered through all the facets and crags of the gemstone tunnels around her, like looking at the sun through a veil of black water. A beacon. Something she could target, if only she could escape her prison.

It called to her, practically shouted her name, desperate to draw her attention.[1]

But she couldn't leave the caves. Or could she? Did the gem she was trapped inside really stop her from crossing the Veil? It would have stopped a normal soul. Of that she was certain. But Janel's hadn't been a normal soul in thousands of years. Xaltorath had lied so many times. The demon had nothing to do with what Janel was. She had tried to corrupt Janel, absolutely, but she had only taken from her. Suless was lamentably right; Xaltorath hadn't turned Janel into a demon.

She'd been a demon from the start.

Janel passed through the Veil. Technically, she died, but technically, she died every night. She was good at it. As soon as she was on the other side, she followed the light and found her way home.

### *(Suless's story)*

"We're leaving," King Kelanis had whispered to Suless, and even she had to admit that seemed like the wisest course of action.

Kelanis had been utterly convinced that they would win this, but that was before Doc had resurrected the Star Court and certainly before Valathea had made her case. Suless had already known which way this was going to go, and she didn't much care if Kelanis survived it or not. She did, however, very much care if *she* did.

That's why she'd convinced him to bring in the army. The vané weren't the most gullible people, but was she not the queen of treachery? It wasn't so difficult to spin a story to the soldiers, to convince them of the necessity of their orders. Wasn't he Terindel the Black, after all? Wasn't Khaeriel in league with Quur? The Star Court could only be imposters, the tricks of an evil prince who still resented that he had never been king. Kelindel's propaganda about his brother, Terindel, suited her needs nicely.

They left quietly along with Miyane and joined the troops waiting outside. The archers. The flamecasters. The shield mages. Wizards and warriors who could, at a word, flatten the Parliament of Flowers and pepper every single person inside with a thousand poisoned arrows.

[1] I suppose this means Senera's glyph did in fact work.

Which was exactly what she was going to make sure King Kelanis ordered them to do.

They'd crossed behind the main barrier when Suless felt it happen. Felt the spells she'd cast trigger and the pure, certain knowledge of it all seep into her. She smiled. Janel had done it. She'd actually done it. That glorious little bitch.

"So that's how it's done," Suless whispered, her voice a combination of triumphant and reverent. She turned to the king. "May I see that dagger?"

Kelanis raised an eyebrow, but plucked the dagger from his belt and handed it to her hilt first. "What do you want it for?"

"Oh, a minor chore."

Suless grabbed the dagger by the hilt, reversed it, and plunged into her heart.

*Kihrin raised an eyebrow. "This is what Senera was talking about, you know. There's no way you actually have an account from Suless."*

*"True," Thurvishar agreed. "That one was what I like to call 'an educated guess.'"*

## *(Janel's story)*

Janel fell to the deck, gasping, a pain ripping through her chest, fire spreading out through her veins. She had moved to repossess her own body, but found it vacant–and dying. Suless must have known Janel wouldn't just abandon this body. She'd left a parting gift.

Janel reached up to her chest and felt the dagger still there. She couldn't breathe. Each movement felt like a brand seared across her body. The world was beginning to darken, but she knew that if she simply pulled the dagger out, she'd die at once. She wasn't ready for it. That bitch had known she wouldn't be. And so Suless bought herself time to escape.

"Suless? Veils! What have you done–" Kelanis's voice cut off with a gurgling noise.

Someone started screaming.

Janel couldn't let herself be distracted. She put her hand around the hilt. As she pulled the dagger free, she concentrated on closing the wound immediately, using the tenyé from the dagger to power the energy she needed. She felt muscle fibers reknit, the pain turn to a dull burning and then a sting. The dagger disintegrated in her hand as she stood, flakes of ash falling to the ground.[2] She felt better. Not perfect, but her heart would keep beating, so that was something.

2 This is disconcertingly similar to effects Vol Karoth creates, so I'm making a special note of it.

Now Janel could pay attention.

She'd been wrong, though; Suless hadn't been trying to escape at all.

Ahead on the walkway, appalled soldiers backed away from the king, while the queen screamed in horror. The king stood wide-eyed, head twisted at an unnatural angle, limbs akimbo. His bones broke and re-formed even as Janel watched, snapping and cracking like he was a doll made of twigs twisted by a child's angry hands. Something writhed under Kelanis's skin, which melted and tore. If there was any mercy in the universe, he was dead by that point.

Kelanis didn't fall. His body continued twisting. Something pushed its way through him, breaking skin, rising up in a shower of gore. The blood made it difficult to see exactly what she looked like, but Janel took it on faith she would be pale-skinned and beautiful, white as snow. Her other, more distinctive features hadn't yet developed, but Suless was brand new to this.

*What's the difference between a human and a demon?*

*Time.*

Janel couldn't help but shudder, looking at the god-queen turned demon. She recognized Suless now, recognized her in a way that had been impossible before Suless had taken this final, irreversible step. She wasn't an identical match–Suless had only eaten a single soul, after all, and not the multitudes of demons, gods, and immortals she might have consumed in a different future–but her core, foundational nature was familiar to Janel. So familiar.

Janel wondered how many thousands of years it would take before Suless dispensed with her birth name and started calling herself simply by her self-anointed title: Queen of Demons.

Xaltorath.

Maybe in *this* timeline, Suless never would. Xaltorath already existed here, after all. But now Janel understood why Grizzst's Binding of the Demons hadn't worked on Xaltorath–because Suless hadn't *been* a demon when he'd performed it.[3]

"Oh, Suless," Janel said, "you may think you've escaped your enemies this way, but I wonder if you have any idea how little tolerance Xaltorath will have for your existence. She won't regard you as some long-lost sister–you're *competition*."

The god-queen looked at her hands and began to laugh. "Xaltorath? Pfft. She's not ready for me. None of you are. Thank you, my dear. This

[3] The real sticking point here is that Suless's demonic nature was self-created, as was Janel's, and that's why neither fell under the sway of the demonic gaeshing, which otherwise affected all the demons who existed at that time and their infected "children" in perpetuity.

is better than I could have dreamed. I hope you don't mind if I devour *your* soul next. Though I'm not asking permission."

Janel just smiled. Suless had no idea.

A dozen guards moved forward as the archers fired.

Suless threw the arrows aside with a gesture while she pulled herself upright, smiling, and waited for the guards, the wizards, all the rest, to attack too. She grinned with satisfaction as she regarded Janel. "Let's do this, my daughter. I'm so going to enjoy the slaughter–"

Suless spasmed forward, surprised, as a razor-sharp tentacle, lined with spikes instead of suckers, erupted from her chest, while another tentacle wrapped around her throat and ripped.

The woman who looked like Miyane pulled her tentacles back into normal hands so quickly that Janel would have missed it if she hadn't been looking directly at her.

"Okay," the mimic said. "I'll start."

Janel raised an eyebrow at the mimic. "Talon?" She only knew the mimic by reputation, but considering what she'd just witnessed, she couldn't imagine who else this could be.

"They've assassinated the king! Arrest them!" someone behind them yelled. The vané probably weren't sure exactly what had just happened, but "arrest everyone and sort it out later" seemed like a sensible first step.

"Oh, I'm so pleased to be recognized," Talon said. "Now, let's run!"

# 101: The Black King

***(Teraeth's story)***

As the crowd began to murmur about the king's disappearance–hardly a good sign–the doors slammed open. Suless and Queen Miyane ran inside. Everyone stood not from respect but because something was so clearly wrong.

The two women ran inside as arrow fire chased them and bounced off the parliament wards. A bloom of energies–fire, ice, lightning's sizzling flash–impacted those same wards like bright, glorious fireworks. For reasons no one could comprehend, the vané army seemed to be trying to kill the two women. The army hadn't succeeded due to the Parliament of Flowers' magical protections.

Suless and Miyane slammed the doors shut and braced themselves on the other side, then glanced back over their shoulders like little girls caught playing a prank on their parents. The two women looked at each other, then slowly turned around, hands still shoved up against the doors.

"It wasn't my fault," Suless declared.

Hope flared in Teraeth's heart. Senera grabbed his arm and squeezed. He pretended not to notice, since it would have only drawn attention to the fact Senera cared what happened to Janel.

"What is the meaning of this?" Daynos's voice shook with outrage. He seemed quite done with this trial's shocks, surprises, and interruptions.

"I can explain–" Queen Miyane started to say, then made a face as if she'd just touched something scalding. "On second thought, she'll explain." The vané queen edged back toward the chairs the king and queen had been using previously.

"Suless" spared the queen a quick glare before she turned a lethal, brilliant smile on Daynos. "I request sanctuary?"

"Janel?" Valathea's voice carried clearly through the room.

Janel waved to her with one hand before slamming it back against the door as it started to open. A loud pounding banged against the other side.

Teraeth hurried down the steps. A second later, the others followed, like ducklings after their mother.

"Move away from the door, young woman," Daynos demanded.

Janel gave one last anxious glance to the door behind her, then raised her hands and backed away to the side. Parliament guards closed in on her and grabbed her arms.

Daynos gestured and the large doors swung open again. The entire vané army stood on the other side, behind several silver-clad soldiers whose faces were nearly purple with rage. "May we enter?" a woman demanded. "The king has been assassinated. The suspects fled into this buildings."

Every eye turned to Janel.

"The assassin was a demon," Janel explained, "who would have killed me if she hadn't stepped in. Ask her." Janel jerked her head in Queen Miyane's direction.

Everyone began shouting, all at once.

*"Be quiet!"*

Megrea slammed her staff against the marble floor, so hard and loud it seemed impossible she hadn't cracked the stone itself.

The hall fell quiet.

"The king is dead?" she asked into that silence.

For a long pause, no one answered, but the same thoughts had to be going through everyone's minds. If the king was dead, then lucky they were about to vote to recognize Khaeriel's and Doc's prior claims, wasn't it?

Teraeth reached the main floor grown increasingly crowded with guards, Founders, and soldiers. He'd fight his way to Janel if he had to. His father saw him and moved to intercept.

"Just give her a minute." Doc had a strange expression on his face, one Teraeth couldn't interpret.

"Yes," Janel answered. "The king is dead. A demon took his soul. I swear I had nothing to do with it."

Megrea gestured toward the center area. "Would you care to step over here and repeat that?"

It didn't take long for the truth to come out, or at least, part of the truth. They never called Queen Miyane–a shuddering, hysterical shell–to testify, but a magical oath made it easy to verify Janel's assertion that she hadn't been responsible for Kelanis's death.

And once they'd done so, they let her go.

Teraeth waited for her. Blood splattered Janel's gown. Her blood, Teraeth thought, but she didn't seem to be in any pain, the wound already healed. Teraeth felt like he didn't have enough air as she took his hand in hers. Her hand wasn't empty, though.

She handed him his arrowhead necklace.

"I think you dropped this," Janel said.

"I must have." He marked her twinkling eyes, the way her mouth turned up, just one corner, her wry smile. He put his hands around her face and leaned down to kiss her. She kissed back, bit him almost immediately, tugging his lower lip between her teeth for a beautifully piercing moment before he kept her tongue too preoccupied for that.

"I guess the glyph worked," Senera said.

Janel immediately broke off the kiss, smiled lovingly at Teraeth, and caressed his jaw. Then the smile went away, and Janel pointed a finger at Senera. "What is she doing here, and why is she still alive?"

Teraeth cleared his throat. "A lot's happened. I promise there's a good explanation."

"It had better be a fantastic explanation." Janel spared Senera a hateful glare. "Or I'm clawing your eyes out as soon as this is over."

Teraeth wasn't entirely sure if that threat was meant for Senera or himself. Possibly both. He put his arm around Janel's waist, grinning. "I've missed you."

Everyone sat down again.

Down on the floor, they seemed to realize that the hearing could continue. Khaeriel looked nervous but happy, and it seemed likely that she had good reason to be. With her brother dead, there was no longer any question that she would end up with the crown.

Doc walked up to Valathea and said something. Then Doc swept Valathea into his arms and kissed her passionately. When they parted, he lifted Chainbreaker[1] from around his neck in one swift, sure motion and set it around hers.

Teraeth felt his blood turn to ice. He removed his arm from around Janel and sat up.

"What . . . ?" He stared in shock.

Why would he do that? Doc would never give up Chainbreaker. It was one of the most powerful artifacts in the whole world. Did he have some reason to think Valathea was in danger?

Valathea tucked the stone under the edge of her dress and returned to her chair.

"What's going on?" Janel asked.

"I thought I knew," Teraeth said.

Megrea came to the center.

"After what was frankly an astonishingly short deliberation," Megrea

[1] Yes, they'd fixed the chain.

said, "we have decided that from henceforth, we shall move forward without the Law of Daynos."

Clamor. Some positive, some negative, depending on individual feelings. Khaeriel slumped back into her chair, clearly relieved.

"However, besides rescinding the Law of Daynos, today's conclusions have troubling implications. While we agree with esteemed Founder Valathea's argument that neither Terindel nor Khaeriel ever properly died and therefore were quite improperly stripped of their crowns, the knowledge of that error brings with it a new danger. We have had five hundred years of peace, but tonight has the potential to split the rule of the vané, a people united, into two divided houses once more. We feel this is to be avoided at all costs."

Khaeriel straightened again, eyes wide.

Teraeth's father had said he didn't want the throne. The only reason Khaeriel had kept Doc by her side was because she'd assumed he wouldn't be a threat to her ambitions. He had promised he had no interest in returning to the throne.

"Had the Law of Daynos never existed, then Terindel would still be king of the Kirpis vané, and his brother, Kelindel, would have never claimed the throne. Terindel was also king of the Kirpis vané before the nation of the Manol ever existed. He is the eldest child of Terrin, and we must acknowledge the superiority of that claim."

A look of growing horror crept over Khaeriel's expression.

"What?" Janel leaned forward. "Is she saying what I think she is?"

"Yes, she is," Teraeth answered. He scowled. His father hadn't been lying when he'd said he was certain the Founders of the Star Court would vote his way. They were clearly far more loyal to him than anyone had credited.

*Don't mess with the plan,* Doc had told Khaeriel, and like a fool, Khaeriel had followed along. So had Teraeth. Except the plan had apparently never been to give the throne back to Khaeriel at all.

Doc was taking the whole damn thing.

And *Doc* had never made any promises to Thaena about performing the Ritual of Night.

"Thus we have carefully weighed the strengths of the two claimants to the throne. Terindel, who was king of the Kirpis vané but has lived for the past five hundred years as a Manol vané, and Khaeriel, daughter of the now-revealed usurper, Kelindel, and the Manol queen, Khaevatz. While we have found Khaeriel's claim significant, we have ultimately decided that the wiser course of action would be to give the throne, whole and entire, over both Kirpis vané and Manol vané, to King Terindel." Daynos then bowed. "Your Majesty."

Khaeriel stood, her face a fury. She turned and stared at Doc.

He gave her a wink. "Better luck next time."

"You son of a–"

"Now, now," Doc wagged a finger at her. "Don't worry. I'm still going to go through with the deal for Thaena on your behalf. You'll keep all your promises. Therin was my friend too."

Khaeriel's expression tightened. "But if you do that–" Anger shifted back into disbelief. Why would Doc go through all this to enact a ritual that would kill him? She turned to look at Valathea, who didn't look at all happy about this outcome. She sat ruler straight, head held high, nostrils flared, every bit of her body language suggesting tight control of a boiling fury. Valathea returned Khaeriel's stare and gave her a single, short nod.

Khaeriel took a deep breath, shuddered, and walked away. She wasn't going to dispute the ruling, although she was muttering something under her breath as she returned to her table.

Teraeth frowned as he took in the scene. He was still missing something. Why would Doc give away Chainbreaker? *Why* would he go ahead with the ritual if he didn't have to? Doc had literally lost his kingdom refusing to perform the Ritual of Night. Doc knew it would cost him his life. Even if he and Therin had been *that* close, why not let Khaeriel do it, since she was the one Thaena was most likely to Return?

"Well," Doc said. "I guess it's time to start planning a particularly lavish coronation."

Which is when Thaena appeared in the middle of the room.

"No, it isn't."

The Goddess of Death was in her full voramer raiment once more, but this time, her white gown was ripped and splattered with gore, her belt and necklace dented from weapon strikes, her hair fins torn. She looked as though she had been fighting nonstop for weeks.

The hall fell silent.

Doc turned and gave Khaeriel a look. "Thanks."

The former queen just glared. Of course she'd prayed to her grandmother. Teraeth felt a wave of dizziness and guilt wash over him. Praying to Thaena is what he *should* have done–and hadn't. He hadn't even thought about doing it. He'd been too busy trying to figure out what his father was up to.

The Goddess of Death walked forward. "I should have known better than to think you wouldn't try something, Terindel. But if you think you can delay this by spending months preparing for your coronation, think again." She snapped her fingers, and several bits of jewelry–necklaces, chains, a tiara–flew off their respective owners and hovered in the air next to her, rearranging themselves into a ragged crown of twisted metal and jewels. She grabbed the result and tossed it down at Daynos's feet. "Crown him. Now. Clear the room and prepare for the ritual."

Off to the side, Valathea quietly stood up and walked out the door.

And everything clicked.

Doc knew his life was forfeit in exchange for performing the ritual. That was if everything went to plan. But what if it didn't? What if Doc *knew* it wouldn't? If Teraeth were in his father's place, there was one scenario under which he'd send Chainbreaker away–send Chainbreaker away on the neck of the woman he loved–and that was if he thought he'd lose both if they stayed. Doc was protecting Valathea . . .

. . . from Thaena.

Which meant that whatever Doc thought would happen next, he already knew it would drive the Goddess of Death into a murderous rage.

# 102: A Pointless Waste

***(Kihrin's story)***

"You know, we have to stop meeting like this," I told Relos Var. "People will start to talk."

He glanced over at me. There was nothing like affection in that expression. This was the man I'd first met back in Kishna-Farriga, the one whose eyes had been filled with only hate and malice. "I should have known you'd be able to convince him to change the plan. Grizzst's never had any stomach for necessary sacrifices."

Relos Var was *angry*. I honestly don't think I'd ever seen him this angry before.

"You did not just say that with a straight face, did you?" Grizzst hopped down from the throne while giving Relos Var a rude gesture. "Because seriously, you wouldn't even be here if it wasn't for me."

"We're not going over this again," Relos Var said. "And you made a promise."

"Oh, under very false pretenses. You hadn't told me what the vané really are."

I blinked. "Wait. What? What do you mean, what the vané really are? What are you talking about?"

Both men ignored me.

Relos Var said, "I'm not going to allow you to interfere with my plans, Gahan. Not this time."

Grizzst shook his head. "Revas, the situation's changed. You need to know what happened when we went to the–"

A lightning bolt hit him square in the chest and sent him flying backward into the wall. If he'd been any normal person, that alone would have killed him, but Grizzst definitely wasn't normal.

Thurvishar and I both dove off the metal stairs we'd been sitting on, just in case. Way too much of this room was outright made of metal.

Before we'd even had a chance to stand, Grizzst pulled something from his waist and pointed. A giant ball of light gathered in the center of the room, focused into a tight beam, and slammed down into Relos

Var in a column of pure energy so bright it obscured him completely from view.

Thurvishar waved a hand, and a giant wall of earth rose up between us and the rest of the fight. I crawled over to the wall and put my back against it. Thurvishar followed. Behind us, a cacophonous sound rose up and then quieted again, followed quickly by what sounded like an inferno coupled with a blast of heat.

"Wow," I said.

From the other side of the wall, Grizzst yelled, "Why haven't you changed back into a dragon yet?" This was followed by an intense sizzling sound and the smell of smoke.

"I'm not a fool. You raised the barrier. Smashing through that would hurt." Then Relos Var laughed. "Besides, I don't need to be a dragon to deal with a toy-based hedge mage like you."

"Toy-based? *Toy-based?* Who bound the demons? Who created the Crown and Scepter of Quur?" Grizzst's voice rose to a pitch that reminded me of a rug dealer arguing with his wife.

"Yes, fine crutches for half-assed wizards of insufficient talent." A large cloud of doves flew overhead.

I turned to Thurvishar. "Doves?"

He shrugged in confusion.

"Oh, that does it!" Grizzst yelled, which was followed by an incredibly loud boom. I had to cover my ears.

"What the hell was that?" Relos Var said.

"Just a little 'toy' I came up with using saltpeter and bat guano."

There was a pause. "Well, shit."

"That's what I said." Grizzst's laughter was maniacal.

"Did someone once tell you that you were funny? They lied." And that was followed by a loud cracking sound and several staggering thuds. A shimmering curtain of cyan-blue energy swept across the room.

I looked over at Thurvishar. "You know Grizzst better than I do. Who do you think is going to win this?"

He winced. "Sadly, Relos Var."

I suspected he was right about that. "Then we'd better do something, don't you think?"

"Have any suggestions?"

I pointed in the direction of the throne, which we could still see from our vantage point. "Why don't we get rid of the reason for the argument." I pointed toward Thurvishar's robes. "I bet Grizzst's wand would do the trick."

Thurvishar pulled himself to his feet. "I suppose it might at that." He pulled the thing out of his sleeve, and pointed it at the crystal.

Nothing happened.

Thurvishar stared at the thing. "He's probably keyed it to only work for himself. It would be the smart thing to do."

"Great." I made a face and then flinched as something very heavy slammed into Thurvishar's earth wall, putting a long crack along its length.

I looked around. There had to be something I could use . . .

My gaze fell back on the slender metal wand in Thurvishar's hands. "Let me see that."

"It's not going to work for you either." But Thurvishar handed it over.

"Oh, it will, just not the way its maker intended." I tested the wand's spring, which was considerable. It made a ringing sound as it snapped back into position. "I can work with this."

Thurvishar looked confused for just the briefest moment, and then comprehension dawned. "Right. I'll try to keep you from being interrupted." He set himself at my back, facing toward where the mage duel was still ongoing.

The theory was the same as what I'd done several times before. This was simple stuff. The only part that was different was that I didn't really know what the hell the crystal was made from. That was easily remedied by looking past the First Veil, letting the innate nature of the crystal show itself. Even if I didn't have a *name* for the material, I still knew enough to break it with the wrong harmonies. While every kind of element split the air just a few dozen feet away, I flicked the wand to produce that ring and let magic and vibration do the work for me.

I have to say that *this* time when that crystal shattered into a thousand pieces, it felt pretty damn good.

*"No!"* Relos Var screamed.

Okay, that felt good too.

The wall between where Thurvishar and I were separated from Grizzst and Relos Var's fight vanished in an instant, disintegrated.

"No, you idiot! Do you know what you've done?" Relos Var rushed over, but it was a little late to stop me. Grizzst followed close behind him. Neither one seemed seriously injured. At best, they were singed around the edges.

I handed the wand back to Grizzst, figuring he could use it if the fighting started up again. "Did you mean that question seriously, or were you just being rhetorical?"

I'd have died right there if Relos Var's expression had been a spell.

"You son of a bitch," he growled.

I ignored the name-calling. He was in a bad mood. "Now you have a choice. You can stop them from performing a pointless ritual, or you can let them go ahead and . . . hey, what happens when all that tenyé energy hits a warding crystal that doesn't exist anymore?"

Relos Var stared at me.

Then he spun around and opened a gate.

# 103: Long Live the King

***(Teraeth's story)***

Doc was coronated quickly. Daynos performed the ceremony, placed the crown upon his brow. Afterward, guards started clearing the room, but Teraeth waved them off. There was no way he was leaving.

"I didn't think this day could become weirder," Janel said. "But here we are."

"No argument from me."

Xivan leaned forward. "Janel, I'm glad that you're back, and I hate to be that person, but . . . what happened to Suless?"

"Oh," Janel said. She paused for a moment. "She escaped."

Xivan's hand clenched around the scabbard of Urthaenriel. Teraeth winced, thinking there was a reasonably good chance that Xivan was at that moment regretting her devotion to friendship.

Plan C would have seen Suless dead.

Janel reached out, clasped Xivan's hand, and squeezed. "She's gone someplace where you can't follow." She looked down for a second before raising her head again. "Xivan, I will destroy her. I promise you that."

Xivan's brow furrowed as though she found that idea difficult to understand. "She had a gem on her. I need it."

Janel frowned and reached down to her belt. She pulled out a small pouch and upended it into her hand. "This? Xivan, this was my tsali. Suless was keeping me imprisoned in it." A single star tear sparkled in the palm of her hand.

Xivan stared at Janel's hand, then slowly reached out and picked up the diamond. "She was lying, then." Xivan's lips thinned. "Of course she was. Why did I let myself think any differently?"

"Whatever else," Teraeth said, "we can always count on Suless to be as petty and spiteful as possible."

"I am so sorry," Janel said.

Xivan closed her eyes, nodding.

Talea leaned out past Xivan. "It really is good to have you back, Janel. I'm so glad we were able to help."

Janel cocked her head. "Wait. You're here because of me?"

Talea nodded vigorously. "Oh yes. Senera brought us."

The woman in question cleared her throat, although Senera didn't look in Janel's direction. The wizard gestured toward the main floor. "Mind if we switched to closer seats?"

Teraeth nodded. "Agreed. I'd like to talk to my father."

When Doc stood, he turned to the Founders. "Your loyalty humbles me. I do not deserve it, but thank you." He stopped himself from whatever he'd been about to say next and started again. "I'm going to need the ritual."

One of the Founders rushed out of the room, presumably to fetch it.

While that happened, Teraeth and the others made their way down to the area normally reserved for only the most important vané. Funny how no one tried to stop them.

Doc walked over to the desk where Valathea had kept her supplies, pulled out an envelope, and handed it to a guard. "Give that to Her Majesty, please." He motioned toward Queen Miyane.

"Oh, I should have mentioned that's Talon," Janel said.

"What?" Teraeth said. "Yeah, that might have been important."

"No, not really," Senera murmured.

The guard walked over to the woman. "For you, Your Majesty." He handed her the envelope.

Queen Miyane looked confused, but she opened up her piece of paper. A look of anger crossed her face. "Why you–" She fell unconscious before she could finish the sentence.

Doc waved a hand, and the paper shriveled and turned to dust. "That's not Queen Miyane. I believe you'll find that's a mimic. We do still have cells that will hold mimics, don't we? Please put her in one before she wakes."

"I honestly wasn't sure that would work on a mimic," Senera whispered next to Teraeth.

Teraeth frowned. "He asked you to do that?"

She nodded. "We both felt it was safer."

It didn't make Teraeth feel any better. Just how much of this had his father planned in advance? Teraeth made his way forward. "Father, I need to speak to you."

"Later," Thaena said.

Teraeth stared at his mother. "There won't *be* a later for him."

Thaena sighed and motioned for Teraeth to go ahead. He walked over to his father. "Damn it, whatever you're about to do, *don't,*" Teraeth said.

Doc smiled at him. "I'm keeping my word. It's what your mother wants."

"No, there's something else going on." Teraeth reached out and touched his father's arm. "Explain it to Thaena. Whatever it is, she'll believe you."

The smile on Doc's face slipped. He returned the motion, clasping Teraeth's shoulder. "No, not me. Anyone but me. We've too much history, I'm afraid. I couldn't trust Khaeriel to do it correctly, and with Senera here . . ." Doc squeezed his hand. "Have I told you I love you? I really should have."

Teraeth felt his throat close up. He didn't know what to say.

"*Trust me,* Teraeth. I'm doing this for Kihrin," Doc said. Then he laughed and leaned over. "And by the way, if you don't marry that boy, I'll never forgive you."

Teraeth *really* didn't know what to say. "Uh, but . . . wait. Kihrin? What did Kihrin tell you?"

But his father had already turned away. Daynos had walked up with a large metal-bound book in his hands.

"Where'd you get this copy?" Doc asked. "It's not the one I owned."

"Grizzst provided us with another," Daynos said. "Just in case."

"Right. Just in case." Doc laughed bitterly as he flipped through the pages. Each one looked like an onionskin rubbing, like someone had rubbed charcoal over an engraved stone. He stopped at one passage and snorted.[1] Then he closed the book and handed it back. "Thank you."

Daynos looked confused. "Won't you need this?"

"What? No," Doc said. "I have it memorized. Let's clear out the center, please. I'll need room to draw the ritual circle."

*Memorized?* Teraeth was supposed to believe his father had *memorized* the ritual he'd infamously refused to perform? He walked back over to Janel and the others. He started to say something to her, but realized that Senera, Xivan, and Talea were standing right next to them. Doc had said Senera's presence was part of why he hadn't explained himself. And Senera seemed to want the ritual to proceed.

Ergo, one could assume Relos Var wanted the ritual to proceed.

"It's a trap," Teraeth murmured. "This was planned." But which ritual was doctored? The one in the book or the one Doc was about to perform from memory?

"Before I start," Doc said, "please bring Therin back." He must have thought Thaena was about to say no, because he added, "I *promise* you that I will perform the ritual. I will do it tonight. I will do it here. But bring Therin back first."

[1] I believe this was the moment Doc realized the ritual had been altered by Grizzst. Knowing the correct ritual so well, he likely identified the substitution of the glyphs right away.

Thaena stared at him. Then she nodded. "Very well. Do you have the body?"

Terindel gestured to the side. A pair of vané left the room and quickly entered again, carrying a stretcher, covered in cloth. It was an easy guess what was under that cloth.

Thaena stared at the body for a second, and Therin sat up, gasping.

It was as easy as that. Teraeth noticed that they'd at least changed him out of the clothes he'd died in, which was considerate. Those had been a mess.

Khaeriel rushed over to him. "Hey. Careful there. Can you stand?"

Therin blinked. "What hap–" He saw Thaena and froze.

"Hello, Therin," Thaena said, smiling.

"What's going on here?" Therin asked, eyes wide and skin pale. It wasn't an atypical reaction, all things considered.

"What's going on here is that you've been Returned," Doc said. "You can thank Khaeriel. She was willing to give her life to have you brought back. So if you ever had a second's doubt that Khaeriel really is in love with you, now you know." His gaze landed on Khaeriel. "However, I think you are far too much like me, little mouse, and I can't have you nibbling at my crown while I'm busy elsewhere. So you and Therin will be escorted to the edge of the country and from there you may go"–he shrugged–"wherever you like. Just not here."

Khaeriel blinked at him. "Wait. What? Are you seriously . . . Are you exiling us?"

"Yes, I am," Doc said. "Get the fuck out. Right now. Before I come to my senses and order something worse than exile." He motioned for the guards.

"Doc, what kind of garbage is this . . . ?" But Therin's protest fell on deaf ears, and the guards politely but firmly pulled him outside, even as his expression was a battlefield of shock, betrayal, and anger.

"And that gets *them* out of the room," Teraeth whispered. Was there any way he could stop this?

If only he knew what *this* even was.

"What?" Janel turned to him. She looked slightly wide-eyed.

"Something's wrong," Teraeth said. "Something's *very* wrong. You see what he's done? He's removed anyone from the room who might be used as a hostage. Thaena wouldn't kill *us*. We're not expendable."

Senera pulled the Name of All Things out of her bodice and began writing furiously.

"That was unexpected," Thaena told Doc.

The once-again vané shrugged. "A lesson I learned a long time ago. I don't share power. Now why don't you let me fulfill my end of the bargain."

Thaena stepped back and gestured for him to begin.

Which he did. He drew out a series of nested octagons on the ground and called for specific supplies, drew intricate glyphs at all the corners. He called for volunteers to help with the ritual; most of the people who answered that call were members of his old court who had themselves only been alive for a very short time. Not all, though. Daynos stepped forward. So did Megrea.

Teraeth found his throat growing tight; all those people were going to die. It wasn't just the person who led the ritual who would have their life claimed. It was every single person who assisted. Every single member of the Star Court, only just returned to life.

They watched as Teraeth's father worked through each stage of the ritual, each time the light growing brighter, the effect growing more intense. The room was soon shuddering from the strength of the tenyé in the room.

"Shit," Senera cursed.

Teraeth focused on her immediately. "What? Quickly!"

She flipped over the journal and showed him both question and answer.

*Can the Ritual of Night King Terindel is enacting on the vané people succeed?*

*No.*

Not a predictive question. Not a question from the future. A question very much grounded in what was possible now. What Doc was doing wouldn't work. Doc was the one who had changed the ritual, and that's why he'd sent Therin away—so Thaena would be less likely to immediately take back the life she'd just granted.

Teraeth turned back to his father just as all the accumulated tenyé in the room dissipated. Doc lowered his arms, looking exhausted and resigned.

Teraeth stood. He wasn't the only one, but he wasn't paying attention. He didn't feel any different. Would he notice losing his immortality? *Would* he feel different?

But more tellingly, all the Founders in the room were still alive, and he *knew* that wasn't right at all.

"Did it work?" Janel asked.

"No," Teraeth said. "It didn't."

Thaena stepped forward. She tilted her head to the side, closed her eyes, as if she was listening to something far away. Then she shook her head. "That did nothing."

Doc shrugged. "I did everything I promised. I cast the Ritual of Night as requested."

Thaena looked around the chamber. There was still a large crowd present; vané who wanted to witness this very singular event if nothing else. She ignored the crowd and turned back to Doc. "You sabotaged it somehow. What did you do?"

"I swear by all I hold dear, I performed the ritual perfectly," Doc said.

Teraeth ran over to Daynos. "Let me see that." Without waiting, he yanked the large book out of the man's hands and ran over to a table. He opened the book and began flipping through the fragile pages, comparing it to what was on the floor. The easiest explanation, of course, was that he'd just made a mistake, that Doc's memory had been less than perfect after all.

Thaena moved fast. She had her hand around Doc's throat, although it was clear she wasn't yet squeezing. She stared at his eyes. "Say, 'Hear my words, for I will tell no lies.'"

Teraeth looked up. "Mother, stop it!"

Doc thrashed in her grip. "Fuck you."

"You were always so willful," Thaena growled. "Say, 'Hear my words, for I will tell no lies.'"

"Thaena!" Janel stood. "What are you doing?"

"Stay out of this, child," Thaena said without turning her head. "Say it!"

Doc let out a strangled cry. "Hear my words, for I will tell no lies!"

"Why didn't it work?" Thaena asked her former lover.

Janel ran over to Teraeth. "What is going on? She's . . . this is thorra." Bullying. The strong taking advantage of the weak. He remembered enough of her lessons on Jorat to know it was the lowest of insults.

Teraeth couldn't find a mistake. The ritual was . . . no. There it was. Seven glyphs in the book and only two on the markings on the floor.

Teraeth scowled. That was the spot for the race glyph. There should have only been *one*.

*Both* rituals were wrong.

"It was never going to work," Doc said. Then he laughed. "Put me down, Kay. You want to know? Fine. I'll tell you. No need for all this."

Thaena let go of Doc, but her expression was still something terrible to behold.

Doc rubbed his neck. Then he looked over and stared straight at Teraeth. The corner of his mouth quirked, but his eyes were sad.

Teraeth fought down a feeling of absolute dread.

Doc turned back to Thaena and held out his hands. "It was never going to work because you can't pick the same flower twice, Kay. All the races have *already* had their immortality stripped from them. The last immortal race lost their immortality five hundred years ago when the vordreth stepped up to the bar. It's done."

"You're—" Thaena looked stunned, then incredulous, and finally furious. "The voras. The vané are an offshoot of the voras. But you became a separate race. *You were supposed to be a separate race!*"

"We became a separate *nation,* with a separate culture and a knowledge of magic that allowed us to stretch out our mortal life spans indefinitely. We were so good at it, even *we* didn't realize we stopped being immortal when the voras fell. The reason we live forever is the same reason mimics live forever–because every time we tsali ourselves or change our shape or just heal ourselves, we're reversing the aging process. House D'Mon would probably have noticed the same pattern if they didn't all die violent early deaths the way they do." Doc shrugged. "I didn't find out the truth until I performed the Ritual of Night myself fifteen hundred years ago. I'm sorry, Kay; I *did* try to save the voramer. We all did. It was only when we saw the ritual didn't work that we realized what was going on."

Thaena was a statue. She turned her head lightly. "And you said nothing."

"Naturally," Doc said. "Because we all know how you get when you think humans are trying to 'outlive their allotted hours.' Why would you treat the vané any differently? There are people in this room who have been alive for fourteen thousand years. We didn't want to lose that."

No one in the entire room said a word. Hardly anyone breathed.

"You changed the ritual," Teraeth said, his voice little higher than a whisper.

Both his parents turned to him.

"What was that?" Thaena asked.

Teraeth swallowed and pointed to the book. "You changed the ritual. If you knew the ritual wouldn't work, why did you change it?"

Doc shook his head. "Because that ritual was already changed. Relos Var's work, I've been told. If I'd used the ritual in *that* book, it wouldn't have targeted the vané. It would have drained power from you, Kay. From you and all the other Guardians, and it would have smashed Vol Karoth's prison wide open. That's why I had to take the throne away from Khaeriel; she'd have performed the sabotaged ritual. So you're welcome."

Teraeth looked over at Senera. The look of surprise on her face made Teraeth suspect Relos Var hadn't let her in on this part of the plan.

"So I have been made a fool by all sides, then," Thaena said with a voice straight from the crypt.

Teraeth's attention whipped back to his mother. He knew that voice. That voice was a terrible sign. "Mother, no!" Teraeth let go of Janel's hand and started running forward.

"Yeah, I guess so," Doc said calmly, "but you have to admit, you made it easy."

Thaena's eyes blazed. The corner of her lip curled in a hateful sneer. She held out her hand and made a fist.

Doc dropped to the ground with horrible, awful finality.

Dead.

All Teraeth could think of as he ran forward was that Doc had known. His father had absolutely known. Known how Thaena would react, known what that cost would be.

This was why he'd sent everyone else away.

Teraeth made it to his father's corpse just a second after the man fell. He stared up at his mother. "You didn't have to do that!"

"But I did. He deceived me," Thaena growled. She turned her head and glared at Janel, who had followed Teraeth down to the center. "Don't you dare judge me. He's doomed all of us. I've spent five hundred years chasing a phantom solution that was *never going to work*!"

"Bring him back," Janel said. "You made your point. Now bring him back."

"No," Thaena growled. Tears were rolling down her cheeks, but Teraeth rather suspected that they were more a sign of rage than sadness. "I'll throw his souls to the demons of Hell myself before I Return him or allow him to set one single foot in the Land of Peace. I'll feed him to the hellhounds myself!"

Janel's nostrils flared. "Khaemezra, he should have told you, but that's not–"

"Do not question me," Thaena growled. "Do not make me doubt my decision to spare you, *demon*!"

Janel closed her mouth and drew back.

"Mother–" Teraeth took a deep breath. He couldn't believe–

He couldn't believe this was happening.

Teraeth honestly spent a second wondering if this was real, if this wasn't an illusion spun by Chainbreaker. A nightmare. Anything but what was actually happening.

Thaena turned to the court. "Crown my son."

Teraeth raised his head. *"What?"*

Thaena ignored him. "Terindel was king. He had a son. Terindel is dead, thus his son is heir. *Crown his son king.*"

Megrea licked her lips nervously. "I don't think it's quite that simple–"

Thaena closed her fist again, and Megrea died.

The whole hall surged up. Thaena raised her arm, and a barrier of energy sprang up all around the hall, blocking everyone in the audience from the floor and those few still there. Teraeth. Janel. A few Founders.

Teraeth looked over to where he'd been sitting. Xivan had drawn Urthaenriel.

Thaena turned to Daynos. "How many more have to die before it *becomes* simple?"

The Founder stared at her in utter and total shock and then motioned to the other. "Fetch the crown."

Teraeth stood. "Mother, no. This isn't . . . I don't want this!"

"I don't care what you want," Thaena growled. "You will do as you're told." She looked at him, and he felt her pull on the servitor link. She did not do so gently. He gasped and found himself on his knees.

Teraeth heard the sound of someone running in his direction. He looked up, saw it was Janel, and held out a hand. "No. Don't." His voice was the barest whisper, but she stopped. Her expression was full of horror.

He knew Daynos was talking, but he couldn't hear the words. Maybe he didn't want to hear the words. This was all a surreal nightmare.

His mother had just killed his father.

She wasn't done.

Light bloomed to the side, the impossible signature of someone opening a gate. He didn't look over to see who it was.

Teraeth flinched as Daynos put the crown on his head. The vané founder's voice was shaking as he said, "–crown you king of the vané people. Long may you reign."

No. No, no, no, no.

Teraeth felt his mother grab him by the arm and yank him to his feet. "Now you'll earn your place."

She teleported them both out of the room.

# PART III

## Rituals of Death

# 104: The Other Side

***(Kihrin's story)***

I stepped out of the gate just a few seconds too late. Just in time to see Thaena vanish, taking Teraeth with her. Just in time to hear the shocked silence of a crowd that still didn't quite understand what had happened but knew that it was something terrible.

Immediately, I heard Urthaenriel's singing. *What?* I wondered if I had developed an impromptu fever; there was simply no way Xivan could be here in the Manol capital.

Then I heard Senera's voice. "Lord Var?"

Really, you'd think I would have learned not to assume anything impossible.

"Kihrin!"

I had exactly that much warning before Janel was in my arms, which, while not unpleasant, was clearly not a happy reunion.

There was a clamor. Orders were shouted out and people told to leave the area. The few guards allowed inside the building, knowing only that outsiders had appeared in a time and place where that should have been impossible, were heading our way.

"What happened?" I asked Janel.

She had tears in her eyes while managing to maintain an expression of murderous rage. "The Ritual of Night doesn't work. And when Khaemezra realized that, she killed Terindel"–her voice broke–"had them crown Teraeth king, and . . . she took him. I don't know what happens next. Nothing good. Kihrin, she's not thinking clearly."

"Wait. The Ritual of Night didn't work?" Relos Var's voice boomed through the hall. "You performed it?" He stood in the center of the hall, looking down at the marks etched in the floor left over from the rite in question. "Oh. You performed it *correctly.*"

Senera's voice answered, "Terindel performed the unaltered ritual, sir. He said he'd memorized it."

Grizzst started laughing. There was a note of hysteria to the sound.

"No one move!" ordered one of the guards, who had somehow decided that this was an excellent time to restore some order and figure out what was going on. I felt sorry for him.

"Put your weapons down, damn it!" some important-looking vané ordered.[1] "It's far too late for that foolishness."

I stared at the spot where Teraeth had stood just a moment before as his mother teleported them both away from the Mother of Trees. I felt like I could feel the lingering echo, the hollow space in my soul emptied out by Teraeth's absence, by the sense of loss that absence promised. The echo matched up perfectly with the reality of Doc's lifeless body, staring up with empty eyes at the vaulted ceiling above.

I buried my despair, pushed it down deep before Vol Karoth could feel it and reach out through that wound to touch the world outside his prison. My heart pounded, the blood in my veins raged, my focus centered on that single truth: Thaena had taken Teraeth.

I wasn't naïve enough to think she had any good intentions toward her newly crowned son. On some level, she must have predicted this possibility. Thaena must have suspected that something might go wrong with the Ritual of Night, that somehow her enemies might find a way to sabotage the ritual. Surely, it hadn't been coincidence that she'd put Teraeth in a position to stand in as sympathetic tie-in to the Manol nation. He was their king, after all.

She'd made contingency plans, finally come due.

The betrayal filled my mouth with bile. I'd trusted her. I'd trusted Thaena even though I'd known she'd been willing to gaesh and sell her own granddaughter–my mother–into slavery. I'd trusted her even though she'd refused to Return so many people, even though she'd lied and manipulated again and again. Somehow, I'd actually let myself believe she was somehow different from Relos Var. But she wasn't any different at all. Even if she hadn't started off like he had, she'd eventually convinced herself that it was acceptable to kill or betray any number of people for the "greater good"–whatever that meant. She'd taken a duty and turned it into an entitlement, an excuse for her own power. Who had the right to tell Thaena she was wrong to sacrifice her son or the entire vané people, if she felt it was the only way to save everyone else.

*I'll carve my way through nations.* Teraeth had told me, *But don't ask me to kill you.*

Egotistical as it may seem, I felt like the whole universe teetered on that moment, and I watched the pendulum waver and then swing in the other direction.

"What's Rev'arric doing here?" Janel said the name like it was a curse word.

[1] I believe that was Daynos.

I glanced down at her. She'd called both Thaena and Relos Var by their real names, which wasn't like her. "He was here to stop the ritual," I said. "My doing. I promise I'll explain."

"There's only one reason that Thaena would demand her son crowned and then take him with her," Valathea said. She stood at the entrance to the room, and just behind her, I saw both my parents–my father alive and well. Valathea walked into the room, never once looking down at Doc's body. My parents did, though, and I saw guilt and anguish cross Khaeriel's face.

"They'll sympathetically link Teraeth to the nation, not the race. Our deaths would be enough tenyé to power the warding crystal."

"Right," Grizzst said, still rubbing his jaw. "Tie it to a country instead of a race. That would work."

"Yes," Relos Var said. "I imagine you gave her the idea with what you did to Quur." He spared a brief glare for Valathea but seemed unwilling to stop and make polite introductions.

"What did Grizzst do to Quur–?" Thurvishar started to ask.

"But the warding crystal's destroyed," I said. "It won't work."

"It *will* work," Relos Var corrected. "If she performs the ritual correctly–and there's no reason to think she won't–it's perfectly capable of wiping out every vané who is part of the Manol nation. It will simply accomplish *nothing*."

"Oh, that's not quite true," I said. "Seriously, what happens if all that energy goes to a warding crystal that doesn't exist?"

"I would imagine it blows up Atrine, destroys Demon Falls, and empties out Lake Jorat on to Marakor," Relos Var answered. "And then millions die . . . while *still* accomplishing nothing." He looked like he'd tasted something foul. "Best-case scenario, she actually stops and *thinks* for long enough to check the crystal, realizes it's broken, and has Argas fix it. Then it imprisons Vol Karoth and still wipes out the vané."

"All that takes time," Thurvishar said. "Thaena would need time to adapt the ritual, figure out the right marks. That's weeks of planning."

"Have you forgotten Shadrag Gor exists already?" Senera said. "While we've stood here talking, she'd already had *days*."

"We can't be certain she even knows about–" Thurvishar stopped himself. "Fine. You're right."

Everyone began to condense, as those with an interest or even just curiosity in what was going on gravitated toward Valathea, Relos Var, and Grizzst.

I looked around the floor of the room. The normally pristine wood floor was deeply gouged with all the marks of the failed Ritual of Night. "Small consolation, but there isn't enough room in the Lighthouse at Shadrag Gor to do this sort of work. That means she'll need to leave it if she plans to perform the actual ritual or some variant." I looked over at Senera. "Can you find out where the ritual's going to be held?"

She looked sick as she shook her head. "No," she said. "That's the future. The Name of All Things can't see the future. If there was only one place possible, it would be different, but–"

"It doesn't matter," Khored said. "We know where she'll go."

A nearly collective inhalation of shock heralded the entrance of the God of Destruction. I hadn't noticed Khored's arrival. No open gates, no teleport flashes. And he wasn't alone either.

Taja, Goddess of Luck, and Tya, Goddess of Magic, flanked him.

It slapped me like a physical blow that both Khored and Taja were vané who might have personal reasons to not want to see their people destroyed. I couldn't even be sure that Thaena's ritual wouldn't affect them in some manner. That wasn't even counting the fact that while Thaena may not have been historically fond of Atrin Kandor, the emperor's patron god, Khored, *was*–and that same Khored was also Teraeth's grandfather. They had stakes in this outcome. Plenty of them.

*People will do stupid things when they're scared, Kihrin.* Taja had been talking about Thaena, and she'd been right to do so.

I was less certain why Tya had chosen to be present, but it was possible she just wasn't a big fan of genocide.

Khored removed his helmet, revealing a black-skinned Manol vané who looked enough like Teraeth to make me grind my teeth.

"We're here to help," Khored said.

The silence in the parliament hall was truly stunning. Here was a group of people–many of the most powerful in the world, including gods–who absolutely hated each other. And the rules were changing so fast.

I found myself wondering just who had switched sides.[2]

Not Relos Var, of course. I still didn't trust him, but if I was sure of one thing, it was this: he sure as hell wasn't in league with Khaemezra. To believe otherwise was to give him credit for a long con that would have put his performance in Atrine to shame.

Also, that fact would have been the answer to the question Thurvishar had forced Senera to ask.

Anyway, Khored and the others had made a hell of an entrance as well as a declaration, so I took the bait. "Okay, where would Thaena perform the ritual?"

Taja gave me a tight, grim smile. "What's the only location intricately tied to all things vané, the center without which our entire people become lost?"

[2] Kihrin's mistake here was thinking that there were ever sides at all.

Oh. "The Well of Spirals."

I heard the words echo around the room. A whole lot of people had come to the same conclusion at the same time.

Relos Var nodded. "Of course." He narrowed his eyes as he looked at three gods. "Are any more of you coming?"

The two goddesses pretended they simply hadn't heard Relos Var, but Khored stopped. The God of Destruction met Relos Var's eyes. The expression on the god's face was unreadable–cold and distant as the moons. They stared at each other for several long, tense seconds.

Then Khored turned to me and said, "Thaena's had Argas fix the crystal. Naturally, Galava and Ompher will be helping her defend their position."

Relos Var's jaw clenched.

"'Naturally'?" My father came to stand next to me, put his hand on my shoulder. I put my hand over his.

"They used to be married," Tya murmured.

"Which ones?" I asked her. "Thaena and–?"

"All of them," Taja said, shrugging as if to say, "You know how it is." "Thaena, Galava, and Ompher. They stayed close, even after Thaena left the marriage."

"Oh," I said. "I see." I glanced over at Janel. She didn't seem to think the idea was particularly strange.

My father squeezed my shoulder, which I took as a reminder to focus even if he hadn't meant it that way. "Galava helped me once. It's hard to believe–" He exhaled. "She seemed nice."

"She *is* nice," Tya said bitterly. "But she's convinced herself resealing Vol Karoth's prison is worth the price. A price *she* won't be paying."

"But the vané can't pay it either," I protested. "Isn't that the whole point? They *already did.*"

"They're not sacrificing our race's immortality," Khored answered. "They're sacrificing the *nation*–the lives of every man, woman, and child–and they're telling themselves it's only fair since we've all long outlived our 'human' life spans. When my grandson finishes the ritual, he'll kill himself and in doing so will also kill the millions sympathetically linked to him. And Vol Karoth's prison will be resealed."

An uneasy silence answered this. Most of the people in the room qualified as Manol "citizens."

Which meant they would die.

"Have they already started?" Relos Var said.

"Sixty-three percent chance," Taja replied.

After a beat of hesitation, Relos Var nodded. "Then let's do this."

"No, wait–!" I started to say that we needed to do a little planning of our own, perhaps figure out a battle strategy.

But no. He opened the gate underneath the entire parliament floor. The whole area that the ritual carvings had taken up and a bit more, so all of us–*all* of us–fell through.[3]

I wasn't prepared.

As we landed, I felt a moment of profound disorientation. I'd expected the Well of Spirals: a beautiful manicured garden of reflecting pools under an illusionary blue sky, filled with green-gowned attendants and luxurious calm.

All that was gone.

The redwoods of the Kirpis had been cleared for miles in every direction. A giant slab of granite had been raised up out of the ground in the distance, leveled off and (I presumed) carved with the necessary symbols for the ritual. I didn't see any of the Well of Spirals priests, but I took it as given that they were very likely dead.

A figure danced on that platform in the distance. I felt my gut twist. I knew it would be Teraeth and, worse, knew he danced a variation of the Maevanos.

Janel liked to talk about being groomed by Relos Var, but that was nothing compared to what Thaena had done to her son.

And in between us and him?

Armies.

I had barely a second to comprehend what I saw. Not just armies of people, although that too, but animals, monsters. Gryphons and giant thriss lizards, massive white elephants that glowed ethereally, betraying their otherworldly natures. The trees hadn't been cut down but had simply moved themselves to the side. Thriss armies. Black Brotherhood assassins. So many and so varied that I couldn't even comprehend the full array of forces, never mind label their nature or numbers.

Three figures stood near the edge of the plateau, and I recognized them all: Galava dressed in green; Ompher, who looked like there was no difference between where the rock stopped and he began; Argas, hallowed in mathematics, surrounded by a swirling field of weapons instead of his normal books.

And towering above all of them . . .

"You know," I said, "I forgot Thaena knows how to change into a dragon."

From a distance, she both did and didn't resemble her son Sharanakal. No lava showed between cracks in her skin. No molten rock

[3] I have to assume Taja, Khored, and Tya might have chosen not to pass through the gate, but it was going where they intended.

dripped from her mouth. She was black-scaled and glossy, trimmed in silver that matched her eyes.

I looked around me. Besides the core group of us, Relos Var had scooped up everyone who'd been on the floor. Founders were there, guards, people from the crowds who'd just wandered too close. My parents. No more than a hundred people in total. People who certainly hadn't asked for this and probably wouldn't survive it.

But no matter how much I wanted to get them away from this, if we didn't stop this ritual, they were all dead.

"So it begins," Thaena said.

She gave us no time, of course. Thaena breathed fire even as Black Brotherhood archers loosed a hail of death into the sky. The ground began to shake, whether from earthquake or elephants, I couldn't tell. Trees near us began to move.

Their armies surged forward.

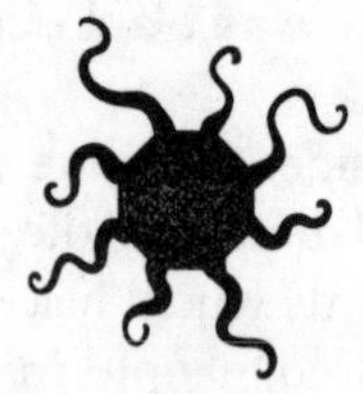

# 105: The Uninvited Guests

***(Janel's story)***

Taja shouted, "Stop the ritual! We'll take care of the others!"

Janel didn't need to be told twice. She grabbed Kihrin's hand and started running. Out of the corner of her eye, Janel saw Thurvishar and Senera break off from the main group and follow.

The ground heaved under their feet as a giant obelisk of stone punched up from the ground in front of them and began falling in their direction. Just as quickly, the stone shattered and fell to pieces, giant shards missing them by minuscule, lucky inches. Janel glanced over her shoulder to see Khored pointing his glass sword in their direction before returning his attention to the stone figure that had suddenly appeared in front of the god: Ompher.

A roar shook the field of battle as an opal-colored white dragon slammed into Thaena, teeth clenched around her throat. They both rolled, knocking over entire trees and crushing at least three elephants.

"Damn," Kihrin said, and Janel knew he'd seen that too.

Janel thought turning into a dragon was a tactical mistake on Thaena's part, but in all likelihood, Thaena hadn't expected Relos Var to show up to this fight. So now she was fighting someone every bit as powerful in a form he was far more comfortable with than she probably was. It wasn't playing to her strengths, whereas Relos Var couldn't say the same.

Janel made herself focus; as tempting as it was to watch that sort of battle, they had slightly more pressing concerns. Like saving Teraeth's life. As well as that of every vané and half of Quur.

Janel heard a closer roar and realized that one of the thriss lizards—vaguely like a drake, only much, much larger—was rushing at them with a mouthful of daggerlike teeth. Thurvishar held up the gem in his hand, and a giant stomping tree tripped, flailed, and fell on top of the animal. A hail of arrows from Thaena's holy hunters loosed in their direction, impacting harmlessly against walls of magical energy Senera summoned.

"We have to keep going!" Kihrin shouted as he pulled his sword from a Black Brotherhood assassin. Two more replaced the dead man, and he was clearly feeling the frustration of having their way blocked.

Janel twisted to the side as another Black Brotherhood assassin lunged at her. "I'm sure if we just explain that we can't stop and play, they'll"–she shoved the man's dagger out of the way and slammed her sword through his torso–"be happy"–Janel spun and ripped her sword up and through the spine of someone trying to approach Kihrin from the side–"to let us go!"

Kihrin moved so gracefully, it almost didn't seem like he was even trying. He ducked under the swing of a thriss curved sword, danced to the side, disarmed the man, and slit his throat in the same motion. "Wait until they start standing back up again."

Janel exhaled. He was right. She'd forgotten that the enemies they fought were Black Brotherhood. Did Thaena have to be paying attention to Return them back to life? "You know what would be helpful right now? Horses!"

"Hey, Senera!" Kihrin shouted. "Any chance you know that smoke horse trick Relos Var used in Atrine?"

Senera looked back from where she had just finished firing a volley of hunter arrows back at their targets. "What? No!"

"Damn."

To the side, a gryphon swooped down and picked up a struggling vané man before flying him up into the sky and releasing him. The man dropped a few feet and then flew up, gesturing with his arms. The gryphon screeched in panic as its feathers burst into flame.

At least five giants of one kind or another were on the field, along with pillars of fire or ice. Lightning bolts slammed out of the heavens. Some of it was probably an illusion, but Janel had no way to tell what was real and what wasn't.

A wall of thorns rose up in front of them, and just as quickly withered and died. More stones erupted from the ground and tried to smash them.

"I don't want to alarm anyone," Kihrin said, "but I think Ompher and Galava have noticed us!"

"Fortunately, so have the gods on our side!" Senera said and then seemed to catch herself. She grumbled something under her breath.[1]

Cracks began appearing in the air in front of them, and Janel's heart froze as she recognized the signs.

"No," she cursed. "Damn it all, *no*!"

Demons poured out of the cracks, laughing maniacally.

In the distance, a familiar form emerged through the Veil. Xaltorath

1 She said, "I can't believe I just said that."

didn't look in her direction. The demon had her eyes focused on a different target. Grinning widely, she started running toward where Thaena and Relos Var battled. The two dragons seemed quite oblivious to anything but each other.

"Kihrin! Xaltorath's here. If she was ever going to have a chance to eat an immortal's soul, this is the place!"

Kihrin stopped and turned in the direction Janel was pointing. "Shit." He grimaced. "I can't. Go! Keep that bastard from making this worse." Kihrin gestured toward Senera and Thurvishar. "You two go with her."

"No," Thurvishar protested. "We're the only thing keeping you alive!"

A giant column of stone took that moment to fall an inch to Kihrin's right. He looked down at the rock, then back up at Thurvishar.

"Right," Thurvishar said, "you'll be fine." He tapped Senera on the shoulder. "Let's go."

Janel was already running.

# 106: When Luck Runs Out

***(Talea's story)***

Almost as soon as the fighting started, a giant crack in the ground separated Talea and her companions from the others. Xivan held up Urthaenriel and pushed Talea behind her, just as a giant fireball tried to form on their location. Before the spell could hit them, some force or wind pushed it away, so it exploded high overhead.

"Xivan! Talea!" a familiar voice called out. "Over here!"

Talea looked over to see Queen Khaeriel–former queen Khaeriel, she supposed–lowering her hands from spellcasting. Next to her stood High Lord Therin D'Mon, not exactly one of Talea's favorite people. He didn't have any weapons, but Talea could assume he was a healer.

Xivan seemed to welcome someone she recognized. Twisting vines tried to grow from the ground and wrap around their feet, but Xivan sliced Urthaenriel through them and they fell away.

The ground shook violently, and all four fought to keep their balance.

"We're going to work triage!" Therin shouted. "Cover us?"

Talea exhaled in relief when Xivan said, "Of course. Let's go."

It's not that Talea feared fighting, but some battles could be won and others only survived. And then only if one was very, very lucky. Talea knew exactly where she stood on a battlefield with gods.

Helping the injured would be dangerous enough.

Despite the miraculous close calls that many on the battlefield seemed to be experiencing, there were plenty of injured to be found. And also plenty of enemies willing to add her to the list.

Talea found herself fighting off a lion with a scorpion tail and a snake-headed man while Xivan at her back was dealing with a Thaenan priest who had died earlier and was now apparently being possessed by a demon. She was starting to feel mildly concerned about the outcome when one of her foes tripped on a piece of rubble created by the remains of a stone pillar Ompher had been tossing around. She speared him, spun up and over his corpse to kick the lion and then used that moment to free her weapon and bring it down on the animal's head.

"Nicely done," Xivan said as she finished dismembering her attacker.

Therin gestured over to a clear spot. "This way!"

They all ran. Khaeriel used the winds to blow away some opportunistic arrows, while Therin broke bones and made enemies bleed if they came too close.

When they reached the clearing, Talea realized that it wasn't perfectly clear of people. A light-skinned vané woman stood there, watching the fighting. She had silver curly hair and wide, white wings, and she looked exhausted.

"Taja," whispered Talea.

"Don't distract her," Khaeriel said. "This is no shelter. Therin, we need to leave! If another god shows themselves–"

A loud, grinding noise filled the air, and a second later, several dozen large razor-edged wheels rolled through the clearing. Xivan pulled Talea to the side a second before she would have been slaughtered. Khaeriel lifted herself and Therin into the air.

A brown-robed man with a circle of spinning razors rotating around him landed in front of Taja. Symbols, shapes, numbers made a similar, if less lethal, halo around his head. He held an open book in one hand and wore wore a small but satisfied smile on his face.

Taja sighed. "Argas."

"–then we shall be in trouble," Khaeriel finished.

"Taja, why are you doing this?" The smile slipped a little, but Argas didn't take any notice of the rest of them; his attention focused purely on the goddess he'd known for millennia. "There's no reason to let Vol Karoth go free."

"No reason?" Taja murmured. "My people are *no reason*?"

"You know I didn't mean it like that. Damn it, stop twisting my words!" Argas's expression turned ugly, hurt, the frustration of a thousand years of conversational barbs pricking against his souls. "Isn't humanity's survival worth the cost? We sacrifice a small percentage to save the whole. This math is easy, Taja."

"That's the problem, Argas," Taja said. "One of the people you're going to kill is standing right in front of you, and you haven't even looked at her." She gestured toward Khaeriel, who seemed rightfully terrified. "But all you can see is the math. Did you ever see the people?"

He pressed his lips together in a tight, thin line. "I fixed the crystal, Taja–"

"Ah, did Thaena have to show you how?" Taja's voice mocked.

He abandoned whatever he'd been about to say, whatever he'd been about to do. Rage filled Argas's eyes, but his voice remained calm and even. "Help me satisfy one more curiosity, then, would you, Taja?" He said it with a tone Talea knew too well, from long experience. A voice that comes just seconds before "lessons" and fists and the red-blood fury of terrible violence.

"What is it, Argas?" Taja's words were resigned, tired. She already knew the answer to her question.

Talea grabbed Xivan's arm. "Get down."

"What does it take to kill you?" Argas asked. Without waiting on her answer, the weapons spinning around him stopped moving, paused, and then all flew at Taja, all at once. A second group immediately replaced them, but this set exploded outward–not just at the Goddess of Luck but at everyone nearby. Including them.

Talea heard screaming as she felt the projectiles hit the ground all around them, a slice of pain across one leg as a razor didn't miss, another one in her side. She realized the screaming was hers.

And the screaming was Taja's.

# 107: Battlefield Dance

***(Kihrin's story)***

As soon as the others left, I turned myself invisible. It meant less than nothing versus wizards of a certain power level or the Eight Immortals themselves. But against animals, monsters, demons, and the Black Brotherhood? Invisibility was effective. I made much better time through the battlefield.

Well, sort of.

As I said, the Eight Immortals could still see me just fine. I assumed Thaena had given the others strict instructions against letting anyone—but me in particular—near her son. Fortunately, I had three gods watching my back. When Ompher would try to smash me with boulders, Khored would disintegrate them. When Galava tried to trip me with vines, Taja made sure I was always just a little too fast for the plants to catch. If the ground opened up under my feet, Tya paved it over with fields of rainbow energy.

In the distance, Grizzst fought demons and humans alike with a thin wand in his hand, summoning up magical beams to freeze and shatter. Across the battlefield, Tya created fountains of multicolored lights, sending out scintillating waves that evaporated enemies as they passed over them.

The other side wasn't exactly letting themselves be pushed over, however. Ompher opened cracks in the earth, crashed them closed on people who fell inside. Galava moved the entire forest and every animal in it against us, and that wasn't counting her control over bodies. And Argas—

Actually, I wasn't sure where Argas was or whether that was a good thing.

Then I tripped on a tree branch and nearly went sprawling. I paused, staring blankly at the offending branch. It wasn't an animated branch, mind you. It hadn't been reaching for me. I'd just tripped. Call it clumsiness.

Or bad luck.

I fought down a terrible feeling of dread.

"Taja," I whispered, but if she was in any position to answer, she didn't.

The whole world seemed to hold its breath. I kept running. Whatever had happened—and something must have—it had distracted the gods.

Twice while climbing I almost fell, and I felt a sense of . . . vulnerability . . . to which I was unaccustomed. As if luck might not always turn in my favor. I pushed down my panic. I reached the plateau and climbed to the top.

I found Teraeth.

He looked dazed, his eyes expressionless. He held a dagger. Occult markings were engraved into the floor, but I knew they wouldn't be the same as the Ritual of Night. This was something new, something Thaena had devised. She'd used something familiar: her own holy rites. I knew the Maevanos well enough to recognize Teraeth was almost finished.

When he plunged that dagger into his chest, the vané people would die.

# 108: The Enemy of Our Enemy

***(Janel's story)***

Janel sprinted toward Xaltorath, aware she had two wizards behind her, one of whom she couldn't trust.[1] But Xaltorath seemed intent on taking down Relos Var, so Senera's motives would be straightforward, at least on this one occasion.

Traversing the battlefield proved to be a frustrating experience in more ways than one for Janel. The problem was memory.

She remembered everything. But knowledge didn't equal skill. Casting spells required mnemonic memory, muscle memory, practiced to the point of automatic reflex. Which she hadn't done. Janel would start to cast a spell and then remember *she* didn't know what to do. C'indrol knew; Janel didn't. In many ways, she'd have been better off abandoning her mortal body and roaming as a demon, but that wasn't an acceptable option for several reasons. Least of which because any demons on the field were fair targets for all sides.

So Janel mostly ended up cutting down enemies with her sword. Which wasn't her sword at all–it belonged to King Kelanis. At least the sword had a nice balance, but she would have preferred something twice as large.

"Up ahead!" Senera pointed.

Relos Var and Thaena had both vanished. A second later, a large explosion blasted the area; they hadn't vanished, just turned back to human size.

Dragon-size targets were awfully easy to hit.

"I see!" Janel dodged out of the way of a giant tentacle-limbed demon grabbing for her, but one of the creature's curling limbs wrapped around her sword arm, barbs sinking into her flesh. She moved to set the thing on fire, but as she did, a slender curved sword cleaved down through the demon's head, so fast the monster didn't have time to make a noise before her attacker fell to pieces. She turned back, expecting to shout a thank-you to Talea or Xivan–

[1] I shall assume she meant Senera.

But it was Xaltorath's shadow demon, darkness wrapped around him like a thick, black cloak.

The creature paused for just a moment, giving off the impression he stared at her. The demon nodded at her–just once–before he vanished and reappeared farther away, assassinating another demon from the shadows before vanishing again.

*He's killing demons,* she thought. *He's only attacking demons.*

Janel almost laughed. How perfectly appropriate. Xaltorath had given her a brother, of a sort. And here he was, lashing out at the other demons, the same way she always had. Janel knew nothing about this demon–who he'd been as a human, if he'd been driven insane like most demons or had somehow escaped that curse too–but in that split second, she felt a warm flare of kinship. Then she pushed her curiosity aside and concentrated on the battle.

Most of Thaena's forces had fled the area, and those who hadn't were dead. Relos Var had transformed back into a human shape, fighting both Thaena and Xaltorath simultaneously. The energies streaming around them were astonishing and terrifying. Off to the side, the stranger who'd come through the portal with Relos Var, Kihrin, and Thurvishar fought a separate but potentially overlapping battle involving a colossal demon swarm who seemed unusually focused on him.

Janel saw the issue immediately: Relos Var was losing. If they just left this whole thing alone, Xaltorath and Thaena would rid the world of Var in just a few short seconds. Which she'd have gladly accepted if only Xaltorath or Thaena winning were any better.

"I can't believe I'm about to do this." Janel watched as one of Xaltorath's claw strikes dropped Relos Var to his knees.

"We have to do something!" Senera was already starting to spellcast, but Janel could easily understand why even a wizard of Senera's skill level might find herself intimidated at the thought of wading into that battle.

Janel gave the woman a contemptuous stare. "No," she said. "We don't have to do a thing." She turned back, sighing. "But we're going to."

Janel debated her options, none of which were good. It wasn't a matter of which was the most dangerous–they were all dangerous–but which of the three Janel might survive fighting. Thaena could kill with a glance.

That was a problem.

So she melted the ground under Xaltorath's feet to catch her attention.

"Hey, Xaltorath!" she shouted. "Can anyone play this game?"

Just then, Thaena paused and looked off into the distance. Her quicksilver eyes widened.

The Goddess of Death vanished.

"What just happened?" Senera looked around.

Thurvishar also scanned the area. "There's always a chance that was a good thing?" He sounded uncertain.

Meanwhile, Xaltorath raised her head and grinned. ***OH YES. THIS PARTY IS ALWAYS READY FOR MORE DANCERS.*** She started moving in Janel's direction.

# 109: Books and Coins

***(Talea's story)***

Talea pulled herself slowly to her feet, assessing the damage. Khaeriel had knocked aside the majority of blades; she and Therin looked fine. Which made Talea glad, because she was absolutely going to bleed out if they didn't heal her. Xivan had taken some injuries, but she was tough to hurt permanently.

But Taja . . .

The Goddess of Luck lay on the ground, with multiple stab wounds from Argas's razors. Crimson stained the front of her otherwise silver gown.

The God of Knowledge wasn't smiling as he looked down at the dying goddess. "You spread yourself too thin, Taja. Tried to save too many people on the battlefield. Bet you never saw this outcome."

Xivan transformed Urthaenriel into a spear and swept it forward through Argas's spinning wheel. A thousand razors that would have sliced a human–living or dead–into fine strips of flesh instead shattered against Godslayer. The spearpoint punched through Argas's heart and burst out the other side. In one quick, smooth motion, Xivan pulled the weapon back and returned it to a black sword.

Argas looked surprised. The spinning razors fell to the ground. The halo vanished. The book was apparently just a book; it landed next to Argas with a wet, dull slap as the God of Knowledge collapsed to the ground, dead.

"Actually," Taja whispered, "I did."

The whole battlefield fell silent.

Talea didn't think it was her imagination. All fighting paused. Talea felt certain that each of the other Eight Immortals had felt that death. They knew one of their own had fallen.

"Therin!" Talea screamed. "Help her!" She scrambled over to where the goddess lay on the ground, ignoring her own injuries.

Taja's breathing was labored. The blades pinned the goddess to the ground; Talea didn't dare pull them out. They were killing Taja and also the only thing keeping her alive.

Therin knelt beside Taja and raised a hand out over the woman.

"Don't bother," Taja whispered. "Argas was . . . right. I overextended myself. You can't give me enough tenyé to fix this. Tell Kihrin to remember what I said–don't play by their rules. He can make his own." She reached out a hand, blindly, not able to look down for whatever she was trying to find.

Talea grabbed her hand. "What? What do you need?"

Taja's hand closed on her own. Talea felt something cold and hard slip between her fingers, and she looked down in surprise to see that Taja had palmed a coin into her hand. "Keep it." A smile lingered ghostly on Taja's lips. "For luck."

Talea stared blankly at the coin, her vision going blurry from the tears in her eyes. "No, no, no. Khaeriel, fix this! Therin, *fix her*!"

Khaeriel had a hand between her teeth. She shook her head, made a wounded, animal sound. "I . . . I cannot . . . Her aura–"

Taja's hand on Talea's loosened its grip and fell away. Her eyes stared blindly.

The Goddess of Luck died.

*Thurvishar stopped his recitation, eyes searching Kihrin's face. "I can stop if you like. I know–"*

*Kihrin wiped his eyes. "No, it's fine. I mean, it's not fine. It's nowhere even close to the definition of* fine.*" He stared off at a far wall for a few seconds, lost. "Do you think she did see it coming at the end?"*

*"I think she knew the odds," Thurvishar answered cautiously.*

*"That's not really an answer," Kihrin said.*

*"But it's the only one I have."*

# 110: Logical Fallacies

***(Kihrin's story)***

I rushed forward. "Teraeth!" I screamed at him, but he danced on, oblivious. Sweat slicked his body. He must have been exhausted, but he couldn't stop dancing. His mother's magic wouldn't allow it.

I pulled my hands into fists. I refused to let this continue. This ritual wasn't a solution. It was, at best, nothing more than a stopgap. And not worth the lives it would take in payment.

I hadn't realized until that moment how much Vol Karoth terrified Thaena. That she was willing to do this just to put off facing him for a few more centuries.

As if summoned because I thought her name, Thaena appeared.

"I don't think I'm going to let you interfere this time," Thaena said.

I turned to face her. I won't lie–I was pretty scared myself. I wasn't holding Urthaenriel. I didn't have a Cornerstone. My own magical defenses were decent, and I hadn't neglected my talismans, but against Thaena?

She could kill me whenever she liked. With a snap of her fingers. With a wave of her hand.

I sheathed my sword. Why pretend?

She looked a little puzzled, but she didn't kill me instantly, so I took it as a good sign.

"Come on, Khaemezra," I said. "You don't have to do this. He's your son. Doesn't that matter to you?"

"Of course it does," Thaena said. "You think I wanted this to be the way things turned out? I'm doing what I have to do. The fact that I don't enjoy it doesn't change its necessity."

"Except it's not necessary." I spread my arms. "Thurvishar and I have another way to power the crystal. You don't have to do this."

Those hard, unyielding mirror eyes reflected no expression at all.

"I don't believe you," Thaena spat. "Argas is dead. Taja is dead. I refuse to accept that they've died for no reason!"

I inhaled a jagged, painful breath. Taja was dead. Oh, that hurt. "You can bring them back, though, right?"

She started laughing. "Oh, little fool. I was never the one who brought anyone back. I'm the Goddess of Death, not Life." A look of horror came over her features. Thaena looked to the side, as if seeing something a long way away. She shuddered and then scoffed. "And now Galava's dead too."

It felt like being kicked. How could *Galava* be dead? "You can fix it, right? There must be something . . ."

Thaena regarded me coldly. "There is. And I'll take care of it right after I take care of *you*."

She unsheathed her swords.

# 111: Rescues

***(Talea's story)***

Xivan pulled Talea to her feet. "I know it hurts, but we have to go."

"You need to stand still for a damn minute, that's what you need to do." Therin rushed over and immediately started looking at Talea's wounds. "Let me stop the bleeding."

Talea blinked away tears. "Go where?"

Xivan pointed to the platform. Even from this distance, Talea saw several figures standing there. No, not standing: fighting.

"Is my son up there?" Khaeriel said.

"Probably," Talea said.

"Can you carry her?" Khaeriel asked Talea, pointing to Xivan.

"Yes?" Talea answered, but then she understood. "You can fly."

"Close enough to it. Hold her in case that sword dislikes my spell." Khaeriel walked over to Therin and put her arm around his waist. "Apologies, my love, but this will not be gentle."

He smiled grimly. "Sometimes I prefer it that way."

She laughed, just once, caught off guard by the gallows humor. Then Khaeriel began casting.

Talea picked up Xivan. "I know this isn't dignified . . ."

Xivan smiled and buried her head in the crook of Talea's neck. "Don't care."

Talea contemplated the possibility that if they sailed through the air toward the platform, some archer who'd survived this long would find that temptation too much to resist.

She rubbed the coin in her hand. "For luck."

An incredibly strong gust of wind sent everyone hurtling into the sky. It wasn't exactly flight. For one thing, Talea had no control whatsoever over the trajectory. Wind pushed her and wind slowed her, and the whole time, she could only hope Khaeriel wouldn't let them fall to their deaths.

No one fired at them, though.

When they landed, Talea saw Kihrin, desperately trying to survive a sword fight with the Goddess of Death. Thaena was taking her time killing him. He had several cuts on his cheeks, his arms, long, shallow cuts along his legs, chest, and stomach. All of his wounds were bleeding.

Needless to say, Kihrin was losing.

# 112: What Is Owed

***(Janel's story)***

Janel met Xaltorath's swing with her sword. Despite her strength, she almost didn't manage to block the blow. "If anyone sees a shield around here, let me know!" she shouted back over her shoulder, but she didn't expect anything from it.

***THIS IS FUN, BUT I'M NOT HERE FOR YOU.***

Xaltorath began backing away.

"Now don't be like that," Janel said. "I'll start to think you don't really love me."

"No!" Thurvishar yelled out. He ran forward.

Janel didn't have to take her eyes off Xaltorath to see the problem. The man who'd come in with Relos Var, the one no one had bothered to introduce. He had a small shield with the Quuros crown inscribed on it and a wand in his free hand. He fired beams of light from the wand, and everything those beams touched died. The small buckler emitted a much larger opalescent shield, which he used to block attacks. He seemed capable, but the demons were targeting him. A great many demons.

"Who is that?" Janel asked to the side.

"Grizzst," Senera answer.

"Holy—" Janel shook her head and returned her attention to Xaltorath and Relos Var. She was fighting on a field with actual gods. Perhaps this wasn't the right time to be overwhelmed by a famous wizard's presence.

Galava appeared some distance away from Relos Var, presumably to fill in the gap left by Thaena's absence. She attacked Var with a cresting emerald wave while plants and flowers and every green thing tried to tangle his feet.

Behind Var, a truly staggering number of demons rushed Grizzst, too many for him to block with the shield. One of them did something: that deadly wand sailed through the air to land in the mud close to where Relos Var and Galava fought.

"Throw him back the wand!" Thurvishar screamed, this time at

Relos Var. He used Wildheart to pull up flowers and vines to try to grab it, but Galava gave him a dry look and withered every one.

Var could have just picked up the damn wand and tossed it. Or used it to destroy enough demons to give Grizzst a chance to regroup. Something.

Senera targeted demons herself, but there were so many. *Every* demon had to be on the field.

Var held out his hand; the wand snapped into it.

"Throw it!" Thurvishar called out one more time.

Var aimed the wand–

–and hit Galava, who doubled over in pain.[1] She raised her eyes, taking in Relos Var with clenched teeth. "Damn you," she said. "I'm not *that* easy to kill."

Thurvishar rose up stone blocks, made them liquid, tried to use it crush and trap the demons. Janel summoned a roaring, spinning column of fire–normally too much temptation for any demon, but not this time. Not against the wizard who had gaeshed them for a thousand years.

Xaltorath paid no attention to that fight. What did she care what happened to Grizzst? He hadn't gaeshed *her,* after all.

A horrible noise crackled as the energy field protecting Grizzst broke apart. Then a yowling mass of demons buried the wizard, and he was lost from sight.

Thurvishar looked anguished. He continued fighting demons with a ferocity unlike his normal methodical spellcasting. They began to scatter.

Janel glanced up from her own slaughter in time to see Xaltorath summon a glowing red glass bar resembling Khored's sword–

*No, that* was *Khored's sword–*

***AREN'T YOU?*** Xaltorath stepped up behind Galava and impaled her through the back. The wound didn't just bleed–it immediately began to burn, blackening the edges in a widening arc. A melting line of rainbow energy moved up Galava's body at the same time, a magical assault.

Xaltorath had absorbed Immortals. Now it used that power to kill another.

"No!" Janel couldn't stop her fighting to close with Xaltorath, no matter how much she wanted to.

Xaltorath made a pulling motion with a hand and ripped Galava's souls free from her body. She let the Goddess of Life's corpse fall to the

[1] I honestly don't know if Grizzst had enchanted the wand so Relos Var could use it, or if Var simply overwhelmed whatever ward of protection would have prevented it.

ground. The demon queen grinned spitefully and turned to Relos Var, who looked shocked, as if even he couldn't believe what had just happened.

As Xaltorath raised her sword to strike again, a whirling glow of rainbow energy spun around her, twisted in the air, and formed into Tya. She looked down at Galava's body, horrified.

"Mother, look out!" Janel called out.

Xaltorath changed targets. As she swung at the Goddess of Magic, Tya gave Xaltorath a contemptuous look and caught the edge of the glass sword between thumb and forefinger, stopping it cold. The sword shuddered and started to disintegrate, until Xaltorath dropped it and stepped away.

"You're not Khored," Tya said, "don't get ideas."

"We have to kill her," Janel called out. "She's taken Galava's souls!"

Xaltorath gave Janel a pout, as if this was some sort of betrayal. The demon stepped backward, away from Tya and Relos Var. ***NEXT TIME, THEN.***

The demon queen vanished.

Janel ground her teeth and returned to killing the other demons. Tya helped. It wasn't what she wanted to do. She wanted to scream at Relos Var, and scream at Senera, and most of all scream at herself.

Janel should've let Relos Var die. She should have killed him herself when she had the chance. If Var hadn't ignored Grizzst in order to injure Galava . . .

And then, all at once, the demons vanished. She stood panting for breath on a twisted, nightmare battlefield, next to Galava's dead body. Where Grizzst's corpse should have been was . . . blood. And a broken buckler strapped to a ragged, severed arm. The demons had eaten everything else.

Fighting continued in the distance, the trees shaking, explosions lighting up the sky.

Khored and Ompher, in all likelihood. There was no one else left.

Tya turned to face Relos Var, her face awash with complex emotions, but mostly rage. She raised her hand, magic swirling around it, even as Relos Var mirrored her movements, wand raised high. He glanced at the wand and then dropped it–apparently deciding it was useless against this enemy.

"Senera," Relos Var said, not looking away from the Goddess of Magic. "It's time to go."

Senera's gaze flickered over to Thurvishar and then back to Relos Var. Just a second's hesitation.

"Yes, my lord," Senera said. She began opening a portal.

Thurvishar ground his teeth and looked away.

"It's over," Relos Var said softly, "don't you think, Irisia?" He wrapped his voice around Tya's real name like the softest velvet.

"Not yet," Tya said, "not even slightly over."

"True," Relos Var agreed, "but I think there's been enough killing for one day. Even for me, losing Rol'amar's been a bit much." He dropped the name with all the skill of a perfectly placed knife sliding across a vein.

Tya's eyes widened. "What?"

Janel hid her confusion, but Thurvishar must have understood better, because he cursed out loud.

"What's happened to Rolan?" Tya demanded.

"They didn't tell you about our son?" Relos Var began slowly walking backward, toward Senera. "Your 'hero' Kihrin killed him. Perhaps forever. In any event, the only person who knows how to bring him back, how to restore his mind is . . ." He shrugged. ". . . me."

Rol'amar. Janel's stomach flipped. She hadn't realized . . . how would she ever have realized that the dragon who'd killed Therin was her . . . gods . . . her *brother.*

"He's lying," Thurvishar growled.

"Just go," Tya said.

"No! He can't just leave!" Janel screamed at Relos Var. "You owe me that much, Revas!" She used his real name without thinking, without considering what it betrayed.

Relos Var stopped and turned back. He gazed at Janel fondly. "I wish you could've been there to see the look on my face when Senera told me who you used to be. It's a name I haven't heard in a long time. It's good to have you back, C'indrol."

"That's a dead person's name," Janel said numbly. She felt her mother come up to her, wrap an arm around her shoulder, hold her close. And she wanted nothing more than to return that embrace, but not . . . now.

"Yes," Var said. "I suppose so. But so's Revas, in a way. We're done here."

"Of course you're done here," Janel said. "You got exactly what you wanted. Again."

Relos Var raised his hands in a "What can you do?" gesture as Senera opened a portal behind him. If any barrier roses had ever protected this area of the Kirpis, they'd been long since destroyed.

"I always do, my dear," Relos Var assured her. "I always do." He spared a glance at Thurvishar, who studied him, eyes narrowed, expression hateful. Relos Var nodded once at his grandson.

Then he and Senera walked through the portal and closed it behind them.

# 113: The Last Dance

***(Kihrin's story)***

I was getting my ass kicked.

Janel had once described how fast Thaena was in combat, but I'd never reconciled the old woman I'd first met at the auction block in Kishna-Farriga with the graceful avatar of death. Experience proved an unforgiving teacher. Often, Thaena wasn't much more than a blur. If I could no longer thank Taja for my survival, I'll just point out I had a fantastic sword teacher.

But I wasn't holding my own. Thaena didn't even need to use magic to kill me. She was doing it the old-fashioned way, slice by painful slice.

I tried my damnedest to fight her off, but it wasn't going to be enough. I didn't have a reach on her, she had two swords to my one, and she was *better.*

I managed to land a cut along her arm, but that hardly compared to the razor marks crisscrossed over me. I started to hear Urthaenriel's song, but I had no idea where Xivan was or if she'd reach me in time. I might well bleed out before the fight was over.

I studied Thaena as much as I could, looking for any opening, any weakness. It wasn't just my life on the line. I pushed one sword up high, dodged around the second, and came down hard on her hand. Thaena dropped a sword, looking shocked.

"Did you forget who trained me?"

"I tire of these games," she growled, "and now we've reached the end of the performance."

I glanced toward Teraeth, behind her, as she lunged forward. Weird as it seemed, I felt like he'd actually taken too long. As if he'd started over at least once.

I barely parried her sword strike. It slid against my upper arm instead of causing a much more fatal wound. But then she did something too fast to follow. I fell to the ground; my sword landed to my left.

I scrambled over toward it while Thaena followed slowly. She was in no rush.

Urthaenriel's pommel slid across the stone ground until the sword stopped right next to me.

"You dropped that," Xivan said.

I rolled, picking up the sword as I stood to my feet. Urthaenriel turned into a gleaming silver bar, singing harmonies in my mind, a soaring choir.

Thaena frowned at me, then looked around. She was trying to figure out where the sword had come from.

And Xivan stood right there. Right out in the open. Thaena couldn't *see* her.

I immediately knew what that had to mean. Valathea was here somewhere, wearing a Cornerstone capable of fooling an Immortal–Chainbreaker. I hadn't seen her at all during the battle, but she'd been in the parliament hall when Relos Var had created his gate. Then a rush of tenyé poured into me, giving me energy, healing my wounds.

My parents had made it to the platform. If anyone knew how to heal from a distance, it was those two.

I didn't want to give Thaena too much time to contemplate who else might be up on the platform with us. I attacked, coming in fast, shifting Urthaenriel through various lengths as I still tried with all my might not to end up impaled on her sword.

But this was a whole new dance. Now I held Urthaenriel, which meant Thaena faced a genuine threat. One that she took seriously. Now I was landing my own strikes, using Godslayer's shifting nature to work past her defenses.

Maybe it would have mattered, if I'd remembered being S'arric. But I didn't. She was thousands of years old. I was twenty.

She feinted and shoved my hand aside. Thaena summoned a new sword in her off hand and sliced down across my wrist. She severed the tendons I needed to hold anything, let alone a weapon. Urthaenriel dropped with agonizing slowness from my twitching fingers.

Thaena caught it before it hit the ground.

"It's time to be done with this." Thaena examined the sword in her hand with distaste, then threw it to the ground behind her. She grabbed my throat and lifted, squeezing. "We'll try again. We'll re-imprison Vol Karoth and buy ourselves the centuries we need to find heroes who will *do what they're told*–"

A blast of energy struck her. Thaena dropped me as she staggered backward.

"You talk too much," Valathea said.

"There you are," Thaena said. "I wondered. Thank you for saving me the effort of chasing you down."

I clutched at my hand, trying to at least stop the bleeding. Valathea had bought me a few seconds. I intended to use them wisely.

"*Listen to yourself,* Khaemezra," Valathea said. "How far have you fallen from the woman I knew. But I wanted you to know I'm going to find my husband, and I'm going to bring him back."

Thaena sneered and started to say something. Started. She blinked and looked surprised instead. A split second later, a silver sword's gleaming point erupted from Thaena's chest along with a spray of blood. Thaena looked down at herself as if she couldn't quite believe what had just happened.

Teraeth stood behind her, holding Urthaenriel.

Thaena's control over him must have broken the moment she grabbed the sword. Then she'd thrown it behind herself. Toward him.

"There's nothing you can do to stop me," Valathea finished.

"Teraeth–" Thaena turned toward her son.

He moved his arm again, a single sharp, efficient motion. Thaena's head came away from her shoulder. Both fell to the ground.

Teraeth stood there for a few seconds–each one a Shadrag Gor-worthy eternity–staring at his mother's corpse. Then he fell to his knees.

We all started running. Me to Teraeth, my parents to me.

I threw my arms around Teraeth and held him to me.

"It's over," I whispered. "It's over."

# 114: Epilogue

***(Kihrin's story)***

Of the four immortals we'd fought, only Ompher survived. With Taja, that meant fully half of the Eight Immortals had been slain. Galava and Thaena were the only immortals who could have resurrected them, and Grizzst, the only wizard who knew how to resurrect her, had also died.

The Well of Spirals was destroyed, although the Founders who had been brought back to the living through the Star Court knew how to rebuild it. Which one assumes the vané will do, given time.

We didn't stick around for the Quuros military to show up and start screaming at everyone. Thurvishar opened the gates; to the Manol for Valathea and my parents, to Yor for Xivan and Talea, and to Grizzst's workshop for himself, Janel, Teraeth, and me. We harbored some faint hope we might find something among Grizzst's notes to show us how to Return Galava. If we can find Grimward, the Mother of Trees still exists to be used as a temporary body for the goddess. It's possible.

Also, I don't for one second believe Grizzst is really dead. Call it naïve on my part, or just overly optimistic, but that bastard seems too crafty to have gone down so easily. I guess we'll see.

Anyway, that brings us here.

Kihrin stopped talking, sighed, and filled his teacup. "So that's that, I suppose."

Thurvishar nodded and set aside his papers. "Quite. I think that's . . . more than enough to send to Tyentso. Although we do have a decision to make."

Kihrin blinked. "You mean besides the one I'm already making?"

Thurvishar sighed. "It's just . . . Argas *did* fix the crystal. And Janel *does* remember being C'indrol. She may not remember the specific method C'indrol developed to tap tenyé, but she will eventually."

Kihrin slumped in his chair, his expression an ugly growl. "You mean we could still do the Ritual of Night. We could still reseal Vol Karoth. We have enough tenyé to do it without wiping out whole nations."

"Yes."

Kihrin chewed on his lower lip, eyes focused on anything but Thurvishar's face. "Whoever performs the ritual will still die, though. It's not the ritual that kills them–it's the strain of holding on to all that tenyé." He slowly shook his head. "And Grizzst wasn't wrong about Vol Karoth. The prison protects him. We lock him away again and all we can do is wait for Relos Var to figure out some other way to break him free. I refuse to play by my brother's rules."

"So we're going through with it." Thurvishar didn't look happy, and he hadn't asked a question.

"Yeah."

"Have you told Teraeth yet?"

"No. And I'm not going to."

Thurvishar frowned at him. "And does he know he remains king?"

Kihrin raised an eyebrow. "No. He's still recovering." Which was an understated way of saying Teraeth hadn't quite stopped staring blankly at walls yet. "I'm sure as soon as he finds out, he'll abdicate and then–" He made a disgusted face.

"Then the honor of being the vané crown prince falls to you," Thurvishar said.

"Hmm. My mother will love that." Kihrin studied the piles of paperwork and sighed. "I'd hoped I would spot a way out. Some flaw . . . something. But maybe that's for the best. I don't know how I would cope with knowing I could have saved them if I'd just done things differently."

"We did everything we could," Thurvishar said mournfully.

"I know," Kihrin said. "I know. But it wasn't enough, was it?"

"No." Thurvishar stood up and left the room.

Kihrin put his head in his hands.

That last bit might have been a sad place to end this chronicle. It was true enough; it happened, basically as written. But the conversation didn't *end* there. And whether or not one considers this true ending sad, tragic, or nihilistic will, I suppose, greatly depend on how it all turns out in the end.

But then, that's so often the case, isn't it?

Even though I am taking steps to make sure Senera never reads this next bit, the spirit of her scholastic presence compels me to admit much of what follows must be considered fabrication. I wasn't there for it. I can't know for certain how events unfolded. I am guessing.

Possibly I am *hoping.*

But this will not be far off the mark. I can only pray what we are doing works.

And that the rest of you can forgive us.

* * *

The vané had a special prison cell that they hardly ever used. It had bars, but those were largely superfluous, a vestigial symbol of the magical energy that kept its prisoner trapped. Talon needed all her energy just to keep a coherent form–never mind shape-change–pushing back against the cell's intense magical pressure. She was effectively helpless.

Something jangled at the door. The guard outside said, "Of course, Your Highness."

A second later, Kihrin walked inside the observation room. "Hey, Talon."

The mimic looked up, and her expression brightened. "Kihrin! Have you come to say hello before my execution? That was sweet of you."

"They're not executing you," Kihrin said.

She rolled her eyes. "They're making me into a tsali and transferring me into a new body. A new not-a-mimic body. And then kicking me out of the Manol. That's an execution, ducky. It's just taking a century to carry out."

Kihrin chuckled and looked to his side. A thumping sound came from outside, followed by the door opening. Thurvishar stepped into the room, dragging the guard's body behind him. "We'll need to do this quickly. They patrol quite often on this level."

Kihrin nodded. Then he unsheathed Urthaenriel and examined the bars. "Looks simple enough to disable."

Talon stood. "Um, I'm sorry, but are you two about to break me out of jail? There's no way the king's pardoned me." She raised an eyebrow. "He's never warmed up to me for some reason."

Kihrin held up his palms. "I'd have gotten you a pardon, but then I'd have to explain why and . . . probably best if we don't."

"Besides," Thurvishar said to Kihrin, "this will be a low point on Teraeth's list of reasons to be upset with you."

"Isn't that the truth?"

Talon looked back and forth between both men. "I'm officially intrigued."

Kihrin gestured toward her with his free hand. "I want to hire you to impersonate someone. It'll be a long-term assignment–weeks, if not months–and you can't drop character for a second. No peppering speech with that 'ducky' tell of yours. The only reason Relos Var won't be able to figure out your real identity using the Name of All Things will be if he doesn't think to have Senera ask. Therefore, you mustn't give him even the slightest reason to question your identity."

Talon tilted her head. "This sounds serious. But, uh . . . you do understand what you're asking, don't you? I can't do that kind of impersonation superficially. You're going to have to give me the corpse–*the brain*–of whoever you want me to impersonate. If your plan is to have me provide an alibi for someone, that's not going to work."

"Well, it might work under specific–" Thurvishar stopped as Kihrin gave him a glare. "Sorry."

"It's fine," Kihrin told her. "We understood the cost before we stepped inside this room."

He stepped forward and slashed, once up, then down. The bars gently fell downward to clatter against the ground. The magical barrier vanished. "Call it a gesture of good faith."

Thurvishar looked toward the door, as if prepared to deal with anyone responding to the sound.

"Bright-Eyes, I raised you better than that. Never give up your best bargaining chip at the beginning of negotiations. What will you offer me now?"

Kihrin gave her a bitter, lopsided smile. "Promise you'll help, and I'll let you kill me and eat the body."

Talon stared at him.

She stared harder.

"Is that . . . Is that a joke?" Her mouth fell open in shock. "You know I can't read your mind when you're wearing Urthaenriel."[1]

"I thought you said you don't use magic to read minds?" Kihrin quirked an eyebrow.

"Ducky, I lie a lot, remember?" Talon chewed on her lip as she studied him. Her eyes chased him over to Thurvishar and then back again. "But you're not serious. You're just toying with me. This is a *prank*."

"No," Kihrin said. "Pardon the pun, but I'm dead serious. You agree to do this–*you promise me you'll do this*–and I'll let you kill me and eat the body. *I'm* the person you'll be impersonating." He paused. "I'd appreciate it if you made the death quick. Been there, done that, don't need the long, drawn-out version."

Talon blinked several times.

"Isn't this what you *want*?" Kihrin asked her.

Talon shook her head. "I don't even know what to say. You–" She quirked an eyebrow. "You want me to impersonate *you*?"

"Yes," Kihrin said. "Exactly. You're going to impersonate me. Perfectly."

"I'll know the truth," Thurvishar told her. "So will Teraeth and Janel."

"Oh, but if you didn't tell them, there'd be less chance–" Talon complained.

[1] Yes, Teraeth gave it back to Kihrin. I currently have it hidden somewhere safe.

"Them sleeping with you thinking that you're me isn't a line I'm willing to cross," Kihrin said. "So they will know the truth. Not negotiable." He looked over at Thurvishar. "They're never going to forgive me as it is."

Thurvishar looked ill. "No, probably not. I don't even want to think about what they're going to do to me. We *should* tell them now."

Kihrin shook his head. "I'll lose my nerve. Trust me on this."

Talon started laughing. "Oh, I get it. You're going to make a soul tsali and then have them build a new body for you at the Well of Spirals once that's rebuilt. That way, no one will realize who you really are. That's clever."

Kihrin blinked. "Damn. That would be clever. Wish I'd thought of it."

Thurvishar pondered the idea. "Maybe we can restore you . . . ?"

"Let's note that for later, then." Kihrin turned back to Talon. "Do we have a deal?"

Talon's eyebrows shot up. "You never struck me as the suicidal type."

"That's because I'm not." Kihrin made a moue. "Seriously, I thought you wanted this."

"I do," Talon said, "but you can't blame me for thinking it's a trap."

"Oh, it *is* a trap," Kihrin reassured her. "Just not a trap for you."

She thought about it for a minute. "Well, when you put it like that, how can I refuse?"

Thurvishar had come along as a precaution. As the person assigned to remove Urthaenriel and hide the sword after Kihrin and Talon left, he wasn't needed for the next step. Indeed, he would probably have only been a hindrance for the next step. This was where they parted.

Quite possibly forever, depending on what happened next.

"Can you turn into something small?" Kihrin asked Talon. "It's best if I carry you."

She shifted into a small tabby cat, which he picked up.

"Good." Kihrin looked over at Thurvishar. "This is going to work." He wasn't precisely sure who he was encouraging.

"We're either about to do something completely brilliant or something that will make Relos Var's mistakes look like quaint grammatical errors," Thurvishar said.

Kihrin found himself laughing. "Oh, Thurvishar. It *can* be both." He paused.

"You're frightened."

"Terrified," Kihrin admitted. "You know what Janel said to me this morning? She said that she and Teraeth had been handed their greatest fears–her a demon, him in authority–so she was really glad that I'd managed to avoid that."

Thurvishar closed his eyes and rubbed his mouth with a hand.

"I should go," Kihrin said, "before I change my mind."

He closed his eyes and imagined fear. Being trapped. Enclosed spaces. He remembered Tyentso possessing him, being a prisoner in his own body. He pictured his fathers dying–Surdyeh, then Therin.

He felt despair.

Kihrin didn't even have to open his eyes to know when the shift happened. He tasted it in the air. And when he opened his eyes, what he saw was no surprise at all.

The cat slipped off his shoulders and began to shift. "Uh, ducky . . ."

"This is Kharas Gulgoth," Kihrin explained. "I should warn you that it's important you don't cast any ranged spells. So opening a gate–if you can do that–isn't a good idea. You'll have to leave on your own. Thurvishar will meet you an hour south of Stonegate Pass once you're outside the Blight. There's a landmark there called the Eight Columns."

Talon looked around the ruins, wide-eyed. The streets were dead of all life. The nearest buildings were worn away, as if an invisible tornado had ground away the city's center for millennia. Which, in a sense, it had.

Talon held up a hand. The tips of her fingers started to turn black and flake away. "Ducky–"

"We should hurry," Kihrin said. "As soon as you have what you need from me, run."

"But you–"

"Do it *now,* Lyrilyn!"

She stabbed him in the heart with her hand, hard and fast, so quickly the shock killed Kihrin instantly.

Talon found she was crying. She didn't . . . understand. She didn't understand at all.

But she would soon enough. It was her nature.

Talon took only what she needed, changed into a cheetah, and followed Kihrin's orders.

She ran.

Kihrin watched Talon go.

More accurately, his ghost watched Talon leave. Janel had once told him the line between the Living World and the Afterlife thinned to transparency in Kharas Gulgoth. He hoped that was true or this all would be embarrassingly in vain.

Kihrin knew what Relos Var wanted. He knew (somewhat more vaguely) what Xaltorath wanted. And in both cases, they meant to use Vol Karoth to obtain their goals. In Xaltorath's case by keeping Vol Karoth weakened and lost. In Relos Var's case by using Urthaenriel to control him.

If Kihrin was Vol Karoth's Cornerstone, Urthaenriel was the god's gaesh, the only one with no reliance on the Stone of Shackles. But Urthaenriel *couldn't* be used to control Kihrin, or Xivan would have done so by accident while they'd traveled together.

Which had given Kihrin the idea. Taja would've been proud; it was the last thing anyone would expect.

Kihrin turned toward the central university hall, which now held an imprisoned dark god. Or, as Kihrin had begun to suspect, an imprisoned dark god *child*. One who was lonely and scared and knew only fear and despair–the whole reason Vol Karoth always sensed Kihrin when their moods aligned.

Relos Var had created Vol Karoth to be a tool. He'd messed up and made a broken god instead. Thaena and the others, having felt that broken god's wrath, had feared him most. But Vol Karoth wasn't the real problem. Vol Karoth was, as Relos Var had claimed, just a tool.

Maybe the thing to do wasn't to lock the tool away or destroy it, but *mend* it.

"All right. You wanted me to come back? Here I am. I'm home."

Kihrin walked into the building.

# Glossary

**A**

Aeyan'arric (EYE-ann-AR-ik)—a dragon associated with ice, cold, and storms.

Afterlife, the—a dark mirror of the living world; souls go to the Afterlife after death, hopefully to move on to the Land of Peace.

agolé (a-GOAL-lay)—a piece of cloth worn draped around the shoulders and hips by both men and women in western Quur.

Alavel (A-la-VEL)—home city of the wizards' school known as the Academy.

Arasgon (AIR-as-gon)—a fireblood, Talaras's brother.

Arena, the—a park in the center of the Capital City that serves as battleground for the choosing of the emperor.

Argas (AR-gas)—one of the Eight Immortals. Considered the god of invention and innovation.

Atrine (at-rin-EE)—capital of the dominion of Jorat, originally built by Emperor Atrin Kandor.

**B**

Baelosh (BAY-losh)—a dragon, best known for the size of his hoard of treasure.

Bahl-Nimian (BALL-nim-ee-AHN)—one of the Doltari Free States, this particular city-state dedicated to Vilfar.

barrier roses—a magical ward preventing teleportation or gate-creation magics anywhere inside the Manol. Nine individuals are known to be able to ignore the barrier roses: the Immortals, Relos Var, and Grizzst, who created them.

Bevrosa (BEV-roz-AH)—a Dry Mother, leader of the morgage tribe living in the center of Kharas Gulgoth, holder of a Cornerstone, Wildheart.

Bezagor (bez-ah-GORE)—a demon lord.

Bikeinoh (beh-KEEN-oh)—Duke Kaen's second wife, now a member of the Spurned.

## C

Chainbreaker–a Cornerstone, associated with the Manol vané. Has powers dealing with illusions.

Cherthog (cher-THOG)–a god of winter and ice, primarily worshipped in Yor.

Cimillion (seh-MIL-e-on)–the original birth name of Emperor Sandus's son, Thurvishar.

Citadel, the–headquarters of the Quuran imperial military.

City, the–a.k.a. the Capital City. Originally a city-state under the control of the god-king Qhuaras, its original name (Quur) now applies to the whole empire.

cloudcurl hair–originally a vané trait, now common in areas like Kirpis and Khorvesh, of hair so curly that it is cloudlike. While both vané groups can have cloudcurl hair, the Kirpis vané were especially famous for it.

Copper Quarter–the mercantile district of the Lower Circle of the Capital City.

Cornerstones, the–eight magical artifacts. The Stone of Shackles and Chainbreaker are two of these.

Court of Gems, the–slang for the royal families of the Upper Circle, represented by twelve different kinds of gemstones.

Crown and Scepter, the–famous artifacts that may only be wielded by the emperor of Quur. Created by Grizzst.

Culling Fields, the–a tavern and inn situated just outside the Arena.

## D

D'Aramarin (day-ar-a-MAR-in)–the first ranked Royal House. House D'Aramarin controls the Gatekeepers, the guild of wizards primarily responsible for running and maintaining the gate system. They are thus responsible for and control almost all inter-dominion trade.

Havar (hav-AR)–High Lord of House D'Aramarin.

D'Erinwa (day-er-in-WAY)–a Royal House, primarily associated with slavery.

D'Kard (day-KARD)–a Royal House, primarily associated with crafting.

D'Lorus (du-LOR-us)–a Royal House, primarily associated with paper, books, schools, and education.

Cedric (KED-rik)–High Lord of House D'Lorus. Father of Gadrith.

Gadrith (GAD-rith)–an infamous necromancer and wizard, also known as Gadrith the Twisted. Was killed permanently by Kihrin D'Mon, using Urthaenriel.

Thurvishar (thur-vish-AR)–Gadrith D'Lorus's adopted son, Lord Heir of House D'Lorus.

D'Mon (day-MON)–a Royal House, primarily associated with the healing arts.

Bavrin (BAV-rin)–deceased son of High Lord Therin D'Mon.

Darzin (DAR-zin)–deceased son of High Lord Therin D'Mon and former lord heir, slain by his younger brother Kihrin D'Mon.

Devyeh (DEV-yeh)–deceased son of High Lord Therin D'Mon.

Galen (GAL-len)–Lord Heir of House D'Mon after the death of his father, Darzin.

Gerisia (ger-IS-see-ah)–youngest daughter of Therin D'Mon, married to the Duke of Khorvesh's second-oldest son.

Kihrin (KEAR-rin)–youngest child of High Lord Therin D'Mon and only child of Queen Khaeriel of the vané. Also, the reincarnation of S'arric, one of the Eight Immortals.

Saerá (SAY-ra)–eldest daughter of Darzin D'Mon.

Sheloran (shel-LOR-ahn)–Galen D'Mon's wife, previously of House D'Talus.

Therin (THER-rin)–High Lord of House D'Mon.

Tishar (tish-AR)–Therin D'Mon's aunt, killed by Gadrith prior to the Capital Hellmarch.

Tishenya (tish-EN-ya)–oldest child of Therin D'Mon.

D'Talus (day-TAL-us)–the Royal House in charge of the smelter and smith's guild, known as the Red Men.

Damaeris (dah-MARE-is)–an acolyte at the Well of Spirals.

Dana (dan-AY)–god-queen of Eamithon, still worshipped as the goddess of wisdom and virtue.

Daughter of Laaka (LAKE-ay)–a.k.a. kraken, an enormous immortal sea creature.

Demon Falls–the artificial dam constructed by Atrin Kandor to form Lake Jorat, called such because the spillways are shaped like demon mouths.

demons–an alien race from another dimension that can, through effort, gain access to the material world. Famous for their cruelty and power. See: Hellmarch.

Devoran Prophecies, the–a many-book series of prophecies that are believed to foretell the end of the world.

Devors (de-VORS)–island chain south of the Capital City, most famous as the home of the Devoran priests and their prophecies.

dhole (dol)–a form of wild dog, domesticated in Jorat and also found throughout Marakor.

Doc–see: Terindel.

Dolgariatz (dol-GAR-ee-atz)–a Manol vané Founder.

Doltar (dol-TAR)–a distant country believed populated by people having pale skin and light-colored hair and eyes. In reality, a patchwork collection of city-states populated by a diverse range of ethnicities and ruled by squabbling god-kings.

Dorna (DOR-na)–an elderly Joratese woman who served as Janel Theranon's nanny in childhood.

Dragonspires, the–a mountain range running north–south through Quur, dividing the dominions of Kirpis, Kazivar, Eamithon, and Khorvesh from Raenena, Jorat, Marakor, and Yor.

dreamweaver–a Kirpis vané sorcerer specializing in illusions.

Drehemia (DRAY-hem-EE-ah)–a dragon.

dreth (dreth)–see: vordreth.

drussian (drus-E-an)–a rare metal superior to iron that can only be created through superhot magical fires.

Dry Mothers, the–the elders of the morgage, who rule the various tribal groups.

Dyana (DEE-an-ah)–a vordreth woman, married to Emperor Sandus, murdered by Gadrith the Twisted. Thurvishar D'Lorus's biological mother.

## E

Eamithon (AY-mith-ON)–a dominion just north of the Capital City, the oldest of the Quuros dominions and considered the most tranquil.

Eidolons–magical sentries guarding the abandoned vané capital of Serafana.

Eight Immortals, the–eight beings of godlike power created by a ritual performed by Relos Var.

Elgestat (EL-ges-stat)–a dreth ruler who died performing the Ritual of Night.

Empire of Quur (koor)–see: Quur.

Eshimavari (esh-EEM-ah-VAR-ee)–the real name of the Goddess of Luck; see: Taja.

Esiné (eh-SIN-ah)–a Manol vané clan that communicates through hand movements.

## F

Feonila (FEE-oh-nih-LAY)–a small town in Khorvesh.

Filoran (FILL-or-an)–dean of the Academy of wizards in Quur.

firebloods–a race originally related to horses but modified by the god-king Khorsal to possess extraordinary size, power, resilience, loyalty, and intelligence. Firebloods are omnivorous, and although they don't possess fingers, some are capable of manipulating tenyé. They have an average life expectancy of eighty years or more.

Founders–in vané society, Founders are members of the race who founded the vané nation, meaning any Founder is at least fourteen thousand years old. Founders have specific legislative powers.

Four Races, the–four immortal, powerful races that once existed. Only the vané still exist in their original, immortal forms, with the other races having devolved into the morgage, dreth, and human races.

## G

gaesh (gaysh), pl. gaeshe (gaysh-ay)–an enchantment created using the Stone of Shackles that forces the victim to follow all commands given by the person who physically possesses their totem focus, up to and including commands of suicide. Being unable or unwilling to perform a command results in death.

Galava (gal-ah-VAY)–one of the Eight Immortals. Goddess of life and nature.

gate–a.k.a. portal. The magical connection of two different geographic locations, allowing for quick travel across great distances. Only powerful wizards can typically create Gatestone-independent portals.

Gatekeepers–the guild who controls and maintains gate travel. Ruled by House D'Aramarin.

Gatestone–a specially inscribed section of stone that somehow makes gate travel much less magically onerous. Exactly how this is accomplished is a proprietary, heavily protected House D'Aramarin secret.

gender, Joratese–Joratese customs define gender separately from sex or sexual orientation, falling into three categories–stallion, mare, and gelding. Stallions can roughly be considered "men" and mares "women." Geldings are those who refuse to define themselves within this otherwise binary system (which has all the flaws one might expect of a polarized gender system). Thus, it is possible to have a "mare" who is biologically male or a "stallion" who is biologically female, and "gelding" has nothing to do with whether or not one is capable of sexual reproduction. See: sexuality, Joratese.

god-kings–immortal wizards who have made themselves passive receivers for tenyé energy dedicated to them (offerings). God-kings turned out to be an excellent example of how power corrupts.

Godslayer–see: Urthaenriel.

god-touched–a "gift" or "curse" (depending on whom one asks) handed down by the Eight Immortals to the eight Royal Houses of Quur. Besides giving each house a distinctive eye color, the curse on the Royal Houses forbids them from making laws.

Gorokai (GORE-o-kai)–a dragon.

goschal (gohs-CHAHL)–morgage word meaning *sacred* or *holy.*

Grimward–one of the Cornerstones, with the ability to bring the dead back to life.

Grizzst (grizt)–falsely attributed to being one of the Eight Immortals; famous wizard, sometimes considered a god of magic, particularly demonology. Believed to be responsible for binding demons as well as making the Crown and Scepter of Quur.

Gryphon Men, the–a secret organization ultimately working for the emperors of Quur, since both Sandus and his predecessor Gendal seem to have had connections to this group. Their goals are unclear, but they seem to be working toward fulfilling the Devoran Prophecies, although that seems counterproductive considering how many of those prophecies predict the destruction of Quur.

Guarem (GOW-rem)–the primary language of Quur.

## H

haerunth (HAIR-runth)–a nutritionally complete grain used by the Kirpis vané to make porridge.

Hanik Mir (HAN-ik MEER)–see: Ompher.

Hell–distinct from the Land of Peace in the Afterlife; it marks the primary dimensional breach the demons used to invade this universe.

Hellmarch–the result of a powerful demon gaining access to the physical world, freely summoning demons and possessing corpses. This usually creates in a runaway path of death and devastation. This typically happens when a demon escapes a summoner's control. Before the breaking of the Stone of Shackles, demons could only be summoned to the Living World by corporeal entities (such as humans or vané). But demons quickly discovered they could exploit a loophole by possessing a living body and forcing that body to summon more of their kind. Demons can also possess corpses in the Joratese/Marakori area but cannot summon more demons in this manner. Famous Hellmarches include the Lonezh Hellmarch and the Capital City Hellmarch.

Hellwarrior–a prophesied villain who will rise up to destroy the Empire of Quur and possibly the world. Also a prophesied hero who will rise up to save the world. Also a group of heroes will do either of the previous two.

## I

idorrá (id-DOR-ray)–a Joratese concept of authority, dominance, and control. Roughly analogous to responsibility, duty, and authority, idorrá can be lost if the holder fails to protect or defend it.

Inalea (INN-a-lee-AH)–a Doltari slave. Senera's mother, deceased.

Ir'amar, (IR-ah-mar), a.k.a Irisia Amar (ir-RIS-ee-ah ah-MAR)–see: Tya.

## J

Jhelora, Fayrin (zah-LOR-ah, FAY-rin)–imperial liaison of the High Council and Ogenra of House D'Jorax. Notoriously corrupt libertine.

Jorat (jor-AT)–a dominion in the middle of Quur of varying climates and wide reaches of grassy plains; known for its horses.

## K

Kaen (kane)–the Yoran ducal line.

Azhen (AHJ-en)–Duke, or Hon, of Yor, grandson of the Joratese Quuros general who conquered the region. Had been keeping the god-queen Suless enslaved by gaesh and was kidnapped by her when the gaesh broke.

Exidhar (EX-eh-DAR)–only child of Azhen and Xivan Kaen, also kidnapped by Suless.

Nexara (Necks-a-RAY)--Exidhar & Veixizhau's infant daughter.

Veixizhau (vex-e-SHAU)–Exidhar Kaen's wife, formally Azhen's wife, but was divorced from her original husband after it was discovered she'd been having an affair with, and was pregnant by, Exidhar.

Xivan (JI-van)–Azhen Kaen's first wife; her Khorveshan ancestry made her unpopular with the Yoran people, and she was eventually killed in an assassination attempt meant for her husband. She was animated by Relos Var and continues to exist as a free-willed undead being who must sustain herself with massive doses of tenyé (souls are the typical source).

Kandor (KAN-dor)

Atrin (AT-rin)–an emperor of Quur who significantly expanded the borders of the empire; most famous for invading the Manol, which resulted in the destruction of virtually the entire Quuros army and the loss of Urthaenriel. Past life of Teraeth.

Elana (e-LAN-ay)–a musician from Khorvesh who married Atrin Kandor. After his death, she returned to using her maiden name, Milligreest, and journeyed into the Korthaen Blight to negotiate a peace settlement with the invading morgage people; responsible for freeing S'arric. Past life of Janel Theranon.

Karolaen (KAR-o-lane)–former name of Kharas Gulgoth.

Kazivar (KAZ-eh-var)–one of the dominions of Quur, north of Eamithon.

kef (kef)–a style of trouser common in western Quur.

Kelanis (KEL-a-nis)–son of Khaevatz and Kelindel, younger brother of Khaeriel; now king of the vané.

Kelindel (KEL-in-del)–the Kirpis vané king who married the Manol vané queen Khaevatz and united the vané people.

Khaemezra (kay-MEZ-rah)–a.k.a. Mother, the High Priestess of Thaena, and leader of the Black Brotherhood; Teraeth's mother; the true name of Thaena. See: Thaena.

Khaeriel (kay-RE-el)–queen of the vané, assassinated by her brother, Kelanis. Because Khaeriel was wearing the Stone of Shackles, she ended up in the body of her assassin and was later gaeshed and sold into slavery to Therin D'Mon by her grandmother, Khaemezra. Kihrin D'Mon's mother.

Khaevatz (KAY-vatz)–deceased Manol vané queen, famous for resisting Atrin Kandor's invasion. She later married Kirpis vané king Kelindel. Khaemezra's daughter and Teraeth's half sister, she and her husband both died fighting a god-king in the Doltari Free States.

Kharas Gulgoth (KAR-as GUL-goth)–a ruin in the middle of the Korthaen Blight; believed sacred (and cursed) by the morgage; prison of the corrupted god Vol Karoth.

Khital (kit-TAL)–a god-king. See: Lord of Little Houses, the.

Khored (KOR-ed)–one of the Eight Immortals, God of Destruction.

Khoreval (KOR-e-val)–a magic spear wielded by Janel Theranon. Particularly efficacious against demons. It was destroyed during the Battle of Atrine by the dragon Morios.

Khorsal (KOR-sal)–god-king who ruled Jorat. He was particularly obsessed with horses and modified a great many of the people and animals under his power. Responsible for the creation of the fireblood horse lines and centaurs.

Khorvesh (kor-VESH)–a dominion to the south of the Capital City, just north of the Manol Jungle.

Kirpis, the (KIR-pis)–a dominion to the north of Kazivar, primarily forest. Most famous for being the original home of one of the vané races, as well as the Academy.

Kishna-Farriga (kish-na fair-eh-GA)–an independent city-state south of Quur, past the Manol Jungle; Kishna-Farriga is used as a trading entrepôt by many neighboring Doltari city-states.

kolyenro mold (KOL-yen-RO)–a mold that can damage and infect silk farms.

Korthaen Blight, the (kor-THANE)–also called *the Wastelands,* a cursed and unlivable land that is (somehow) home to the morgage.

## L

Laaka (LAKE-ay)–goddess of storms, shipwrecks, and sea serpents.

laevos (LAY-vos)–a Joratese hairstyle consisting of a strip of hair down the center of the head and shaved sides, echoing a horse's mane. Some Joratese grow their hair this way by default; it's considered a sign of nobility.

Lake Eyamatsu (EY-ah-mat-sew)–a large lake inside the Manol Jungle.

Lake Jorat–a large lake formed by the Demon Falls dam.

Land of Peace, the–Heaven, the place of reward souls go after they die and are judged worthy by Thaena. Home to the Font of Souls, from which all new souls are created, and all souls go to be reincarnated.

Laudvyis (LAWD-vey-is)–a vané acting as a body double for King Kelanis.

Lefoarnan's (leh-FOUR-nan's)–an exclusive entertainment club located in the Mother of Trees.

Lesinuia power station (le-SIN-yu-ah)–a facility where Grizzst worked prior to the destruction of Karolaen, purpose unknown.

Lord of Little Houses, the–a god-king operating in the I've only seen Doltari Free States whose sphere of influence centers on the bathroom and associated bodily functions.

Lorgrin (LOR-grin)–chief physicker of House D'Mon, murdered by Gadrith.

Lower Circle–the area of the Capital City that exists outside of the safety of the tabletop mesa of the Upper Circle, thus making it vulnerable to flooding.

Lyrilyn (LIR-il-in)–a slave girl owned by Pedron D'Mon, later transformed by the Stone of Shackles into the mimic Talon. She was Khaeriel's handmaiden and tasked with smuggling Khaeriel's newborn son, Kihrin, back to the Manol, a task she failed to carry out.

## M

Maevanos (MAY-van-os)–1. an erotic dance; 2. a holy rite of the Black Gate, the church of Thaena.

Manol, the (MAN-ol)–an area of dense jungle in the equatorial region of the known world; home to the Manol vané.

Marakor (MARE-a-kor)–the Quuros dominion to the southeast of the empire.

mare–a Joratese person who identifies as a woman (note: different from being sexually female, see: gender, Joratese) and expresses "mare" attributes such as housekeeping, child rearing, farming, crafting, art, and cooking and embraces teamwork, family, and subordinate values.

Meahwa (ME-ah-wah)–a vané member of the Black Brotherhood who runs a silk farm.

Milligreest (mill-eh-GREEST)

Eledore (EL-ah-DOOR-ee)–daughter of Qoran Milligreest.

Jarith (JAR-ith)–only son of Qoran; like most Milligreests, served in the military; killed by Xaltorath during the Capital Hellmarch.

Kalindra (KAL-ind-rah)–the widowed wife of Jarith Milligreest, who died during the Capital Hellmarch. Secretly, a member of the Black Brotherhood, of Khorveshan and Zheriasian descent.

Nikali (ni-KAL-i)–cousin of Qoran Milligreest, famous for his skill with a sword. See: Terindel.

Qoran (KOR-an)–high general of the Quuros Army, considered one of the most powerful people in the empire. Janel Theranon's father.

Taunna (TAWN-ay)–a cousin of Qoran Milligreest, adopted and raised by Nikali; current owner of the Culling Fields.

mimics–although commonly believed to be an entire race, mimics are actually a small number (either twelve or sixteen) survivors of a vané experiment in spell imprinting, which gave them all the ability for extremely fast shape-change, telepathy, and memory absorption (through consumption of brain matter). They all promptly went insane. It's unknown how many of them now work as assassins or spies. See: Talon.

misha (MEESH-ah)–a long-sleeved shirt worn by men in Quur.

Mithraill (MEETH-rail)–Khored's son and Sovereign Khaevatz's consort, Mithraill was killed while attacking King Terindel (who was wearing the Stone of Shackles), who afterward found himself in Mithraill's body.

Mithros (MEETH-ros)–leader of the Red Spears, a mercenary company selling their services to the highest bidder for tournaments in Jorat; a Manol vané. The real name of Khored, God of Destruction.

Miya (MY-ah)–see: Miyathreall.

Miyane (MY-an-ee)–queen of the vané, wife of King Kelanis and previously wife of Queen Khaeriel. Note that Miyane is Miyathreall's biological sister.

Miyathreall (MY-ah-threel)–a.k.a. Miya; a handmaiden to Queen Khaeriel, secretly a member of the Black Brotherhood. Miya was slain while assassinating Queen Khaeriel (who wore the Stone of Shackles), and Khaeriel, trapped in Miya's body, was gaeshed and sold to Therin D'Mon.

Molas (MOO-las)–a beggar from Bahl-Nimian

moolthras (MOOL-thras)–a large reptilian pack animal used by the thriss.

Morasan (MOR-ah-san)–a vané acolyte working at the Well of Spirals.

Morea (MOR-e-ah)–Talea's twin sister, who was murdered by Talon.

morgage (mor-gah-GEE)–a savage race that lives in the Korthaen Blight and makes constant war on its neighbors. These are mainly Quuros living in the dominion of Khorvesh, but they hold a special hatred for the vané.

Morios (MORE-ee-os)–a dragon, also Mithros's brother.

## N

Name of All Things, the–a Cornerstone, currently owned by Senera, which will truthfully answer any question the owner asks while holding it. It cannot predict the future, answer questions earlier than its own creation, or interpret opinions.

Nameless Lord, the–the Joratese name of the eighth of the Eight Immortals. See: S'arric.

Nathera, Ola (na-THER-ah, O-la)–a.k.a. Raven. A former slave and owner of the Shattered Veil Club in Velvet Town, Ola was killed accidentally by Thurvishar D'Lorus during Kihrin's attempt to run away. She was later consumed and impersonated by Talon.

Nemesan (NEM-es-an)–a deceased god-king.

Nerikan (NAIR-eh-kahn)–a Quuros emperor.

Nezessa (nez-es-SAY)–a member of the Spurned.

## O

Octagon, the–the main slave auction house of the Capital City.

Ogenra (O-jon-RAY)–an unrecognized bastard of one of the Royal Houses. Far from being unwanted, Ogenra are considered an important part of the political process because of their ability to circumvent the god-touched curse.

Old Man, the–see: Sharanakal.

Ompher (OM-fur)–one of the Eight Immortals, god of the world.

ord (ord)–the main monetary unit of Kishna-Farriga.

Oxun, Nevesi (OH-chewn, nev-es-EYE)–member of the Quuros High Council.

## Q

Qown, Brother (kown)–an acolyte of the Vishai Mysteries, now apprenticed to Relos Var.

Quarry, the–a prison used by the vané.

Quur, the Great and Holy Empire of (koor)–a large empire originally expanded from a single city-state (also named Quur), which now serves as the empire's capital.

Quuros High Council–the ultimate ruling body of Quur, composed of representatives nominated from the Royal Houses. Theoretically, the emperor has authority over them, but no emperor has attempted to enforce that authority since Emperor Kandor. It's widely believed that emperors are gaeshed when receiving the Crown and Scepter, hamstringing their powers.

## R

Raenena (RAY-nen-ah)–a dominion of Quur, nestled in the Dragonspires to the north.

Rainbow Lake–a small lake in Eamithon famous for being the home of Grizzst's workshop, although no one has ever found it.

raisigi (RAY-sig-eye)–a tight-fitting bodice worn by women.

Return–to be resurrected from the Afterlife, always with the permission of the Goddess of Death, Thaena.

Rev'arric (rev-AR-ik)–see: Var, Relos.

Rindala (RIN-dah-lah)–a Kirpis vané dreamweaver who acts as warden of the prison known as the Quarry.

Ritual of Night, the–a voras ritual designed to drain the immortality from an immortal race and use that power to recharge the eighth warding crystal keeping Vol Karoth imprisoned. The ritual kills its participants.

Rol'amar–a dragon.

Rook–see: D'Mon, Kihrin.

## S

S'arric (sar-RIC)–one of the Eight Immortals, mostly unknown (and deceased); god of sun, stars, and sky; murdered by his older brother, Rev'arric. Past life of Kihrin D'Mon. Was corrupted during a magical ritual and turned into Vol Karoth.

sallí (sal-LEE)–a hooded, cloak-like garment designed to protect the wearer from the intense heat of the Capital City.

Sandus (SAND-us)–a farmer from Marakor, later emperor of Quur.

sejin (seh-JIN)–an anise-flavored milky liquor popular in Kishna-Farriga.

Selanol (SELL-an-al)–the solar deity worshipped as part of the Vishai Mysteries.

Senera (SEN-er-AY)–a former slave of Doltari ancestry, now acting as an agent for Relos Var. Owner of the Name of All Things.

Serafana (ser-AH-fawn-NAY)–former capital of the vané nation of Kirpis.

sexuality, Joratese–Joratese society defines sexual identity around partner preference. So, for example, anyone who prefers biologically female sexual partners "runs with mares" regardless of their own biological sex. People who "run with stallions" prefer male sexual partners, and people who "run with the herd" would be considered bisexual. Asexuals simply "don't run." All of these options are accepted without discrimination in Joratese society.

Shadowdancers, the–an illegal criminal organization operating in the Lower Circle of the Capital City.

Shahara (shah-HAR-ray)–a voramer ruler who died performing the Ritual of Night.

shanathá (shan-NA-tha)–a light, hard metal used to make some kinds of armor and weapons.

Sharanakal (SHA-ran-a-KAL)–a dragon.

Simillion (SIM-i-le-on)–first emperor of Quur. Past life of Thurvishar D'Lorus.

sky trees–A native species of Ompher, very few of these trees remain outside of the Manol Jungle. They grow to colossal size. While they block out almost all sunlight within the Jungle, they also act as a support mechanism for life under the canopy.

Soaring Halls, the–the imperial palace in the Capital City of Quur. Emperors have rarely used the palace as actual living space, although it has happened.

Spurned, the–an all-female warrior company under the command of Xivan Kaen.

stallion–a Joratese person who identifies as a man (note: different from being sexually male, see: gender, Joratese) and expresses "stallion" attributes such as leadership, assertiveness, guardianship, entertaining, contests, and combativeness.

star tears–a kind of rare blue diamond; also, the tsali of any soul not originally from this universe.

Stone of Shackles, the–one of the eight Cornerstones, ancient artifacts of unknown origin. The Stone of Shackles has power over souls, including the ability to exchange its wearer's soul with that of their murderer. The Stone of Shackles was destroyed, at least temporarily, by Kihrin D'Mon using Urthaenriel, which freed all gaeshe made using it (namely, almost all of them).

Suless (SEW-less)–god-queen of Yor, associated with witchcraft, deception, treachery, and betrayal; also associated with hyenas. Suless was the very first god-king, who was gaeshed by and forced to marry Cherthog. She was freed from her gaesh when the Stone of Shackles was destroyed.

sundew–a bioluminescent sap harvested from sky trees that allows plants and animals below the canopy layer of the Manol Jungle to conduct photosynthesis.

Surdyeh (SUR-de-yeh)–a wizard and minstrel secretly working for the Gryphon Men who raised Kihrin D'Mon. Surdyeh was murdered and consumed by Talon.

Szarrus (sah-ZAR-us)–a thriss weapon master and member of the Black Brotherhood.

## T

Taja (TAJ-ah)–one of the Eight Immortals, Goddess of Luck.

Talea (tal-E-ah)–Morea's sister. A slave girl formerly owned by Baron Mataris, now second in command of the Spurned.

talisman–an otherwise normal object whose tenyé has been modified to vibrate in sympathy with the owner, thus reinforcing the owner's tenyé against enemies who might use magic to change it into a different form. This also means it's extremely dangerous to allow one's talismans to fall into enemy hands. Since talismans interfere with magical power, every talisman worn weakens the effectiveness of the wearer's spellcasting.

Talon–a mimic assassin who was "taken over" by Lyrilyn because of the Stone of Shackles. She promptly went insane (as is tradition) but has since continued pursuing a garbled set of sometimes contradictory goals as her multiple personalities clash with each other. See: Lyrilyn.

tenyé (ten-AY)–the true essence of an object, vital to all magic.

Teraeth (ter-RAYTH)–hunter of Thaena; a Manol vané assassin and member of the Black Brotherhood; son of Khaemezra and Terindel. Reincarnation of Atrin Kandor.

Terindel (TER-in-del)–an infamous Kirpis vané king who was forced out of the Kirpis by Atrin Kandor and later sparked a civil war in the Manol. Was killed by Mithraill, but because Terindel was wearing the Stone of Shackles, he switched bodies with his killer. Married to first Valathea, then Elana Milligreest.

Thaena (thane-AY)–one of the Eight Immortals. Goddess of Death.

Theranon (ther-a-NON)–a noble family from Jorat.

Janel (jan-EL)–a demon-tainted warrior who goes to the Afterlife when she sleeps. Adopted daughter of Xaltorath, real daughter of Qoran Milligreest and the goddess Tya. Reincarnation of Elana Milligreest and C'indrol.

Ninavis (NIN-a-vis)–a former outlaw staging a curious rebellion in Jorat. Adopted by Janel Theranon and became Count of Tolamer after Janel's abdication. Is likely about to become Duke of Jorat.

thorra (THOR-ah)–Joratese term for a person who abuses idorrá privileges; bully or tyrant, lit. "a stallion who is not safe to leave with other horses."

Three Sisters, the–either Taja, Tya, and Thaena, or Galava, Tya, and Thaena; also, the three moons in the night sky.

thudajé (thu-DAJ-ay)–Joratese term of respect, humility, and submission; thudajé is considered an essential and positive Joratese trait. No matter how high in idorrá someone is, the Joratese believe there will always be someone to whom they owe thudajé.

Tillinghast, Professor (TIL-in-gast)–a professor who teaches at the Academy in Kirpis. Infamous for giving very boring lectures.

Tolamer (TOL-a-mear)–a canton in northeastern Jorat, ruled by the Theranon family for almost five hundred years.

Traitor's Walk, the–a vané form of execution where the condemned is gaeshed to prevent them from leaving the Korthaen Blight and then released there without food or water.

tsali stone (zal-e)–a crystal created from the condescended soul of a person.

Twin Worlds, the–name for the combination of the Living World and Afterlife, when referring to both realms as part of a larger whole.
Tya (TIE-ah)–a.k.a. Irisia. One of the Eight Immortals, the Goddess of Magic.
Tya's Veil–an aurora borealis effect visible in the night sky.
Tyentso (tie-EN-so)–formerly Raverí D'Lorus, now the emperor of Quur; the first woman to ever be emperor.

## U

Uisigi (YOU-sig-eye)–undergarments, specifically underpants or loincloths.
Upper Circle–the mesa plateau in the center of the Capital City that is home to the Royal Houses, temples, government, and the Arena.
Urthaenriel (UR-thane-re-EL)–a.k.a. Godslayer, the Ruin of Kings, the Emperor's Sword. A powerful artifact that is believed to make its wielder completely immune to magic and thus is capable of killing gods.

## V

Valathea (val-a-THEE-uh)–a harp passed through the Milligreest family. Also, a deceased queen of the Kirpis vané, Terindel's wife, who was sentenced to the Traitor's Walk after her husband's death.
Valrashar (val-ra-SHAR)–vané princess, daughter of Kirpis vané king Terindel and Queen Valathea. Therin D'Mon's grandmother.
Vamara, Mother (va-MAR-ah)–one of the Dry Mothers.
vané (van-AY)–a.k.a. vorfelané. An immortal, magically gifted race known for their exceptional beauty. Vané appearance is mutable and can be changed as the vané desires (although not quickly). Vané tend to keep the skin colors they were born with unless they are making a big statement (as happened when the Manol vané split from the Kirpis and the entire population of the new nation deliberately darkened their skin).
vané, Kirpis–a fair-skinned, immortal race who once lived in the Kirpis forest. They were driven south to eventually relocate in the Manol Jungle.
vané, Manol–the vané who settled in the Manol Jungle, in part as protest against Kirpis vané isolationism and unwillingness to pay attention to both the Blight and the threat of humanity.
Var, Relos (VAR, REL-os)–a powerful wizard, believed responsible for the ritual that created the Eight Immortals and also the ritual that created both the dragons and Vol Karoth.
Vayldeba (VALE-deb-ah)–a vané Founder.
Veil, the–1. the aurora borealis effect sometimes seen in the nighttime

sky; 2. the state of perception separating seeing the "normal" world from seeing the true essence or tenyé of the world, necessary for magic.

velsanaund (VEL-san-ound)–a large lizard, originally developed by the thriss, now used by the vané for transportation.

Velvet Town–the red-light district of the Lower Circle. Those who engage in the sex trade are commonly described as *velvet* (i.e. velvet boys or velvet girls).

Vimor (vim-OR)–a Doltari slave. Senera's father, deceased.

Visallía (viz-ALL-e-ah)–a march in Jorat.

Vishai Mysteries, the (vish-AY)–a religion popular in parts of Eamithon, Jorat, and Marakor; little is known about their inner workings, but their religion seems to principally center around a solar deity named Selanol; usually pacifistic; members of the faith will often obtain licenses from House D'Mon to legally practice healing.

Vol Karoth (VOL ka-ROTH)–a.k.a. War Child or Warchild. A demon offspring crafted by demons to counter the Eight Immortals; alternately, a corrupted remnant of the sacrificed god of the sun, S'arric.

voramer (vor-a-MEER)–a.k.a. vormer. An extinct water-dwelling race believed to be the progenitors of the morgage and the ithlakor; of the two, only the ithlakor still live in water. Many Zheriasians have ithlakor ancestors, which is part of the reason they have a reputation for being "undrownable."

voras (vor-AS)–a.k.a. vorarras. Extinct race believed to have been the progenitors of humanity, who lost their immortality to imprison Vol Karoth.

vordreth (vor-DRETH)–a.k.a. vordredd, dreth, dredd, dwarves. An underground-dwelling race known for their strength and intelligence. Despite their nickname, not short. Believed to have been wiped out when Atrin Kandor conquered Raenena, but in fact, the largest dreth population lives under the Doltar region, which has more than its share of dreth-blooded inhabitants.

## W

Warmonger–a Cornerstone whose power seems to involve manipulating loyalty and anger over large populations.

Watchmen–the guards tasked with policing the Capital City.

Well of Spirals, the–a location sacred to vané, where they imprint their children and perform a number of miraculous biological magics. The mimics were created there.

Wenora, Vornel (WEN-or-ay, vor-NEL)–a member of the High Council.

Wilavir, Silvat (wil-a-VIR, SIV-at)–author of *Siege Tactics of the Yoran Invasion.*

Wildheart–a Cornerstone that allows its owner to control plant and animal life, as well as manipulate earth and rocks.

Winding Sheet, the–a velvet house specializing in providing lethal entertainments for those with sufficient wealth to afford them.

witch–anyone using magic who hasn't received formal, official training and licensing; although technically gender neutral, usually only applied to women.

witchhunter–imperial soldiers specifically trained to track down and eliminate witches. Known for wearing their talismans in the form of coins they wear as scale armor.

Worldhearth–a Cornerstone with the power to allow its user clairvoyance through heat sources.

## X

Xaloma (ZAL-o-may)–a dragon, associated with souls.

Xaltorath (zal-tor-OTH)–a demon prince who can only be summoned through the sacrifice of a family member. Self-associated with lust and war. Gender neutral but identifies as female when dealing with her adopted daughter, Janel.

## Y

Ynis (YIN-is)–a god-king who once ruled the area now known as Khorvesh. Associated with death and snakes.

Yor (yor)–one of Quur's dominions, the most recently added and the least acclimated to imperial rule.

## Z

Zaibur (ZAI-bur)–1. the major river running from Demon Falls and Lake Jorat all the way to the ocean, dividing Jorat from Marakor; 2. a strategy game.

Zajhera, Father (zah-JER-ah)–leader of the Vishai Faith / Vishai Mysteries. Personally exorcised the demon Xaltorath, who possessed Janel Theranon when she was a child. An alias used by Relos Var.

Zherias (ZER-e-as)–A large island to the southwest of Quur. Independent from Quur and anxious to stay that way. Famous for their skill at piracy and trade. Contains a high proportion of voramer ancestry, so that it's not uncommon for Zheriasians to go to sea when they're older.

# Family Trees

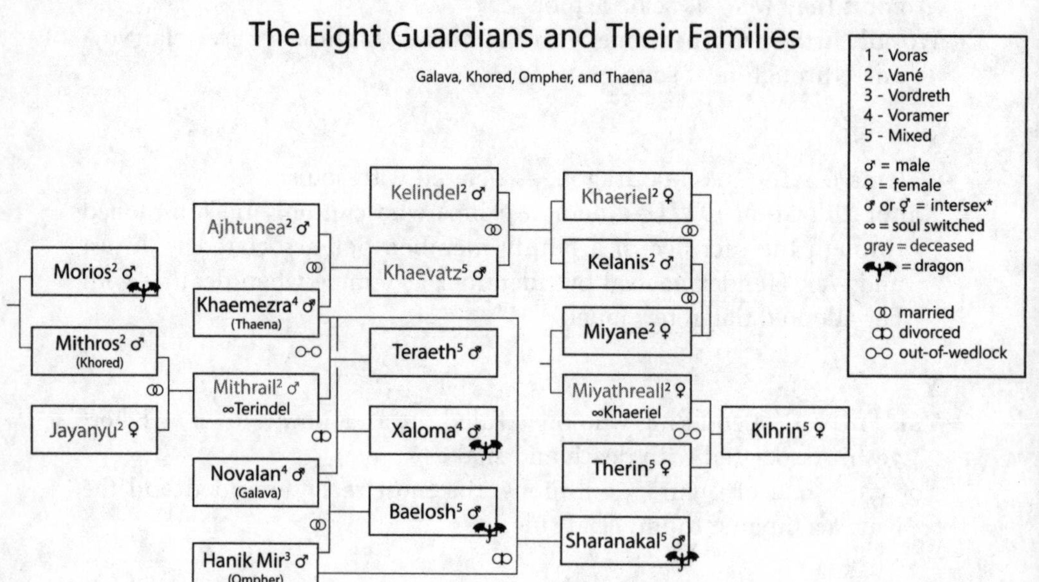


*⚦ mark voramer, who are born male, and become female during the later part of their life cycle. They are capable of reproduction during both stages. ⚥ indicates a non-voramer intersex status.

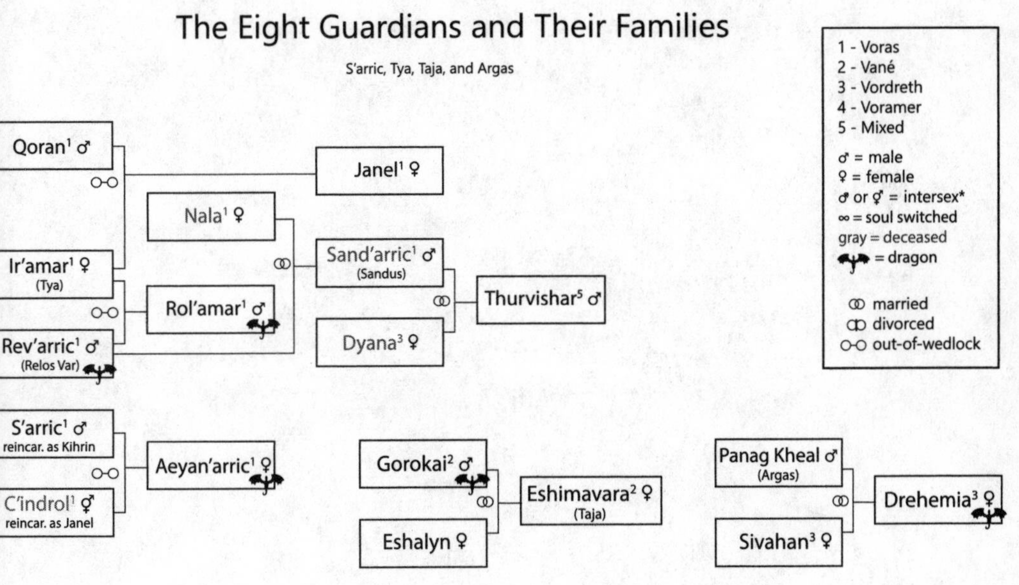


*⚦ mark voramer, who are born male, and become female during the later part of their life cycle. They are capable of reproduction during both stages. ⚥ indicates a non-voramer intersex status.

# Time Line

12416 PQ — Original settlement of Ompher: the voras settle on Nythrawl, the vordreth on Tyga, and the voramer in the oceans.

12291 PQ — A group of voras activists split off and settle on Vala, calling themselves the vorfelane or vané.

1756 PQ — Dimensional rift first noticed on Nythrawl.

1728 PQ — Demon invasion begins in Nythrawl. The demons are capable of retreating across dimensional barriers where no one can follow.

1645 PQ — The voras are forced to flee Nythrawl, relocating to Vala and Tyga. Millennia of technology and infrastructure is lost, never to be recovered.

1572 PQ — Rev'arric devises a magical ritual to imbue people with power to fight the demons. Rev'arric expects to be allowed to use the ritual on himself. Instead, the ritual is used on eight specific individuals, including Rev'arric's brother, S'arric. The Eight Guardians immediately begin winning huge successes.

1390 PQ — Rev'arric "improves" the Ritual of Eight, or so he claims, but the ritual backfires, turning his brother, S'arric, into Vol Karoth and turning all the ritual participants, himself included, into dragons. The Cornerstones are also created. Vol Karoth immediately seeks out and slays the other seven Guardians before he is imprisoned by the Assembly using a hastily created and devastating ritual called the Ritual of Night. The ritual strips the voras of their immortality, but the person who was holding Urthaenriel during the ritual, a man named Grizzst, is unaffected and remains immortal.

1389 PQ — The Age of God-Kings begins. A voras researcher named Su'less develops the god-king spell map. A voras named Cher'thog finds the Stone of Shackles and, upon discovering what it does, uses it to gaesh Su'less, forces her to show him the god-king spell, and forces her to marry him. Su'less teaches her daughter Ca'less the spell before Cher'thog thinks to forbid it, and Ca'lessa teaches anyone who cares to learn.

1380 PQ The god-kings keep the voras alive, but at the cost of humanity's enslavement.

1302 PQ A faction of vané who are disquieted by the creation of Vol Karoth and the god-kings split from the Kirpis and relocate to the Manol under the leadership of two children of the Eight Guardians: Khaevatz and her consort, Mithraill.

66 PQ Grizzst successfully cures Rev'arric of his insanity and allows him to take a human form. Grizzst successfully resurrects the Eight Guardians.

65 PQ Grizzst, with the help of Tya and Argas, creates the Crown and Scepter and uses them and the Stone of Shackles to bind the demons.

64 PQ First known appearance of Xaltorath. Also the first known mention of the prophecies.

5 PQ The Eight Immortals decide to start doing something about the god-kings. Taja finds a young man named Simillion who just lost his family to god-king soldiers and instructs him to find Grizzst, the keeper of Urthaenriel.

1 PQ Simillion finally tracks down Grizzst in a brothel, but Grizzst takes the boy under his wing and eventually takes him to the god-queen Dana, whom Grizzst entrusted with Urthaenriel.

1 QR Simillion uses Urthaenriel to slay the god-king Qhuaras (with some help from Qhauras's consort, Caless).

2 QR Simillion marries Dana, merging Eamithon and the City-State of Quur.

4 QR After returning from skirmishing with God-King Nemesan, Simillion is assassinated by the richest merchant families of Quur. The Eight curse the families responsible in retaliation.

5 QR Ynis invades Quur. The families end up fighting to decide who will be the next emperor, and the winner, Nerikan D'Talus, slays Ynis and adds Khorvynis, renamed Khorvesh, to the empire. Khorvynis's thriss citizens are either put to the sword or driven from their home.

43 QR Nerikan is slain by Nemesan. This time, Grizzst arrives and formally codifies ground rules for the succession using the Crown and Scepter.

683 QR Vol Karoth wakes. He attempts to free himself by pulling a

giant plume of plasma from the sun directly to the planet. Tya blocks the effects by creating the magical barrier known as Tya's Veil, but the Veil's presence changes the color of the sky from blue to teal. The voramer become mortal.

1506 QR Atrin Kandor becomes emperor.

1533 QR Kandor conquers Raenena, mostly by virtue of sticking a flag in the mountains and claiming it.

1612 QR Atrin Kandor kills Khorsal and conquers Jorat, in the process creating Lake Jorat and the city of Atrine.

1699 QR Kandor turns his attention to the Kirpis vané and forces them to abandon the Kirpis forest.

1707 QR Atrin Kandor buys Elana Milligreest from her parents and marries her.

1708 QR Vol Karoth wakes again. King Terindel refuses to conduct the ritual, forcing the vordreth to shoulder that burden.

1709 QR Civil war erupts among the vané, while Kandor decides to invade the Manol. Terindel's brother stages a coup with the help of Queen Khaevatz and leads his brother into a trap, but because Terindel is wearing the Stone of Shackles, he ends up in the body of his killer, Mithraill. Meanwhile, the combined vané forces succeed in killing Atrin Kandor, while Terindel's daughter, Valrashar, is gaeshed and sold into slavery and his wife, Valathea, is sentenced to the Traitor's Walk.

1710 QR With Kandor dead, the morgage of the Blight invade Quur. Kandor's widow, Elana, has a vision that tells her only she can stop the fighting, and so, even though she's pregnant with Atrin's child, she travels to the Blight to parlay. She encounters Valathea while traveling, and they become lovers. However, during the trip, Valathea is poisoned and, to avoid the normally uncurable effects, turns herself into a harp. Elana promises to keep Valathea safe, while she bargains with the Dry Mothers and eventually frees S'arric's soul from Vol Karoth.

1712 QR The Celestial Concord is struck.

1720–
1962 QR The conquest of the City-States of Zaibur occurs.

2044 QR Emperor Gendal finishes conquering Yor, marking the last of the Quuros dominions to be added to the empire.

2113 QR Queen Khaeriel is assassinated. Like her uncle, Terindel, she's wearing the Stone of Shackles, and like him, she ends up in the body of her killer. However, this was anticipated, and so Khaeriel is captured, gaeshed, and sold to Therin D'Mon.

2119 QR The Affair of the Voices occurs, in which Nikali and Qoran Milligreest, Therin D'Mon, and a Marakori wizard named Sandus uncover a plot to gaesh and control Imperial Voices. When the smoke clears, Therin D'Mon discovers he is now High Lord of House D'Mon. The four friends drift apart: Therin and Qoran because of their new responsibilities, and Sandus to spend time with his new wife, Dyana.

2120 QR Therin's wife, Nora, dies in childbirth; Thaena refuses to Return her. Racked by guilt, Therin begins drinking heavily and eventually sleeps with Khaeriel under conditions of extremely dubious consent. She becomes pregnant.

2121 QR Kihrin D'Mon is born. Khaeriel sends him away with her handmaiden, Lyrilyn, giving Lyrilyn the Stone of Shackles so she can't be magically tracked. This backfires when Lyrilyn is attacked and killed by the mimic Talon, turning Lyrilyn into a mimic. In the aftermath, a man named Surdyeh finds Kihrin, puts the Stone of Shackles on the baby, and takes him to be raised by Ola Nathera.

2136 QR Kihrin breaks into the wrong house.

# Acknowledgments

I'd like to thank my agent, Sam Morgan, for once again being the perfect agent, and for encouraging my often very strange antics. I'd also like to thank my editors, Devi Pillai and Bella Pagan, for all their hard work and encouragement. (I could not have done this without you.) I'd also like to give all the love to everyone in the author sack–Alex, Macey, Rekka, Ev, Sam, Miri, and Alyshondra–for your help keeping me sane. I'd especially like to thank Freya Marske for her assistance in making sure this was indeed a kissing book. And lastly, and always, my thanks to my husband Mike, who fills my life with joy.